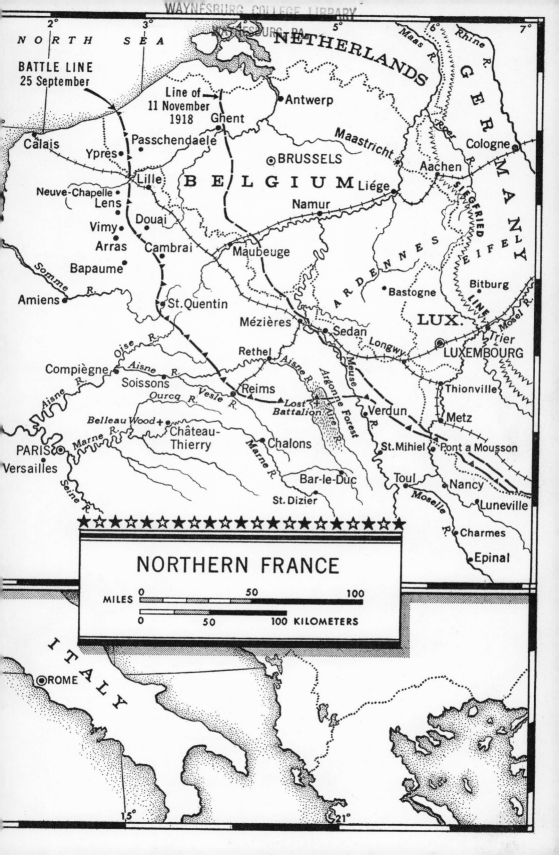

2°   3°   4°   5°   6°   7°

N O R T H   S E A

NETHERLANDS

Maas R.

Rhine R.

G E R M A N Y

BATTLE LINE
25 September

Line of
11 November
1918

Antwerp

Ghent

Cologne

Passchendaele

Maastricht

Aachen

Calais

Ypres

Roer R.

Liége

⊙BRUSSELS

B E L G I U M

Lille

SIEGFRIED

Neuve-Chapelle

Namur

Lens

Douai

E I F E L

Vimy

Cambrai

Maubeuge

Arras

A R D E N N E S

Bastogne

Bitburg

Bapaume

Mosel R.

Somme R.

St. Quentin

LINE

Amiens

LUX.

Oise R.

Mézières

Sedan

Longwy

Trier

Rethel

⊙LUXEMBOURG

Compiègne

Aisne R.

Soissons

Reims

Argonne Forest

Meuse R.

Thionville

Ourcq R.

Vesle R.

Lost
Battalion

Verdun

Metz

Belleau Wood

Château-
Thierry

Aire R.

St. Mihiel

Pont a Mousson

PARIS⊙

Marne R.

Chalons

Toul

Nancy

Versailles

Marne R.

Bar-le-Duc

Luneville

Seine R.

St. Dizier

Moselle R.

Charmes

Epinal

★☆★☆★☆★☆★☆★☆★☆★☆★☆★☆★☆★☆★

NORTHERN FRANCE

MILES   0   50   100

0   50   100 KILOMETERS

I T A L Y

⊙ROME

15°   21°

American Men at Arms

American Men at Arms

✗

Selected and Introduced by

F. VAN WYCK MASON

LITTLE, BROWN AND COMPANY • BOSTON • TORONTO

COPYRIGHT NOTICES AND ACKNOWLEDGMENTS

Grateful acknowledgment is made to the following for permission to reprint copyrighted material:

CURTIS L. ANDERS — "Orders: Plans and Execution" from THE PRICE OF COURAGE by Curt Anders. Copyright © 1957 by Curtis L. Anders.

APPLETON-CENTURY — "Life in the Foxholes" from THE BIG WAR by Anton Myrer. Copyright © 1957 by Anton Myrer. By permission of Appleton-Century.

CROWN PUBLISHERS — "The Killing" from THE SLOT by John Clagett. Copyright 1958 by John Clagett. Used by permission of Crown Publishers, Inc.

THE JOHN DAY COMPANY — "The Lost Battalion" and "Corpsman!" from KNOWN BUT TO GOD by Quentin Reynolds. © 1960 by Quentin Reynolds. Reprinted by permission of The John Day Company, Inc., Publisher.

DODD, MEAD & COMPANY — "Letters From a Rookie" from DERE MABLE by Edward Streeter. Copyright, 1918, 1919, 1941, by Edward Streeter. "Queenstown Patrol" from S-54 by Edward Ellsberg. Copyright, 1930, 1931, 1932, 1959, by Commander Edward Ellsberg. "The Hunter and the Hunted" from WOLFPACK by William M. Hardy. Copyright © 1960 by William M. Hardy. All reprinted by permission of Dodd, Mead & Company.

JOHN DOS PASSOS — "Waiting" and "The Argonne" from THREE SOLDIERS by John Dos Passos. Copyright 1921 and 1948 by John Dos Passos. Published by Houghton Mifflin Company and reprinted by permission of the author.

DOUBLEDAY & COMPANY — "First Wave" from DO NOT GO GENTLE by David MacCuish. Copyright © 1960 by David MacCuish. "Mutiny" from THE CAINE MUTINY by Herman Wouk. Copyright 1951 by Herman Wouk. "Beyond the Call of Duty" from THE LOCUST FIRE by Eugene Brown. Copyright © 1957 by Eugene Brown. All reprinted by permission of Doubleday & Company, Inc.

Contents

✗

WORLD WAR I (1917-1918)

✗

WORLD WAR II (1941-1945)

Attack and Counterattack

The E.T.O.

There Was Also Time for Laughter

The War in the Pacific

KOREA (1950-1953)

Introduction

✂

It is only by pure coincidence that this anthologist should find himself preparing an introduction to a secondary anthology of war stories, almost twenty years after THE FIGHTING AMERICAN, which was published while World War II was nearing the peak of its fury.

Of course, during the passage of these twenty years, profound changes have taken place in the political and social attitudes of men and women who served in World War I, World War II and in the Korean conflict.

One also suspects that the taste and viewpoint of the reading public have altered greatly — certainly this is true of the anthologist.

Through the medium of carefully considered stories and excerpts from novels by outstanding authors I have attempted to demonstrate how the American soldier, gradually and unwillingly, abandoned his deeply in-grained mistrust of professional soldiers in particular and military authority in general to evolve into the efficient, if disillusioned, GI of the 1900's.

This change in the American's attitude toward service with the Armed Forces I think had its inception during World War I, which, by the way, was the last war in which our men genuinely were inspired by patriotic slogans, flag-waving and the hoary fable that sheer valor on the part of hastily trained militia and semi-irregular troops inevitably must prevail over the enemy no matter what the odds — which on several occasions proved to be an almost fatal misconception.

In AMERICAN MEN AT ARMS are offered fictional accounts of episodes and combat characteristic of World War I, World War II, and the wretched Korean conflict in which American armies again prevailed only to see hard-won victories nullified by the shortsightedness of well-intentioned but purblind politicians.

The Korean conflict, in particular, demonstrated that, at long last, Americans, both civilian and military, had come to face the fact that modern wars can only be won when fought by well-trained, fully equipped troops led by skilled generals, in turn directed by forward-looking statesmen dedicated to the long-term safety of their country.

Can one picture raw militia regiments such as ran, all too often, before British regulars back in 1812 able to conduct, in good order, an operation as hazardous, agonized and protracted as our Army's mid-winter retreat from the Reservoirs in Korea?

Imagine the courageous but ill-disciplined, untrained and haphazardly equipped conscripts of 1861 and 1862 being able to storm successfully ashore in Asia, North Africa, Sicily and Normandy! Almost certainly such troops, even though lacking tactical, technical and administrative know-how, would have been quite ready to make such an attempt as they did — with disastrous results — against Fort Fisher, North Carolina, in 1865.

As to why this editor decided to include or to omit certain short stories and to make categorical excerpts from novels by his esteemed fellow writers, he can only plead that his judgment may have become a trifle biased through the fact that he has served under fire overseas in two world wars and readily admits to impatience with politically biased or precious writers of *belles lettres* who attempt, with psychiatric tremolos, to reproduce the supposed reactions of American soldiers in battle.

As a member of a family which proudly has worn the uniforms of the United States Armed Forces through seven generations the editor must retain toward such efforts — whatever their literary merit — a degree of ironic skepticism.

Possibly at this point it might be advisable to mention some of this anthologist's qualifications as a selector of war stories.

I departed for World War I at the age of sixteen — of course I had lied about my years — to drive an ambulance for the French and in this capacity was present at the siege of Verdun where my fluent knowledge of the French language was to prove invaluable — to me at least. It is amazing, even at this late date, that I can recall with surprising clarity so many sights, smells, sounds and incidents of that horrible experience.

The business of serving as a mere noncombatant having become increasingly distasteful, I enrolled in the Artillery School at Fontainbleau and was about to be commissioned an *aspirant* in the French Service when the United States entered the War.

The moment I was allowed to resign from the French Army I went to Paris and enlisted in the AEF. Despite my tender years — seventeen — I was at once made a sergeant, which was only due to my above-mentioned knowledge of French and a certain gift of understanding how to get things done with our Gallic friends.

For a time I served in the U. S. Army's Corps of Interpreters and was attached in succession to various French, French-Colonial and American headquarters. Especially after I was commissioned in our service as a "shave-tail" — or second lieutenant — I had the opportunity of observing operations while they were being fought on various fronts and sectors. Thus I was afforded, I believe, what must have been an unusually varied and comprehensive view of certain campaigns of World War I.

Aside from the grim aspects, I recall occasional amusing incidents: one of these I have recounted as "The Goldfish Mutiny," which is included in this volume.

Long after the Armistice I had the pleasure of meeting and comparing recollections with certain authors who had written so well about that so-called "war to end wars" and am proud here to include some of their works; among them were Leonard Nason, John Dos Passos, Laurence Stallings and that tough, gifted and unforgettable U. S. Marine, Major John Thomason.

Between the wars I served for many years with various National Guard units — including the celebrated Squadron A of New York — and so was offered an opportunity to appreciate at first hand the strengths and weaknesses inherent in our National Guard system.

When the Second World War broke out I had resigned my commission in the artillery, but telegraphed for reinstatement on the afternoon of Pearl Harbor. Twenty days later I was recommissioned a major and ordered to report for duty with the War Department's Bureau of Public Relations in Washington, D.C.

Thus commenced a hiatus in my writing career which continued for almost four years, but this was far from time wasted — during that interval I was enabled to observe a great deal of what transpired on some of our Army's higher staffs.

After successfully disentangling myself from a well-hated desk in the Pentagon, I arrived in London early in 1943 to serve at ETOUSA Headquarters with G–5 — a division of the General Staff which occupied itself with the planning and conduct of Civil Affairs and Military Government.

Later that year I was fortunate enough to be appointed to G–5 COSSAC (Chiefs of Staff to the Supreme Allied Commander) which was the designation of SHAEF before General Eisenhower was selected to be the Supreme Allied Commander in the European Theater.

In my capacity as Chief Historian for G–5 SHAEF I operated on a Presidential directive which ordered me to "collect, preserve and collate" the material from which histories relative to the operations of Civil Affairs and Military Government would be written. To accomplish this I was assigned a staff of some forty American, British and French historians — for the most part Americans.

This assignment inevitably brought me into contact with a good many famous figures, among them Field Marshal Bernard Montgomery, who, I regret to report, was most ungracious and noncooperative about honoring the directive which required that G–5 historians be attached to his principal headquarters.

I shall never forget my interview with the late Lieutenant General George Patton, Jr., who had started out as even more hostile toward my mission than had Montgomery himself.

Midway through my interview the General suddenly leaned over his desk and bellowed, "Say, you're not the Mason who wrote THREE HARBOURS and STARS ON THE SEA?"

Diffidently, I admitted that I might be held responsible.

"Well, I'll be damned!" he said. "You don't look much like a quill pusher, but it seems like you know something about history. Question is, how much?" The fierce white brows merged. "Tell me, Colonel, what's the only battle that was fought between two generals world-famous at the time, who'd their best troops with 'em, who occupied exactly the terrain they'd selected and who fought the battle as they'd planned? When was it and who won?"

To this day I don't know what turned over in my memory and prompted me to reply: "Sir, I believe you are referring to the battle of Zama which was fought outside Carthage during the Third Punic War around 202 B.C. between Scipio Africanus and Hannibal." I couldn't help adding, "Guess you know that the Romans won a decisive victory!"

"Now, by God," roared Patton, "that shines! Damned if it don't." Presently he became wary once more. "Say, Colonel, do you propose to hand any of the stuff you may come across over to the god-damn newspapers?"

Joyfully and hastily I assured the General that in all probability no material collected by the Historical Branch G–5 would be printed until long after the war was over. From that moment the Historical Section G–5 never had more generous or intelligent cooperation.

Curiously enough, I found myself under fire many more times during World War II than in the First Unpleasantness because, in order to prevent the destruction, mutilation or suppression of vitally important documents, I needed to advance with attacking units much more often than I had any desire.

It was because of this necessity that I participated in the capture of several POW camps and also such ghastly concentration camps as Belsen, Buchenwald and Ravensbruck. I also was present at the immensely moving liberation of Amsterdam by the Canadian Army and later got involved in the thick of the street fighting that went on during the capture of Augsburg.

One amusing recollection which comes to mind is that when Leipzig was captured I was assigned a billet in the Headquarters Officers' barracks and what should I find lying open on the cot but a pirated German edition of THREE HARBOURS!

Undoubtedly this anthology includes selections from novels which may or may not be considered great literature but which have been reprinted because, in this anthologist's opinion, they most accurately portray the emotions of Americans serving their country.

In cases where an excerpt has been taken from a long book, the editor has deleted paragraphs and even pages not directly pertinent to the particular situation or action being described and has attempted to present such selections as structually balanced and complete.

The editor has not, as in a preceding anthology, limited his selections to descriptions of actual combat; in this collection the reader, among other subjects, will find some examples of humor for, even under the worst of conditions, the American soldier always has found a time for laughter.

Also included are a good many non-battlefield yarns concerning training camps, the noncombatant services and the Medical Corps — there is even one descriptive of a VD hospital.

It also seemed important to describe the varying reactions of American POW's captured in North Africa, Europe and in the Far East. All in all, an earnest effort has been made to present to the reader a well-rounded and comprehensive picture of Americans serving with the Armed Forces.

Here are offered fifty-six selections representing the work of forty-seven different fiction writers. From the work of these authors some twenty motion pictures have been made, one vastly successful musical comedy, two fine plays and a great many TV shows.

It is the anthologist's hope that the reader, if and when he finishes this book, will feel that he has been well entertained and, at the same time, possibly has obtained a more complete understanding of the nation's altered attitude toward the use and training of its armed forces.

It is perhaps ironical that the most widely read words ever written by the editor — a professional novelist for over thirty years — should have been a piece of non-fiction.

They were the Communiqué No. 1, released during the D-Day landings, which read as follows: "Under the command of General Eisenhower, Allied naval forces, supported by strong air forces, began landing Allied armies this morning on the north coast of France."

I had been borrowed from Military Government especially to write the first dozen odd-numbered communiqués issued by Supreme Headquarters Allied Expeditionary Forces.

F. van Wyck Mason
"Hampton Head"
Southampton
Bermuda

World War I

(1917 – 1918)

✗

Letters from a Rookie

✕

from *Dere Mable*

by EDWARD STREETER

Dere Mable:

Having nothin better to do I take up my pen to rite.

We have been here now three weeks. As far as I am concerned I am all ready to go. I told the Captain that I am ready any time. He said yes, but that wed have to wait for the slow ones cause they was all goin together. I says was I to go out to drill with the rest. He said yes more for the example than anything else. Its kind of maddening to be hangin round here when I might be over there helpin the Sammies put a stop to this thing.

In the mean time I been doin guard duty. Seems like I been doin it every night but I know what there up against and I don't say nothin. Guard duty is something like extemperaneus speakin. You got to know everything your goin to say before you start. Its very tecknickle. For instance you walk a post but there aint no post. An you mount guard but you dont really mount nothin. An you turn out the guard but you dont really turn em out. They come out them selves. Just the other night I was walkin along thinkin of you Mable an my feet which was hurtin. It made me awful lonesome. An officer come up and he says why dont you draw your pistol when you here someone comin. An I says I dont wait till the sheep is stole I drew it this afternoon from the Supply sargent. An I showed it to him tucked inside my shirt where no one could get it away from me without some tussel, you bet, Mable. But it seems that you got to keep on drawin it all the time. Then later I here footsteps. I was expectin the relief so I was right on the job. An a man come up and I poked my pistol right in his face an says Halt. Who goes there? And he says Officer of the day. An bein disappointed as who wouldnt be I says Oh hell. I thought it was the relief. An he objected to that. The relief, Mable — but whats the use you wouldnt understand it.

Theres some mistake up north about the way were built, Mable. Its kind of depresin to think that you could forget about us so quick. Everyones gettin sweters without sleeves and gloves without fingers. We still got everything we started with Mable. Why not sox without feet and pants without legs. If your makin these things for after the war I think your anticipatin a little. Besides its depresin for the fellos to be reminded all the time. Its like givin a fello a life membership to the Old Soldiers home to cheer him up when he sails. I was sayin the other day that if the fellos at Washington ever got onto this theyll be issuin soleles shoes and shirtles sleves.

Its gettin awful cold. No wonder this is a healthy place. All the germs is froze. I guess there idea of the hardenin proces is to freeze a fello stiff. The Captain said the other day we was gettin in tents of trainin. Thats all right but Id kind of like to see those fellos that go swimmin in the ice in winter. I guess thed like our shouer baths. They say Cleanliness is next to Godliness, Mable. I say its next to impossible.

I started this letter almost a weak ago. I just found it in my bakin can. They call it a bakin can but its too small to bake nothin. I keep my soap in it. I got some news for you. The regiment is to be dismantled. The Captain called me over this mornin and asked me where Id like to be transferred. I said home if it was the same to him. So there goin to send me to the artillery. This is a very dangerous and useful limb of the servus, Mable. I dont know my address. Just write me care of the General.

I got the red muffler that your mother sent me. Give her my love just the same

yours relentlessly,
Bill.

✗

Mon Cherry Mable:

Thats the way the French begin there love letters. Its perfectly proper. I would have rote you sooner but me an my fountin pens been froze for a week. Washington will never know how lucky he was that he got assigned to valley Forge instead of here. It got us out of drill for a couple of days. Thats somethin. I guess Id rather freeze than drill. Its awful when they make you do both though.

Two of my men has gone home on furlos. Me bein corperal I took all there blankets. The men didnt like it but I got a squad of men to look out for an my first duty is to keep fit. Duty first. Thats me all over. I got so many blankets now that I got to put a book mark in the place I get in at night or Id never find it again.

We spent most of our time tryin to find somethin to burn up in the Sibly stoves. A sibly stove, Mable, is a piece of stove pipe built like the leg of a sailurs trowsers. Old man Sibly must have had a fine mind to think it out all by hisself. They say he got a patent on it. I guess that must have been a slack winter in Washington. The government gives us our wood but I guess that the man who decided how much it was goin to give us had an office in the Sandwitch Islands. I says the other day that if theyd dip our allowance in fusfrus wed at least have some matches, eh Mable? I'm the same old Bill, Mable. Crackin jokes an keepin everybody laffin when things is blackest.

I was scoutin round for wood today an burned up those military hair brushes your mother gave me when we came away. I told her theyd come in mighty handy some day.

They say a fello tried to take a shouer the other day. Before he could get out it froze round him. Like that fello in the bible who turned into a pillo of salt. They had to break the whole thing offen the pipe with him inside it and stand it in front of the stove. When it melted he finished his shouer an said he felt fine. Thats how hard were gettin, Mable.

I bought a book on Minor Tackticks the other day. Thats not about underaged tacks that live on ticks as you might suppose, Mable. Its the cience of movin bodies of men from one place to another. I thought it might tell of some way of gettin the squad out of bed in the morning but it doesnt. All the important stuff like that is camooflaged sos the Germans wont get onto it.

Camooflage is not a new kind of cheese Mable. Its a military term. Camooflage is French for cauliflower which is a disguised cabbage. It is the same thing as puttin powder on your face instead of washin it. You deceive Germans with it. For instance you paint a horse black and white stripes an a German comes along. He thinks its a picket fence an goes right by. Or you paint yourself like a tree an the Germans come an drink beer round you an tell military sekruts.

Well I guess its time to say Mery Xmas now Mable. I guess it wont be a very Mery Xmas withut me there, eh? Cheer up cause Im goin to think of you whenever I get time all day long. Im pretty busy nowdays. I got to watch the men work. It keeps a fello on the jump all the time. I like it though, Mable. Thats me all over. Isnt it?

Dont send me nothin for Christmas, Mable. I bought something for you but Im not going to tell you cause its a surprize. All that I can say is that it cost me four eighty seven ($4.87) which is more than I could afford. An its worth a lot more. But you know how I am with money. A spend drift. So dont send me anything please although I need an electric flash light, some cigarets, candy an one of them sox that you wear on your head. Ill spend my last sent on anyone I like but I dont want to be under no obligations. Independent. Thats me all over.

You might read this part to your mother. I dont want nothin from her ether.

Rite soon an plain, Mable, cause I dont get much chance to study.

Yours till the south is warm,

Bill.

Your mothers present cost me three seventy seven ($3.77).

✗

Mon Ami:

Sounds like a scourin pouder, doesnt it, Mable? As a matter of fact its the way a French lady talks to a fello shes awful fond of.

Im not an officer any more. I was just goin to resine anyways. The Captins been watchin me rise an he didnt like it. He knew I knew more than him as well as me. Always askin me questions. Id always tell him cause I knew he had a wife and children in Jersey City an so I was sorry for them. Soft. Thats me all over. But the other day when I was on guard duty he says, "Corperal, whats the General orders?" an I says, "Captin if you dont kno them now you never will and I wouldnt be doin no service to my country if I told you." Cold but civil, Mable. You kno how I can be.

The Captin just felt cheap an walked away. I kind of felt sorry for him. Almost told him so once or twice. Then I went on guard again. I go on guard a lot. The men like me to be corperal of the guard because when the relief goes out I take all there blankets an go right to sleep instead of standin outside an watchin them freeze. Men hate to be watched when they are freezin.

But I happened to be outside for some reason, goin to dinner I guess, an I saw the Colonel coming. I says "Turn out the guard." (No one really turns em out, Mable. They come out themselves.) The Colonel sees who it is an waves an says "Never mind the guard, Corperal." So I thanks him an goes back to the company an goes to bed.

As soon as the Captin sees that the Colonel is savin me up for over there he gets sore. His plan has been to kill me before we left here. He said he was goin to reduce me. Thats not the same way your father reduces when he cuts out beer with his meals an sits in a Turkish all day. I never said you will or you wont. Just waited till he got outside an thumbed my nose at him. High spirited. Thats me all over.

An English officer came over the other day an told us all about the war. He didnt quite finish it cause he only had three quarters of an hour.

They was quite a few things I didnt kno even at that. He said that the heavy artillery was commanded by the C.C.O.D.A. an the light artillery by the C.O.A. An theres a special N.C.O. who has nothin to do but look after the S.A.A. Just imagine, Mable. I wish Id studied chemistree more when I was in school. It would make things a lot easier for me now. Then he said that a man always got into his O.O. to observe the action of the 75s. These English are always great for dress an that formal stuff.

Im glad there tellin us this before we go over. It would have been awful embarassing to have tried to observe the action of the 75s in my B.V.Ds. I asked him if they had any trouble with the B.P.O.Es. When he left he said "Cheero." Without winkin a hair I says "Beevo." Same old Bill, eh Mable?

They said the other day that my name was on a list to go to school an learn all about liason. I said there wasnt much use in there doin that cause I was pretty well up on that stuff. At home, I says, I had a reputashun for a devil with the wimen. Nobody knows better than you, eh Mable? I guess thats a little over your head though, Mable. I try to be as simple as I can. If Im not just tell me.

Im ritin this letter with my shoes off. I hope youll excuse my bein so informal but Im havin the old trouble with my feet. They never been right since that winter I taught you to dance. I went to the doctor with them an he said to keep offen them as much as I could. So they put me to work scrubbin the mess shack on my hans and nees. I bet if a fello had both legs shot off theyd prop you up against the walk an put you peelin onions.

I got to quit now. They got a thing called retreat they have every night. I always like to be there just to show the Captin Im behind him regardless.

Im sendin you my pictur in a uniform pointin to an American flag. Its kind of simbolical the man said, if you know what that is. I thought youd like to put it on the mantle in a conspikuous place sos to have somethin to be proud of when your girl friend comes in to talk. Id ask you for your pictur only I havent got much room for that kind of thing down here.

yours exclusively

Bill.

Waiting

X

from *Three Soldiers*

by JOHN DOS PASSOS

At the brow of the hill they rested. Chrisfield sat on the red clay bank and looked about him, his rifle between his knees. In front of him on the side of the road was a French burying ground, where the little wooden crosses, tilting in every direction, stood up against the sky, and the bead wreaths glistened in the warm sunlight. All down the road as far as he could see was a long drab worm, broken in places by strings of motor trucks, a drab worm that wriggled down the slope, through the roofless shell of the village and up into the shattered woods on the crest of the next hills. Chrisfield strained his eyes to see the hills beyond. They lay blue and very peaceful in the noon mist. The river glittered about the piers of the wrecked stone bridge, and disappeared between rows of yellow poplars. Somewhere in the valley a big gun fired. The shell shrieked into the distance, towards the blue, peaceful hills.

Chrisfield's regiment was moving again. The men, their feet slipping in the clayey mud, went downhill with long strides, the straps of their packs tugging at their shoulders.

"Isn't this great country?" said Andrews, who marched beside him.

"Ah'd liever be at an O.T.C. like that bastard Anderson."

"Oh, to hell with that," said Andrews. He still had a big faded orange marigold in one of the buttonholes of his soiled tunic. He walked with his nose in the air and his nostrils dilated, enjoying the tang of the autumnal sunlight.

Chrisfield took the cigarette, that had gone out half-smoked, from his mouth and spat savagely at the heels of the man in front of him.

"This ain't no life for a white man," he said.

"I'd rather be this than . . . than that," said Andrews bitterly. He tossed his head in the direction of a staff car full of officers that was stalled at the side of the road. They were drinking something out of a Thermos bottle that they passed round with the air of Sunday excursionists. They waved, with a conscious relaxation of discipline, at the men as they passed. One, a little lieutenant with a black mustache with pointed ends, kept

crying: "They're running like rabbits, fellers; they're running like rabbits."
A wavering half-cheer would come from the column now and then where
it was passing the staff car.

The big gun fired again. Chrisfield was near it this time and felt the
concussion like a blow in the head.

"Some baby," said the man behind him.

Someone was singing:

> "Good morning, Mister Zip Zip Zip,
> With your hair cut just as short as,
> With your hair cut just as short as,
> With your hair cut just as short as mi-ine."

Everybody took it up. Their steps rang in rhythm in the paved street that
zigzagged among the smashed houses of the village. Ambulances passed
them, big trucks full of huddled men with gray faces, from which came
a smell of sweat and blood and carbolic.

Somebody went on:

> "O ashes to ashes
> An' dust to dust . . ."

"Can that," cried Judkins, "it ain't lucky."

But everybody had taken up the song. Chrisfield noticed that Andrews's eyes were sparkling. "If he ain't the damnedest," he thought to
himself. But he shouted at the top of his lungs with the rest:

> "O ashes to ashes
> An' dust to dust;
> If the gasbombs don't get yer
> The eighty-eights must."

They were climbing the hill again. The road was worn into deep ruts
and there were many shell holes, full of muddy water, into which their feet
slipped. The woods began, a shattered skeleton of woods, full of old
artillery emplacements and dugouts, where torn camouflage fluttered from
splintered trees. The ground and the road were littered with tin cans
and brass shell-cases. Along both sides of the road the trees were festooned,
as with creepers, with strand upon strand of telephone wire.

When next they stopped Chrisfield was on the crest of the hill beside a
battery of French seventy-fives. He looked curiously at the Frenchmen,
who sat about on logs in their pink and blue shirt-sleeves playing cards
and smoking. Their gestures irritated him.

"Say, tell 'em we're advancin'," he said to Andrews.

"Are we?" said Andrews. "All right. . . . Dites-donc, les Boches cour-
rent-ils comme des lapins?" he shouted.

One of the men turned his head and laughed.

"He says they've been running that way for four years," said Andrews. He slipped his pack off, sat down on it, and fished for a cigarette. Chrisfield took off his helmet and rubbed a muddy hand through his hair. He took a bite of chewing tobacco and sat with his hands clasped over his knees.

"How the hell long are we going to wait this time?" he muttered. The shadows of the tangled and splintered trees crept slowly across the road. The French artillerymen were eating their supper. A long train of motor trucks growled past, splashing mud over the men crowded along the sides of the road. The sun set, and a lot of batteries down in the valley began firing, making it impossible to talk. The air was full of a shrieking and droning of shells overhead. The Frenchmen stretched and yawned and went down into their dugout. Chrisfield watched them enviously. The stars were beginning to come out in the green sky behind the tall lacerated trees. Chrisfield's legs ached with cold. He began to get crazily anxious for something to happen, for something to happen, but the column waited, without moving, through the gathering darkness. Chrisfield chewed steadily, trying to think of nothing but the taste of the tobacco in his mouth.

The column was moving again; as they reached the brow of another hill Chrisfield felt a curious sweetish smell that made his nostrils smart. "Gas," he thought, full of panic, and put his hand to the mask that hung round his neck. But he did not want to be the first to put it on. No order came. He marched on, cursing the sergeant and the lieutenant. But maybe they'd been killed by it. He had a vision of the whole regiment sinking down in the road suddenly, overcome by the gas.

"Smell anythin', Andy?" he whispered cautiously.

"I can smell a combination of dead horses and tuberoses and banana oil and the ice cream we used to have at college and dead rats in the garret, but what the hell do we care now?" said Andrews, giggling. "This is the damndest fool business ever. . . ."

"He's crazy," muttered Chrisfield to himself. He looked at the stars in the black sky that seemed to be going along with the column on its march. Or was it that they and the stars were standing still while the trees moved away from them, waving their skinny shattered arms? He could hardly hear the tramp of feet on the road, so loud was the pandemonium of the guns ahead and behind. Every now and then a rocket would burst in front of them and its red and green lights would mingle for a moment with the stars. But it was only overhead he could see the stars. Everywhere else white and red glows rose and fell as if the horizon were on fire.

As they started down the slope, the trees suddenly broke away and they saw the valley between them full of the glare of guns and the white light of star shells. It was like looking into a stove full of glowing embers. The hillside that sloped away from them was full of crashing detonations and yellow tongues of flame. In a battery near the road, that seemed to crush their skulls each time a gun fired, they could see the dark forms of the artillerymen silhouetted in fantastic attitudes against the intermittent red glare. Stunned and blinded, they kept on marching down the road. It seemed to Chrisfield that they were going to step any minute into the flaring muzzle of a gun.

At the foot of the hill, beside a little grove of uninjured trees, they stopped again. A new train of trucks was crawling past them, huge blots in the darkness. There were no batteries near, so they could hear the grinding roar of the gears as the trucks went along the uneven road, plunging in and out of shellholes.

Chrisfield lay down in the dry ditch, full of bracken, and dozed with his head on his pack. All about him were stretched other men. Someone was resting his head on Chrisfield's thigh. The noise had subsided a little. Through his doze he could hear men's voices talking in low crushed tones, as if they were afraid of speaking aloud. On the road the truck drivers kept calling out to each other shrilly, raspingly. The motors stopped running one after another, making almost a silence, during which Chrisfield fell asleep.

Something woke him. He was stiff with cold and terrified. For a moment he thought he had been left alone, that the company had gone on, for there was no one touching him.

Overhead was a droning as of gigantic mosquitoes, growing fast to a loud throbbing. He heard the lieutenant's voice calling shrilly:

"Sergeant Higgins, Sergeant Higgins!"

The lieutenant stood out suddenly black against a sheet of flame. Chrisfield could see his fatigue cap a little on one side and his trench coat, drawn in tight at the waist and sticking out stiffly at the knees. He was shaken by the explosion. Everything was black again. Chrisfield got to his feet, his ears ringing. The column was moving on. He heard moaning near him in the darkness. The tramp of feet and jingle of equipment drowned all other sound. He could feel his shoulders becoming raw under the tugging of the pack. Now and then the flare from aeroplane bombs behind him showed up wrecked trucks on the side of the road. Somewhere a machine gun spluttered. But the column tramped on, weighed down by the packs, by the deadening exhaustion.

The turbulent flaring darkness was calming to the gray of dawn when Chrisfield stopped marching. His eyelids stung and his eyeballs were flaming hot. He could not feel his feet and legs. The guns continued incessantly like a hammer beating on his head. He was walking very slowly in a single file, now and then stumbling against the man ahead of him. There was earth on both sides of him, clay walls that dripped moisture. All at once he stumbled down some steps into a dugout, where it was pitch-black. An unfamiliar smell struck him, made him uneasy; but his thoughts seemed to reach him from out of a great distance. He groped to the wall. His knees struck against a bunk with blankets in it. In another second he was sunk fathoms deep in sleep.

When he woke up his mind was very clear. The roof of the dugout was of logs. A bright spot far away was the door. He hoped desperately that he wasn't on duty. He wondered where Andy was; then he remembered that Andy was crazy — "a yaller dawg," Judkins had called him. Sitting up with difficulty he undid his shoes and puttees, wrapped himself in his blanket. All round him were snores and the deep breathing of exhausted sleep. He closed his eyes.

He was being court-martialed. He stood with his hands at his sides before three officers at a table. All three had the same white faces with heavy blue jaws and eyebrows that met above the nose. They were reading things out of papers aloud, but, although he strained his ears, he couldn't make out what they were saying. All he could hear was a faint moaning. Something had a curious unfamiliar smell that troubled him. He could not stand still at attention, although the angry eyes of officers stared at him from all round. "Anderson, Sergeant Anderson, what's that smell?" he kept asking in a small whining voice. "Please tell a feller what that smell is." But the three officers at the table kept reading from their papers, and the moaning grew louder and louder in his ears until he shrieked aloud. There was a grenade in his hand. He pulled the string out and threw it, and he saw the lieutenant's trench coat stand out against a sheet of flame. Someone sprang at him. He was wrestling for his life with Anderson, who turned into a woman with huge flabby breasts. He crushed her to him and turned to defend himself against three officers who came at him, their trench coats drawn in tightly at the waist until they looked like wasps. Everything faded, he woke up.

His nostrils were still full of the strange troubling smell. He sat on the edge of the bunk, wriggling in his clothes, for his body crawled with lice.

"Gee, it's funny to be in where the Fritzies were not long ago," he heard a voice say.

"Kiddo! We're advancin'," came another voice.

"But, hell, this ain't no kind of an advance. I ain't seen a German yet."

"Ah kin smell 'em though," said Chrisfield, getting suddenly to his feet.

Sergeant Higgins's head appeared in the door. "Fall in," he shouted. Then he added in his normal voice, "It's up and at 'em, fellers."

Chrisfield caught his puttee on a clump of briers at the edge of the clearing and stood kicking his leg back and forth to get it free. At last he broke away, the torn puttee dragging behind him. Out in the sunlight in the middle of the clearing he saw a man in olive-drab kneeling beside something on the ground. A German lay face down with a red hole in his back. The man was going through his pockets. He looked up into Chrisfield's face.

"Souvenirs," he said.

"What outfit are you in, buddy?"

"143rd," said the man, getting to his feet slowly.

"Where the hell are we?"

"Damned if I know."

The clearing was empty, except for the two Americans and the German with the hole in his back. In the distance they heard a sound of artillery and nearer the "put, put, put" of isolated machine guns. The leaves of the trees about them, all shades of brown and crimson and yellow, danced in the sunlight.

"Say, that damn money ain't no good, is it?" asked Chrisfield.

"German money? Hell, no. . . . I got a watch that's a peach though." The man held out a gold watch, looking suspiciously at Chrisfield all the while through half-closed eyes.

"Ah saw a feller had a gold-handled sword," said Chrisfield.

"Where's that?"

"Back there in the wood"; he waved his hand vaguely. "Ah've got to find ma outfit; comin' along?" Chrisfield started towards the other edge of the clearing.

"Looks to me all right here," said the other man, lying down on the grass in the sun.

The leaves rustled underfoot as Chrisfield strode through the wood. He was frightened by being alone. He walked ahead as fast as he could, his puttee still dragging behind him. He came to a barbed-wire entanglement half embedded in fallen beech leaves. It had been partly cut in one place, but in crossing he tore his thigh on a barb. Taking off the torn puttee, he wrapped it round the outside of his trousers and kept on walking, feeling a little blood trickle down his leg.

Later he came to a lane that cut straight through the wood where there were many ruts through the putty-colored mud puddles. Down the lane in a patch of sunlight he saw a figure, towards which he hurried. It was a young man with red hair and a pink-and-white face. By a gold bar on the collar of his shirt Chrisfield saw that he was a lieutenant. He had no coat or hat and there was greenish slime all over the front of his clothes as if he had lain on his belly in a mud puddle.

"Where you going?"

"Dunno, sir."

"All right, come along." The lieutenant started walking as fast as he could up the lane, swinging his arms wildly.

"Seen any machine-gun nests?"

"Not a one."

"Hum."

He followed the lieutenant, who walked so fast he had difficulty keeping up, splashing recklessly through the puddles.

"Where's the artillery? That's what I want to know," cried the lieutenant, suddenly stopping in his tracks and running a hand through his red hair. "Where the hell's the artillery?" He looked at Chrisfield savagely out of green eyes. "No use advancing without artillery." He started walking faster than ever.

All at once they saw sunlight ahead of them and olive-drab uniforms. Machine guns started firing all round them in a sudden gust. Chrisfield found himself running forward across a field full of stubble and sprouting clover among a group of men he did not know. The whiplike sound of rifles had chimed in with the stuttering of the machine guns. Little white clouds sailed above him in a blue sky, and in front of him was a group of houses that had the same color, white with lavender-gray shadows, as the clouds.

He was in a house, with a grenade like a tin pineapple in each hand. The sudden loneliness frightened him again. Outside the house was a sound of machine-gun firing, broken by the occasional bursting of a shell. He looked at the red-tiled floor and at a chromo of a woman nursing a child that hung on the whitewashed wall opposite him. He was in a small kitchen. There was a fire in the hearth where something boiled in a black pot. Chrisfield tiptoed over and looked in. At the bottom of the bubbling water he saw five potatoes. At the other end of the kitchen, beyond two broken chairs, was a door. Chrisfield crept over to it, the tiles seeming to sway underfoot. He put his finger to the latch and took it off again suddenly. Holding in his breath he stood a long time looking at the door. Then he pulled it open recklessly. A young man with fair hair was sitting at a table, his head resting on his hands. Chrisfield felt a spurt of joy when he saw that the man's uniform was green. Very coolly he pressed the spring, held the grenade a second and then threw it, throwing himself backwards into the middle of the kitchen. The light-haired man had not moved; his blue eyes still stared straight before him.

In the street Chrisfield ran into a tall man who was running. The man clutched him by the arm and said:

"The barrage is moving up."

"What barrage?"

"Our barrage; we've got to run, we're ahead of it." His voice came in wheezy pants. There were red splotches on his face. They ran together down the empty village street. As they ran they passed the little red-haired lieutenant, who leaned against a whitewashed wall, his legs a mass of blood and torn cloth. He was shouting in a shrill delirious voice that followed them out along the open road.

"Where's the artillery? That's what I want to know; where's the artillery?"

The woods were gray and dripping with dawn. Chrisfield got stiffly to his feet from the pile of leaves where he had slept. He felt numb with cold and hunger, lonely and lost away from his outfit. All about him were men of another division. A captain with a sandy mustache was striding up and down with a blanket about him, on the road just behind a clump of beech trees. Chrisfield had watched him passing back and forth, back and forth, behind the wet clustered trunks of the trees, ever since it had been light. Stamping his feet among the damp leaves, Chrisfield strolled away from the group of men. No one seemed to notice him. The trees closed about him. He could see nothing but moist trees, gray-green and black, and the yellow leaves of saplings that cut off the view in every direction. He was wondering dully why he was walking off that way. Somewhere in the back of his mind there was a vague idea of finding his outfit. Sergeant Higgins and Andy and Judkins and Small — he wondered what had become of them. He thought of the company lined up for mess, and the smell of greasy food that came from the field-kitchen. He was desperately hungry. He stopped and leaned against the moss-covered trunk of a tree. The deep scratch in his leg was throbbing as if all the blood in his body beat through it. Now that his rustling footsteps had ceased, the woods were absolutely silent, except for the dripping of dew from the leaves and branches. He strained his ears to hear some other sound. Then he noticed that he was staring at a tree full of small red crab apples. He picked a handful greedily, but they were hard and sour and seemed to make him hungrier. The sour flavor in his mouth made him furiously angry. He kicked at the thin trunk of the tree while tears smarted in his eyes. Swearing aloud in a whining singsong voice, he strode off through the woods with his eyes on the ground. Twigs snapped viciously in his face, crooked branches caught at him, but he plunged on. All at once he stumbled against something hard that bounced among the leaves.

He stopped still, looking about him, terrified. Two grenades lay just under his foot; a little further on a man was propped against a tree with his mouth open. Chrisfield thought at first he was asleep, as his eyes were closed. He looked at the grenades carefully. The fuses had not been sprung. He put one in each pocket, gave a glance at the man who seemed to be asleep, and strode off again, striking another alley in the woods, at the end of which he could see sunlight. The sky overhead was full of heavy purple clouds, tinged here and there with yellow. As he walked towards the patch of sunlight, the thought came to him that he ought to have looked in the pockets of the man he had just passed to see if he had any hard bread. He stood still a moment in hesitation, but started walking again doggedly towards the patch of sunlight.

Something glittered in the irregular fringe of sun and shadow. A man was sitting hunched up on the ground with his fatigue cap pulled over his eyes so that the little gold bar just caught the horizontal sunlight. Chrisfield's first thought was that he might have food on him.

"Say, Lootenant," he shouted, "d'you know where a fellow can get somethin' to eat."

The man lifted his head slowly. Chrisfield turned cold all over when he saw the white heavy face of Anderson; an unshaven beard was very black on his square chin; there was a long scratch clotted with dried blood from the heavy eyebrow across the left cheek to the corner of the mouth.

"Give me some water, buddy," said Anderson in a weak voice.

Chrisfield handed him his canteen roughly in silence. He noticed that Anderson's arm was in a sling, and that he drank greedily, spilling the water over his chin and his wounded arm.

"Where's Colonel Evans?" asked Anderson in a thin petulant voice.

Chrisfield did not reply but stared at him sullenly. The canteen had dropped from his hand and lay on the ground in front of him. The water gleamed in the sunlight as it ran out among the russet leaves. A wind had come up, making the woods resound. A shower of yellow leaves dropped about them.

"First you was a corporal, then you was a sergeant, and now you're a lootenant," said Chrisfield slowly.

"You'd better tell me where Colonel Evans is. . . . You must know. . . . He's up that road somewhere," said Anderson, struggling to get to his feet.

Chrisfield walked away without answering. A cold hand was round the grenade in his pocket. He walked away slowly, looking at his feet.

Suddenly he found he had pressed the spring of the grenade. He struggled to pull it out of his pocket. It stuck in the narrow pocket. His arm and his cold fingers that clutched the grenade seemed paralyzed. Then a warm joy went through him. He had thrown it.

Anderson was standing up, swaying backwards and forwards. The explosion made the woods quake. A thick rain of yellow leaves came down. Anderson was flat on the ground. He was so flat he seemed to have sunk into the ground.

Chrisfield pressed the spring of the other grenade and threw it with his eyes closed. It burst among the thick new-fallen leaves.

A few drops of rain were falling. Chrisfield kept on along the lane, walking fast, feeling full of warmth and strength. The rain beat hard and cold against his back.

He walked with his eyes to the ground. A voice in a strange language stopped him. A ragged man in green with a beard that was clotted with mud stood in front of him with his hands up. Chrisfield burst out laughing.

"Come along," he said, "quick!"

The man shambled in front of him; he was trembling so hard he nearly fell with each step.

Chrisfield kicked him.

The man shambled on without turning round. Chrisfield kicked him again, feeling the point of the man's spine and the soft flesh of his thighs against his toes with each kick, laughing so hard all the while that he could hardly see where he was going.

"Halt!" came a voice.

"Ah've got a prisoner," shouted Chrisfield still laughing.

"He ain't much of a prisoner," said the man, pointing his bayonet at the German. "He's gone crazy, I guess. I'll take keer o' him . . . ain't no use sendin' him back."

"All right," said Chrisfield still laughing. "Say, buddy, where can Ah git something to eat? Ah ain't had nothin' fur a day an a half."

"There's a reconnoiterin' squad up the line; they'll give you somethin'. . . . How's things goin' up that way?" The man pointed up the road.

"Gawd, Ah doan know. Ah ain't had nothin' to eat fur a day and a half."

The warm smell of a stew rose to his nostrils from the mess kit. Chrisfield stood, feeling warm and important, filling his mouth with soft greasy potatoes and gravy, while men about him asked him questions. Gradually he began to feel full and content, and a desire to sleep came over him. But he was given a gun, and had to start advancing again with the reconnoitering squad. The squad went cautiously up the same lane through the woods.

"Here's an officer done for," said the captain, who walked ahead. He made a little clucking noise of distress with his tongue. "Two of you fellows go back and git a blanket and take him back to the crossroads. Poor fellow." The captain walked on again, still making little clucking noises with his tongue.

Chrisfield looked straight ahead of him. He did not feel lonely any more now that he was marching in ranks again. His feet beat the ground in time with the other feet. He would not have to think whether to go to the right or to the left. He would do as the others did.

The Wildcat

X

by ALBERT PAYSON TERHUNE

When Cassius Wyble came down from his mountains to the 2000-population metropolis of Clayburg on his half-yearly trip for supplies, he thought the old custom of Muster Day had been revived. No fewer than eleven men in khaki were lounging round the station platform or sitting on the steps of the North America general store. Enlistment posters, too, flared from windows and walls.

These posters — except for their pretty pictures — meant nothing at all to Cash Wyble. For, as with his parents and grandparents, his knowledge of the written or printed word was purely a matter of hearsay.

Yet the sight of the eleven men in newfangled uniform — so like in color to his own butternut homespuns — interested Cash. "What's all the boys doin' — togged up thataway?" he demanded of the North America's proprietor. "Waitin' for the band?"

"Waiting to be shipped to Camp Lee," answered the local merchant prince, adding, as Cash's burnt-leather face grew blanker, "Camp Lee, down in Virginia, you know. Training camp for the war."

"War?" queried Cash, preparing to grin, at prospect of a joke. "What war?"

"What war?" echoed the dumfounded storekeeper. "Why, *the* war, of course! Where in blazes have you been keeping yourself?"

"I been up home, where I belong," said Cash sulkily. "What with the hawgs, an' crops an' skins an' sich, a busy man's got no time traipsin' off to the city every minute. Twice a year does me pretty nice. An' now suppose you tell me what war you're blattin' about."

The storekeeper told him. He told him in the simplest possible language. Yet half — and more than half — of the explanation went miles above the listening mountaineer's head. Cash gathered, however, that the United States was fighting Germany.

Germany he knew by repute for a country or a town on the far side of the world. Some of its citizens had even invaded his West Virginia mountains, where their odd diction and porcelain pipes roused much derision among the cultured hill folk.

"Germany?" mused Cash, when the narrative was ended. "We're to war with Germany, hey? Sakes, but I wished I'd knowed that yesterday! A couple of Germans went right past my shack. I could a shot 'em as easy as toad pie."

The North America's proprietor valued Cash Wyble's sparse trade, as he valued that of other mountaineers who made Clayburg their semi-annual port of call. If on Cash's report these rustics should begin a guerilla warfare upon their German neighbors, more of them would presently be lodged in jail than the North America could well afford to spare from its meager customer list.

Wherefore the proprietor did some more explaining. Knowing the mountaineer brain, he made no effort to point out the difference between armed Germans and noncombatants. He merely said that the government had threatened to lock up any West Virginian who should kill a German — this side of Europe. It was a new law, he continued, and one that the revenue officers were bent on enforcing.

Cash sighed and reluctantly bade farewell to an alluring dream that had begun to shape itself in his simple brain — a dream of "laying out" in cliff-top brush, waiting with true elephant patience until a German neighbor should stroll, unsuspecting, along the trail below and should move slowly within range of the antique Wyble rifle.

It was a sweet fantasy, and hard to banish. For Cash certainly could shoot. There was scarce a man in the Cumberlands or the Appalachians who could outshoot him. Shooting and a native knack at moonshining were Cash's only real accomplishments. Whether stalking a shy old stag or potting a revenue officer on the skyline, the man's aim was uncannily true. In a region of born marksmen his skill stood forth supreme.

He felt not the remotest hatred for any of these local Germans. In an impersonal way he rather liked one or two of them. Yet, if the law had really been off . . .

The zest of the manhunt tingled pleasantly in the marksman's blood. And he resented this unfair new revenue ruling, which permitted and even encouraged the killing of Germans in Europe and yet ordained a closed season on them in West Virginia. Still, there was no sense in a busy man's risking jail or a fine by indulging his sporting tastes. So Cash tried to forget the temptation, and proceeded to the more material task of trafficking for his next half-year's supplies.

A few months later the draft caught Cash Wyble and carried him away in its swirling flood, depositing him in due time, with a quantity of similar mountaineer flotsam, in the training mill of Camp Lee.

No half-grown wildcat dragged by the scruff of the neck from the sanctuary of its tree hole was ever one-tenth so ragingly indignant as was Cash at his impressment into his country's service. Born and bred of fellow illiterates in the wildest corner of the Cumberland Range, thirty-two miles from the nearest railroad, he knew nothing and cared less about the affairs of the world that lay beyond the circling blue mountain walls.

To Cash all persons who lived outside that circle were foreigners, even if their habitat was the adjoining county of his own state. He had heard of England and of France and of Europe, in much the same vague fashion as he had heard of Germany. He knew the name of the President of the United States; of the governor of West Virginia; of the mayor of Clayburg. Also of the political party whose ticket his father had always voted, and which Cash, in consequence, voted. He knew there had been a Civil War and — from pictures and from paternal description — he knew the types of uniforms each side had worn. The foregoing facts comprised his total knowledge of American politics and of world history.

As to the causes and the occasion and the stakes of the present war, he had not an inkling. Nor could the explanations of slightly better-informed recruits make the matter much clearer to him. It most certainly roused no trace of enthusiasm or of patriotism in his indignant breast. All he knew or was interested in was that he had been forced to leave his shack and his straggly mountainside farm and his hidden moonshine still, at the very worst possible season for leaving any of them.

He had been coerced into riding innumerable miles to a foreign state that seemed all bottomland, and there was herded with more men than he had known were on earth. He had been dressed in an amazing suit; made to wear socks and underclothes for the first time in his life; and daily put through a series of physical evolutions whose import was a sealed book to him. In all weathers, too, he must wear shoes.

Like the aforesaid caught wildcat, Cash Wyble rebelled at every inch of the way. For his first two months of captivity he spent more time in the guardhouse than out of it. On his first day at camp he tried to thrash a lieutenant who was lining up a rawly shambling company and who spoke with unwelcomed sharpness to the mountaineer. Scarce had Cash atoned for this crime when he succeeded in giving a very creditable thrashing to a sergeant who was teaching his squad the mysteries of about face.

Hearing that the nearby city of Petersburg was larger than Clayburg — which he knew to be the biggest metropolis in America — Cash set out to nail the lie by a personal inspection of Petersburg. He neglected to apply for leave, so was held up by the first sentinel he met.

Cash explained very politely his reason for quitting camp. But the pig-headed sentinel still refused to let him pass. Two minutes later a fast-summoned corporal and two men were using all their strength to pry Wyble loose from the luckless sentry. And again the guardhouse had Cash as a transient and blasphemous guest.

He was learning much more of kitchen-police work than of guard mount. At the latter task he was a failure. The first night he was assigned to beat pacing, the relief found him restfully snoring, on his back, his rifle stuck up in front of him by means of his bayonet thrust into the ground. Cash had seen no good reason why he should walk to and fro for hours when there was nothing exciting to watch for and when he had been awake since early morning. Therefore he had gone to sleep. And his subsequent guardhouse stay filled him with uncomprehending fury.

The salute, too, struck him as the height of absurdity — as a bit of tom-foolery in which he would have no part. Not that he was exclusive, but what was the use of touching one's forelock to some officer one had never before met? He was willing to nod pleasantly and even to say "Howdy, Cap?" when his company captain passed by him for the first time in the morning. But he saw no use in repeating that or any other form of salutation when the same captain chanced to meet him a bare fifteen minutes later.

Cash Wyble's case was not in any way unique among Camp Lee's thirty thousand new soldiers. Hundreds of mountaineers were in still worse mental plight. And the tact as well as the skill of their officers was strained well-nigh to the breaking point in shaping the amorphous backwoods rabble into trim soldiers.

Not all members of the mountain draft were so fiercely resentful as was Cash. But many others of them were like unbroken colts. The strange frequency of washing and of shaving and the wearing of underclothes were their chief puzzles.

The company captain labored with Cash again and again, pointing out the need of neat cleanliness, of promptitude, of vigilance; trying to make him understand that a salute is not a sign of servility; seeking to imbue him with the spirit of patriotism and of discipline. But to Cash the whole thing was infinitely worse and more bewildering than had been the six months he had once spent in Clayburg jail for mayhem.

Three things alone mitigated his misery at Camp Lee: the first was the shooting; the second was his monthly pay — which represented more real money than he ever had had in his pocket at any one time; the third was the food — amazing in its abundance and luxurious variety to the always hungry mountaineer.

But presently the target shooting palled. As soon as he had mastered

carefully the intricacies of the queer new rifle they gave him, the hours
at the range were no more inspiring to him than would be, to Paderewski,
the eternal playing of the scale of C with one finger.

To Cash, the target shooting was child's play. Once he grasped the rules
as to sights and elevations and became used to the feel of the army
rifle, the rest was drearily simple. He could outshoot practically every
man at Camp Lee. This gave him no pride. He made himself popular
with men who complimented him on it by assuring them modestly that
he outshot them not because he was such a dead shot but because they
shot so badly.

The headiest colt in time will learn the lesson of the breaking pen. And
Cash Wyble gradually became a soldier. At least he learned the drill and
the regulations and how to keep out of the guardhouse — except just after
payday; and his lank figure took on a certain military spruceness. But under
the surface he was still Cash Wyble. He behaved, because there was no in-
centive at the camp that made disobedience worth while.

Then after an endless winter came the journey to the seaboard and the
embarkation for France; and the awesome sight of a tossing gray ocean a
hundred times wider and rougher than Clayburg River in freshet time. Followed a week of agonized terror, mingled with an acute longing to die.
Then ensued a week of calm water, during which one might refill the
oft-emptied inner man.

A few days later Cash was bumping along a newly repaired French railway in a car whose announced capacity was forty men or eight horses.
And thence to billet in a half-wrecked village, where his regiment was
drilled and redrilled in the things they had toiled so hard at Camp Lee
to master, and in much that was novel to the men.

Cash next came to a halt in a network of trenches overlooking a
stretch of country that had been tortured into hideousness — a region
that looked like a Doré nightmare. It was a waste of hillocks and gullies
and shellholes and blasted big trees and frayed copses and split boulders
and seared vegetation. When Cash heard it was called no man's land
he was not surprised. He well understood why no man — not even an
ignorant foreigner — cared to buy such a tract.

He was far more interested in hearing that a tangle of trenches, somewhat like his regiment's own, lay three miles northeastward, at the limit
of no man's land, and that those trenches were infested with Germans.

Germans were the people Cash Wyble had come all the way to France to
kill. And once more the thrill of the manhunt swept pleasantly through
his blood. He had no desire to risk prison. So he had made very certain
by repeated inquiry that this particular section of France was in Europe;
and that no part of it was within the boundaries or the jurisdiction of the
sovereign state of West Virginia. Here, therefore, the law was off on Ger-

mans, and he could not get into the slightest trouble with the hated
revenue officers by shooting as many of the foe as he could go out and
find.

Cash enjoyed the picture he conjured up — a picture of a whole bevy
of Germans seated at ease in a trench, smoking porcelain pipes and con-
versing with one another in comically broken English; of himself stealing
toward them, and from the shelter of one of those hillock boulders
opening a mortal fire on the unsuspecting foreigners.

It was a quaint thought, and one that Cash loved to play with. Also it
had an advantage that most of Cash's vivid mind pictures had not. For, in
part, it came true.

The Germans, on the thither side of no man's land, seemed bent on
jarring the repose and wrenching the nerve of their lately arrived Yankee
neighbors. Not only were those veteran official entertainers Minnie and
Bertha, and their equally vocal artillery sisters, called into service for the
purpose, but a dense swarm of snipers was also impressed into the task.

Now this especial reach of no man's land was a veritable snipers' para-
dise. There was cover — plenty of it — everywhere. A hundred sharpshooters of any scouting prowess at all could deploy at will amid the tumble of
boulders and knolls and twisted tree trunks and battered foliage and craters.

The long spell of wet weather had precluded the burning away of
undergrowth. There were treetops and hill summits whence a splendid
shot could be taken at unwary Americans in the lower front-line trenches
and along the rising ground at the rear of the Yankee lines. Yes, it was a
stretch of ground laid out for the joy of snipers. And the German sharpshooters took due advantage of this bit of luck. The whine of a high-power
bullet was certain to follow the momentary exposure of any portion
of khaki anatomy above or behind the parapets. And in disgustingly many
instances the bullet did not whine in vain. All of which kept the newcomers from getting any excess joy out of trench life.

To mitigate the annoyance there was a call for volunteer sharpshooters
to scout cautiously through no man's land and seen to render the Boche
sniping a less safe and exhilarating sport than thus far it had been. The
job was full of peril, of course. For there was a more than even chance
of the Yankee snipers' being sniped by the rival sharpshooters, who were
better acquainted with the ground.

Yet at the first call there was a clamorous throng of volunteers. Many
of these volunteers admitted under pressure that they knew nothing of
scout work and that they had not so much as qualified in marksmanship.
But they craved a chance at the Boche. And grouchily did they resent the
swift weeding-out process that left their services uncalled for.

Cash Wyble was the first man accepted for the dangerous detail. And
for the first time since the draft had caught him his burnt-leather face

expanded into a grin that could not have been wider unless his flaring ears had been set back.

With two days' rations and a goodly store of cartridges he fared forth that night into no man's land. Dawn was not yet fully gray when the first crack of his rifle was wafted back to the trenches. Then the artillery firing, which was part of the day's work, set in. And its racket drowned the noise of any shooting that Cash might be at.

Forty-eight hours passed. At dawn of the third day Cash came back to camp. He was tired and horribly thirsty; but his lantern-jawed visage was one unmarred mask of bliss.

"Twelve," he reported tersely to his captain. "At least," he continued in greater detail, "twelve that I'm dead sure of. Nice big ones, too, some of 'em."

"Nice big ones!" repeated the captain in admiring disgust. "You talk as if you'd been after wild turkeys!"

"A heap better'n wild-turkey shootin'!" said Cash with a grin. "An' I got twelve that I'm sure of. There was one, though, I couldn't get. A he-one, at that. He's sure some German, that feller! He's as crafty as they make 'em. I couldn't ever come up to him or get a line on him. I'll bet I threwed away thirty cartridges on just that one Dutchy. An' by-an'-by he found out what I was after. Then there was fun, Cap! Him and I did have one fine shootin' match! But I was as good at hidin' as he was. And there couldn't neither one of us seem to get to the other. Most of the rest of 'em was as easy to get as a settin' hen. But not him. I'd a laid out there longer for a crack at him, but I couldn't find no water. If there'd been a spring or a water seep anywheres there I'd a stayed till dooms-day but what I'd a got him. Soon's I fill up with some water I'm goin' back after him. He's well worth it. I'll bet that cuss don't weigh an ounce under two hundred pound."

Cash's smug joy in his exploit and his keen anticipation of a return trip were dashed by the captain's reminder that war is not a hunting jaunt; and that Wyble must return to his loathed trench duties until such time as it should seem wise to those above him to send him forth again.

Cash could not make head or tail out of such a command. After months of grinding routine he had at last found a form of recreation that not only dulled his sharply constant homesickness but made up for all he had gone through. And now he was told he could go forth on such delightful excursions only when he might chance to be sent!

Red wrath boiled hot in the soul of Cash Wyble. Experience had taught him the costly folly of venting such rage on a commissioned officer. So he hunted up Top Sergeant Mahan of his own company and laid his griefs before that patient veteran.

Top Sergeant Mahan — formerly of the regular army — listened with true sympathy to the complaint; and listened with open enthusiasm to the tale of the two days of forest skulking. But he could offer no help in the matter of returning to the battue.

"The cap'n was right," declared Mahan. "They wanted to throw a little lesson into those Boche snipers and make them ease up on their heckling. And you gave them a man's size dose of their own physic. There's not one sniper out there today, to ten who were on deck three days ago. You've done your job. And you've done it good and plenty. But it's done — for a while anyhow. You weren't brought over here to spend your time in prowling round no man's land on a still hunt for stray Germans. That isn't Uncle Sam's way. Don't go grouching over it, man! You'll be remembered, all right. And if they get pesky again, you'll be the first one sent out to abate them. You can count on it. Till then, go ahead with your regular work and forget the sniper job."

"But, Sarge!" pleaded Cash. "You don't get the idea. You don't get it at all. Those Germans will be shyer than scat, now that I've flushed 'em. An' the longer the news has a chance to get around among 'em, the shyer they're due to get. Why, even if I was to go out there straight off it ain't likely I'd be able to pot one where I potted three before. It's the same difference as it is between the first flushin' of a wild-turkey bunch an' the second. An' if I've got to wait long there'll be no downin' *any* of 'em. Tell that to the cap. Make him see if he wants them cusses he better let me get 'em while they're still gettable."

In vain did Top Sergeant Mahan go over and over the same ground, trying to make Cash see that the company captain and those above him were not out for a record in the matter of ambushed Germans.

Wyble had struck one idea he could understand, and he would not give it up. "But, Sarge," he urged desperately, "I'm no good here foolin' around with drill an' relief an' diggin' an' all that. Any mudback can do them things if you folks is set on havin' 'em done. But there ain't another man in all this outfit who can shoot like I can; or has the knack of 'layin' out'; or of stalkin'. Pop got the trick of it from Grandfather. An' Grandfather got it off the Injuns in the old days. If you folks is out to get Germans I'm the feller to git 'em for you. Nice big ones. If you're here just to play soldier, any poor fool can play it for you as good as me."

"I've just told you," began the sergeant, "that we —"

"Another thing!" suggested Cash brightly. "These Germans must have villages somewheres. All folks do. Even Injuns. Some place where they live when they ain't on the warpath. Get leave an' rations an' cartridges for me — for a week, or maybe two — an' I'll guarantee to scout till I find one of them villages. The Dutchies won't be expectin' me. An' I can likely pot a whole mess of 'em before they can get to cover.

"Say!" he went on eagerly, a bit of general information flashing into his memory. "Did you know Germans was a kind of Confed? The fightin' Germans, I mean. Well, they are. The whole twelve I got was dressed in gray Confed uniform, same as Pop used to wear. I got his old uniform to home. Lord, but Pop would sure lay into me if he knowed I was pepperin' his old side partners like that! I'd figured that all Germans was dressed like the ones back home. But they've got regular uniforms. Confed uniforms, at that. I wonder does our general know about it?"

Again the long-suffering Mahan tried to set him right; this time as to the wide divergence between the gray-backed troops of Ludendorff and the Confederacy's gallant soldiers. But Cash merely nodded cryptically, as always he did when he thought his foreigner fellow soldiers were trying to take advantage of his supposed ignorance. And he swung back to the theme nearest his heart.

"Now about that snipin' business," he pursued, "even if the cap don't want too many of 'em shot up, he sure won't be so cantankerous as to keep me from tryin' to get that thirteenth feller! I mean the one that kept blazin' at me whiles I kept blazin' at him; an' the both of us too cute to show an inch of target to the other or stay in the same patch of cover after we'd fired. That Dutchy sure can scout grand! He's a born woodsman. An' you all don't want it to be said the Germans has got a better sniper than what we've got, do you? Well, that's just what will be said by everyone in this here county unless you let me down him. Come on, Sarge! Let me go back after him! I been thinkin' up a trick Grandfather got off of the Injuns. It oughter land him sure. Let me go try! I believe that feller can't weigh an ounce less than two-twenty. Leave me have one more go after him, and I'll bring him in to prove it!"

Top Sergeant Mahan's patience stopped fraying, and ripped from end to end. "You seem to think this war is a cross between a mountain feud and a deer hunt!" he growled. "Isn't there any way of hammering through your mind that we aren't here to pick off unsuspecting Germans and make a tally of the kill? And we aren't here to brag about the size of the men we shoot, either. We're here, you and I, to obey orders and do our work. You'll get plenty of shooting before you go home again, don't worry. Only you'll do it the way you're told to. After all the time you've spent in the hoosegow since you joined, I should think you'd know that."

But Cash Wyble did not know it. He said so — loudly, offensively, blasphemously. He said many things — things that in any other army than his own would have landed him against a blank wall facing a firing squad. Then he slouched off by himself to grumble.

As far as Cash Wyble was concerned the war was a failure — a total failure. The one bright spot in its workaday monotony was blurred for him by the orders of his stupid superiors. In his vivid imagination that elusive

German sniper gradually attained a weight not far from three hundred pounds.

In sour silence Cash sulked through the rest of the day's routine. In his heart boiled black rebellion. He had learned his soldier trade, back at Camp Lee, because it had been very strongly impressed upon him that he would go to jail if he did not. For the same reason he had not tried to desert. He had all the true mountaineer horror for prison. He had toned down his native temper and stubbornness, because failure to do so always landed him in the guardhouse — a place that, to his mind, was almost as terrible as jail.

But out here in the wilderness there were no jails. At least Cash had seen none. And he had it on the authority of Top Sergeant Mahan himself that this part of France was not within the legal jurisdiction of West Virginia — the only region, as far as Cash actually knew, where men are put in prison for their misdeeds. Hence the rules governing Camp Lee could not be supposed to obtain out here. All of which comforted Cash not a little.

To him *patriotism* was a word as meaningless as was *discipline*. The law of force he recognized — the law that had hog-tied him and flung him into the army. But the higher law which makes men risk their all, right blithely, that their country and civilization may triumph — this was as much a mystery to Cash Wyble as to any army mule.

Just now he detested the country that had dragged him away from his lean shack and forbade him to disport himself as he chose in no man's land. He hated his country; he hated his army; he hated his regiment. Most of all he loathed his captain and Top Sergeant Mahan.

At Camp Lee he had learned to comport himself more or less like a civilized recruit, because there was no breach of discipline worth the penalty of the guardhouse. Out here it was different.

That night Private Cassius Wyble got hold of two other men's emergency rations, a bountiful supply of water, and a stuffing pocketful of cartridges. With these and his adored rifle he eluded the sentries — a ridiculously easy feat for so skilled a woodsman — and went over the top and on into no man's land.

By daylight he had trailed and potted a German sniper. By sunrise he had located the man against whom he had sworn his strategy feud — the German who had put him on his mettle two days before.

Cash did not see his foe. And when from the edge of a rock he fired at a puff of smoke in a clump of trees no resultant body came tumbling earthward. And thirty seconds later a bullet from quite another part of the clump spatted hotly against the rock edge five inches from his head. Cash smiled beatifically. He recognized the tactics of his former opponent. And once more the merry game was on.

To make perfectly certain of his rival's identity, Cash wiggled low in the undergrowth until he came to a jut of rock about seven feet long and two feet high. Lying at full length behind this low barrier, and parallel to it, Cash put his hat on the toe of his boot and cautiously lifted his foot until the hat's sugar-loaf crown protruded a few inches above the top of the rock.

On the instant, from the tree clump, snapped the report of a rifle. The bullet, ignoring the hat, nicked the rock comb precisely above Cash's upturned face. He nodded approval, for it told him that his enemy was not only a good forest fighter but that he recognized the same skill in Wyble.

Thus began two days of delightful pastime for the exiled mountaineer. Thus, too, began a series of offensive and defensive maneuvers worthy of Natty Bumppo and Old Sleuth combined.

It was not until Cash abandoned the hunt long enough to find and shoot another German sniper and appropriate the latter's uniform that he was able, under cover of dusk, to get near enough to the tree clump for a fair sight of his antagonist. At which juncture a snap shot from the hip ended the duel.

Cash's initial thrill of triumph, even then, was dampened. For the sniper — to whom by this time he had credited the size of Goliath, at the very least — proved to be a wizened little fellow, not much more than five feet tall.

Still Cash had won. He had outgeneraled a mighty clever sharpshooter. He had gotten what he came out for, and two other snipers, besides. It was not a bad bag. As there was nothing else to stay there for, and as his water was gone, as well as nearly all his cartridges, Cash shouldered his rifle and plodded wearily back to camp for a night's rest.

There, to his amazed indignation, he was not received as a hero, even when he sought to recount his successful adventures. Instead, he was arrested at once on a charge of technical desertion, and was lodged in the local substitute for a regular guardhouse.

Bewildered wrath smothered him. What had he done, to be arrested again? True, he had left camp without leave. But had he not atoned for this peccadillo fiftyfold by the results of his absence? Had he not killed three men whose business it was to shoot Americans? Had he not killed the very best sniper the Germans could hope to possess?

Yet they had not promoted him. They had not so much as thanked him. Instead, they had stuck him here in the hoosegow. And Mahan had said something about a court-martial.

It was black ingratitude! That was what it was. That and more. Such people did not deserve to have the services of a real fighter like himself. Which started another train of thought.

Apparently — except on special occasions — the Americans did not send men out into the wilderness to take pot shots at the lurking foe. And apparently that was just what the Germans always did. He had full proof, indeed, of the German custom. For had he not found a number of the graybacks thus happily engaged? Not for one occasion only, but as a regular thing?

Yes, the Germans had sense enough to appreciate a good fighter when they had one. And they knew how to make use of him in a way to afford innocent pleasure to himself and much harm to the enemy. That was the ideal life for a soldier — "laying out" and sniping the foe. Not kitchen-police work and endless drill and digging holes and taking baths. Sniping was the job for a he-man, if one had to be away from home at all. And in the German ranks alone was such happy employment to be found.

When Cash calmly and definitely made up his mind to desert to the Germans, he was troubled by no scruples at all. Even the dread of the mysterious court-martial added little weight to his decision. The deed seemed to him not a whit worse than was the leaving of one farmer's employ, back home, to take service with another who offered more congenial work. Wherefore, he deserted.

It was not at all difficult for him to escape from the elementary cell in which he was confined. It was a mere matter of strategy and luck. So was his escape to no man's land.

Unteroffizier Otto Schrabstaetter an hour later conducted to his company commander a lanky and leather-faced man in khaki uniform, who had accosted a sentry with the pacific plea that he be sworn in as a member of the German Army.

The sentry did not know English; nor did Unteroffizier Otto Schrabstaetter. And though Cash addressed them both in a very fair imitation of the guttural English he had heard used by the West Virginia Germans — and which he fondly believed to be pure German — they did not understand a word of his plea. So he was taken to the captain, a man who had lived for five years in New York.

With the Unteroffizier at his side and with two armed soldiers just behind him, Cash confronted the captain, and under the latter's volley of barked questions told his story. Ten minutes afterward he was repeating the same tale to a flint-faced man with a fox-brush mustache — Colonel von Scheurer, commander of the regiment that held that section of the first-line trench.

A little to Cash's aggrieved surprise, neither the captain nor the colonel seemed interested in his prowess as a sharpshooter or in his ill-treatment at the hands of his own army. Instead, they asked an interminable series of questions that seemed to have no bearing at all on his case.

They wanted, for instance, to know the name of his regiment; its quota of men; how long they had been in France; what sea route they had taken in crossing the ocean; from what port they had sailed; and the approximate size of the convoy. They wanted to know what regiments lay to either side of Cash's in the American trenches; how many men per month America was sending overseas and where they usually landed. They wanted to know a thousand things more, of the same general nature.

Cash saw no reason why he should not satisfy their silly curiosity. And he proceeded to do so to the best of his ability. But as he did not know so much as the name of the port whence he had shipped to France, and as the rest of his tactical knowledge was on the same plane, the fast-barked queries presently took on a tone of exasperation.

This did not bother Cash. He was doing his best. If these people did not like his answers that was no affair of his. He was here to fight, not to talk. His attention wandered.

Presently he interrupted the colonel's most searching questions to ask "You all don't happen to be the Kaiser, do you? I suppose not though. I'll bet that old Kaiser must weigh . . ."

A thundered oath brought him back to the subject at hand, and the cross-questioning went on. But all the queries elicited nothing more than a mass of misinformation, delivered with such palpable genuineness of purpose that even Colonel von Scheurer could not doubt the man's good faith. And at last the two officers began to have a very fair estimate of the mountaineer's character and of the reasons that had brought him thither.

Still it was the colonel's mission in life to suspect — to take nothing for granted. And after all, this yokel and his queer story were no more bizarre than was many a spy trick played by Germany upon her foes. Spies were bound to be good actors. And this lantern-jawed fellow might possibly be a character actor of high ability. Colonel von Scheurer sat for moment in silence, peering up at Cash from beneath a thatch of stiff-haired brows. Then he ordered the captain and the others to leave the dugout.

Alone with Wyble the colonel still maintained his pose of majestic surveillance. Then with no warning he spat forth the question, "*Wer bist du?*"

Not the best character actor unhung could have simulated the owlish ignorance in Cash's face. Not the shrewdest spy could have had time to mask a knowledge of German. And, as Colonel von Scheurer well knew, no spy who did not understand German would have been sent to enlist in the German Army.

The colonel at once was satisfied that the newcomer was not a spy. Yet, to make doubly certain of the recruit's willingness to serve against his own country, von Scheurer sought another test. Pulling toward him a scratch pad, he picked up a pencil from the table before him and proceeded to make a rapid sketch. When the sketch was complete he detached the top sheet and showed it to Cash. On it was drawn a rough likeness of the American flag.

"What is that?" he demanded.

"Old Glory," answered Cash, after a leisurely survey of the picture, adding in friendly patronage, "and not bad drawed, at that."

"It is the United States flag," pursued the colonel, "as you say. It is the national emblem of the country where you were born — the country you are renouncing to become a subject of the All Highest."

"Meanin' God?" asked Cash.

He wanted to be sure of every step. While he did not at all know the meaning of *renounce*, yet his attendance at mountain camp-meeting revivals had given him a possible inkling as to what "All Highest" meant.

"What?" inquired the puzzled colonel, not catching his drift.

"The 'All Highest' is God, ain't it?" said Cash.

"It is His Imperial Majesty the Kaiser," sharply retorted the scandalized colonel.

"Oh!" exclaimed Cash, much interested. "I see. In West Virginia we call him God. An' over in this neck of the woods your Dutch name for Him is Kaiser. What a ninny I am! I'd always had the idea the Kaiser was just a man, with somethin' the same sort of job as President Wilson's. But . . ."

"This picture represents the flag of the United States," resumed the impatient von Scheurer, waiving the subject of theology for the point in hand. "You have renounced it. You have declared your wish to fight against it. Prove that. Prove it by tearing that sketch in two — and spitting upon it!"

"Hold on!" interposed Cash, speaking with tolerant kindness as to a somewhat stupid child. "Hold on, Cap! You got me wrong. Or maybe I didn't make it so very clear. I didn't ever say I wanted to fight Old Glory. All I said I wanted to do was to fight that crowd of smart alecks over yonder who jail me all the time an' won't let me fight in my own way. I've got nothin' against the old flag. Why, that there's the flag I was borned under! Me an' Pop an' Grandfather an' the whole lot of us — as far back as there was any America, I reckon. I don't go round wavin' it none. That ain't my way. But I sure ain't goin' to tear it up. And I ain't goin' to spit on it. I . . ."

He checked himself. Not that he had no more to say, but because to his astonishment he found he was beginning to lose his temper. This phenomenon halted his speech and turned his wondering thoughts inward.

Cash could not understand his own strange surge of choler. He had not been aware of any special interest in the American flag. A little bunting representation of the Stars and Stripes — now faded close to whiteness — hung on the wall of his shack at home, where his grandmother, a rabid Unionist, had hung it nearly sixty years earlier, when West Virginia had refused to join the Confederacy. Every day of his life Cash had seen it there, had seen without noting or caring.

Camp Lee, too, had been ablaze with American flags. And after he had learned the rules as to the flag salute, Cash had never given the banners a second thought. The regimental flags, too, here in France, had seemed to him but a natural part of the army's equipment, and no more to be venerated than the twin bars on his captain's tunic.

Thus he could not in the very least account for the fiery flare of rebellion that gripped him at this ramrodlike Prussian's command to defile the emblem. Yet grip him it did. And it held him there, quivering and purple, the strange emotion waxing more and more overpoweringly potent at each passing fraction of a second. Dumb and shaking, he glowered down at the amused colonel.

Von Scheurer watched him placidly for a few moments; then with a short laugh he advanced the test. Reaching for the sheet of paper whereon he had sketched the flag, the colonel held it lightly between the fingers of his outstretched hands.

"It is really a very simple thing to do," he said carelessly, yet keeping a covert watch upon the mountaineer. "And it is a thing that every loyal German subject should rejoice to do. All I required was that you first tear the emblem in two and then spit upon it — as I do now."

But the colonel did not suit action to words. As his fingers tightened on the sheet of paper the dugout echoed to a low snarl that would have done credit to a Cumberland catamount. And with the snarl, six feet of lean and wiry bulk shot through the air across the narrow table that separated Cash from the colonel.

Von Scheurer with admirable presence of mind snatched his pistol from its temporary resting place in his lap. With the speed of the wind he seized the weapon. But with the speed of the whirlwind Cash Wyble was upon him, his clawlike fingers deep in the colonel's full throat, his hundred and sixty pounds of bone and gristle smiting von Scheurer on chest and shoulder.

Cash had literally risen in air and pounced on the Prussian. Under the impact von Scheurer's chair collapsed. Both men shot to earth, the colonel undermost and the pistol flying unheeded from his grasp. Over, too, went the table, and the electric light upon it. And the dugout was in pitch blackness.

There in the dark Cash Wyble deliriously tackled his prey, making queer and hideous little worrying sounds now and then far down in his throat, like a dog that mangles its meat. And there the sentry from the earthen passageway found them when he rushed in with an electric torch, and followed by a rabble of fellow soldiers.

Cash at sound of the running footsteps jumped to his feet. The man he had attacked was lying very still, in a crumpled and yet sprawling heap — in a posture never designed by nature.

With one wild sweep of his windmill arms Cash grabbed up the sheet of paper on which von Scheurer had made his life's last sketch. With a simultaneous sweep he knocked the glass-bulbed torch from the sentinel, just as a rifle or two were centering their aim toward him; and, head down, he tore into the group of men who blocked the dugout entrance.

Cash had a faintly conscious sense of dashing down one passageway and up another, following by forestry instinct the course he noted when he was led into the colonel's presence. He collided with a sentinel; he butted another from his flying path. He heard yells and shots — especially shots. Once something hit him on the shoulder, whirling him half round without breaking his stride. Again something hot whipped him across the cheek. And at last he was out, under the foggy stars, with excited Germans firing in his general direction and loosing off star shells.

Again instinct and scout skill came to the rescue as he plunged into a bramble thicket and wriggled through long grass on his heaving stomach.

An hour before dawn Cash Wyble was led before his sleepy and unloving company commander. The returned wanderer was caked with dirt and blood. His face was scored by briers. Across one cheek ran the red wale of a bullet. A very creditable flesh wound adorned his left shoulder. His clothes were in ribbons.

Before the captain could frame the first of a thousand scathing words, Cash broke out pantingly, "Stick me in the hoosegow if you're a mind to, Cap! Stick me there for life. Or wish me onto a kitchen-police job forever! I'm not kickin'. It's coming to me, all right, after what I done.

"I get the drift of the whole thing now. I'm on to what it means. It — it means Old Glory! It means — *this!*"

He stuck out one muddy hand wherein was clutched a wad of scratch-pad paper.

Then the company commander did a thing that stamped him as a genius. Instead of administering the planned rebuke and following it by sending the wretch to the guardhouse, he began to ask questions.

"What do you make of it all?" dazedly queried the captain of Top Sergeant Mahan, when Cash had been taken to the trench hospital to have his shoulder dressed.

"Well, sir," reported Mahan meditatively, "for one thing, I take it, we've got a new soldier in the company. A soldier, not a varmint. For another thing, I take it, Uncle Sam's got a new American on his list of nephews. And — and, unless I'm wrong, Kaiser Bill is short one crackajack sniper and one perfectly good Prussian colonel, too. War's a funny thing, sir."

Queenstown Patrol

x

from S-54

by EDWARD ELLSBERG

"Your last chance, Mr. Parker!"

Commander Wilson fairly snapped out his words.

"One more breakdown on the L–18, and back you go to Annapolis, instructing midshipmen; that is, if they'll have you there. Otherwise you'll go to Guam till this war's over!"

Lieutenant Parker nervously twisted the visor of his cap, with red face and clenched teeth listened silently to the stinging reprimand.

The irate commander caught his breath, added, "Two boats in this flotilla are already wearing chevrons for sinking U-boats, while all you've done is to break down on three patrols and get towed in!" He glowered up at the L–18's skipper, paused again.

Parker waited a moment for Commander Wilson to continue, then looking into the stern face before him, hesitantly began to explain. He was curtly interrupted.

"Wartime, Mr. Parker. No excuses!" The flotilla commander turned abruptly in his chair, started to examine the chart spread on the table before him. The interview was over.

The dazed lieutenant paused in the midst of his explanation, stared at the broad back before him; then his jaws clicked firmly to. "Aye, aye, sir!" He turned on his heel, stumbled out of the cabin.

His last chance! Parker looked across the deck of the mother ship, his eyes sweeping for an instant the hills that circled the Irish Queenstown harbor, then gazed down hopelessly at the L–18 moored alongside the tender. What ailed that damn pig, anyway? It was not his fault, nor his crew's either, if the mass of junk that had been squeezed into that sleek hull below there was continually breaking down.

Parker stepped to the port rail, looked overboard. A tangle of lines led from a cargo port in the high side of the *Melville*, disappeared down an open hatch just forward of the L–18's conning tower. Through those lines the submarine was sucking compressed air, distilled water, electricity for her batteries; storing up the vital energy necessary for her next patrol. Outboard of the L–18 were three sister submarines, and on the *Melville's* starboard side were two more — her litter of pigs, sucking greedily away at the mother ship's lines.

Parker ducked through the rail, seized the top rung of the Jacob's ladder, scrambled down, the rope ladder swaying violently against the steel plates of the *Melville* as he descended.

Dungarees smeared with grease, white cap oil-soaked and hardly recognizable as ever having been the starched and gold-laced headgear of a once smart naval officer, face grimy with dirt and perspiration, Lieutenant Parker painfully dragged his strained body off the top of the starboard diesel engine, where, jammed between the sloping inner hull of the submarine and the cylinder heads, he had been struggling to adjust the fuel-oil sprays.

Abaft him, in the passage, a weary gang of machinist's mates surveyed the maze of cams and valves on the engines, turned tired eyes on their skipper as he slid off the cylinder and landed on the floor plates alongside them.

"Well, Mac, they look O.K. to me." Parker, his neck still aching from his cramped position over the diesels, faced his chief machinist's mate, nodded stiffly.

"They oughta be, Captain," replied McCarthy. "Since the *Walton* towed us in the night before last, there ain't a man in this gang's had an hour's sleep. We been working on them engines steady, and whatever else breaks down on the next patrol, it ain't gonna be them diesels."

"It had better not be *anything* else, either," said Parker ruefully. "The old man just got through chewing me out on the *Melville*. Said we were a disgrace to the Navy — broken down at sea now on three patrols straight — and if it happened again, he'd put someone aboard that knew how to operate a pigboat. What ails this tub, anyway? The other pigs have managed to keep on moving."

"The way she's built, I guess," answered McCarthy. "She's a war baby. Some shipyard made a record on her, built her complete in four months from duct keel to conning tower, sorta stunt to show how they were doing their bit to win the war. And this is the result. Nothing's right. When it's not one thing busting down, it's two. I wish I was back on a battlewagon, or one of them boats they built in peacetime when they had time to do a job. This bucket's gonna be our finish sure."

"Not if I know it," snapped out the skipper. "You carried out your orders, Mac?"

"Yeh, I done what you said. There ain't a piece of machinery inside this hull that us engineers ain't gone over to make sure she's right. Up forward, Wilson and the torpedo gang have done the same for their gear, and

Sparks here has gone over the electric outfit from stem to stern. Nothing in the boat that we could get hands on ain't been overhauled; only the rudders and the gear outside is left. If you want that inspected you'll have to put the boat in dry dock. And lemme tell you, Captain, the crew's all shot. They ain't had no rest for forty-eight hours; the first thing you know, they'll be going to sleep standing up."

"No, Mac, we can't dry-dock her. Orders are to sail at dusk. Turn all hands in except the watch; let them get what rest they can till we get out. There'll be mighty little rest for them once we're out playing hide-and-seek with Fritzie!"

A vague mass loomed in the darkness off the starboard side. Lieutenant Parker glanced up hastily at it. Daunt Rock. They were passing through the rocky cleft that formed the entrance to Queenstown harbor.

"Right a little!"

"Right a little, sir!" echoed the quartermaster, swinging the steering control over for a moment.

"Steady now. Follow the lights."

"Aye, aye, sir!"

Ahead in the darkness, two faint points, perhaps a hundred yards apart, gleamed fitfully, bobbing up and down against the black background of the night — the hooded stern lights of the two minesweepers clearing a safe passage to the open sea for the L–18. Between those boats a wire cable sawed through the depths, sweeping for mines sowed by enemy submarines outside the harbor.

Anxiously Parker watched the steering, keeping always in the wake of that sweep. At half speed the L–18 plowed through the night, a safe mile astern of her shepherding convoy.

The submarine started to pitch sluggishly as she met the ocean waves; spray broke over the chariot bridge, drenched the quartermaster, soaked the officer crouching behind him in the confined space between the binnacle and the periscope shears; a trickle of water ran down the open hatch at their feet, gathered in a little pool in the control room below. Parker pulled the helmet of his windbreaker lower over his forehead, wiped the salt spray from his eyes, peered steadily ahead over the binnacle, conning the ship to keep it squarely between those protecting lights.

A thud, a distant roar, a cloud of white foam shone for an instant against the black water ahead. The light on their port bow danced violently a few seconds. The L–18 shook uneasily a moment, then settled down again to the steady pounding of her diesels.

"Another egg," muttered Parker. "Funny how the Heinies always know when a ship's coming out!"

"Easy enough, skipper," growled the quartermaster, his eyes glued on the patch of froth ahead where the mine had exploded. "Queenstown's full of spies. Lucky for us we had them sweeps. That egg was right in our path!"

Parker nodded. Lucky, yes. For the L–18 was steaming squarely through a roiled mass of foam, standing out sharply in the dark ocean. He glanced ahead. There were the twin lights, a hundred yards apart, moving steadily on through the night as if nothing had happened. He owed his luck to the minesweepers, unromantic trawlers manned by fishermen, steaming unconcernedly through the minefields clearing a path for the fighting ships. Parker shook his head. A tough life on those sweeps. Fine chance of striking mines themselves. Of course, their light draft allowed them to steam right over a mine without contacting it. That is, if Heinie had his mines all set at the right depths. But occasionally he didn't, and one floated too close to the surface for even a light-draft trawler to pass over. A tough life on those mine sweeps. He shook his head again. Not for him.

"We're clear, Captain. The sweeps is heading back!" mumbled the helmsman.

Parker turned, looked over the edge of the chariot bridge. The lights had veered to port, stopped while they heaved in their kites and reeled in the sweep wire. A sharp flicker of light pierced the darkness. A blinker tube was flashing at them from the wheelhouse of the nearest vessel. In dots and dashes came the message: "Good luck."

The flickering ceased, the dim guide lights on the trawlers were suddenly turned off, the L–18 pounded ahead through the darkness into the open sea. They were clear, in water so deep the Germans could not anchor mines. A brief command, the L–18 turned to starboard, headed for the seas to the west of Ireland where the troopships of America, jammed full of doughboys, were rushing reinforcements to the hard-pressed western front.

"Good luck!" Parker repeated the message gloomily, strained his eyes ahead where the low bow of his submarine plunged into the sea. Good luck! The L–18 had meant anything but that to him so far. Would she hang together this cruise? His last chance. Disconsolately he wondered what a tour on Guam was like. A mere speck in the Pacific, no place for an officer in wartime. He gripped the rail, stared ahead into the night. No tour on Guam for him!

"Silence in the boat!"

At diving stations, the crew of the L–18 leaned tensely over their controls. The pounding of the diesels ceased suddenly. A strange quiet gripped the hull, broken only by the sharp hiss of air whistling out of the vents as the L–18 went awash.

In the center of the control room, McCarthy heaved around on a huge valve wheel, screwing home the main air inlet to the diesels. A bang. The quartermaster above slammed closed the conning-tower hatch, slid down the ladder into the control room, gripped the steering lever.

With his eyes glued to the depth gauge on the port bulkhead, Parker watched as the needle registered their sinking.

McCarthy gave his valve a final twist, reported, "Outboard ventilation valve secured, sir!"

Parker nodded. Twenty feet, the deck was just going under.

"Ready on the main motors, sir!"

"One third ahead!" Without taking his eyes from the gauge, the skipper stepped to the periscope, watched their rapidly increasing depth.

The hiss of air ceased; a tiny jet of water shot out the telltale from the ballast vent line. A seaman hastily closed the cock, called out, "Ballast tanks flooded, sir."

"Aye, aye. Close all the vents!"

More valves were hurriedly screwed down, reported closed. The L–18 kept sinking. Forty feet on the gauge.

"Enough!" called Parker sharply. "Hold her at forty! Standard speed, both motors!"

Diving wheels twirled, down went the controllers, the whir of electric motors filled the boat. Parker pressed a button. A slight grinding broke out as the periscope tube rose slowly from the well at his feet, came to full elevation, stopped. He pressed his face against the rubber eyepiece, looked out.

A few faint streaks of red glowed in the east, lighted dimly the dark circle of sky and sea visible through the periscope. The day was breaking. He swung his lens around, swept the horizon. Nothing in sight.

For the hundredth time Parker looked at the crumpled radio message on the chart board. He knew it by heart now.

> FROM: C IN C, QUEENSTOWN.
>
> TO: USS L–18.
>
> U–6 REPORTED OPERATING IN YOUR SQUARE STOP USE UTMOST EN-
> DEAVORS TO MAKE CONTACT

Parker smiled ruefully. Only too well he realized the U–6 was there. Would he ever forget those drifting corpses he had glimpsed yesterday, the sightless eyes staring down his periscope, the gray sea dotted with the bloated bodies of men and horses through which he had picked his way gingerly as the L–18 swam slowly through the wreckage where the torpedoed *Morentic* had gone down? Yes, the U–6 was in his square.

And if it had not been for that destroyer, he might have made the contact the C in C was so anxious about. He groaned at the recollection. Infernal luck! Midnight, the L–18 was cruising slowly awash, her engines barely turning over, all hands on the bridge straining their ears for the noise of pounding diesels. Their enemy, they knew, must be on the surface somewhere, running engines full power, recharging batteries for his next day's work. The L–18 had caught her radio code signals, reporting no doubt to faroff Germany her success in sinking the horse transport; had heard her chattering the gossip of the war zone with sister U-boats scattered over the seas off Ireland. Strong signals — she was close to them. Cautiously Parker had zigzagged back and forth, seeking the bearing on which his antennae caught the signals loudest, then headed carefully in on that bearing. He remembered the sudden thrill when a familiar throb came to them faintly across the heaving seas, when through his night glasses he had picked up the vague outline of a distant conning tower silhouetted against the dark horizon.

And he had made a perfect approach. With engines stopped to prevent any noise which might alarm the enemy, he had stealthily crept in on his motors to within a mile, submerged to periscope depth to avoid any chance of being seen, and full speed had moved in to make his attack on his unsuspecting prey, torpedoes ready, his finger on the firing button, his target broadside on, success assured.

C'est la guerre! He bit his lip at the recollection. His radioman, white-faced, had stumbled out of the little soundproof booth abaft him with startling news. A destroyer! The high pitched note of her propellers was ringing in his microphones!

And almost before the breathless operator had blurted out his message, Parker, his eye still pressed to the periscope, saw a streak of fire flash through the darkness, a brilliant glare as the tracer shell burst, and in that flash of light the U–6 brilliantly outlined with men madly scrambling down her conning tower, while she moved slowly ahead, started to settle in a crash dive. Then darkness again.

In anguish, Parker had taken a wild chance, hurriedly pressed the trigger, fired a torpedo at his vanishing prey. He had missed. Range too long, aim bad, poor run on his torpedo? He never knew. The U–6 had disappeared before he could fire again. In the rush of events that followed, only the L–18 had occupied his thoughts.

"Hard dive!"

With diving planes at full depression, they had plunged suddenly from periscope depth to eighty feet. And just in time.

A sharp explosion. The L–18 shook violently; her white-faced crew clung to their controls to save themselves. A depth bomb. Was it meant for them or the U–6? Who knew? To a destroyer every submarine was an enemy. Shoot first, investigate afterward.

A little sick, Parker had hesitated a moment. Should he come up? A salvo of four-inch shells might come crashing into his hull before he could get the lid open and his Very recognition signals bursting in the air.

Another crash, and then at brief intervals a series of them. The L–18 quivered with each shock. The destroyer was laying a pattern of depth bombs as she whirled in a figure eight over the spot where the U–6 had disappeared. Soon she would stop, listen for propellers. And if she picked them up instead of the U–6 a shower of depth bombs would come raining down on them. Parker's indecision vanished.

"Stop the motors!"

Without headway to overcome her negative buoyancy, the L–18 commenced sinking. One hundred feet, two hundred feet, two hundred and fifty feet. In agony Parker had watched the gauge. Bottom at fifty fathoms according to the chart. Two hundred feet was their working depth, three hundred feet their safe limit. Was the chart accurate? Three hundred feet, still sinking. Petrified, the men gripped their controls, watched the gauge. And then, at three hundred and five feet, a gentle bump, the L–18 came softly to rest in the mud. A sigh of relief echoed audibly through the control room; tense limbs relaxed; his crew breathed once more.

The shocks of the depth bombs were fainter now, ceased shortly. Crouched alongside the operator in the tiny radio booth, receivers jammed over his ears, Parker listened on the microphones to the shrill note of the propellers on the surface, singing in his ears one moment as the destroyer darted ahead, then ceasing abruptly as she stopped her engines to listen. Back and forth, it seemed endlessly, that note rang through the sea as the destroyer searched the depths, then faded gradually as the baffled ship swung in ever-widening circles, trying to pick up the trail of her submerged enemy.

But in vain. Somewhere in the depths, nestling quietly in the mud like himself, Parker visioned the U–6, shuddered at the thought. The vessel which a few minutes before he had been ready to blow out of the water, was now, like the L–18, a hunted fugitive, her crew crouching in terror like his own in their cramped compartments, shaking at the fear that something might float up, give their hiding place away, send a hurtling bomb, set to burst at the bottom, down on the hull to crush their fragile shell, bury them forever in the mud and the ooze of the ocean floor.

But it had not happened. The destroyer had vanished, seeking a submarine still under way. After two hours on the bottom, Parker had partly blown his safety tank, floated up to thirty feet, pushed up his periscope, made a careful search to insure that neither friend nor foe was in sight on the surface, then hastily blown the rest of the safety tank to get his conning tower fully out of water.

With the lid open to get air for the engines, he had hurried full speed through the night to put at least five miles between himself and the scene of the battle, lest the U–6 should bob up and catch him unawares. Then, with propellers disconnected and engines working full power, the L–18 spent the rest of the dark hours recharging storage cells, while her thankful crew took turns, four at a time, in clambering up on the little bridge, hardly six feet out of water, and breathing in the free air of heaven.

Once more Lieutenant Parker swept the horizon with his periscope, scanned the waves as the dawn broke over the sea. Nothing in sight on the surface — the destroyer had vanished.

At dead-slow speed, the L–18 swam through the sea, using only enough of her precious electricity to give her diving planes control and hold the depth against the slight positive buoyancy which Parker was carrying on the boat for safety's sake. Slowly the minutes dragged on, grew to hours. The sun rose high in the heavens, no longer threw a blinding glare into the periscope eye as it swung around. The submarine wheeled gradually in a high spiral, the search curve on which Parker hoped to find his enemy.

Inside the boat, the air grew thicker; the odor of oil, of acid fumes from the batteries, permeated the control room; the atmosphere became laden with carbon dioxide from being breathed over and over again. Parker noted that the air of alertness with which his men had taken the boat under, was gradually vanishing; heads drooped over the controls, lackluster eyes gazed vacantly at gauges, pored uncomprehendingly over the switchboard. His own head started to ache; his eyes, strained by the high-powered lenses in the periscope, burned in their sockets; his head felt heavy, his mind thick. Six hours under; eight more to go before darkness settled again and they could safely come up. He wondered vaguely what had become of the U–6. She must be taking it easier. Unaware of the presence of another submarine, she would spend part of her time, at least, awash with her lid open, taking a fresh supply of air every hour or so, perhaps even running on her diesels to conserve her batteries, safe in the thought that she could spot a surface ship and dive long before such a small object as her conning tower could be seen by any approaching vessel. Parker thanked his luck for that unawareness; at least he had not given himself away by coming up and firing recognition signals while the U–6 was still around. Unquestionably the Germans had dived the night before without the slightest knowledge that the sudden rush of that hurtling destroyer was all that had saved them from certain disaster.

Well, it was nearly over. With the night, his patrol was finished; the L–18 would move hastily out of that square, get well clear before the L–7, relieving them, came on the patrol in the morning. A grim situation, all right. Once his relief arrived, if he was still there submerged, she would certainly blow him out of the water if she sighted his periscope; if he ran on the surface and disclosed his identity as an Allied man-of-war, then a torpedo from the lurking U–6 was almost certain to do the same. A rotten life in the pigs — fair game for everybody, submerged or afloat, with that blasted air to eat your lungs out while under water, and the deafening roar of diesels to ruin your sleep and drive you crazy while you charged at night; and always in the background of your mind, while running submerged, that gnawing fear of the sea, lying in wait to crush your boat and flatten you out if your pig went out of control for a brief instant and sank just a few feet too deep before you caught her.

Parker shook his head, tried to throw off the weight that seemed to press in on his throbbing temples. He was lucky — his last day on patrol. Tonight when they broke surface, and the engines started to pound again, it would be to drive them home to Queenstown, not to charge batteries for another day of torture in the depths.

And nothing had broken down. He could face Commander Wilson on the *Melville*; his men, instead of overhauling engines, could spend their time in port on liberty. Cork, even Queenstown, after a week jammed inside this pig, would be heaven for a sailor. No breakdowns. Perhaps the jinx was shaken at last. With an effort, the dopey skipper pulled his thoughts back from the rest that awaited him in Queenstown, pressed his eye against the lens in front of him.

A vista of gray waves met his sight, undulating gently, capped with patches of white foam here and there, merging in the distant haze with a cloudy sky. Slowly he revolved the periscope tube, scanned the horizon, searched the intervening sea. Nothing in sight — no ships, no smoke, only the vast sweep of the deserted ocean. Perfunctorily he finished his inspection, pressed the motor button, started to house the periscope.

A glint of sunshine flashed into his eye. Queer. The sun was too high for that. He stopped housing, squinted out the lens. His heart skipped a beat.

There, half a mile off on the starboard bow, its tapering length glistening in the sun, was a periscope!

Parker leaned forward, punched a voice-tube button, shouted excitedly, "Torpedo room! Stand by. U-boat on the starboard bow!"

As if jolted by an electric current, the drooping figures around the control room stiffened suddenly, looked toward their skipper. Forgotten were the bad air, the cramped quarters. Tense figures gripped the controls again; eager eyes scanned their instruments, ready for action. The enemy was in sight!

His temples throbbing wildly, Parker pressed his face again to the eyepiece, looked hurriedly at the bearing. Forty degrees on his starboard bow. They must bring her dead ahead.

"Ten degrees right rudder!" His voice sounded strange, far-off, as, eye glued to the periscope, the words hissed out.

"Ten right, sir," echoed the helmsman just forward of him.

The L-18 started to swing. Parker dared not even for an instant take his gaze off that thin steel finger dancing in the faroff waves; if he lost it in the whitecaps, he might never pick up that gleam again. Slowly he walked his periscope round as the submarine answered her rudder and the bearing of his target drew ahead. The L–18 heeled gently in her turn. Parker clung tightly to the handles to maintain his balance. Only ten degrees on the bow now.

"Meet her!"

Hurriedly Lieutenant Parker tried to estimate the course of that periscope. Was the U–6 bows-on to him or was she broadside? Only in the latter case would a slim submarine offer target enough for a decent shot. Tensely he watched the wisps of spray play round the distant tube, caught a tiny wake on its far side, switched in the high-magnification lens to study it. The field of view in his periscope narrowed; the distant waves seemed suddenly to leap closer; he was startled to see that the eye of the enemy periscope was pointing directly at him, that the two submarines were headed for each other!

For an instant, his blood froze, his jaw dropped, he stared open-mouthed, hypnotized by that tiny lens gleaming at him across half a mile of tossing seas.

"Steady on the course now." The quartermaster's voice broke the silence of the control room.

With a jerk, Parker came back to life. No more maneuvering, he must get his torpedo in first!

He fumbled for the firing pistol, stared out the lens. The enemy periscope was dead ahead; his boat had steadied. Parker's fingers gripped the firing handle, started to squeeze the trigger. A vague recollection; he paused. The torpedo room had not reported ready.

For the first time since sighting the enemy, Parker tore his eye from the rubber shield, stooped hastily, and looked forward through the open watertight doors into the torpedo room, where, outboard of the shining bronze covers of the tubes, he glimpsed the broad back of his chief torpedo man straining frenziedly over a wheel.

Parker straightened up, punched a button, sang out into the voice tube, "Torpedo room there! What's wrong?"

The reply fell like a bludgeon on his ear.

"The bow cap's jammed, Captain! We can't rotate it to uncover any of the torpedo tubes outside."

Parker's heart sank like lead. The bow cap — the spherical outside fairwater over his nest of torpedoes, with a solitary opening which had to register with the mouth of the tube to be fired before the missile could be ejected — jammed! And with none of his four tubes in line with the opening.

Parker stooped, stared forward into the torpedo room where his men were struggling with the rotating gear. A brawny seaman seized a spoke, added his weight to the chief's on the wheel.

Broken down again! In a daze, the stunned skipper watched the straining torpedo men while the full meaning of the accident sank into his brain. The glistening bodies of his torpedoes, the grim warheads full of TNT that a moment before, so he thought, had needed but the pressure of his finger to spring from his tubes toward the U–6 — imprisoned now behind that fatal cap, impossible of release! The L–18 had suddenly become impotent, unable to attack, helpless even to defend herself. The shock of that destroyer's depth bombs last night must have sprung the shafting, jammed the operating gears.

As he watched, a third seaman sprang forward with a huge monkey wrench, slipped its jaws over the rim of the wheel for a lever, flung his body hard down on the handle. No use. The wheel refused to turn; the bow cap was frozen tight with all the tubes sealed off.

Stunned by the situation, Parker turned to find terrified faces staring at him from all sides; the afterend of the room was filled with engineers. Like a flash the news of their disaster had spread through the boat; unconsciously the men were starting to edge toward the escape hatch beneath the conning tower.

Escape! A cracked laugh died in his throat. Why worry over the hatches? The U–6 was close aboard. Another few seconds and the quickest way out would be through their smashed side.

"Hard dive!"

The order burst from his parched lips, echoed like a bomb through the room. Diving wheels spun madly, controllers went over to "Full speed ahead." The L–18 started to seek safety in the depths. Ignoring his crew, Parker flung himself at the periscope, got a fleeting glimpse of that deadly eye staring at him not two hundred yards away, saw a fine cloud of spray spout through the surface, a streak of bubbles form in the waves, race for him. Then the sea washed over his periscope, suddenly blotted out everything.

"They've fired!" groaned Parker. He twisted his head from the useless lens, looked feverishly over his shoulder at the depth gauge. Still forty feet, the needle hardly starting to move. Would they never get down? Blanched faces, wild eyes all around followed his glance; trembling lips muttered curses watching that dial.

A few seconds now, the torpedo would strike. Parker looked despairingly toward his torpedo room, at the men still struggling there. "One more breakdown and back you go to . . ." Commander Wilson's threat flashed through his mind. "Annapolis." One more breakdown. How deep was the ooze on the ocean bottom? "Or Guam till this war's over." Wilson was wrong. A shattered submarine buried in the mud. Forty-five feet on that gauge now. No hope. How many seconds since the U–6 had fired? Only ten seconds needed by a torpedo to cover that distance. His gaze wandered over the side of the submarine, covered everywhere with intricate machinery. Where would their hull suddenly burst open, let the ocean come pouring through? One more breakdown. He cursed the builders of this pig-boat.

A deafening crash, the L–18 heeled drunkenly to port, the bow shot up at a sharp angle. The end. Curses, prayers, a tangle of arms and legs, a knot of crazed seamen struggling for the ladder to the conning tower; then a sudden silence as the fighting men stopped, looked wonderingly around for the rushing water that should be flooding the boat.

Parker, in a daze, extricated himself from the Kingston levers in the port bilges, groped his way uncertainly back to his station. The water! Where was it? Which compartment had that torpedo torn apart?

Incredulously he shot a glance through the forward bulkhead, then aft through the quivering hull. The deck was badly heeled; mattresses, men, tools, charts, were sprawled out everywhere; but there was no cataract of water rushing toward him — yet.

What had happened? That explosion, the shock that had tossed them through the seas like a bubble? The torpedo had hit somewhere; in a damaged boat Parker dared not stay submerged.

"Blow all ballast! Hard rise!"

His sharp command rang through the control room. Bewildered men, startled to find themselves still alive, untangled themselves from the manifolds, scrambled out of the bilges, staggered back to their controls. The shrill whistle of compressed air, the grinding of gears, the whir of motors echoed through the boat as the men of the L–18 fought to check their descent, to rise to the surface, escape from their prison. Ballast water poured overboard, propellers drove viciously ahead, diving planes at full elevation shot the trembling shell upward.

An instant, then their conning tower burst clear, the submarine rocked unsteadily in the seaway. Parker scrambled up the ladder into the conning tower, tripped the lever. The hatch flew back, he crawled through. Water was still pouring off the chariot bridge; his low deck was just breaking from the sea. Swiftly his eye ran along the hull from the jagged net cutter in the bow to the tapering stern. Unbelievingly his glance swept back. No damage anywhere.

And yet, that explosion. The torpedo had certainly struck something. What?

Half a ship length ahead, a spreading patch of oil caught his eye. He stared, thunderstruck. That was where the U–6 had been!

Something rubbed his legs. He looked down. McCarthy was squeezing through the hatch. Below him, Parker caught a glimpse of the conning tower jammed with men, struggling to get out. In a trice, his chief machinist's mate was alongside him; seamen were pouring out the hatch, crowding the chariot bridge, clambering down the outside of the conning tower to the half-awash deck below.

A huge bubble of air rose through the sea into the middle of the slick, frothed a moment, then subsided as the oily ring widened out, a patch of water strangely smooth in an ocean of tossing waves and spray-tipped crests. Anxiously Parker scanned the sea — no periscope anywhere. But there in the bubbles and the froth, a few bits of oil-soaked wreckage were breaking surface, shattered fragments of a submarine's deck!

"Look, skipper, this pile of junk rates a chevron on her conning tower from now on. We're heroes! The L–18's sunk a U-boat!" McCarthy pointed excitedly at the bits of wood and huge globules of oil gushing upward near their bow.

Lieutenant Parker nodded slowly. "Guess you're right, Mac, she's gone. But what under the sun's happened? I saw that torpedo start for us."

"The gyro in the tail of that torpedo must have stuck with the rudder hard over, and made it run in a circle so it curved round and socked the U–6 instead of us. I seen that happen once in target practice, but never with a war shot." He mopped the beads of sweat off his forehead. "I guess pigboats and tin fish ain't no more reliable in the Heinie navy than they are in your Uncle Sam's."

Parker looked forward to his bow, in full surface trim now, vaguely made out just below the water line the rounded outlines of the torpedo-tube cap, watched a moment his torpedo gang clustered on the forecastle, futilely staring down at the iron hemisphere.

He shook his head, gripped the engine telegraph, turned a strained face toward McCarthy. "Well, Mac, we'd better get under way for home now while we're still live heroes. Our patrol's about over, and we're helpless anyway with that bow cap jammed."

"Aye, aye, sir," said McCarthy with a grin. "Let's make knots for Queenstown before this pig breaks down, or Commander Wilson will be after us!"

The Goldfish Mutiny

※

by F. VAN WYCK MASON

It was about eleven o'clock of a drizzling and cheerless fall morning that Company D of the 333rd Machine Gun Battalion, with Brownings, carts, mules and all, trudged into the so-called rest billets at Beauville. The sodden khaki-clad column came to a halt as their captain was hailed by a red-faced, portly major who appeared to be the billeting officer for the village.

"Well, well, captain, not very spruce-looking are you?" the major greeted in a bluff, jovial voice that grated on the ears of the footsore column. After two weeks of unrelieved duty in the lines, enduring a relentless hammering by the exceedingly well-directed German artillery, D Company was not feeling the least bit jovial or bluff.

"Well, well!" continued the major, as he shook hands with the hollow-eyed captain. "You boys certainly look like you'd been to war. Big casualty list? Well, well, you'll come around fine with the nice quarters and the fine hot food we're going to give you here."

The mud-covered, hollow-cheeked men brightened perceptibly at the mention of food. By the vagaries of the gods of war, D Company had completely lost contact with its ration base for the last three days of their sojourn in the trenches.

"Food!" they cried, licking their unshaven chops in anticipation. "Chow! Nice, thick, rest-area steaks — carrots, and French fries, all brown and hot! Baby boy!"

After the long and meager diet of corned willy and goldfish, alias corned beef and salmon, D Company was desperately glad of the prospect of a change.

"Man," grunted a lanky, red-haired Southerner, a corporal, shivering in the front rank, "if I ever lays eyes on another hunk of goldfish, I'll go over the hill, so help me Hannah!"

"Steaks!" muttered the sodden ranks. "Sweet music, oh, lead me to 'em for a honest-to-God feed at last!"

"Yeh?" A bandy-legged private, whose flat cauliflower-eared face was dominated by a broken and flattened nose, looked up with swift suspicion, then spat resoundingly. "What wise guy slipped yuh de low-down we goin' to get steak 'stead of more o' Uncle Sam's favorite fruit?"

The tall corporal who had first spoken said nothing, but shifted his pack and hunched the sodden slicker higher on his neck as mechanically he tilted his dripping helmet forward to rid it of chilly, transparent drops that formed persistently on its brim.

"Aw," said he, and swallowed with a jerk of his prominent Adam's apple, "they's mean men in this man's army, but they-all ain't got the heart to feed us no more monkey meat and sa'mon. We been fightin' the whole Kraut army for two weeks, and we sho'ly rates a good feed. Say, boy, will you bend yore eyes over that?"

Followed by the voracious glances of the halted machine gunners, a white-aproned cook with hairy red arms skirted the edge of the road, a squawking chicken clutched firmly in his plump, chapped hand.

At the sound of the fowl's despairing swan song, the tall corporal wheeled sharply and his washed-out blue eyes followed the executioner from sight.

"Boy, there goes some cunnel's eats. Chicken!" There was a world of wistfulness in the lanky corporal's sigh.

"Yeh," observed the short ex-pug gloomily, "when youse gets to be a colonel, Jake, youse can rate chicken, too."

Ankle-deep in a mixture of mud and richly pungent manure, Jake's platoon clumped down the street with sagging shoulders and stumbling feet. In passing, they gazed curiously at the ancient white-walled houses and slopping red-tiled roofs that loomed to either side through the drizzle.

"Well, boys," remarked the sergeant when the men had disposed of their sodden belongings about a drafty barn which, if one were to judge from its scurrilous chalked inscriptions, had sheltered many other units of the A.E.F. "We're goin' to lean into a real feed. I heard the major slipping the info to the C.O."

Blasphemous and sulphuric language greeted the announcement.

"It's damn well time," snarled one as he struggled out of his pack. "I could eat a horse and chase the driver."

Presently there was a pleasing clank and clatter of mess kits as the top sergeant's whistle shrilled in the street. Foremost in the line-up were Corporal Jake Tourneur and the short, broad-shouldered blond battler known as Tug Schmalz, their faces alight with hope and anticipation.

"Hey, soldier, where-at do we tie on the nose-bag?" Jake demanded of the sergeant.

"Last shack on the right, in the courtyard," snapped the sergeant with a malevolent snicker. "Hurry up, boys, or the minute steaks and artichokes will be gettin' cold and the vol-au-vents spoiled."

"Hi-yah!" shouted the corporal, and started down the street at a head-long run with other members of the platoon stringing out behind like a ravenous comet's tail. Jake covered the distance, slippery footing and all, in something under half a minute, and arrived at the low stone wall over which drifted the tantalizing smell of frying meat and wood smoke.

"Baby," panted Jake, his slicker streamed out horizontally behind, "what I'm goin' to do to them steaks is a caution!"

He skidded round the corner and bolted through the gate, his aluminum oval shaped mess kit already unfolded and his coffee cup's handle secure. There, greeting his gladdened eyes, was the welcome outline of a chow gun, dimmed by saliva-inducing clouds of smoke and steam hovering and hanging low about it. Nearby toiled the cooks and K.P.'s.

"Come and get it, 'fore I trun it out!" bawled the cook, as though Jake and the hungry rest needed any encouragement! How welcome was the sight of broad khaki-clad backs bending laboriously over pans that gave off clouds of succulent vapor.

"One side, guy! One side, or a leg off," gasped Jake, pushing his way through the K.P.'s clustered about the stove for warmth. Confidently he held out his mess kit, a broad grin on his dirty, unshaven face.

Quite suddenly that smile vanished, never to return, for into the polished aluminum flopped a solitary golden-red chunk of bony salmon. Beside it a greasy K.P. forked a single slab of thick, fat pork. Dazedly incredulous, Jake stared, too outraged to speak while a single mealy white potato splashed into the oily salmon sauce.

"All right, youse, dat's all; on your way," snapped the cook. "Whaddaya t'ink dis is, Delmonico's? On your way, bum, on your way."

Momentarily crushed by cruel disillusionment, the tall corporal allowed himself to be shouldered aside while a consuming, blinding rage of bitter resentment was born in his brain, growing until he shook like an aspen. Nerves overtaut from the trenches grew dangerously evident and his pale face worked spasmodically as about him rang the heartfelt curses of the others.

"Steak!" they snarled. "Of all the damn gyp deals they ever was!"

Then Corporal Jake Tourneur got going. He burst into such a stream of profanity as one may hope to accumulate after years of research along the waterfronts. From his lips poured a stream of withering, scorching invectives that omitted not a single person in the A.E.F. He delved into the rich, colorful vocabulary of the mule-skinner, of the bucko mate and the longshoreman, until, with breathless and white fury, he towered over the thoroughly frightened cook, his black eyes blazing and his lips twitching.

"Take this whole damned mess and stuff it up your shirt," he snarled. "I've had enough of it."

Loud grew the uproar, and a riot trembled on the edge of existence; then, from a nearby doorway emerged a spruce lieutenant, his tiny mustache trembling with agitation. Unerringly seeking out Jake as the source of the rebellion, he loftily elbowed his way through the crowd.

"What's this?" demanded the pink-cheeked one aggressively.

"Hawg wash, suh," grunted the tall corporal sullenly, pointing a dirty forefinger at the repellent mess kit of salmon. "And damn pore hawg wash at that!"

The lieutenant turned a deep shade of crimson and snatched a mess kit from one of the lowering doughboys who had encircled the chow gun. He tasted the salmon sauce.

"I find this fish perfectly delicious," he stated coldly. "Here, eat that!" He thrust out the mess kit at the tall Southerner.

"All right," snarled Jake, a species of madness seizing him, "if you like it so damn much, take it all!" So saying, he hurled the contents of his mess kit into that smooth pink-and-white face, drenching the tremulous little mustache and the natty whipcord uniform.

A gasp of horror went up from the assembled machine gunners as the unhappy lieutenant cursed and tried to claw the gluey, orange-hued mess from his eyes.

"I'll have you court-martialed! Arrest that man!" he shrilled. But Jake, a moment before, had spun on his heel and, parting the crowd like a snowplow, stalked out of the gate with Tug Schmalz trotting along behind him. On the battered red face of the shorter man was a beatific expression of wonder.

"Gee, guy," he remarked, "I sure hearn some fancy cussin' in my life, but dey was Sunday School lessons compared to dat song youse sung." Hopeful that the corporal might begin again, the erstwhile prizefighter followed, his mess kit yet filled with the sorry mess.

Then, as they reached the main village street once more, a private girt in a spotless white apron passed them, a covered dish in his hands.

"What you got there?" growled Jake savagely.

"G'wan, fry your fat face," was the retort of the messenger. "Whaddaya want to know for? You ain't gonna —"

Without a word Corporal Tourneur's red bony fist shot out and caught the orderly by the collar. With the other hand he raised the cover of the dish. There, cozily nestled on a carpet of French fries, lay a roasted chicken with savory gravy eddying about it.

For a long moment the Southerner hesitated on the brink of violence but, from behind, came the angry shouts of the lieutenant.

"Arrest that man!"

Down the street an M.P., scenting trouble, whirled about and pricked up his ears.

"Stop that man!"

"Beat it!" implored Tug, and pulled at Jake's sleeve. "Beat it, guy, or yuh'll break rocks at Leavenworth de rest o' yer life! You struck a officer; in wartime dat's a shootin' offense."

The M.P., now thoroughly aroused, was running toward the two mutineers.

Reluctantly Jake freed the terrified mess orderly and dived down a side street to disappear in a dark tangle of woods looming behind the village. Behind them rose the cries of their pursuers.

"Now, you tore it high, wide and handsome," grunted Tug, when, breathless and with faces lashed in red wales by the moist twigs of the forest, the two paused in a little clearing. "You an' me is fixed for a fine go in stir, and no bondsmen handy."

"Listen to me, big boy," announced Jake with smoldering eyes. "Right now I'm goin' to tell you somethin'. Inside of fo'ty-eight hours I'm fixin' to sink these here molars in the best chicken dinner you ever hear of."

"G'wan," grunted Tug. "You're cockeyed. You ain't got no more chanst of eating chicken than I got of bein' next welterweight champeen. Bet you t'ree months' pay youse don't come near enough to chicken to slip it a fistful o' corn."

"O.K., big boy," grumbled Jake. "When Jake Tourneur craves chicken, he's sure fixin' to git it. Your mazuma's as good as lost, son."

His voice died away abruptly, for the underbrush was crackling dangerously near. Accordingly he listened a moment, then trotted off down a narrow path through the dark, dripping woods.

At the end of a half-hour's trudging among the glistening trunks of the trees, the two emerged from the shelter of the forest and beheld before them another little town as exactly like the one they had quitted as two lumps of coal.

The corporal lifted his long, dark head and sniffed the wind eagerly, much in the manner of his own "houn' dawgs."

"Ah," he said, "they-all's throwin' some eats into the crowd down there. Maybe there'd be a chance of hornin' in on a real feed."

"Fergit it, guy," objected the other mournfully. "They's probably a phone from dat boig we was in over to dis one. Don't youse fergit we're A.W.O.L. now and fair meat fer the gat o' every ornery son-of-a-gun of a M.P. in this sector." The prize fighter peered about uneasily, his small blue eyes resting fearfully upon the village. "Looks nice and restful, but yuh can't tell. I ain't felt this way since I was ham 'n' eggin' out in Chicago."

The lanky Southerner sniffed the breeze once more.

"Come on," he urged, "let's take a chance. I'm that hungry I could eat polecat *an' like it!*" So saying, he straightened his forage cap and marched boldly into the quagmire of a road that led to the little white-walled hamlet seen, like a vision of hope, through the drifting rain, mist and fog.

With a masterly assumed air of innocence, the two hungry outcasts tramped toward the loom of red-tiled roofs and low, white-walled structures that made up the village. Tug swore furiously as, on the edge of town, a convoy of high-sided, camouflaged Mack trucks, loaded with elephant iron and barbed wire, went clanking by, splattering the sticky yellow mud of the roadway high into the air.

The begoggled driver of the leading truck, as he caught the blast of Private Schmalz's profanity, leaned far out over the side and wagged a reproving finger.

"Bad boys," he said in a high falsetto, "does your mamma know you have run away from home an' taken to swearing?"

"If mah belly wahn't gratin' on mah backbone," shouted Jake furiously, "I'd aim to take a fall out o' that damned mechanic."

But they were even too weary to scrape off the new accumulation of mud and disconsolately tramped into the village street, casting hungry glances to the right and left. Everything betokened the occupancy of American troops — O.D. painted motorcycles, camionettes, and scrawled notices in English.

"Hey, *soldat*," inquired Jake of a private who crouched out of the rain in a doorway, wielding a busy toothpick, "where-at does they-all deal the eats in this dump? Me and the big boy heah is on our way to ketch up to our outfit at Beauville. We ain't been eatin' much lately, and I reckon we'd like to get a mouthful afore we-all goes on."

"Grub pile is over, Johnny Reb," grunted the doughboy, twiddling the toothpick and eyeing the strangers suspiciously. "Maybe the food butcher's got a few scraps left lying around."

"Whadja have for chow?" inquired Tug hopefully. "Was it a real feed?"

"Sure," replied the private, with a sigh as he extracted a shred of meat, eyed it, then ate it. "We got a A-one mess sergeant. They's only thirty of us parkin' in this burg, and believe it or not, that guy rounded up enough chicken —"

"Chicken!" Jake's long jaw dropped at the word.

"Yeh," continued the private, and waved the toothpick amiably. "You c'n call me a liar if you want, but we had chicken all right. They was kinda sophisticated and old, but man alive, they sure tasted like a million bucks after all the salt horse and dunderfunk we've been feeding on. If you fellers hurry up," he suggested, "they might be a wing or two left."

His eyes widened in amazement as the two mud-splashed strangers fairly sailed down the village street, heading with unerring instinct toward the house from which came that heaven-sent aroma.

"Hey, youse guys," shouted a sergeant of M.P.'s. "What do you bums think this is, a race course?" He jumped aside just in time to avoid being hurled to the ground by Jake's maddened rush.

"Boy," panted the Southerner over his shoulder, "did you hear that? Chicken! You ain't got no chance for your money now."

With hope beating high in his heart, Jake pushed through the stragglers of the meal. As he passed he glanced at the mess kits and waved a triumphant hand to call Tug's attention.

There was no mistaking the shape of those slender, delicate bones that rested in the aluminum containers. The repast undoubtedly had been chicken.

"What you guys want?" A very fat cook looked up in a belligerent fashion.

"Have a heart, buddy," pleaded the corporal, his mouth watering as he beheld the indubitable evidence that a chicken dinner had been distributed. "We-all ain't had nothing to eat for two days. We done got left behind when our outfit come out of the lines."

"What outfit was dat?" inquired a burly, unshaven sergeant with a suspicious glare. "Youse guys look more to me like a couple of A.W.O.L.'s."

"D Company, 333rd Machine Gun," snapped Jake, and exhibited tarnished collar ornaments in substantiation.

"That's right," volunteered a figure from a dark corner. "That outfit went through here early this morning. They're on the level, Hank."

Tug gave a realistic sigh of relief. "Give us anyt'ing youse got," he pleaded. "Salt horse, goldfish, or anyt'ing. I ain't been so hungry since I was ridin' the rods."

"You guys *do* look kinda tuckered out and white around the gills," admitted the jovial cook, "and since you seem to be regular fellers, I'll —"

Corporal Jake stood trembling on the brink of ecstasy, and his whole hungry being seemed filled with a gracious flood of thanksgiving when the fat man behind the stove continued:

"I'll fry you up a hunk of chicken apiece. Just park your dogs out of the way over there."

The local soldiers began heaving themselves up one by one, and grunting sympathetic words to the waiting pair, made their way out into the persistent, soul-killing drizzle.

With borrowed mess kits in their hands, the two adventurers waited like cats about a fish cart, scarcely able to credit their senses. The whole smelly room spun about Jake's head like an immense top.

"A.E.F., where are you?" was Tug's continual remark. "Gee, dis just can't be de Ass End First! Don't nobody snap his fingers and wake me up."

In a delighted daze the two sodden, hollow-cheeked scarecrows watched the stout performer drop two heavy half chickens in the sizzling fat on the stove. It hissed and spluttered bravely, playing the sweetest of gastronomic melodies in Jake's ears.

"In two shakes of a lamb's tail you guys can sink your molars in the best slab of chicken meat served this side of Paris." The cook shuffled across the kitchen and produced a handful of cold fried potatoes. These he dumped into the pan with the chicken.

Every hiss and crackle of that fat played sweet symphonies in Jake's large red ears. With the gaze of a man who sees his soul's salvation before him, he feasted his eyes upon that piece of chicken now turning a golden brown. Around the knife and fork his muddied, chapped fingers opened and closed spasmodically and a continual fountain of water formed in his mouth. Finally, the cook turned the chicken over for the last time and indicated a pile of French fried potatoes which lay steaming to one side.

"All right, youse guys," he said, "come and git it, and eat hearty. Don't they feed you up in the lines? How's it like up there?"

Transfixed with joy, the two arose, but from the doorway came a loud, startled cry.

"Hey, Mose, pipe the United States Marines policing up — I wonder who those M.P.'s are after."

"Look out," cried another, "they're coming here. You should have married that girl, I tell you."

M.P.'s! The tall corporal stood frozen in his tracks, an agonizing doubt in his mind.

"Beat it," hissed Tug, "the coppers is after us. Beat it, if you don't want to make little ones outa big ones from here to Leavenworth! That damn looey's sicked the Publicity Boys on us!"

The cook, instantly alarmed at the prospect of having sheltered — and comforted, as the phrase goes — two possible criminals, caught up a cleaver and with warning cries mounted guard over the stove. Behind him hissed and crackled the frying chicken, so near and yet so infinitely far.

But even as the lanky Southerner weighed his chances against the cook, there came a loud clatter of hobnails and the sound of imperious voices at the door but a few feet away.

"Where are they?" panted a harsh voice. "They went in here?"

"In there."

Then with visions of a court-martial and subsequent unpleasant proceedings rising in dreadful clarity before his eyes, Jake turned and, casting a forlorn farewell look at the stove, leaped through the back door with Tug a stride behind.

"There they go! Stop 'em! Halt! Halt!"

Like alley cats pursued by terriers, the fugitives fairly sailed over a low wall that enclosed the backyard, though its top was studded with broken bottles.

"Halt or I fire!" There was no mistaking the menacing tone of that shouted threat, and Jake ducked frantically as an automatic pistol uttered its dry staccato bark. Just an inch or so over his head whined a hungry bullet.

"Stop! Stop!"

Before the howling M.P.'s could fire another shot, the fugitives dropped to temporary shelter behind the mud-splashed wall. Tug, at that moment, rose valiantly to the emergency, a different person. His coarsened features took on a look of furtive cunning as, without an instant's hesitation, he turned down a little alley.

"Foller me!" he snapped. "I know how to duck coppers."

Jake ran as hard as he could, but could not resist stealing a glance over his shoulder.

There were two red-faced M.P.'s just astride the wall, their red brassards showing up strongly as they raised their pistols for another shot. Snap! Crack! *Zo-e-e-e!* bullets went keening by.

"Deserters!" bawled the pursuers at the top of their lungs. "A.W.O.L.'s, murderers! Stop 'em! Everybody out! Get 'em, dead or alive!"

From all sides of that previously serene village rose startled shouts. Figures in blue, khaki, and black poured out of every house, gripping varied weapons, apparently determined to cut off the retreat of the bewildered chicken hunters. The fierceness of this pursuit puzzled and depressed the fugitives; that looey must have raised a terrible stink. Perhaps it was a very serious military offense to spill salmon over a lieutenant?

Jake turned paler and paler as the blood cry swelled. Tug evidently knew what he was doing, for with incredible speed he vaulted another wall and darted into a house, scattering startled peasants right and left.

A hair-raising scream arose as the foremost of the fugitives trod squarely on the family cat. The women of the household drowned out the unhappy feline's wails in a united shriek of terror.

Jake hesitated in a dark passage, momentarily lost, bewildered in the gloom and by the earsplitting screams of the peasant women. Then, ahead, he saw a door bang open and the chunky figure of Tug dash out across the farther street.

A doughboy, evidently billeted with the family, foolishly tried to cut off the harassed corporal's retreat.

"One side!" grunted the fugitive. "Ah aims to go places and do things." His large, horny fist shot out and with the impetus of his stride behind it caught the ambitious doughboy a terrific blow on the side of the face that sent him staggering and rolling among the rows of copper pots and pans behind. They caused a gorgeous uproar.

Jake was running at top speed now and breath was coming with difficulty into his chest. Furthermore, the flapping slicker cut down his best speed. Behind, he could hear the shouts of the rising hue and cry. Once more on the glistening cobbles of the village street, Jake hurdled a steaming manure pile, a sleeping pig or two, and followed the fleeting form of the ex-boxer into the shelter of the woods again where they promptly were screened by a thick growth of friendly underbrush, but the pursuit remained stern and unremitting, with almost the entire population of the village taking part. Twigs cracked and branches snapped ominously on all sides of the two lost sheep from D Company.

"Dem low-lifes is goin' to put de collar on us after all," panted Tug, his battered features sweating and scarlet with exertion. "Sounds like dey want to lynch us, all fer one hunk o' goldfish!"

"No, suh, they ain't goin' to get me till Ah has my chicken dinner," snarled the corporal with something of a fanatic's fire in his eyes. "When Ah want chicken, Big Boy, Ah want it terrible bad."

"Yeh," gasped the private, "and youse won't like losin' three months' pay, neither — if you don't owe it all in stoppages."

The wet twigs lashed their faces like tiny whips and their slickers caught and tore in the underbrush as they bolted onward. Then, quite suddenly, to Jake's profane dismay, they once more beheld the familiar outlines of the red village roofs through the trees before them. His heart stopped dead.

"Gee!" gasped Tug. "We've run in a circle. What the hell we goin' to do? The bulls'll be here in a minute. Think fast, you big bum, you got me into dis."

For a moment the breathless, hopeless runners paused — but only for a moment. Behind rose the crashing progress of their pursuers who, realizing that the fugitives unconsciously were returning toward the village, had redoubled their efforts.

"Look!" panted the Southerner. "There's a dugout of some kind — no, it's a root cellar. 'Tain't much, but it's our best bet."

Amid a tangle of shrubbery the wild-eyed fugitives could barely distinguish the outline of a low door. It was not a ruin, but a vegetable cellar, built almost invisibly into a rise of the earth.

With the silence of Indians on the warpath, the two crept on hands and knees into the cold, damp darkness and there crouched fearfully, while the doughboys lugging Springfields, M.P.'s brandishing ugly, black-snouted automatics, and gangling peasant lads armed with manure forks and scythes tore by — all bellowing for the blood of the hunted. They seemed disconcertingly confident that at any moment they might find their quarry.

Jake placed his mouth close to his companion's leatherlike ear, deformed into a hideous cauliflower by years of leather-pushing. "Gone by," he whispered. "Maybe we'll still excape with a hull skin."

"What I don't t'ink of youse and yer damn chickens!" replied Tug with feeling. "What for was I sap enough to come wit' youse, anyhow?"

"I didn't invite you, what I remember," grunted Jake gloomily. "But you can't go back now. That looey I decorated with the Order of the Golden Fish will sho'-nuff send us up the rocky road till hell freezes three-foot thick. If you was to show up in Beauville now, you would be welcome like a skunk in a church lawn party so you better traipse along with Uncle Jake and have a nice second joint when —" there was a note of steel in the corporal's voice — "when I get that chicken. And so help me Hannah I'm sho' fixin' to have it afore noon tomorry if I have to murder every cunnel in this Gawd-forgot sector."

For some time longer the two lay on their bellies breathlessly listening to the baffled coming and going of the irate and evidently murderously inclined M.P.'s.

"I cain't understand," objected the Southerner, "why them sailors' Pee Poles should get so blamed steamed up over a pore little no-'count mess kit o' salmon."

As if in answer to his query, two Marine M.P.'s halted just outside the door. Jake could see their thick, putteed legs on a level with his eyes.

"They was hard eggs," observed one of the policemen. "The A.M.P. from Roosty told us to shoot 'em on sight. They're the guys that did them murders over at Malincourt. These birds fit the description O.K. One big, ugly black-haired cuss looks like a Missouri mule what's been kicked — and the other short, sportin' a phiz only a mother could love. Cauliflower ear, too."

The other M.P. shifted his weight and cursed as a trickle of water dripped from his glistening helmet down the neck of his uniform.

"Yeh, Donovan was tellin' me there's a big reward out for 'em — dead or alive. They can't get away — Captain Gohagan's got a dragnet out and believe me, kid, I ain't takin' no chances; when I sees 'em, I fire first and ask questions at the post mortem. Remember, it's dead or alive and I likes 'em *dead!*" He laughed grimly.

Tug shivered and Jake drew a deep, quivering breath. So that was how the land lay! At last the two police tramped off, leaving a pair of thoroughly alarmed machine gunners behind.

"Can yuh tie a tag to that?" groaned Tug, his battered face working. "Seems to me we stands about the same chance Frank Moran had against Willard." He stiffened spasmodically as he felt Jake's hand close upon his arm. "What is it? Are dey comin' back?" he breathed in swift dismay.

"Look!" There was a quivering note in the Southern Corporal's voice. "Look! A hen yard!"

There indeed was a little chicken house and a run some fifty yards away on the extreme edge of the village. Watching the feeding hens sat a little dirty-faced, barefoot girl. But the interest of Private Tug Schmalz was not in chickens any longer. Before his fearful, sunken eyes rose a vision of Tug Schmalz stretched cold and dead on his face with an M.P.'s bullet in his back.

"We're goin' to git it," he murmured, "and git it right."

"Bet yo' life, big boy," agreed Jake dreamily. "The one I aims to get is that big black one with the white tail feathers."

"White tail feathers hell!" Tug relapsed into disgusted silence.

The cheerless afternoon rolled on toward cold twilight. The rain finally abated and a sickly yellow sunset tinted the white plaster walls of the farmhouses. Then, to Jake's acute dismay, an elderly Frenchman in a patched and soiled blue smock came out and, with the help of the child, noisily herded the hens toward the village. One belated straggler suddenly appeared from the little hen house and careered along after the others with its neck outstretched and its wings spread, as though it could read the bitter thoughts of the tall, black-headed man crouching despondently among the dusty cobwebs of the vegetable cellar.

"Dere goes de only supper we're like to eat," said Tug with a bitter laugh. "Why in hell is a Frog chicken one o' de family and livin' at home? Now we're like to get our pants shot off wit'out no excuse."

Stony-faced, Jake stared off into the misty night. He felt very old and tired and he was very hungry. Tantalizingly the lights of the village houses came to him. There was food and warmth and shelter from the biting north wind that had begun to moan through the tree tops.

"Come on, big boy," he said when Tug dropped to the ground beside him, "we can't go into that burg — we'll just have to find another."

Like fantastic garlands, streamers of roast chicken danced before his eyes, turning, turning — juicy breast, plump legs and all. Like luscious will-o'-the-wisps they glowed among the steadily dripping trees and even the sighing of the wind bore a marked resemblance to the satisfied, sleepy clucking of chickens.

"Going goofy, I guess," he told himself. "And chicken is the only cure!"

The Lost Battalion

✂

from *Known But to God*
by QUENTIN REYNOLDS

The first sight which met the 308th when their transport landed at Liverpool was a huge sign advertising Spratt's Dog Cakes. "After the food we've had on this ship, even dog cakes will be a relief," Peter Grange said.

It had been an uncomfortable trip. Six thousand men had been packed into accommodations that before had berthed only eighteen hundred. Mess supplies had been spoiled, and during the later stages of the voyage they had had to resort to army rations, not the steaks and chicken they had grown accustomed to at Camp Upton, but the inevitable beans and canned corned beef. They had gone through two submarine scares, but now the ship was anchored in the Mersey and barges were coming out to take them ashore. They were quickly transferred to the little six-wheeled compartment cars and the train headed south. There had been rumors that they would train for a month or two at Winchester, which suited the men fine. It would give them a chance to become acquainted with England and to investigate the report that the girls of England were fond of Yanks. They sped through tidy, red-roofed villages of the north and stopped at more populous cities such as Leicester, where girls at canteens served hot coffee and where crowds cheered them happily. The Yanks had arrived.

Hours later, they were not at Winchester but at Dover, which meant there would be no pleasant interval before leaving for France. There were disquieting reports in Dover. Mont Kemmel had fallen, and it looked as if the Germans would take Calais. Could it be that they would immediately be thrown into combat in an attempt to save Calais? Not only the men but officers worried that night. The next morning they went aboard transports and headed for the French coast. The Channel was far worse than any weather they had encountered on the Atlantic crossing. Only those with the strongest stomachs escaped seasickness. It was raining when they reached Calais. From the landing, a British Tommy looked up at the waxen, pale faces at the rail. "You blokes goin' to war? You look dead already."

Danny's first letter from the front read in part:

Our first night in France wasn't very glamorous. We landed at
a channel port (the censor tells us we can't name cities), and
were given a few hours off to investigate the town. The place had
been bombed several times and the sight of wrecked homes gave
us our first feeling that we were in the war zone. But the French
have a real sense of humor, even in a city like this that has been
almost demolished. There was a sign outside of one bistro saying:

English spoken here
American Understood

The French beer was warm and tasteless. We tried French cigarettes and choked on them. The town was filled with kids selling
bitter chocolate and sugarless cookies, but they were laughing,
good-natured kids, all of whom had picked up some English. That
night we slept in tents, a dozen men to each tent. The German
celebrated our arrival by bombing us from the air at dawn. It was
odd to hear the planes above us, knowing they were enemies.
When they dropped their bombs they exploded with a dull "or-r-
umph" sound, and in our ignorance we didn't know if they were
landing far away or on the next tent. We found later they'd
landed four miles from us in an open field.

Our camp was on the outskirts of the city. Near us there was a
compound which held several hundred German prisoners of war.
They didn't look very frightening in their drab prisoners' uniforms.
To add to this international flavor, there were some two hundred
Chinese laborers hired to dig water ditches, prepare ground for
tents and throw up sheds to protect our equipment in case of rain.
The Chinese were awakened by the bombing (the twelfth time
in two weeks), and were so mad about it that they grabbed their
pickaxes and shovels, broke into the compound and started a tong
war with the prisoners. Before the French guards could get them
under control, half a dozen Germans had busted skulls. What was
done to the Chinese? Nothing. Around here laborers are more important than soldiers.

During the first two weeks, our instructors in advanced training
were British. Some of the boys didn't like taking orders from the
"limeys" but we had to learn from them about new items of equipment we'd been given which they had used in combat. Some were
weapons, others, complicated gadgets like the Lucas 14cm daylight
signal lamp. We've had a few brawls with the limeys in the cafés
at night. It doesn't take much to ignite a spark. A lot of the

French and some British have given us the nickname "Sammies"; logically enough, they derive it from Uncle Sam, but the boys hate it. They prefer to be called Yanks.

The Division was gradually being shaken down, readied for combat. The forced marches, carrying full pack, the maneuvers simulating real fighting conditions with live ammunition being used, were all part of a plan to harden the men and put them into mental and physical condition for front-line duty. The expected attack against Calais did not materialize, and one day they received their marching orders. Every man was a member of a squad, a platoon, a company, a battalion, and the 77th Division itself was too huge to be anything but an impersonal mass. Private Cannon was a member of Company A. First Battalion, 308th Infantry. He and the others by now had identified themselves with their company and with their battalion. The First Battalion boarded freight cars marked ominously QUARANTE HOMMES, HUIT CHEVAUX (forty men, eight horses), for which the American Legion club was later named, and headed for what most of them hoped would be the front. They skirted Paris, which tantalizingly lingered before their eyes just long enough for them to see the Eiffel Tower, then they headed for Nancy. There they remained in the freight yards until the tempting sight of the beautiful city was rudely snatched away from them. Finally, they detrained at two towns, Charmes and Portieux. From now on they would march. They marched to Migneville in Lorraine, a town which had been occupied by the Germans and which showed scars of the fierce fighting for it that had taken place. Civilians had been removed from the city and the men of the First Battalion were billeted in the homes, churches, barns, that were still serviceable. Units of the great "Rainbow Division," the fighting 42nd Division of the U. S. Army, first to arrive in France, began streaming in. They'd been in the lines only a few miles ahead for ninety days, and as they marched through the town they threw cheerful insults at the men of the First Battalion, who would relieve them.

"What they'll do to you when you get up there!" they'd cry tauntingly. It was Sergeant Hopkins, master of invective, who bellowed out, "Every German prisoner of war we've seen is singing. 'I'm Always Chasing Rainbows.'" The men quickly improvised verses more insulting than lyrical, which caused a number of Rainbow platoons to break ranks and fight it out.

Finally, only a French division stood between the 77th and the actual front lines.

Danny Cannon, the other six members of his squad, and a second squad of seven were quartered in a large "comfortable" barn just north of Migneville. They had fixed the larger holes in its roof, had cleaned it thoroughly, and, except for the always present threat of a German breakthrough, life wasn't too hard. Pete Grange had shown a genius for scrounging. He had a fondness for rising at dawn and disappearing for a few hours, usually bringing back with him a few bottles of wine, a freshly killed chicken, French cigarettes. His father had sent him off well-heeled with American one-dollar bills, which had considerable attraction for the French peasants. When he couldn't buy, he would borrow; when he couldn't borrow, he would "liberate." Even Sergeant Hopkins looked up to him as the ideal man to serve the platoon. "That Grange is a real soldier," he once said to Danny with admiration. "He'll steal anything."

A group of British sergeants had been assigned temporarily to the battalion. All were veterans of three years of combat and they told the untried Americans stories of their experience. It was Sergeant Hopkins who had met the British sergeant Alfie Clayton and brought him to the barn. He was a wiry little Cockney who had become expert in the handling of unexploded shells. Clayton had been one of the original members of "Kitchener's Contemptibles" and had survived three years of warfare without a scratch. When he talked about war, even Hopkins remained mute.

"When you get up front, mates," he'd say, "first thing to do is to find out who you're fightin'. A good officer will send out a squad at night just to nab one prisoner. All you want to know is the name of his outfit. Maybe it's a Prussian regiment. If it is and you're in a trench like you will be, always keep your napper below the parapet and keep duckin'. With the bloody Prussians, it's always bang-bang, the war is on twenty-four hours a day. But if they're Bavarians or Saxons, you can take it easy. They only come at you when there's a big push. They're gentlemen, they are. Now it's sure that Bavarians or Saxons are holding the line opposite us. That one defending French division is strung out thin, and still the Boche hasn't tried to break through. Sure, they throw a few Minnies and whizz-bangs at us every day, but that's just to keep us honest. We got nothin' to worry about.

"The worst thing," he went on, "is when you're sent out on night patrol in No Man's Land. Until you learn the drill. Trouble is, at first you usually get lost. Crawl on your belly until you come to barbed wire. Maybe it's yours; maybe it's the Boche's. Keep crawling until you find one of the poles supporting the wire. If it's iron, hold your breath and move away. The Boche uses iron stakes — we use wooden ones. The Boche does everything by the book. We Tommies don't know any better, so we do things unexpected like. I reckon you Yanks will be the same when we get up further."

Sergeant Clayton liked to sing. "Everytime we get close enough for them to hear us, we sing this song," he said, "and those blokes usually know some English:

"We beat you at the Marne
We beat you at the Aisne
We gave you hell at Neuve-Chapelle
And here we are again.

"Ain't many of us still around who went through those three awful
battles, but I'm one of them. I'm a lucky Cockney born in the sound of
the bells."

The month in Lorraine gave the division a gentle initiation into the fighting war, but then it was ordered to relieve the 4th Division on the southern
bank of the Vesle River. The 4th was taking a murderous beating. They
were staged against the first-class veteran Germans, and now the untried and untested 77th was told that it would be thrown against what
was probably the most efficient fighting force the German war machine
could present.

The men were loaded into trucks, each carrying full fighting equip-
ment, including a rifle, the usual pack, two extra bandoliers of .30-caliber
ammunition. Their route lay through Fère-en-Tardenois to the Fort de
Wesle, where they left their trucks and scurried into the concealing forest.
Now, for the first time, they heard the cacophony of war, the thunderous
concerto of big German guns. The next morning they took over the line.
There were no trenches, only hurriedly dug foxholes. The men of the 4th
Division didn't say much as they filed by on their way to the rear. Every
soldier looked exhausted. Danny and every other man in his division
knew that this time they were fighting for real.

Their first unpleasant experience was an attack by mustard gas. To
Danny, it smelled much like crushed onions. Happily, a crosswind had
diverted most of it, and when it arrived the gas had so thinned out
as to be nonlethal. The Germans decided to give these replacements a
noisy welcome. All day they threw "ashcans," "iron cigars," "Minnies,"
and the "88's" which the men called "whizzbangs." They were to
learn everything the hard way those few days. They learned about shell
splinters; for instance, if a high explosive shell burst four hundred yards
away, they must throw themselves flat, knowing that ragged four-pound
chunks of red-hot iron could reach them even at that distance. They
learned about "iron maidens," huge trench mortar shells with steel fins to
maintain correct position during flight. The Germans kept lobbing these
into that portion of the riverbank held by the First Battalion. They
received their initiation into phosphorized cartridges, or "tracer" bullets. At night these would often streak the air with a startling flicker of
streaming lights looking like an army of racing fireflies.

Hopkins said, "They're throwing everything at us except their own
trenches."

During the first few days these new men took a savage beating and took it well. The 77th learned one distasteful lesson that shocks every man when he first finds himself in combat — dead horses smell exactly like dead men. Even when the shelling stopped, the horrible odor of death remained. The heat intensified the discomfort of the troops; the large canvas water bags had been exhausted of cool if chlorinated water, and they had to depend upon the few streams along the line. Danny's platoon was stationed at Ville Savoie, where there was a fine fountain. It was under sporadic fire.

"Sarge, I've timed their fire," he said to Hopkins. "They fire for two minutes, then stop for two minutes. When they stop again, why don't I run out there, hang a water bag at the fountain and then run back. The next time they stop, I'll dash out and get the bag. We need water bad."

"Okay, Danny, but don't get hit."

"Death is for suckers," Cannon laughed. He was beginning to be filled with the confidence some veterans never attain. He had a strong feeling that although everyone else in his battalion might "get it" — he wouldn't. Men who can acquire that comforting if spurious state of mind make the best soldiers — and during those days on the Vesle, Danny Cannon was proving to be a very good soldier indeed.

For five days, the Germans had complete air superiority and during the daylight hours their planes raked the Allied positions with machine-gun fire and dropped bombs accurately on gun emplacements. Observation planes were sending reports back about the position of gun batteries and these were under constant shelling. This lasted for two weeks and Danny knew now what it was like to see friends blown to bits only yards away. But it only strengthened his resolve; he was growing more and more like Hopkins. He could eat spoiled canned salmon without becoming too sick. He could pick the maggots out of his "corned willie" and down the rest with relish. He could drink warm, brackish water without getting dysentery.

It was the French under General Mangin who exerted such a severe flanking pressure to the northwest that the Germans had to retire. They retired well with strong supporting troops, artillery, and the ever-present planes covering them. Then one morning the 77th crossed the Vesle and could draw its first easy breath in some time. The First Battalion was relieved and sent back to Sergy, some twenty miles to the rear.

"As I remember, there's a stream there," Lieutenant John Parker told his platoon. "Grange and I will find billets for us. The rest of you run like hell for that stream. It's small, so get there first. Fill your canteens, then shed your lousy clothes and hit that water."

"Smart fellow," Hopkins said to Danny.

They wallowed in the cool water and picked cooties from their uniforms, which they then soaked in the stream. By the time the platoon had finished washing, the thin trickling stream was a dirty gray. Hot meals were cooked that night and men who had slept little for ten days collapsed in the straw of barns or, for that matter, anywhere they happened to be. All except Private Pete Grange. He disappeared for two hours to return with three bottles of wine and two large rolls of sausage.

Inevitably, the time came to advance again. This time it was to the River Aisne. It was another tough battle and casualties were high, but again the 77th gained ground. It was now a compact, hard-fighting, tough regiment. The replacements were men from the Midwest, from New England, from the South, and at first they called the veterans of the 77th "the city boys." Half a dozen fights later, they still called them "city boys" but with respect.

And then came the Argonne.

Major Charles W. Whittlesey, tall, bespectacled commander of the First Battalion, had briefed his men well. A lawyer in civilian life, he had been meticulous in explaining the importance of the offensive (it had been planned by General Foch) and had not minimized the dangers to be faced.

"This could be the offensive that wraps up the war for us," he said grimly. "Our goal is the Sedan-Mezières railroad, the main line of supply for the Germans on the whole Western Front. If that can be cut, it will mean a general retirement by the Germans. This is our biggest offensive; we are throwing every available division into it. That means" — he hesitated — "one million two hundred thousand American troops. Keep that in mind if you ever feel alone. Every man we have will be fighting. The French will be on our left flank. The big obstacle between us and the enemy is the Argonne Forest. That *must* be taken."

Things went pretty well according to plan for the first three days. The First Battalion was in the region of Le Mort Homme, a German war cemetery. That night it rained hard and Danny and his platoon dug foxholes and tried to find shelter from the driving late September rains. At dawn they were given bacon, butter, and bread, and then came the order to advance. The orders from Brigade Headquarters were: "North, straight ahead, then bear westward up the ravine that climbs from the valley of Charlevaux Brook. On the crest lies the Giesler Stellung, the main German line. Take it; push on to the road on the opposite slope above Charlevaux Valley and take La Palette Hill. There the regiment will reorganize and wait for further advance."

The First would be the advance battalion. They reached the western edge of the forest, comforting at first because the trees and heavy shrubbery afforded some cover. But the Germans were somewhere ahead and because of the heavy forest, Headquarters couldn't pinpoint their position and order a barrage.

"This may not be as tough as we thought," Danny said to Pete Grange.

"It will be if you guys don't shut up," Sergeant Hopkins snapped.

Whispered orders came from Whittlesey, to be relayed down the line, and the men, shadowy brown figures against brown trees, moved leftward among the caves and crannies at the foot of La Palette Hill. Bullets chipped against the limestone shelves and men fell in the ankle-deep mud crying "Medic." They turned the corner and started up the hill and the machine guns opened. The fire seemed to the men to be a perfectly horizontal hailstorm of lead. They flung themselves on the ground and crawled, firing occasionally, which only advertised their presence without any result.

"You can't hit what you can't see," Hopkins snarled. "Save it."

Whittlesey phoned Brigade Headquarters. "Impossible to take La Palette. How about Hill 198, the other side of the ravine?"

Permission was granted, and perhaps three hundred lives were saved. They veered to the right, away from the murderous firing. There were snipers atop Hill 198, but nothing heavy coming at them.

"The command is forward," Lieutenant John Parker in charge of the platoon barked. They inched their way up the hill, not in formation but singly or by twos and threes. And then they stumbled into a trench. It had been dug long ago but it was a properly revetted permanent line, camouflaged by nature with weeds and creeping growths and with drainage sumps, firing platform machine-gun posts. This was part of the Giesler Stellung. Whittlesey hurried up with Larney, his signal man, and with Richards and Tollefson carrying pigeon cages. If all communications to Regiment and Brigade were cut off, there was always a chance that pigeons could carry messages back. He called for his officers. The temptation to linger in the relative safety of the trench was great, but he was too good an officer to succumb to it.

"Take your men forward across Charlevaux Brook," he ordered.

They skidded, slid, slipped, down the slope. They had to cross an open field two hundred yards wide, and the machine guns from La Palette opened up in the fading dusk. And then they were across the stream. Officers gave orders quickly. Machine guns were set up facing La Palette. Positions were allotted to the twenty automatic rifles. Canteens were filled at the stream and men munched on their "corned willy" and hardtack.

"It wasn't too bad," Danny said.

"If the French give us decent support and our artillery can find the Germans, and if everybody on the whole front is moving as fast as we've moved," Hopkins said, "we'll be all right."

"The major brought this off," Hopkins added. "He got orders to reach this spot and here we are. Yeah, this is the best war I was ever in."

Lieutenant Parker said, "Sure. A fine war. We're sitting here, six hundred men with no blankets, no rations, no trench mortars, no tents, no tanks, and damn little ammo for what guns we do have."

"That means they don't expect us to slug it out," Sergeant Hopkins said. "The heavy stuff and supplies ought to be on the way now, don't you think?"

"Who can read the mind of Brigade Headquarters?" Lieutenant Parker didn't like the situation.

Neither did Whittlesey. He knew that the Germans usually attacked at dawn. If they did he had nothing much with which to defend except human flesh. The big attack didn't come at dawn, neither did the reserves Whittlesey was frantically asking for. But at dawn, the hated *Minenwerfer* started lobbing mines into the section held by the First Battalion. The doughboys called them Minnies. They were relatively slow-moving mortar shells which made no noise until they landed and exploded. They were invented by Professor Karl Kultur of Berlin and were horribly effective at close range. Danny and his pals huddled into the now friendly muddy ground to escape them, but when they burst they threw bits of steel in all directions. The Minnies were being thrown in a haphazard manner; the Germans hadn't as yet gotten their target coordinates straightened out. Now a few shells from 88's started coming in. Whittlesey sent a runner back with a message: *Being shelled by German artillery. Fire coming from northwest. Can we have artillery support?* To supplement the message carried by the runner, he had Richards send off a pigeon with the same message. Neither arrived.

At dawn General Alexander, at the 77th Division Headquarters, felt that things were going pretty well. He knew something that Major Whittlesey didn't know: that the First Battalion had broken the German line. The First were far ahead of anyone else in the sector, and so far he had received no messages to indicate that Whittlesey was in a precarious spot. But experienced Alexander, a stocky, square-jawed, aggressive regular army man, knew that the Germans would soon be attracted by the breakthrough made by Whittlesey and his battalion. He ordered an attack by the 305th Infantry on Whittlesey's right flank, and ordered the 307th to renew pressure on the left flank. He knew that Whittlesey and the First Battalion were about to write the most heroic saga of World War I. They weren't calling it the "Lost Battalion" yet.

The day went slowly. Danny, Peter Grange, Hopkins, Lieutenant Johnny Parker, were good men with a rifle. They huddled in the mud looking for quick flashes which would show the position of enemy snipers, and often their four rifles roared simultaneously. Other squads were doing the same, but although they killed a number of snipers the range of their rifles wasn't great enough to get the men who handled the trench mortars — the Minnies. They didn't know that the French on the left flank had been pushed back, that the reserves General Alexander had ordered were bogged down at the foot of Hill 198, now held by strong German detachments with machine guns and 88's. But they did feel alone. They *were* alone.

No one slept much that night. A messenger had arrived from Regimental Headquarters with a message that at early light a heavy barrage would be laid on the Germans to prevent any counterattack. The attack barrage started on schedule. It sounded great. There was the preliminary screech — familiar now — and then the ear-splitting explosions. It was great until the men of the First Battalion realized that the shells were falling too close to them. They knew the shells came from their own artillery; they came from the south but they were bursting two hundred yards in front of their brook. And then the first landed among them, and Danny, twenty yards away, saw Cavanaugh go down. He saw Bill Johnson and Sergeant Mile Greally and Abe Bienstock and the Indian, Jamie Rainwater, blown to bits, and Danny involuntarily said out loud, "Lay off us. We're on your side." There was quiet for a moment and then he heard a strange noise. Danny turned to Pete Grange and said, "What is that?"

"It's those pigeons," Grange shouted. "They're scared too."

"If they aren't, they're crazy." Danny, for some odd reason, wasn't really scared. His boxing helped him now. "We're losing the first couple of rounds," he said to himself. "So what! We'll nail this guy pretty soon."

Whittlesey couldn't send runners back to Headquarters, and his telephone had been cut. He had to depend on the pigeons. His message read:

WE ARE ALONG THE ROAD PARALLEL CHARLEVAUX BROOK. OUR OWN ARTILLERY IS DROPPING A BARRAGE DIRECTLY ON US. FOR GOD'S SAKE STOP IT.

                                                          WHITTLESEY

He wrote it in duplicate and gave the two notes to Richards. "Send this with two of your pigeons," he ordered and when Richards said, "I have only two left, sir," he nodded and repeated his order. Richards hurriedly attached the messages to the legs of his two pigeons. One was named Jacques, the other Cher Ami. He released them and the two birds circled uncertainly. Then Jacques flew off in a straight line north. Cher Ami, understandably confused by the noise of exploding shells, flew to a tree and clung perched on a low branch. Richards waved his arms frantically at the frightened bird, and yelled at him. Then he remembered that this was a French bird. "*Va-t-en*," he shouted, and the bird appeared to understand. He circled once and headed south. It was only three miles (as a bird flies) to Headquarters. It took Cher Ami four hours to make the trip. Somewhere along the line he was hit. When he reached the regimental headquarters pigeon loft, he had lost an eye, had a broken breastbone, and had lost a leg. Corporal George Gault in charge of the loft looked unbelievingly at the trembling bird and said, "Youngster, you deserve a medal." (They gave Cher Ami a medal, retired him, found him a wife, and he lived for two more years.) Gault hurried the message to Alexander, who turned white when he read it. There was nothing he could do now, the barrage had been completed an hour before.

He ordered supplies (food, blankets, medical supplies, ammunition) to be dropped to the First Battalion. Four planes were hurriedly loaded. They took off. One was shot down over La Palette, two dropped their supplies into the German lines, the fourth pilot came back to report he couldn't identify the American battalion.

"Damn it all, they're lost somewhere out there," the pilot said. "And I didn't want to risk dropping stuff that the Germans might get."

Danny Cannon knew only one thing: for the first time in his life he was hungry. He crawled some thirty yards to where Richards was sitting with his two empty pigeon cages.

"All your birds gone?" Cannon said.

Richards nodded numbly. He felt lost now without his birds. He had had a brief spell at basic training before they discovered that he had been a pigeon fancier in Brooklyn, but they had never bothered to teach him how to use a rifle.

"Is there any bird food left?" Cannon asked.

Richards looked surprised at the question and then said, "Yes, Corporal."

"Then what are we waiting for?"

Richards pulled six packages of pigeon food from his pocket. He handed three of them to Danny. The firing had lessened now and the two men sat in the shelter of a tree eating cracked corn, split peas, and birdseed.

"Your pigeons eat better than we do," Cannon said and then crawled back to his platoon. By some miracle not one member of his platoon had been hit. It was dusk and everyone, including the Germans, the elements, and a fading sun seemed tired. Cannon noticed that Lieutenant Parker was reading a small book.

"Is that a mystery, Lieutenant?" Danny asked him.

The lieutenant shook his head and held out the volume. Danny looked at the gold title on the cover, *Science and Health* by Mary Baker Eddy.

"This is food and drink to me," Parker said and his voice was confident. "It is a comfort when things are bad. In a spot like this I guess we all need a crutch."

Pete Grange pulled a rosary from his tunic and said, "Lieutenant, this is my crutch," and then he turned to Danny Cannon and said, "What's yours, chum?"

Danny picked up his Springfield. "My faith's in God and life, I guess, and my gun and the four grenades I've got hung on my belt. I never tried to bribe God in peacetime. I'm not going to try to bribe him now. I have a mother back home who almost became a nun. She's probably spending twenty-four hours a day praying for me. If her prayers don't work, I don't know that mine will." Danny was really thinking aloud when he realized that he might have hurt the feelings of two men he liked and respected very much. "I don't mean any disrespect, Lieutenant, and I hope the rosary works for you, Pete."

That night Major Whittlesey sent two runners back to report the desperate position of their battalion. One was killed and the other forced to return — for the first time Whittlesey and his officers knew that the battalion was surrounded. Strangely enough, Regimental, Brigade, Corps and Army Headquarters already knew this. The reports of the plight of the First Battalion had seeped through to Paris and alert Fred Ferguson of the United Press had sent a dispatch to New York about the "Lost Battalion." He could not, at that time, identify it, but his story appeared in the hundreds of newspapers served by the United Press, and suddenly all America was talking about the "Lost Battalion." But the men (there were less than four hundred of them now) who occupied only four hundred yards of French soil along the Charlevaux Brook didn't know this. They knew only that they were wet and hungry and felt very much alone. They knew now they were in a pocket, a small untenable bit of ground covering less than two acres, completely surrounded by the enemy.

Major Whittlesey didn't sleep that night. He walked from foxhole to foxhole saying calmly to his men, "We'll get out of here all right. Keep in mind that there are two million men on our side on their way up here; keep your heads down; don't fire at anything you can't see." He was not the kind of man to indulge in pep talks. His lawyer's approach was cerebral rather than emotional, but there was a confidence in his voice that gave new strength to the tired men to whom he spoke.

Another man who didn't sleep that night was Captain George C. McMurtry, second-in-command of the Battalion. The troops respected Major Whittlesey; they would go to confession to big, warmhearted McMurtry. He, too, walked up and down the four-hundred-yard line and the men felt better when he talked to them. It was McMurtry who stopped to give orders to Lieutenant John Carter. Captain McMurtry was not much for bothering with rank. He called all of the officers and half of the noncommissioned officers by their first names. "Johnny," he said to Lieutenant Parker, "I hate to ask you to do this, but I want you to take three men out there. We've noticed that the Boche are sending out single-man patrols, trying to find out how strong we are. The Major wants a couple of prisoners. If you run into one, treat him gently and bring him back alive. Incidentally, I seem to remember you have a boy named Cannon who knows some German. Take him with you. It's quiet out there tonight and he might hear something. Okay, Johnny?"

Sergeant Hopkins looked up and said, "Captain, I'm the only pro in this platoon. I never volunteered for anything in my life but I want in on this mission. I trained everybody in this group including, if he'll forgive me," he added with a straight face, "Lieutenant Parker. Okay, sir?"

McMurtry grinned, "How about it, Johnny?" he asked Parker.

Parker said, "I don't like to admit it to him, Captain, but I think Hopkins is the best soldier in the American Army. I'd like to take him, Cannon, and Pete Grange. If Grange doesn't do anything else he may bring back some German rations. He's the best scrounger in the outfit."

Ten minutes later the four men crawled out to what was their own little No Man's Land, a distance of about six hundred yards. They crawled two hundred yards through the slimy mud and not a sound came from the German trenches. They had crawled another hundred yards when Lieutenant Parker whispered to Hopkins, "You and Cannon go to the right; Grange and I will go to the left. Don't advance more than another two hundred yards. Then wait, and maybe one of those Huns will come into your arms. If this happens, shove your Colt into his belly and just say to him, 'Be quiet and you stay alive,' then make him crawl back to our lines."

Hopkins and Danny obeyed orders and waited. They were very close to the Germans. Danny could hear German phrases spoken, not loudly, and cautiously. Hopkins whispered, "I don't think we're more than sixty yards from their advanced trenches. I wish we could each throw two grenades. We'd kill a lot of those jokers, but that ain't in our orders, is it?"

Danny Cannon chuckled, reached out a hand and pressed Hopkins's shoulder. "It's good being with you, Sarge," he said simply. "I said a stupid thing to Lieutenant Parker and Pete Grange today. I said my gun was my crutch. But it is you who have always been my crutch — ever since that day when we fought it out in the Y.M.C.A. hut at Camp Upton. You taught me how to take a loss like a man, and it has been a comfort ever since. It helps now."

It was then that Danny felt something pressing against his back. It was then that he heard a voice saying in German, "Surrender or die." He heard Hopkins grunt and knew that the same thing had happened to him. They had been taken from the rear by German soldiers smarter than themselves. Danny's muscles tensed. He heard Hopkins turn in the mud to get at the German nearest him, and the sound of a rifle butt striking flesh. He knew that the sergeant was dead or near it. He realized

then that there were three men behind him. They took his gun and grenades and told him to crawl straight ahead. They reached a trench and
one of the Germans called out "Beethoven," the password for the night.
He was pushed into the trench and a handkerchief tied over his eyes. They
led him through the crisscross trench system that led to the German command post. When they stopped, one of the Germans ran his hands over
him, looking for concealed weapons; then he snatched Cannon's identification disks from his neck. He was led down a flight of steps and the
blindfold removed. He found himself in a warm, well-lighted bunker. Behind a desk sat a German officer who introduced himself in German.

"*Sprechen Sie Deutsch?*" he asked.

Cannon mumbled, "*Ja, ich spreche Deutsch.*"

"Oh, let's talk your language." The German colonel smiled. "Sit down.
We German officers know the rules and obey them. I am not going to ask
you anything, Corporal, that you cannot answer in good conscience. You
have nothing to fear from us."

"Where is my sergeant?" Danny blurted out.

"He's all right. We've sent him to the rear. He'll have nothing worse
than a headache tomorrow."

"I'll give you my name, rank, and serial number, nothing else," Cannon
said stubbornly.

The German officer nodded and said casually, "That's all right. I don't
need even that from you. You see, we know everything about your outfit,
including the fact that the New York newspapers are referring to it as the
'Lost Battalion.' I want to speak to you about the — what is it — four hundred men who are still alive in your battalion. I know you are the
308th Infantry with a few units from the 307th. I know your battalion is
out of food and supplies, and that it is completely cut off from your headquarters. Your battalion has put up a good fight. Here is something you
do not know. It is now two A.M. At six A.M. we are going to make a flamethrower attack against you. We have enough flame throwers to destroy
everything within the four hundred yards where your men have dug in. I
want you to take a message back to Major Whittlesey asking him to surrender his command. If he does, not one of his men will be hurt. If he does
not, not one of you will be left alive."

"I'll take the message to my commanding officer," Danny said.

The way back was not difficult. The Germans had stopped firing and
the battalion was not wasting its own precious ammunition tonight. He
crossed the stream, gave the password, and reported directly to Major Whittlesey. Captain McMurtry was with him. The major cleaned his glasses and
read the note. Wordlessly he passed it on to his second in command.

McMurtry chuckled. "We've got them licked or they wouldn't have sent this. How can a man who hits you with flame throwers talk of human decency?"

"We've two alternatives," Whittlesey said, thinking aloud. "We can try to retreat. If we go south in single file, most of the men will make it. Or, we can surrender. By now, Regiment, Brigade, Army, all know the spot we're in and I know well General Alexander is pushing to relieve us. I think," he said softly, "that we'll ignore this message. Now, Cannon, tell me the whole story."

Danny did. He told them of the password "Beethoven." He told of how Hopkins had been hit and captured, and then he went back to his squad. He told the men of his experience and of the surrender note.

"What did the major say?" one of the men asked.

"He told them to go to hell," Danny said, not knowing that his words would be in the headlines of the New York newspapers within a few hours. The word spread from foxhole to foxhole, from tree to tree, from boulder to boulder. Within fifteen minutes every man in the battalion had heard it.

"The major told them to go to hell," tired men chuckled.

Head-weary, starving, wounded, half-deafened, half-hysterical men were transformed into a wild rage, a furious desire for vengeance. Tired men, sick, starving, half-deafened, almost hysterical men sat up and sharpened bayonets on limestone. Wounded men who hadn't fired a rifle in two days pulled themselves out of holes and began to hunt for cartridges. All along the line, men too weak to talk bristled with a new determination.

Whittlesey asked German-born Private Dietz to attempt to break through with a message to headquarters telling of the impending attack. Within an hour he came in contact with units of the 307th Infantry Division. Fifteen minutes later he had delivered the message to Colonel Spencer Martin. Martin relayed it to Division, which relayed it to Corps. Corps relayed it to Army, and at Army Headquarters, an alert correspondent relayed it to his wire service in Paris, which relayed it to New York. The New York *Times* was just going to press. It was put on page one and the headline over it read:

LOST BATTALION SPURNED
OFFER OF SAFETY

"Go to Hell," shouted Major Whittlesey when
Germans sent note pleading for surrender

But the men crouched along the banks of Charlevaux Brook didn't know that. They didn't know that General Alexander had ordered the 307th Infantry to break through at all costs and relieve the battalion. They didn't know that a dozen airplanes were already loaded with food, medical supplies, and ammunition ready to take off at dawn. They only knew one thing. They knew that a lot of them would be dead before this day ended.

The planes did come over before the attack began. For the first time they found their target. Sergeants and corporals hurriedly distributed the precious ammunition; medicos pounced on the morphine and bandages; there was not time now for food. Then it came. The German commanding officer knew that his troops south of the "Lost Battalion" were taking a bad beating. He knew the Americans would break through in time. This assault had to be the final one. He had made one serious miscalculation: the weather was very good that morning and the dawn broke at 4:45 A.M. This gave the twelve airplanes a chance to drop their supplies before the 6 A.M. ultimatum was reached. It was that interval of an hour and fifteen minutes which gave the Americans the chance to rearm. Throwing everything he had when no white flag appeared at 6 A.M., the German used *Minenwerfer*, grenades, machine guns, 88's, and flame throwers. But his men were not prepared for the fierce, angry repulse of this attack. The men of the First were still sustained by the strange alchemy that had made them forget their wounds, their weariness. The Germans were not prepared for the deadly fire which cut down the men who hurled the flame throwers. At best a flame thrower has a range of a hundred yards and cannot be used from a trench. The flame throwers did not inflict one casualty. At 9 A.M. Major Whittlesey turned to Captain McMurtry and said calmly, "They're slowing up."

"The Boche machine guns are firing too high; they aren't hurting us much," McMurtry said. Then he added, "But there are three on our right flank. They are liable to smarten up soon and lower their sights. I would like permission to send a squad of riflemen out to cut them off. The underbrush out there to the right is very heavy. It will give them some protection."

"Go ahead, Captain."

McMurtry hurried to where Danny Cannon was firing at anything that moved. McMurtry told him to pick four men, try to outflank the machine-gun nest without being observed, and wipe it out. "If you can do it with your rifles, fine. But the heavy shrubbery will probably obscure your view. If you can get close enough without being spotted, your grenades will do the job. Okay, Cannon?"

"Okay, sir," Cannon said.

He led his detail a hundred and fifty yards to the right. Cannon could hear the firing of the machine guns. He knew where they were — about four hundred yards ahead. Cautiously, taking advantage of every tree trunk, every bit of shrubbery, he led them closer to the nest. They were within a hundred yards of it but couldn't see it well enough to use their rifles.

"Keep in single file, five paces apart, and don't shoot or throw a grenade till I tell you to. Follow me," he said to them. "They haven't seen us yet. We'll crawl another fifty yards and when you see me throw a grenade, all of you toss yours. Then move quickly to the rear. Pass the word along."

They inched forward slowly. Finally Danny saw the gunners. There were four machine guns, inexcusably grouped closely together. He detached a grenade from his belt, and said, "I'm going to lob one right into their laps. Everybody is on his own."

He waited twenty seconds, pulled the pin, counted to ten, and threw it. It landed just short of the startled machine gunners. His men immediately hurled grenades that exploded in bright golden flashes. The rhythmic rat-a-tat-a-tat of the guns stopped. Danny tried to get closer now. He could see a dozen men in German uniforms. He knew that within ten seconds those machine guns would be swiveled around to him. He ran forward five yards and threw another grenade and then another one. Both landed exactly where he had aimed. The machine guns had stopped. Only one machine gun was still barking. Then Danny threw his last grenade. Six hundred yards away a German gunner launched a trench mortar in the general direction of the First Battalion. It fell nearly four hundred yards short of its objective. It fell at the feet of Danny Cannon.

Danny Cannon died without knowing that eight hours later Major Houghton, leading the First Battalion of the 307th Regiment, would break through to relieve Major Whittlesey and his men, or that later in the day when the American breakthrough came to the south, all of the survivors of the "Lost Battalion" were sent to the rear. Of the 600 who had started out to occupy the position along Charlevaux Brook, only 194 were alive. He never knew that when General Alexander came to Charlevaux Brook he said to Major Whittlesey, "Now I can see, Major, why our airplanes couldn't find this place."

Whittlesey's lips tightened. His face looked like a mask. He hadn't slept or shaved for three days and he had hardly eaten anything. He said nothing, but Lieutenant Joseph Paine, standing near, blurted out, "But, General, your artillery found it all right."

"Oh no, that was French artillery," Alexander said without batting an eyelash.

Danny never knew that eight members of his Battalion (including Whittlesey and McMurtry) were awarded Congressional Medals of Honor. He never knew that when Major Whittlesey returned home he was given a hero's reception. He never knew (nor did anyone else) what went on in the tortured mind of Charles W. Whittlesey, or that two years after the war was over Charles Whittlesey, back again in civilian life as a lawyer, boarded the steamer *Toloa* for a vacation in Cuba. Danny Cannon never knew that when the ship was twenty-four hours out of New York, Charles Whittlesey disappeared over the rail. His body was never recovered.

Captain Flagg – Sergeant Quirt

✗

from *What Price Glory?*
by LAURENCE STALLINGS
and MAXWELL ANDERSON

ACT II

A cellar in a disputed town, a typical deep wine cellar of a prosperous farmhouse on the edge of a village in France. It resembles half of a culvert thirty feet in diameter, with a corresponding curved roof and walls. One end is open, and the other is walled up, admitting a narrow and rather low door in the center, through which a flight of stairs extends to the ground floor above. This cellar is lit dimly by two candles placed at either side of the front stage and held in bottles on small bully-beef boxes. The rear wall can only barely be discerned. Along the sides of this culvert are dirty white ticks stuffed with straw for sleeping quarters, the sort of ticks headquarters detachment men carry about with them. There are four on each side, arranged with all the litter of miscellany a soldier carries about tucked at their heads, and with the foot of these pallets extending into the center of the culvert. The effect is not unlike in design that of a hospital ward, with feet toward the center aisle. Back of FLAGG's *bunk all manner of stuff — first-aid kits, bandages, chocolates, sticks, pistols and rifles, notes, books of memoranda, etc.*

Two men are asleep, snoring gently — gas masks at alert on chests, tin hats on back of heads, and heads on floor. They are indescribably dirty, and with six or eight days' beard.

The two men are SPIKE *and* KIPER. KIPER *is on second bunk at left,* SPIKE *on third bunk at right.* GOWDY *enters. Stirs* SPIKE *with his foot.*

GOWDY.   All right. Heave out and lash up. Lively now. Rations are in. Go draw for ten. At the gray stable tonight. Take that sack there. [*Points to a muddy sack on the floor near by.*]

SPIKE. What time is it? Rations in?

GOWDY. You heard me, Spike. Shake a leg and go draw rations for ten men, at the gray stable near the square. It's after two o'clock.

SPIKE. Where's Captain Flagg?

GOWDY. Down tying up Mr. Aldrich.

SPIKE. So they got him. Bad?

GOWDY. I'll say they did. A ticket home. Right arm torn all to hell.

SPIKE. A damned dirty shame. He's lucky, though, to get out with an arm. I'd sell 'em mine, and at the same price. What was it — that one-pounder again?

GOWDY. No. Fuse cap from a grenade. Made a hell of a mess on Mr. Aldrich. He was crawling on the embankment near the railway station, and somebody inside threw him a present.

SPIKE [now up and re-winding a spiral legging]. A damned swell officer, if you ask me. Taking him out tonight?

GOWDY. No. The skipper is bringing him here. Send him tomorrow night. He's lost too much blood to walk it before dawn. God, it's getting on my nerves.

KIPER [who has been awakened]. Who? Mr. Aldrich hit bad?

GOWDY. Pretty bad. Arm. Make a bunk for him, willya? Shake it down and pile another in the back. He'll want to sit up with it. Make up Harry's bunk.

SPIKE [at door, about to go upstairs, turns at this]. Harry's bunk? Why, Harry?

GOWDY. Harry's through with bunks.

SPIKE. Bumped off?

GOWDY. Worse. In the belly crossing the square. [SPIKE goes out.]

KIPER. Where is he?

GOWDY. The skipper rushed him back an hour ago. No use, though; Harry was unconscious — halfway — holding half his guts in his bare hands and hollering for somebody to turn him loose so he could shoot himself.

KIPER. Captain Flagg want me?

GOWDY. He said not to wake you. Might need you later on.

KIPER. A good job for me, I suppose. Jeez, with this daylight saving I ain't going to live forever, that's sure. I think I'll go crazy and get the doc to gimme a ticket.

GOWDY. Flagg's crazy now. Raving crazy. Hasn't slept for five nights. We'll be sitting on him in another night like he's had tonight.

KIPER. The whole damned universe is crazy now.

* * *

[A commotion at head of stairs. Enter CAPTAIN FLAGG supporting ALDRICH by gripping ALDRICH's uninjured wrist over his shoulder and *easing him gently down steps.* ALDRICH *is not groaning. After all, it won't hurt for fifteen minutes or so. But he is weak from loss of blood and soaked through, and is in an indescribable mess of dried blood and dirt, which appears black.* FLAGG, *who is unkempt, has no leggings or laces in his breeches, these flapping in the most disillusioning fashion about his bare legs. His blouse, an old army blouse many sizes too big and without a sign of any insignia, is tied with a piece of twine. He is bareheaded — no tin hat and no accoutrements of any sort. He is a very weary-looking man. He wears belt and holster with automatic bound to leg. As* FLAGG *enters, followed by* MATE, GOWDY *jumps up and spreads blanket on bunk.*]

FLAGG.   Right here, Aldrich. [*Lowers him down on bunk. The* PHAR-MACIST'S MATE *follows him.* FLAGG *kneels above* ALDRICH. *The* MATE *stands.*]   Gimme a stick of that dope, Holsen.

MATE.   They are quarter grains, Captain.

FLAGG [*to* ALDRICH, *lying down*].   Take these two now. [*He puts two tablets from a tiny vial in the wounded officer's mouth.*] I'm putting these in your blouse. Get somebody to give you one every three hours until you are carried out.

ALDRICH.   What are they?

FLAGG.   Morphine — quarter grains ——

ALDRICH [*not dramatic, just casual*].   What if I take them all when your back is turned?

FLAGG [*turning his back and crossing to his own bunk down left; sits on bunk*].   Go ahead. It's your affair.

[*After* FLAGG *is seated on his bunk a strange sob is heard at the head of the stairs.* LIEUTENANT MOORE, *last seen in company headquarters, rushes in and goes straight over to* ALDRICH, *where he stands and looks down at his arm, and not his face.*]

MOORE.   Oh, God, Dave, but they got you. God, but they got you a beauty, the dirty swine. God DAMN them for keeping us up in this hellish town. Why can't they send in some of the million men they've got back there and give us a chance? Men in my platoon are so hysterical every time I get a message from Flagg, they want to know if they're being relieved. What can I tell them? They look at me like whipped dogs — as if I had just beaten them — and I've had enough of them this time. I've got to get them out, I tell you. They've had enough. Every night the same way. [*He turns to* FLAGG.] And since six o'clock there's been a wounded sniper in the tree by that orchard angle crying "Kamerad! Kamerad!" Just like a big crippled whippoorwill. What price glory now? Why in God's name can't we all go home? Who gives a damn for this lousy, stinking little town but the poor French bastards who live here? God damn it! You talk about courage, and all night long you hear a man who's bleeding to death on a tree calling you "Kamerad" and asking you to save him. God damn every son of a bitch in the world who isn't here! I won't stand for it. I won't stand for it! I won't have the platoon asking me every minute of the live-long night when they are going to be relieved. . . . Flagg, I tell you you can shoot me, but I won't stand for it. . . . I'll take 'em out tonight and kill you if you get in my way. . . . [*Starts sobbing again.*]

[GOWDY *and* KIPER *sit up.*]

FLAGG [*rising quickly as though he might kill the man, and then putting his arm around the chap, who has clearly gone smash for a few minutes. He speaks in a quiet, chastening tone, with a gentility never before revealed*]. Here, boy, you can't do this before all these men. [*Walks him.*] They are rubbed up, too. You are all tuckered out with your side of the line. Don't worry about your platoon. We'll get them out. You turn in here. [*Walks him to bunk on the left side of the room.* KIPER *crosses and throws blanket on him; stops at bunk nearest entrance.*] And dope off for a little while . . . that's it, give him a blanket, Kiper . . . and now take it easy a while, and you can go back to your platoon in time to stand to. Sleep it off, boy, sleep it off. . . . You're in a deep wide hole, and shells can't get you. Sleep it off. [FLAGG *crosses to his own bunk, lights cigarette at candle, seats himself on bunk.* GOWDY *rests head on arm.* QUIRT *kneels on floor, gets a piece of chocolate out of his pocket; rises, as though his legs were asleep. He carries his helmet. He crosses and tosses candy to* MOORE.]

QUIRT. Just a little chocolate I bought off a Y.M.C.A. wagon down at the base. [QUIRT *is sympathetic and begins to talk nervously.*] I got hit myself once. In Nicaragua. We were washed up before we made a landing. I was a corporal, and when we were scrubbing down and putting on clean uniforms — doctors' orders, you know, so they wouldn't have to wash us when we were hit — [*turns to* GOWDY] a bird said to me — it was old Smoke Plangetch, who was killed in 1913 in a Chippie joint in Yokohama — Smoke said to me: "You'd better swab down, you son of a sea-bitch, because I dreamed last night they wrote your name on a bullet." I said to him, "The bullet ain't been cast that can shoot Micky Quirt." He said, "If your name is on one, it will turn the corner and go upstairs to find you." Jeez! That afternoon when we made a landing and hit the beach, the spigs was on a hill five hundred yards offshore. We started up the hill — they weren't many of us dropping — and I came to a log I had to jump [QUIRT *illustrates this*] and I lost my balance and threw my hand up in the air. [QUIRT *extends his wrist.*] Look, right through the God damn fin, as pretty as a pinwheel. . . . Smoke saw it. "Oh, yeah, you wisenheimer son of a Chinese tart," he says to me, "your name was on that one and you had to reach up for it." [GOWDY *laughs.* QUIRT *is obviously embarrassed by having spoken of himself so much. He turns and recollects his business and goes over to* FLAGG. *Crosses to the foot of* FLAGG's *bunk.*] Rations detail in, sir. Lost the two Jameson boys in the ravine going down. Both badly hit.

Lost Fleischman and Rosenthal in the dump. Both slight. Brought back all the ammunition and two sacks of bread, one of canned willie, French; I carried a sack of beet sugar on my back. Got a piece of shrapnel in it where they are shelling the crossroads — stopped it square. In the next war, I'm going to wear a suit of beet sugar and stand forest fire watch in the Rocky Mountains. [*He turns, and then remembers and comes back.*] Oh, I brought up two of those thirty-day wonder lieutenants from a training camp. Sent up by divisional for instruction.

FLAGG.   By God, I won't stand for it. They wipe their damned dirty feet on this company. They can give my men all their damned good jobs. They can keep us in the line all during the whole damned war. But I'll be damned if my sergeants have got time to teach army lieutenants how to button their pants in the dark.

QUIRT.   They are in my hole now, sir. Pretty badly shaken up by the ravine. First time up, you know. Shall I send them to you, sir?

FLAGG.   Send them to me, and for God's sake, don't call me sir any more tonight.

QUIRT [*to* GOWDY].   All right. You heard him. Hit the deck. You'll find 'em in my hole. [GOWDY *goes.*] Those Huns in the railway station again?

FLAGG.   Try to cross the town square when there's a flare up, and you'll see.

QUIRT.   You get a visit from brigade headquarters tonight. I saw their party in the ravine as we were going down to the dump.

FLAGG.   The old man says we've got to drive them off the embankment. Huh! He can give me five general courts and I'll not waste another man at that business. It will take a brigade action to get them out for good.

QUIRT.   Do you mind if I take a look around there now? I'd like to see this damned war some. For six days I've been a lousy bakery wagon — haven't seen a spiggoty yet, except stinking dead ones — I never see soldiers stink like these Heinies.

FLAGG.   All right. Go get your blooming can blown off. But bury yourself, while you're about it. The burying detail is in for the night.

QUIRT.   Gosh, I wish to hell I was home.

FLAGG.   Go get one of those Alsatian lootnants then, and you'll get a leave.

QUIRT.   I don't want to die yet, thanking you just the same. Well, here goes. [*Exit.*]

FLAGG.   Well, keep your head down. I can't waste any gravediggers on sergeants. [FLAGG *shrugs his shoulders and walks over to above* ALDRICH.] Sorry Moore blew up that way, Aldrich . . . you are a damned sight luckier than he is, but he doesn't know it. I'll have you out tomorrow night with the ration detail, and you'll be parking your body in a big white bed in another two days. Good luck. . . . You've been a damned good man. I wish you could get a ribbon for this town.

[As FLAGG *leaves,* GOWDY *enters with two lieutenants. They are just like tailor's dummies of a Burberry outfit, slicked to the notch and perky and eager. As they enter,* FLAGG *steps on his cigarette and stands facing them. The* LIEUTENANTS *come down and stand side by side.*]

FLAGG [*starts back in mock admiration and salaams deeply as they come forward*]. So *this* is the last of the old guard, eh? In the name of the holy sweet Jumping, are you gentlemen bound for a masked ball, that you come disguised as officers? Or do you wish to save the snipers the trouble of picking you off with a glass, that you wear signboards? [*He goes nearer them, inspecting their clothes.*] Can't you go without those trench coats even to the trenches? How long will you last in those boots? Take 'em off before you even part your hair in the morning. . . . [*He changes to a thundering staccato.*] My name is Flagg, gentlemen, and I'm the sinkhole and cesspool of this regiment, frowned on in the Y.M.C.A. huts and sneered at by the divisional Beau Brummells. I am a lousy, good-for-nothing company commander. I corrupt youth and lead little boys astray into the black shadows between the lines of hell, killing more men than any other company commander in the regiment, and drawing all the dirty jobs in the world. I take chocolate soldiers and make dead heroes out of them. I did not send for you, Mister . . . [*he leans forward, and the first officer salutes and speaks:* "Cunningham, sir"] nor for you . . . ["Lundstrom, sir," *also salutes*]; and I confess I am in a quandary. Four days ago I should have been more hospitable, for I had four gunnery sergeants then. Now I have two, and can't spare them to teach little boys how to adjust their diapers. I've no doubt that one of you was an all-American halfback and the other the editor of the college paper, but we neither follow the ball nor the news here. We are all dirt, and we propose to die in order that corps headquarters may be decorated. I should be happy to receive suggestions as to what should be done with you. Ah, I have it! There are two German gunners over in the enemy railway station. Two bright young men might get them out and cut their throats before dawn; then no more could get in the station all day. Two bright young men, who know very little of anything just yet. I have two bright ones, but they are far too valuable. They are corporals with ten years' experience. [*The* LIEUTENANTS *are speechless. There is not a smile in the cellar.* CUNNINGHAM, *who is the bigger of the two, finally answers, in a slow Southern drawl.*]

CUNNINGHAM. I'll do anything you will. Where is the railway station and the two bucks that have got you buffaloed?

FLAGG. Why, it's Frank Merriwell! All right, Frank. You and me will be playing ball in hell by three o'clock this morning.

LUNDSTROM. Put me in too, sir.

FLAGG. Oh, no, no, no! We must have officers left. Rule of the game. Must have officers. Men would get right up and go home, and then there wouldn't be any war at all. Besides, three would be a crowd, and I hate crowds early in the morning around the railway station. They are so noisy, and they die so fast. [*He turns to* GOWDY.] Gowdy! Take Mr. Lundstrom to the fourth platoon sergeant, and tell him that here's his new officer. [RUNNER *and* LUNDSTROM *move to door.* FLAGG *is all business now.*] And by the way, Mr. Lundstrom, they filter through and bomb twice a week, small parties slipping down that ravine you'll find on your left. Watch it closely, or you'll all have your throats cut before you know it. And let that sergeant sleep for the next two days. Remember, he'll do no details until he's rested. Of course you can wake him for advice. That's all. Shove off. [RUNNER *and* LUNDSTROM *salute, and go out.* CUNNINGHAM *sits down.* QUIRT *enters with his helmet on, limping; steals forward quietly, and sits down on his bunk. There is a nice bloody mess on his right calf.* FLAGG *happens to turn, sees what's going on, sits up, watches* QUIRT. QUIRT *looks back, finally grins, then tries to open a first-aid pack.*]

FLAGG. What's the matter with you?

QUIRT. Got a can opener?

FLAGG. You crook!

QUIRT. I say, Captain, got a can opener?

FLAGG. Those things are supposed to be opened with the teeth.

QUIRT. You don't say! Well, this'n wasn't. This here can was evidently made for the Red Cross by the Columbia Red Salmon Company. Like as not instead of bandages I'll find the God damnedest mess of goldfish in it.

FLAGG [*rises, crosses to* QUIRT, *takes can away from him*]. Where were you? [*He comes over, strains at the tin. He is looking daggers.*] Where were you?

QUIRT. Just looking around.

FLAGG. Here. [*Hands him tin, opened.*]

QUIRT. Thanks.

FLAGG. Where were you, I said.

QUIRT [*takes out bandage*]. In the vegetable garden, pulling turnips. [*Starts wiping leg.*]

FLAGG. God damn you, Quirt, I believe you stuck your leg out. [*Goes back and sits on bunk.*]

QUIRT. Like hell I did. If I'd wanted to stick my leg out don't you think I've had plenty of chances to do it before? No, sir, I stuck my head out and some bird in the church tower took a shot at me. There she is. In and out without touching the bone. Just let me squeeze the juice out and she'll be all right. Ain't she the prettiest little damn puncture you ever saw, Captain? Ain't she a beauty?

FLAGG. I suppose you think you're going back to Cognac Pete's, huh?

QUIRT. How'd you guess it? Yes, sir, back to my little skookum lady you tried to make me a present of. Am I happy? Am I happy? Oh, boy! Ask me, Captain, am I happy?

FLAGG. You mean to say you aren't cured of Charmaine yet?

QUIRT. Cured of Charmaine? No, sir, I ain't even getting better. Oh, Captain Flagg, ain't you proud of yourself, ain't you a wizard? God, ain't I sorry to leave you all alone here in this mess? Think of her sitting on my lap, lighting my pipe in the kitchen, and you dodging machine guns. I wonder I don't bust out crying. You know, I wouldn't wonder if you got bumped off and never came back. As a matter of fact, I hope you damn well get your head blown off.

FLAGG. Yeah, you always did have a charming disposition.

QUIRT [squeezing his wound gently]. Oh, pretty baby, papa doesn't mean to hurt you. Lookit, Captain. By God, I wouldn't take a hundred dollars Mex. for that little bumblebee that flew in there.

FLAGG. Feel pretty cocky, don't you? Well, you can't go out tonight. I guess you can work all right with that. You'll wait here till Cunningham and I get back with that Alsatian shavetail from the railroad embankment. Then I get leave, the company gets a rest, and we go back together, see?

QUIRT. Not much, I don't see. I've got a very important engagement back to Pete's place. Can't be postponed, not even for the pleasure of your enjoyable company, such as it is. I don't wait for nothing in the world but a medical tag.

[Enter PHARMACIST'S MATE; stands on steps, leans head in door.]

MATE. Heard your first sergeant was hit in that turnip patch. [FLAGG indicates QUIRT. MATE crosses to QUIRT; kneels.] Let's have a look. Um. Night soil in that patch, and you, like a damned fool, crawl after they hit you, and now you're full of that muck. Can you walk, Sergeant?

QUIRT [lying back]. Well, depends on what I see.

MATE [helps up QUIRT, who carries helmet]. Go to the sick bay at once for a shot of tetanus, and then get out of here. [Takes his arm, and both cross.] You can reach a collecting station before you're done.

QUIRT. Ain't this heartbreaking, Flagg? Well, duty calls. But my eyes fill with tears at the thought of leaving my old company commander. I don't know as I can go through with it.

FLAGG. Make it snappy, Quirt, or you'll find the door locked.

QUIRT. Yeah? What door?

FLAGG. Charmaine's.

QUIRT. Are you wounded, too, Mr. Flagg?

FLAGG. No, but inside ten minutes I'm going to be wounded or bumped off or have that God damned prisoner for the Brig.

QUIRT. Try to get killed, will you? To please me — just this once? [QUIRT and the MATE go out.]

FLAGG. Mr. Cunningham . . . I guess you thought I was joking when I proposed that little expedition to the railroad embankments?

CUNNINGHAM. I did not. When do we start? [*Coming to* FLAGG.]

FLAGG. Well, I was. I was kidding hell out of you. I'd no more let you go in there, boy, than I'd knife you in the back. The air is full of steel this side of that embankment, and a green man has about as much chance as a cootie on Fifth Avenue.

CUNNINGHAM. You going?

FLAGG. I've got official reasons for going, see? The Brig wants a prisoner, and he also wants that nest wiped out. Also, I got private and personal reasons for wanting to catch up with that baboon that got the little present through his leg.

CUNNINGHAM. If you're going, that suits me. I ain't no green man. I can crawl on my belly.

FLAGG. Yeah?

CUNNINGHAM. I'm a locomotive engineer and I've been crawling under trains for fifteen years. Had several engines shot out from under me likewise. You think you can scare me with this here war? Christ! you ought to see a few railroad wrecks!

FLAGG. Well, Mr. Cunningham, I'm inclined to think you'll do.

CUNNINGHAM. You're God damn right, I'll do.

FLAGG. What do you say we black our faces and give a little party, now the guests will be asleep?

CUNNINGHAM. Sure. I like the cut of your jib, and you can lead me to it. Show me which one is the lootenant, so I won't hurt him.

FLAGG. You from Texas?

CUNNINGHAM. You hit it.

FLAGG. Now I get you. So we've got another damned Texan in this outfit, wanting to fight anybody that ain't from Texas.

CUNNINGHAM. Yep, and I ain't no God damn college boy, either.

FLAGG. Good stuff! Now throw away them fancy-dress clothes of yours and dip in here. [*He offers a can of lampblack.*]

CUNNINGHAM. Sure. [*Takes off overcoat.*] I was a locomotive engineer on the Louisiana Midland. Three wrecks in my division last year. Christ, but this war shore is a great relief to me. [*Both black their faces.*] I'm an engineer officer attached to infantry. My brother's still driving an engine back home. Had a letter last month from him. He says, "You dirty yellow sapsucker, quitting your job on the Louisiana Midland. I knew you always were a yellow dog, but I didn't think you'd go back on the road thataway."

FLAGG. Now if I only had a pretty little engine. [*Suddenly there is a scream upstairs, a shout in a burly strange tongue. "Heraus!" and three bombs explode.* FLAGG, *the* RUNNERS, *and all save* ALDRICH *dash for the door.*] Marines! Marines! Marines! [*The lieutenant who had been put to sleep stirs uneasily. After a brief tumult, the people of the cellar descend stairs,* FLAGG *holding a German officer by the collar. He takes him straight to the candle.*] Let me have a look at you, sweetheart, let me have a look! Boys, he's an Alsatian lieutenant! He couldn't wait for us to go after him, so he came over. [*He embraces his captive.*] Oh, sweetheart — you're the sweetest sight I've seen since Charmaine! Here, Kiper [*pushes him to* KIPER] — take care of him for me, and for God's sake don't scare him to death, because he's our ticket of leave!

LEWISOHN [*screams, outside*]. Captain Flagg . . .

FLAGG. Who's that?

LIPINSKY. It's little Lewisohn, sir.

[LEWISOHN *is carried in by* GOWDY *followed by* PHARMACIST'S MATE, *and he is crying monotonously for* CAPTAIN FLAGG.]

LEWISOHN. Captain Flagg. Captain Flagg. Stop the blood. Stop the blood.

FLAGG [*takes him from* GOWDY *and puts him on floor*]. I can't stop it, Lewisohn. I'm sorry. [*He examines wound in left side.*]

LEWISOHN. Oh, Captain Flagg, stop the blood.

FLAGG. Fix him with your needle, Mate. [MATE *gives him needle in arm.*]

LEWISOHN. Oh, Captain Flagg, can't you please, sir, stop the blood?

FLAGG [*puts hand behind* LEWISOHN's *head and gently lowers him to floor*]. You'll be all right, boy. You'll be all right. You'll be all right.

[LEWISOHN *sighs and relaxes his body.*]

CURTAIN

The Argonne

X

from *Three Soldiers*

by JOHN DOS PASSOS

It was purplish dusk outside the window. The rain fell steadily making long flashing stripes on the cracked panes, beating a hard monotonous tattoo on the tin roof overhead. Fuselli had taken off his wet slicker and stood in front of the window looking out dismally at the rain. Behind him was the smoking stove into which a man was poking wood, and beyond that a few broken folding chairs on which soldiers sprawled in attitudes of utter boredom, and the counter where the "Y" man stood with a set smile doling out chocolate to a line of men that filed past.

"Gee, you have to line up for everything here, don't you?" Fuselli muttered.

"That's about all you do do in this hell-hole, buddy," said a man beside him.

The man pointed with his thumb at the window and said again:

"See that rain? Well, I been in this camp three weeks and it ain't stopped rainin' once. What d'yer think of that fer a country?"

"It certainly ain't like home," said Fuselli. "I'm going to have some chauclate."

"It's damn rotten."

"I might as well try it once."

Fuselli slouched over to the end of the line and stood waiting his turn. He was thinking of the steep streets of San Francisco and the glimpses he used to get of the harbor full of yellow lights, the color of amber in a cigarette holder, as he went home from work through the blue dusk. He had begun to think of Mabe handing him the five-pound box of candy when his attention was distracted by the talk of the men behind him. The man next to him was speaking with hurried nervous intonation. Fuselli could feel his breath on the back of his neck.

"I'll be goddamned," the man said, "was you there too? Where d'you get yours?"

"In the leg; it's about all right, though."

"I ain't. I won't never be all right. The doctor says I'm all right now, but I know I'm not, the lyin' fool."

"Some time, wasn't it?"

"I'll be damned to hell if I do it again. I can't sleep at night thinkin' of the shape of the Fritzies' helmets. Have you ever thought that there was somethin' about the shape of them goddamn helmets . . . ?"

"Ain't they just or'nary shapes?" asked Fuselli, half turning round. "I seen 'em in the movies." He laughed apologetically.

"Listen to the rookie, Tub, he's seen 'em in the movies!" said the man with the nervous twitch in his voice, laughing a croaking little laugh. "How long you been in this country, buddy?"

"Two days."

"Well, we only been here two months, ain't we, Tub?"

"Four months; you're forgettin', kid."

The "Y" man turned his set smile on Fuselli while he filled his tin cup up with chocolate.

"How much?"

"A franc; one of those looks like a quarter," said the "Y" man, his well-fed voice full of amiable condescension.

"That's a hell of a lot for a cup of chauclate," said Fuselli.

"You're at the war, young man, remember that," said the "Y" man severely. "You're lucky to get it at all."

A cold chill gripped Fuselli's spine as he went back to the stove to drink the chocolate. Of course he mustn't crab. He was in the war now. If the sergeant had heard him crabbing, it might have spoiled his chances for a corporalship. He must be careful. If he just watched out and kept on his toes, he'd be sure to get it.

"And why ain't there no more chocolate, I want to know?" the nervous voice of the man who had stood in line behind Fuselli rose to a sudden shriek. Everybody looked round. The "Y" man was moving his head from side to side in a flustered way, saying in a shrill little voice:

"I've told you there's no more. Go away!"

"You ain't got no right to tell me to go away. You got to get me some chocolate. You ain't never been at the front, you goddamn slacker." The man was yelling at the top of his lungs. He had hold of the counter with two hands and swayed from side to side. His friend was trying to pull him away.

"Look here, none of that, I'll report you," said the "Y" man. "Is there a noncommissioned officer in the hut?"

"Go ahead, you can't do nothin'. I can't never have nothing done worse than what's been done to me already." The man's voice had reached a singsong fury.

"Is there a noncommissioned officer in the room?" The "Y" man kept looking from side to side. His little eyes were hard and spiteful and his lips were drawn up in a thin straight line.

"Keep quiet, I'll get him away," said the other man in a low voice. "Can't you see he's not . . . ?"

A strange terror took hold of Fuselli. He hadn't expected things to be like that. When he had sat in the grandstand in the training camp and watched the jolly soldiers in khaki marching into towns, pursuing terrified Huns across potato fields, saving Belgian milkmaids against picturesque backgrounds.

"Does many of 'em come back that way?" he asked a man beside him.

"Some do. It's this convalescent camp."

The man and his friend stood side by side near the stove talking in low voices.

"Pull yourself together, kid," the friend was saying.

"All right, Tub; I'm all right now, Tub. That slacker got my goat, that was all."

Fuselli was looking at him curiously. He had a yellow parchment face and a high, gaunt forehead going up to sparse, curly brown hair. His eyes had a glassy look about them when they met Fuselli's. He smiled amiably.

"Oh, there's the kid who's seen Fritzie's helmets in the movies. . . . Come on, buddy, come and have a beer at the English canteen."

"Can you get beer?"

"Sure, over in the English camp."

They went out into the slanting rain. It was nearly dark, but the sky had a purplish-red color that was reflected a little on the slanting sides of tents and on the roofs of the rows of sheds that disappeared into the rainy mist in every direction. A few lights gleamed, a very bright polished yellow. They followed a boardwalk that splashed mud up from the puddles under the tramp of their heavy boots.

At one place they flattened themselves against the wet flap of a tent and saluted as an officer passed waving a little cane jauntily.

"How long does a fellow usually stay in these rest camps?" asked Fuselli.

"Depends on what's goin' on out there," said Tub, pointing carelessly to the sky beyond the peaks of the tents.

"You'll leave here soon enough. Don't you worry, buddy," said the man with the nervous voice. "What you in?"

"Medical Replacement Unit."

"A medic, are you? Those boys didn't last long at the Château, did they, Tub?"

"No, they didn't."

Something inside Fuselli was protesting: "I'll last out though. I'll last out though."

"Do you remember the fellers went out to get poor ole Corporal Jones, Tub? I'll be goddamned if anybody ever found a button of their pants." He laughed his creaky little laugh. "They got in the way of a torpedo."

The "wet" canteen was full of smoke and a cosy steam of beer. It was crowded with red-faced men, with shiny brass buttons on their khaki uniforms, among whom was a good sprinkling of lanky Americans.

"Tommies," said Fuselli to himself.

After standing in line a while, Fuselli's cup was handed back to him across the counter, foaming with beer.

"Hello, Fuselli," Meadville clapped him on the shoulder. "You found the liquor pretty damn quick, looks like to me."

Fuselli laughed.

"May I sit with you fellers?"

"Sure, come along," said Fuselli proudly, "these guys have been to the front."

"You have?" asked Meadville. "The Huns are pretty good scrappers, they say. Tell me, do you use your rifle much, or is it mostly big gun work?"

"Naw; after all the months I spent learnin' how to drill with my goddamn rifle, I'll be a sucker if I've used it once. I'm in the grenade squad."

Someone at the end of the room had started singing:

"O Mademerselle from Armenteers,
    Parley voo!"

The man with the nervous voice went on talking, while the song roared about them.

"I don't spend a night without thinkin' o' them funny helmets the Fritzies wear. Have you ever thought that there was something goddamn funny about the shape o' them helmets?"

"Can the helmets, kid," said his friend. "You told us all about them oncet."

"I ain't told you why I can't forgit 'em, have I?"

"A German officer crossed the Rhine;
    Parley voo?
A German officer crossed the Rhine;
He loved the women and liked the wine;
    Hanky Panky, parley voo . . ."

"Listen to this, fellers," said the man in his twitching nervous voice, staring straight into Fuselli's eyes. "We made a little attack to straighten out our trenches a bit just before I got winged. Our barrage cut off a bit of Fritzie's trench an' we ran right ahead juss about dawn an' occupied it. I'll be goddamned if it wasn't as quiet as a Sunday morning at home."

"It was!" said his friend.

"An' I had a bunch of grenades an' a feller came runnin' up to me, whisperin', 'There's a bunch of Fritzies playin' cards in a dugout. They don't seem to know they're captured. We'd better take 'em pris'ners!'

"'Pris'ners, hell,' says I, 'We'll go and clear the beggars out.' So we crept along to the steps and looked down. . . ."

The song had started again:

"O Mademerselle from Armenteers,
    Parley voo?"

"Their helmets looked so damn like toadstools I came near laughin'. An' they sat round the lamp layin' down the cards serious-like, the way I've seen Germans do in the Rathskeller at home."

"He loved the women and liked the wine,
    Parley voo?"

"I lay there lookin' at 'em for a hell of a time, an' then I clicked a grenade an' tossed it gently down the steps. An' all those funny helmets like toadstools popped up in the air an' somebody gave a yell an' the light went out an' the damn grenade went off. Then I let 'em have the rest of 'em an' went away 'cause one o' 'em was still moanin'-like. It was about that time they let their barrage down on us and I got mine."

> "The Yanks are havin' a hell of a time,
> Parley voo?"

"An' the first thing I thought of when I woke up was how those god-damn helmets looked. It upsets a feller to think of a thing like that." His voice ended in a whine like the broken voice of a child that has been beaten.

"You need to pull yourself together, kid," said his friend.

"I know what I need, Tub. I need a woman."

"You know where you get one?" asked Meadville. "I'd like to get me a nice little French girl a rainy night like this."

"It must be a hell of a ways to the town. . . . They say it's full of M.P.'s too," said Fuselli.

"I know a way," said the man with the nervous voice, "Come on; Tub."

"No, I've had enough of these goddamn Frog women."

They all left the canteen.

As the two men went off down the side of the building, Fuselli heard the nervous twitching voice through the metallic patter of the rain:

"I can't find no way of forgettin' how funny those guys' helmets looked all round the lamp . . . I can't find no way . . ."

Bill Grey and Fuselli pooled their blankets and slept together. They lay on the hard floor of the tent very close to each other, listening to the rain pattering endlessly on the drenched canvas that slanted above their heads.

"Hell, Bill, I'm gettin' pneumonia," said Fuselli, clearing his nose.

"That's the only thing that scares me in the whole goddamn business. I'd hate to die o' sickness . . . an' they say another kid's kicked off with that — what d'they call it? — menegitis."

"Was that what was the matter with Stein?"

"The corporal won't say."

"Ole Corp looks sort o' sick himself," said Fuselli.

"It's this rotten climate," whispered Bill Grey, in the middle of a fit of coughing.

"For cat's sake quit that coughin'. Let a feller sleep," came a voice from the other side of the tent.

"Go an' get a room in a hotel if you don't like it."

"That's it, Bill, tell him where to get off."

"If you fellers don't quit yellin', I'll put the whole blame lot of you on K.P.," came the sergeant's good-natured voice. "Don't you know that taps has blown?"

The tent was silent except for the fast patter of the rain and Bill Grey's coughing.

"That sergeant gives me a pain in the neck," muttered Bill Grey peevishly, when his coughing had stopped, wriggling about under the blankets.

After a while Fuselli said in a very low voice, so that no one but his friend should hear:

"Say, Bill, ain't it different from what we thought it was going to be?"

"Yare."

"I mean fellers don't seem to think about beatin' the Huns at all, they're so busy crabbin' on everything."

"It's the guys higher up that does the thinkin'," said Grey grandiloquently.

"Hell, but I thought it'd be excitin' like in the movies."

"I guess that was a lot o' talk."

"Maybe."

Fuselli went to sleep on the hard floor, feeling the comfortable warmth of Grey's body along the side of him, hearing the endless, monotonous patter of the rain on the drenched canvas above his head. He tried to stay awake a minute to remember what Mabe looked like, but sleep closed down on him suddenly.

The bugle wrenched them out of their blankets before it was light. It was not raining. The air was raw and full of white mist that was cold as snow against their faces still warm from sleep. The corporal called the roll, lighting matches to read the list. When he dismissed the formation the sergeant's voice was heard from the tent, where he still lay rolled in his blankets.

"Say, Corp, go an' tell Fuselli to straighten out Lieutenant Stanford's room at eight sharp in Officers' Barracks Number Four."

"Did you hear, Fuselli?"

"All right," said Fuselli. His blood boiled up suddenly. This was the first time he'd had to do servants' work. He hadn't joined the army to be a slavey to any damned first loot. It was against army regulations anyway. He'd go and kick. He wasn't going to be a slavey. . . . He walked towards the door of the tent, thinking what he'd say to the sergeant. But he noticed the corporal coughing into his handkerchief with an expression of pain on his face. He turned and strolled away. It would get him in wrong if he started kicking like that. Much better shut his mouth and put up with it. The poor old corp couldn't last long at this rate. No, it wouldn't do to get in wrong.

At eight, Fuselli, with a broom in his hand, feeling dull fury pounding and fluttering within him, knocked on the unpainted board door.

"Who's that?"

"To clean the room, sir," said Fuselli.

"Come back in about twenty minutes," came the voice of the lieutenant.

"All right, sir."

Fuselli leaned against the back of the barracks and smoked a cigarette. The air stung his hands as if they had been scraped by a nutmeg grater. Twenty minutes passed slowly. Despair seized hold of him. He was so far from anyone who cared about him, so lost in the vast machine. He was telling himself that he'd never get on, would never get up where he could show what he was good for. He felt as if he were in a treadmill. Day after day it would be like this, — the same routine, the same helplessness. He looked at his watch. Twenty-five minutes had passed. He picked up his broom and moved round to the lieutenant's room.

"Come in," said the lieutenant carelessly. He was in his shirtsleeves, shaving. A pleasant smell of shaving soap filled the dark clapboard room, which had no furniture but three cots and some officers' trunks. He was a red-faced young man with flabby cheeks and dark straight eyebrows. He had taken command of the company only a day or two before.

"Looks like a decent feller," thought Fuselli.

"What's your name?" asked the lieutenant, speaking into the small nickel mirror, while he ran the safety razor obliquely across his throat. He stuttered a little. To Fuselli he seemed to speak like an Englishman.

"Fuselli."

"Italian parentage, I presume?"

"Yes," said Fuselli sullenly, dragging one of the cots away from the wall.

"Parla Italiano?"

"You mean, do I speak Eyetalian? Naw, sir," said Fuselli emphatically, "I was born in Frisco."

"Indeed? But get me some more water, will you, please?"

When Fuselli came back, he stood with his broom between his knees, blowing on his hands that were blue and stiff from carrying the heavy bucket. The lieutenant was dressed and was hooking the top hook of the uniform carefully. The collar made a red mark on his pink throat.

"All right; when you're through, report back to the Company." The lieutenant went out, drawing on a pair of khaki-colored gloves with a satisfied and important gesture.

Fuselli walked back slowly to the tents where the Company was quartered, looking about him at the long lines of barracks, gaunt and dripping in the mist, at the big tin sheds of the cook shacks where the cooks and K.P.'s in greasy blue denims were slouching about amid a steam of cooking food.

Something of the gesture with which the lieutenant drew on his gloves caught in the mind of Fuselli. He had seen people make gestures like that in the movies, stout dignified people in evening suits. The president of the company that owned the optical goods store, where he had worked, at home in Frisco, had had something of that gesture about him.

And he pictured himself drawing on a pair of gloves that way, importantly, finger by finger, with a little wave of self-satisfaction when the gesture was completed. . . . He'd have to get that corporalship.

> "There's a long, long trail a-winding
> Through no man's land in France."

The company sang lustily as it splashed through the mud down a gray road between high fences covered with great tangles of barbed wire, above which peeked the ends of warehouses and the chimneys of factories.

The lieutenant and the top sergeant walked side by side chatting, now and then singing a little of the song in a deprecating way. The corporal sang, his eyes sparkling with delight. Even the somber sergeant who rarely spoke to anyone, sang. The company strode along, its ninety-six legs splashing jauntily through the deep putty-colored puddles. The packs swayed merrily from side to side as if it were they and not the legs that were walking.

> "There's a long, long trail a-winding
> Through no man's land in France."

At last they were going somewhere. They had separated from the contingent they had come over with. They were all alone now. They were going to be put to work. The lieutenant strode along importantly. The sergeant strode along importantly. The corporal strode along importantly. The right guide strode along more importantly than anyone. A sense of importance, of something tremendous to do, animated the company like wine, made the packs and the belts seem less heavy, made their necks and shoulders less stiff from struggling with the weight of the packs, made the ninety-six legs tramp jauntily in spite of the oozy mud and the deep putty-colored puddles.

It was cold in the dark shed of the freight station where they waited. Some gas lamps flickered feebly high up among the rafters, lighting up in a ghastly way white piles of ammunition boxes and ranks and ranks of shells that disappeared in the darkness. The raw air was full of coal smoke and a smell of freshly cut boards. The captain and the top sergeant had disappeared. The men sat about, huddled in groups, sinking as far as they could into their overcoats, stamping their numb wet feet on the mud-covered cement of the floor. The sliding doors were shut. Through them came a monotonous sound of cars shunting, of buffers bumping against buffers, and now and then the shrill whistle of an engine.

"Hell, the French railroads are rotten," said someone.

"How d'you know?" snapped Eisenstein, who sat on a box away from the rest with his lean face in his hands staring at his mud-covered boots.

"Look at this," Bill Grey made a disgusted gesture towards the ceiling. "Gas. Don't even have electric light."

"Their trains run faster than ours," said Eisenstein.

"The hell they do. Why, a fellow back in that rest camp told me that it took four or five days to get anywhere."

"He was stuffing you," said Eisenstein. "They used to run the fastest trains in the world in France."

"Not so fast as the 'Twentieth Century.' Goddamn, I'm a railroad man and I know."

"I want five men to help me sort out the eats," said the top sergeant, coming suddenly out of the shadows. "Fuselli, Grey, Eisenstein, Meadville, Williams . . . all right, come along."

"Say, Sarge, this guy says that Frog trains are faster than our trains. What d'ye think o' that?"

The sergeant put on his comic expression. Everybody got ready to laugh.

"Well, if he'd rather take the side-door Pullmans we're going to get aboard tonight than the 'Sunset Limited,' he's welcome. I've seen 'em. You fellers haven't."

Everybody laughed. The top sergeant turned confidentially to the five men who followed him into a small well-lighted room that looked like a freight office.

"We've got to sort out the grub, fellers. See those cases? That's three days' rations for the outfit. I want to sort it into three lots, one for each car. Understand?"

Fuselli pulled open one of the boxes. The cans of bully beef flew under his fingers. He kept looking out of the corner of his eye at Eisenstein, who seemed very skillful in a careless way. The top sergeant stood beaming at them with his legs wide apart. Once he said something in a low voice to the corporal. Fuselli thought he caught the words: "privates first-class," and his heart started thumping hard. In a few minutes the job was done, and everybody stood about lighting cigarettes.

"Well, fellers," said Sergeant Jones, the somber man who rarely spoke, "I certainly didn't reckon when I used to be teachin' and preachin' and tendin' Sunday School and the like that I'd come to be usin' cuss words, but I think we got a damn good company."

"Oh, we'll have you sayin' worse things than 'damn' when we get you out on the front with a goddamn German aeroplane droppin' bombs on you," said the top sergeant, slapping him on the back. "Now, I want you five men to look out for the grub." Fuselli's chest swelled. "The company'll be in charge of the corporal for the night. Sergeant Jones and I have got to be with the lieutenant; understand?"

They all walked back to the dingy room where the rest of the company waited huddled in their coats, trying to keep their importance from being too obvious in their step.

"I've really started now," thought Fuselli to himself. "I've really started now."

The bare freight car clattered and rumbled monotonously over the rails. A bitter cold wind blew up through the cracks in the grimy splintered boards of the floor. The men huddled in the corners of the car, curled up together like puppies in a box. It was pitch-black. Fuselli lay half asleep, his head full of curious fragmentary dreams, feeling through his sleep the aching cold and the unending clattering rumble of the wheels and the bodies and arms and legs muffled in coats and blankets pressing against him. He woke up with a start. His teeth were chattering. The clanking rumble of wheels seemed to be in his head. His head was being dragged along, bumping over cold iron rails. Someone lighted a match. The freight car's black swaying walls, the pack piled in the center, the bodies heaped in the corners where, out of khaki masses here and there gleamed an occasional white face or a pair of eyes — all showed clear for a moment and then vanished again in the utter blackness. Fuselli pillowed his head in the crook of someone's arm and tried to go to sleep, but the scraping rumble of wheels over rails was too loud; he stayed with open eyes staring into the blackness, trying to draw his body away from the blast of cold air that blew up through a crack in the floor.

When the first grayness began filtering into the car they all stood up and stamped and pounded each other and wrestled to get warm.

When it was nearly light, the train stopped and they opened the sliding doors. They were in a station, a foreign-looking station where the walls were plastered with unfamiliar advertisements. "V-E-R-S-A-I-L-L-E-S"; Fuselli spelt out the name.

"Versales," said Eisenstein. "That's where the kings of France used to live."

The train started moving again slowly. On the platform stood the top sergeant.

"How d'ye sleep," he shouted as the car passed him. "Say, Fuselli, better start some grub going."

"All right, Sarge," said Fuselli.

The sergeant ran back to the front of the car and climbed on.

With a delicious feeling of leadership, Fuselli divided up the bread and the cans of bully beef and the cheese. Then he sat on his pack eating dry bread and unsavory beef, whistling joyfully, while the train rumbled and clattered along through a strange, misty-green countryside — whistling joyfully because he was going to the front, where there would be glory and excitement, whistling joyfully because he felt he was getting along in the world.

It was noon. A pallid little sun like a toy balloon hung low in the reddish-gray sky. The train had stopped on a siding in the middle of a russet plain. Yellow poplars, faint as mist, rose slender against the sky along a black shining stream that swirled beside the track. In the distance a steeple and a few red roofs were etched faintly in the grayness.

The men stood about balancing first on one foot and then on the other, stamping to get warm. On the other side of the river an old man with an oxcart had stopped and was looking sadly at the train.

"Say, where's the front?" somebody shouted to him.

Everybody took up the cry: "Say, where's the front?"

The old man waved his hand, shook his head and shouted to the oxen. The oxen took up again their quiet processional gait and the old man walked ahead of them, his eyes on the ground.

"Say, ain't the Frogs dumb?"

"Say, Dan," said Bill Grey, strolling away from a group of men he had been talking to. "These guys say we are going to the Third Army."

"Say, fellers," shouted Fuselli. "They say we're going to the Third Army."

"Where's that?"

"In the Oregon forest," ventured somebody.

"That's at the front, ain't it?"

At that moment the lieutenant strode by. A long khaki muffler was thrown carelessly round his neck and hung down his back.

"Look here, men," he said severely, "the orders are to stay in the cars."

The men slunk back into the cars sullenly.

A hospital train passed, clanking slowly over the cross-tracks. Fuselli looked fixedly at the dark enigmatic windows, at the red crosses, at the orderlies in white who leaned out of the doors, waving their hands. Somebody noticed that there were scars on the new green paint of the last car.

"The Huns have been shooting at it."

"D'ye hear that? The Huns tried to shoot up that hospital train."

Fuselli remembered the pamphlet "German Atrocities" he had read one night in the Y.M.C.A. His mind became suddenly filled with pictures of children with their arms cut off, of babies spitted on bayonets, of women strapped on tables and violated by soldier after soldier. He thought of Mabe. He wished he were in a combatant service; he wanted to fight, fight. He pictured himself shooting dozens of men in green uniforms, and he thought of Mabe reading about it in the papers. He'd have to try to get into a combatant service. No, he couldn't stay in the medics.

The train had started again. Misty russet fields slipped by and dark clumps of trees that gyrated slowly waving branches of yellow and brown leaves and patches of black lace-work against the reddish-gray sky. Fuselli was thinking of the good chance he had of getting to be corporal.

At night. A dim-lighted station platform. The company waited in two lines, each man sitting on his pack. On the opposite platform crowds of little men in blue with mustaches and long, soiled overcoats that reached almost to their feet were shouting and singing. Fuselli watched them with a faint disgust.

"Gee, they got funny lookin' helmets, ain't they?"

"They're the best fighters in the world," said Eisenstein, "not that that's sayin' much about a man."

"Say, that's an M.P.," said Bill Grey, catching Fuselli's arm. "Let's go ask him how near the front we are. I thought I heard guns a minute ago."

"Did you? I guess we're in for it now," said Fuselli.

"Say, buddy, how near the front are we?" they spoke together excitedly.

"The front?" said the M.P., who was a red-faced Irishman with a crushed nose. "You're 'way back in the middle of France." The M.P. spat disgustedly. "You fellers ain't never goin' to the front, don't you worry."

"Hell!" said Fuselli.

"I'll be goddamned if I don't get there somehow," said Bill Grey, squaring his jaw.

A fine rain was falling on the unprotected platform. On the other side the little men in blue were singing a song Fuselli could not understand, drinking out of their ungainly-looking canteens.

Fuselli announced the news to the company. Everybody clustered round him cursing. But the faint sense of importance it gave him did not compensate for the feeling he had of being lost in the machine, of being as helpless as a sheep in a flock.

Hours passed. They stamped about the platform in the fine rain or sat in a row on their packs, waiting for orders. A grey belt appeared behind the trees. The platform began to take on a silvery gleam. They sat in a row on their packs, waiting.

The Prisoners

X

from *Company K*

by WILLIAM MARCH

SERGEANT JULIUS PELTON

On the afternoon of the fourth day we fell back to the edge of the wood and dug in, and the First Battalion passed over our heads and continued the attack. In front of us stretched a wheat field and a wrecked farmhouse, and beyond that the wood started again. The wood before us seemed intact and unhurt, but the wood in which we lay was littered with toppling trees and torn branches, still green. To our left was a gravel pit, long abandoned, with one narrow opening; and back of that a ravine ran straight for a hundred yards and stopped blindly against a bank of clay.

From where I was lying I could see the gravel pit, with Johnny Citron on guard at the gap, watching the twenty-two prisoners we had taken that day. Then Captain Matlock came over to me. "What'll we do with them, Sergeant?" he asked.

"I don't know, sir," I said.

"The easiest thing would be to train a machine gun on the gravel pit," he added; "that would be the simplest way."

"Yes, sir," I answered, and laughed, not taking him seriously.

"No," he said after a minute's thought; "the gap is too narrow and the sides are dug in so it would be pretty hard for the gunners. . . ."

I seen then that he was not joking.

"We'd better take them into the ravine and do it there," he said. . . .

I listened to what he was saying, keeping my mouth shut, but while he was talking I kept thinking: "I've been in the service since I was a kid eighteen years old. I've seen a lot of things that would turn an ordinary man's stomach. I guess I shouldn't be particular now. . . . But this is raw! — This is the rawest thing I ever heard of!"

When Captain Matlock stopped talking, I saluted him. "Yes, sir," I said.

"You'd better take Corporal Foster and his automatic rifle squad. I think Foster is the right man to do it."

"Yes, sir," I said, "yes, sir; I think he is."

"You'd better tell Foster to get it over with before dark."

"Yes, sir," I said.

Later, when I was talking to Foster, I felt ashamed. . . . "Christ! but this is raw," I thought. . . . "Christ! but this is the rawest thing I ever heard of!" . . . Then I remembered what my old drill sergeant had told me in boot camp, twenty years before. "Soldiers ain't supposed to think," he said. "The theory is, if they could think, they wouldn't be soldiers. Soldiers are supposed to do what they are told, and leave thinking to their superior officers."

"Well," I said to myself, "I guess it's none of my business. I guess I'm here to carry out instructions." Then I walked to where Foster was and repeated Captain Matlock's orders.

CORPORAL CLARENCE FOSTER

"That's an old trick," I said. "I remember reading about it in the paper back home before I enlisted: "The Germans send men over in droves, to give themselves up, and after a while there are more prisoners back of the line than soldiers. Then the Germans make an attack, which is a signal for the prisoners to overpower their guards and come up from the rear. It's an old gag!" I said; "and it generally works. Those Prussians are smart babies, don't ever forget that! — They've pulled that trick on the French time and time again. . . . I'm surprised you never heard about it, Sergeant," I said.

"I've heard a lot of hooey in my time," he answered.

"Well, this is straight dope," I said. "I've seen it all written up in the newspapers."

"Do you believe all the tripe you read in the newspapers?" asked Sergeant Pelton.

"Well, I believe *that!*" I said; "I wouldn't put anything dirty past a German."

Sergeant Pelton began to laugh. "Captain Matlock said you were the right man for the job."

"I take his confidence in me as a compliment," I answered. . . . "Christ almighty! — This is *war!* . . . What did you think it was? A Sunday-school picnic? . . . Take these Germans now. — Burning churches and dashing out the brains of innocent babies. — You've got to fight fire with fire," I said. "This is the only sort of treatment a German can understand. . . ."

Sergeant walked away. "All right. Be ready in half an hour," he said. "Let's get it over with quick." Then I walked back to the trench where my squad was and told them Captain Matlock's orders. I realized a great many people, who did not understand the necessity for such an act, would censure Captain Matlock for shooting prisoners, but under the circumstances, there was no other way out. I expected an argument from Walt Drury and that sea-lawyer, Bill Nugent, and I got it. "Don't tell me," I said; "if the arrangement don't suit you, tell your troubles to Captain Matlock!"

"He wouldn't dare do a thing like that," repeated Nugent; "not a dirty thing like that. . . ."

"What do you birds think this is?" I asked. "This is war! . . . Why didn't you bring along your dolls and dishes to play with! . . ."

PRIVATE WALTER DRURY

Corporal Foster told us to load our rifles and go to the gravel pit. There were some prisoners there, and Captain Matlock had ordered us to take them into the ravine, and shoot them. . . . "I won't do it!" I said. — "I might kill a man defending my own life, but to shoot a human being in cold blood . . . I won't do that! — I won't do it!" I said. . . .

"You'll do what the Captain says or you'll get a court-martial. Then they'll stand you up and shoot you too. — Maybe you'd like that!"

"I won't do it!" I said.

"All right," said Corporal Foster. "Use your own judgment, but don't say I didn't warn you."

Then we took our rifles and walked to the gravel pit. There were about two dozen prisoners, mostly young boys with fine, yellow fuzz on their faces. They huddled together in the center of the pit, their eyes rolling nervously, and spoke to one another in soft, frightened voices, their necks bending forward, as if too frail to support the heavy helmets they wore. They looked sick and hungry. Their uniforms were threadbare and torn, and caked with mud, and their bare toes protruded through crevices in their boots. Some were already wounded and weak from loss of blood, and could hardly stand alone, swaying back and forth unsteadily.

Then suddenly my own knees got weak. "No," I said; "no. — I won't do it. . . ." Corporal Foster was getting the prisoners lined up in a single file, swearing angrily and waving his hands about. . . . "Why don't I refuse to do this?" I thought. "Why don't all of us refuse?" If enough of us refuse, what can they do about it? . . ." Then I saw the truth clearly: "We're prisoners too. We're all prisoners . . . No!" I said. "I won't do it!"

Then I threw my rifle away, turned and ran stumbling through the woods. I heard Corporal Foster calling to me to come back; I heard Dick Mundy and Bill Nugent shouting, but I ran on and on, dodging behind trees and falling into shell holes, hiding and trembling and then running forward again. Finally I came to an old barn and hid there behind a pile of refuse and tried to think of what I had done. I had no friends to shield me. I could not speak French. I didn't have a chance. I would be picked up by the military police sooner or later and tried as a deserter. That was inevitable, I knew. . . . "Better give myself and get it over with," I decided; "maybe I'll get off with twenty years. — Twenty years isn't such a long time." I thought, "I'll only be forty-two, when I come out, and I can start life all over again. . . ."

Private Charles Gordon

When we got the prisoners lined up, and had started them out of the pit, Walt Drury made a funny noise, threw his rifle away and ran through the woods. . . . "Walt!" I called. — "Walt!"

"Let him alone," said Corporal Foster, "he'll get his later."

Then the prisoners came out of the pit stolidly with their heads lowered, neither looking to the right nor the left. The wood had been raked by artillery fire but recently, and the leaves that clung to the shattered trees and the pendant branches were still green. In places the trunks of the trees had been scored by shrapnel, leaving strips of bark, gnawed-at and limp, dangling in the wind; leaving the whitish skin of the trees exposed, with sap draining slowly . . .

"Come on," said Foster. "Come on. Let's get going before dark."

We picked our way through the wrecked wood, lifting aside the trailing branches, kicking with our boots the leaves that had rained down and made a green carpet. When we reached the entrance to the ravine, the prisoners drew back, frightened, and began to talk excitedly amongst themselves, then, glancing apprehensively over their shoulders, they entered, one by one, and huddled against the far bank.

One of the prisoners had very blue eyes and didn't seem frightened at all. He began to talk to his comrades, smiling and shaking his head. I couldn't understand what he was saying, but I had an idea he was telling them not to worry because there was nothing to fear. . . . "These men are wearing different uniforms and they speak a different language, but they are made out of the same flesh and blood that we are," I imagined him saying. "There's nothing to fear. They aren't going to hurt us."

Suddenly the blue-eyed man looked at me and smiled, and before I knew what I was doing, I smiled back at him. Then Sergeant Pelton gave the signal to fire and the rifles began cracking and spraying bullets from side to side. I took steady aim at the blue-eyed man. For some reason I wanted him to be killed instantly. He bent double, clutched his belly with his hands and said, "Oh! . . . Oh!" like a boy who had eaten green plums. Then he raised his hands in the air, and I saw that most of his fingers were shot away and were dripping blood like water running out of a leaky faucet. "Oh! . . . Oh!" he kept saying in an amazed voice. . . . "Oh! Oh! Oh!" Then he turned around three times and fell on his back, his head lower than his feet, blood flowing from his belly, insistently, like a tide, across his mud-caked tunic: staining his throat and his face. Twice more he jerked his hands upward and twice he made that soft, shocked sound. Then his hand and his eyelids quit twitching.

I stood there spraying the bullets from side to side in accordance with instructions. . . . "Everything I was ever taught to believe about mercy, justice and virtue is a lie," I thought. . . . "But the biggest lie of all are the words 'God is Love.' That is really the most terrible lie that man ever thought of."

Private Roger Inabinett

When the last prisoner quit kicking, my squad went out of the ravine and back to their trench. I stepped behind a fallen tree, and they passed on ahead without missing me. For a while I could hear them moving through the wood, rustling the leaves with their feet, but after a time everything was quiet again. Then I went back and began going through the pockets of the dead men, but it was hardly worth the trouble. Most of them had paper marks and a few metal coins with square holes punched in them. I put these in my pocket. They might have some value: I didn't know. Then there were a lot of letters and photographs which I tore up and threw in a pile. Some of the men were wearing regimental rings which I took off their fingers — they're worth three or four francs each — and one had a fine, hand-carved cigarette lighter, shaped like a canteen, but there wasn't much of anything else.

What I was really looking for were Iron Crosses. They're worth real money back in the S.O.S. They make fine souvenirs and the boys buy them to send back to their sweethearts. Sometimes they bring as much as 150 francs each. The squareheads generally wear them pinned to their under-shirts, under their tunics, but if there was a single decoration among those prisoners, I couldn't find it.

When I was almost through, I looked up and saw Sergeant Pelton watching me steadily, without moving his eyes.

"I'm looking for Iron Crosses," I said.

Then he caught me by the collar and pulled me up. "Put that stuff back," he said.

"What's the sense in that, Sarge?" I asked. "We got more right to it than anybody else. If we don't get it, somebody else will." Then I took the cigarette lighter and offered it to him. "Here, you can have this, if you want it," I said.

For a moment I thought he was going to hit me, but he thought better of it. He turned me loose suddenly and walked away. "Get on back to your squad," he said.

"All right," I said; "if that's the way you feel about it, it's all right by me. — But there's no use you getting sore."

"Get on back to your squad!" he said.

Private Richard Mundy

I decided to take my rifle apart and clean it thoroughly. I didn't want to think about those prisoners any more, but as I sat there with my squad in the shallow trench, with the rifle parts scattered about me, I couldn't help thinking about them. Corporal Foster was opening cans of monkey meat with a bayonet and Roger Inabinett divided the meat and the hardtack into eight equal parts.

Charlie Gordon got out his harmonica and began to play a lively tune, but Everett Qualls stopped him. Then Foster passed out the rations and each man took his share. At sight of the food, Bill Nugent took sick. He went to the edge of the trench and vomited. When he came back his face was white. Jimmy Wade had a canteen of cognac which he passed over to him and Bill took a big swig of it, but immediately he got up and vomited again. Then he lay stretched out and trembled.

"What's the matter with you, Bill?" asked Foster.

"Nothing," he said.

"They've pulled that trick on the French a thousand times, and got away with it, too!" said Foster. "These Germans are smart hombres. You got to watch them all the time."

Ahead of us in the wheat field, the rays of the late sun lay flat on the trampled grain, but in the wood it was almost dark. Inabinett was playing with a cigarette lighter he had found in the wood. He kept snapping it with a clicking sound. "All it needs is a new flint," he said. "It'll be as good as new with another flint."

I put my rifle back together and rubbed the butt with oil. I kept seeing those prisoners falling and rising to their knees and falling again. I walked to the end of the trench and looked over the top. A long way ahead was the sound of rifle fire and to the west there was intermittent shelling, but here, in the wood, everything was calm and peaceful. "You wouldn't know we were in the war at all," I thought.

Then I had an irresistible desire to go to the ravine and look at the prisoners again. I climbed out of the trench quickly, before anybody knew what I was going to do. . . .

The prisoners lay where we had left them, face upward mostly, twisted in grotesque knots like angleworms in a can, their pockets turned outward and rifled, their tunics unbuttoned and flung wide. I stood looking at them for a while, silent, feeling no emotion at all. Then the limb of a tree that grew at the edge of the ravine swayed forward and fell, and a wedge of late sunlight filtered through the trees and across the faces of the dead men. . . . Deep in the wood a bird uttered one frightened note and stopped suddenly, remembering. A peculiar feeling that I could not understand came over me. I fell to the ground and pressed my face into the fallen leaves. . . . "I'll never hurt anything again as long as I live," I said. . . . "Never again, as long as I live. . . . Never! . . . Never! . . . Never! . . ."

THE UNKNOWN SOLDIER

We were returning from a wiring party that quiet night and the men were in high spirits. Then two Maxims opened a deadly, enfilading fire, and one of my companions threw his hands up and fell without a sound. I stood there confused at the sudden attack, not knowing which way to turn. Then I heard someone shout: "Look out! Look out for the wire!" and I saw my companions, flat on their frightened bellies, scattering in all directions. I started to run, but at that moment something shoved me, and something took my breath away, and I toppled backward, and the wire caught me.

At first I did not realize that I was wounded. I lay there on the wire, breathing heavily. "I must keep perfectly calm," I thought. "If I move about, I'll entangle myself so badly that I'll never get out." Then a white flare went up and in the light that followed I saw my belly was ripped open and that my entrails hung down like a badly arranged bouquet of blue roses. The sight frightened me and I began to struggle, but the more I twisted about, the deeper the barbs sank in. Finally I could not move my legs any more and I knew, then, that I was going to die. So I lay stretched quietly, moaning and spitting blood.

I could not forget the faces of the men and the way they had scurried off when the machine guns opened up. I remembered a time, when I was a little boy and had gone to visit my grandfather, who lived on a farm. Rabbits were eating his cabbages that year, so Grandfather had closed all the entrances to his field except one, and he baited that one with lettuce leaves and young carrots. When the field was full of rabbits, the fun began. Grandfather opened the gate and let in the dog, and the hired man stood at the gap, a broomstick in his hand, breaking the necks of the rabbits as they leaped out. I had stood to one side, I remembered, pitying the rabbits and thinking how stupid they were to let themselves be caught in such an obvious trap. — And now as I lay on the wire, the scene came back to me vividly. . . . *I* had pitied the rabbits! — I, of all people . . .

I lay back, my eyes closed, thinking of that. Then I heard the mayor of our town making his annual address in the Soldiers' Cemetery of our town. Fragments of his speech kept floating through my mind: "These men died gloriously on the Field of Honor! . . . gave their lives gladly in a Noble Cause! . . . What a feeling of exaltation was theirs when Death kissed their mouths and closed their eyes for an Immortal Eternity! . . ." Suddenly I saw myself, too, a boy in the crowd, my throat tight to keep back the tears, listening enraptured to the speech and believing every word of it; and at that instant I understood clearly why I now lay dying on the wire. . . .

The first shock had passed and my wounds began to pain me. I had seen other men die on the wire and I had said if it happened to me, I would make no sound, but after a while I couldn't stand the pain any longer and I began to make a shrill, wavering noise. I cried like that for a long time. I couldn't help it. . . .

Towards daybreak a German sentry crawled out from his post and came to where I lay. "Hush!" he said in a soft voice. "Hush, please!"

He sat on his haunches and stared at me, a compassionate look in his eyes. Then I began to talk to him: "It's all a lie that people tell each other, and nobody really believes," I said. . . . "And I'm a part of it, whether I want to be or not. — I'm more a part of it now than ever before: In a few years, when war is over, they'll move my body back home to the Soldiers' Cemetery, just as they moved the bodies of the soldiers killed before I was born. There will be a brass band and speech making and a beautiful marble shaft with my name chiseled on its base. . . . The mayor will be there also, pointing to my name with his thick, trembling forefinger and shouting meaningless words about glorious deaths and fields of honor. . . . And there will be other little boys in that crowd to listen and believe him, just as I listened and believed!"

"Hush," said the German softly. "Hush! . . . Hush!"

I began to twist about on the wire and to cry again.

"I can't stand the thought of that! I can't stand it! . . . I never want to hear military music or high-sounding words again: I want to be buried where nobody will ever find me — I want to be wiped out completely. . . ."

Then, suddenly, I became silent, for I had seen a way out. I took off my identification tags and threw them into the wire, as far as I could. I tore to pieces the letters and the photographs I carried and scattered the fragments. I threw my helmet away, so that no one could guess my identity from the serial number stamped on my sweatband. Then I lay back exultant!

The German had risen and stood looking at me, as if puzzled. . . . "I've beaten the orators and the wreath-layers at their own game!" I said. . . . "I've beaten them all! — Nobody will ever use me as a symbol. Nobody will ever tell lies over my dead body now! . . ."

"Hush," said the German softly. "Hush! . . . Hush!"

Then my pain became so unbearable that I began to choke and bite at the wire with my teeth. The German came closer to me, touching my head with his hand. . . .

"Hush," he said. . . . "Hush, please. . . ."

But I could not stop. I thrashed about on the wire and cried in a shrill voice. The German took out his pistol and stood twisting it in his hand, not looking at me. Then he put his arm under my head, lifting me up, and kissed me softly on my cheek, repeating phrases which I could not understand. I saw, then, that he too, had been crying for a long time. . . .

"Do it quickly!" I said. "Quickly! . . . Quickly!"

He stood with trembling hands for a moment before he placed the barrel of his pistol against my temple, turned his head away, and fired. My eyes fluttered twice and then closed; my hands clutched and relaxed slowly.

"I have broken the chain," I whispered. "I have defeated the inherent stupidity of life."

"Hush," he said. "Hush! . . . Hush! . . . Hush! . . ."

PRIVATE CHARLES UPSON

The first thing we noticed was the silence of the German artillery. Then our own artillery quit firing. We looked at each other, surprised at the sudden quietness and wondered what was the matter. A runner came up, out of breath, with a message from Divisional: Lieutenant Bartelstone, in command of our company, read it slowly and called his platoon sergeants together. "Pass word to the men to cease firing, the war is over," he said.

CORPORAL STEPHEN WALLER

Company K went into action at 10:15 P.M. December 12, 1917, at Verdun, France, and ceased fighting on the morning of November 11, 1918, near Bourmont, having crossed the Meuse River the night before under shellfire; participating, during the period set out above, in the following major operations: Aisne, Aisne-Marne, St. Mihiel and Meuse-Argonne.

A number of men were cited for bravery, the following decorations having been actually awarded for meritorious service under fire: 10 Croix de Guerre (four of them with palms); 6 Distinguished Service Crosses; 2 Medailles Militaires and 1 Congressional Medal of Honor, the latter being awarded to Private Harold Dresser, a man of amazing personal courage.

The percentage of casualties in killed, wounded in action, missing or evacuated to hospital suffering from disease, was considerably higher than average (332.8 per cent).

Our commanding officer, Terence L. Matlock, Captain, was able and efficient and retained throughout the respect and the admiration of the men who served under him.

World War II

(1941 – 1945)

World War II: Attack and Counterattack

Pearl Harbor

⚔

from *The Pistol*

by JAMES JONES

When the first bombs lit at Wheeler Field on December 7, 1941, Pfc Richard Mast was eating breakfast. He was also wearing a pistol. From where Mast sat, amidst the bent heads, quiet murmur, and soft, cutlery-against-china sounds of breakfast, in a small company mess in one of the infantry quadrangles of Schofield Barracks, it was perhaps a mile to Wheeler Field, and it took several seconds for the sound of the explosions, followed soon after by the shockwave through the earth, to reach his ears. Obviously, as far as Mast was concerned during those few seconds, the United States was still at peace, although in actual fact she was already, even then, at war. Consequently, during those moments, Mast had no idea at all of getting to keep the pistol he was wearing.

In one way it was unusual for a soldier in peacetime to be wearing a pistol at breakfast, but in another way it was not. The day before, on Saturday's duty roster, Mast and three other men had been named to go on Interior Guard duty. This guard duty lasted from four in the afternoon to four in the afternoon, twenty-four hours, and the men assigned to it daily from the various companies drew pistols, pistol belts, arm brassards and pistol lanyards from their company supply rooms. They were required to sign for these, required to wear them at all times when they were not actually sleeping, and, twenty-four hours later when they came off guard, required to turn them back immediately. This was a strict rule. No exceptions to it were allowed in any form. There was a good reason for it.

In our Army, back in those now-dead, very far-off times, pistols were at a premium. The regulation .45-caliber automatic pistol adopted by the Army was a beautiful thing; it was also a potent weapon at close range. But perhaps even more important, it was small enough to steal. It would be pretty hard for any soldier who was being discharged to steal a rifle, even if he dismantled it completely. Not so with the pistol, and any man would have dearly loved to get his hands on a loose one, without signed records following it around. This, however, was next to impossible to do. Not only was very careful track kept of them, but they were also very scarce in an infantry regiment, since they were issued only to Headquarters personnel, officers, and members of machine-gun squads. As a result, about the only time a straight duty rifle private like Mast ever got to put his hands on one was the twenty-four hours when he went on guard.

All this, of course, went into Mast's enjoyment of wearing, handling and possessing, for twenty-four hours at least, a pistol. But for Mast, who was nineteen and imaginative, there was an even greater pleasure in it. Wearing a pistol on his hip made him feel more like a real soldier, seemed to give him an unbroken lineal connection with the Army of the days of the West and Custer's Cavalry, made him feel that he was really in the Army, a feeling Mast did not often have in what to himself he termed this crumby, lazy outfit. It was almost enough to offset his irritation at having his weekend pass spoiled by guard duty on Sunday.

After the first rack of bombs went off and the sound and shockwave reached the little company mess, there was almost a full minute of thoughtful silence during which everyone looked at everyone else. "Dynamiting?" somebody said. Then another rack fell and exploded and at the same time the first plane came screeching over the quadrangle, its machine guns going full blast. After that there wasn't any doubt and the entire mess jumped up to rush outside.

Mast, being careful to catch up his Sunday half pint of milk so no one could steal it, went too, his pistol riding reassuringly on his hip. A pistol obviously wasn't much good against strafing airplanes, but just the same it felt good to him to have it. It gave Mast a sort of swaggery confidence. He wished rather wistfully, as he watched the next plane come over, that he did not have to turn it in tonight when he went off guard.

It was pretty exciting outside the quadrangle in the street. Out here you could see a big column of black smoke beginning to rise up through the bright morning air from down at Wheeler Field where they were bombing the planes. You could see them twinkling up there in the sun. They looked innocent, as though they had nothing to do with the destruction going on below.

Every few minutes a fighter with the red discs painted on the wings and fuselage would come screeching and blasting over, his MG fire raking the street. Then everyone would surge back against the building. As soon as he was gone, they would surge right back out again and stand staring at the smoke column as if they were personally responsible for it and proud of their achievement. They looked as though they wanted to take credit for the whole thing themselves, without giving the Japs any at all.

Mast, surging backward and forward with them, had an excited feeling of being in on history, of actually seeing history made, and he wondered if any of the other men felt that way. But Mast doubted if they did. Most of them weren't too bright, or very educated.

Mast happened to be one of three high school graduates in his company, and this fact often worked against him, in many ways. Of the other two, one was company clerk and a sergeant, and the other had been carried off on special duty to work in battalion intelligence and was a tech sergeant. But Mast had steadfastly refused to be inveigled into any such job. If he had wanted to be a clerk, he could have enlisted in the Air Corps. As a result, Mast was the only high school graduate doing straight duty as a rifle private in his company, and in a company like this, where almost nobody had completed grade school, almost no one liked or trusted a man who had finished high school.

For a moment, excitedly, Mast thought of drawing his pistol and taking a few blasts at the low-flying planes as they came over, but he was afraid of looking absurd or ridiculous so he didn't. Even though he had made Expert in pistol on the range, he was reasonably sure he would never hit one. But, boy! Mast thought, what if he did hit one? did bring one down single-handed all by himself with his pistol? What a hero he would be, and at only nineteen! Hell, maybe he'd even get a medal. He could imagine the whole thing in his mind as he allowed himself to be jostled back by the men in front as another plane screamed over: the general, the regimental band playing the parade on the division parade ground, the whole business. Boy, what would they think about *that* back home in Miseryville? Even so, he was still too embarrassed, too afraid of being laughed at, to haul the pistol out.

Actually, Mast was the only man present with a weapon, since the other three men on guard with him had to stay over at the guardhouse and sleep there. That was where Mast himself would have been, if he had not been picked as orderly at guardmount yesterday. Wishing he dared draw it, Mast let his hand fall down to his side and massaged the holster flap of his pistol he knew he would have to turn back this evening.

Just then a heavy hand was laid on his shoulder. Startled, Mast turned around to see First Sergeant Wycoff, a big man in his thirties, looking at him with angry eyes and the same numb, stupid, half-grinning expression on his face that all the others had, including his own.

"Mast, aren't you on guard orderly today?"

"What? Oh. Yeah. Yeah, I am."

"Then you better get your tail on over to Headquarters and report," the First Sergeant said, not unkindly. "They'll probably be needing you for carrying messages."

"Okay," Mast said; "yes, sir," and began to shoulder his way back inside through the press, finishing his bottle of milk as he went. Now why the hell hadn't he thought of that himself? he wondered.

Inside the quadrangle, after he had gone back through the building, Mast found men were running everywhere. Whenever a plane came roaring, sliding over they broke and scattered like bowling pins. Then they would get back up and go back to their running. Mast saw one man actually get shot in the leg. It was unbelievable. He simply fell down and lay there with his head up, beating his fists on the ground, whether in anger or anguish Mast could not tell. After the planes passed he was helped to the sidelines by two men who ran out, dragging his leg for all the world like an injured football player being helped out of the game.

Up on the roofs of the quadrangle men had begun to appear with machine guns and BAR's and were now firing back at the planes as they came over, and from his vantage point under the porch Mast watched them, envying them hungrily. Of all days, he would have to be on guard today; and not only that, would have to get himself picked as guard orderly.

Mast had been on guard plenty of times in the past, but he had never before been chosen orderly. This was because he always became nervous when it came to answering the General Orders questions. He always looked as polished at inspection as everyone else, and he had the General Orders memorized. But whenever the Officer of the Day asked him the questions he would freeze, and his mind would go blank.

And now today of all days, Mast thought regretfully, he would have to make it for orderly. Usually it was the most coveted job, because all you had to do was sit around Headquarters all day outside the Colonel's office and you got your whole night off to yourself, while the rest of them had to stand two hours on and four off, around the clock.

Well, that was just about what he might have expected, Mast thought sadly, have figured on, his customary luck: guard orderly on the day the dirty Japs attacked Oahu.

Standing in under the covered porch and watching the scene before him, a sad, bitter melancholy crept over Mast. It was a feeling that even the longest life was short and the end of it was death and extinction and then rotting away, and that about all a man could expect along the way was frustration, and bitterness, and phoniness in everybody, and hatred. Perhaps being a high school graduate in a company of oafs contributed to it a little bit.

Disdaining to run like the rest of them, even though he could not help feeling a certain nervousness, Mast composed his face into a contemptuous smirk and came out from under the protection of the porch and walked slowly around the square, his pistol swaying bravely on his hip. Twice as he walked flame-spitting planes came sliding over, churning up twin rows of dust across the grass and ricocheting screamingly off the brick, and Mast could feel the muscles of his back twitch, but he refused to let himself run or even walk faster.

From under one of the porches of the 3rd Battalion an officer yelled at him, angrily, indignantly, outraged: "Hey, you silly son of a bitch! Get out of there! Are you crazy? Move! Run! That's an order!"

Mast turned his head to look at him, but he did not stop or change his gait. Then suddenly emotion spurted out of him like blood gushing out of a wound. "Go to hell," he shouted happily, knowing that for once he was invulnerable even to an officer. Just then a third plane came screeching, blasting over and his eyes began to blink themselves rapidly, as if that act in itself would offer him protection. Then it was gone, just like that, off over the quad. In some odd way of possessive ownership, of just knowing it was there, the pistol on his hip helped shore up Mast's courage. He sure wished he didn't have to turn it in tonight. It wasn't like a rifle. Didn't give you the same feeling at all. What the damned government *ought* to do was issue every trooper a rifle and pistol both. They used to. In the Cavalry.

In the Headquarters building upstairs outside the Colonel's office, when Mast got there, everything was in an uproar. Officers were running all over the place, bumping into each other, getting in each other's way. They all had the same numb, stupid, excited look the men in Mast's company had had, the same look Mast could feel on his own face, and once again Mast was struck with that awareness that he was actually *seeing* history made.

When he finally saw the Adjutant coming out of the Old Man's office, he reported to him and told him he was here.

"What? Oh," the middle-aged first lieutenant said, looking numbly excited, as well as harassed. "Well, stick around. May have something for you to do. Messages or something." He hurried off. Mast sat back down. What a way to spend the bombing of Hawaii. Outside the Jap fighters continued to scream over the quad, blasting. Inside, high-ranking officers continued to bump into each other in their hurry. And Mast sat.

It was some time after the attack was over, several hours, before the Adjutant found time to release Mast and send him back to his company.

They would not need him further. In the interim he had been sent out with a series of messages from the Colonel to the various battalion and company commanders about moving out, and twice he was sent by the Adjutant to the motor pool to find out what was holding the trucks up, but that was all.

Slowly Mast trudged back across the quad that was now swarming with activity. Not only had he missed almost all of the attack, but this release of the guard to take the field meant that he would have to turn in the pistol, and all Mast could think of was that if the Japs were landing (or *had* landed), what a wonderful personal defense weapon that pistol would be. Especially against those Samurai sabers of the officers, about which he had read so much. Because as soon as the other three men on guard reported back also, they would all be required to turn in their pistols for which they'd signed. Gloomily he kicked at a clod ahead of him that a Jap MG had churned up from the green.

When he got back to the company area the first thing Mast found out, however, from one of the disgruntled privates who had been detailed to help load the kitchen truck, was that the other three men from the company were staying behind. The entire Interior Regimental Guard with the sole exception of the orderly, which was himself of course, had been ordered to stay behind and continue their guarding duties until some provision for relieving them could be organized.

For a moment, as he heard this, Mast thought of just going on upstairs and hiding the pistol away in his full-field pack. It would certainly go unnoticed, perhaps for a long time, in this confusion. Perhaps forever. That was what he wanted to do. But what good would the pistol do him if the Japs were on the beaches and it was in his pack? Anyway, he thought with defeat, he had signed his name for it. And some essential of Mast's childhood training, some inherent nervousness at the idea of going against authority, some guilt, and the shame of getting caught, refused to let him do what he desired. Now, if he hadn't signed his name — Hell, it wasn't even simple honesty, Mast raged at himself, it was just plain fear.

But he still couldn't make himself do it. So instead he temporized. Still wearing the pistol and the other accouterments of guard duty, he went into the Orderly Room to report to the First Sergeant, to see what might happen. Maybe the First wouldn't even notice it.

"What? Oh," First Sergeant Wycoff said, looking up with harassed eyes. He was behind his desk packing files and report books. "Released you? Well, turn in your gear and go upstairs and pack, Mast," he said, not unkindly. "Field uniform, full field pack, one barracks bag."

"Yes, sir." Mast's spirits fell. He turned to go.

"And Mast," First Sergeant Wycoff said sharply.

Mast turned around, his heart in his mouth from guilt. He was caught. "Sir?"

"Don't worry about time," the First Sergeant said bitterly, without even looking up. "There'll be plenty of goddamned time for you to pack." He slammed his Morning Report book into a musette bag.

"Yes, sir."

Outside, Mast tried to analyze it. The First had told him to turn in his gear. Okay. That was obviously more or less an order. On the other hand, Wycoff had not mentioned the pistol specifically or even looked at it. But then perhaps that was because he always wore one himself when the company was in the field. In addition to his rifle, Mast remembered bitterly. Well, he couldn't very well turn in the other stuff without the pistol. Reluctantly, loving the feel of the pistol on him and in his hand more now than ever before — especially when he thought about those Samurai sabers, Mast turned toward the supply room.

He was saved by the supply clerk. This soldier, a long, thin stringbean of an Italian Pfc who had been in the Army at least twelve years, was now in charge of another disgruntled detail drafted at random to load the supply truck, sitting in the street behind the kitchen truck. He only snarled.

"For God's sake, Mast! Don't bother me with a lousy pistol and brassard," he screamed, shaking at Mast a .30-caliber watercooled he was carrying. "I got *impor*tant things to do. Them goddam beaches are probably crawling with Jap infantry right now."

"Okay, I'm sorry," Mast said, and carefully veiled his surprised happiness under a look of hurt vanity.

Morally exonerated now, and relieved, although not without a certain nervousness at the thought of those beaches crawling with Jap infantry (crawling: like ants: all over you), he went upstairs to pack. The pistol still rode his hip heavily, a weight pregnant with compressed power, symbolic of an obscure personal safety. No wonder everybody wanted pistols. And he himself could not be held accountable for thievery: he had tried to give it back.

The second floor squadroom was alive with movement of men kneeling and straining at pack-straps, men stooping to stuff barracks bags with extra clothes. Moving out! As he rolled his own pack, Mast thought once again about packing the pistol away so no one would see it. If he did, maybe nobody would *ever* remember it. But if the Japs *were* on the beaches, already, he would want it immediately. And if the company dropped their packs going into action as they surely would, and the pistol was in his pack —

Well aware that he was taking a real chance of eventually losing it back to the supply room, Mast decided to gamble and wear it anyway. What good would it do him, what protection, lying in a barracks bag or pack? Luckily it was a regulation holster and not the kind the MP's wore. All he had to do was unhook it off the web pistol belt, hook it into his rifle cartridge belt, and stuff the extra clips into the cartridge pockets above it. The brassard and lanyard he packed in the bottom of the barracks bag with the pistol belt. Then, wearing his tin hat with a jauntiness he did not entirely feel when he thought about what might be in store for them, Mast carted everything downstairs to the yard where the company was slowly forming. Sergeant Wycoff had certainly been right about the time. There was another full hour and a half to wait, and it was nearly three o'clock before the personnel trucks of the Regiment began to move.

On the way down to the beaches in the trucks Mast received only one comment on the pistol. A Private 1st Class in the same truck but from another platoon, a huge blue-jowled black Irishman of twenty-two named O'Brien, asked him enviously where did he get the pistol?

"That?" Mast said coolly, but with his mind working swiftly. "Oh, I've had that a long time. Bought it off a guy."

O'Brien moved his big dark face inarticulately, wrinkling his broad forehead and moistening his lips, then flexed his hamlike hands a couple of times where they dangled from his knees. He stared at the holstered pistol hungrily, almost abjectly. Then he turned his huge dark head with the pale green eyes and stared off levelly from the back of the open truck with its hastily mounted MG on the cab roof, toward where the sea was. Mast had seen him engaged in some tremendous, almost Herculean fist fights since he had been in the company, but he did not look tough now. He turned back to Mast. "Want to sell it?" he said huskily.

"Sell it? Hell, no. That's why I bought it."

O'Brien reached one big-fingered hand up and unbuttoned his shirt pocket and pulled out a wad of bills. "Made some money on craps last night," he said almost wistfully. "Give you fifty bucks for it."

Mast was astonished, and did not think he had heard right. He had had no idea his new possession would be so valuable — not to anyone but himself. But there was O'Brien, and there was the money. Nobody else in the truck was paying any attention.

"No," Mast said. "Nosir. I want it for myself."

"Give you seventy," O'Brien said quietly, almost beseechingly. "That's all I got."

"No dice. I told you. That's why I bought it in the first place. So I could have it for myself."

"Well, hell," O'Brien said hopelessly, and slowly put his useless money back in the pocket and buttoned the flap. Unhappily he clutched his rifle, and out of the broad, dark, brooding face with its pale green eyes stared off in the direction of the sea again.

But that was the only comment. No one else noticed the pistol apparently, not even Mast's own squad leader. They were all too concerned with thinking about what they might find on the beaches. Mast could not help feeling rather smugly sorry for O'Brien, somewhat the same feeling a man who knows he has salvation experiences for one who knows he has not; but Mast did not know what he could be expected to do. There was only one pistol. And through fate, or luck, and a series of strangely unforeseeable happenings, it had been given to him, not O'Brien.

Mast and O'Brien were not the only ones who kept looking off toward where the sea was. If the colonel knew that the Japanese forces had not landed, he might possibly have told the Company Commander. But if he had, the Company Commander had not seen fit to tell his troops. Perhaps the truth was that nobody knew. At any rate, the men in the truck did not. And as the convoy, moving by fits and starts, wound its way down off the high central plateau of the island, there were places between the hills where the men could get clear glimpses far away below them of the smoking shambles of Pearl Harbor and Hickham Field. The sight made them even more thoughtful. As far away as they could see, a mile-long line of trucks was worming its way down bumper to bumper, carrying them at a pace a man could walk, toward Honolulu and they knew not what else.

Actually, long before they ever reached the city everybody knew the Japanese had not landed. The word was shouted back from truck to truck, traveling far faster than the trucks themselves went forward. But the knowledge reassured nobody. If they didn't land today, they would tomorrow, or the next day. And going through the city there was very little friendly response by the men in the trucks to the wildly cheering civilians who only so recently as last night had wanted nothing to do with soldiers except take their money.

The method in which the trucks had been loaded back at Schofield by Regimental Order was planned in advance so that the men and equipment for each beach position would be loaded all on the same truck, or trucks. Consequently, the little section of the miles-long convoy which was Mast's company (whose sector ran from Wailupe east through Koko Head to Makapuu Head), having split off from the main trunk highway and made its way through the city on back roads, found itself alone out on Kamehameha Highway going east, its trucks peeling off one by one from the head of the column as it came abreast of their positions, until finally only four were left: the four trucks for the company's last and biggest position at Makapuu Point, one of which trucks was Mast's. The effect was weird, if not downright enervating: From a huge, powerful convoy of unnumbered men and vehicles they had dwindled down to just four trucks, alone, moving along a deserted highway between the mountains and the sea and filled with thirty-five puny men and eighteen puny machine guns, all that was left, apparently, to fight the war alone against the entire might of the Imperial Japanese war machine. Or so they felt. Mast could not help feeling a shiver, in spite of his pleasure over his new pistol.

Makapuu Head, and Point, was acknowledgedly the worst position in the company sector. For one thing, there were no civilian homes within miles, such as the majority of the company's position had, and hence no civilians by whom to be admired, and from whom to bum food. For another, it was at the very extreme end of the company chow line and by the time the little weapons carriers that brought the food got to them, the food itself in the big aluminum pots was so cold the grease would be congealed on top of it. For a third, Makapoo (as they came at once to call it) was the only position in the company sector large enough to have a truly autonomous military organization; most of the positions had four, or five, or even seven, men and were run by a single sergeant or corporal; not Makapoo: it had thirty-five, its own private lieutenant, six sergeants, and at least four corporals. And, as every soldier knows, a sergeant who has an officer observing him does not act at all the same as a sergeant who is on his own.

For a fourth thing, Makapuu Point was the very hub and apex of what the Islanders preferred to call the "Windward" side of Oahu. Jutting far out into the sea all by itself, there was nothing between it and San Francisco, and the wind that poured against the Pali and shot straight up, strongly enough to keep more than one would-be suicide from obtaining more than a couple of broken legs by a fall of more than a hundred feet, poured across it also, a living river of air, a tidal ocean of it. "Windward" was a pretty lax term for such a wind, if you had to live in it without relief. And at Makapoo you were never free of it. It never ceased. Even in the pillboxes cut into the living rock in November, the wind seeped in like water and made chilling eddies of air among the shivering men who tried to sleep there.

And if these were not enough to earn Makapoo its title of "A-hole of the Universe," for a fifth thing, there was not a single building there to take shelter in; nor was there enough loose dirt on top the solid rock to drive a tentpeg into. This was the beach position Richard Mast, with his customary luck, had managed to get himself assigned to; and this was the beach position they scrambled out of the trucks that first day to try and make, first, militarily defensible, and then, second, livable.

The first week of both of these attempts was hectic, what with the Japanese expected every day, and also ridiculous. It consisted mainly (after having first got the MG's set up in their proper fields of fire in the pillboxes) of putting up all day barbed wire which far more often than not the sea washed away, of standing guard half the night, and of having one's shelterhalf and two blankets blown off of one during the rest of the night by the wind. There was consequently very little sleep. No matter how tightly and carefully a man might wrap up, the wind, testing here, trying there, eventually would find a loose corner somewhere with which to begin its endless and seemingly diabolical tug of war. There was not room enough for most of the men to sleep "indoors," if the rock floors of the pillboxes could be called that, and most of them had to lie down outside on the stony ground in the full force of the wind. No one had thought to try to provide sleeping shelter for the men.

But even all of this discomfort, together with the excitement of the anticipated invasion and the bad news about the Philippines, did not stir up half as much interest at Makapoo as Mast's loose pistol, once it became known generally that he had it. Everybody wanted it. In the first five days after the attack Mast had no less than seven separate offers to buy it, as well as two nocturnal attempts to steal it from him as he slept. He could not remember having had so much attention since he first came into this company over a year ago.

Quite plainly O'Brien had talked about it. About this free-floating, unrecorded pistol loose at Makapoo in Mast's hands. Out of his hunger for it, plus his lack of success in getting hold of it, O'Brien had talked about it to somebody, if not everybody. How else would anyone know? And Mast began to realize his error in having lied about it and said he'd bought it. He had done that out of sheer instinct, and because he did not want it brought to the attention of the supply room that he still had it; and after two years in the Army Mast was cynically suspicious that there existed more than one man who would go to the supply room and tell, just simply because he himself did not have one. And for the purpose he had used it, the lie had sufficed. The supply room apparently was still totally unaware it had a pistol missing. But in succeeding, the lie had created other problems. It had, in effect, thrown the possession of Mast's pistol open to the field: anyone who had it, owned it.

Actually, Mast was willing to accept possession of his pistol under those circumstances; or any other circumstances. Having worn and cared for it those days since the attack had made it his in a peculiar way that he could not possibly have felt that Sunday when he knew he had to turn it back in twenty-four hours. And from there, it was only one step to believing that he *had* bought it after all, the only logical step to take, in fact. He knew of course that somewhere there existed a paper with his signature on it saying that he owed God, or the Army, one pistol. And while the knowledge registered with him, it also somehow did not register. He *had* bought it. He could even, when pressed, remember the face of the man from the 8th Field Artillery who had sold it to him. So in one way the pistol had become what everyone believed it was. And Mast was prepared to defend it on those terms. From any source of jeopardy.

The offers to buy it ranged in price from twenty dollars to sixty dollars, none as high as the seventy dollars O'Brien had offered him under the stress of that first day. O'Brien himself was out of the bidding now, having lost nearly all of his seventy dollars in a poker game in one of the pillboxes. Poker was just about the only recreational facility left them now, and since it was clear that money was not going to be of use to any of them for some time to come, almost everybody who had any cash played; and the young lieutenant in charge of the position was powerless to stop it. And usually, whenever anyone won a wad of money, the first thing they did was go to Mast and make an offer for his pistol. Mast, naturally, refused them all.

As for the two attempts to steal it, Mast was lucky in being able to circumvent them both. The first occurred on the third night after the attack. Up to then Mast had been used to sleeping with his cartridge belt, and the holstered pistol, under his head for a sort of makeshift pillow and he woke up from a fitful sleep in the unceasing ear-beating wind to feel his belt, with the pistol on it, being stealthily withdrawn from under his head. He made a grab for it, caught it and yanked, and retained his pistol. But when he raised up to look, all he could see in the moonless darkness was the retreating back of a crouched running figure, its footfalls silent because of the loudly buffeting wind. After that, he decided to sleep with his belt on, around his waist. And after someone, whose retreating back he could also see but not identify, tried two nights later to sneak the pistol out of its holster while he again slept, he slept after that with the pistol itself tucked into his waist belt under his buttoned-down shirt and zippered field jacket while still wearing the riflebelt outside. This made for difficult sleeping, but then sleeping at Makapoo was difficult at best, and he didn't care. Now that he had his pistol he meant to keep it.

It was interesting to speculate upon just why everyone was so desirous of possessing this particular pistol, and Mast did speculate on it, a little. Everybody had always wanted pistols, of course, but this was somehow becoming a different thing, he felt. But he was so busy working all day long, trying to sleep at night, and above all trying to keep and protect his pistol, that he really had very little time left to speculate on anything.

Certainly, a lot of it had to do with the fact that it was free, unattached. All the members of the machine-gun platoon at Makapoo carried pistols too, but theirs had been assigned to them and so nobody tried to steal them. It was pointless, because the serial numbers were registered to them. But because Mast had bought his (Had he? Yes! He had. He distinctly had.), instead of signing a requisition for it, it was unrecorded and therefore anyone who could come into possession of it would own it.

And yet, despite that very strong point, there seemed to be something else, something Mast, certainly, could not put his finger on. Everybody seemed to be getting frantic to possess his pistol. And Mast was unable to account for it, or understand it.

All Mast knew was the feeling that the pistol gave him. And that was that it comforted him. As he lay rolled up in his two blankets and one shelterhalf at night with the rocky ground jabbing him in the ribs or flanks and the wind buffeting his head and ears, or as he worked his arms numb to the shoulder all day long at the never-ending job of putting up recalcitrant barbed wire, it comforted him. Thy rod and thy staff. Perhaps he had no staff — unless you could call his rifle that — but he had a "rod." And it would be his salvation. One day it would save him. The sense of personal defensive safety that it gave him was tremendous. He could even picture the scene: lying wounded, and alone, his rifle lost, himself unable to walk, and a Jap major bearing down on him with a drawn saber to split him in half: then his pistol would save him. The world was rocketing to hell in a bucket, but if he could only hold onto his pistol, remain in possession of the promise of salvation its beautiful blue-steel bullet-charged weight offered him, he could be saved.

Give 'Em Hell, Boys

✗

from *See Here, Private Hargrove*

by MARION HARGROVE

The Japanese attack on Pearl Harbor this afternoon came as stunning news to the men at Fort Bragg. There had been a rumor, one day a couple of months ago, that Germany had declared war on the United States to beat us to the draw, and since it was merely a rumor, there was no confirmation or denial over the radio all day long. That supposed news back then had been taken with a philosophic shrug and the thought, "Well, it's what we've been expecting."

This today caused a different war feeling. It was not what we had been expecting. To the soldiers here, whose only attention to the newspapers is a quick glance at the headlines, it was startling and dreadful.

The men who heard the news announcement over the radio this afternoon at the Service Club were, for the most part, new to the Army, with less
than a month of training behind them. Their first feeling of outrage gave
way to the awful fear that they would be sent away, green and untrained
and helpless, within a week.

The rumor mill began operation immediately. New York and Fort Bragg
will be bombed within the month, the rumors said. Probably, by that time,
all of us will be in Hawaii or Russia or Persia or Africa. Green and untrained and helpless. This business of teaching a man for thirteen weeks in
a replacement center will be dispensed with, now that war is upon us.
You're a civilian one day and a rookie member of a seasoned fighting outfit
the next.

Except for a few for whom the radio held a terrible fascination, the men
thought first of communicating with their families, their friends, their
sweethearts. They immediately went for writing materials and for the two
public telephones of the club. Almost all of the 64,000 men of Fort Bragg
were trying to reach their homes through the eight trunk lines which ran
out of the pitifully overburdened little telephone exchange in Fayetteville.

Miss Ethel Walker, who was acting as senior hostess for the Replacement
Center's Service Club, had planned an entertainment program for the
evening, but when she looked out at the tension in the social hall, she despaired. She telephoned her boss, Major Herston M. Cooper, the special
services officer.

"There's no use trying to put on the show tonight," she said. "Shall I
cancel it? And may I turn off the radio?"

"If it's a good program, keep it," said the major. "And by all means leave
the radio on. Just hang on; I'll be there in five minutes."

The major, a former criminologist and schoolteacher in Birmingham, was
a lean and mischievous-looking infantry officer with a gift of gab and a
camaraderie with the enlisted men. He sauntered into the Service Club,
noised it about that he was going to talk, and hooked up the public address
microphone.

"Here it comes," said an unhappy acting corporal. "Here comes the
higher brass, to tell us the worst."

The major cleared his throat and looked over the crowd which gathered
about him. "I know that this is your Service Club," he said, "and that I'm a
staff officer barging in on you. Before I was an officer, I was an enlisted
man. And, as an enlisted man, I've done more KP than any man in this
room."

A little of the tension passed and the major lapsed into one of his con-
veniently absent-minded rambles. "In fact, I went on KP every time they
inspected my rifle. Couldn't keep the thing clean."

He paused. "The main thing that has us worrying this afternoon is the very same thing we're being trained to protect. It's what they call the American Way — and they spell it with capitals.

"I have my own ideas about the American Way. I think the American Way is shown in you boys whose parents paid school taxes so that you could know what it was to cut hooky. It's shown in the men who pay two dollars to see a wrestling match, not to watch the wrestlers but to boo the referee. It's the good old go-to-hell American spirit and you can't find it anywhere but here.

"You and I both, when we were called into the Army, brought our homes with us. We've been thinking less about war than about getting back home after a while — back to our girls and our wives and our civilian jobs.

"Well, we know now where we stand and we don't have to worry about whether we're in for a long stretch or a short vacation. That should be cleared up now. We know that we've got only one job now and we haven't time to worry about the one at home.

"You're worrying because you're not prepared soldiers, you're not ready to fight yet. When the time comes for you to go, you'll be ready. You'll have your fundamental training before you leave the Replacement Center.

"Even if war is declared tomorrow, you'll be taught for a while here. And if war were declared tonight, we'd still have our Service Club and our movies and our athletics. During our off hours, we would. That's part of the American Way.

"Spending your duty hours at work and your leisure hours at worry — that's no good. That's what the enemy wants for you."

The major stopped again and looked at the soldiers seated at writing tables and the ones waiting for the telephones. "Someone once told me that the best thing to do with a letter you're not sure should be sent is to hang on to it for twenty-four hours. You might apply that to those letters you're writing now. I'm not going to write my family until tomorrow.

"Don't write or telephone home when you're under a strain like this. Your parents and friends are worrying about you now and there's no need to feed their worries. The letters most of you are writing are going to disturb your people back home, and they're going to write letters back that will react on you. Nobody's going to get anywhere like that.

"Relax for a while. Have a beer somewhere or get into a good argument or just go home and sleep it off. Then write home when you've had time to think it over. Let your letters be reassuring; you owe it to your folks.

"I guess that's all, boys."

He turned to leave the microphone, but returned as if he had suddenly remembered something.

"The regular variety show will go on tonight at eight o'clock," he said.

They come and they go from the Replacement Center more quickly now, or perhaps it merely seems that they do. The training cycles have not been cut down much, but the turnover of men seems greater. Perhaps it's just that we notice the arrivals and departures more, now that war has given them grimness.

We call the train — the one that brings in recruits and takes out soldiers — the Shanghai Express. The term probably was used first by some disgruntled soldier who put into it the bitterness of a difficult transition from civilian to soldier. Now the term is used with a certain tender fondness by the permanent personnel of the Center, we who watch the men come and go.

The melancholy moan of a train whistle is heard in the distance of the night and a sergeant clicks his teeth wistfully. "Here she comes, boys," he says. "Here comes that Shanghai Express." The sound of the whistle identifies all that touches the heart of a soldier.

There was a group of new men coming in this morning, down at the railroad siding. Their new uniforms hung strangely upon them, conspicuous and uncertain and uncomfortable — new uniforms on new soldiers.

They were frightened and ill at ease, these men. A week ago they had been civilians and the prospect of the Army had probably hung over some of them like a Damoclean sword. They had been told, by well-meaning friends, that the Army wouldn't be so bad once they got used to it. The Army will make you or break you, they had been told. The Army really isn't as bad as it's painted, they had heard. All of this, in a diabolically suggestive way, had opened conjectures to terrify the most indomitable.

This morning, they still hadn't had time to get over their fears. They still had no idea of what Army life was going to be like. Most of all and first of all, they wondered, "What sort of place is this we're coming into?"

Their spirits were still at their lowest point — past, present, or future.

The Replacement Center band, led by wizened little Master Sergeant Knowles, was there to greet them with a welcome that might dispel from from the feeling that they were cattle being shipped into the fort on consignment. First there were the conventional but stirring military marches, the "Caisson Song" and all the rest. And then there was a sly and corny rendition of the "Tiger Rag," a friendly musical wink that said, "Take it easy, brother."

A little reassured but still suspicious, the men went from the train to the theater, where they would see a program of entertainment and possibly hear a short and casual welcoming address by General Parker.

This afternoon the sound of marching feet came up Headquarters Street from the south and a battery of departing soldiers approached. As they neared the headquarters building, there came the order, "Count cadence — command!" and two hundred voices took up a chant. They passed, counting their footsteps in ringing ordered tones.

Laden with haversacks, they passed in perfect order. Their lines were even, their marching co-ordinated and confident. Their uniforms no longer bore the awkward stamp. Their caps were cocky but correct and their neckties were tucked between the right two buttons.

The cadence count is the scheme of the battery commander who feels proud of the men he has trained, who wants to show them off to the higher-ups in Center Headquarters. "The general might be standing by his window now, watching my men pass," they say. "If he isn't, we should attract his attention."

Just as their arrival marks an emotional ebb, their departure is the flood tide. The men who came in a few weeks ago, green and terrified, leave now as soldiers. The corporal whom they dreaded then is now just a jerk who's bucking for sergeant. Although they are glad that they have been trained with other men on the same level here, the training center which was first a vast and awful place is now just a training center, all right in its way — for rookies. They themselves have outgrown their kindergarten.

The band is at the railroad siding, this time to see them off with a flourish. They pay more attention to the band this time. They know the "Caisson Song." They know their own Replacement Center Marching Song, composed by one of their number, a quiet little ex-music teacher named Harvey Bosell. They hum the tune as they board the Shanghai Express.

They see the commanding general standing on the sidelines with his aide. He is no longer an ogre out of Washington who might, for all they know, have the power of life and death over them to administer it at a whim. He is the commanding general, a good soldier and a good fellow, and it was damned white of him to come down to see them off.

They board the train and they sit waiting for it to take them to their permanent Army post and their part in the war.

As a special favor and for old times' sake, the band swings slowly into the song that is the voice of their nostalgia, "The Sidewalks of New York." Yankee or Rebel, Minnesotan or Nevadan, they love that song.

You can see their faces tightening a little, and a gently melancholy look come into their eyes as the trombone wails beneath the current of the music. Their melancholy is melancholy with a shrug now. Home and whatever else was dearest to them a few months ago are still dear, but a soldier has to push them into the background when there's a war to be fought.

With the music still playing, the train pulls slowly out and Sergeant Knowles waves it good-bye with his baton.

An old sergeant, kept in the Replacement Center to train the men whose fathers fought with him a generation ago, stands on the side and watches them with a firm, proud look.

"Give 'em hell, boys," he shouts behind them. "Give 'em hell!"

Dress Rehearsal

X

from *The Steel Cocoon*

by BENTZ PLAGEMANN

On the following day, Monday, the *Ajax* was assigned a position as flank guard to the *Jove*, the aircraft carrier, for practice flight maneuvers. The *Ajax* also drew the crash-boat duty, which meant that she must be prepared at a moment's notice to launch the small boat in a rescue operation for any young pilot who might miss the flight deck and plunge into the sea.

It had been a busy morning for Williams, since, on the night before, during the run of a movie on the forecastle, almost one-third of the crew had been struck with food poisoning. It did not take Doctor Claremont long to track down the guilty agent. After the baseball game on the beach the cooks, coming back late to the ship, had served up as part of an impromptu supper the remainder of the cold meat and potato salad that they had taken ashore for lunch.

It was not a serious disorder, but under the circumstances it was certainly uncomfortable and inconvenient, even if not without its comic aspects. Boys sat on watch with pails beside them, the heads were crowded with a passing stream of groaning, retching victims, and in the still, tropical night the entire ship had a distinct and unpleasant odor, like an untidy children's nursery during an epidemic of colic. Doctor Claremont felt that no extraordinary steps were indicated, but he did post Williams to a special watch on the dishwasher, to make certain that the mess boys, in their eagerness to finish this disagreeable task in the steaming quarters below deck, would not fail to leave the serving trays in the washer for the length of time required to sterilize them.

After that it was a relief for him to take up his appointed place on the deck beside the small boat, with his life belt and first-aid bag. In case of emergency the small boat was to be launched with McNulty, MacDougal, Clancy, Chief Bullitt, and Williams, and they stood together by the rail, watching in silence.

From the deck of the *Ajax* the *Jove* looked enormous, a whole metal microcosm. While they rose and fell with the sea, the *Jove* merely sat, like a solid in a solid. On its landing deck planes manned by young, inexperienced pilots, untried by war, took off and landed in sequence, in an atmosphere of tension that communicated itself even as far as the *Ajax*. From their distance, watching with hands cupped over their eyes against the sun, the men on the *Ajax* could see only dimly the organized activity on the *Jove*, the planes moving into place for takeoff, the landing planes braked into place abruptly on the deck, the men walking or running, the signal pennants flashing. When the *Jove* wheeled about majestically in the blue, tropical water, it left an ever-widening swath of lighter turquoise, swirling with masses of bubbles rising from the stern.

Suddenly, from out of the glare of the sun, a plane came in uncertainly, wobbling a bit in its flight, as if flown by an extremely inexperienced pilot. It overshot the flight deck of the *Jove* and plunged, in a spray of foam, into the space of water between the *Ajax* and the *Jove*.

In a matter of minutes, with shouted instructions from McNulty, the small boat, the crew aboard, was lowered, the falls let go, the sea-painter cast off, and with MacDougal at the tiller they sped toward the place where the plane had come down.

The plane had sunk almost at once upon hitting the water, going down like a stone, but they could see the pilot afloat. He had freed himself, and he bobbed in the water in his life jacket, but by the time they had reached him he had gone into shock. His head, held above water, fell listlessly to one side. They brought the small boat as near to him as they could, while Clancy stripped down to his shorts. He dived over the side and held the young pilot, propelling him toward the boat, where McNulty and MacDougal pulled him aboard. A Stokes stretcher waited in readiness, lined with blankets, and with a pillow in one end; they placed him in this gently and covered him with the blankets.

It was impossible to determine if he was injured at all beyond shock. Unconscious, the young pilot looked absurdly young, wet, like a fledgling from the shell. He had close-cropped blond hair, ears well set against his head, classical features pale under his tan, like a fallen Ganymede asleep, his full young lips parted over flawless teeth. Chief Bullitt, stooping over him as the small boat sped toward the shore, raised one eyelid with the side of his thumb. The pupil of the eye was not dilated, which would seem to indicate an absence of head injury. Bullitt felt his pulse beneath the blanket. It was low but steady, as his respiration was, except for a deep sigh now and then, as if he struggled for more air. Wordlessly, Bullitt took a small bottle of brandy from the first-aid pack and broke the seal. No liquid could be given to an unconscious man, for fear that he might choke, but Bullitt held the open flask beneath the pilot's nostrils, and presently his eyes opened, astonishingly blue in his clear young face.

"Where am I?" he asked.

"In the men's bar at the Ritz, of course," Bullitt said briskly, holding the brandy to the young man's lips, "and, really, next time, please try to think of a more original line."

The young pilot drank the brandy. Color returned to his cheeks. He moved and tried to rise, but Bullitt held him back. "Lie still," he said. "You will need all of your strength for your court-martial."

The pilot sighed. In such an instance, with a plane lost, he would have to answer in court for his possible negligence. Reminded of this, an expression of pain crossed his face, and he closed his eyes again. The small boat sped on, back through the bay, through the channel, and toward the boat landing of the Marine base. Ahead of them they could see an ambulance with a red cross painted on its side, summoned to the dock by message from the *Ajax* for the emergency.

Returning to the *Ajax* in the small boat, Williams felt a sense of mysterious depression, a kind of anxiety and apprehension. The downed pilot, Kerensky's throat, the boys vomiting in the head, Pawling's hand — a sequence of mishaps, none of them of fatal consequence, yet all of them seeming in some way to threaten the fabric of their life, as if even Captain Thompson's ready authority, the youth and vigor of the crew, and the sustaining comfort of the daily routine could not really stand between them and protect them from the dangers and the impermanence and the unpredictability of life. The injury to Pawling's hand was a sort of symbol — the hand, stretched out toward experience and life, maimed and rebuked in its reach. And underneath all this was a feeling of guilt from which he could not free himself. He had not told Doctor Claremont the night before about the injury to Pawling's hand. When Bullitt had gone back to his quarters, Williams had remained behind in the sick bay to clean it up. He delayed this job, hopeful that Doctor Claremont would return while he was there, and he would have reason to explain what had happened. After he had finished the job he went out to the deck and stood, in the early dusk, at the rail near the gangway, torn by indecision. It was not his place, certainly, to report his immediate superior to their superior above. His code of behavior rebelled at such a thought. He was not a tale-bearer, a child running to teacher. But which was more important, a principle, perhaps superficial in concept, or the state of a man's hand? His indecision angered him; he resented the position in which he found himself, mostly, perhaps, because he had created it himself, by his defense of Bullitt in the beginning. And still Doctor Claremont did not come back. He had stayed ashore for dinner at the hospital, and when he did return, finally, the confusion brought about by the sudden onset of food poisoning in the crew had made it impossible to tell him about Pawling. Williams had been relieved of the necessity of telling him, but this mechanical solution to his indecision instead of relieving him of his feeling of guilt seemed only to increase it. Today it seemed to him that his failure to tell Doctor Claremont about the injury to Pawling's hand had been an act of moral cowardice which made him an accomplice in Bullitt's default.

Suddenly, for the first time, Williams longed to be finished with training and practice. He was impatient for the action of war, and he wondered idly if perhaps this accounted, in part, for the recurrence of major wars. As if, every now and again, in rebellion against their inability to govern their own lives, men found it easier to live with a larger burden than with many small ones, as a householder might, in desperation, borrow from a bank to pay his creditors, so that all his small debts might be submerged in a single debt of greater magnitude.

But the day was not yet finished with them. When the ship secured from maneuvers that afternoon, a small boat approached them from the base and the Reverend Luther Foss, Protestant chaplain of the base, climbed the accommodation ladder. In the small Georgia town in which she had been born, and in the house where she had borne Stud, Mrs. Artemus Clancy had died. The word had come to Guantánamo Bay through the routine channel of the American Red Cross Home Service, with a request for leave.

Captain Thompson had Stud brought to his cabin, and when he arrived the captain excused himself and went to the bridge. Captain Thompson was a man of simple and profound religious belief, but he shared this conviction with an impatient and vague dislike of most ministers of the Gospel. Too many of them, he felt, became lesser men in the process of serving God, as if they feared to approach Him, or felt it inappropriate to approach Him with the full vigor of their manliness. It was his opinion that most of them smiled too much, and too easily, and the words they used, words such as "fellowship," seemed to Captain Thompson to be almost meaningless, like old coins that had had their value effaced by too much handling. When Captain Thompson attended religious service he sat erect in the pew, with his chin pulled in and his neck and head straight. He feared God, but he held it to be his moral obligation to remember that he had been created in God's image, and for that reason it was necessary to respect himself, and not be sappy and soft, as he might have phrased it, in his relationship with his Creator. He remembered how he had felt when his own mother had died, and he hoped that the Reverend Foss wouldn't make it too hard for poor Stud. A man needed to be alone at a time like that, especially to face the decisions that always went along with tragedy. He supposed he would be asked to sign an emergency leave for Stud, so that he could fly to Georgia for the funeral, but he wished that Stud would not ask for leave. A funeral, Captain Thompson felt, was nothing but an effort to comfort the living, and it was his first belief that the best comfort for the living in their loss was simply to go ahead doggedly with whatever work was at hand.

After fifteen minutes or so, Mr. Foss sought Captain Thompson out on the bridge. Mr. Foss was an example of the sort of minister most trying to Captain Thompson. Even in the uniform of a Marine Corps officer he was unmistakably a minister. He was slender and fair, and, although certainly not effeminate in manner, he seemed sexless, and the healthy coloring of his face seemed to be there not as a result of a life of action but rather as the product of a life of abstention. He wore a look of careful, impersonal solicitude, and because, as is usual in such circumstances, he could sense Captain Thompson's disapproval, he was also somewhat nervous. "Seaman Clancy thinks he will not ask for emergency leave," the chaplain said. His tone was uncertain, as if he did not quite know whether to accept this decision as being proper or improper, and whether or not Captain Thompson would be pleased or displeased.

Captain Thompson, accustomed to concealing his feelings, was of no help to Mr. Foss, since he did not allow himself to reveal his sense of relief and approval at the news that Stud had elected to stay on board.

"Where is he now, Chaplain?" Captain Thompson asked.

"He has gone below," Chaplain Foss said. "I believe the bos'n is with him."

"Good," Captain Thompson said. "Good."

McNulty had taken Stud to the boatswain's locker in the forward hold, because it was one of the few small places in the ship where a man could be alone. He left him there when he went to look for Williams.

"He's taking it bad, Doc," he said. It was the first time McNulty had come to Williams about anything since they had left Boston, but his manner was completely natural, as if the greater need for their mutual services in the traditional roles they occupied on board ship suspended or made unimportant the issue about Bullitt. "He's crying now, Doc, and I thought maybe you could give him something that would sort of quiet him down."

Williams went to Doctor Claremont, in his cabin, and he gave him the key to the medical locker, and permission to take a phenobarbital to Clancy.

At the boatswain's locker, Williams shut the door behind him. Stud was lying, sprawled face down, on a coil of heavy line, crying with childlike sobs. Williams sat down next to him on an overturned pail. When Stud heard him he turned his tear-stained, swollen face toward him in silence, with his twisted mouth half-open, like a mask of tragedy.

"I've brought you a pill," Williams said. "It will make you feel better."

"She's dead," Stud said. "I ain't never going to see her no more."

"I know," Williams said. "You take this pill."

Stud turned his body to one side, facing Williams, and rested his head on his folded arm. "I couldn't stand to go see her put in the ground," he said. "Do you think I done right?"

"I think you did," Williams said. "You can remember her as she was when you saw her."

"But I've been so bad," Stud said, chokingly. "Do you reckon she knows that now, how bad I was?"

"It doesn't matter," Williams said. "You've been no worse than anyone else. Mothers can forgive anything."

"She forgive me anything," Stud said. "No matter what I done. Like the time about the cake."

"The cake?" Williams asked.

"There was this cake, see, on the table in the pantry, cooling," he said. "It had thick icing on it, like I like. You know, chocolate. I seen it there, and when she went out to feed the chickens I picked up this butcher knife, see, and scooped off a hunk of icing and put it in my mouth." He paused a moment to catch his breath. "And then she come in and seen it, and she said, 'Tim' — that's my real name, Tim — she said, 'Tim, that cake was pretty for the company, and now you spoiled it,' and I said, innocent like, you know, 'I didn't do nothing,' and she said, 'Stick out your tongue, Tim,' and I stuck out my tongue, and the knife had cut it, and the blood commence to run down my chin. Oh, it was funny," he said, his face contorted with anguish. "She's dead," he said, crying harshly, "and I didn't never even tell her. I didn't never tell her that I loved her! I loved her more than anybody else in the whole world, and I didn't never even tell her, and now she's dead!"

"You didn't have to tell her that," Williams said. "She knew. Take the pill, Stud. McNulty wants you to take it. Do it for him, Stud."

Clancy raised himself up on the coil of line, and took the pill Williams held out to him. He swallowed it with a sip of water from the mug Williams had brought.

"Drink it all, Stud," Williams said. "When you cry, you lose a lot of moisture. You've got to put it back."

"Is that a fact?" Stud said.

"It's a fact," Williams said.

"It don't matter," Stud said, falling back on the coil of line, his face suddenly empty. "She's dead."

First Wave

X

from *Do Not Go Gentle*

by DAVID MacCUISH

There was a time, and a beginning, and a morning velveted with the remnants of hard voices now reduced to whispers as the light grew. There was the press of men around him, milling and turning; shoulders pushing against his chest and back, gently bearing him across steel plates of a deck to the ship's railing.

A hand grabbed the shovel fastened to his combat pack, tugging it downward.

Hudge behind the mocking whisper, "Black as a witch's tit, eh, guy?"

He nodded, not wanting to talk. He wished Hudge would not stand so close to him, as his thighs were quivering with a cold dread. He gripped the sling of his rifle tighter, bearing down on the weight of it, the leather biting into his shoulder.

"Tulagi, Florida, Guadalcanal!"

The strange names he had heard at briefing. "The first to go against the enemy." "The first to land on enemy soil in this war!" "The honor has been given to us —"

Ah, yes, the honor. All the honor.

They were to land on Florida Island.

The guns of the task force rippled into a steady crash, driving the sound into his throat.

In the Solomons.

Something somber in the name. Something somber in the eyes of the men dressing under the yellow lights in the steaming quarters. Their faces growing into hard angles as they packed their gear. Late summer in the air, but something of the autumn in their faces.

And around him now was the silent movement of men, bodies arched in forced casualness, all lumps and hollows in their helmets and combat packs. The smell of them, thick with strange and familiar odors: fresh dungarees and oil against the sea smell, moist with darkness, bearing something of rotting grass and leaves.

Norman reached for a cigarette in his breast pocket, easing the pack strap aside, his fingers tangling in his dog-tag chain. He tucked the metal under his tee shirt, the cold touch of them making him shiver.

"You okay, buddy boy?"

The fast whisper of Hudge again.

He half turned in exasperation. "What the hell ya want me to do, Hudge, sing a song?"

A quiet run of laughter, low and muffled around him, alien and sad in the shuffling dark. The lumping figures flickering on and off as the bombardment streamed its fire into blackness and yellow periods blossomed out on the sea.

"Hey, Hudge —" He tried to turn to the figure hunched next to him. His rifle struck something soft.

A bitter voice behind him snarling, "Watch it, ya sonofabitch!"

"Sorry," he mumbled.

They must not see his fear. The battle was starting and he was committed, and now he must remember his friends and Tango, too, because part of this was for him.

He tried to swallow but could not.

Slowly his eyes began to make out greater details: the brown and mottled greens of the uniforms around him, the color like the polka-dot horses on the merry-go-round with that long-ago tune playing, and Tango's eyes in sudden pain. He tried to remember how the music went but he could not.

The ship creaked under him, motionless in the water. The corrugated metal of the deck an echoing steel; the breathing of the men, deep and steady.

All the faces seemed different somehow and the voices, too. An isolation was stealing over him as though the disappearing darkness were drawing a familiar warmth away to leave him naked and exposed.

There was a stirring in the men, a leaning forward to the railing. He stared. Red and white lights were winking at them from the black mass of the islands ahead, now sliding out of the water as the dawn came. There was a sudden run of sweat under his arms as the puttering whine of the Higgins boats approached. The bull horn snarled high over them, and a voice shouted over the P.A.: "Marines to points of debarkation! Marines to the cargo nets!"

Hudge's voice behind him in the shuffle of feet. "It's pucker-up time, girls. Keep yer legs crossed!"

Then over the side in a sweeping rush of men, gear clattering and boots stomping on the metal. Down the moist net, and it swaying and pitching, held by several men in the boat far below. All the voices calling now and shouting; the net crawling with figures, their boots starting to shine as the light came, and the helmets and rifles glittered and tossed.

Do it like at La Jolla, he said over and over to himself. Like at La Jolla in the early summer. Hands on vertical lines. Watch feet above. Can bust fingers. Move 'em fast, and don't look down. Don't look down!

Like at La Jolla in the summer, with the California coast shimmering under the white houses on the cliffs. Riding toward them through the warm surf, pretending a Sunday game of war.

Then he was in the boat, stumbling against boxes of ammo, lurching against the sides of it as the other men poured down. A strange pressure gripping his chest in pulsing waves of growing fright. The rusty side of the transport looking massive and secure, and they were leaving it. He wanted to climb back up into the steel of its protection. The bobbing boat threw him from side to side. He braced his legs and swallowed rapidly against a rush of saliva in his throat.

"Ho!"

"Yaw!"

"Ho!"

Someone shouting things, and the churning men yelling and stamping over the gulping of the engine.

"McLeod!"

Someone calling his name from far away. His heart jumped. Maybe he was wanted back on ship. He stared up at the railing. Two sailors were waving at him. The nets were empty now and falling back against the ship.

"McLeod!" Again the voice.

An elbow jabbed him. "Sound off, jerk!"

He stared aft. Larko, the platoon sergeant, glaring.

"Ho!" he shouted, his voice shrill.

Larko's helmet shook with disgust.

"Shipley!"

"Ya hoo!"

"Hudgins!"

"Pres — unt!"

He turned to Hudge. The face was prickled with growing excitement, black eyes glittering and the full mouth pulled back into a set smile. His new mustache was a pencil smudge over the white of his teeth, and the eyes meeting his were bold with assurance, the lean body rocking easily with the boat.

"Don't — worry — baby — Hudge'll — save —" The words being split by the growing bellow of the engine. Norman leaned against the steel side and hunched low, bowing his head, his helmet bobbing against the pack in front of him; jumping inwardly from the jabs of canteens, scabbards, shovels and buckles as they pitched and heaved.

"Looks — jus' — like — California!" A shout from Hudge. He glanced up. The figure was peering over the side, eyes slitted against the wind and water.

That crazy smile, Norman thought, trying to recall who else once smiled that way. Someone before — at a time when he had been afraid. That weird smile!

"Wunnerful day — cruise!" Hudge grinned down at the crouching figures.

"Get — gawdamn — head —" Larko's bellow in the rolling sounds. Norman shoved his breath in and out. Suddenly he wanted to choke and cry, to fall down and tell them he could not go in. He looked frantically at the side of the boat.

If he fell over — !

But he could not get out without the others seeing him. He could not do that. His mind raced searching for an excuse, and hating himself for the growing desperation.

"Sealark — Channel!" a little-boy voice was chanting. "They — call this — Sealark!"

"Ooooo — waaaaaa!" The mine-whistle moan of the shells passing over them.

Norman stared at the white face of Hawkins next to him. There was vomit on the pouting lips, and fear spreading across the violet eyes like fire. The boy nodded slowly to him. " 'At's what — Sealark!"

Norman suddenly hated him for talking, for pointing the words at him. "Shut — !" He trembled with a fierce rage, wanting to strike the pale face that seemed a mirror of his own fear, but the head jerked forward suddenly, the helmet fell off, and the boy sprayed vomit into his hands.

Good! Norman thought savagely. Good, good! Then staring at the white hair of the boy in the stepping shadows and grasping his pack harness to steady him.

"What — Christ's name — ?" The sagging face of Buzzaro turning in anger. "Puke — on — self!"

A gasping "Sorry!"

Norman fumbled for the boy's helmet and placed it on his head. "Better — Hawk?"

The boy nodded. Hudge leaned over and patted his shoulder. " 'S all right, buddy. Make anybody — flash — hash!"

Hudge grinned at him, his rifle like an exclamation mark at the end of his shoulder. "Gonna be — breeze!"

Norman looked away. The Semper Fi Zachary Scott, mustache and all. "Ever — tell — 'bout this — broad — Tijuana?"

Norman shook his head not answering, taking his breath in and out in rhythm with the pulsing engine. They were moving fast now, and the spray was coming in.

"Said — she was — daughter — Pancho Villa!"

He didn't want to joke. He could not laugh with a mouth turning into stone. Leave me alone, he wanted to say, but he did not dare to look up.

"Lock and load!"

He jumped with the snap of the command from aft.

"Lock and load!"

He fumbled for the bolt, his fingers wet on the metal, the copper shell glinting in the breech as he threw it open.

To kill!

My God, he thought, to kill.

Hudge leaned to him. "Cha — starin' at — hoss? Gotta — girlie picture — there?"

He drove the bolt home and checked the safety, then fumbled for his cartridge belt and tugged at one of the pockets where his clips were. His hands like wax and no strength in them at all, but a trembling starting in his shoulders and moving to his fingers.

The coxswain behind him was shouting strange words at Lieutenant Libby, and then the men were rising and moving in a writhing coil of shouts and thumping clamor.

An odd silence then above the blast of the engine and the sea pour.

The shelling had stopped. They were close in.

"On feet! On — feet!" Libby calling in a high wail.

He staggered to his feet, gripping the rifle fiercely, watching the barrels ahead flashing now in the sunlight like tubes of ribboned glass.

The engine changing its sound. Slowing down. The air hot and smelling of thick trees and mud.

He braced himself as they ground to a halt; the men lurching forward with shouts and curses plunging and falling. Then over the boat railing and the water cold on his thighs, with an utter weariness seeping through his legs and into his body. The water falling away to his leggings then, and the sand only.

He was running into a hot silence broken only by the thud of many feet around him, the jingle of equipment, distant calls and grunting explosions of breath. He did not look up. The sweat felt like oil on his face as he squinted against the glare of coral sand, very white, sounding like sandpaper under his feet.

"Here — here!"

A whispered shout. He raised his head and stared, trying to focus against the glare, his body a sea of inward cringes.

From behind a log at the jungle's edge, high up on the beach, Hudge waving to him. He spurted up and fell behind the frayed wood, the sweat now stinging his eyes into blinking terror.

Hudge laughed deep in his throat. "Jus' like La Jolla. What'd I tell ya, hoss?"

Not a shot had been fired.

Norman wiped his eyes and stared into the undulating greens and blacks ahead. They'd be in there. They were in there waiting.

Voices were calling. He looked back, squinting in the yellow light. Many boats were bobbing in the surf, some coming in with droning power, others swirling about to return to the far transports. There was thunder on the two islands in the bay. He shifted his glance. Up and down the beach men were running in apelike crouches, calling and waving.

Hudge grinned at him. "How come ya walked in, hoss?"

"What?"

"Ya looked like you was strollin' through Balboa Park."

"Hell, I ran —"

Hudge looked at his pants distastefully. "You piss yer pants, too?"

"Big joke! I felt like it, though."

Larko was waving from behind a clump of brush. Hudge touched his arm. "Let's move out, ole track star!" The eyes gleamed.

They ran in a weaving crouch. It was all silent and very strange.

Larko spoke rapidly, his heavy jowls trembling with sweat. "We're movin' out now. Gotta make Halavo village." His fingers moved over the map and small drops fell on it. "Right here's where we are. We move off to our left." His narrowed eyes lifted to Norman. "What the hell's the matter? You got asthma or sumphin'?"

Norman closed his mouth, his teeth coming together.

"Now ya guys stay close to the point. We run inta anythin', jus' stay loose." His rifle lowered to Hudge. "You're point."

Norman moved his eyes to the boy. One thick eyebrow moved up and the head jerked in a nod. The smile stayed.

Up and down the beach groups of men were disappearing into the jungle. Lieutenant Libby called and waved to their right, his arm sweeping them toward the darkness of the trees.

Larko heaved to his feet, the sand squealing. "Move out!"

There were myriad tunnels of green darkness deepening into black, smelling of rot and perpetual decay. Birds called sounds ominous with shrill intent, and the ground sucked and tugged at his feet. Water shimmered from the leaves and the fronds, trickled down vines and warped trunks. Pools of water everywhere, and the sound of it seeping into his ears and flecking his body with tiny drops that burned like sulphur and made him wince and tremble. He was walking alone on a journey into night, and the tunnels were all around him with their mouths of cannon, and the steel in his hands was heavy and sharp but not meant to cut into the earth. No, this steel was not meant for that.

"Never thought Florida —"

He half whirled as Hawkins whispered behind him, almost dropping his rifle in sudden terror.

"Knock off chatter!" The bitter whisper from Larko in the green heat behind.

Norman wanted to smash the young boy. He stumbled forward, his heart staggering. He watched the tiger movements of Hudge a few yards ahead, the slim figure slipping in and out of the shadows, the head revolving back and forth as though on oiled bearings. Then the hand shot up and the figure froze. Norman slipped to his knees, fumbling for the trigger, the rifle an enormous weight suddenly. He stared, trying to see beyond the shadows.

The water oozed under his knees in the silence punctuated by the bird warnings. Mosquitoes hummed about his mouth and throat. He tried to breathe silently but the sound was hissing in his throat. The arm fell and they moved ahead. Once Hudge looked back, his eyes lost in the darkness of his helmet, but his teeth gleamed.

He's enjoying it, Norman thought. My God, he's enjoying it! And the bird cries seemed to grow more insane, and the greens shimmered into yellow and blue, then back to green again, the fronds speckled with moisture whispering over them as they passed; and each step seemed to fling him deeper into an inner isolation.

He stepped into a pothole up to his ankles and nearly vomited from the gaslike odor that swirled into his mouth. It was the earth secreting a small portion of horror in a smell. The earth warning him with liquid decay that smelled of death under the green shadows that licked at him with fire. He knew the farther he walked into it, step by step, the less he would ever know of sun again. Then he saw Larko closing in to him from his right.

The sergeant's wet hand bit into his arm, and the eyes glittered above the furious whisper: "Look, poet, you keep yer fuckin' head movin'. Knock off the dreams, see!"

The hand threw him forward. Norman glanced back, wetting his mouth. Larko's rifle arced in command for him to keep moving.

He paced along carefully, moving his head from side to side, watching the trees and pulsing bushes.

They came into the village an hour later, circling it in a run of silent dread, then into the one street, with arms waving frantically for covering fire if the need be; moving through the few deserted huts.

The place was deserted.

In a gesturing crouch Larko and Lieutenant Libby talked briefly, then ordered them back to the beach.

There was the sound of gunfire like a deep growling far out at sea. That would be Guadalcanal, he thought. They're going in on Guadalcanal. It had a funny sound to it. He smoked a cigarette in the pacing silence, watching the grace of Hudge, still at point, his fatigue jacket black with sweat, glinting green and silver shadows.

They regrouped on the beach at noon and watched the bombardment of Gavutu Island, two miles away in the channel. There was a steady crackle of fire from Tulagi on their left, and that island seemed to tremble in a fire of smoke.

He felt very tired as he crouched in the hot shade of a eucalyptus tree and stared with the other men from their cover at the jungle's edge.

"Bet they're catchin' hell, eh?" A voice from the tangled thicket, and another answering, "Sounds like a real go and we're outa it. Sonofabitch!"

Attack!

✕

from *The Naked and the Dead*
by NORMAN MAILER

At 0400, a few minutes after the false dawn had lapsed, the naval bombardment of Anopopei began. All the guns of the invasion fleet went off within two seconds of each other, and the night rocked and shuddered like a great log foundering in the surf. The ships snapped and rolled from the discharge, lashing the water furiously. For one instant the night was jagged and immense, demoniac in its convulsion.

Then, after the first salvos, the firing became irregular, and the storm almost subsided into darkness again. The great clanging noises of the guns became isolated once more, sounded like immense freight trains jerking and tugging up a grade. And afterward it was possible to hear the sighing wistful murmur of shells passing overhead. On Anopopei the few scattered campfires were snubbed out.

The first shells landed in the sea, throwing up remote playful spurts of water, but then a string of them snapped along the beach, and Anopopei came to life and glowed like an ember. Here and there little fires started where the jungle met the beach, and occasionally a shell which carried too far would light up a few hundred feet of brush. The line of beach became defined and twinkled like a seaport seen from a great distance late at night.

An ammunition dump began to burn, spreading a rose-colored flush over a portion of the beach. When several shells landed in its midst, the flames sprouted fantastically high, and soared away in angry brown clouds of smoke. The shells continued to raze the beach and then began to shift inland. The firing had eased already into a steady, almost casual, pattern. A few ships at a time would discharge their volleys and then turn out to sea again while a new file attacked. The ammo dump still blazed, but most of the fires on the beach had smoldered down, and in the light which came with the first lifting of the dawn there was not nearly enough scud to hide the shore. About a mile inland, something had caught fire on the summit of a hill, and back of it, far away, Mount Anaka rose out of a base of maroon-colored smoke. Implacably, despite the new purple robes at its feet, the mountain sat on the island, and gazed out to sea. The bombardment was insignificant before it.

In the troop holds, the sounds were duller and more persistent; they grated and rumbled like a subway train. The hold electric lights, a wan yellow, had been turned on after breakfast, and they flickered dully, throwing many shadows over the hatches and through the tiers of bunks, lighting up the faces of the men assembled in the aisles and clustered around the ladder leading up to the top deck.

Martinez listened to the noises anxiously. He would not have been surprised if the hatch on which he was sitting had slid away from under him. He blinked his bloodshot eyes against the weary glare of the bulbs, tried to numb himself to everything. But his legs would twitch unconsciously every time a louder rumble beat against the steel bulkheads. For no apparent reason he kept repeating to himself the last line from an old joke, "I don't care if I do die, do die, do dy." Sitting there, his skin looked brown under the jaundiced light. He was a small, slim and handsome Mexican with neat wavy hair, small sharp features. His body, even now, had the poise and grace of a deer. No matter how quickly he might move the motion was always continuous and effortless. And like a deer his head was never quite still, his brown liquid eyes never completely at rest.

Above the steady droning of the guns, Martinez could hear voices separating for an instant and then being lost again. Separate babels of sound came from each platoon; the voice of a platoon leader would buzz against his ear like a passing insect, undefined and rather annoying. "Now, I don't want any of you to get lost when we hit the beach. Stick together, that's very important." He drew his knees up tighter, rolled back farther on his haunches until his hip-bones grated against the tight flesh of his buttocks.

The men in recon looked small and lost in comparison to the other platoons. Croft was talking now about the landing craft embarkation, and Martinez listened dully, his attention wavering. "All right," Croft said softly, "it's gonna be the same as the last time we practiced it. They ain't a reason why anything should go wrong, and it ain't goin' to."

Red guffawed scornfully. "Yeah, we'll all be up there," he said, "but sure as hell, some dumb sonofabitch is going to run up, and tell us to get back in the hold again."

"You think I'll piss if we have to stay here for the rest of the war?" Sergeant Brown said.

"Let's cut it out," Croft told them. "If you know what's going on better than I do, *you* can stand up here and talk." He frowned and then continued. "We're on boat-deck station twenty-eight. You all know where it is, but we're goin' up together just the same. If they's a man here suddenly discovers he's left anythin' behind, that'll be just t.s. We ain't gonna come back."

"Yeah, boys, don't forget to take your rubbers," Red suggested, and that drew a laugh. Croft looked angry for a second, but then he drawled, "I know Wilson ain't gonna forget his," and they laughed again. "You're fuggin ay," Gallagher snorted.

Wilson giggled infectiously. "Ah tell ya," he said, "Ah'd sooner leave my M-one behind, 'cause if they was to be a piece of pussy settin' up on that beach, and Ah didn't have a rubber, Ah'd just shoot myself anyway."

Martinez grinned, but their laughter irritated him. "What's the matter, Japbait?" Croft asked quietly. Their eyes met with the intimate look of old friends. "Aaah, goddam stomach, she's no good," Martinez said. He spoke clearly, but in a low and hesitant voice as if he were translating from Spanish as he went along. Croft looked again at him, and then continued talking.

Martinez gazed about the hold. The aisles between the bunks were wide and unfamiliar now that the hammocks were lashed up, and it made him vaguely uneasy. He thought they looked like the stalls in the big library in San Antonio and he remembered there was something unpleasant about it, some girl had spoken to him harshly. "I don't care if I do die, do die," went through his head. He shook himself. There was something terrible going to happen to him today. God always let you know things out of his goodness, and you had to . . . to watch out, to look out for yourself. He said the last part to himself in English.

The girl was a librarian and she had thought he was trying to steal a book. He was very little then, and he had got scared and answered in Spanish, and she had scolded him. Martinez's leg twitched. She had made him cry, he could remember that. Goddam girl. Today, he could screw with her. The idea fed him with a pleasurable malice. Little-tit librarian, he would spit on her now. But the library stalls were still a troop hold, and his fear returned.

A whistle blew, startling him. "Men for boat-deck fifteen," a voice shouted down, and one of the platoons started going up the ladder. Martinez could feel the tension in everyone around him, the way their voices had become quiet. Why could they not go first? he asked himself, hating the added tension which would come from waiting. Something was going to happen to him. He knew that now.

After an hour their signal came, and they jogged up the ladder, and stood milling outside the hatchway for almost a minute before they were told to move to their boat. The decks were very slippery in the dawn, and they stumbled and cursed as they plodded along the deck. When they reached the davits which held their landing boat, they drew up in a rough file and began waiting again. Red shivered in the cold morning air. It was not yet six A.M., and the day had already the depressing quality which early mornings always had in the Army. It meant they were moving, it meant something new, something unpleasant.

All over the ship the debarkation activities were in different stages. A few landing craft were down in the water already, filled with troops and circling around the ship like puppies on a leash. The men in them waved at the ship, the flesh color of their faces unreal against the gray paint of the landing craft, the dawn blue of the sea. The calm water looked like oil. Nearer the platoon, some men were boarding a landing craft, and another one, just loaded, was beginning its descent into the water, the davit pulleys creaking from time to time. But over most of the ship men were waiting like themselves.

Red's shoulders were beginning to numb under the weight of his full pack, and his rifle muzzle kept clanging against his helmet. He was feeling irritable. "No matter how many times you wear a goddam pack, you never get used to it," he said.

"Have you got it adjusted right?" Hennessey asked. His voice was stiff and quivered a little.

"Fug the adjustments," Red said. "It just makes me ache somewhere else. I ain't built for a pack, I got too many bones." He kept on talking, glancing at Hennessey every now and then to see whether he was less nervous. The air was chill, and the sun at his left was still low and quiet without any heat. He stamped his feet, breathing the curious odor of a ship's deck, oil and tar and the fish smell of the water.

"When do we get into the boats?" Hennessey asked.

The shelling was still going on over the beach, and the island looked pale green in the dawn. A thin wispy line of smoke trailed along the shore.

Red laughed. "What! do ya think this is gonna be any different today? I figure we'll be on deck all morning." But as he spoke, he noticed a group of landing craft circling about a mile from them in the water. "The first wave's still farting around," he reassured Hennessey. For an instant he thought again of the Motome invasion, and felt a trace of that panic catching him again. His fingertips still remembered the texture of the sides of the rubber boat as he had clung to it in the water. At the back of his throat he tasted salt water again, felt the dumb whimpering terror of ducking underwater when he was exhausted and the Jap guns would not stop. He looked out again, his shaggy face quite bleak for a moment.

In the distance the jungle near the beach had assumed the naked broken look which a shelling always gave it. The palm trees would be standing like pillars now, stripped of their leaves, and blackened if there had been a fire. Off the horizon Mount Anaka was almost invisible in the haze, a pale gray-blue color almost a compromise between the hues of the water and the sky. As he watched, a big shell landed on the shore and threw up a larger puff of smoke than the two or three that had preceded it. This was going to be an easy landing, Red told himself, but he was still thinking about the rubber boats. "I wish to hell they'd save some of that country for us," he said to Hennessey. "We're gonna have to live there." The morning had a raw expectant quality about it, and he drew a breath, and squatted on his heels.

Gallagher began to curse. "How fuggin long we got to wait up here?"

"Hold your water," Croft told him. "Half the commo platoon is coming with us, and they ain't even up yet."

"Well, why ain't they?" Gallagher asked. He pushed his helmet farther back on his head. "It's just like the bastards to have us wait up on deck where we can have our fuggin heads blown off."

"You hear any Jap artillery?" Croft asked.

"That don't mean they ain't got any," Gallagher said. He lit a cigarette and smoked moodily, his hand cupped over the butt as though he expected it to be snatched away from him any moment.

A shell sighed overhead, and unconsciously Martinez drew back against a gunhousing. He felt naked.

The davit machinery was complicated, and a portion of it hung over the water. When a man was harnessed into a pack and web belt and carried a rifle and two bandoliers and several grenades, a bayonet and a helmet, he felt as if he had a tourniquet over both shoulders and across his chest. It was hard to breathe and his limbs kept falling asleep. Climbing along the beam which led out to the landing craft became an adventure not unlike walking a tightrope while wearing a suit of armor.

When recon was given the signal to get into its landing boat, Sergeant Brown wet his mouth nervously. "They could've designed these better," he grumbled to Stanley as they inched out along the beam. The trick was not to look at the water. "You know, Gallagher ain't a bad guy, but he's a sorehead," Stanley was confiding.

"Yeah," Brown said abstractedly. He was thinking it would be a hell of a note if he, a noncom, were to fall in the water. My God, you'd sink, he realized. "I always hate this part," he said aloud.

He reached the lip of the landing craft, and jumped into it, the weight of his pack almost spilling him, jarring his ankle. Everyone was suddenly very merry in the little boat which was swaying gently under the davits. "Here comes old Red," Wilson yelled, and everybody laughed as Red worked gingerly along the beam, his face puckered like a prune. When he reached the side he looked over scornfully at them and said, "Goddam, got the wrong boat. They ain't no one stupid-looking enough here to be recon."

"C'mon in, y'old billygoat," Wilson chuckled, his laughter easy and phlegmy, "the water's nice and cold."

Red grinned. "I know one place on you that ain't cold. Right now it's red-hot."

Brown found himself laughing and laughing. What a bunch of good old boys there were in the platoon, he told himself. It seemed as if the worst part were over already.

"How's the General get into these boats?" Hennessey asked. "He ain't young like us."

Brown giggled. "They got two privates to carry him over." He basked in the laughter which greeted this.

Gallagher dropped into the boat. "The fuggin Army," he said, "I bet they get more fuggin casualties out of guys getting into boats." Brown roared. Gallagher probably looked mad even when he was screwing his wife. For an instant he was tempted to say so, and it made him laugh even more. In the middle of his snickering he had a sudden image of his own wife in bed with another man at this exact moment, and there was a long empty second in his laughter when he felt nothing at all. "Hey, Gallagher," he said furiously, "I bet you even look pissed-off when you're with your wife."

Gallagher looked sullen, and then unexpectedly began to laugh too. "Aaah, fug you," he said, and that made everyone roar even more.

The little assault craft with their blunt bows looked like hippopotami as they bulled and snorted through the water. They were perhaps forty feet long, ten feet wide, shaped like open shoe boxes with a motor at the rear. In the troop well, the waves made a loud jarring sound beating against the bow ramp, and already an inch or two of water had squeezed through the crevices and was sloshing around the bottom. Red gave up the effort to keep his feet dry. Their boat had been circling for over an hour and he was getting dizzy. Occasionally a cold fan of spray would drop on them, shocking and abrupt and a trifle painful.

The first wave of soldiers had landed about fifteen minutes ago, and the battle taking place on the beach crackled faintly in the distance like a bonfire. It seemed remote and insignificant. To relieve the monotony Red would peer over the side wall and scan the shore. It still looked untenanted from three miles out but the ornament of battle was there — a thin foggy smoke drifted along the water. Occasionally a flight of three dive bombers would buzz overhead and lance toward shore, the sound of their motors filtering back in a subdued gentle rumble. When they dove on the beach it was difficult to follow them, for they were almost invisible, appearing as flecks of pure brilliant sunlight. The puff their bombs threw up looked small and harmless and the planes would be almost out of sight when the noise of the explosions came back over the water.

Red tried to ease the weight of his pack by compressing it against the bulkhead of the boat. The constant circling was annoying. As he looked at the thirty men squeezed in with him, and saw how unnaturally green their uniforms looked against the blue-gray of the troop well, he had to breathe deeply a few times and sit motionless. Sweat was breaking out along his back.

"How long is this gonna take?" Gallagher wanted to know. "The goddam Army, hurry up and wait, hurry up and wait."

Red had started to light a cigarette, his fifth since their boat had been lowered into the water, and it tasted flat and unpleasant. "What do you think?" Red asked. "I bet we don't go in till ten." Gallagher swore. It was not yet eight o'clock.

"Listen," Red went on, "if they really knew how to work these kind of things, we woulda been eating breakfast now, and we woulda got into these crates about two hours from now." He rubbed off the tiny ash which had formed on his cigarette. "But, naw, some sonofabitchin' looey, who's sleeping right now, wanted us to get off the goddam ship so he could stop worrying about us." Purposely, he spoke loud enough for the Lieutenant from the communications platoon to hear him and grinned as the officer turned his back.

Corporal Toglio, who was squatting next to Gallagher, looked at Red. "We're a lot safer out in the water," Toglio explained eagerly. "This is a pretty small target compared to a ship, and when we're moving like this it's a lot harder to hit us than you think."

Red grunted. "Balls."

"Listen," Brown said, "They ain't a time when I wouldn't rather been on that ship. I think it's a hell of a lot safer."

"I looked into this," Toglio protested. "The statistics prove you're a lot safer here than any place during an invasion."

Red hated statistics. "Don't give me any of those figures," he told Corporal Toglio. "If you listen to them you give up taking a bath 'cause it's too dangerous."

"No, I'm serious," Toglio said. He was a heavyset Italian of about middle height with a pear-shaped head which was broader in the jaw than the temple. Although he had shaved the night before, his beard darkened all of his face under his eyes except for his mouth, which was wide and friendly. "I'm serious," he insisted, "I saw the statistics."

"You know what you can do with them," Red said.

Toglio smiled, but he was a little annoyed. Red was a pretty good guy, he was thinking, but too independent. Where would you be if everybody was like him? You'd get nowhere. It took co-operation in everything. Something like this invasion was planned, it was efficient, down to a timetable. You couldn't run trains if the engineer took off when he felt like it.

The idea impressed him, and he pointed one of his thick powerful fingers to tell Red when suddenly a Jap shell, the first in half an hour, threw up a column of water a few hundred yards from them. The sound was unexpectedly loud, and they all winced for a moment. In the complete silence that followed, Red yelled loud enough for the whole boat to hear, "Hey, Toglio, if I had to depend on you for my safety, I'd a been in hell a year ago." The laughter was loud enough to embarrass Toglio, who forced himself to grin. Wilson capped it by saying in his high soft voice, "Toglio, you can figger out more ways to make a man do something, and then it turns out all screwed up anyway. Ah never saw a man who was so particular over nothin'."

That wasn't true, Toglio said to himself. He liked to get things done right, and these fellows just didn't seem to appreciate it. Somebody like Red was always ruining your work by making everybody laugh.

The assault boat's motors grew louder suddenly, began to roar, and after completing a circle, the boat headed in toward shore. Immediately the waves began to pound against the forward ramp, and a long cascade of spray poured over the troops. There was a surprised groan and then a silence settled over the men. Croft unslung his rifle and held one finger over the muzzle to prevent any water from getting into the barrel. For an instant he felt as though he were riding a horse at a gallop. "Goddam, we're going in," someone said.

"I hope it's cleaned up at least," Brown muttered.

Croft felt superior and dejected. He had been disappointed when he had learned weeks before that recon was to be assigned to the beach detail for the first week. And he had felt a silent contempt when the men in the platoon had shown their pleasure in the news. "Chickenshit," he muttered to himself now. A man who was afraid to put his neck out on the line was no damn good. Leading the men was a responsibility he craved; he felt powerful and certain at such moments. He longed to be in the battle that was taking place inland from the beach, and he resented the decision which left the platoon on an unloading detail. He passed his hand along his gaunt hard cheek and looked silently about him.

Hennessey was standing near the stern. As Croft watched his white silent face, he decided that Hennessey was frightened and it amused him. The boy found it hard to be still; he kept bobbing about in his place, and once or twice he flinched noticeably at a sudden noise; his leg began to itch and he scratched it violently. Then, as Croft watched, Hennessey pulled his left trouser out of his legging, rolled it up to expose his knee, and with a great deal of care rubbed a little spittle over the irritated red spot on his knee. Croft gazed at the white flesh with its blond hairs, noticed the pains with which Hennessey replaced his trouser in the legging, and felt an odd excitement as if the motions were important. That boy is too careful, Croft told himself.

And then with a passionate certainty he thought, "Hennessey's going to get killed today." He felt like laughing to release the ferment in him. This time he was sure.

But, abruptly, Croft remembered the poker game the preceding night when he had failed to draw his full house, and he was confused and then disgusted. You figure you're getting a little too smart for yourself, he thought. His disgust came because he felt he could not trust such emotions, rather than from any conviction that they had no meaning at all. He shook his head and sat back on his haunches, feeling the assault boat race in toward land, his mind empty, waiting for what events would bring.

Martinez had his worst minute just before they landed. All the agonies of the previous night, all the fears he had experienced early that morning had reached their climax in him. He dreaded the moment when the ramp would go down and he would have to get out of the boat. He felt as if a shell would swallow all of them, or a machine gun would be set up before the bow, would begin firing the moment they were exposed. None of the men was talking, and when Martinez closed his eyes, the sound of the water lashing past their craft seemed overwhelming as though he were sinking beneath it. He opened his eyes, pressed his nails desperately into his palms. "Buen Dios," he muttered. The sweat was dripping from his brow into his eyes, and he wiped it out roughly. Why no sounds? he asked himself. And indeed there were none. The men were silent, and a hush had come over the beach; the lone machine gun rapping in the distance sounded hollow and unreal.

A plane suddenly wailed past them, then roared over the jungle firing its guns. Martinez almost screamed at the noise. He felt his legs twitching again. Why didn't they land? By now he was almost ready to welcome the disaster that would meet him when the ramp went down.

In a high piping voice, Hennessey asked, "Do you think we'll be getting mail soon?" and his question was lost in a sudden roar of laughter. Martinez laughed and laughed, subsided into weak giggles, and then began laughing again.

"That fuggin Hennessey," he heard Gallagher say.

Suddenly Martinez realized that the boat had ground to a stop. The sound of its motors had altered, had become louder and a little uncertain, as if the propeller were no longer biting the water. After a moment he understood that they had landed.

For several long seconds, they remained motionless. Then the ramp clanked down, and Martinez trudged dumbly into the surf, almost stumbling when a knee-high wave broke behind him. He walked with his head down, looking at the water, and it was only when he was on shore that he realized nothing had happened to him. He looked about. Five other craft had landed at the same time, and the men were stringing over the beach. He saw an officer coming toward him, heard him ask Croft, "What platoon is this?"

"Intelligence and reconnaissance, sir, we're on beach detail," and then the instructions to wait over by a grove of coconut trees near the beach. Martinez fell into line, and stumbled along behind Red, as the platoon walked heavily through the soft sand. He was feeling nothing at all except a conviction that his judgment had been delayed.

The platoon marched about two hundred yards and then halted at the coconut grove. It was hot already, and most of the men threw off their packs and sprawled in the sand. There had been men here before them. Units of the first wave had assembled nearby, for the flat caked sand was trodden by many feet, and there was the inevitable minor refuse of empty cigarette packs and a discarded ration or two. But now these men were inland, moving somewhere through the jungle, and there was hardly anyone in sight. They could see for a distance of about two hundred yards in either direction before the beach curved out of view, and it was all quiet, relatively empty. Around either bend there might be a great deal of activity, but they could not tell this. It was still too early for the supplies to be brought in, and all the troops that had landed with them had been quickly dispersed. Over a hundred yards away to their right, the Navy had set up a command post which consisted merely of an officer at a small holding desk, and a jeep parked in the defilade where the jungle met the beach. To their left, just around the bend an eighth of a mile away, the Task Force Headquarters was beginning to function. A few orderlies were digging foxholes for the General's staff, and two men were staggering down the beach in the opposite direction, unwinding an eighty-pound reel of telephone wire. A jeep motored by in the firm wet sand near the water's edge and disappeared beyond the Navy's CP. The landing boats which had beached near the colored pennants on the other side of Task Force Headquarters had backed off by now and were cruising out toward the invasion fleet. The water looked very blue and the ships seemed to quiver a little in the mid-morning haze. Occasionally one of the destroyers would fire a volley or two, and half a minute later the men would hear the soft whisper of the shell as it arched overhead into the jungle. Once in a while a machine gun would start racketing in the jungle, and might be answered soon after with the shrill riveting sound of a Japanese light automatic.

Sergeant Brown looked at the coconut trees which were shorn at the top from the shelling. Farther down, another grove had remained untouched, and he shook his head. Plenty of men could have lived through that bombardment, he told himself. "This ain't such a bad shelling, compared to what they did to Motome," he said.

Red looked bitter. "Yeah, Motome." He turned over on his stomach in the sand, and lit a cigarette. "The beach stinks already," he announced.

"How can it stink?" Stanley asked. "It's too early."

"It just stinks," Red answered. He didn't like Stanley, and although he had exaggerated the faint brackish odor that came from the jungle, he was ready to defend his statement. He felt an old familiar depression seeping through him; he was bored and irritable, it was too early to eat, and he had smoked too many cigarettes. "There ain't any invasion going on," he said, "this is practice. Amphibious maneuvers." He spat bitterly.

Croft hooked his cartridge belt about his waist, and slung his rifle. "I'm going to hunt for S-four," he told Brown. "You keep the men here till I get back."

"They forgot us," Red said. "We might as well go to sleep."

"That's why I'm going to get them," Croft said.

Red groaned. "Aaah, why don't you let us sit on our butts for the day?"

"Listen, Valsen," Croft said, "you can cut all the pissin' from here on."

Red looked at him warily. "What's the matter?" he asked, "you want to win the war all by yourself?" They stared tensely at each other for a few seconds, and then Croft strode off.

"You're picking the wrong boy to mess with," Sergeant Brown told him.

Red spat again. "I won't take no crap from nobody." He could feel his heart beating quickly. There were a few bodies lying in the surf about a hundred yards from them, and as Red looked a soldier from Task Force Headquarters began dragging them out of the water. A plane patrolled overhead.

"It's pretty fuggin quiet," Gallagher said.

Toglio nodded. "I'm going to dig a hole." He unstrapped his entrenching tool, and Wilson snickered. "You just better save your energy, boy," he told him.

Toglio ignored him and started digging. "I'm going to make one too," Hennessey piped, and began to work about twenty yards from Toglio. For a few seconds the scraping of their shovels against the sand was the only sound.

Oscar Ridges sighed. "Shoot," he said, "Ah might as well make one too."

He guffawed with embarrassment after he spoke, and bent over his pack. His laughter had been loud and braying.

Stanley imitated him. "Waa-a-aaah!"

Ridges looked up and said mildly, "Well, shoot, Ah just cain't help the way Ah laugh. It's good enough, Ah reckon." He guffawed again to show his good will, but the laughter was much more chastened this time. When there was no answer, he began to dig. He had a short powerful body which was shaped like a squat pillar, for it tapered at neither end. His face was round and dumpy with a long slack jaw that made his mouth gape. His eyes goggled placidly to increase the impression he gave of dull-wittedness and good temper. As he dug, his motions were aggravatingly slow; he dumped each shovelful in exactly the same place, and paused every time to look about before he bent down again. There was a certain wariness about him, as though he were accustomed to practical jokes, expected them to be played on him.

Stanley watched him impatiently. "Hey, Ridges," he said, looking at Sergeant Brown for approbation, "if you were sitting on a fire, I guess you'd be too lazy to piss and put it out."

Ridges smiled vaguely. "Reckon so," he said quietly, watching Stanley walk toward him, and stand over the hole to examine his progress. Stanley was a tall youth of average build with a long face which looked vain usually and scornful and a little uncertain. He would have been handsome if it had not been for his long nose and sparse black mustache. He was only nineteen.

"Christ, you'll be digging all day," Stanley said with disgust. His voice was artificially rough like that of an actor who fumbles for a conception of how soldiers talk.

Ridges made no answer. Patiently, he continued digging. Stanley watched him for another minute, trying to think of something clever to say. He was beginning to feel ridiculous just standing there, and on an impulse kicked some sand into Ridges's foxhole. Silently, Ridges shoveled it out, not breaking his rhythm. Stanley could feel the men in the platoon watching him. He was a little sorry he had started, for he wasn't certain whether the men sided with him. But he had gone too far to renege. He kicked in quite a bit of sand.

Ridges laid down his shovel and looked at him. His face was patient but there was some concern in it. "What you trying to do, Stanley?" he asked.

"You don't like it?" Stanley sneered.

"No, sir, Ah don't."

Stanley grinned slowly. "You know what you can do."

Red had been watching with anger. He liked Ridges. "Listen, Stanley," Red shouted, "wipe your nose and start acting like a man."

Stanley swung around and glared at Red. The whole thing had gone wrong. He was afraid of Red, but he couldn't retreat.

"Red, you can blow it out," he said.

"Speaking of blowing it out," Red drawled, "will you tell me why you bother cultivating that weed under your nose when it grows wild in your asshole?" He spoke with a heavy sarcastic brogue which had the men laughing before he even finished. "Good ol' Red," Wilson chuckled.

Stanley flushed, took a step toward Red. "You ain't going to talk to me that way."

Red was angry, eager for a fight. He knew he could whip Stanley. There was something which he was not ready to face, and he let his anger ride over it. "Boy, I could break you in half," he warned Stanley.

Brown got to his feet. "Listen, Red," he interrupted, "you weren't spoiling that damn hard to have a fight with Croft."

Red paused, and was disgusted with himself. That was it. He stood there indecisively. "No, I wasn't," he said, "but there ain't any man I won't fight." He wondered if he had been afraid of Croft. "Aaah, fug it," he said, turning away.

But Stanley realized that Red would not fight, and he walked after him. "This ain't settled for me," he said.

Red looked at him. "Go blow, will ya."

To his amazement Stanley heard himself saying, "What's the matter, you going chickenshit?" He was positive he had said too much.

"Stanley," Red told him, "I could knock your head off, but I ain't gonna fight today." His anger was returning, and he tried to force it back. "Let's cut out this crap."

Stanley watched him, and then spat in the sand. He was tempted to say something more, but he knew the victory was with him. He sat down by Brown.

Wilson turned to Gallagher and shook his head. "Ah never thought old Red would back down," he murmured.

Ridges, seeing he was unmolested, went back to his digging. He was brooding a little over the incident, but the satisfying heft of the shovel in his hand soothed him. Just a little-bitty tool, he told himself. Pa would git a laugh out of seein' somethin' like that. He became lost in his work, feeling a comfortable familiarity in the labor. They ain't nothin' like work for bringin' a man round, he told himself. The hole was almost finished, and he began to tamp the bottom with his feet, setting them down heavily and evenly.

The men heard a vicious slapping sound like a fly-swatter being struck against a table. They looked around uneasily. "That's a Jap mortar," Brown muttered.

"He's very near," Martinez muttered. It was the first thing he had said since they had landed.

The men at Task Force Headquarters had dropped to the ground. Brown listened, heard an accelerating whine, and buried his face in the sand. The mortar shell exploded about a hundred and fifty yards away, and he lay motionless, listening to the clear terrifying sound of shrapnel cutting through the air, whipping the foliage in the jungle. Brown stifled a moan. The shell had landed a decent distance away, but . . . He was suffering an unreasonable panic. Whenever some combat started there was always a minute when he was completely unable to function, and did the first thing that occurred to him. Now, as the echo of the explosion damped itself in the air, he sprang excitedly to his feet. "Come on, let's get the hell out of here," he shouted.

"What about Croft?" Toglio asked.

Brown tried to think. He felt a desperate urgency to get away from this stretch of beach. An idea came to him, and he grasped it without deliberation. "Look, you got a hole, you stay here. We're gonna head down about half a mile, and when Croft comes back, you meet us there." He started gathering his equipment, dropped it suddenly, muttered, "Fug it, get it later," and began to jog down the beach. The other men looked at him in surprise, shrugged, and then Gallagher, Wilson, Red, Stanley and Martinez followed him, spread out in a long file. Hennessey watched them go, and looked over at Toglio and Ridges. He had dug his hole only a few yards away from the periphery of the coconut grove, and he tried to peer into the grove now, but it was too thick to be able to see more than fifty feet. Toglio's foxhole on his left was about twenty yards away but it seemed much farther. Ridges, who was on the other side of Toglio, seemed a very great distance away. "What shall I do?" he whispered to Toglio. He wished he had gone with the others, but he had been afraid to ask for fear they would laugh at him. Toglio took a look around, and then crouching, ran over to Hennessey's hole. His broad dark face was sweating now. "I think it's a very serious situation," he said dramatically, and then looked into the jungle.

"What's up?" Hennessey asked. He felt a swelling in his throat which was impossible to define as pleasant or unpleasant.

"I think some Japs sneaked a mortar in near the beach, and maybe they're going to attack us." Toglio mopped his face. "I wish the fellows had dug holes here," he said.

"It was a dirty trick to run off," Hennessey said. He was surprised to hear his voice sound natural.

"I don't know," Toglio said, "Brown's got more experience than I have. You got to trust your noncoms." He sifted some sand through his fingers. "I'm getting back in my hole. You just sit tight and wait. If any Japs come, we've got to stop them." Toglio's voice was portentous, and Hennessey nodded eagerly. This was like a movie, he thought. Vague images overlapped in his mind. He saw himself standing up and repelling a charge. "Okay, kid," Toglio said, and clapped him on the back. Crouching again, Toglio ran past his own hole to talk to Ridges. Hennessey remembered Red's telling him that Toglio had come to the platoon after the worst of the Motome campaign. He wondered if he could trust him.

Hennessey squatted in his hole and watched the jungle. His mouth was dry and he kept wetting his lips; every time there seemed to be a movement in the bushes, his heart constricted. The beach was very quiet. A minute went by, and he began to get bored. He could hear a truck grinding its gears down the beach, and when he took a chance and turned around, he could see another wave of landing craft coming in about a mile from shore. Reinforcements for us, he told himself, and realized it was absurd.

The harsh slapping sound came out of the jungle and was followed by another discharge and another and another. That's the mortars, he thought, and decided he was catching on fast. And then he heard a screaming piercing sound almost overhead like the tearing squeals of a car braking to avert a crash. Instinctively he curled flat in his hole. The next instants were lost to him. He heard an awful exploding sound which seemed to fill every corner of his mind, and the earth shook and quivered underneath him in the hole. Numbly he felt dirt flying over him, and his body being pounded by some blast. The explosion came again, and the dirt and the shock, and then another and another blast. He found himself sobbing in the hole, terrified and resentful. When another mortar landed, he screamed out like a child, "That's enough, *that's enough!*" He lay there trembling for almost a minute after the shells had stopped. His thighs felt hot and wet, and at first he thought, I'm wounded. It was pleasant and peaceful, and he had a misty picture of a hospital bed. He moved his hand back, and realized with both revulsion and mirth that he had emptied his bowels.

Hennessey froze his body. If I don't move, I won't get any dirtier, he thought. He remembered Red and Wilson talking about "keeping a tight ass-hole," and now he understood what they meant. He began to get the giggles. The sides of his foxhole were crumbling, and he had a momentary pang of anxiety at the thought that they would collapse in the next shelling. He was beginning to smell himself and he felt a little sick. Should he change his pants? he wondered. There was only one other pair in his pack, and he might have to wear them for a month. If he threw these away, they might make him pay for them.

But no, that wasn't true, he told himself; you didn't have to pay for lost equipment overseas. He was beginning to get the giggles again. What a story this would make to tell Pop. He saw his father's face for a moment. A part of him was trying to needle his courage to look over the edge of his hole. He raised himself cautiously, as much from the fear of further soiling his pants as from an enemy he might see.

Toglio and Ridges were still beneath the surface of their slit-trenches. Hennessey began to suspect he had been left alone. "Toglio, Corporal Toglio," he called, but it came out in a hoarse croaking whisper. There was no answer; he didn't ask himself whether they had heard him. He was alone, all alone, he told himself, and he felt an awful dread at being so isolated. He wondered where the others were. He had never seen combat before, and it was unfair to leave him alone; Hennessey began to feel bitter at being deserted. The jungle looked dark and ominous like a sky blacking over with thunderclouds. Suddenly, he knew he couldn't stay here any longer. He got out of his hole, clutched his rifle, and started to crawl away from the hole.

"Hennessey, where you going?" Toglio shouted. His head had suddenly appeared from the hole.

Hennessey started, and then began to babble. "I'm going to get the others. It's important, I got my pants dirty." He began to laugh.

"Come back," Toglio shouted.

The boy looked at his foxhole, and knew it was impossible to return to it. The beach seemed so pure and open. "No, I got to go," he said, and began to run. He heard Toglio shout once more, and then he was conscious only of the sound of his breathing. Abruptly, he realized that something was sliding about in the pocket of his pants made as they bellied over his leggings. In a little frenzy, he pulled his trousers loose, let the stool fall out, and then began to run again.

Hennessey passed by the place where the flags were up for the boats to come in, and saw the Navy officer lying prone in a little hollow near the jungle. Abruptly, he heard the mortars again, and then right after it a machine gun firing nearby. A couple of grenades exploded with the loud empty sound that paper bags make when they burst. He thought for an instant, "There's some soldiers after them Japs with the mortar." Then he heard the terrible siren of the mortar shell coming down on him. He pirouetted in a little circle, and threw himself to the ground. Perhaps he felt the explosion before a piece of shrapnel tore his brain in half.

Red found him when the platoon was coming back to meet Toglio. They had waited out the shelling in a long zigzag trench which had been dug by a company of reserve troops farther along the beach. After word had come that the Jap mortar crew had been wiped out, Brown decided to go back. Red didn't feel like talking to anybody, and unconsciously he assumed the lead. He came around a bend in the beach and saw Hennessey lying face down in the sand with a deep rent in his helmet and a small circle of blood about his head. One of his hands was turned palm upward, and his fingers clenched as though he were trying to hold something. Red felt sick. He had liked Hennessey, but it had been the kind of fondness he had for many of the men in the platoon — it included the possibility that it might be ended like this. What bothered Red was the memory of the night they had sat on deck during the air raid when Hennessey had inflated his life belt. It gave Red a moment of awe and panic as if someone, *something*, had been watching over their shoulder that night and laughing. There was a pattern where there shouldn't be one.

Brown came up behind him, and gazed at the body with a troubled look. "Should I have left him behind?" he asked. He tried not to consider whether he were responsible.

"Who takes care of the bodies?"

"Graves Registration."

"Well, I'm going to find them so they can carry him away," Red said.

Brown scowled. "We're supposed to stick together." He stopped, and then went on angrily. "Goddam, Red, you're acting awful chicken today, picking fights and then backing out of them, throwing a fit over . . ." He looked at Hennessey and didn't finish.

Red was walking on already. For the rest of this day, that was one part of the beach he was going to keep away from. He spat, trying to exorcise the image of Hennessey's helmet, and the blood that had still been flowing through the rent in the metal.

The platoon followed him, and when they reached the place where they had left Toglio, the men began digging holes in the sand. Toglio walked around nervously, repeating continually that he had yelled for Hennessey to come back. Martinez tried to reassure him. "Okay, nothing you can do," Martinez said several times. He was digging quickly and easily in the soft sand, feeling calm for the first time that day. His terror had withered with Hennessey's death. Nothing would happen now.

When Croft came back he made no comment on the news Brown gave him. Brown was relieved and decided he did not have to blame himself. He stopped thinking about it.

But Croft brooded over the event all day. Later, as they worked on the beach unloading supplies, he caught himself thinking of it many times. His reaction was similar to the one he had felt at the moment he discovered his wife was unfaithful. At that instant, before his rage and pain had begun to operate, he had felt only a numb throbbing excitement and the knowledge that his life was changed to some degree and certain things would never be the same. He knew that again now. Hennessey's death had opened to Croft vistas of such omnipotence that he was afraid to consider it directly. All day the fact hovered about his head, tantalizing him with odd dreams and portents of power.

First Blood

✕

from *The Thin Red Line*

by JAMES JONES

Billions of hard, bright stars shone with relentless glitter all across the tropic night sky. Underneath this brilliant canopy of the universe, the men lay wide awake and waited. From time to time the same great cumuli of the day, black blobs now, sailed their same stately route across the bright expanse blotting out portions of it, but no rain fell on the thirsting men. For the first time since they had been up in these hills it did not rain at all during the night. The night had to be endured, and it had to be endured dry, beneath its own magnificent beauty. Perhaps of them all only Colonel Tall enjoyed it.

Finally, though it was still black night, cautionary stirrings and whispers sibilated along the line from hole to hole as the word to move out was passed. In the inhuman, unreal unlight of false dawn the grubby, dirty-faced remnants of C-for-Charlie sifted from their holes and coagulated stiffly into their squads and platoons to begin their flanking move. There was not one of them who did not carry his cuts, bruises or abrasions from having flung himself violently to the ground the day before. Thick fat rolls of dirt pressed beneath the mudcaked fingernails of their hands, greasy from cleaning weapons. They had lost forty-eight men or just over one-fourth of their number yesterday in killed, wounded or sick; nobody doubted they would lose more today. The only question remaining was: Which ones of us? Who exactly?

Still looking dapper although he was now almost as dirty as themselves, Colonel Tall with his little bamboo baton in his armpit and his hand resting on his rakishly lowslung holster strode among them to tell them good luck. He shook hands with Bugger Stein and Brass Band. Then they trudged away in the ghostly light, moving away eastward back down the ridge to face their new day while thirst gnawed at them. Before dawn lightened the area, they had crossed back over the third fold — where they had lain so long in terror yesterday, and where the familiar ground now looked strange — and had traversed the low between the folds to the edge of the jungle where they were hidden, where Col Tall would not let them go yesterday, and where not a single Japanese was in sight. Approaching it cautiously with scouts out, they found nobody at all. A hundred yards inside the jungle they discovered a highly passable, much used trail, its mud covered with prints of Japanese hobnailed boots, all pointing toward Hill 210. As they moved along it quietly and without trouble, they could hear the beginning of the fight on the ridge — where they had left the previously four, but now five volunteers with Captain Gaff.

Tall had not waited long. B-for-Baker now manned the line of holes behind the ledge. Tall sent them forward to the ledge itself, and as soon as it was light enough to see at all, sent the middle platoon forward in an attack whose objective was to wheel right in a line pivoted on the ledge so that they would be facing the strongpoint. This would place them in a position to aid Gaff.

But the middle platoon's move was not successful. MG fire from the strongpoint, and other hidden points nearby, hurt them too badly. Four men were killed and a number of others were wounded. They were forced to return. That was the noise of the fight C-for-Charlie heard; and its failure left everything up to Gaff and his now five volunteers. They would have to take the strongpoint alone. Tall walked over to them where they lay.

This fifth volunteer with Gaff was Pfc Cash, the icy-eyed taxi-driver from Toledo with the mean face, known in C-for-Charlie as "Big Un." Earlier, before C-for-Charlie moved out, Big Un had come up to Tall in the dark and in a ponderous voice had asked to be allowed to stay behind and join Gaff's assault group. Tall, who was not used to being approached by strange privates anyway, could hardly believe his ears. He could not even remember ever having seen this man. "Why?" he asked sharply.

"Because of what the Japs done to them two guys from 2d Battalion three days ago on Hill 209," Big Un said. "I ain't forgotten it, and I want to get myself a few of them personally before I get knocked off or shot up without getting a chance to kill some. I think Capn Gaff's operation'll be my best oppratunity."

For a moment Tall could not help believing he was being made the victim of some kind of elaborate and tasteless hoax, perpetrated by the wits of Charlie Company who had sent this great oaf up to him deliberately with this stupid request for personal, heroic vendetta. 1st Sgt Welsh, for one, had a mind capable of such subtle ridicule.

But when he looked up (as he was forced to do; and Tall was by no means a small man) at this huge, murderous face and icy, if not very intelligent eyes, he could see despite his flare of anger that the man was obviously sincere. Cash stood, his rifle slung not from one shoulder but across his back, and carrying in his hands one of those sawed-off shotguns and bandolier of buckshot shells which some fool of a staff lieutenant had had the bright idea of handing out for "close quarter work" the night before the attack — which meant that Cash had hung onto the damned thing all through the danger of yesterday. Tall thought they had all been thrown away. A sudden tiny thrill ran through Tall despite himself. The brute really was big! But his own reaction made him even more angry.

"Soldier, are you serious?" he snapped thinly. "There's a war on here. I'm busy. I've got a serious battle to fight."

"Yes," Big Un said, then remembering his manners added, "I mean: Yes, sir: I'm serious."

Tall pressed his lips together. If the man wanted to make such a request, he should know he was supposed to go through channels: through his Platoon Leader and his Company Commander to Gaff himself; not come bothering the Battalion Commander with it when the Battalion Commander had a battle to fight.

"Don't you know —" he began in frustration, and then stopped himself. Tall prided himself on being a professional and such requests for personal vendetta offended and bored him. A professional should ignore such things and fight a battle, or a war, as it developed on the ground. Tall knew Marine officers who laughed about the jars of gold or gold-filled Japanese teeth some of their men had collected over the campaign, but he preferred to have nothing to do with that sort of thing. Also, though his protégé Gaff had lost two men yesterday evening, they had decided between them that the experience and the knowledge of the terrain gained by the survivors more than made up for the adding of two green replacements who would probably be more liability than help. Still . . .

And anyway, here this great oaf still stood, waiting dumbly, as though his wishes were the only ones in the world, and blocking Tall's path with his huge frame so Tall could not see anything that was going on.

After biting the inside of his lip, he snapped out coldly, "If you want to go with Captain Gaff, you'll have to go talk to him about it and ask him. I'm busy. You can tell him that I don't object to your going. Now, God damn it, *go away!*" he yelled. He turned away. Big Un was left holding his shotgun.

"Yes, sir!" he called after the Colonel. "Thank you, sir!" And while Tall had continued with getting C-for-Charlie moving, Cash had gone in search of Gaff.

Big Un's cry of thanks after the Colonel had not been without his own little hint of sarcasm. He had not been a hack pusher all his life not to know when he was being deliberately snubbed by a social better, high intelligence or low. As far as intelligence went, Big Un was confident he could have been as intelligent as any — and more intelligent than most — if he had not always believed that school and history and arithmetic and writing and reading and learning words were only so much uninteresting bullshit which took up a man's time and kept him from getting laid or making an easy buck. He still believed it, for his own kids as well as for himself. He had never finished his first year of high school and he could read a paper as well as anybody. And as for intelligence, he was intelligent enough to know that the Colonel's statement about not objecting was tantamount to acceptance by Gaff. In fact, all the time he was talking there to the Colonel, Big Un had intended to tell Gaff that, anyway. Now he could tell him truthfully.

So, in the still dark predawn, Gaff and his four volunteers were treated to the awesome spectacle of Big Un looming up over them through the dark, still clutching his shotgun and bandolier of shells which he had clung to so dearly all through the terror of yesterday in his US-made shell-hole among the 1st Platoon. Stolidly and without excitement, Big Un made his report. As he had anticipated, he was immediately accepted — although Gaff, too, looked at his shotgun strangely. All he had left to do was find Bugger Stein and report the change, then come back and lie down with the others to wait until B Company's middle platoon made its attack and it was their own turn. Big Un did so with grim satisfaction.

There was little for them to do but talk. During the half hour it took the middle platoon of B Company to fail and come tumbling and sobbing back over the ledge with drawn faces and white eyes, the six of them lay a few yards back down the slope behind B's right platoon, which in addition to holding the right of the line along the ledge was also acting as the reserve. It was amazing how the longer one lasted in this business, the less sympathy one felt for others who were getting shot up as long as oneself was in safety. Sometimes the difference was a matter of only a very few yards. But terror became increasingly limited to those moments when you yourself were in actual danger. So, while B's middle platoon shot and were shot, fought and sobbed thirty yards away beyond the ledge, Gaff's group talked. Cash the new addition more than made his presence felt.

Big Un himself did very little of the talking, after explaining his reason for wanting to come with them, but he made himself felt just the same. Unslinging his rifle, he arranged it and the shotgun carefully to keep their actions out of the dirt, and then simply lay, toying with the bandolier of shotgun shells and slipping them in and out of their cloth loops, his face a stolid, mean mask. The slingless shotgun was a brandnew, cheap-looking automatic with its barrel sawed off just behind the choke and a five shell magazine; the shot shells themselves were not actually buckshot at all, but were loaded with a full load of BB shot capable of blowing a large, raw hole clear through a man at close range. It was a mean weapon, and Cash looked like the man to use it well. Nobody really knew very much about him in C-for-Charlie. He had come in as a draftee six months before and while he had made acquaintances, he had made no real friends. Everybody was a little afraid of him. He kept to himself, did most of his drinking alone, and while he never offered to challenge anybody to a fight, there was something about his grin which made it plain that any challenges he received would be cheerfully and gladly accepted. Nobody offered any. At six foot four and built accordingly, in an outfit where physical fighting prowess was considered the measure of a man's stature, nobody wanted to try him. Except for Big Queen (over whom he towered by five inches, though he did not weigh as much) he was the biggest man in the company. There were those who were not above trying slyly to promote this battle of the giants between Big Un and Big Queen, just to see who *would* win; and many bets might have been taken, except that nothing ever came of it. Curiously enough, the nearest Big Un ever came to having a real friend was Witt the Kentuckian, who hardly came up to his waist, and who used to go on pass with him before Witt was forcibly transferred. This turned out to be because in Toledo Big Un had known and admired so many Kentuckians who had come up north to work in the factories, and had liked their strong, hardheaded sense of honor which showed itself in drunken brawls over women or fist fights over particular prize seats at some bar. But now, today, he did not even speak to Witt beyond a perfunctory grunt of greeting. The rest of them watched him and his shotgun curiously. Despite the fact that they were now seasoned veterans of this particular assault and could look down on Big Un from this height of snobbery, they were all somehow a little reluctant to try it.

John Bell, for one, had forgotten all about the Japanese torture killing of the two George Company men three days before. It was too long ago and too much had happened to him since. When Big Un recalled it with such surprise to them all, Bell found it didn't really matter so much any more. Guys got killed, one way or another way. Some got tortured. Some got gut-shot like Tella. Some got it quick through the head. Who knew how much those two guys suffered, really? Only themselves; and they no longer existed to tell it. And if they no longer existed, it didn't either and was no longer important. So what the fuck? A wall existed between the living and the dead. And there was only one way to get over it. That was what was important. So what was all this fuss about? Bell found himself eyeing Big Un coolly and wondering what his real angle was, behind all this other crap. The others in the little group obviously felt the same way, Bell noted, from the peculiar looks on their faces; but nobody said anything. Thirty-five yards away beyond and above the little protective ledge the middle platoon of Baker still fired and fought and now and then yelled just a little bit. If Bell was any judge by the sound of it, what was left of them would be coming back pretty quickly. A rough fingernail of excitement picked at his solar plexus when he thought what this would mean soon for himself. Then, suddenly, like a bucket of cold water dashed in his face, his own supreme callousness smashed into his consciousness and shook him with a sense of horror at his own hardened brutality. How would Marty like being married to this husband, when he finally did get home? Ah, Marty! so much is changing; everywhere. Therefore, when the middle platoon of B did come rolling and tumbling and cursing and sobbing back over the ledge with their white eyeballs in their faces and their open mouths, Bell watched them with an anguish which was perhaps out of all proportion even to their own.

How the others in the assault group felt about the return of the platoon, Bell could not tell. From their faces they all, including Cash, seemed to feel the same cool, guarded callousness he himself had just been feeling, and now was so desperately wanting not to feel. The Baker Company men lay against the ledge staring at nothing and seeing nobody and breathing in long painful gasps through their parched throats. There was no water to give them and they needed water badly. Though the day was not yet really hot, they were all sweating profusely, thus losing even more precious moisture. Making a noise like a battery of frogs in a swamp two of them rolled up their eyeballs and passed out. Nobody bothered to help them. Their buddies couldn't. And the assault group only lay and watched them.

This lack of water was becoming a serious problem for everybody, and would be more of one as the glaring equatorial sun mounted, but whatever the reason — though there was plenty of it in the rear — no water could be got this far forward to them. Curiously enough, it was little Charlie Dale the insensitive, rather than Bell or Don Doll, who voiced it for all of them in the assault group. Imaginative or not he was animal enough to know what his belly told him and be directed by it. "If they don't get us some water up here soon," he said loud enough to be heard by everybody in the vicinity, "we ain't none of us going to make it to the top of this hill." Abruptly, he rolled over to face the looming shape of Hill 209 in their rear and began to shake his fist at it. "Dirty Fuckers! Dirty bastards! Pig bastards! You got all the fucking water in the world, and you drinking ever fucking drop of it, too! You ain't lettin any of it get past you up to us, are you! Well you better get some of it up here to your goddam *fightin men*, or you can take your goddam fucking battle and shove it up your fat ass and lose it!" He had yelled this much of his protest, and it verberated off along the ledge where nobody, least of all the middle platoon of B, paid any attention to it. The rest of it tapered away, into an intense, unintelligible mutter which, as Colonel Tall now sauntered toward them from his command hole baton in hand, became a respectful and attentive silence.

The Colonel, whose walk was leisurely and erect — as straight up as he could get, in fact — condescended to squat while he talked in a low serious voice to Gaff. Then they were off and crawling again along the by now so familiar ledge — familiar to the point of real friendliness almost, John

Bell thought, which could be a bad trap if you believed it — as it curved away out of sight around the hill's curve, Gaff in the lead.

Bell crawled around Charlie Dale in the second spot and touched the Captain on the behind. "You better let me take the point, sir," he said respectfully.

Gaff turned his head to look at him with intense, crinkled eyes. For a long moment the two, officer and ex-officer, looked honestly into each other's eyes. Then with an abrupt gesture of both head and hand Gaff admitted his small error and signaled Bell to go on past him. He let one more man, Dale, pass him and then fell into the third spot. When Bell reached the point where the trough began and Lieutenant Gray had died, he stopped and they all clustered up.

Gaff did not bother to give them any peptalk. He had already explained the operation to them thoroughly, back at the position. Now all he said was, "You all know the job we've got to do, fellows. There's no point in my going over it all again. I'm convinced the toughest part of the approach will be the open space between the end of the trough here and the shoulder of the knob. Once past that I think it won't be so bad. Remember that we may run into smaller emplacements along the way. I'd rather bypass them if we can, but we may have to knock some of them out if they block our route and hold us up. Okay, that's all." He stopped and smiled at them looking each man in the eyes in turn: an excited, boyish, happy, adventuresome smile. It was only slightly incongruous with the tensed, crinkled look in his eyes.

"When we get up to them," Gaff said, "we ought to have some fun."

There were several weak smiles, very similar to his own if not as strong. Only Witt's and Big Un's seemed to be really deep. But they were all grateful to him. Since yesterday all of them, excepting Big Un, had come to like him very much. All last evening, during the night, and again during the predawn movements, he had stayed with them except during his actual conferences with Colonel Tall, spending his time with them. He kidded, cajoled and boosted them, cracking jokes, telling them cunt stories about his youth at the Point and after, and all the kooky type broads he had made — had in short treated them like equals. Even for Bell who had been one it was a little thrilling, quite flattering to be treated as an equal by an officer; for the others it was moreso. They would have followed Gaff anywhere. He had promised them the biggest drunk of their lives, everything on him, once they got through this mess and back down off the line. And they were grateful to him for that, too. He had not, when he promised, made any mention about "survivors" or "those who were left" having this drunk together, tacitly assuming that they would all be there to enjoy it. And they were grateful for that also. Now he looked around at them all once more with his boyish, young adventurer's eager smile above the tensed, crinkled eyes.

"I'll be leading from here on out," he said. "Because I want to pick the route myself. If anything should happen to me, Sergeant Bell will be in command, so I want him last. Sergeant Dale will be second in command. They both know what to do.

"Okay, let's go." It was much more of a sigh than a hearty bellow.

Then they were out and crawling along the narrow, peculiarly sensed dangerousness of the familiar trough, Gaff in the lead, each man being particularly careful of the spot where the trough opened out into the ledge and Lieutenant Gray the preacher had absentmindedly got himself killed. Big Un Cash, who was new to all this, was especially careful. John Bell, waiting for the others to climb out, caught Charlie Dale staring at him with a look of puzzled, but nonetheless hateful enmity. Dale had been appointed Acting Sergeant at least an hour before Bell, and therefore should have had the seniority over him. Bell winked at him, and Dale looked away. A moment later it was Dale's turn to go, and he climbed out into the trough without a backward look. Only one man, Witt, remained between them. Then it was Bell's own turn. For the — what was it? third? fourth? fifth time? Bell had lost track — he climbed out over the ledge and crawled past the thin screen of scrub brush. It was beginning to look pretty bedraggled now from all the MG fire which had whistled through it.

In the trough ahead with his head down Charlie Dale was thinking furiously that that was what you could always expect from all goddam fucking officers. They hung together like a pack of horse thieves, busted out or not. He had broke his ass for them all day yesterday. He had been appointed Acting Sergeant by an officer, by Bugger Stein himself, not by no fucking platoon sergeant like Keck. And about a hour before. And look who got command? You couldn't trust them no further than you could throw them by the ears, no more than you could trust the governmint itself to do something for you. Furiously, outraged, keeping his head well down, he stared at the motionless feet of Doll in front of him as if he wanted to bite them off.

Up ahead Gaff had waited, looking back, until they were all safely in the trough. Now there was no need to wait longer. Turning his head to the right he looked off toward the strongpoint, but without raising his head high enough to see anything above the grass. Were they waiting? Were they watching? Were they looking at this particular open spot? He could not know. But no need in spotting them a ball by exposing himself if they were. With one last look back directly behind him at Big Un Cash, who favored him with a hard, mean, gimleteyed grin that was not much help, he bounced up and took off with his rifle at high port, running agonizingly slowly and pulling his knees up high to clear the matted kunai grass like a football player running through stacks of old tires. It was ludicrous to say the least, not a dignified way to be shot, but not a shot was fired. He dived in behind the shoulder of the knob and lay there. After waiting a full minute he motioned the next man, Big Un, to come on. Big Un, who had moved up, as the others had moved up behind him, took right off at once running in the same way, his rifle pounding against his back, the shotgun in his hands, his helmet straps flapping. Just before he reached the shoulder a single machine gun opened up, but he too dived to safety. The machine gun stopped.

The third man, Doll, fell. He was only about five yards out when several MGs opened up. They were watching this time. It was only twenty or twenty-five yards across, the open space, but it seemed much longer. He was already breathing in ripping gasps. Then his foot caught in a hole in the mat of old grass and he was down. Oh, no! Oh, no! his mind screamed at him in panic. Not me! Not after all the rest that's happened to me! Not after all I've lasted through! I won't even get my medal! Blindly, spitting grass seeds, and dust, he clambered up and staggered on. He only had ten yards more to go, and he made it. He fell in upon the other two and lay sobbing for breath and existence. The bright, washed sun had just come up over the hills in the east.

By now in the early morning sunshine and stark shadows all the MGs from the strongpoint were firing, hosing down the trough itself as well as the open space. Bullets tore over the heads of Charlie Dale, Witt and Bell in bunches which rattled and bruised the poor thin little bushes. It was now Dale's turn to go, and he was still furious at Bell. "Hey, wait!" Bell yelled from behind him. "Wait! Don't go yet! I got an idea!" Dale gave him one hate-filled contemptuous look and got to his feet. He departed without a word, chugging along solidly like a little engine, in the same way he had gone down and come back up the slope in front of the third fold yesterday. By now a sort of semi-path had been pushed through the grass, and this aided him some. He arrived behind the shoulder and sat down, apparently totally unmoved, but still secretly angry at Bell. Nothing had touched him.

"You must be out of your mind!" Captain Gaff shouted at him.

"Why?" Dale said. Maliciously, he settled himself to see what fucking Bell would do now. Heh heh. Not that he wanted him to get hurt, or anything.

Bell demonstrated his idea immediately. When he and Witt had crawled to the end of the trough, the MGs still firing just over their heads, Bell pulled the pin on a grenade and lobbed it at the strongpoint. But he did not throw it straight across; he threw it into the angle formed by the ledge and the trough, so that it landed in front of the bunker but further back much closer to the ledge. When the MGs all swung that way, as they did immediately, he and Witt crossed in safety before they could swing back. Cleary the three of them could have done it just as easily, and when he threw himself down grinning in the safety behind the shoulder, Bell winked at Charlie Dale again. Dale glowered back. "Very bright," Gaff laughed. Bell winked at Dale a third time. Fuck him. Who did he think he was? Then suddenly, after this third wink, like some kind of a sudden stop, Bell realized the fear he had felt this time had been much less, almost none at all, negligible. Even when those bullets were sizzing just over his head. Was he learning? Was that it? Or was he just becoming inured. More brutalized, like Dale. The thought lingered on in his head like an echoing gong while he sat staring at nothing, then slowly faded away. And so what? If answer is yes, or if question does not apply to you, pass on to next questionnaire. What the hell, he thought. Fuck it. If he only had a drink of water, he could do anything. The MGs from the strongpoint were still hosing and belaboring the empty trough and its poor straggly bushes as the party moved away.

Gaff had told them that he thought the rest of the route would be easier once they were past the open space, and he was right. The terrain mounted steeply around the knob which jutted out of the ridge and up here the mat of grass was not quite so thick, but now they were forced to crawl. It was next to impossible to see the camouflaged emplacements until they opened up, and they could not take any chances. As they moved along in this snail's way, sweating and panting in the sun from the exertion, Bell's heart — as well as everybody else's — began to beat with a heavier pulse, a mingled excitement and fear which was by no means entirely unpleasant. They all knew from yesterday that beyond the knob was a shallow saddle between the knob and the rock wall where the ledge ended, and it was along this saddle which they were to crawl to come down on the Japanese from above. They had all seen the saddle, but they had not seen behind the knob. Now they crawled along it, seeing it from within the Japanese territory. They were not fired upon, and they did not see any emplacements. Off to the left near the huge rock outcrop where the seven Japanese men had made their silly counterattack early yesterday, they could hear the tenor-voiced Japanese MGs firing at Baker Company at the ledge; but nothing opened up on them. When they reached the beginning of the saddle, sweating and half-dead from the lack of water, Gaff motioned them to stop.

He had to swallow his dry spittle several times before he could speak. It had been arranged with Colonel Tall that the commander of Baker's right platoon would move his men along the ledge to the trough and be ready to charge from there at Gaff's whistle signal, and because of this he unhooked his whistle from his pocket. The saddle was about twenty or twenty-five yards across, and he spaced them out across it. Because of the way it fell the strongpoint below was still invisible from here. "Remember, I want to get as close to them as we can before we put the grenades to them." To Bell's mind, overheated and overwrought, the Captain's phraseology sounded strangely sexual; but Bell knew it could not be. Then Gaff crawled out in front of them, and looked back.

"Well, fellows, this is where we separate the men from the boys," he told them, "the sheep from the goats. Let's crawl." He clamped his whistle in his teeth and, cradling his rifle while holding a grenade in one hand, he commenced to do so.

Crawling along behind him, and in spite of his promise of a big beer-bust, everything paid for by him, Gaff's volunteers did not take too kindly to his big line. Shit, I could have done better than that myself, Doll thought, spitting out yet another grass seed. Doll had already entirely for-gotten his so near escape crossing the open space, and suddenly for no ap-parent reason he was transfixed by a rage which ranged all through him like some uncontrollable woods fire. Do not fire until you see the red of their assholes, Gridley. You may shit when ready, Gridley. Damn the tor-pedoes, full crawl ahead. Sighted Japs, grenaded same. There are no athe-ists in foxholes, Chaplain; *shit* on the enemy! He was — for no reason at all, except that he was afraid — so enraged at Gaff that he could have put a grenade to him himself right now, or shot him. On his left, his major competition Charlie Dale crawled along with narrowed eyes still hating all officers anyway and as far as he was concerned Gaff's final line only proved him right. Beyond Dale, Big Un Cash moved his big frame along con-temptuously, his rifle still on his back, the fully loaded shotgun cradled in his arms; he had not come along on this thing to be given dumb slogans by no punk kid officers — sheeps and goats my ass, he thought and there was no doubt in his hard hackpusher's mind about which side he would be on when the count came. Witt, beyond Big Un and himself the extreme left flank, had merely spat and settled his thin neck down into his shoul-ders and set his jaw. He was not here for any crapped up West Point heroics, he was here because he was a brave man and a very good soldier and because his old outfit C-for-Charlie needed him — whether *they* knew it or not; and Gaff could spare him the conversation. Slowly, as they crawled, the extreme left of the strongpoint came into view fifty yards away and about twenty yards below them.

On the extreme right of the little line John Bell was not thinking about young Captain Gaff at all. As soon as Gaff had made his bid for an im-mortal line Bell had dismissed it as stupid. Bell was thinking, instead, about cuckoldry. Why that subject should come into his mind at a time like this Bell didn't know, but it had and he couldn't get rid of it. Thinking about it seriously, Bell discovered that under serious analysis he could only find four basic situations: sad little husband attacking big strong lover, big strong lover attacking sad little husband, sad little husband attacking big strong wife, big strong wife attacking sad little husband. But always it was a sad little husband. Something about the emotional content of the word automatically shrunk all cuckolded husbands to sad little husbands. Undoubtedly many big strong husbands had been cuckolded in their time. Yes, undoubtedly. But you could never place them in direct connection with the emotional content of the word. This was because the emotional content of the word was essentially funny. Bell imagined himself in all four basic situations. It was very painful, in an exquisitely unpleasant, but very sexual way. And suddenly Bell knew — as well and as surely as he knew he was crawling down this grassy saddle on Guadalcanal — that he was cuckold; that Marty was stepping out, was sleeping with, was fucking, somebody. Given *her* character and *his* absence, there was no other possibility. It was as though it were a thought which had been hanging around the borders of his mind a long time, but which he would never allow in until now. But with one man? or with several? Which did one prefer, the one man which meant a serious love affair? or the several which meant that she was promiscuous? What would he do when he got home? beat her up? kick her around? leave her? Put a goddamned grenade in her bed maybe. Ahead of him the entire strongpoint was visible by now, its nearer, right end only twenty-five yards away, and only a very few yards below their own height now.

And it was just then that they were discovered by the Japanese.

Five scrawny bedraggled Japanese men popped up out of the ground holding dark round objects which they lobbed up the hill at them. Fortunately only one of the five grenades exploded. It lit near Dale who rolled over twice away from it and then lay huddled as close to the ground as he could get, his face turned away. None of its fragments hit him, but it made his ears ring.

"Pull and throw! Pull and throw!" Gaff was yelling at them through the noise of the explosion, and almost as one man their six grenades arched at the strongpoint. The five Japanese men who had popped up out of the ground had by now popped back down into it. But as the grenades lit, two other, unlucky Japanese popped up to throw. One grenade lit between the feet of one of these and exploded up into him, blowing off one of his feet and putting him down. Fragments put the other one down. All of the American grenades exploded.

The Japanese with his foot off lay still a moment then struggled up to sit holding another grenade as the blood poured from his severed leg. Doll shot him. He fell back dropping the ignited grenade beside him. It did not go off.

"Once more! Once more!" Gaff was yelling at them, and again six grenades arched in the air. Again all of them exploded. Doll was a little late getting his away because of the shot, but he got it off just behind the others.

This time there were four Japanese standing when the grenades lit, one of them carrying a light MG. The exploding grenades put three of them down, including the man with the Nambu, and the fourth, thinking better of it, disappeared down a hole. There were now five Japanese down and out of action in the little hollow.

"Go in! Go in!" Gaff cried, and in a moment all of them were on their feet running. No longer did they have to fret and stew, or worry about being brave or being cowardly. Their systems pumped full of adrenaline to constrict the peripheral blood vessels, elevate the blood pressure, make the heart beat more rapidly, and aid coagulation, they were about as near to automatons without courage or cowardice as flesh and blood can get. Numbly, they did the necessary.

The Japanese had shrewdly taken advantage of the terrain to save themselves digging work. Behind the holes into the emplacements themselves was a natural little low area where they could come out and sit in cover when they were not actually being shelled, and it also served as a communication trench between the holes. Now in this hollow the scrawny, bedraggled Japanese rose with rifles, swords and pistols from their holes to meet Gaff and his crew. At least, some of them did. Others stayed in the holes. Three tried to run. Dale shot one and Bell shot another. The third was seen to disappear in a grand broadjump over the edge of the rockface, where it fell clear, sixty or eighty feet to the jungle treetops below. He was never seen again and no one ever learned what happened to him. The others came on. And Gaff and his troops, the Captain blowing his whistle shrilly with each exhalation of breath, ran to meet them, in clear view of Baker Company at the ledge until they passed out of sight into the hollow.

Big Un killed five men almost at once. His shotgun blew the first nearly in two and tore enormous chunks out of the second and third. The fourth and fifth, because the gun was bucking itself higher each time he fired, had most of their heads taken off. Swinging the empty shotgun like a baseball bat, Big Un broke the face of a sixth Japanese man just emerging from a hole, then jerked a grenade from his belt, pulled the pin and tossed it down the hole after him into a medley of voices which ceased in the dull roaring boom of the constricted explosion. While he struggled to unsling the rifle from his back, he was attacked by a screaming officer with a sword. Gaff shot the officer in the belly from the hip, shot him again in the face to be positive after he was down. Bell had killed two men. Charlie Dale had killed two. Doll, who had drawn his pistol, was charged by another screaming officer who shouted "Banzai!" over and over and who ran at him whirling his bright, gleaming sword around his head in the air. Doll shot him through the chest so that in a strange laughable way his legs kept right on running while the rest of him fell down behind them. Then the torso jerked the legs up too and the man hit the ground flat out with a tremendous whack. Doll shot him a second time in the head. Beyond him Witt had shot three men, one of them a huge fat sergeant wielding a black, prewar U. S. Army cavalry saber. Taking the overhead saber cut on the stock of his rifle, cutting it almost to the barrel, Witt had buttstroked him in the jaw. Now he shot him where he lay. Suddenly there was an enormous quiet except for the wailing chatter of three Japanese standing in a row who had dropped their weapons. There had been, they all realized, a great deal of shouting and screaming, but now there was only the moans of the dying and the hurt. Slowly they looked around at each other and discovered the miraculous fact that none of them was killed, or even seriously damaged. Gaff had a knot on his jaw from firing without cheeking his stock. Bell's helmet had been shot from his head, the round passing through the metal and up and around inside the shell between metal and fiber liner and coming out the back. Bell had an enormous headache. Witt discovered he had splinters in his hand from his busted riflestock, and his arms ached. Dale had a small gash in his shin from the bayonet of a downed and dying Japanese man who had struck at him and whom he subsequently shot. Numbly, they stared at each other. Each had believed devoutly that he would be the only one left alive.

It was clear to everyone that it was Big Un and his shotgun which had won the day, had broken the back of the Japanese fight, and later when they discussed and discussed it, that would remain the consensus. And now in the strange, numb silence — still breathing hard from the fight, as they all were — Big Un, who still had not yet got his rifle unslung, advanced snarling on the three standing Japanese. Taking two by their scrawny necks which his big hands went almost clear around, he shook them back and forth gaggling helplessly until their helmets fell off, then grinning savagely began beating their heads together. The cracking sound their skulls made as they broke was loud in the new, palpable quiet. "Fucking murderers," he told them coldly. "Fucking yellow Jap bastards. Killing helpless prisoners. Fucking murderers. Fucking prisoner killers." When he dropped them as the others simply stood breathing hard and watching, there was no doubt that they were dead, or dying. Blood ran from their noses and their eyes were rolled back white. "That'll teach them to kill prisoners," Big Un announced, glaring at his own guys. He turned to the third, who simply looked at him uncomprehendingly. But Gaff jumped in between them. "We need him. We need him," he said, still gasping and panting. Big Un turned and walked away without a word.

It was then they heard the first shouts from the other side, and remembered they were not the only living. Going to the grassy bank they looked out over and saw the same field they themselves had tried to cross last evening. Coming across it at a run, the platoon from Baker was charging the strongpoint. Back beyond them, in full view from here, the other two platoons of B had left the ledge and were charging uphill, according to Colonel Tall's plan. And below Gaff and his men the first Baker platoon charged on, straight at them, yelling.

Whatever their reason, they were a little late. The fight was already over. Or so everyone thought. Gaff had been blowing his whistle steadily from the moment they first had gone in right up to the end of the fight, and now here came the heroes. Preparing to wave and cheer ironically and hoot derision at their "rescuers," Gaff's men were prevented by the sound of a machine gun. Directly below them in one of the apertures, a single MG opened up and began to fire at the Baker Company platoon. As Gaff's men watched incredulously, two Baker Company men went down. Charlie Dale, who was standing nearest to the door of the embrasure which was firing, leaped over with a shocked look on his face and threw a grenade down the hole. The grenade immediately came flying right back out. With strangled yells everyone hit the dirt. Fortunately, the grenade had been thrown too hard and it exploded just as it fell over the lip of the rockface, where the broadjumping Japanese had also disappeared, hurting nobody. The MG below continued to fire.

"Look out, you jerk!" Witt cried at Dale, and scrambled to his feet. Pulling the pin on a grenade and holding it with the lever depressed, he grabbed his rifle and ran over to the hole. Leaning around the right side of it, holding his rifle like a pistol in his left hand with the stock pressed against his leg, he began to fire the semi-automatic Garand into the hole. There was a yell from below. Still firing, Witt popped the grenade down the hole and ducked back. He continued to fire to confuse the occupants. Then the grenade blew up with a dull staggering roar, cutting off both the scrabble of yells and the MG, which had never stopped firing.

Immediately, others of the little force, without any necessity of orders from Gaff, began bombing out the other four holes using Witt's technique. They bombed them all, whether there was anyone in them or not. Then they called to the Baker Company platoon to come on. Later, four Japanese corpses were found huddled up or stretched out, according to their temperaments, in the small space Witt had bombed. Death had come for them and they had met it, if not particularly bravely, at least with a sense of the inevitable.

So the fight for the strongpoint was over. And without exception something new had happened to all of them. It was apparent in the smiling faces of the Baker Company platoons as they climbed up over the emplacement leaving five of their guys behind them in the kunai grass. It was apparent in the grinning face of Colonel Tall as he came striding along behind them, bamboo baton in hand. It showed in the savage happiness with which Gaff's group bombed out the empty bunkers using Witt's safety technique: one man firing while another tossed the grenades. Nobody really cared whether there was anyone in them or not. But they hoped there were hundreds. There was a joyous feeling in the safety of killing. They slapped each other on the back and grinned at each other murderously. They had finally, as Colonel Tall was later to tell newsmen and correspondents when they interviewed him, been blooded. They had, as Colonel Tall was later to say, tasted victory. They had become fighting men. They had learned that the enemy, like themselves, was killable; was defeatable.

Alligator

✕

from *Tales of the South Pacific*

by JAMES A. MICHENER

One day in November, 1942, a group of admirals met in the Navy Building, in Washington. They discussed the limited victory at Coral Sea. They estimated our chances on Guadalcanal. They progressed to other considerations, and toward the end of the meeting the officer who was serving as improvised chairman said, "We will take Kuralei!"

It was a preposterous decision. Our forces at that moment were more than a thousand enemy-held miles from Kuralei. We barely had enough planes in the Pacific to protect the Marines on Guadalcanal. Our ability to hold what we had grabbed and to digest what we held was uncertain. The outcome in the Pacific was undecided when the men in Washington agreed that next day they would take Kuralei.

Equally fantastic men in Russia made equally fantastic decisions. They forgot that Von Paulus was at the gates of Stalingrad. They were saying, "And when we have captured Warsaw, we will sweep on directly to Poznań. If necessary, we will bypass that city and strike for the Oder. That is what we will do."

And in London, Americans and British ignored Rommel at the threshold of Alexandria and reasoned calmly, "When we drive Rommel out of Tunisia, and when you Americans succeed in your African venture, we will land upon Sicily in this manner."

That each of these grandiose dreams came true is a miracle of our age. I happened to see *why* the Kuralei adventure succeeded. It was because of Alligator. I doubt if anything that I shall ever participate in again will have quite the same meaning to me. Alligator was a triumph of mind, first, and then of muscle. It was a rousing victory of the spirit, consummated in the flesh. It was to me, who saw it imperfectly and in part, a lasting proof that democratic men will ever be the equals of those who deride the system; for it was an average group of hard-working Americans who devised Alligator.

First the admirals in Washington conveyed their decision to their subordinates. "We will take Kuralei!" One of the subordinates told me that his head felt like a basket of lead when the words were spoken. "Take Kuralei!" he laughed in retrospect. "It was as silly as suggesting that we sail right in and take Rabaul, or Truk, or Palau. At that time it was a preposterous imagination."

But he and perhaps sixty other high-ranking officers set out to take Kuralei. Specialists of all branches of the service studied Kuralei day and night, to the exclusion of all else. Map-makers were called in to make complete maps of Kuralei . . . and four other islands so that no one could say for sure, "Kuralei is next." It was soon discovered that there were no maps of the island that could be trusted. Months later, lonely aircraft stole over Kuralei at great speed, and unarmed. They photographed the island . . . and four other islands, and some were never seen again. A submarine one night put six men ashore to reconnoiter a Kuralei beach. They returned. The men who crept ashore on another island did not return, but even in the moments of their darkest torture those men could not imperil the operation, for they knew nothing. In five months the first maps of Kuralei were drawn. They proved to be sixty per cent accurate. Hundreds of lives paid for each error in those maps; hundreds more live today because the maps contained so much accurate information.

The admiral in charge of providing the necessary number of destroyers for the operation studied eighteen or twenty contingencies. *If* the submarine menace abates within four months; *if* we could draw twelve destroyers from the Aleutians; *if* we had only eight carriers to protect; *if* we can insist upon using only those transports that make sixteen knots; *if* we can rely upon complete outfitting in Brisbane; *if* Camden and Seattle can finish outfitting the cruisers we need; *if* the job between here and Ascension can be turned over to destroyer escorts; *if* the African experiment needs all the destroyers allocated to it; *if* we could draw heavily upon MacArthur's fleet for the time being; *if* reports from Korea four weeks previous to D-day continue favorable as to the disposition of the Jap fleet; *if* we decide to knock out most of the shore batteries by aerial bombardment; *if* we have a margin of safety at Midway; *if* we have an air cover as powerful as we plan; *if* we can suspend all convoys south of Pearl Harbor, and so on until a truly perplexing number of possibilities had been considered. But when a man whose life has been planned to the sea, whose whole purpose for living is meeting an emergency like this, spends four months on the problem of destroyers at Kuralei, one has a right to expect a judicious decision.

The medical corps attacked their problem somewhat differently. They made a study of all amphibious landings of which there was any history. Landings by a large force, by a small force. Landings with a ground swell and in calm water. Landings with air cover and without. Landings with fierce air opposition and with moderate. Landings with no air opposition. Landings in the tropics, in the arctic, and in temperate climate. Landings with hospital ships available and with hospital ships sunk. In fact, where no experience was available to draw upon, the doctors spent hours imagining what might conceivably happen. Slowly and with much revision, they proceeded to draw up tables. "Against a beach protected by a coral reef, with a landing made at high tide against effective but harassed enemy opposition, casualties may be expected as follows . . ." Specialists went to work upon the tentative assumptions. "Of any 100 casualties suffered in this operation, it is safe to predict that the following distribution by type will be encountered." Next research doctors computed the probable percentages of leg wounds, stomach wounds, head wounds, arms shattered, faces blown away, testicles destroyed, eyes lost forever, and feet shot off. Then the hospital men took over. "It can be seen from the accompanying table that xx hospital ships with xx beds must be provided for this operation. Of the xx beds, no less than xx per cent must be adjustable beds to care for wounds in categories k through r." Next the number of surgeons required was determined, the number of corpsmen, the number of nurses and their desired distribution according to rank, the number of enterologists, head specialists, eye men, and genito-urinary consultants. The number of operating tables available was determined, as were all items of equipment. A survey was made of every available hospital and medical facility from Pearl Harbor to Perth. "By the time this operation commences, it is reasonable to assume that we shall have naval hospitals on Guadalcanal, the Russells, Munda; that we shall have increased facilities in the New Hebrides and Noumea; and that projects already under way in New Zealand and Australia will be completed. This means that at the minimum, we shall have . . ." Four medical warehouses were completely checked to see that adequate supplies of all medicines, plasma, bandages, instruments, and every conceivable medical device would be available. "If, as is reasonable to suppose, we have by that time secured an effective airstrip, say at some point like Konora, we will have available fourteen hospital planes which should be able to evacuate critically wounded men at the rate of . . ." At this point a senior naval doctor interrupted all proceedings.

"Let us now assume," he said, "that this operation is a fiasco. Let us imagine for the moment that we have twenty-five per cent casualties. That our schedule for operations is doubled. That head wounds are increased two hundred per cent. What will we do then?" So the doctors revised their tables and studied new shreds of past experience. About this time a doctor who had commanded a medical unit for the Marines on Guadalcanal returned to Washington. Eagerly, his fellow physicians shot questions at him for three days. Then they revised their estimates. A British doctor who was passing through Washington on a medical commission that would shortly go to Russia was queried for two days. He had been on Crete. Slowly, with infinite pains, ever cautiously, but with hope, the doctors built up their tables of expectancy. Long before the first ship set sail for Kuralei, almost before the long-range bombers started softening it up, the medical history of the battle was written. Like all such predictions, it was bloody and cruel and remorseless. Insofar as our casualties fell short of the doctors' fearful expectations, we would achieve a great victory. And if our losses amounted to only one half or one third of the predictions, hundreds upon hundreds of homes in the United States would know less tragedy than now they could expect to know. In such an event Admiral Kester would be able to report on the battle in those magic words: "Our losses were unexpectedly light." It was strange. The men who would make up the difference between the expected dead and the actual dead would never know that they were the lucky ones. But all the world would be richer for their having lived.

About this time it was necessary to take more and more men into the secret of Kuralei. Seven months had passed. An inspiring whisper was sweeping the Navy: "A big strike is on." Everyone heard the whisper. Stewards' mates in Australia, serving aboard some harbor tug, knew "something was up." Little Japanese boys who shined shoes in Pearl Harbor knew it, and so did the French girls who waited store in Noumea. But *where* was the strike directed? *When* was it timed to hit? More than half a year had passed since the decision had been reached. Evidences of the decision were everywhere, but the ultimate secret was still protected. A manner of referring to the secret without betraying it was now needed.

Alligator was the code word decided upon. It was the Alligator operation. Now the actual printing of schedules could proceed. Wherever possible, names were omitted. Phrases such as this appeared: "Alligator can be depended upon to suck the Japanese fleet . . ." "Alligator will need not less than twenty personnel planes during the period . . ." "Two weeks before Alligator D-day, hospitals in the area south of . . ." The compilation of specific instructions had begun. Mimeograph machines were working, and over certain offices an armed guard watched night and day. Alligator was committed.

The day upon which the Kuralei operation was named, Captain Samuel Kelley, SC, USN, left Washington for the island of Efate, in the New Hebrides. He was instructed to assume full command of all supply facilities in that area and to be prepared to service a major strike. "Nothing," he was told, "must interfere with the effective handling of this job. Our entire position in the Pacific depends upon the operation."

At the same time a captain close to Admiral King was dispatched with verbal instructions to Admiral Kester, to the top-flight officers at Pearl Harbor, and to General MacArthur. This captain did not know of Captain Kelley's commission, and the two men flew out to the South Pacific in the same plane, each wondering what the other was going to do there.

Meanwhile, in Washington plans had gone as far as they could. In minutely guarded parcels they were flown to Pearl Harbor, where Admiral Nimitz and his staff continued the work and transmuted it into their own.

No commitments had been made as to when D-day should be, but by the time the project was turned over to Admiral Nimitz, it did not look half so foolish as when it was hatched in Washington. By the time I heard of it much later, it seemed like a logical and almost inevitable move. The subtle difference is that when I saw how reasonable it was, the plan was already so far progressed that only a major catastrophe could have disrupted it. I think that therein lies the secret of modern amphibious warfare.

In Pearl Harbor the mimeograph machines worked harder and longer than they had in Washington. Day by day new chapters were added to the pre-history of Alligator. Old ones were revised or destroyed, and yet there was no printed hint as to where Alligator would strike. All that could be told for certain was that a tremendous number of ships was involved. The super-secret opening sections of Alligator had not yet been printed, nor would they be until the last few weeks before the inevitable day.

At this stage of developments I was sent to Pearl Harbor on uncertain orders. I had a suspicion that I might be traveling there in some connection or other with the impending strike. I thought it was going to be against some small island near Bougainville. For a few electric moments I thought it might even be against Kavieng. Kuralei never entered my head.

I landed at the airfield and went directly to Ford Island, where I bunked with an old friend, a Lieutenant English. Sometime later Tony Fry flew up on business, and the two of us lay in the sun, swapped scuttlebutt, and waited in one dreary office after another. Since I was a qualified messenger and had nothing to do, I was sent out to Midway with some papers connected with Alligator. The island made no impression on me. It was merely a handful of sand and rock in the dreary wastes of the Pacific. I have since thought that millions of Americans now and in the future will look upon Guadalcanal, New Georgia, and Kuralei as I looked upon Midway that very hot day. The islands which are cut upon my mind will be to others mere stretches of jungle or bits of sand. For those other men cannot be expected to know. They were not there.

Finally Tony Fry left for Segi Point, an infinitesimal spot in the Solomons. English had to go on a trip somewhere, and I was alone in the rooms on Ford Island. Young officers reported in by the hundreds in those exciting days prior to the big strike, and after brief interviews, hurried on to islands they had never heard of, to ships they had never known. I stayed, and stayed, and stayed. I did the usual things one did in Pearl Harbor, but somehow the crowds appalled me, and an evil taste never left my mouth. Other men have had similar experiences, in California, or New York, or Oklahoma. They were home, yet there was an evil taste in their mouths; for not even Chicago or Forth Worth can solace a man who has been in the islands and who knows another great strike is forming. His wife and his mother may tell him that he is home now, and order him to forget the battles, but he knows in his heart that he is not home.

It was in this mood that I reported one day to fleet headquarters. That time the call was not in vain. I was given a medium-sized briefcase, unusually heavy. I was told that if our plane went down at sea, I must throw the case into the water. It was guaranteed to sink in eight seconds. I was given a pistol, and a Marine sergeant as an armed guard. With an armed escort I was taken to a waiting airplane. Seven other officers were in the plane, and I was certain that at least one of them was a guard assigned to watch me, but which officer it was I could not ascertain.

We stopped that night at Funafuti, a speck in the ocean. Two guards were stationed at my quarters, which were shared with no one. In the morning the procedure of the previous day was repeated, and we left Funafuti, a truly dismal island, for sprawling New Caledonia.

When we were about an hour away from Noumea, where Admiral Kester had his headquarters, an unfavorable weather report was received, and we were directed to land at Plaine des Gaiacs, an airstrip some distance from Noumea. We made what I considered a pretty hazardous landing, for we were well shaken up. We had a difficult decision to make. Should we fly to Noumea in a smaller plane? Should we go down by jeep? Or should we lay over until morning? It was decided to wait an hour and to try the first alternative.

A TBF took us down, and it was then that I learned which of my fellow officers was my extra guard. It was a jay-gee who looked exactly like a bank clerk. In the crowded TBF we never acknowledged that either knew why the other was there. At Magenta we made a wretched landing, and both the jay-gee and I were obviously frightened when we left the plane. Bad weather was all about us, and we wondered how the pilot had felt his way through the clouds.

Again an armed car was waiting, and we proceeded directly to Admiral Kester's headquarters. There the admiral was waiting. Three of us, the jay-gee, the Marine, and I, presented the briefcase to him.

Admiral Kester took the case into his room and opened it. It contained a mimeographed book, eight and one-half inches by fourteen. The book contained six hundred and twelve pages, plus six mimeographed maps. The most startling thing about the book was the first page. The first sentence designated the forthcoming operation as Alligator. The second sentence was short. It said simply, "You will proceed to Kuralei and invest the island."

Slowly, like one who had acquired a Shakespeare folio after years of dreaming, Admiral Kester leafed idly through the super-secret first pages. The warships of his task force were named. The points of rendezvous indicated. The location of every ship was shown for 1200 and 2400 hours of each of the five days preceding the landings. The barrages, the formation of the landing craft, the composition of aerial bombardment, code words for various hours, radio frequencies, location of spotting points, and every other possible detail which might ensure successful operations against the enemy — all were given in the first few pages. Only the time for D-day was missing.

The admiral passed over the opening pages and dipped at random into the massive volume. Page 291: "At this time of year no hurricanes are to be expected. There is, however, record of one that struck three hundred and eighty miles southwest of Kuralei in 1897. Assuming that a hurricane does strike, it will be certain to travel from . . ."

On page 367 Kester read that "the natives on Kuralei should be presumed to be unfriendly. Long and brutal administration under the Germans was not modified by the Japanese. Instead of finding the natives opposed to Japanese rule, American forces will find them apathetic or even hostile. Under no circumstances should they be used as runners, messengers, or watchers. They should, however, be questioned if captured or if they surrender."

On page 401 the admiral was advised that fruit on Kuralei was much the same as that on islands farther south and that in accordance with the general rule of the South Pacific, "if something looks good, smells good and tastes good, eat it!"

It was on page 492 that the admiral stopped. "Casualties may be expected to be heavy. The landing on Green Beach will probably develop an enfilading fire which will be aimed high. Chest, head, and face casualties are expected to be above that in any previous operation. If barbed wire has been strung at Green Beach since the reconnoiters of December, casualties will be increased. Every precaution must be made to see that all hospital ships, field hospital units, and base hospitals in the area are adequately staffed to handle an influx of wounds in the head and chest. This is imperative."

On page 534 a clear night was predicted from the hours of 0100 on until about 0515. Depending upon D-day, the moon might or might not be bright enough to completely silhouette the fleet. It was to be noticed, however, that even a crescent moon shed enough light to accomplish that purpose. The brighter planets were sometimes sufficiently strong, in the tropics, to outline a battleship.

Admiral Kester closed the book. Alligator, it said on the brown stiff-paper cover. At that moment similar Alligators were being studied by men responsible for submarine patrols, aircraft operations, battleship dispositions, and supply. Each of the men — and it is easy to understand why — said, as he closed the book after his first cursory study of it, "Well, now it's up to me."

D-day would be selected later, and some officer-messenger like me would fly to various islands and move under heavy guard. He would, like me, be some unlikely candidate for the job, and to each copy of Alligator in circulation he would add one page. It would contain the date of D-day. From that moment on, there would be no turning back. A truly immense project would be in motion. Ships that sailed four months before from Algiers, or Bath, or San Diego would be committed to a deathless battle. Goods that had piled up on wharves in San Francisco and Sydney would be used at last. Blood plasma from a town in Arkansas would find its merciful destination. Instruments from London, salt pork from Illinois, diesel oil from Louisiana, and radio parts from a little town in Pennsylvania converged slowly upon a small island in the remote Pacific.

Men were on the move, too. From Australia, New Zealand, the Aleutians, Pearl Harbor, Port Hueneme, and more than eight hundred other places, men slowly or speedily collected at appointed spots. Marines who were sweating and cursing in Suva would soon find themselves caught in a gasping swirl which would end only upon the beach at Kuralei, or a mile inland, or, with luck, upon the topmost rock of the topmost hill.

Each of the remaining bits of gossip in this book took place after the participants were committed to Kuralei. That is why, looking back upon them now, these men do not seem so foolish in their vanities, quarrels, and pretensions. They didn't know what was about to happen to them, and they were happy in their ignorance.

The intensity, the inevitability, the grindingness of Alligator were too great for any one man to comprehend. It changed lives in every country in the world. It exacted a cost from every family in Japan and America. Babies were born and unborn because of Alligator, and because of Alligator a snub-nosed little girl in Columbia, South Carolina, who never in a hundred years would otherwise have found herself a husband, was proposed to by a Marine corporal she had met only once. He was on the first wave that hit the beach, and the night before, when he thought of the next day, he cast up in his mind all the good things he had known in life. There was Mom and Pop, and an old Ford, and Saturday nights in a little Georgia town, and being a Marine, and being a corporal, and there wasn't a hell of a lot more. But there was that little girl in Columbia, South Carolina. She was plain, but she was nice. She was the kind of a girl that sort of looked up to a fellow. So this Marine borrowed a piece of paper and wrote to that girl: *"Dear Florella, Mabe you dont no who i am i am that marine Joe Blight brot over to see you. You was very sweet to me that night Florella and i want to tell you that if i . . ."*

But he didn't. Some don't. To Florella, though, who would never be married in a hundred years anyway, that letter, plus the one the chaplain sent with it . . . well, it was almost as good as being married.

"You Can't Live Without 'Em"

ℵ

from *Battle Cry*

by LEON URIS

The small, thin and graying Army general paraded in front of the large wall map with a pointer in his hand. Brigadier General Pritchard, a fatherly-appearing man, was now the commander of all forces on Guadalcanal. Before him stood and sat an array of majors, lieutenant colonels and colonels, cigarette smoking, cigar smoking, and pipe smoking. He laid the pointer on his field desk, rubbed his eyes, and faced the men before him.

"I am extremely anxious to get this drive under way." He turned to the small group of Marine officers near the tent flap. "The Camdiv — combined Army and Marine division — will be unique in this operation. And, I might add, the Pentagon and the Navy are watching with extreme interest. This is the first real offensive of the war. There is much, as I have pointed out, that will be novel and experimental, and it will have a great bearing on future operations. We shall have a testing ground, so to speak. Naval gun-fire in support of advancing land troops, flame throwers, close air support and air reconnaissance on short objectives, to name a few new wrinkles." He picked up the pointing stick and tapped it in his hand, restlessly. "Are there any questions? No? Very well, gentlemen. All further information will be relayed through channels. We jump off at zero six four five on the tenth. Good luck to all of you."

A buzz arose from the officers as they filed out and headed for the jeeps. Sam Huxley stood by the opening until all were gone except Pritchard and his aide. Huxley shifted his helmet and approached the field desk. Pritchard looked up from a map.

"Yes?"

"Major Huxley, Second Battalion, Sixth Marines, sir."

"What is it, Huxley?"

"May I have the General's indulgence for a few minutes?"

"Something not clear, Major?"

"Everything is quite clear, sir."

"What's on your mind?"

"General Pritchard, is a suggestion out of order?"

Pritchard put down the magnifying glass and relaxed in his canvas field chair, tilting it back on its rear legs and swinging it gently. "Sit down, Major. A suggestion is never out of order in my command."

Huxley remained standing. He drew a deep breath and leaned over the desk. "General Pritchard, keep the Sixth Marines off the lines."

The General nearly fell over backwards. He caught the desk and brought the chair to a still position. "What!"

"I said, sir, don't use the Sixth Marines in this operation."

"You're way off base, Major. That is not a matter for a junior officer."

Huxley fidgeted nervously for a moment. "May I speak freely, sir?"

The General tapped his small wrinkled fingers on the field map, eyed the large rawboned man before him and said, "By all means, Huxley, say your piece."

"I believe," Huxley said, "that our senior officers are in a state of constant intoxication and don't grasp the situation. Or, perhaps they do grasp it and have decided to get intoxicated."

"Kindly get to the point."

Huxley clenched his fist, "General," he cried, "the Sixth Marines are too good to waste on this type of operation."

"I beg your pardon?"

"Do you know the history of this outfit, sir?" he rambled on quickly. "General, you command all the forces in the area. You know the situation. They are planning strikes farther up the Solomons."

"What has that to do —"

"You have ample Army forces. Two divisions and the elements of another for this drive on Guadalcanal. I beg you, General, give us an island to hit farther up the line. This Regiment is for assault. We've worked hard and we're well trained. We deserve a better break."

Pritchard smiled softly. "I know the history of the Sixth Marines quite well, Major," he said. "I was captain in the last war. A Marine corporal kept a bayonet up my butt all the way through Belleau Woods."

His appeasing humor did not seem particularly funny to Huxley. "Then give us an island, sir. You can do it. Just recommend that we be held for landing duty in the next operation."

The General's soft mood changed. "Huxley, tell me something. Do you honestly think your men are too good to tramp through the jungle for thirty miles, digging them out of caves, blowing up bunkers, and slushing through the mud? Or isn't there enough glory in it for you?"

"It's not our cup of tea, sir. You have more than enough Army. . . ."

"In other words, Huxley, the dirty grind is for the dogfaces. You'd rather have a little more blood."

Huxley turned crimson. The words stuck coming out.

"I'll answer for you, Huxley," Pritchard said. "You think you are too good to fight beside us, don't you? You think that your regiment is worth my division?"

"Exactly! There are a thousand islands out there. If the Army wants to fart around for six weeks, it's their business. We'll never get this war finished, especially if you take one of the few decent outfits you have and waste them. We're fighters, we want a beachhead."

"Suppose we let Washington figure out how long this war is going to last."

"May I leave, sir?"

"No! Sit down, dammit!" The little general drew himself to his full five-foot-seven-inch height and marched up and down before the chair where Huxley sat. "I've been damned lenient with you, Huxley. You wouldn't be so liberal with one of your own officers. War is a dirty business, Major, and one of the dirtiest things you Marines are going to have to take is orders from the Army. If you are anxious to get your head blown off, we'll get you transferred to assault some choice real estate.

"I do not know, and never will agree with your psychology of fighting this war. By using this Marine regiment, I will save more men, both yours and mine. We are going to drive to Esperance and we're going to do it slowly and surely. We'll not use men where we can use artillery, if we have to wait a month for the artillery to get there. No blood-hungry Marine is going to tell me how to run my campaign. I've warned you, Major, and I warn you again, that I don't want the Marines running a horse race down that coast. You are going to keep your flank intact and you are going to move with us. Now get back to your outfit!"

Sam Huxley arose, trembling with white anger as Pritchard returned to his desk. He glanced up. "You look as if you might blow a gasket, Major. Go on, say it."

"I am thinking, General Pritchard, that you can take the whole goddam Army and shove it you know where." He stormed from the tent.

The General's aide, who had remained silent in the wake of Huxley's anger, rushed to the General. "Surely, sir," he said, "you aren't going to let that man keep his command?"

For several moments Pritchard seemed steeped in thought. Finally he spoke. "If I fire or court-martial that Marine, there'll be hell to pay. Any co-operation we have or expect to get from the Navy will blow sky high. Thank God, we've only got a regiment of them. There's going to be a real donnybrook before this war is over. Our thinking is too far apart."

"My sympathy certainly rests with the men," the aide said, "having people like that for officers."

"I don't know," Pritchard answered, "I don't know. They're a queer breed. You and I will really never know what makes them tick. But if I was on the lines fighting for my life and I had my choice of whom I wanted on my right and my left, I'd call for a couple of Marines. I suppose they're like women . . . you can't live with 'em and God knows you can't live without 'em."

No Prisoners!

✕

from *Walk into Hell*

by RICHARD C. HUBLER

They crawled in open order, each man perhaps five yards from the other. Inching along on their elbows with their carbines cradled, using their knees to push, the wide skirmish line went forward in the jungle like the undulating body of a snake. On the sodden leaf mold which was the soil outside Sangai their progress was noiseless. In the darkness, thick as a hand laid across heaven, they could not be seen nor could they see the Japanese. They must be within a hundred yards of the camp proper, fifty yards from the clearing.

They could hear the enemy talking. The high, rising syllables and the singsong carry-overs of the voices came to them clearly. Evidently this main bivouac of the enemy had not been officially alerted. It was incredibly careless. There was the sound of metal clanking and the flicker of a torch through the leaves.

The advancing line kept on. Canadeau heard the strange sounds of the enemy before him. To him, it felt as if the whole group were in a gigantic warehouse, hearing people, strangers, talking behind the boxes which filled it — but could not see them. The Japanese voices had the same hollow echoes and ghostly quality of sounds underseas, an illusion increased by the night. They could not be more than twenty yards away.

Still they advanced. Suddenly, on Canadeau's left, there sounded a stifled pop. A thin, dripping stream of fire rose through the thin tops of the trees. The sky burst into the white brilliance of a magnesium flare. Instantly other Very pistols popped. The sky was covered with light. Canadeau saw his stark shadow before him on the ground. He stopped and cowered. So did the rest: it was the signal.

The jabbering of the Japanese was silenced. There was a rising hurry and confusion in the Sangai camp. The flares floated almost motionless above both contingents, burning with their dropping bits of flaming magnesium.

Like magic, the Japanese began to appear. *We were wrong*, thought Canadeau, as he fired desperately. *Not twenty yards; ten, at the most.* Rifles began their spasmodic chugging all along the line, the echoes of their usual definitive cracking muffled by the underbrush. The Japanese began to yell in high-pitched, meaningless shrieks. Grenades went end over end through the air, their tumbling shadows sharply defined for a second on the ground, then vanishing in a red, menacing flash. They exploded in a sound which was lost in the excitement of the hearing which could not comprehend more than had already impacted the brain.

Full in the stark light, at the thirty-foot range, the whole battle unfolded as though it were contained in a theater. The tough, green leaves, ripped from their stems by bullets and shrapnel, fell unceasingly on both sides as though it were autumn. It was noticeable that more fell on the Marines than on the Japanese. That was good: it meant the enemy was firing high.

A panting figure came running up almost beside Canadeau. The Sergeant wriggled a few feet away and kept firing. He saw from the corner of his eye that it was Burke, back to his old position in a light machine-gun squad. The little Irishman did not recognize Canadeau; it was doubtful if he saw him. He was working furiously.

He had been carrying the unmounted, perforated barrel of a light .30-caliber machine gun. Evidently there had been no time to wait for the bearer of the tripod to come up, or perhaps he had been killed. Burke, half kneeling, half standing, was bracing the gun against his own body, putting in with sure, quick hands a long belt of bullets. In a moment he raised the barrel with his left hand and pressed the trigger release.

The rattling discharge came to Canadeau dimly like a great riveting gun. He saw Burke's slight figure jerk with every report. He almost seemed caught in the convulsions of a tortured St. Vitus's dance. But he kept on firing.

At length the belt ran through. Burke dropped the machine gun. Tears were running down his face. He wore an expression of agony. Canadeau knew why: the barrel of the machine gun, after the fifth shot, had been red-hot. The flesh of Burke's left hand must have been burned in those few seconds until it looked like the crisp brown skin of a holiday turkey.

The Sergeant had no more time to see Burke. He reached for his own rifle. A bullet spatted on a rock beside him. The fragments pierced Canadeau in his wounded arm and cheek. He rolled over on his back and caught a shaking in the fronds of the palm above him. He fired, cross-shoulder, and fired again until the slender muzzle of his gun felt hot in his hand. There was a slumping weight in the palm top when he was finished. Canadeau knew it was the dead-hung corpse of the sniper, belted into his post, camouflaged by paint and fronds until he was impossible to see. He rolled back onto his belly just in time.

Burke's machine gun had been put out of action. Not by the enemy but by Burke's rapid firing: the barrel had got so heated that it was useless. There were no replacements. Canadeau saw Burke fling it away and dive headlong toward the body of a dead Marine which lay a yard from him. He fumbled with the dead man's belt. It was a demolition kit.

Canadeau knew what he wanted it for. The Japanese had some previously prepared positions on the jungle side of their encampment. They were not many but they were well placed and deadly. Most of them were deep dugouts excavated between the high, ten-foot-thick roots of the immense jungle trees.

One especially troublesome such nest was directly before them. It seemed to be full of Japanese snipers who sprang up, fired, and ducked down again. Grenades seemingly had no effect on them. The enemy either flung them back or else the explosions had apparently no effect — perhaps because of the grenade-hole trick which Canadeau and Burke had already used.

Canadeau saw a squinting face peering out of the bushes three yards from Burke, who was still working to loosen the demolition belt. It was a Japanese, his face just being contorted into the peculiar expression of a man taking infinitely careful aim. The shadows from the sinking flares added to his ghastly expression.

The Sergeant had no time for more than a quick hip shot. His bullet, sped by luck, took the Jap squarely between his eyes. He tumbled back, slowly, like a man sinking into molasses, and disappeared. Burke did not notice what had happened. His fingers flew. He had the belt free.

By this time, concentrated firepower was keeping the enemy snipers in the banyan dugout undercover except for a few stray shots. Canadeau, seeing Burke's intention, added his own fire to the others'. Burke, vainly trying to unloose a six-block unit of TNT in the belt, finally in anger lit a fuse. He made a looping toss of the whole kit of twenty-four blocks into the dugout of the enemy.

It must have been a short fuse. It exploded almost immediately, just as the flares expired. In the impenetrable darkness the flare of the TNT was like a red fan of surprising intensity. The sound was subterranean but no less deafening. Against the torched impression of the explosion on his brain, Canadeau saw the giant tree totter and begin to fall, wrenching out its cables of lianas from the trees, dragging a whole surrounding area to its destruction.

Burke's coup had destroyed not only the sniper's nest. It had also breached the whole front of the Japanese defense. Corbett must have seen it instantly. More rockets went up. Flares again lighted the sky. Canadeau heard the Colonel's voice booming: "Get moving, you bastards, get forward!" He no longer referred to his men as "gentlemen." The tree lay with its roots sprawled upward like a wall. The vines were like ropes. But it offered no shelter to the enemy. Nor did the attackers use it for cover.

The Marines and the Rangers went around both sides in an irresistible torrent. The Colonel's voice lifted them out of their scraped foxholes and sent them rushing forward. Three or four went down, jerked like dropped puppets, and lay still. More flares went up and burst in glowing arcs. The rest of the line, weaving and broken, pushed up to the margin of the Sangai camp. The odor of raw earth hit Canadeau's nostrils as he ran forward with the rest.

The charge stopped there. They dug in again. Now they were under the fire of the second line of Japanese emplacements. This seemed to be a line of heavy machine guns, rather than the lighter Nambus which they had first encountered. The bursts were longer. They came more often. The Japanese were using their heavier mortars, too.

Canadeau did not think, as he moved up with the rest, that much was to be feared from the heavier equipment of the enemy. It was not as good as their light stuff. The knee mortars, for example, were a lot better than the Japanese sixty-millimeter jobs.

For the first time he worried about Bouchard and Nina. Back in the cubby between the stalks of the sheltering banyan they were probably safe, but Canadeau could not be sure. There was the curiosity of Nina. Bouchard, despite his self-accusation of cowardice after the fight in his living room, could hardly be accounted as afraid after his work on the trail back. They would want to know what was going on.

Gouts of flames sprang up to the right and left of the Sergeant. Canadeau scrabbled into the moss and detritus under him. He could get no deeper unless he actually dug in with the entrenching tools which he did not have. He was not willing to get up on one knee and expose himself. He knew what was happening: he was being bracketed by mortar fire.

There was no reason for it. He was not a command post, an object of desire to the Japanese GQ. It was merely one of those senseless incidents which occurred in any sort of melee. The blasts of the detonating shells were coming closer. Canadeau could smell the burned powder sharply in his nose. It gagged him with the metallic taste of his fear.

As suddenly as it had begun, the barrage ceased. Perhaps they thought they had the area spotted well enough. Now that the detonations no longer deafened him, Canadeau could tell that the focus of the battle had moved even farther forward. There was only one way to tell that in the night: by the noise and the spurts of light in the jungle foliage.

Canadeau, pushing himself forward with trembling knees, came to a small crater made by a mortar shell. It was not deep. The explosions of this weapon were antipersonnel. Such a crater offered to anyone wise in the ways of artillery a shelter which was comforting in its implications. One rarely saw two craters in the same place; lightning rarely struck twice. It was a good bet to hide in the midst of the torn and still stinking earth. Canadeau crouched and peered ahead.

Their own mortars were poufing away behind them. Their shells exploded with heartening regularity in their flat blasts ahead. Canadeau wondered if the Japanese would fall back still farther and begin the usual type of Pacific fighting: the bunker-pillbox-cave kind of warfare at which the enemy had become adept. It was a problem, too, as to what they would do to the foe after they had driven them back to the beach. Such a climax might be more damaging to them than to the enemy if they were able to bring up waterborne reinforcements.

Slightly ahead and to the right of Canadeau three machine guns were being set up in the oily mud. The squads handled them like automatons. There was no hesitation; no mistakes of fitting the barrel onto the tripod. A housewife might make a mistake in the quiet of her kitchen adjusting the top of a fruit jar. Here in the jungle and battle there was nothing of the kind, even with infinitely more delicate machinery. The belts were snapped in. They began feeding through like cloth in a sewing machine.

They had been set up just in time. The Japanese were ready to attempt another charge. Their own rockets — not all of them white, some red — added to the ghastly appearance of the battle with their tinged light. The enemy uprose from every corner of the great room of the jungle ahead. Shrieking imprecations, they came on at a slipping, staggering run toward the Marines.

The machine guns rattled steadily, not increasing their tempo. The rifle fire increased in sound noticeably. Canadeau, wriggling up a little, took the position of cover for the machine guns. He fired and fired again. He had lost sight of Corbett.

The Japanese kept on. Huge gaps appeared in their shadowy ranks. Their shouting, now hoarse and incoherent, was slackening, but not their progress. Suddenly Canadeau's brain shut off the sound and fury of the attack. He saw the oncoming enemy only as cartoons, unreal caricatures in the night. The flares were fading. One came down directly before the Sergeant and struck an advancing Japanese. He had been wounded and was crawling on his hands and knees. The still burning flare landed on his back and stuck. Canadeau saw his mouth open but the scream of agony did not come to his sealed brain.

Not even the firing of his own gun penetrated to his eardrums. In the great, eerie silence of his realization, he found his sight amplified. His eyes caught gradations of sight out of his pupils' focus which were forms of the enemy in the growing night. The sputter of the machine guns and the slight flares from the firing rifles, the detonations of grenades and the muzzle blasts of mortars took over the illumination of the battle. Still Canadeau could not hear.

As quickly as it had vanished his hearing came back, just as the Japanese attack subsided for the second time. As the remnants of the enemy began to waver and fall back, there was a simultaneous rising on the left flank of the Marines' position. The Colonel must have been holding some men in reserve. What seemed to be a whole platoon to Canadeau's startled eyes and newly acute hearing sprang out of the earth. They shouted louder than the Japanese.

"God's sake, shut up!" It was one of the machine gunners on Canadeau's right. "Those sons of bitches are mad enough already!"

It was a single touch of humor, unconscious enough, in the whole macabre affair. Again the firing rose to its crescendo and more rockets went up, what must have been the last of the supply. The bazookas, somewhere forward, began their peculiar hissing like a gigantic piece of silk being torn in half. A dim illumination came through the trees.

The damn Japanese camp, thought Canadeau. *It's burning!*

The red light grew. It illumined every cranny of the jungle. Canadeau could see the Japanese falling back. As they did, he noticed, certain of the enemy troops detached themselves and scrambled up the trees like monkeys. They used their feet and their hands as if they were spurred. Their grotesque bodies disappeared quickly into the treetops.

The Marine advance stopped. The few cheers which had broken out at the burst of flame from the main camp subsided. They knew the job of those men in the trees. They were snipers, hiding to take what toll they could of the attackers.

Canadeau saw Corbett's small figure moving rapidly among the advance units. One or two of the light machine guns were trained upward, far above their normal field of fire. They began spraying in the palm tops. Others concentrated on the few thickets of mangrove which signaled the nearness of the coast. The snipers would concentrate on just such personnel as the Colonel. They had orders to pick off the key men of the enemy. Next in order in the priority of death were noncommissioned officers. Third, they picked the corpsmen.

A grenade went forward over Canadeau's head. It revolved in the air like an expertly tossed football in a forward pass. Canadeau saw it fall between four Japanese. Instantly the group flung itself to the ground like a single unit. The grenade did not explode. It was a dud.

The act seemed to have attracted the attention of most of the men around the Sergeant. Though the Japanese formed an attractive target in their momentary grouping, none had fired at them. Now, as they rolled away from the grenade, Canadeau, like the rest, turned his fire on them. He saw the bodies jerk, roll, try to stand, and collapse. All of them were killed before they could reach safety behind jutting rocks or the near-by tree trunks.

The heat of the fire in the burning Japanese camp could be almost felt, Canadeau fancied. The place was a mass of flame and explosions. Seen through the barred trunks of the trees, it presented almost a gala scene. There were little volcanoes of exploding ammunition. Bullets ricocheted aimlessly about, digging up the ground, burrowing into the trees with smacking sounds. A few rockets roared upward into the sky. The explosion flung up burning festoons of bandages into the air like serpentine on New Year's.

Canadeau, rising to a crouch, went forward in a stooping run. He had been taken with an idea. He found the Colonel with a runner, issuing hurried instructions.

"Corbett," panted Canadeau, mindful of instructions that no man was to be addressed by his title, "I've got an idea how to pin these guys right against the shore!"

"How?" Corbett had no time to greet him.

"Send around a flanking column. Take 'em in the rear, grind 'em up."

Canadeau could see the grim flicker of a smile on the Colonel's face. He started to crawl away.

Canadeau was disappointed with the kind of violent disappointment which takes a man who feels that his vital advice had been disregarded. But the next moment he discovered why the Colonel had not bothered to reply.

There was a whooping shout from the other side of the fire. The demoralized Japanese faltered. The cries were unmistakably the cries of Marines.

Canadeau himself shouted in answer. His heart was in his throat. He got up so hastily that his shoulder wound, until now quiescent with its throbbing ache barely noticed in the excitement of battle, began to send sharp stabs of pain through his body. His arm would no longer support action. Nevertheless, a three-legged beast, Canadeau went forward. Forward with the rest who were crouching and running now, as hard as they could, stooping, clambering, leaping over rocks and through the jungle masses of foliage.

The snipers were forgotten. The remaining Japanese troops were overwhelmed by the charge. Corbett's astonishingly loud voice was everywhere, cheering, exhorting, encouraging. The unmistakable sound of a bazooka, whooshing through the night, began to be heard. The conflagration's light increased.

Canadcau felt exultant and ashamed. He knew what had happened, that he ought to have trusted to the Colonel's judgment. Now he knew why the Marines he had met had seemed so few, even with the addition of Myers's forces. The whole scheme of attack came clear.

Corbett had divided his forces into two columns. One, with which Canadeau was now ducking, running, crawling ahead in its triumphant charge, was the mountain column. It had swung up into the hills, traveled along the precipitous ridge, and descended on the road. Breaking through whatever Japanese cordon it encountered, the force had swung back toward the coast.

Meanwhile, the second column had threaded its way through the sinks of the mangrove swamps and the coral reefs along the beach. The attack had been timed precisely. By H-hour the flares had gone up both as light and as a signal to the beach column. The whole expeditionary group must have been set and moved out. The Colonel was not just driving the Japanese into the sea. He had caught the camp at Sangai in a gigantic nutcracker. The enemy was the nut, caught inextricably between the two crushing attacks. Corbett had a good chance of wiping them out, barring the dozen or so that might escape by the flanks into jungle concealment.

The whole plan had been executed with consummate surprise. The enemy, it was apparent, had already dissolved into shouting, defiant components which had no longer the similitude of organized resistance. It was only a matter of minutes before they would be wiped out. *No prisoners*, thought Canadeau as he stumbled along, *no prisoners!* His thought was as savage as his instinct. He was panting for slaughter.

The Landing at Kuralei

✕

from *Tales of the South Pacific*
by JAMES A. MICHENER

Jap intelligence officers brought the colonel sixty-page and seventy-page reports of interrogations of American prisoners. They showed him detailed studies of every American landing from Guadalcanal to Konora. They had a complete book on Admiral Kester, an analysis of each action the admiral had ever commanded. At the end of his study Lieutenant Colonel Hyaichi ruled out the possibility of our landing at the promontory. "It couldn't be done," he said. "That coral shelf sticking out two hundred yards would stop anything they have."

But before the colonel submitted his recommendation that all available Jap power be concentrated at the northern bays, a workman in Detroit had a beer. After his beer this workman talked with a shoe salesman from St. Louis, who told a brother-in-law, who passed the word on to a man heading for Texas, where the news was relayed to Mexico and thence to Tokyo and Kuralei that "General Motors is building a boat that can climb over the damnedest stuff you ever saw."

Lieutenant Colonel Hyaichi tore up his notes. He told his superiors: "The Americans will land on either side of the promontory." "How can they?" he was asked. "They have new weapons," he replied. "Amphibious tanks with treads for crossing coral." Almost a year before, Admiral Nimitz had decided that when we hit Kuralei we would not land at the two bays. "We will hit the promontory. We will surprise them."

Fortunately for us, Lieutenant Colonel Hyaichi's superiors were able to ignore his conclusions. It would be folly, they said, to move defenses from the natural northern landing spots. All they would agree to was that Hyaichi might take whatever material he could find and set up secondary defenses at the promontory. How well he did his job you will see.

At 0527 our first amphibs hit the coral shelf which protruded underwater from the shore. It was high tide, and they half rode, half crawled toward land. They had reached a point twenty feet from the beach, when all hell ripped loose. Lieutenant Colonel Hyaichi's fixed guns blasted our amphibs right out of the water. Our men died in the air before they fell back into the shallow water on the coral shelf. At low tide their bodies would be found, gently wallowing in still pools of water. A few men reached shore. They walked the last twenty feet through a haze of bullets.

At 0536 our second wave reached the imaginary line twenty feet from shore. The Jap five-inch guns ripped loose. Of nine craft going in, five were sunk. Of the three hundred men in those five amphibs, more than one hundred were killed outright. Another hundred died wading to shore. But some reached shore. They formed a company, the first on Kuralei.

It was now dawn. The LCS-108 had nosed in toward the coral reef to report the landings. We sent word to the flagship. Admiral Kester started to sweat at his wrists. "Call off all landing attempts for eighteen minutes," he said.

At 0544 our ships laid down a gigantic barrage. How had they missed those five-inch guns before? How had anything lived through our previous bombardment? Many Japs didn't. But those hiding in Lieutenant Colonel Hyaichi's special pillboxes did. And they lived through this bombardment, too.

On the small beach to the west of the promontory 118 men huddled together as the shells ripped overhead. Our code for this beach was Green, for the one to the east, Red. The lone walkie-talkie on Green Beach got the orders: "Wait till the bombardment ends. Proceed to the first line of coconut trees." Before the signal man could answer, one of our short shells landed among the men. The survivors re-formed, but they had no walkie-talkie.

At 0602 the third wave of amphibs set out for the beach. The vast bombardment rode over their heads until they were onto the coral shelf. Then a shattering silence followed. It was full morning. The sun was rising. Our amphibs waddled over the coral. At the fatal twenty-foot line some Japs opened up on the amphibs. Three were destroyed. But eight got through and deposited their men ashore. Jap machine gunners and snipers tied into tall trees took a heavy toll. But our men formed and set out for the first line of coconut trees.

They were halfway to the jagged stumps when the Japs opened fire from carefully dug trenches behind the trees. Our men tried to outfight the bullets but could not. They retreated to the beach. The coconut grove was lined with fixed positions, a trench behind each row of trees.

As our men withdrew they watched a hapless amphib broach to on the coral. It hung suspended, turning slowly. A Jap shell hit it full in the middle. It rose in the air. Bodies danced violently against the rising sun and fell back dead upon the coral. "Them poor guys," the Marines on the beach said.

At 0631 American planes appeared. F6F's. They strafed the first trench until no man but a Jap could live. They bombed. They ripped Green

Beach for twelve minutes. Then the next wave of amphibs went in. The first two craft broached to and were blown to shreds of steaming metal. "How can those Japs live?" the man at my side said. In the next wave four more amphibs were sunk.

So at 0710 the big ships opened up again. They fired for twenty-eight minutes this time, concentrating their shells about sixty yards inland from the first row of coconut stumps. When they stopped, our men tried again. This time they reached the trees, but were again repulsed. Almost four hundred men were ashore now. They formed in tight circles along the edge of the beach.

At 0748 we heard the news from Red Beach, on the other side of the promontory. "Repulsed four times. First men now safely ashore!" Four times! we said to ourselves. Why, that's worse than here! It couldn't be! Yet it was, and when the tide started going out on Red Beach, the Japs pushed our men back onto the coral.

This was fantastic! When you looked at Alligator back in Noumea you knew it was going to be tough. But not like this! There were nine rows of coconut trees. Then a cacao grove. The edge of that grove was Line Albany. We had to reach the cacaos by night. We knew that an immense blockhouse of sod and stone and concrete and coconut trees would have to be reduced there before night. We were expected to start storming the blockhouse by 1045. That was the schedule.

At 1400 our men were still huddled on the beach. Kester would not withdraw them. I don't think they would have come back had he ordered them to do so. They hung on, tried to cut westward but were stopped by the cliffs, tried to cut eastward but were stopped by fixed guns on the promontory.

At 1422 Admiral Kester put into operation his alternative plan. While slim beachheads were maintained at Red and Green all available shock troops were ordered to hit the rugged western side of the promontory. We did not know if landing craft could get ashore. All we knew was that if they could land, and if they could establish a beach, and if they could cut a path for men and tanks down through the promontory, we might flank each of the present beachheads and have a chance of reaching the cacaos by dark.

At 1425 we got our orders. "LCS-108. All hands to Objective 66." The men winked at one another. They climbed into the landing barges. The man whose wife had a baby girl. The young boy who slept through his leave in Frisco. They went into the barges. The sun was starting to sink westward as they set out for shore.

Lieutenant Colonel Hyaichi's men waited. Then two fixed guns whose sole purpose was to wait for such a landing fired. Shells ripped through the barges. One with men from 108 turned in the air and crushed its men to death. They flung their arms outward and tried to fly free, but the barge caught them all. A few swam out from under. They could not touch bottom, so they swam for the shore, as they had been trained to do. Snipers shot at them. Of the few, a few reached shore. One man shook himself like a dog and started into the jungle. Another made it and cried out to a friend. "Red Beach! Green Beach! Sonova Beach!" You can see that in the official reports. "At 1430 elements from LCS-108 and the transport *Julius Kennedy* started operations at Sonova Beach."

The hidden guns on the promontory continued firing. Kester sent eight F6F's after them. They dived the emplacements and silenced one of the guns. I remember one F6F that seemed to hang for minutes over a Jap gun, pouring lead. It was uncanny. Then the plane exploded! It burst into a violent puff of red and black. Its pieces were strewn over a wide area, but they hurt no one. They were too small.

At 1448 a rear admiral reported to Kester, "Men securely ashore at Objective 66." The admiral diverted all available barges there. Sonova Beach was invaded. We lost three hundred men there, but it was invaded. Barges and men turned in the air and died alike with hot steel in their guts, but the promontory was invaded. Not all our planes nor all our ships could silence those damned Jap gunners, but Sonova Beach, that strip of bleeding coral, it was invaded.

At 1502 Admiral Kester sent four tanks ashore at Sonova with orders to penetrate the promontory and to support whichever beach seemed most promising. Two hundred men went along with axes and shovels. I watched the lumbering tanks crawl ashore and hit their first banyan trees. There was a crunching sound. I could hear it above the battle. The tanks disappeared among the trees.

At 1514 came the Japs' only airborne attack that day. About thirty bombers accompanied by forty fighters swept in from Truk. They tried for our heavy ships. The fleet threw up a wilderness of flak. Every ship in the task force opened up with its five-inchers, Bofors, Oerlikons, three-inchers and .50 calibers. The air was heavy with lead. Some Jap planes spun into the sea. I watched a bomber spouting flames along her port wing. She dived to put them out. But a second shell hit her amidships. The plane exploded and fell into the ocean in four pieces. The engine, badly afire, hit the water at an angle and ricocheted five times before it sank in hissing rage.

One of our transports was destroyed by a Jap bomb. It burst into lurid flame as it went down. Near by, a Jap plane plunged into the sea. Then, far aloft an F6F came screaming down in a mortal dive. "Jump!" a thousand voices urged. But the pilot never did. The plane crashed into the sea right behind the Jap bomber and burned.

A Jap fighter, driven low, dived at the 108 and began to strafe. I heard dull spats of lead, the firing of our own guns, and a cry. The Jap flashed past, unscathed. Men on the 108 cursed. The young skipper looked ashen with rage and hurried aft to see who had been hit.

The Japs were being driven off. As a last gesture a fighter dived into the bridge of one of our destroyers. There were four explosions. The superstructure was blown away with three dozen men and four officers. Two other fighters tried the same trick. One zoomed over the deck of a cruiser and bounced three times into a boiling sea. The other came down in a screaming vertical spin and crashed deep into the water not far from where I stood. There were underwater explosions and a violent geyser spurting high in the air.

Our planes harried the remaining Japs to death, far out at sea. Our pilots, their fuel exhausted, went into the sea themselves. Some died horribly of thirst, days later. Others were picked up almost immediately and had chicken for dinner.

While the Jap suicide planes were crashing into the midst of the fleet, a Jap shore battery opened up and hit an ammunition ship. It disintegrated in a terrible, gasping sound. Almost before the last fragments of that ship had fallen into the water, our big guns found the shore battery and destroyed it.

Meanwhile power had been building up on Green Beach. At 1544, with the sun dropping lower toward the ocean, they tried the first row of coconut trees again. They were driven back. This time, however, not quite to the coral. They held onto some good positions fifteen or twenty yards inland.

At 1557 Admiral Kester pulled them back onto the coral. For the last time that day. He sent the planes in to rout out that first trench. This time, with noses almost in the coconut stumps, our fliers roared up and down the trenches. They kept their powerful .50's aimed at the narrow slits like a woman guiding a sewing machine along a predetermined line. But the .50's stitched death.

At 1607 the planes withdrew. At a signal, every man on that beach, every one, rose and dashed for the first trench. The Japs knew they were coming, and met them with an enfilading fire. But the Green Beach boys piled on. Some fell wounded. Others died standing up and took a ghostly step toward the trench. Some dropped from fright and lay like dead men. But most went on, grunting as they met the Japs with bayonets. There was a muddled fight in the trench. Then things were quiet. Some Americans started crawling back to pick up their wounded. That meant our side had won.

Japs from the second trench tried to lead a charge against the exhausted Americans. But some foolhardy gunners from a cruiser laid down a pinpoint barrage of heavy shells. Just beyond the first trench. It was dangerous, but it worked. The Japs were blown into small pieces. Our men had time to reorganize. They were no longer on coral. They were inland. On Kuralei's earth.

At 1618 Admiral Kester made his decision. Green Beach was our main chance. To hell with Red. Hang on, Red! But everything we had was thrown at Green. It was our main chance. "Any word from the tanks?" "Beating down the peninsula, sir." It was no use banging the table. If the tanks could get through, they would.

At 1629 about a hundred amphibs sped for Green Beach. They were accompanied by a tremendous barrage that raked the western end of the beach toward the cliffs. Thirty planes strafed the Jap part of the promontory. A man beside me started yelling frantically. A Jap gun, hidden somewhere in that wreckage, was raking our amphibs. "Get that gun!" he shouted. "It's right over there!" He jumped up and down and had to urinate against the bulkhead. "Get that gun!" Two amphibs were destroyed by the gun. But more than ninety made the beach. Now, no matter how many Japs counterattacked, we had a chance to hold the first trench.

"A tank!" our lookout shouted. I looked, but saw none. Then, yes! There was a tank! But it was a Jap tank. Three of them! The Jap general had finally conceded Lieutenant Colonel Hyaichi's point. He was rushing all moveable gear to the promonotory. And our own tanks were still bogged down in the jungle.

"LCS-108! Beach yourself and use rockets!" The order came from the flagship. With crisp command the young skipper got up as much speed as possible. He drove his small craft as near the battle lines as the sea would take it. We braced ourselves and soon felt a grinding shock as we hit coral. We were beached, and our bow was pointed at the Jap tanks.

Our first round of rockets went off with a low swish and headed for the tanks. "Too high!" the skipper groaned. The barrage shot into the cacao trees. The Jap tanks bore down on our men in the first ditch. Our next round of rockets gave a long hissss. The first tank exploded loudly and blocked the way of the second Jap.

At this moment a Jap five-incher hit the 108. We heeled over to port. The men at the rocket-launching ramps raised their sights and let go with another volley. The second rank exploded. Japs climbed out of the manhole. Two of them dived into the cacaos. Two others were hit by rifle fire and hung head downward across the burning tank.

The third Jap tank stopped firing at our men in the first trench and started lobbing shells at LCS-108. Two hit us, and we lay far over on the coral. The same foolhardy gunners on the cruiser again ignored our men in the first trench. Accurately they plastered the third tank. We breathed deeply. The Japs probably had more tanks coming, but the first three were taken care of.

Our skipper surveyed his ship. It was lost. It would either be hauled off the reef and sunk or left there to rot. He felt strange. His first command! What kind of war was this? You bring a ship all the way from Norfolk to stop two tanks. On land. You purposely run your ship on a coral reef. It's crazy. He damned himself when he thought of that Jap plane flashing by. It had killed two of his men. Not one of our bullets hit that plane. It all happened so fast. "So fast!" he muttered. "This is a hell of a war!"

At 1655 the Marines in trench one, fortified by new strength from the amphibs, unpredictably dashed from the far western end of their trench and overwhelmed the Japs in the opposite part of trench two. Then ensued a terrible, hidden battle as the Marines stolidly swept down the Jap trench. We could see arms swinging above the trench, and bayonets. Finally, the men in the eastern end of trench one could stand the suspense no longer. Against the bitterest kind of enemy fire, they rushed past the second row of coconut stumps and joined their comrades. Not one Jap survived that brutal, silent, hidden struggle. Trench two was ours.

At 1659 more than a thousand Jap reinforcements arrived in the area. Not yet certain that we had committed all our strength to Green Beach, about half the Japs were sent to Red. Lieutenant Colonel Hyaichi, tight-lipped and sweating, properly evaluated our plan. He begged his commanding officer to leave only a token force at Red Beach and to throw every ounce of man and steel against Green. This was done. But as the reserves moved through the coconut grove, the skipper of the LCS-108 poured five rounds of rockets right into their middle. Results passed belief. Our men in trench two stared in frank astonishment at what the rockets accomplished. Then, shouting, they swamped the third Jap trench before it could be reinforced.

At 1722, when the sun was beginning to eat into the treetops of Kuralei, our tanks broke loose along the shore of the promontory. Sixty sweating foot-slogging axmen dragged themselves after the tanks. But ahead lay an unsurmountable barrier of rock. The commanding officer of the tanks appraised the situation correctly. He led his ménage back into the jungle. The Japs also foresaw what would happen next. They moved tank destroyers up. Ship fire destroyed them. We heard firing in the jungle.

At 1740 our position looked very uncertain. We were still six rows from Line Albany. And the Japs had their blockhouse right at the edge of the cacaos. Our chances of attaining a reasonably safe position seemed slight when a fine shout went up. One of our tanks had broken through! Alone, it dashed right for the heart of the Jap position. Two enemy tanks, hidden up to now, swept out from coconut emplacements and engaged our tank. Bracketed by shells from each side, our tank exploded. Not one man escaped.

But we soon forgot the first tank. For slowly crawling out of the jungle came the other three. Their treads were damaged. But they struggled on. When the gloating Jap tanks saw them coming, they hesitated. Then, perceiving the damage we had suffered, the Japs charged. Our tanks stood fast and fired fast. The Japs were ripped up and down. One quit the fight. Its occupants fled. The other came on to its doom. Converging fire from our three tanks caught it. Still it came. Then, with a fiery gasp, it burned up. Its crew did not even try to escape.

At 1742 eleven more of our tanks landed on Sonova Beach. You would have thought their day was just beginning. But the sun was on their tails as they grunted into the jungle like wild pigs hunting food.

An endless stream of barges hit Green Beach. How changed things were! On one wave not a single shot from shore molested them. Eight hundred Yanks on Kuralei without a casualty. How different that was! We got Admiral Kester's message: "Forty-eight minutes of daylight. A supreme effort."

At 1749 the Japs launched their big counterattack. They swept from their blockhouse in wild assault. Our rockets sped among them, but did not stop them. It was the men in trench three that stopped them.

How they did so, I don't know. Japs swarmed upon them, screaming madly. With grenades and bayonets the banzai boys did devilish work. Eighty of our men died in that grim assault. Twelve had their heads completely severed.

But in the midst of the melee, two of our three tanks broke away from the burning Jap tanks and rumbled down between trench three and trench four. Up and down that tight areaway they growled. A Jap suicide squad stopped one by setting it afire. Their torches were their own gasoline-soaked bodies. Our tankmen, caught in an inferno, tried to escape. From trench three, fifty men leaped voluntarily to help them. Our men surrounded the flaming tank. The crewmen leaped to safety. In confusion, they ran not to our lines but into trench four. Our men, seeing them cut down, went mad. They raged into trench four and killed every Jap. In a wild spontaneous sweep they swamped trench five as well!

Aboard the LCS-108 we could not believe what we had seen. For in their rear were at least a hundred and twenty Japs still fighting. At this moment reinforcements from the amphibs arrived. The Japs were caught between heavy fire. Not a man escaped. The banzai charge from the blockhouse had ended in complete rout.

At 1803 Admiral Kester sent his message: "You can do it. Twenty-seven minutes to Line Albany!" We were then four rows from the blockhouse. But we were sure that beyond trench seven no trenches had been dug. But we also knew that trenches six and seven were tougher than anything we had yet tackled. So for the last time Admiral Kester sent his beloved planes in to soften up the trenches. In the glowering dusk they roared up and down between the charred trees, hiccuping vitriol. The grim, terrible planes withdrew. There was a moment of waiting. We waited for our next assault. We waited for new tanks to stumble out of the promontory. We waited in itching dismay for that tropic night. We were so far from the blockhouse! The sun was almost sunk into the sea.

What we waited for did not come. Something else did. From our left flank, toward the cliffs, a large concentration of Jap reinforcements broke from heavy cover and attacked the space between trenches one and two. It was seen in a flash that we had inadequate troops at that point. LCS-108 and several other ships made an instantaneous decision. We threw all our fire power at the point of invasion. Rockets, five-inchers, eight-inchers and intermediate fire hit the Japs. They were stopped cold. Our lines held.

But I can still see one flight of rockets we launched that day at dusk. When the men in trench two saw the surprise attack coming on their flank, they turned sideways to face the new threat. Three Americans nearest the Japs never hesitated. Without waiting for a command to duty they leaped out of their trench to meet the enemy head on. Our rockets crashed into the advancing Japs. The three voluntary fighters were killed. By their own friends.

There was no possible escape from this tragedy. To be saved, all those men needed was less courage. It was nobody's fault but their own. Like war, rockets once launched cannot be stopped.

It was 1807. The sun was gone. The giant clouds hanging over Kuralei turned gold and crimson. Night birds started coming into the cacao grove. New Japs reported to the blockhouse for a last stand. Our own reinforcements shuddered as they stepped on dead Japs. Night hurried on.

At 1809, with guns spluttering, eight of our tanks from Sonova Beach burst out of the jungle. Four of them headed for the blockhouse. Four tore right down the alleyway between trenches five and six. These took a Jap reinforcement party head on. The fight was foul and unequal. Three Japs set fire to themselves and tried to immolate the tank crews. They were actually shot into pieces. The tanks rumbled on.

At the blockhouse it was a different story. Tank traps had been well built in that area. Our heavies could not get close to the walls. They stood off and hammered the resilient structure with shells.

"Move in the flame-throwers. Everything you have. Get the blockhouse." The orders were crisp. They reached the Marines in trench five just as the evening star became visible. Eight husky young men with nearly a hundred pounds of gear apiece climbed out of the trench. Making an exceptional target, they blazed their way across six and seven with hundreds of protectors. They drew a slanting hailstorm of enemy fire. But if one man was killed, somebody else grabbed the cumbersome machinery. In the gathering darkness they made a weird procession.

A sergeant threw up his hands and jumped. "No trenches after row seven!" A tank whirled on its right tread and rumbled over. Now, with tanks on their right and riflemen on their left, the flame-throwers advanced. From every position shells hit the blockhouse. It stood. But its defenders were driven momentarily away from the portholes. This was the moment!

With hoarse cries our flame-throwers rushed forward. Some died and fell into their own conflagration. But three flame-throwers reached the portholes. There they held their spuming fire. They burned away the oxygen of the blockhouse. They seared eyes, lips, and more than lungs. When they stepped back from the portholes, the blockhouse was ours.

Now it was night! From all sides Japs tried to infiltrate our lines. When they were successful, our men died. We would find them in the morning with their throats cut. When you found them so, all thought of sorrow for the Japs burned alive in the blockhouse was erased. They were the enemy, the cruel, remorseless, bitter enemy. And they would remain so, every man of them, until their own red sun sank like the tired sun of Kuralei.

Field headquarters were set up that night on Green Beach. I went ashore in the dark. It was strange to think that so many men had died there. In the wan moonlight the earth was white like the hair of an old woman who has seen much life. But in spots it was red, too. Even in the moonlight.

Unit leaders reported. "Colonel, that schedule for building the airstrip is busted wide open. Transport carrying LARU-8 hit. Heavy casualties." I grabbed the man's arm.

"Was that the transport that took a direct hit?" I asked.

"Yes," he said, still dazed. "Right in the belly."

"What happened?" I rattled off the names of my friends in that unit. Benoway, in the leg. The cook, dead. The old skipper, dead. "What happened to Harbison?" I asked.

The man looked up at me in the yellow light. "Are you kidding, sir?"

"No! I know the guy."

"*You* know him? Hmmm. I guess you don't! You haven't heard?" His eyes were excited.

"No."

"Harbison pulled out four days before we came north. All the time we were on Efate he couldn't talk about anything but war. 'Hold me back, fellows. I want to get at them!' But when our orders came through he got white in the face. Arranged it by airmail through his wife's father. Right now he's back in New Mexico. Rest and rehabilitation leave."

"That little Jewish photographic officer you had?" I asked, sick at the stomach.

"He's dead," the man shouted. He jumped up. "The old man's dead. The cook's dead. But Harbison is back in New Mexico." He shouted and started to cry.

"Knock it off!" a Marine colonel cried.

"The man's a shock case," I said. The colonel came over.

"Yeah. He's the guy from the transport. Fished him out of the drink. Give him some morphine. But for Christ's sake shut him up. Now where the hell *is* that extra .50-caliber ammo?"

The reports dragged in. We were exactly where Alligator said we should be. Everything according to plan. That is, all but one detail. Casualties were far above estimate. It was that bastard Hyaichi. We hadn't figured on him. We hadn't expected a Cal Tech honors graduate to be waiting for us on the very beach we wanted.

"We'll have to appoint a new beachmaster," a young officer reported to the colonel.

"Ours get it?" the colonel asked.

"Yessir. He went inland with the troops."

"Goddam it!" the colonel shouted. "I told Fry a hundred times . . ."

"It wasn't his fault, sir. Came when the Japs made that surprise attack on the flank."

There was sound of furious firing to the west. The colonel looked up.

"Well," he said. "We lost a damned good beachmaster. You take over tomorrow. And get that ammo in and up."

I grabbed the new beachmaster by the arm. "What did you say?" I whispered.

"Fry got his."

"Tony Fry?"

"Yes. You know him?"

"Yes," I said weakly. "How?"

"If you know him, you can guess." The young officer wiped his face. "His job on the beach was done. No more craft coming in. We were attacking the blockhouse. Fry followed us in. Our captain said, 'Better stay back there, lieutenant. This is Marines' work.' Fry laughed and turned back. That was when the Japs hit from the cliffs. Our own rockets wiped out some of our men. Fry grabbed a carbine. But the Japs got him right away. Two slugs in the belly. He kept plugging along. Finally fell over. Didn't even fire the carbine once."

I felt sick. "Thanks," I said.

The colonel came over to look at the man from LARU-8. He grabbed my arm. "What's the matter, son? You better take a shot of that sleeping stuff yourself," he said.

"I'm all right," I said. "I was thinking about a couple of guys."

"We all are," the colonel said. He had the sad, tired look that old men wear when they have sent young men to die.

Looking at him, I suddenly realized that I didn't give a damn about Bill Harbison. I was mad for Tony Fry. That free, kind, independent man. In my bitterness I dimly perceived what battle means. In civilian life I was ashamed until I went into uniform. In the States I was uncomfortable while others were overseas. At Noumea I thought, "The guys on Guadal! They're the heroes!" But when I reached Guadal I found that all the heroes were somewhere farther up the line. And while I sat in safety aboard the LCS-108 I knew where the heroes were. They were on Kuralei. Yet, on the beach itself only a few men ever really fought the Japs. I suddenly realized that from the farms, and towns, and cities all over America an unbroken line ran straight to the few who storm the blockhouses. No matter where along that line you stood, if you were not the man at the end of it, the ultimate man with his sweating hands upon the blockhouse, you didn't know what war was. You had only an intimation, as of a bugle blown far in the distance. You might have flashing insights, but you did not know. By the grace of God you would never know.

Alone, a stranger from these men who had hit the beaches, I went out to dig a place to sleep. Two men in a foxhole were talking. Eager for some kind of companionship, I listened in the darkness.

"Don't give me that stuff," one was saying. "Europe is twice as tough as this!"

"You talk like nuts," a younger voice retaliated. "These yellows is the toughest fighters in the world."

"I tell you not to give me that crap!" the older man repeated. "My brother was in Africa. He hit Sicily. He says the Krauts is the best all-round men in uniform!"

"Lend me your lighter." There was a pause as the younger man used the flameless lighter.

"Keep your damned head down," his friend warned.

"If the Japs is such poor stuff, why worry?"

"Like I said," the other reasoned. "Where did you see any artillery barrage today? Now if this was the Germans, that bay would of been filled with shells."

"I think I saw a lot of barges get hell," the young man argued.

"You ain't seen nothing! You mark my words. Wait till we try to hit France! I doubt we get a ship ashore. Them Krauts is plenty tough. They got mechanized, that's what they got!"

"You read too many papers!" the second Marine argued. "You think when they write up this war they won't say the Jap was the toughest soldier we ever met?"

"Look! I tell you a thousand times. We ain't met the Jap yet. Mark my words. When we finally tangle with him in some place like the Philippines . . ."

"What were we doin' today? Who was them little yellow fellows? Snow White and the Seven Dwarfs? Well, where the hell was Snow White?"

"Now wait! Now wait just a minute! Answer me one question. Just one question! Will you answer me one question?"

"Shoot!"

"No *ifs* and *ands* and *buts?*"

"Shoot!"

"All right! Now answer me one question. Was it as tough as you thought it would be?"

There was a long moment of silence. These were the men who had landed in the first wave. The young man carefully considered the facts. "No," he said.

"See what I mean?" his heckler reasoned.

"But it wasn't no pushover, neither," the young man defended himself.

"No, I didn't say it was. But it's a fact that the Nips wasn't as tough as they said. We got ashore. We got to the blockhouse. Little while ago I hear we made just about where we was expected to make."

"But on the other hand," the young Marine said, "it wasn't no picnic. Maybe it *was* as tough as I thought last night!"

"Don't give me that stuff! Last night we told each other what we thought. And it wasn't half that bad. Was it? Just a good tough tussle. I don't think these Japs is such hot stuff. Honest to God I don't!"

"You think the way the Germans surrendered in Africa makes them tougher?"

"Listen, listen. I tell you a hundred times. They was pushed to the wall. But wait till we hit France. I doubt we get a boat ashore. That's one party I sure want to miss."

There was a moment of silence. Then the young man spoke again. "Burke?" he asked. "About last night. Do you really think he'll run for a fourth term?"

"Listen! I tell you a hundred times! The American public won't stand for it. Mark my words. They won't stand for it. I thought we settled that last night!"

"But I heard Colonel Hendricks saying . . ."

"Please, Eddie! You ain't quotin' that fathead as an authority, are you?"

"He didn't do so bad gettin' us on this beach, did he?"

"Yeah, but look how he done it. A slaughter!"

"You just said it was easier than you expected."

"I was thinkin' of over there," Burke said. "Them other guys at Red Beach. Poor bastards. We did all right. But this knuckle-brain Hendricks. You know, Eddie, honest to God, if I had a full bladder I wouldn't let that guy lead me to a bathroom!"

"Yeah, maybe you're right. He's so dumb he's a colonel. That's all. A full colonel."

"Please, Eddie! We been through all that before. I got a brother wet the bed till he was eleven. He's a captain in the Army. So what? He's so dumb I wouldn't let him make change in my store. Now he's a captain! So I'm supposed to be impressed with a guy that's a colonel! He's a butcher, that's what he is. Like I tell you a hundred times, the guy don't understand tactics."

This time there was a long silence. Then Eddie spoke, enthusiastically. "Oh, boy! When I get back to Bakersfield!" Burke made no comment. Then Eddie asked, "Tell me one thing, Burke."

"Shoot."

"Do you think they softened this beach up enough before we landed?"

Burke considered a long time. Then he gave his opinion: "It's like I tell you back in Noumea. They got to learn."

"But you don't think they softened it up enough, do you, Burke?"

"Well, we could of used a few more bigs ones in there where the Japs had their guns. We could of used a few more in there."

Silence again. Then: "Burke, I was scared when we hit the beach."

"Just a rough tussle!" the older man assured him. "You thank your lucky stars you ain't goin' up against the Krauts. That's big league stuff!"

Silence and then another question: "But if the Japs is such pushovers, why you want me to stand guard tonight while you sleep?"

Burke's patience and tolerance could stand no more. "Goddammit," he muttered. "It's war! If we was fighting the Eyetalians, we'd still stand guard! Plain common sense! Call me at midnight. I'll let you get some sleep."

The Killing

✗

from *The Slot*

by JOHN CLAGETT

On December seventh, Jim Print waited in the dark by the boat. He smoked one cigarette after another. The courier boat was in and the envelope with the dope lay in the radio shack with the captains. Print fretted with the waiting, but at last he caught sight of the little group of officers walking toward him. There was no joking or laughing among them; that was bad. But then he already was sure the Express would run this night.

"Jim?" Noble said. "There you are. Okay, we've got ten of them on the way down. The airedales hit them but didn't do much good. We're all that's left, and we'll have to take them on."

He sounded serene, almost pleased, Print thought. This bird is glad about it!

The lines came in. Print had the wheel. "Take her away, Jim," Charlie said pleasantly, and the Ninety-Seven, one of the eight PT's going out to fight ten destroyers, was on her way down the harbor.

The sky held no moon and when the Ninety-Seven reached Savo Island the Bay was pitch black, and rough as well, with occasional whitecaps driving into the cockpit, and thunder sounding from the northwest. The Ninety-Seven's patrol was from the southeast corner of Savo to Cape Esperance. It was, as Charlie cheerfully told the crew, the hotspot of the evening, and they should be the first to find the enemy. At midnight, the Ninety-Seven was on a leg of the patrol course from Savo to Guadal, a half mile out from the smaller island. Noble was standing beside Print, binoculars at his eyes. The engines were purring away; no one was speaking. Not a star was showing, but the rain had stopped and there was a slight transparency to the night.

"Jim," Noble said excitedly. "I see them. They're just coming into the Bay, and we're on a good course for a shot."

"Where are they?" Print tried to match the skipper's voice.

"Just follow my glasses." Print did so, and on the dark line of the ocean he saw the fleeting, nearly invisible shapes of the invaders.

"Okay," Jim said hoarsely. "I've got them. Seven, maybe eight. All destroyers, I guess."

"Keep your glasses on them. Hill! Stay on our present course, and set the throttles for 1250 RPM, twenty knots."

"Present course, 1250 RPM, aye, aye, sir."

"Everard, broadcast this warning: 'All Preps from Prep Charlie; Scotch in water, eight of them, riding the rails. Over.'"

Print heard Everard repeating the words into the mike. Christ Almighty! he thought; what's got into Charlie? He sounds like this was some game.

"In about five minutes we'll be in position for a good bow shot," Nobel said quietly.

Sonofabitch! Print thought. Maybe you're not scared, but by God I am! I don't want to go in that close on eight destroyers. Noble's calm and easy manner was infuriating when he, Print, was shaking and scared to hell and gone.

All right, Noble whispered to himself; I got that sentence out. My voice sounded strange to me but at least I kept it steady. Wish I could say the same for my hands and my gut. Feel like I'd swallowed a tray of ice cubes and half of them stuck in my throat. He knew perfectly well that the Japs might already have seen the boat, that at any second the shells might start coming over; he knew, further, that he had to wait five minutes before arriving at a range that would give the old World War I torpedoes a chance to hit. Death was over there in those dark shapes; almost worse, mutilation was there as well. A leg torn off; arms gone; face gone; your testicles shot off. It happened more often than people liked to admit. He remembered men that he had picked up from the *Northampton* who had been gone from the waist down, just shreds of flesh and white bone below the life jackets. That was Noble's nightmare, and beside it almost nothing in the world mattered. Coward — hell yes, I'm a coward. Court-martial? Stuff it; the worst you can do is shoot me cleanly dead. Medals and pretty ribbons? Hell with them. But something he couldn't understand kept him standing there with his glasses at his eyes, watching the Japs; kept him from changing course, from speeding up to get in quicker, from slowing down to reduce the wake. He was pushing on each foot to keep his knees from shaking. He didn't know what it was that kept him fast. Maybe it was memory of his terror when the motors failed; maybe it was, far behind him, the warm bed with the soft flesh and the love he had to be worthy of. Maybe even it was Jim Print, who stood there like a rock, glasses to his eyes, his voice steady and quiet. Christ! Noble thought; I envy Jim his courage.

Noble didn't change the course; he set the torpedo director for a range of 600 yards and kept going. He had the sights lined up, and as soon as the bow of the first destroyer came into view over the notch he would fire torpedoes, put the rudder hard right, and try to sneak away. It was impossible that the Japs didn't see them, they were getting so close. Noble closed his hands on the grab rail until they hurt; he bit his lips, he held in physically the cold and growing turmoil in his belly. Print, right beside him, was softly whistling "The Old Chisholm Trail." That lucky sonofabitch, to be born without nerves! Noble was getting sick. He was going to vomit. . . . Wait! There. Coming close.

"Stand by!" Noble said, and Print unlocked the firing circuit.

Notch, foresight, and destroyer lined up; Noble held on to composure and ordered:

"Fire one! Fire two!"

The boat jolted; a heavy whoosh sounded from starboard and port, and with a clang and rasp of metal the two long, dark shapes shot out of the tubes and splashed heavily into the water. Powder-smoke and the stench of hot oil blew over Noble.

"Fire three! Fire four!"

One torpedo splashed into the water, but there was no sign of the other.

"Percussion!" Noble rasped and heard the thwock of Stern's mallet on the firing-pin again and again. Hell with that fish!

"Hard left rudder!" Noble grated, still hanging on. He heard the exhaled breaths of everyone around him. Still the Jap line came on, dark and silent. The Ninety-Seven was forever turning; now she was parallel to the enemy, now and at last heading away from them at right angles. Jim pointed and Noble saw another PT, a hundred yards away, also coming around in a turn. So two sets of fish must be under way toward the enemy. Now the Ninety-Seven was all the way around. How Noble yearned to take a chance and throw off mufflers, shove the throttles forward as far as they would go, build up speed, and get away. He couldn't stand this much longer. . . .

An orange light glowed alongside the leading Jap destroyer. Noble stared back at her, open-mouthed with suspense. The orange glow grew, expanded, climbed, and with it a high column of black and white water. Orange glow became vivid flash, then flame, and the volcanic upsurge illuminated the long gray vessel beneath it, and briefly, the careening shapes of the others astern. The white column of water fell back into the sea but the flames still climbed. The sound of the explosion was low and rumbling and Noble could feel it in his body, quivering up from the disturbed ocean. He gazed stupidly around his boat; he expected the crew to be shouting with joy, yet in each face that he could see by the light of the burning ship he found only the stunned apprehension that small boys might feel, on finding that their campfire had spread all over the vacant lot. The Ninety-Seven was close, too damned close; the second destroyer in line sparkled redly, viciously, fore and aft; elevated trains rushed toward Noble and shell spouts were flung from the water halfway between the two retreating PT's.

Noble signaled the mufflers off; then gently but steadily he shoved the throttles forward. Lightened of her torpedoes, and as if weary of muffled creeping, the Ninety-Seven stuck her nose up and tore through the water as Noble ordered Hill to turn hard right toward the shell spouts. The other boat had done the same, and the two PT's came within ten yards of each other for a brief instant. The next shell struck to port, so close that Noble could hear the sharp crack of the splitting air, and something smacked viciously into the bow of his boat. He pushed Hill from the wheel and started zigzagging. With his free hand he drew his forty-five and fired two shots into the air — the signal for smoke. Behind the Ninety-Seven guns were thundering all along the Japanese column, and Noble felt each crash in his belly; but it was better now that he was running at full speed, doing something. . . . Where the hell was the smoke? Hadn't Sterns heard his signal? Noble looked aft again and cried out with relief at sight of the funnel of white smoke boiling up from the wake.

The moment of greatest danger came as Noble swung hard left, running perpendicular to the previous course, with the boat's location made perfectly evident by the moving, forward end of the rising wall of smoke. But at this speed he didn't need to hold the course long. One shell came close as he swung right again, reversing course, going behind the smoke screen, holding this reversed course until the boat reached the center of it. Then he turned away from the enemy and streaked it for the southernmost end of Savo. Behind him, the wall of smoke billowed slowly upward, illuminated by enemy searchlights. They could not see the PT at all, and no shells were even close any more.

"Thank God for that smoke!" Print gasped.

Noble didn't answer; he had to devote all his energies to keeping his knees stiff. The boys were yelling now, and he heard snatches of exultant chatter. He should throttle down now, put on mufflers, and creep, but he wanted so damned badly to be out of the action area. Savo was just off the port bow, and the Ninety-Seven was beginning to swing around the point to safety.

"*Watch out!*" Print screamed. "Charlie, LOOK!"

Dead ahead, 300 yards away, just rounding the southern end of Savo, was a Jap destroyer. The enemy had sent a sleeper south of Savo in hopes of doing just what had been done. Noble spun the wheel madly, the boat careened and skidded through the water, dragging her long tail of wake and smoke around in a 180-degree turn.

Whrramm! went the destroyer's bow gun, and a white splash climbed into the air, so close that the concussion jarred Noble's feet from the deck of the boat. The PT was still making smoke, and Noble had the throttles wedged against the forward end of their quadrants, praying for more speed. Back the PT streaked, heading northwest now, only a hundred yards from Savo's beaches, with the destroyer after her like a hawk. The smoke was billowing up and blinding the Jap gun crew forward; otherwise the Ninety-Seven would have been finished, for the enemy kept up a heavy fire through the smoke. Tracers swept forward through the smoke, passing over and around the Ninety-Seven, making spaced rows of white in the water.

"Depth charges!" Noble shouted, and Jim lunged out of the cockpit. As he did so, the Jap searchlight came on, and she was so close that the light seemed high in the sky, as if coming from a two-story building from across a street. From its high position the light beam just skimmed the top of the smoke and settled on the PT. Christ! Noble could have counted the individual hairs on the backs of his hands; the light seemed to burn, he was so exposed. He glanced back and in the light saw Print and Sterns kick a depth charge over the side, just as the gunners commenced firing at the light. It all happened at once: the bath of light, the splashing depth charges, and the roll and spaced rattle of the twin fifties and the 20-mm. The destroyer's bow gun fired again through the smoke, the PT's tracers found the bridge, and the light went out. Then, even in the new dark, Noble saw the heaven-reaching pillars of white water from the two depth charges rising just off the destroyer's bow, and felt the concussion of the water's turmoil.

"I'll bet that shook up his sake for him!" Hill shouted. The destroyer fell farther behind now, still wrapped in smoke, but Noble's relief was brief. From out in the bay, the still-moving column of the enemy, now well past the burning hulk of their leader, opened fire on the Ninety-Seven. Marked by the spreading smoke behind and outlined against the dark island, with her tracers fanning backward toward the destroyer, the PT made a good target. Spouts rose before her bows, shells slammed into the wake, once, Noble was sure, hitting alongside and bouncing over his head. Shells exploded in the surf and among the palm trees ashore. The long enemy line was a winking, snapping stream of fire. The Ninety-Seven needed four minutes to run the length of Savo and gain relative safety, but in that moment Noble lost all hope of making it.

Jim was back in the cockpit clutching Noble's arm; he could hear his exec cursing; anyway, no more whistling, Noble thought savagely. Noble was cutting the land close, terribly close, for he wasn't going to waste any distance. At forty-five knots, the land streamed past; the boat's wake lay in the outer surf, she was so close. The mountain echoed back the sound of the engines and the crack of gunfire. The boat rocked violently in the ridged white surf that caught her abeam. Noble held his breath, wondering wildly what it was like to have a shell explode beneath your feet; surely at any second they would get it. The air was a rushing wall; white spray streamed over him, blinding him. Which would it be? A coral rock tearing out the bottom, or a bursting shell?

A point of land jutted out ahead; Noble swung left to increase clearance, slamming by the point so close that for a moment he thought he was lost, and whirled around the point, fishtailing inward. Another point ahead; the Ninety-Seven tore around it, with the trees and rocks a blur of motion as from a railway window at night, and, unbelievably, the boat was around the end of the island and safe! The firing died away, noise cut off suddenly by the shoulder of the mountain.

"We made it!" Print gasped. Noble was beyond speech or feeling in that moment, drowned in a vast relief. He kept the engines at full speed, and pulled himself together.

"Keep a close watch on that point," he ordered. "He may still be after us." He dragged out the forty-five and signaled to Sterns to stop making smoke. For an endlessly long space of time the boat roared on through the black waters toward the northeast.

"Guess he didn't follow us, Charlie," Print said at last. "No sign of him."

Print's relief was plain in his voice, and the skipper was sure that his own showed equally clearly.

"Good. Now watch the other end of the island. They might send another sleeper around."

For another three minutes Noble maintained speed, taking the boat well clear of the battleground before dropping the engines down to 1200 RPM and ringing for the mufflers. Silence blessedly flowed over the Ninety-Seven. Noble's knees were so weak that he gave the wheel to Hill and climbed to his under-way seat, remaining there nerveless and limp, his head rolling on his shoulders with the motion of the boat. The crew was very quiet. "Jesus Christ!" Noble heard Johnson say in a pained voice. Hill took out a handkerchief and mopped his face, keeping one hand on the wheel. Print turned around and looked up at Noble, his face a blur in the darkness.

"Charlie," he said. "Skipper, I guess we got us a destroyer."

It was only then that the cheering started. Noble brought his attention back to the radio; he had been barely conscious of its constant uproar and interchange while the Ninety-Seven was being chased around the island; now it was relatively quiet, perhaps because of Savo's blanketing influence. Then he heard Ollie reporting to base that the Japs had pulled out without landing troops, leaving one destroyer behind and taking a cripple with them. Noble slid down to the deck and picked up the mike.

"Prep Ollie from Prep Charlie," he said. "I have Bakered, I have Bakered. Request permission to take a drink of rye whiskey. Over."

"Prep Charlie from Prep Ollie. Affirmative, boy, and I do mean affirmative. You can paint a scalp on your cockpit, bud. Over."

"Okay, boys." Noble had to speak loudly to break through their cheering. We've got no boats down and no survivors to worry about, so let's go home."

The bow swung, and the Ninety-Seven went over the rippled, clutching waters, going home to safety and rest.

The Sacrificed Regiment

✕

by WILLIAM CHAMBERLAIN

The night came down, bringing a dusty breeze which blew from the south, and bringing white moonlight which washed across the escarpment to spill against the rough shapes of the mountains beyond. It touched the scrub with a gray sheen and caressed the sad ghosts of burned-out tanks and lingered over the broken ground where Task Force George lay, resting and licking its wounds and waiting. For what it waited, Task Force George didn't know. Didn't care much. It was enough that it rested for a little while.

The task-force commander's CP was in a trailer parked above one of the countless *wadis* — dry stream beds — which fanned down into the broken plain which Task Force George had crossed that day. Not in a roaring, sledging dash as the books said. No, foot by bloody foot and yard by bloody yard.

And now the infantry clung to the broken ground at the edge of the hills and the tanks huddled in the shelter of the *wadis* while Task Force George hung grimly onto the ground that it had bought so dearly. For tomorrow Rommel's legions would come slamming in again. That was the way it went.

Mark Stringer was thinking of this as he went on toward the general's CP absently slapping his riding crop against his booted leg — for he was a man who still clung to the dress to which he had become accustomed through the years. A dry, brief-spoken officer with the lean frame of a cavalryman who wore the thirty years of his service easily. Gray had marked his temples with a heavy brush and the habit of command had marked his mouth, leaving it thin and a little impatient — and a little sad. Colonel Mark Stringer, Class of '14.

The general was waiting for him in front of the trailer's hooded doorway; he led the way in. There was a bunk at one end, neatly made up and covered with a gray blanket with the West Point mark in the center. A map table which folded down. A gasoline lantern and two folding chairs and a helmet and a gas mask and a belted pistol hanging from hooks. The general waved to one of the chairs.

"Sit down, Mark," he said. "I'm glad you came."

He took a bottle from a trunk locker beneath the bunk and poured small drinks into two tumblers; he handed one to Mark, then sat on the bunk, turning the other glass in his fingers. He and Mark had once roomed together, but that was a long time ago and a lot of water had gone under the bridge since then.

Mark said, "Well, Jim," and they drank.

The general sighed heavily and placed his empty glass on the map table. He was a big man, with a face heavily lined, and his manner was oddly diffident.

"I just heard about Bill," he said. "I'm sorry, Mark. Have you any details?"

Mark shook his head. "Not many. He was leading an assault wave when his tank took a direct hit from an Eighty-eight. It burned," he said, his voice betraying nothing — not even the fierce pride which tempered his grief a little. "That's about all, Jim."

The general nodded and a silence fell between them for a little. They were remembering the same things, Mark thought absently. Things in the past. That day — thirty years gone now — when together they had reported in at old Fort Manley. Two new second lieutenants, eager and faintly scared, and with their brides with them.

And they were seeing Bill again as he had toddled about the quarters which they had shared during that school year at Ripley. Or watching Bill, towheaded and eleven, on the day that he had won the junior jumping event at Fort McArdle. Many posts and many memories, but a long time ago now.

The general laid a hand on Mark's shoulder for a moment; then poured another small drink into the glasses. "I'm sorry, Mark," he said, and both knew that the subject was closed. It had to be that way with Task Force George clinging to the edge of the mountains and another red day even now in the making.

Then the general said, "How's The Regiment, Mark?" and the tension eased in Mark a little.

"As it's always been, Jim," he said.

They both understood that, for The Regiment — they had thought of it in capitals since their second-lieutenant days — had been home to both of them for more than half the years of their service. And they remembered it as it had been at first. Guidons fluttering in the wind and troop horses dancing and sabers clattering above the singing of the trumpets as the squadrons passed in review. It was a grimmer, less glamorous regiment now, roaring along in steel-hulled machines. But still The Regiment.

The general's face had settled back into heavy lines as he got up and pulled a map toward him across the table. "How about your casualties today, Mark?" he asked.

"Heavy," Mark told him. "Not crippling. We can still fight."

A captain put his head through the blackout curtain in the doorway and the general beckoned him in. "What have you got, Eddie?" he asked. "Mark, you know Eddie Herdon, my S-2?"

Mark nodded and the captain gave him a quick, harried look and spread a paper on the map table. "The air report, sir," he said to the general. "It just came in. I thought you ought to see it."

The general picked it up in his thick fingers; studied it for a long moment and then nodded. "What we were afraid of," he said. "It's confirmation that they're moving up a fresh tank outfit. How soon can they get to the Sidi Behr side of the pass, Eddie?"

"By about eight o'clock tomorrow morning, sir."

The general nodded again. "O.K., Eddie. Nothing more that you can do right now. Get some sleep."

The captain went on back into the night and the general tapped the paper with his fingers for a moment before he turned back to Mark. "Things are fouled up, Mark," he said. "Bad."

"I guessed it," Mark told him. "What happened, Jim?"

The general spread his big hands a little. "Poor intelligence, I guess. A snafu somewhere up the line. Task Force George was supposed to make an end run — get through the pass fast and clear the way for the corps attack day after tomorrow. There was supposed to be nothing in front of us except weak Italian outposts. Well, you saw what we ran up against today."

"I saw," Mark agreed, tight-lipped.

"We ran smack into two of their crack divisions," the general went on, half to himself. "Germans, not Eyeties. Task Force George got itself a bloody nose today, Mark. It's liable to get worse than that tomorrow. Look here."

He leaned over to put a big finger on the map. "That report that Eddie just brought indicates that they're concentrating a fresh regiment of armor here at Sidi Behr. You heard what he said — they can close in there by eight o'clock tomorrow."

Mark said nothing — there was nothing to say — as the general fell silent for a moment. Both of them knew well enough what would happen if that fresh regiment came roaring through Sidi Behr pass to slam into Task Force George. It could be bad — very bad.

A sergeant came to the door of the trailer and put his head through the curtain. "Would the general like some coffee, sir?" he asked, and the general carefully put the report down.

"Why, yes," he said. "Please, Hoskins."

The sergeant came in and placed two mugs on the table, taking care to keep them clear of the maps, and poured coffee that was black and steaming. Mark waited until the man was gone.

He said then, "The Regiment can take care of that concentration, Jim. That'll ease your pressure here."

The general picked up the thick mug and looked at Mark across the brim. "How, Mark?" he asked.

Mark Stringer bent over the map to trace a line with his finger. "There's a smaller pass north of Sidi Behr," he said. "One of my reconnaissance parties discovered it an hour ago. It's bad going, but I think I can get the tanks through — hit the Germans at Sidi Behr tomorrow before they get organized."

The general sat for a long moment, sipping his coffee and staring at the map while the lines deepened in his face. The gasoline lantern burned with a drowsy hiss and outside a battery was firing with a steady *thump* . . . *thump* . . . *thump*.

"It's a long chance, Mark," the general said at last. "It would be a devil of a march — a devil of a fight if you got through. You'd have to run naked. No supply vehicles. No rear echelon. No nothing — just tanks and the gas that they can carry."

"I know that," Mark said tightly.

"That's the only way you could possibly get through in time." The general stopped again: he looked at his empty cup and put it down. "And there'd be no help coming up from behind, Mark. Likely Task Force George will be fighting for its life here in front of the pass. The Regiment will be out into the blue."

"It's one of those things," Mark said, clipping his words a little. "Do you know of any better scheme, Jim?"

The general placed his hands flat on the map and stared at them, and Mark knew the things that were going through the other's mind. He believed that he was sending The Regiment out to die — as part of a sister regiment had once died on the Little Big Horn. He was sending it straight into the middle of Rommel's army on a mission from which it had scant chance to return.

"Can you get through, Mark?" he asked at last.

"We'll get through."

The general's face suddenly hardened and he stood up, a big man with a tired stoop to his shoulders. "All right, Mark," he said. "I guess I've got no choice. You know that I'm sending you beyond the point of no return."

Quick anger suddenly ran through Mark and, for a fleeting second, he saw The Regiment as he had first seen it thirty years ago — guidons snapping and troop horses dancing.

"There's no such thing as a point of no return in The Regiment, Jim," he said, his voice harsh. "We'll go through the pass and we'll come back." He wheeled and went out into the moonlight.

Back at his CP he issued orders to his battalion commanders and his staff in a clipped, precise voice, and saw the sudden shock flow over their faces as they began to realize the thing that he was telling them to do. His own face hardened. These officers were not Old Army. They were men who had been clerks, teachers, businessmen a year, two years ago. They did not understand that this thing was up to The Regiment. That, nasty or not, The Regiment did its job. But they had to learn those things.

"Those are my orders, gentlemen," he said, clipping his words again. "Are there any questions?"

Handy, commanding the second battalion, moved forward a little, his face set. "As I understand it, sir, we're going through the pass with nothing but the tanks?"

"That's right," Mark said.

"And we're going to fight after we get through?"

"Major," Mark said, "this Regiment has only one reason for being. That is to fight. It has been fighting now for a hundred years. It will fight again tomorrow."

Handy's face got a little red and the others shuffled their feet uneasily, glancing at Mark out of the corners of their eyes. They didn't quite understand this lean, fierce man. There was an inner fire which burned in his face and awed them a little; scared them at the same time. And there was still memory of that wicked fight this morning. Uneasy anticipation of tomorrow's battle.

"It seems like a long chance —" Handy began, but his voice trailed away and he wished that he hadn't spoken.

Mark slapped his riding crop against his boot and looked at them, gathered in front of him in the moonlight. Around him, the night was filled with the rumble of tank engines. Farther away that lone battery still fired.

"Gentlemen," he said, and his voice was oddly gentle now, "I do not assume that any task is impossible to this Regiment. Our mission is vital to Task Force George. The Regiment is the only unit that is capable of performing it. That is why I volunteered — volunteered, gentlemen — to make the march through the pass."

He stopped for a moment, looking at them, and through the moonlight their faces seemed to grow older, more assured. Faintly he thought that he could see the stamp of The Regiment begin to set itself on their lips.

"We will go through the pass alone," he added finally. "We will fight whatever stands in our way. We will come back. If there are no further questions, that is all, gentlemen."

They went away through the moonlight and Handy talked with his adjutant as they went. "It doesn't make sense!" he said violently. "He's throwing the outfit away! Volunteered! A flea couldn't get through that damned pass — let alone fight afterwards! What do we use for gas when our tanks are empty? Tell me that!"

"I left my crystal ball back home in the States," the adjutant said. "How would I know what makes a West Pointer tick?"

Handy kicked viciously at a stone in his path. "Well, this washes up a good outfit," he said bitterly. "It's been nice knowing you, Pete."

Two men sat with their backs against the treads of their tank — Betty Ann — and spooned beans out of C-ration cans while they talked in desultory voices. The night was full of noises around them — the uneasy sounds made by many men and vehicles moving restlessly at their chores: the clank of cans as gas tanks were filled; the distressed roaring of a stalled truck; the steady thump of a battery firing from the shelter of the hill.

Corporal Coombs, the tank driver, tossed his empty can away. He was lanky and redheaded and just past twenty. Grease had smeared his face in clownish markings, but his eyes were bright and untroubled as he fished for a cigarette. He had none.

"Heck of a note," he said cheerfully. "Cigarette me, Denny. How can a man fight a war without a smoke?"

Dennison, the gunner, passed a pack across in the moonlight. He was ten years older than Coombs — a dark, intense man with eyes set far back into his head. He had been studying music before a war had come to snatch him away from his piano and drop him down here among the dray *wadis* of Tunisia.

"It's a symphony," he said under his breath. "There's a great chord running through it if a man could only write it down."

Coombs got his cigarette lighted and looked curiously at his companion. "What's a great chord running through?" he asked.

Dennison made a vague gesture toward the moonlight. "That. All of that out there. Don't you hear it?"

"I hear it all right," Coombs said cheerfully. "And you can have it. You can have all of it, Denny boy. I'll give you my share. Just say the word."

"It's alive," Dennison said. "All music must live or else it isn't music. It's just sound without meaning. This is real."

"My old man used to be a musician," Coombs said dreamily. "He played the accordion. Just let him get a skinful of red wine and he'd play your leg off."

A sergeant, the tank commander, came through the shadows. "Up off your duffs," he said heavily. "We're movin' out."

"Where to, Sarge?" Coombs wanted to know.

The sergeant spat. "How should I know where to? They don't ask me where I want to go. They just tell me."

"Maybe we got a choice," Coombs said, struggling to his feet. "Me, I want to go back to San Francisco. Can you arrange it, Sarge?"

"Climb into the can," the sergeant said. "I'm fresh out of tickets to San Francisco right now."

Mark Stringer came through the moonlight, and the three men stiffened as he stopped in front of them; stood for a moment, slapping the crop against his boot. There was a thin flintiness in his face, but his voice was vaguely gentle as he spoke.

"How are things?" he asked.

"O.K., sir — I guess," the tank commander said. "We're just loadin' up, Colonel."

"You've done well today," Mark Stringer said. "The Regiment has done well. I expected that. I'm not surprised."

"Yes, sir," the sergeant said vaguely.

"Good luck!" Mark said abruptly and wheeled away through the mottled shadows. The three stared after him.

"Old Hell on Wheels, himself," Coombs said finally. "Now what do you suppose he was stopping to pass the time of day with us for? The only time he ever spoke to me before was to chew my head off once because Betty Ann was stuck in a ditch."

"He's all right," Dennison said mildly. "He can hear the music in all this. I could see the look in his eyes."

Corporal Coombs snorted and spat. "How crazy can you get?" he asked. "All that old goat ever heard is bugles. I know about him — the sergeant major was telling me one day back in the States. He's been in this Regiment since he was a pup. I'll bet that he used to chase Indians with it back in the days when it still had horses. I don't trust that kind, Mac. They get you into trouble."

"Load up. Load up," the sergeant said in his heavy voice. "Maybe he's got things on his mind. His kid was killed this morning when we come up over the escarpment."

"Everybody's got to die," Coombs said stubbornly. "Even colonels' sons. You sure we ain't going back to San Francisco, Sarge? My mamma would be glad to see me."

A hooded lantern burned dimly in the CP trailer as Mark entered. Edison Merritt, his executive, was there, bending over the map table. A dry, humorless man who had been a statistician before the war. Mark liked him.

"The regiment will be ready to roll in a half hour, sir," Merritt said. "The battalions have all checked in."

Mark nodded. "You'll stay here with the echelon, Edison," he said, and began to buckle on his equipment with practiced fingers. "I'll go with the column."

"I don't like it, sir," Merritt said suddenly. "Heaven knows, I'm no soldier; I'm a statistician. Figures are the only things that I know, but figures are sure. They give you the right answers when you add them up — and these don't add up."

Mark smiled faintly as he settled his pistol on his hip. "What doesn't add up, Edison?"

"Nothing adds up. Going through the pass this way. The Air Force boys have got a word for it. You're reaching for the point of no return, sir. If anything goes wrong, you won't come back."

Odd, Mark thought, that his executive should use the same phrase that the general had used. He turned it over in his mind — apt words, he decided. The point of no return. But just words. Words to describe a chimera, a hobgoblin — and a thing which The Regiment didn't know. It would return.

"We'll come back, Edison," he said and went on out to where Lieutenant Simms, his assistant S-3, was waiting with the jeep.

The racket of engines made a steady roar above the scrub now and the night was full of the snuffling of steel machines as the tanks moved into formation. A quick thrill went through Mark and he paused for a moment to listen. He could feel The Regiment gathering itself like a great cat in the moonlight.

Bud Simms, bright and eager as a new blade, turned his head and grinned as Mark slid into the jeep beside him. "Sounds swell, doesn't it, sir?" he said.

Mark smiled faintly, shoving away the sudden stab which Simms's youthful face reawakened in him. Bill had used to grin like that. "Let's go, Bud," he said.

They passed the point where the lead battalion waited and Mark swung his arm in a gesture long unused. "Forward!" he said, and knew that his words were lost in the growling clatter of the engines, but it didn't matter.

It was good, he thought, to be riding here at the head of the column again, his squadron — no, it was battalions now, wasn't it? — strung out behind him. In his mind's eye he could see them, but the moonlight played tricks. He could swear that guidons fluttered there and horses tossed their heads.

It was an hour later when they left the escarpment and turned into the black gut which opened in the hills. A chill wind had freshened and it whipped against Mark's face as he sat in the jeep and watched The Regiment go by to be swallowed up in the canyon.

They marched well, Mark thought, pride tugging at him. But then The Regiment had always marched well. Fought well too. The big tanks lumbered on by, snorting angrily as they tipped and swayed over the broken ground. Squat and deadly shadows with the last of the moonlight sliding along the slender barrels of the guns. There were gaps in The Regiment, Mark knew with that sudden stab of pain again, but the gaps had closed and it marched whole again.

Bud Simms said softly, "That's an outfit, sir. The devil himself couldn't stop it."

Mark nodded and looked at the watch on his wrist. Two hours until midnight. They must debouch onto the plains above Sidi Behr by daylight if they were to fight with an even chance of success. So little time.

"Can you get back to the head of the column, Bud?" he asked, clipping his words again.

"I can take this bucket anywhere, sir," Bud Simms answered, and they lurched forward into the shadows again.

Moonlight didn't reach down here as they worked their way deeper into the maw of the pass, and that was good, Mark thought. It hid them from eyes which might pry from the air. The narrow walls threw back the roar of the engines, so that the night was filled with a pulsing, growling thunder. Chunks of rock, fallen from the walls above, blocked the way, and the tanks wound a tortuous way through them, weaving back and forth, but always going forward.

The hands of Mark's watch passed midnight; went steadily on. Bud Simms, silent now, clung grimly to the wheel of the pitching jeep as he leaned far forward to follow the uncertain track. A great slide of detritus blocked them for a half hour, and Mark waited patiently while men labored and swore in the darkness below. Then the lead tank snorted to the top, tipped down the far side and the column went on again. More slides, but the column went on.

Dawn was beginning to break as the column neared the mouth of the pass and ran into the roadblock. There was a sudden spatter of fire and Mark Stringer heard the nasty sound of bullets whining off the rocks above him. Bud Simms spun the jeep away into the safety of the boulders as the leading tanks came up — deployed with hatches buttoned down. The steady *wham . . . wham . . . wham* of their guns was like a giant beating a drum in the morning.

It was over quickly and a few men in the uniforms of Italy were scrambling away through the rocks with the hungry bullets of the machine guns reaching for them. Then the column was on the march again, tanks ghostly in the morning mist as the pass began to widen. A half hour later the plains of Sidi Behr lay in front, with the distant town dimly white on its hill as it guarded the mouth of the big pass ten miles away.

Mark halted the column in the shelter of the canyon; he dismounted from the jeep and sent word back for the battalion commanders to join him. Weariness possessed him suddenly as he waited, slapping his riding crop against his boot, and an uncertainty, alien to him, began to nag at his mind with a little rat's gnaw of worry.

The gas in the tanks would be almost gone now, he thought, and the general's words came back to him. What was that expression that he had used? The point of no return? Confound it, why weren't people more careful with their words? And yet that meant something, didn't it? Suppose he flung The Regiment at that white town on the hill and they didn't go through?

Suppose the time came — this afternoon, tonight, tomorrow morning — when the gas tanks ran dry and the ammunition was gone? When The Regiment lay helpless while it died? And it was his responsibility. His alone. Suddenly he felt very lonely standing there. His was the decision.

They could dig the tanks in here at the mouth of the pass — stop anything that tried to come through — and still get back if things went too badly. Nobody would blame him for such a decision. There was such a thing as a point of no return. Perhaps he had been stupid. A pigheaded old fool who had been deluded by his pride.

But that would not save Task Force George. That would not stop the German armor from piling through the big pass to slam into men already fought out. The chill wind suddenly caressed his face, and he squared his shoulders as the doubts blew away. He had brought The Regiment here to do a job and, by heaven, the job was going to be done! Back in the pass he seemed to see guidons fluttering through the mist where The Regiment waited.

The battalion commanders came up, faces grease-streaked and weary in the dawn. Tiredness in their eyes, but something else there too. The grim satisfaction of men who have accomplished half of a nasty job; who do not flinch from the nastier half to follow. Quick pride in them welled up in Mark as he stepped forward.

"Sidi Behr is there, gentlemen," he said, turning a little to point with his riding crop. "If our intelligence is right, the Germans will reach there in about two hours. We'll be there first."

He paused for a moment; then went on in his clipped, dry voice. Details of the approach. Details of the attack. Formations. Not much. Not much needed for an attack which would be, in its stark reality, an old-fashioned cavalry charge. Mark paused again, not finished, and Handy asked, "How about your CP, sir? Where will it be?"

Mark didn't answer for a moment as he allowed his eyes to turn back to where The Regiment waited. Then he said, his voice flat, "At the head of the assault column, Bert. . . . Are there any other questions, gentlemen? Very well, we'll move out."

The Regiment marched out of the pass, fanned out into its three approach columns as the tanks started their run for the white houses of the town which squatted on its hill. The mists burned away, and Mark, watching through his glasses, knew suddenly that young Eddie Herdon had been wrong in his estimate as to the time it would take the Germans to reach Sidi Behr. They were on its hill already, their armor lying back in wait.

Well, no matter, The Regiment would go on. In war you didn't waste time crying over such things.

The battalions were deploying along the lip of the *wadi* which Mark had named as a line of departure, when the first fire came from the town twenty minutes later. Black shell bursts suddenly gushed in the morning and the air carried the wicked *spang* of the 88's. The air attack came a moment later. One moment the sky was empty — blue with the peace of a new day. Then it was full of screaming dive bombers whose bullets marched viciously across the sand and whose bombs made stinking geysers in the morning. They were gone presently, but they had left their mark behind.

Off to the left a tank burned, pouring clouds of greasy smoke into the sky. Two others were slewed around with their treads trailing behind them like the broken legs of wounded men. Machine-gun bullets had shattered the jeep's windshield and Mark sat very still in his seat, a hand pressed to his side while pain bit into him like a white-hot iron. His mind was suddenly very clear, its perceptions reaching out with grasping fingers.

He saw that the German armor was fanning out from Sidi Behr now. Saw that The Regiment had halted in confusion on the *wadi's* lip. Saw that Bud Simms was looking at him with eyes which were scared.

"You're hit, sir!" Bud Simms was saying in a voice which was shocked and disbelieving. "You've been hit!"

"Signal The Regiment to move into the attack," Mark said, keeping his teeth shut tightly as he clung to the jeep's rail. "Then get me out in front there, Bud."

Bud Simms spoke cryptic words into the radio transmitter. Then swung the jeep toward the shelter of a rocky hill which rose to the left. "I'll get you over there behind the rocks where I can have a look at —"

"Get me out in front, Bud!"

"Sir —" Bud Simms began desperately, but Mark's voice, thin and slashing as a steel blade, stopped him. "Bud! Take me out in front!"

He could see the tanks, like fat black bugs, wavering on the lip of the *wadi* while the shells burst among them. The jeep was pulling out in front now, and he knew that the tankers saw him as he waved an arm, clinging to the jeep's rail and gritting his teeth against the pain. Then The Regiment was rolling forward, guns yammering and spinning tracks pawing at the sand. . . .

As The Regiment had gone forward at Monterrey, he thought hazily. And at Gettysburg and in the Valley of Virginia. The way that it had charged through the steaming cogon grass of Mindanao and across the deserts of Mexico and past the painted buttes of the Dakotas.

The white walls of the town on the hill were dancing crazily now, but the jeep was rocking on toward it, and he knew, through the waves of pain which flowed through him, that young Bud Simms was yelling hoarsely and that The Regiment was steaming forward with the resistless sweep of an ocean roller. He could see the guidons fluttering above it in the wind. His Regiment. There would never be a better.

It was nearly dark when consciousness came back into Mark Stringer. He was lying in a house with a shattered wall through which the last of the daylight came, and Edison Merritt was on one knee beside him. Bandages swathed his chest and a young medico was standing to one side, talking with the battalion commanders.

"How do you feel, sir?" Edison Merritt was asking with an eager urgency in his voice. "The doc says you'll be O.K."

"The Regiment?" Mark asked, the words in a whisper.

"It's all right, sir. You gave the Germans a devil of a beating. They pulled south and Task Force George is on its way through the pass now. I brought the echelon on through the north pass."

Mark let his breath go out in a faint sigh and warmth and gladness flowed swiftly into him. His eyes wandered to where the battalion commanders talked, their voices low and the grime of battle still on them. Clerks and schoolteachers and businessmen, he thought with a stark clarity. Soldiers. They were a part of The Regiment — good men — and The Regiment was proud of them.

He lifted his voice so that it carried through the shadows. "Well done, gentlemen," he said clearly. "Very well done. It is the sort of thing that is expected of The Regiment."

Below the town, Corporal Coombs leaned against the hull of his tank and pushed the damp hair out of his eyes. "Cigarette me, boy," he said to Dennison. "I've had a busy day. A very busy day, indeed. That colonel of ours is a hard man, Denny."

"A good man," Dennison said slowly. "He could have been a great musician. I could see that in his eyes."

"He blew the bugles today all right," Corporal Coombs agreed. "He blew 'em hard."

The War Machine

Ӿ

from *E Company*

by FRANK O'ROURKE

Spring came, and the war machine rolled into high gear. Tunisia was surrounded on land by English, Americans, and French. On the sea, never resting, the British Navy patrolled the coasts and was suspicious even of the fish. In the air the planes, gathered together over the winter, roamed the skies and poured over the Germans, their bomb bays opening many times. Captain Dobbs felt the change of tempo, the turning of the tide. Company E was in the advance again, but this time they waited for orders that proposed the most daring gamble of the war.

The general was sending a vast number of men from the south to the north, to catch the Germans with their pants down, drive through the last layers of hills, and come down on Cape Bon for a flying finish. To do this they had to accomplish something that had never been done before, some-thing the logistical experts said should never be attempted — send one army, with all its equipment, across the communication line of another army. But they crossed, and not one hour was lost in the crossing.

Captain Dobbs led Company E, bolstered with a few new replacements he didn't know yet, into position for the last drive. A Lieutenant Harvey had the 1st Platoon, a quiet boy who listened to the advice of Sergeant Maas, now platoon sergeant, and used his head to think with and not to stare at things in the sky. They came up on the line, and across the valley was the enemy, still waiting, weaker now, his claws dulled, but still waiting. The play was coming to the climax; the last-act curtain was going up. This time the orchestra would play a very loud tune, Dobbs knew, with the artillery doing a lot of trumpeting and the planes heavy with the kettle-drums. He was glad he wasn't a German; they were going to get the surprise of their life.

Hickman had his story all ready but for one thing. He wanted to hear these men talk about their love for each other, for the Company, for the things they stood for. He tried once to feel them out, but they would not talk this way. They did not talk about these feelings. Men do not do that;

they would be embarrassed and call themselves and anyone who mentioned such things damned sentimental fools. But they thought, and in the thinking small bits of that love came out: like giving away one cigarette when you had two left, or asking, "Joe, you want some help with that?" or reading their letters to some guy who didn't get one. This had happened to the Company, and Dobbs, feeling it, remembered the old story about the invisible bonds being stronger than all the chains in the world. It was an extraordinary thing that had happened, and perhaps no one realized it more acutely than Max Hickman. The correspondent had stayed with them, eaten with them, slept with them, got wet and cold and hungry with them, prayed with them. Oh, yes, they prayed. Not out loud, maybe, but inside, where a man keeps counsel with his own soul.

Hickman could see this story, and he was sorry he had not been with them from the very beginning, so he could better piece together their friendships and loves and hates, know how they had started back at MacIntosh, where they had drilled, sweated, and worked together. He tried to pick up a little more from Bixler, but it was hard to do. And he was tired; fifty-two is not an age adapted to the punishment they were taking. But his never-ending curiosity to know them and be with them made him stick along; it made him go with Hennessy's platoon to the hill that night because he had never been in a night attack.

Lieutenant Hennessy went up the hill and met a company of Germans, and the fight was something no man liked to remember. They drove the Germans halfway down the reverse slope and held them there, but more Germans came up and kept smashing at the hilltop, throwing grenades and laying mortar fire and sneaking up close on their bellies. Hennessy finally ordered what was left of the platoon — eight men — back to the Company on the next ridge. They refused to go. He ordered them; so they pulled out, crying and swearing, and Hennessy stayed behind on the hill. He looked around, and two guys were still there beside him, watching for movement on the reverse slope. Hennessy told them to get the hell out of there, were their ears stopped up so they couldn't hear an order?

Dobbs got the rest from Reed. Hennessy had known the hill had to be held at all costs until morning. He told them to get out, and then he recognized Smith and Reed, the goldbrick twins. Smith said, "There's no rank up here, sir. I'm staying."

A grenade rolled into the rocks between them, and Hennessy threw it back just in time. It blew ten feet down the hill, splattering them with dirt and rock chips. Reed said, "I can't take this," and ran down the hill. Smith stayed.

They fought it out all night long on that hill, and when morning came and the Company drove up and over, flanked by tanks, they found thirty-seven dead Germans on the reverse slope and on the hill. Hennessy was on his stomach, shot several times through the chest. Smith lived long enough to whisper something to Captain Dobbs. He said, "Sir, tell a girl named Brinky that Lieutenant Hennessy said the phonograph ran down." Smith coughed, and the medic wiped his mouth. He said, "I tried to make up for the craps." Then he died.

They found Max Hickman on the hill and wondered at the smile on his face. They had liked him a lot, and this hurt them a great deal more than most of them cared to admit, even though he wasn't a member of the Company.

Captain Dobbs and the Company went on, over the hills, fighting through the country that was so worthless yet meant so much. When Dobbs got a breather he wrote Hennessy's mother, and Sergeant Debler came over and asked if he could write to Smith's folks in Kansas City and tell them about Smitty. Debler said, "Is Reed all right?" and Dobbs said, "He'll be okay. He turned out pretty good, didn't he, Sergeant?" Reed had been in the first assault wave that came up the hill that morning; he had fought like a madman and was shot three times in the legs. He was in the hospital now.

Debler said, "Yes, sir. He's a lot better than some folks thought he was. He's a lot too good for some others I know."

Dobbs sent Max Hickman's typewriter and duffel to the place directed. He put a little note inside the typewriter. It read: "We were proud to have Max Hickman with us. He was every inch a soldier and a man." He signed it, " 'E' Company."

Sergeant MacDonald spoke to no one for two days after Hennessy's death. He stalked about his kitchen, his face lined with grief, his hands moving convulsively toward the knives and cleavers. The afternoon before the Company attacked another hill, Sergeant MacDonald said, "Sandy, I'm going up there and get in one lick if it kills me. I got to get one guy for Lieutenant Hennessy, just one guy or I'll bust."

Sandy said, "Go on, Mac. I'll take care of things."

"And don't be thinking you're gonna be mess sergeant," MacDonald growled. "I'll be back in the morning, and you better have things going."

So MacDonald, knowing little about guns and nothing about fighting, sneaked up to the Company assembly area in dark coveralls and, when no one was looking, grabbed a rifle and followed Lieutenant Frick's platoon into the night. He didn't know where he was going, but he wanted to get there fast.

The hill was just a number on the maps, but it was the bloodiest fight of the African campaign; it was an ugly mound of dirt and rock, with a stone fence running diagonally across its rump, very little cover on the top, and an old hut on the forward slope. It was the key to the advance; it had to be taken. Company E got the assignment.

Captain Dobbs wrote a letter to his wife the night before they left. He knew that a lot of men had written these letters on other occasions like this, but he was unashamed in writing, writing what he honestly thought would be his last letter to Mary. He tried to tell her how he felt, how he loved her, and that if she got this he wouldn't be coming back. He gave the letter to Sergeant Dorset, who was recovering from the flesh wound he got at the Kasserine, with instructions for mailing.

"You won't need this, sir," Dorset said. "I'll see you in the morning."

"I hope so," Dobbs said. "Good-by, Dorset."

Dorset said, "Good luck, sir."

Lieutenant Svenson moved in with him as they waited for the hour. Svenson said, "We've seen a lot, sir."

Dobbs put his arm around Svenson's shoulders, looking at the big man's face. "Take care of yourself, Oscar," he said tersely. "This may be rough."

"The last stand," Svenson said. "We bust 'em now, they're done."

Dobbs said, "You got something there. Come on, let's be at it."

It was dark when they moved out, and Dobbs didn't have a chance to see the old faces; he wanted to, badly, to smile and shake hands and wish them luck. But it was dark and they were on their way. He moved out, with Sergeant McKay a shadow beside him, always there, always ready for any command. The four runners from the platoons were behind them, indistinct shapes in the night.

They moved up the hill and went into it. Dobbs thought about his men and the enemy as he fought, thinking how here, at last, were the men of one nation with all their beliefs, against the men of another nation, fanatically educated to their twisted, warped ideals. It was a bitter, vicious fight that night, a fight of more than man against man: it was everything in their country against everything in that other country, all piled up and ready to be judged on this night.

When morning finally got around to showing itself, as Debler said weakly, bleeding from four flesh wounds, they had the hill. Company E had reached out for that which it had prepared itself for, and taken it. The training, the work, the maneuvers, the bitching and love and hate had been absorbed for this task, and, having been absorbed, the men had used it bravely and well. They had done their job.

There was no other way to express it, Dobbs thought. They had done their job. He was on the hill when the attack moved around them and passed them by, with Germans breaking everywhere and pulling out.

Lieutenant Colonel Spinner and Major McBride found him there, his right arm in a sling, his head cut, reading McKay's report. He was groggy and not altogether certain he was really alive.

"You did it, Dobbs," Spinner said.

"Yes, sir," Dobbs said. "We did it."

McBride said, "It's all over but the shouting. We'll have 'em in a few days."

Dobbs read the report. Svenson on the way to the hospital with ten slugs in his legs. Sergeants Mason, Hastings, and Hanson dead. Twenty-seven privates missing, dead and wounded. Fifteen more men scarcely fit to go on. He looked up and said, "Sir, Company E is about wiped out. I guess you'd better reorganize."

Those were the words he had never thought he would have to say; so much lay behind saying them.

"Yes," Spinner said. "Don't think about it, Dobbs."

"We've got to go, Colonel," McBride said softly.

Dobbs stood up and they shook hands, gravely, Dobbs with his left hand, and Spinner said, "I'll see you tonight. Bring the Company forward to the new CP. I'll have orders waiting as soon as I get to Regiment and find out what the hell is going on. This is so big and so fast we can't keep up with it."

Sergeant Dorset met Dobbs with the letter in his hands. He was close to crying, he was so happy. He said, "I told you we could tear this up, sir."

Dobbs said, "Tear it up, Dorset."

Dorset tore the letter into a hundred pieces and threw the pieces into the air. He said, "You know what that crazy MacDonald did last night, sir?"

Dobbs said, "What now? Wreck the kitchen truck?"

Dorset said, "Hell, no. He grabbed a rifle and sneaked up there with you. Sergeant Gleason told me he got six of them and was going strong at the end, so blamed mad he was swinging that rifle like a butcher knife at everybody and anything. He's back with the kitchen train now, telling Sandy how to win a war."

"I'm glad he feels better," Dobbs said. "Get some paper, Dorset. Mc-Kay, you got a pen? We've got a lot of letters to write."

When the finish came, so suddenly it caught Von Arnim and the German High Command flat-footed, Captain Dobbs had the Company in a bivouac area outside of Tunis. There were forty-three men in the Company now; half of them were sick, and some of them had small cuts and wounds not bad enough to be taken back to a hospital. They sat around in little groups and talked about furloughs and rest and swimming and beer; and Dobbs walked among them twice a day and talked about the weather. The only trouble was, it was nice every day.

Promenade in North Africa

✂

from *The Gallery*
by JOHN HORNE BURNS

I remember the Sixth General Hospital in Casablanca. It was stuck, as they seem to stick all hospitals, in a school with large windows and many floors. Its doctors and its nurses were mostly from New England, so that the place had an air of efficiency and cold kindness that struck me strange in Casa. The nurses lived in a high apartment like a silo. The GI's had a tent area near Parc Lyautey. On one side was a clearing of French tanks drawn up in rows, the way military force is deceptive and orderly — on review. Between the tanks and the tents there was a cement road where the French used to walk arm in arm in the evenings. Ward boys and dental technicians leaned over their barbed-wire enclosure on nights when they weren't on duty. They called out to all and sundry, as though they felt it necessary to reaffirm their being in a strange land. Their tents were pyramidal. In the daytime the flaps were tucked up, and I could see the mosquito netting looped up over the frames of the cots in a tight ball.

I remember that the nurses at the Sixth General Hospital were plumper and saltier than most ANC's. They talked wistfully of Boston and Taunton and Waltham and Cambridge and Worcester. Army general hospitals are incestuous. They're like a little town in which everyone spies on everyone else, and everyone dates everyone else. The surgical captain has his favorite nurse, while the anesthetist looks on and gnashes his teeth. The patients are well cared for, but they're outside the charmed circle; they're like guests at a summer hotel in the Adirondacks. They never get to see the inside. They lie on their beds and watch the life of the general hospital. They're not a part of it at all, unless some nurse takes a fancy to them on her ward, or some doctor bucking for his majority takes a special interest in their rare disease.

The main ward at the Sixth General was the biggest in the whole world. They'd taken over a lumber shed and a printing plant, and the beds just went on and on. In those acres of beds they could have laid all the sick and wounded of the war. I remember lying in my bed in this ward. I had the GI's because I'd neglected to scald my mess gear with one soapy and two clear. My illness gave me a time schedule all my own. I'd feel the dry spasms of peristalsis in my belly and I'd go tearing to the latrine. Everything came out of me in an agony over which I had no control. Then I'd go back to bed, cured of everything, including my energy and the will to live. Two hours later it would happen all over again. I turned from side to side under my mosquito netting and watched the going and comings on the big ward, the visits, the flirtations. I envied the Georgia ward boys for the easy way they had with the doctors and nurses, the kidding, the rushes with the bedpan, and the goose-necked jars of amber. And because I was an ambulatory patient, I had to make my own bed every morning.

I remember best one of the nurses. She told us to call her Butch. She was from Dorchester and she was the biggest gal I'd ever seen. When she bent over to take my temperature, I thought from her wide breasts and bulging belly that a witty and motherly cow was ministering to me. We loved the lieutenant for her laugh that was cynical and rich. She specialized in making the appendix patients laugh until they all but burst their stitches. There was a smell of cologne and soap about her. One night she had a baby on the stairs of the nurses' quarters. The colonel had to deliver her himself; it was the first time he'd practiced obstetrics in thirty years. He was so mad at her for waking him out of a sound sleep that he shipped her and her baby back from Casa to the States. We smiled in our beds, for after she'd cared for us all, she now had something all her own to love. A parachutist in a near-by bed bet that an Ayrab was the father, but none of us laughed. We were ashamed of the parachutist and devoted to the lieutenant. She'd been the nurse of the Sixth General who'd mitigated for us the somber impersonal excellence of army medical care. She'd had a good word for each of us. Often when we couldn't sleep in the Casablanca nights, she'd given us that pink pill. A truck driver three beds over said that if he ever got back to Boston alive, he'd take out our lieutenant and her baby and set them up to supper and drinks. He added that women like the lieutenant are the salt of the earth.

I remember also the nut ward of the Sixth General in Casa. Not that I was ever in there, except for a visit. It was called the Parker House after the nice old psychiatrist in charge of it. Lieutenant Colonel Parker never knew why so many people smiled at him on the streets of Casablanca. He kept the nuts in a separate building, locked and grated and barred and remote from the other buildings of the Sixth General. Beaucoup GI's and officers ended up in the Parker House. From there they usually went home on a boat, under guard. The officers and GI's were together in one ward. I guessed that when you went off your trolley, you didn't care much whether your insignia was a bar or a stripe.

I remember going to the Parker House to visit a buddy who blew up after a week's sitting and staring at the wall of his tent. He took his tommy gun and fired it at the canvas. Then he lay, after he'd fired his bursts, in a slit trench of his own making until our major came:

"What are you trying to do, Perkins, k-k-k-kill us all?"

And Perkins was taken to the Parker House. It was his theory that his heart was going to stop in the very next minute. Old Colonel Parker told him there was nothing the matter with his heart. Still he moaned and stared at the wall for hours on end. He wasn't the same, I remember, when I went to see him the last night before they shipped him back to the States. He sat on a bench with his head in his hands. He was wearing GI pajamas and a red bathrobe with 6TH GEN HOSP stenciled on the back. They'd taken away the belt of his bathrobe so he couldn't strangle himself. But when he saw me outside the grating, all his apathy dropped, and he came over and hung on the bars, smiling and cavorting, like a monkey praying to be fed.

"They're ZI-ing me. It's one way to get out of all this crap."

He told me about the new truth drug they gave him, and he wondered what he'd talked about under its influence.

"Just like you do when you get crocked," I said reassuringly.

"Well, anyway, I'm getting out of all this crap," he said over and over.

After a while the MP told me I must go. The MP's at the Parker House were a strange gang, gentle and gangling and tender. They used to kid the nuts, and they told me on my way out that many people outside in the army were crazier than some locked up in here.

I remember that outside on the streets of Casa I wondered which of us would go next to the Parker House. I got lower and lower because I knew Perkins wasn't just pretending. So finally I went into the Select Bar and started throwing them down. I got bluer and bluer in spite of the phonograph playing "L'ombre s'enfuit" and the luscious Casablancaise hanging over her cash register and the pigs sitting buxomly on the green leather chairs and waiting till I'd buy them a drink. It was a new sort of drunkenness I hit that evening. I seemed to be a ghost in a roomful of yelling people, all aliver than I.

When they threw me out of the Select at closing time, I lurched through the streets of Casa and got lost. I'd go a few blocks, lean against a doorway, black out, come to, and then blunder on again. It was the only time I'd ever wanted to meet an MP. Once I came to and looked up to see the stars of Casa flickering. I was lying on my back in the rue, and an Ayrab was bending over me. He was removing my cigarettes and franc notes from my pockets. I began to laugh in my stupor as I thought of the GI legend that the Ayrabs will cut off your balls and sew them in your mouth. I laughed although the cognac had paralyzed me. The Ayrab stopped his frisking and kissed me on the forehead.

"Je cherche ce soir un copain du genre féminin."

And knowing I was about to black out again, I gathered up all my forces and yelled. The Ayrab fled laughing into the blue shadows. I remember being trussed into the MP wagon. And I remember waking in an immaculate bed at the Sixth General.

"I want Lieutenant Duffy to give me a pink pill."

"Oh hush your mouth," the nurse said, reversing my ice pack. "You're still as drunk as a skunk."

I remember when it came our turn to go in the forty-by-eights. We sat by the long stubby train in the freight yards of Casa, swatting flies. The officer in charge of the movement bustled about counting noses. We lay on our barracks bags swigging from our canteens.

"This is it. We're going to Italy to fight."

"Ah, blow it. . . . I figure we're going to Oran or Algiers for more of this base section life."

I remember that our officers had two cars of their own up front. We were put with all our equipment into the open latticed horsecars. Guard details were posted in each car. Through the slats the Ayrabs could stick their fingers and remove anything, for we heard that the train went through Morocco at a speed less than a man could run. We made our beds on the floor, where there were still leavings of hay.

I remember how strange and autonomous it was to scud slowly through Morocco in a boxcar. At one end we had a pile of C-rations and a gasoline can of water. On the floor were our packs and blankets. We slept like a litter of kittens. The brown cleft hills swam slowly past; I sat on a ledge with my legs swinging. The crap games started up. The train would stop in the middle of desert spaces where there was nothing to halt for. And Ayrab kids would come out of the nowhere as though they'd inched up from the sand. With them, since we'd been red-lined for months, we did a thriving trade in mattress covers, shirts, and trousers. They brought us vin rouge in leather bottles. At night, lying on the floor, it was hard to sleep. In the moonlight the sandy hummocks drifted past as though I watched them from a magic carpet. Or sometimes I remember that the duty officer would come to our car when the train was taking on water. He wore fatigues and carried his carbine slung on his shoulder. After six months in Casa he figured that these were genuine combat conditions. Who knew but what the Ayrabs would ambush us all by the full of the moon when we were stalled out in the middle of nowhere?

"Remember it's a court-martial offense to sell anything to the Ayrabs, men."

"Yessir," we said in chorus.

In his barracks bag the mess sergeant had beaucoup vin that he'd laid in before we left Casa. He had also a small spirit lamp, a present from his last shackjob. He was a Polack hunky and knew all the angles. He knew how to lick around officers with a bold obsequiousness that made them think he was treating them as a rough and ready equal. With us he was like an SS man in the movies. When drunk, which was always, he'd knock our heads together and let loose on us a stream of obscenities. He said that these phrases excited a shackjob 'more than loving words. Then when we were black and blue, he'd fall into a sort of motherliness towards us and make coffee. He was in his element in that forty-by-eight. Made us bring him his breakfast box of K-ration as he lay yawning in his sack. His buddy the second cook Jacobowski was growing a mustache on the trip.

I remember the sorrows of our officers in their two wagons-lit up front. The French locomotive sooted all over the cars so that they had to sit all day with their windows closed while they read their cases or did crossword puzzles. Our officers fell into types. The Sporting Set had their musette bags full of rum and didn't come out of their haze till we hit Algiers. The Girls had pneumatic mattresses which they inflated every evening at sundown. On the second day out of Casa the officers ordered the French engineer to put their cars at the end of the train. Said they were tired of looking like Negroes. But French engineers take orders from no one but Maréchal Pétain.

Outside of Oran at Mostaganem I remember we stopped on a siding near Prisoner of War Enclosure 131. Shipping to Algiers were all Italian officer P/W who'd decided that they were no longer fascist but wanted to collaborate with us Allies. We got out of our forty-by-eights and stretched our legs. We were warned by the duty officer that we mustn't fraternize with the P/W.

"Fraternize, my arse," the mess sergeant said after the officer had gone. "Who wants to fraternize with an Eyetie? They fired on our boys in Africa, didn't they? And they're doin it now in Italy."

"They did it because they were told to," the pfc said.

He was a liberal and wore horn-rimmed spectacles.

"I say, put the bastards against a wall," the mess sergeant said.

He always shouted his opinions.

"You forget the Geneva Convention," the pfc said gently.

"Sure, we treat em white!" the mess sergeant said, looking at his buddy Jacobowski. "So in twenty years they can declare war on us again. What have they got to lose? They'll live better'n they did in the Eyetalian Army. . . . Friggin wops . . . Dagos . . ."

"Polack," the pfc said, almost inaudibly.

I remember how the Italian officers approached their cars with the MP guards. I thought of the Guineas of Brooklyn and Joisey City with their pimpled faces and their oiled hair and the aggressive spite that made them boxers and corner toughs. For I'd never seen anything of the Italian Army except the explosive tiny Sicilians from Camp 101 who used to wait in the officers' messes of Casa.

"Christ!" screamed the mess sergeant, waving his lumpy fists. "They're gettin parlor cars!"

"The Geneva Convention," the pfc prompted under his breath.

"Those Ginso bastards are gettin parlor cars while we sleep like pigs in a forty-by-eight! Will someone please tell me what this goddam war is about?"

We walked a little closer to have a look at the Italian officers, waiting to mount the train with their gear.

"Gosh, they *are* good-looking men," the company clerk said.

He read the poems in *Stars and Stripes*.

I remember that the Italians struck me with marveling. They looked neither like movie gangsters nor like the sad barbers of Brooklyn. These carried themselves with a certain soft proudness, though I remember arrogant ones among them. A few were blond. But nearly all wore a delicacy of feature and a dignity I'd never seen before. Their noses and their mouths had a different look than Americans'. The Bersaglieri officers had sugarloaf caps with feathers in them. The Alpini officers wore shorts that showed their fine long legs, like the limbs on wrestlers in old statues. And all had sewed, below the left shoulder, a metal boot.

"Well, Musso did all right in his men," the company clerk said.

"Wait till we see the wimmin," the mess sergeant promised. "I'm keepin my C-ration till we get to Italy. Those Ginso signorinas will do anything for food."

"Damn good-looking guys," a corporal said. "But I s'pose they'd put a knife in your back as quick as they'd look at you."

I remember that one of our officers talked Italian. His old man had left Naples and had made a mint in the meat-packing business in Chicago. This was the moment Lieutenant Figarotta'd been sweating out for years, a chance to crap all over the folks from the old country. He stepped forward and offered a cigarette to an officer of the Alpini. When the officer reached out with a smile and a bow, Lieutenant Figarotta tittered and twitched the cigarette out of reach. The Italian officer flushed and stood at rigid attention. This scene angered some of us.

"If you ask me," the pfc with glasses said, "they make some of our officers look sick."

But no one had asked him.

"Pretty boys, ain't they?" the mess sergeant ranted to his following, but not too loudly. "How'd ya like to have ya sisters goin' out on dates with them? Because that's exactly what them P/W are doin' back in the States. And our wimmin are fassenated with that Dago stuff."

And I remember that, as he was getting into his car, a captain of the

Bersaglieri dropped his portfolio at my feet. I hesitated an instant, then I bent and picked it up and handed it to him.

"Grazie infinite," he said.

There was something old and warm in his voice such as I'd never heard before. I felt that beyond all pretense he liked me, that he was lonely and lost. On his lip was a neat mustache. He had clear gray eyes behind lashes longer than any I'd ever seen, except those that girls buy in the five and ten. His breath was sweet. He wavered an instant before me, then vaulted into his car.

The Italian officers hung out of the windows of their cars, talking excitedly to one another like vacationists on an excursion train. Most had blue-gray caps like Mussolini's, with the earflaps tied up over their heads. Some waved cordially to the MP's.

"Addio al reticolato, a quel benedetto recinto!" one called.

The mess sergeant was beside himself with fury. He raved at all the cars of Italian officers:

"If ya hadn't declared war on us, I wouldn't be here lookin' at ya goddam sissy faces."

"They had no more to do with the war than you did," the pfc confided to his spectacles.

I remember that as I lay down again in my sack in the forty-by-eight, I mused on the faces of those Italians. They had fewer lines, fewer splotches than the young men of America. I wasn't quite convinced that their sorrow came because they were defeated. It must be some agony that we as yet knew nothing of. . . . But then they'd declared war on us. They were our enemies. Yet in those young men of Italy I'd seen something centuries old. An American is only as old as his years. A long line of something was hidden behind the bright eyes of those Italians. And then and there I decided to learn something of the modern world. There was something abroad which we Americans couldn't or wouldn't understand. But unless we made some attempt to realize that everyone in the world isn't American, and that not everything American is good, we'd all perish together, and in this twentieth century. . . . My mind kept reverting to the captain of the Bersaglieri. And under different circumstances he'd have ordered me to my death. . . . Something stirred in me that touched me more profoundly than ever before, even in love. And I fell asleep. . . .

World War II: The E.T.O.

Operation Stitch

✕

from *Command Decision*

by WILLIAM W. HAINES

Major Davis interrupted the conference with an unscientific sense of personal importance. He knew the impropriety of this feeling but could not resist it. For weary months he had been summoned and dismissed, like a bellhop. This time he bore information that warranted a voice in affairs. Haley had warned him that Kane himself was in the room. Davis had rejoiced in reminding Haley that there were no data indicating correlation between Kane's whereabouts and incipient Polar Turbulence. Dennis had told him to report change instantly. He had change to report. His confidence was confirmed, upon entrance, by the instant, complete attention he could always command from Dennis . . . for a minute.

"Excuse me, sir. You said if anything special . . ."

"Of course. Go right ahead, Major."

"We've a flash from Iceland, sir. Only preliminary but it does indicate a most interesting condition. A cold mass of a rather exceptional nature has formed eccentrically . . ."

"Never mind the genealogy," said Dennis. "What's it going to do?"

It was always like this. Davis compressed his indignation.

"Blanket the Continent, sir, if . . ."

"When?"

"On present indications late Monday afternoon unless . . ."

"When will it close my bases?"

"Best estimate now, sir, is any time after fifteen hundred Monday."

Davis held his tongue now. They could chew that one over and then ask him. But Dennis did not ask him. He burst out savagely.

"I always said God must love Willi Messerschmitt."

He brooded through a black silence and then, remembering Davis, nodded brief, absent-minded dismissal.

"Bring confirmations or further changes as they come in."

Davis retired with a frustrate and highly unscientific inner imprecation that the Army Air Forces and all their generals could go to hell.

Kane watched the closing of the door with an uneasiness he could only hope he was not showing. His mind had been made up even before he heard the weather. In the long run he knew that the Allies would win this war, jets or no jets. He had resolved to save Dennis for the permanent wars among the services. A man of his force was too valuable to be destroyed by misfortune in a temporary foreign campaign. He told himself now that the only question remaining was how to whip Dennis without breaking his spirit. Even to himself he did not yet admit a deeper uncertainty as to whether he could, in a showdown, whip Dennis at all. As if aware of this himself, the Brigadier was already challenging him again.

"There goes our summer, sir. We'll make it now or bite off our nails waiting for another chance."

"Casey, I'm sorry, but two more days of prohibitive losses just now . . ."

Dennis exploded.

"God damn it, sir, it's *not* a theory any longer. Can't you see why we're having these losses? Do you think the Germans would fight like this if they weren't scared of our bombardment?"

Martin saw Kane himself shake with this blast. But he checked himself and spoke to his aide.

"Homer, make a note of that, for the Chief."

Prescott whipped out a notebook, bent over the map table, and fixed his shocked eyes upon Dennis. The Brigadier, as if conscious of the narrowness of this momentary reprieve, paused for a minute before continuing with an earnest, low-voiced sincerity more moving than any vehemence.

"We've scarcely scratched Germany yet, sir, but look what we're doing to their Air Force. We're doing what no other weapon in this war has done or can do. We're making it fight, on *our initiative*, where it can't refuse in order to rest and rebuild. We are tearing it up *over Germany*. The German Air Force has been the balance of power in this whole war, ever since Munich. It took their Ground Forces everywhere they've been. It beat the Polish Air Force in three days, the Norwegian in three hours; it forced the Maginot Line and beat the French in three weeks . . ."

"Homer," said Kane, "be sure you're getting this."

"The Royal Air Force," continued Dennis, "won a brilliant battle from it but it was a defensive battle, over England. The German Air Force rested a little and then knocked off Yugoslavia and Greece for practice, captured Crete, dominated the Mediterranean, chased the Russians to Moscow and the Volga, and got close enough to that Caspian oil to smell it. They blockaded the North Cape and very nearly cut the Atlantic life line to England itself. Peterson would have done it if Goering had given him two groups instead of one *Staffel*. And even after that they took Rommel to the gates of Alexandria.

"Now where is that German Air Force, sir? Already we've made them convert bomber groups to fighters, we've made them switch their whole production, procurement, and training programs. We've made them pull operational groups off the Russians and away from Rommel to put them over there, across the Channel, against us . . ."

He walked over and banged the map with his fist and his voice was rising again now.

"Now the Russians have been able to mount and sustain a counteroffensive. Our own people, in the Med, have air superiority and they're advancing with it . . ."

"Get every word of this, Homer," breathed Kane.

"Well, get this too, Homer," rasped Dennis. "The Germans know all of this better than we do. They've been willing to loosen their grip on their costliest conquests and break the whole balance of their Air Force for just one thing . . . to defend Germany itself from us. They've done it because they know something else. They know that fighters, Spits and Hurricanes, saved England from either decisive bombardment or invasion. Now they've got a better fighter than those were. They intend to make Europe as impregnable as the British made England. And they're going to do it, just as surely as we sit here with our fingers in our asses and let them!"

Prescott coughed discreetly through the enveloping silence.

"Do you want that in too, sir?"

Kane did not hear Prescott. He had been listening to Dennis. It was the burning sincerity of the plea which had illuminated again for him the old dream. He was seeing in fact the old vision of Air Power itself, the vision he had followed, the vision for which he and his kind had planned and pleaded and promised.

And yet it remained a glittering gamble. Kane knew far better than Dennis how bitterly the levels above him were torn with their own disunities, political, strategic, nationalistic, now that they had achieved the suppression of air power to an auxiliary level. He knew the quarrels and compromises, the delays and disagreements, the wary stalemates between military strategy and international policy, the sacrifices of lives to save faces and of faces to save the fears that were older than any passing war.

Kane looked past the waiting Dennis to the map now, but even as his quickening eyes swept toward Germany they hung on the chalk marks on the loss column of the Ops board. He shook his head heavily and clearly heard Prescott repeat his frightened question.

"No, not that part exactly, Major. Just the sense of it. Casey, I agree with you entirely, my boy, but we've simply got to wait till we're a little stronger."

"Sir," said Dennis, and they could all see him controlling himself with evident effort now, "wars are lost by waiting. If it were a question of potential strength there wouldn't be any wars. It isn't like that. Decisions are won by the margins available at critical times and places. The Allies waited, at Munich. The French and British waited, behind the Maginot Line. The Germans waited, for a little more relative strength to invade England. The Russians waited, until they had to take on the German armies without an ally in the field. We waited, for more strength to coerce Japan.

"Now we're forcing the fighting, at terrible disadvantages of distance, defenses, and weather . . . on a margin so thin we cross ourselves before counting losses . . . with a bomber that thirty-millimeter cannon will make obsolete. But we're doing it. We have, *now*, the advantage of the offensive, precariously, but we've got it. Advantage is cumulative. If we stop now and wait for the cycle to swing again we'll be waiting for them to put a roof on the Continent. I'm not trying to tell you that Operation Stitch will win the war. But no battle anywhere in this war has been won without aerial supremacy. Operation Stitch is the price of that."

He stopped. The muffled drumming of the motors outside and the clacking of the teleprinter in the Ops room filled part of the silence; the rest of it hung heavily over them all. Kane knew now that Dennis was not going to yield. He could relieve him, of course. But Dennis believed these things and would say them elsewhere, anywhere, even in Washington itself if Kane sent him back there. On the other hand, if Washington itself decided to relieve him . . . Kane shook his head and rose with quick decision, the others springing up after him.

"Will you gentlemen wait in the anteroom, please."

He saw Garnett's angry flush at being included with the other ranks but he offered no modification of the order. After a second Garnett followed the others out, closing the door himself.

"Casey, I'm taking Cliff back to my headquarters with me at once and releasing the Division to your discretion."

"Thank you, sir," said Dennis quietly.

Kane hesitated, wishing to say more, remembering that the spoken word cannot be unsaid. Dennis did not need things spelled out for him, but his own deep, haunting anxiety made Kane speak against his wiser instincts.

"Casey, you realize what can happen?"

"Perfectly, sir."

"Well, I hope it doesn't. Good luck, my boy."

He was turning toward the door when Evans stepped in from the Ops room, reluctantly extending a sheet of teleprint paper.

"Top Secret relay from General Kane's headquarters for the General, sir."

After observing Dennis's defense of Goldberg that evening Sergeant Evans had gone to the Top Secret Files and read the plan labeled Operation Stitch. One perusal of it confounded him. The Army, or at least the Fifth Division, did have a sensible, logical plan. Evans was dazed until he remembered what was going on in the next room. That confirmed it all. This plan was so good that it was requiring the exertions of a major general to resist its use.

Evans had shaken his head, wondering why Dennis had not already been court-martialed. And yet Kane was evidently vacillating. Against all previous experience, Evans himself had begun to hope when the reality of the clattering teleprinter spelled out the message he now handed General Kane.

Standing by at attention he watched Kane wilt visibly through a quick reading of it before handing on the message to Dennis.

"It's from Les Blackmer, Casey."

Dennis read aloud slowly: "Impossible contact Chief yet. Considered opinion here implores moderation and low losses during critical three days next especially in view of Part Two which follows. Two; you are again advised imminent visit three high-ranking members House of Representatives Military Affairs Committee, arriving Prestwick probably this night. Contact Embassy at once. Representative Malcolm will particularly wish to see his nephew, Captain Lucius Malcolm Jenks O—886924371 your command. Suggest his assignment special escort duty this visit and must remind how opportune would be decoration Captain Jenks if eligible either presently or prospectively end Washington signal Casey for God's sake find General Kane and tell him wise men from west already Prestwick arriving Croydon daylight Embassy frantic signed Saybold for Kane."

Dennis lowered the paper slowly. But Kane did not wait to hear.

"Sorry, Casey. You will put maximum sorties and tonnage on the safest naval target you can find, under fighter cover, tomorrow. I'll take Jenks with me in my car and make . . . er . . . medical arrangement."

"Sir, this is impossible."

"Nothing's impossible, Casey. We're doing it."

Dennis wheeled on Evans. "Sergeant, get those two officers . . ."

Evans sprang for the door. Kane did not speak until it had closed. His voice was regretful but firm.

"The charges will be quashed. We'll have a formal presentation for the visiting firemen here tomorrow, timed so they can lunch afterward and then watch the return of the mission. You will instruct any plane sufficiently damaged to jeopardize landing to use one of the other stations. I'll have a citation written for Jenks in my office tonight. . . ."

He looked up indignantly as the door opened and two officers wearing medical insignia appeared. Their faces were puffy and their blouses ruffled from sleep but the elder saluted smartly.

"Dayhuff and Getchell reporting as ordered, sir."

"General Kane," said Dennis. "Major Dayhuff is my Division Medical Officer. Captain Getchell is flight surgeon of Jenks's group."

"Well . . ." Kane did not extend his hand.

"Major, tell General Kane exactly what you told me."

"General Kane, there is no satisfactory medical explanation of Captain Jenks's conduct. He acknowledges this and says he expects no medical exoneration."

Thoroughly alert now, Kane studied the doctors closely. A presentiment was warning him to caution, as it had warned him earlier in the evening, against a showdown with Dennis. He spoke more civilly, feeling his way.

"Mightn't that in itself be an indication of neurosis?"

"Doctors can be wrong, sir. In our opinion he's normal."

"Have you made a formal record of this?"

"Not yet, sir. We shall."

"Do you think this is simple fear . . . cowardice, Major?"

"No, sir. Any man in his right mind is afraid to fly these missions. The cowards welcome a medical excuse not to. This man apparently doesn't want one."

"Have you any idea of why he refused to fly?"

Dayhuff nodded a graying head to his junior. Captain Getchell chose his words with slow, conscientious care.

"We don't consider this a medical matter, sir. But Captain Jenks has mentioned some of his ambitions to me, in fact to anyone who would listen. He has been very frank to say that he intends to make something out of this war."

"How?"

"Politically, I believe, sir. At first Jenks made a noticeable effort to be popular in the Group but the effect was . . . well, contrary to his hopes. His operational training phase was not harmonious. By the time we entered combat status he was distrusted by the others and very resentful. When the men rode him he used to say that not only they but the whole army would come begging to his door someday and then they'd learn something about who ran the country."

"Mightn't that, in itself, indicate . . . er . . . instability?"

"Sir," said Dayhuff, "if we took to diagnosing ambition for an aberration we'd be busier than we are."

"Thank you very much, gentlemen," said Kane.

They saluted and withdrew. As they went Dennis noted that Evans had re-entered with them and overheard the conversation. He dismissed the Sergeant with an abrupt nod of his head.

"Casey," asked Kane thoughtfully, "are these doctors our own?"

"No, sir. Civilian reservists."

"Hmmm. Of course we can get Jenks to our own people . . ."

"One of these men is from Mayo and the other from Hopkins, sir. They will sign the report."

Dennis had hoped that he would not have to do this. He knew now that he would and he was a little surprised at the calmness that possessed him.

It had been like this when he was testing. All through the preparation there were doubt and nervousness and tension. Then, with the take-off, those things dropped behind. It became very simple. A man did all he could first to eliminate needless risk. Then he forced the intended risk until something broke . . . sometimes the plane, sometimes the man, sometimes the prevailing boundaries of gravity and momentum. Dennis had done it before; he was going to do it again now. He studied Kane's troubled irresolution as calmly as he had once studied his instruments before nosing down.

"Umm. We've got to do *something*, Casey."

"I know a way, sir."

"What?"

"If Jenks had been acting under direct, secret orders to hold himself in readiness for this escort duty and to discontinue flying missions until he had performed it, he would have been justified in refusing the mission without explanation. If the right orders, suitably dated, had been delayed, in channels, in this headquarters . . ."

Kane got it at once.

"Exactly, Casey, exactly. I won't forget this, my boy."

"I'll attend to the whole thing," said Dennis, "*as soon as I've ordered the Schweinhafen mission for tomorrow.*"

He saw Kane's face twitch.

"Casey, this sounds like blackmail."

"You've told me, sir, that there were times when you forced the Chief's hand."

Kane managed a smile now. "You have your orders."

Dennis looked deliberately at his watch. "Then at five-nineteen I charge Jenks with desertion in the face of the enemy."

"General, I order you to release Captain Jenks to me."

"I understand the order, sir. But the charges will be filed, the evidence heard, and the trial held in this headquarters unless you promise me Schweinhafen tomorrow and Fendelhorst the next day I judge suitable."

"Casey, really, my boy, this is preposterous. If you'll just consider . . ."

"I have considered, sir."

"You realize that I might not be able to . . . protect you?"

"I do, sir."

"Well, if you want to take the personal risk *I can* release the Division. . . . I was really going to anyway before that signal. . . ."

Dennis had already picked up the black Admin phone. He kept his back on Kane while ordering Jenks's release to the Major General's personal custody, so as to give Kane time to collect himself. When Dennis faced him again Kane managed an air of sorrowful gravity.

"In the circumstances, Casey, I'll have to signal Washington the correction on today's strike."

"I understand that, sir."

"Well, don't come to the gate."

With an angry slam of the door Kane was gone. Turning in his tracks Dennis opened the Ops door and shouted for Haley. His face was calm when the startled Colonel appeared.

"Put Stitch, phase two, Schweinhafen, on the printer at once for all groups for tomorrow. Bomb and fuel loadings as before; routes and timing to follow. . . ."

Martin hurried in from the anteroom now.

"Casey, Percent went out of here burning like a fuse. What the hell did you do?"

"Twisted his tail a little. Get going, Haley."

"Sir, you're sure you mean Schweinhafen?"

"Certain. I'll sign it in a minute but get it clicking."

Haley raised appealing eyes to inform the heavens that this was none of his work and hurried out the door.

The door had hardly closed on Haley before Martin's anxiety expressed itself.

"Quit smirking and tell me what you did."

"I traded him Jenks for Schweinhafen and Fendelhorst. Jenks's uncle Malcolm of the House Military Affairs Committee arrives here tomorrow."

"Casey, this is suicide. Percent can phone Washington."

"Well, it was the last card. He might play straight."

"Might."

"You can't tell, Ted. I can remember when Kane had guts. Let's go to work."

He had started for the Ops room door when Martin's voice stopped him.

"Casey, Cliff said Helen wants me to pick a godfather for the kid. Will you take it?"

He was so pleased that he had to hesitate a second to cover his embarrassment.

"You trying to queer it for life?"

"I'm serious, Casey."

"Well, sure."

"And I want you to promise me something."

"What?"

"If he ever wants to join the goddamned army you'll take a club and beat his brains right out through his tail."

"I know what you mean," said Dennis slowly.

Martin walked over to him now, unpinning the wings from his blouse as he came.

"But after you get 'em beaten out he'll probably become a pilot. If he does, give him these."

He extended the wings. Dennis looked from them to Martin's face without moving a hand.

"Nuts. All I owe him's a silver cup and a blameless example through life. You give him those yourself."

"You keep 'em, I might lose 'em."

"No you don't, Ted. You're sitting here, biting your fingernails, tomorrow."

Martin shook his head. "No dice, Casey. Schweinhafen's mine."

Dennis had known this was coming and had meant to prepare himself for final, unequivocal decision but there had not been time. There never was time. He looked at the set face before him and tried to stall until his head cleared.

"Listen, Ted. Any of the others can . . ."

"Not tomorrow. They hear too well."

He knew his own face must be twitching now as Kane's had.

"What do you mean?"

"You know damned well what I mean. Percent can double-cross you with a counterorder from Washington and signal a recall or change of target after we've started."

"I . . . I had thought of that but . . ."

"You won't have to tomorrow. Let's go. I'll get some benzedrine and meet you in the Ops room."

Dennis felt the impact of metal in his palm and tried to speak but no sound followed Martin.

The Triple Two

⚹

from *Hawaii*
by JAMES A. MICHENER

On September 22, 1943, the Triple Two looked forward across the bow of their transport and saw rising in the misty dawn the hills of Italy, and Sergeant Goro Sakagawa thought: "I'll bet there's a German division hiding in there, waiting for us to step ashore."

He was right, and as the Japanese boys climbed down out of their transport to invade the beaches of Salerno, German planes and heavy artillery tried to harass them, but their aim was wild and all the units made it without casualty except one crop-headed private named Tashimoto, who sprained his ankle. The gang passed the word along with the acid comment, "Wouldn't you know it would be a guy from Molokai?"

Salerno lay southeast of Naples and had been chosen because it provided a logical stepping-off place for an encircling movement on Rome, some hundred and fifty miles distant, and on the day of landing, the Two-Two-Two started the long march north. The Germans, knowing both of their coming and of their composition, were determined to halt them. A specific order had been issued by Hitler: "To defeat the little yellow men who are traitors to our ally Japan and who are being cruelly used as propaganda by their Jewish masters in America, is obligatory. If these criminal little men should win a victory, it would be strongly used against us. They must be stopped and wiped out."

The Japanese boys from Hawaii did not know of this order, and after they had met one line of massive German resistance after another, they concluded: "These krauts must be the best fighters in the world. This is a lot tougher than they told us it was going to be." If the Two-Two-Two gained three miles, they did so against the most formidable German resistance: mines killed boys from Maui, tanks overran fighters from Molokai; gigantic shells exploded among troops from Kauai; and dogged, powerful ground forces contested every hill. Casualties were heavy, and the Honolulu *Mail* began carrying death lists with names like Kubokawa, Higa, and Moriguchi.

The furious efforts of the Germans to halt and humiliate the Japanese boys had an opposite effect to the one Hitler wanted; Allied war correspondents, both European and American, quickly discovered that whereas other fronts might not produce good stories, one could always get something exciting with the Two-Two-Two because they were the ones that were encountering the best the enemy could provide. Ernie Pyle, among others, marched for some days with the Hawaii troops, and wrote: "I have come to expect our American boys to continue fighting in the face of great odds, but these short, black-eyed little fighters are setting a new record. They continue slugging it out when even the bravest men would consolidate or withdraw. They form a terrific addition to our team, and dozens of boys from Texas and Massachusetts have told me, 'I'm glad they're on our side.' " So Hitler's determination to hit the Japanese so hard that they would be forced to collapse in shame, backfired because they fought on in glory.

Once Ernie Pyle asked Goro Sakagawa, "Sergeant, why did you push on against that cluster of houses? You knew it was crowded with Germans."

Goro replied in words that became famous both in Italy and America: "We had to. We fight double. Against the Germans and for every Japanese in America." Reported Pyle: "And they're winning both their wars."

September, October, November, December: the beautiful months, the months of poetry and rhythm, with nights growing colder and the soft mists of Italy turning to frost. How beautiful those months were when the boys from Hawaii first realized that they were as good fighting men as any in the world. "We fight double," they told themselves, and when they came to some Italian town, bathed in cloudless sunlight, standing forth against the hills like an etching, each tower clear in the bright glare, they attacked with fury and calculation, and bit by bit they drove the Germans back toward Rome. Colonel Whipple, delighted by the showing of his troops and pleased with the good reports they were getting in the American press, nevertheless warned his men: "It can't go on being as easy as this. Somewhere, the Germans are going to dig in real solid. Then, we'll see if we're as good as they say."

In early December Hitler sent to the Italian front a fanatical Prussian colonel named Sep Seigl, unusual in that he combined a heritage of Prussian tradition and a loyalty to Naziism. Hitler told him simply, "Destroy the Japanese." And when he studied his maps he decided, "I shall do it at Monte Cassino." Colonel Seigl was a bullet-headed young man of thirty-

seven whose promotion had been speeded because of his dedication to Hit-
ler, and on three different battlefronts he had proved his capacities. At
Monte Cassino he was determined to repeat his earlier performances. The
Japanese would be humiliated.

So as December waned and as the Two-Two-Two slogged steadfastly up
the leg of Italy toward Rome, they picked up many signs that their critical
battle was going to be engaged somewhere near the old monastery of
Monte Cassino, and belts tightened as they approached it. At the same
time, from the north Colonel Sep Seigl was moving down to Cassino some
of the ablest German units in Italy, but he did not intend to engage the
Japanese on the slopes of the mountain. His troops were not permitted to
construct their forward positions on that formidable pile of rock; they were
kept down below along the banks of the Rapido River that here ran in a
north-south direction, with the Japanese approaching from the east and
the Germans dug in along the west. Surveying the German might he
now had lined up along the Rapido, Colonel Seigl said, "We'll stop them
at the river."

On January 22, 1944, Colonel Mark Whipple halted his Japanese troops
along a line one mile east of the Rapido and told them, "Our orders
are clear and simple. Cross the river . . . so that troops behind us can
assault that pile of rocks up there. The Germans claim a rabbit can't get
across the approaches without being shot at from six angles. But we're
going across."

He dispatched a scouting party consisting of Sergeant Goro Sakagawa,
his brother Tadao, who was good at sketching, and four riflemen, and
at dusk on the twenty-second of January they crawled out of their hiding
places and started on their bellies across the most difficult single battle
terrain the Americans were to face in World War II. With meticulous
care, Tadao Sakagawa drew maps of the route. Two hundred yards west of
their present positions the Two-Two-Two would come upon an irriga-
tion ditch three feet wide and four feet deep. As they crawled out of it,
they would be facing German machine guns and a marsh some thirty
yards wide, beyond which lay another ditch. Thirty yards beyond hid a
third ditch, twice as deep, twice as wide. As the men climbed out of this
one, they would face a solid wall of machine-gun fire.

When they got this far in the darkness Goro Sakagawa licked his dry
lips and asked his men, "What's that ahead?"

"Looks like a stone wall."

"Jesus," Goro whispered. "You can't expect our boys to negotiate those
three ditches and then climb a wall. How high is it?"

"Looks about twelve feet high."

"This is impossible," Goro replied. "You fellows split up. You go that
way, we'll go this. Let's see if there's a break in the wall."

In the darkness they found none, only a stout, murderous stone wall, twelve feet high and with a jagged top. When they reassembled, Goro said in a rasping whisper, "Christ, how can anybody get over that damned thing? With machine guns everywhere. Sssssh."

There was a sudden chatter of German guns, but the men firing them must have heard a sound in some other direction, for the firing did not come close to Goro and his men. "Well," he said when it ceased, "over we go."

Patiently and with skill, in the darkness of night, the six Japanese boys helped one another over the terrifying wall, and from it they dropped into the eastern half of the dry river bed of the Rapido. It was about seventy-five feet across, about fifteen feet deep, and every spot of its entire cross section was monitored by German machine guns. On their bellies, the six soldiers crept across the dry river and trusted that no searchlights would be turned on. In the cold night they were perspiring with fear.

But when they got to the other side of the Rapido they discovered what fear really was, for both machine guns and searchlights opened up, but the young Japanese managed to secrete themselves in crevices at the foot of the western bank; but what terrified them was not the imperative staccato of the guns or the probing fingers of lights, but the monstrous nature of the river's west bank. It rose fairly straight up from the river bed, sixteen feet high, and was topped by a stout double fence of barbed wire which could be expected to contain mines at two-foot intervals.

"Are you getting this on paper?" Goro whispered to Tadao. " 'Cause when they see this, no general living would dare send men across this river." A passing light illuminated the wild and terrible tangles of barbed wire and then passed on. "You got it?" Goro asked. "Good. Hoist me up. I'm going through it."

Tadao grabbed his older brother's hand. "I have enough maps," he cautioned.

"Somebody's got to see what's over there."

His men hoisted him onto the top of the west bank of the river, where he spent fifteen perilous minutes picking his way inch by inch through the tangled barbed wire. He knew that at any moment he might explode a mine and not only kill himself but doom his five companions as well. He was no longer sweating. He was no longer afraid. He had passed into some extraordinary state known only by soldiers at night or in the heat of unbearable battle. He was a crop-headed, tense-bellied Japanese boy from Kakaako in Honolulu, and the courage he was displaying in those fateful minutes no one in Hawaii would have believed.

He penetrated the wire, leaving on the barbs tiny shreds of cloth which would guide him safely back, and in the darkness he found himself on the eastern edge of a dusty road that led past the foot of Monte Cassino. Hiding himself in the ditch that ran alongside the road, he breathed deeply, trying to become a man again and not a nerveless automaton, and as he lay there, face up, a searchlight played across the countryside, hunting for him perhaps, and it passed on and suddenly illuminated the terrain that rose above him, and although he had seen it from a distance and knew its proportions, he now cried with pain: "Oh, Jesus Christ, no!"

For above him rose an unassailable rocky height, far, far into the sky, and at its crest clung an ancient monastery, and from where he lay Goro realized that he and his men were expected to cross all that he had seen tonight, and that when they got to this road in which he now huddled, other fellows from Hawaii were expected to forge ahead and climb those overpowering rocks that hung above him. In the lonely darkness he shivered with fright; then, as men do at such times, he effectively blocked out of his mind the realization of what Monte Cassino was like. It was not an unscalable height. It was not mined and interlaced with machine guns. It was not protected by the Rapido River defenses, and a gang of Japanese boys were not required to assault it, with casualties that would have to mount toward the fifty-per-cent mark, or even the eighty. Goro Sakagawa, a tough-minded soldier, cleansed himself of this knowledge and crept back to his men, then back to his commanding officer.

"It'll be tough," he reported. "But it can be done."

As he spoke, Colonel Sep Seigl was reviewing the same terrain and he knew far more about it than Goro Sakagawa, for he had maps prepared by the famous Todt Labor Corps, which had built this ultimate defense of Rome. He could see that the first three ditches which the Japanese would have to cross were covered in every detail by mines and machine-gun fire, and he told his men, "I suppose scouting parties are out there right now, but if they miss the mines, they'll be lucky." He saw the plans for defending the river itself, which presented one of the most formidable obstacles any army could encounter, and whereas Goro a few minutes before had been guessing as to where the mines and machine guns were, Seigl knew, and he knew that even his own soldiers, the finest in the world, could not penetrate that defense. And west of the river, of course, lay the exposed road which could be cut to shreds with mortar fire, and beyond that the cliffs of Monte Cassino up which no troops could move. At midnight Colonel Seigl concluded: "They'll try, but they'll never make it. Here is where we bloody the nose of the traitor Japanese. Tomorrow we'll watch them wilt under fire."

January 24, 1944, began with a cold, clear midnight and it was greeted with a thundering barrage of American gunfire which illuminated the bleak river but which did not dislodge the Germans. For forty minutes the barrage continued, and a beginner at warfare might have taken heart, thinking: "No man can live through that." But the dark-skinned men of the Two-Two-Two knew better; they knew the Germans would be dug in and waiting.

At 0040 the barrage stopped and the whistles blew for advance. Goro clutched his brother by the arm and whispered, "This is the big one, kid. Take care of yourself." Progress to the first ditch was painful, for the Germans launched a counter-barrage and the first deaths at Monte Cassino occurred, but Goro and Tadao pushed stolidly ahead in the darkness, and when they had led their unit across the dangerous ditch and onto the edge of the marsh, they told their captain, "We'll take care of the mines," and they set out on their bellies, two brothers who could have been engaged in a tricky football play, and they crawled across the marsh, adroitly cutting the trip wires that would otherwise have detonated mines and killed their companions, and when they reached the second ditch Goro stood up in the night and yelled, "Mo bettah you come. All mines pau!" But as he sent the news his younger brother Tadao, one of the finest boys ever to graduate from Punahou, stepped upon a magnesium mine which exploded with a terrible light, blowing him into a thousand shreds of bone and flesh.

"Oh, Jesus!" Goro cried, burying his face in his hands. No action was required. None was possible. Tadao Sakagawa no longer existed in any conceivable form. Not even his shoes were recoverable, but where he had stood other Japanese boys swept over the marshy land and with battle cries leaped into the next ditch, and then into the next.

It took five hours of the most brutal fighting imaginable for the Japanese troops to reach the near bank of the Rapido, and when dawn broke, Colonel Sep Seigl was slightly disturbed. "They should not have been able to cross those fields. They seem rather capable, but now the fight begins."

Against the troops for which he had a special hatred he threw a wall of bombardment that was almost unbelievable, and to his relief, the advance was halted. No human being could have penetrated that first awful curtain of shrapnel which greeted the Two-Two-Two at the Rapido itself. "Well," Colonel Seigl sighed, "at least they're human. They can be stopped. Now to keep them pinned down. The Japanese cannot absorb casualties. Kill half of them, and the other half will run."

But here Colonel Seigl was wrong. Half of Goro Sakagawa had already been killed; he had loved his clever brother Tadao as only boys who have lived in the close intimacy of poverty and community rejection can love, and now Tadao was dead. Therefore, when the German shelling was at its most intense, Goro said to his captain, "Let's move across the river. I know how."

"We'll dig in," the captain countermanded.

But when Colonel Whipple arrived to inspect the battered condition of his men, Goro insisted that the river could be crossed, and Whipple said, "Go ahead and try." At this point one of the lieutenants from Baker Company, Goro's commanding officer, and a fine young officer from Kansas, said, "If my men go, I go."

"All right, Lieutenant Shelly," Whipple said. "We've got to cross the river."

So Lieutenant Shelly led forty men, with Sergeant Sakagawa as a guide, down into the bed of the Rapido, at nine o'clock on a crystal-clear morning, and they came within six yards of crossing the river, when a titanic German concentration of fire killed half the unit, including Lieutenant Shelly. The twenty who were left began to panic, but Goro commanded sternly, "Up onto that bank and through that barbed wire."

It was a completely insane thing to attempt. The Rapido River did not propose to allow any troops, led by Goro Sakagawa or otherwise, to violate it that day, and when his stubborn muddy fingers reached the barbed-wire embankment, such a furious load of fire bore down upon him that he had to drop back into the river. Three more times he endeavored vainly to penetrate the barbed wire, and each time Colonel Seigl screamed at his men, "Kill him! Kill him! Don't let them get started!" But although tons of ammunition were discharged in the general direction of Sakagawa and his determined men, somehow they were not killed. Huddling in the protection of the far bank of the river, the gallant twenty waited for their companions to catch up with them, when all together they might have a chance of crashing the barbed wire.

But the firepower of the Germans was so intense that the Japanese boys who were still on the eastern bank could not possibly advance. At times the wall of shrapnel seemed almost solid and it would have been complete suicide to move a man into it. "We've got to hold where we are," Colonel Whipple regretfully ordered.

"What about those twenty out there in the river?"

"Who's in charge? Lieutenant Shelly?"

"He was killed. Sergeant Sakagawa."

"Goro?"

"Yes, sir."

"He'll get his men out," Whipple said confidently, and at dusk, after a day of hell, Goro Sakagawa did just that. He brought all of his twenty men back across the river, up the dangerous eastern bank, back through the minefields and safely to headquarters.

"Colonel wants to see you," a major said.

"We couldn't make it," Goro reported grimly.

"No man ever tried harder, Lieutenant Sakagawa."

Goro showed no surprise at his battlefield commission. He was past fear, past sorrow, and certainly past jubilation. But when the bars were pinned to his tunic by the colonel himself, the rugged sergeant broke into tears, and they splashed out of his dark eyes onto his leathery yellow-brown skin. "Tomorrow we'll cross the river," he swore.

"We'll certainly try," Colonel Whipple said.

On January 26 the Japanese troops did try, but once more Colonel Sep Seigl's able gunners turned them back with dreadful casualties. On January 27 the Japanese tried for the third time, and although Lieutenant Goro Sakagawa got his men onto the road on the other side of the river, they were hit with such pulverizing fire that after forty-five minutes they had to withdraw. That night an Associated Press man wrote one of the great dispatches of the war: "If tears could be transmitted by cable, and printed by linotype, this story would be splashed with tears, for I have at last seen what they call courage beyond the call of duty. I saw a bunch of bandy-legged Japanese kids from Hawaii cross the Rapido River, and hold the opposite bank for more than forty minutes. Then they retreated in utter defeat, driven back by the full might of the German army. Never in victory have I seen any troops in the world achieve a greater glory, and if hereafter any American ever questions the loyalty of our Japanese, I am not going to argue with him. I am going to kick his teeth in."

On January 28, Lieutenant Sakagawa tried for the fourth time to cross the Rapido, and for the fourth time Colonel Sep Seigl's men mowed the Japanese down. Of the 1300 troops with which Colonel Whipple had started four days earlier, 779 were now casualities. Dead Japanese bodies lined the fatal river, and men with arms and legs torn off were being moved to the rear. At last it became apparent that the Germans had effectively stopped the advance of the hated Two-Two-Two. That night Colonel Seigl's intelligence reported: "Victory! The Japanese have been driven back. They're in retreat and seem to be leaving the line."

The report was partially correct. Lieutenant Goro Sakagawa's company, and the unit of which it was a part, was being withdrawn. The boys were willing to try again, but they no longer had enough men to maintain a cohesive company and they had to retreat to repair their wounds. As they passed back through a unit from Minnesota coming in to replace them, the Swedes, having heard of their tremendous effort, cheered them and saluted and one man from St. Paul yelled, "We hope we can do as good as you did."

"You will," a boy from Lahaina mumbled.

So the Germans stopped the Two-Two-Two . . . for a few hours, because in another part of the line other units from Hawaii were accumulating a mighty force, and on February 8 Colonel Sep Seigl's intelligence officer reported breathlessly, "The damned Japanese have crossed the river and are attacking the mountain itself!"

With a powerful surge the Japanese boys drove spearheads almost to the top of the mountain. They scaled heights that even their own officers believed impregnable, and they routed out more than two hundred separate machine-gun emplacements. Their heroism in this incredible drive was unsurpassed in World War II, and for a few breathless hours they caught a toehold on the summit of the mountain itself.

"Send us reinforcements!" they radioed frantically. "We've got them licked."

But reinforcements could not negotiate the cliffs, and one by one the Japanese victors were driven back from their dizzy pinnacles. As they stumbled down the steep flanks of Monte Cassino the Germans gunned them unmercifully, but at last the fragments of the force staggered back to camp and announced: "The Germans cannot be driven out." But one fact of triumph remained: the headquarters camp was now on the west bank of the Rapido. The river had been crossed. The way to Rome lay open.

It was in their bruising defeat at Monte Cassino that the Two-Two-Two became one of the most famous units of the war. "The Purple Heart Battalion" it was called, for it had suffered more casualties than any other similar-sized unit in the war. The Mo Bettahs won more honors, more decorations, more laudatory messages from the President and the generals than any other. But most of all they won throughout America a humble respect. Caucasians who fought alongside them reported back home: "They're better Americans than I am. I wouldn't have the guts to do what they do." And in Hawaii, those golden islands that the Japanese boys loved so deeply as they died in Italy, people no longer even discussed the tormenting old question: "Are the Japanese loyal?" Now men of other races wondered: "Would I be as brave?" So although the Prussian Nazi, Colonel Sep Seigl, did exactly what he had promised Hitler he would do — he crushed the Japanese at Monte Cassino — neither he nor Hitler accomplished what he had initially intended: for it was in defeat that the Japanese boys exhibited their greatest bravery and won the applause of the world.

Therefore it is strange to report that it was not at Monte Cassino that the Two-Two-Two won its greatest laurels. This happened by accident in a remote corner of France.

After the Triple Two's had retired to a rear area in Italy, there to lick their considerable wounds and to re-form with fresh replacements from the States — including First Lieutenant Goro Sakagawa's younger brothers Minoru and Shigeo — the Mo Bettah Battalion was shipped out of Italy and into Southern France, where it was allowed to march in a leisurely manner up the Rhone Valley. It met little German opposition, nor was it intended to, for the generals felt that after the heroic performance at Monte Cassino the Japanese boys merited something of a respite, and for once things went as planned. Then, accompanied by a Texas outfit that had also built a name for itself in aggressive fighting, the Two-Two-Two's swung away from the Rhone and entered upon routine mopping-up exercises in the Vosges Mountains, where the easternmost part of France touched the southernmost part of Germany.

The Triple Two's and the Texans moved forward with calculating efficiency until they had the Germans in what appeared to be a final rout. Lieutenant Sakagawa kept urging his men to rip the straggling German units with one effective spur: "Remember what they did to us at Cassino." Hundreds of bewildered Germans surrendered to him, asking pitifully, "Have the Japanese finally turned against us too? Like the Italians?" To such questions Goro replied without emotion: "We're Americans. Move through and back." But if he kept his hard face a mask of indifference, secretly he trembled with joy whenever he accepted the surrender of units from Hitler's master race.

It was understandable, therefore, that Goro Sakagawa, like his superiors, interpreted the Vosges campaign as the beginning of the end for Hitler. But this was a sad miscalculation, for if the young, untrained Nazi troops sometimes faltered, their clever Prussian generals did not. They were now charged with defending the German homeland, and from his epic success at Monte Cassino, Colonel Sep Seigl, now General Seigl, had arrived at the Vosges to organize resistance at that natural bastion. Therefore, if he allowed his rag-tag troops to surrender in panic to the Triple Two's, it was for a reason; and in late October of 1944 this reason became apparent, for on the twenty-fourth of that month General Seigl's troops appeared to collapse in a general rout, retreating helter-skelter through the difficult Vosges terrain; and in so doing they enticed the battle-hungry Texans to rush after them, moving far ahead of American tanks and into the neatest trap of the war.

General Seigl announced the springing of his trap with a gigantic barrage of fire that sealed the bewildered Texans into a pocket of mountains. "We will shoot them off one by one," Seigl ordered, moving his troops forward. "We'll show the Americans what it means to invade German soil." And he swung his prearranged guns into position and began pumping high explosives at the Texan camp. There without food or water or adequate ammunition, the gallant Texans dug in and watched the rim of fire creep constantly closer.

At this point an American journalist coined the phrase the "Lost Battalion," and in Texas radios were kept tuned around the clock. Whole villages listened to agonizing details as the sons of that proud state prepared to die as bravely as their circumstances would permit. A sob echoed across the prairies, and Texans began to shout, "Get our boys out of there! For Christsake, do something!"

Thus what had been intended as respite for the Triple Two suddenly became the dramatic high point of the war. A personal messenger from the Senate warned the Pentagon: "Get those Texans out of there or else." The Pentagon radioed SHAEF: "Effect rescue immediately. Top priority white." SHAEF advised headquarters in Paris, and they wirelessed General McLarney, at the edge of the Vosges. It was he who told Colonel Mark Whipple, "You will penetrate the German ring of firepower and rescue those men from Texas." Lest there be any misunderstanding, another general flew in from Paris, red-faced and bitter, and he said, "We're going to be crucified if we let those boys die. Get them, goddamn it, get them."

Colonel Whipple summoned Lieutenant Goro Sakagawa and said, "You've got to go up that ridge, Goro. You mustn't come back without them."

"We'll bring 'em out," Goro replied.

As he was about to depart, Mark Whipple took his hand and shook it with that quiet passion that soldiers know on the eve of battle. "This is the end of our road, Goro. The President himself has ordered this one. Win this time, and you win your war."

It was a murderous, hellish mission. A heavy fog enveloped the freezing Vosges Mountains, and no man could look ahead more than fifteen feet. As Baker Company filed into the pre-dawn gloom, each Japanese had to hold onto the field pack of the boy in front, for only in this manner could the unit be kept together. From the big, moss-covered trees of the forest, German snipers cut down one Hawaiian boy after another, until occasionally some Japanese in despairing frustration would stand stubbornly with his feet apart, firing madly into the meaningless fog. At other times German machine guns stuttered murderously from a distance of twenty feet. But Goro became aware of one thing: firepower that an hour before had been pouring in upon the doomed Texans was now diverted.

To rescue the Lost Battalion, the Two-Two-Two had to march only one mile, but it was the worst mile in the world, and to negotiate it was going to require four brutal days without adequate water or food or support. The casualties suffered by the Japanese were staggering, and Goro sensed that if he brought his two younger brothers through this assault, it would be a miracle. He therefore cautioned them: "Kids, keep close to the trees. When we move from one to the other, run like hell across the open space. And when you hit your tree, whirl about instantly to shoot any Germans that might have infiltrated behind you."

At the end of the first day the Triple Two's had gained only nine hundred feet, and within the circle of steel wounded Texans were beginning to die from gangrene. Next morning the Japanese boys pushed on, a yard at a time, lost in cold fog, great mossy trees and pinnacles of rock. Almost every foot of the way provided General Seigl's riflemen with ideal cover, and they used it to advantage. With methodical care, they fired only when some Japanese ran directly into their guns, and they killed the Triple Two's with deadly accuracy. On that cold, rainy second day the Japanese troops gained six hundred feet, and nearly a hundred of the trapped Texans died from wounds and fresh barrages.

A curious factor of the battle was that all the world could watch. It was known that the Texans were trapped; it was known that the Two-Two-Two's were headed toward their rescue, and the deadly game fascinated the press. A Minnesota corporal who had fought with the Triple Two's in Italy told a newspaperman, "If anybody can get 'em, the slant-eyes will." In Honolulu newspapers that phrase was killed, but the entire community, sensing the awful odds against which their sons were fighting, prayed.

On the third day of this insane attempt to force the ring of fire, Baker Company was astonished to see trudging up the hill they had just traversed the familiar figure of Colonel Mark Whipple. The men well knew the basic rule of war: "Lieutenants lead platoons against the enemy. Captains stay back and encourage the entire company. Majors and light colonels move between headquarters and the companies. But chicken colonels stay put." Yet here was Colonel Whipple, a West Point chicken colonel, breaking the rule and moving into the front lines. Instinctively the Japanese boys saluted as he passed. When he reached Goro he said simply, "We're going to march up that ridge and rescue the Texans today."

This was a suicidal approach and no one knew it better than Whipple, but it had been commanded by headquarters. "I can't order my boys into another Cassino," he had protested. "This is worse than Cassino," headquarters had admitted, "but it's got to be done." Whipple had saluted and said, "Then I must lead the boys myself." And there he was.

His inspiration gave the Japanese the final burst of courage they needed. With terrifying intensity of spirit the Two-Two-Two moved up the ridge. The fighting was murderous, with Germans firing point-blank at the rescuers. Barrages from hidden guns, planted weeks before at specific spots by General Seigl, cut down the Triple Two's with fearful effect, and at one faltering point Goro thought: "Why should we have to penetrate such firepower? We're losing more than we're trying to save."

As if he sensed that some such question might be tormenting his troops and halting their flow of courage, Colonel Whipple moved among them, calling, "Sometimes you do things for a gesture. This is the ultimate gesture. They're waiting for us, over that ridge." But the men of the Triple Two could not banish the ugly thought that haunted them: "Texans are important and have to be saved. Japanese are expendable." But no one spoke these words, for all knew that the Texas fighters didn't have to prove anything; the Japanese did.

When night fell on the twenty-ninth of October the Japanese troops were still four hundred yards short of their goal. They slept standing up, or leaning against frozen trees. There was no water, no food, no warmth. Outpost sentries, when relieved, muttered, "I might as well stay here with you." There was no bed. Men ached and those with minor wounds felt the blood throbbing in their veins. Hundreds were already dead.

At dawn a German sniper, hidden with Teutonic thoroughness, fired into the grim encampment and killed Private Minoru Sakagawa. For some minutes his brother Goro was not aware of what had happened, but then young Shigeo cried, "Jesus! They killed Minoru!"

Goro, hearing his brother's agonized cry, ran up and saw Minoru dead upon the frozen ground. This was too much to bear, and he began to lose his reason. "Achhhh!" he cried with a great rasping noise in his throat. Two of his brothers had now died while under his command, and the rest of his troops seemed doomed. His right hand began trembling while his voice continued to cry a meaningless "Achhhh."

Colonel Whipple, who knew what was happening, rushed up and clouted the young lieutenant brutally across the face. "Not now, Goro!" he commanded, using a strange phrase: Not now, as if later it would be permissible to go out of one's mind, as if at some later time all men might do so, including Whipple himself.

Goro fell back and his hand stopped trembling. Staring in dull panic at his colonel, he tried vainly to focus on the problems at hand, but failed. He could see only his brother, fallen on the pine needles of the Vosges. Then his cold reason returned, and he drew his revolver. Grabbing Shigeo by the shoulder he said, "You walk here." Then to his men he roared, in Japanese, "We won't stop!" And with appalling force he and his team marched in among the great trees.

It was a desperate, horrible hand-to-hand fight up the last thousand feet of the ridge. Shigeo, following the almost paralyzed fury of his brother, exhibited a courage he did not know he had. He moved directly onto German positions and grenaded them to shreds. He ducked behind trees like a veteran, and when the last roadblock stood ahead, ominous and spewing death, it was mild-mannered Shigeo, the quiet one of the Sakagawa boys — though there were now only two left — who with demonic craftiness went against it, drew its fire so that he could spot its composition, and then leaped inside with grenades and a Tommy gun. He killed eleven Germans, and when his companions moved past him to the ultimate rescue of the Texans he leaned out of the Nazi position and cheered like a schoolboy.

"You're a lieutenant!" Colonel Whipple snapped as he went forward to
join the Texans, and a boy from Maui looked at Shig and said in pidgin,
"Jeez, krauts all pau!"

In rough formation, with Lieutenant Goro Sakagawa at their head, the
Japanese boys marched in to greet the Texans, and a tall Major Burns
from Houston stumbled forward, his ankle in bad shape, and tried to
salute, but the emotion of the moment was too great. He was famished
and burning with thirst, and before he got to Goro he fell in the dust.
Then he rose to his knees and said from that position, "Thank God. You
fellows from the Jap outfit?"

"Japanese," Goro replied evenly. He stooped to help the Texan to his
feet and saw that the man was at least a foot taller than he was. All
the Texans, starving and parched though they were, were enormous
men, and it seemed indecent that a bunch of runty little rice-eaters should
have rescued them.

Against his will, for Major Burns was a very brave man and had kept
his troops alive mainly through the force of his extraordinary character,
the tall Texan began to weep. Then he was ashamed of himself, bit his
lip till it nearly bled and asked, "Could my men have some water?" He
turned to his troops and shouted, "Give these Japs a big welcome."

Goro grabbed the major as if they were two toughs back in Kakaako and
said in sudden, surging anger, "Don't you call us Japs!"

"Goro!" Colonel Whipple shouted.

"What, sir?" He didn't remember what he had just said.

"All right," Whipple snapped. "Let's start down the hill."

The Japanese troops formed two lines at the entrance to the pocket in
which the Texans had been trapped, and as the giant men passed to freedom between the pairs of stubby Triple Two's some of the Texans began to laugh, and soon the pocket was choked with merriment, in which
big Texans began to embrace their rescuers and kiss them and jump
them up into the air. "You little guys got guts," a huge fellow from Abi-
lene shouted. "I thought we was done for."

Lieutenant Sakagawa did not join the celebration. He was watching his
men, and estimated dully that of the original 1200 Japanese boys that had
set out to storm the ridge, fully two-thirds were now either dead or severely wounded. This terrible toll, including his brother Minoru, was almost more than he could tolerate, and he began mumbling, "Why did
we have to lose so many little guys to save so few big ones?" It had
cost 800 Japanese to rescue 341 Texans. Then his mind began to harden
and to come back under control, and to discipline it he began checking off
Baker Company, and he found that of the 183 men who had waded
ashore with him at Salerno in September of 1943 only seven had managed

to stick with the outfit through October of 1944. The rest — all 176 of them — were either dead or wounded.

Now Shigeo rushed up to advise his brother that Colonel Whipple had promoted him on the field of battle, a soldier's sweetest triumph, and the brilliant-eyed youth shouted, "Goro, I guess this time we really showed the world!" But Goro, counting the dead, wondered: "How much more do we have to prove?" And from the manner in which his mind jerked from one image to the next, he realized that he was close to mental collapse, but he was saved by a curious experience. From among the Texans a hysterical medic, his mind deranged by three shells that had exploded while he was trying to cut off a shattered leg, began moving from one Japanese to another, mumbling, "Greater love hath no man than this, that he lay down his life for his brother."

Major Burns heard the speech and yelled, "There goes that goddamned odd-ball again. Please, please, shut him up!"

But the medic had reached Goro, to whom he mumbled, "Lieutenant, indeed it is true. No man hath greater love than this, that he would march up such a fucking ridge to save a complete crock of shit like Major Burns." In his wildness the medic turned to face Burns, screaming hysterically, "I hate you! I hate you! You led us into this death trap, you crazy, crazy beast!"

Almost sadly, Major Burns, pivoting on his good leg, swung on the medic and knocked him out. "He was more trouble than the Germans," he apologized. "Somebody haul the poor bastard out."

Before any of the Texans could get to the capsized medic, Goro had compassionately pulled the unconscious fellow into his arms. A gigantic Texan came along to help, and the odd trio started down the bloody ridge, but when they had returned halfway to safety, General Seigl's last furious barrage enveloped them, and two shells bracketed Colonel Mark Whipple, killing him instantly. Goro, who witnessed the death, dropped his hold on the medic and started toward the man who had done so much for the Japanese, but at long last his nervous system gave way.

The awful "Achhhh" filled his throat, and his hands began trembling. His head jerked furiously as if he were an epileptic and his eyes went vacant like those of an imbecile. "Achhhh! Achhhh!" he began to shout hysterically, and he started falling to his right, but caught himself by clutching air. His voice cleared and he began screaming, "Don't you call me a Jap! Goddamn you big blond Texans, don't you call me a yellow-belly!"

In wild fury he began lashing out at his tormentors, stupidly, ineffectively. He kept shouting irrelevant threats at the Texans whom he had just saved, and was ready to fight even the biggest. One man from Dallas gently held him off as an adult would a child, and it was pathetic to see the

stocky Japanese swinging wildly at the air, unable to reach his giant adversary. Finally he returned to the horrible achhhh sound, and at this point
his brother Shigeo ran up to take command. He pinioned Goro's arms, and
when the latter seemed about to break out once more, Shigeo smashed a
hard right-cut to the jaw and slowed him down.

Now Goro began to whimper like a child, and two men from his outfit
had the decency to cover him with a blanket, so that his disintegration
would not be visible to his own troops, and in this condition they patiently led him, shivering and shuddering, out of the Vosges Mountains
where the Texans had been trapped.

Toward the foothills they passed through a guard unit from their own
battalion, and a young lieutenant from Able Company, a haole boy from
Princeton, asked, "Who you got under the blanket?" and Shigeo replied,
"Lieutenant Sakagawa."

"Was he the one who got through to the Texans?"

"Who else?" Shig replied, and as the cortege of wounded and near-mad
and starved and war-torn passed, the Princeton man looked at Goro Sakagawa's mechanically shuffling feet and muttered, "There goes an American."

Queen Penicillin

✗

from *The Gallery*

by JOHN HORNE BURNS

Awakening these mornings in Naples, he'd turn on his canvas cot, shove
aside his mosquito netting, light a cigarette, and look out at the bell tower
of Maria Egiziana. His consciousness was clear, the way he used to come to
as a child and start thinking of what he'd do today.

But the deliciousness of those awakenings had gone. Up till last week
he'd known them with Marisa. But now she'd gone to Rome. And for days
there'd been something in his mind, something crouching that he could
escape only when he slept. All day long it sat on his shoulder whispering
the red doubts and fears into his ear. He was free only in those first
instants of awaking. But with the first few puffs on his cigarette the Idea
came back. This morning It was especially pressing. Today he'd Know.

He got up and groped down to the latrine. The sunlight hadn't yet come into this corridor, but he knew the passageway drunk or sober. In the latrine he voided his bladder and stood looking at his naked body in the mirror. By the early August sunlight of Naples he looked like a Moor. Marisa'd loved this color of his skin. He examined his flesh, peering over himself with a wild hushed interest. He knew every inch of himself. Then the Idea broke over him more viciously than in the past four days. His dark skin globuled with sweat.

Back in the room he dressed himself quickly. He was shaking. He heard his heart say yes yes yes. And from the other cot Roy was regarding him with sleepy compassion.

"Goin to find out this mornin?"

"Yup."

"Good luck, boy. Ya been sweatin this one out."

His boots clattered on the stairs of the palazzo. Naples too was awakening in the August morning. By the windows the sandflies hung poised in their clouds. And he heard the clatter of the cats in the street and the prickly whispering of the women's brooms as they swept the sidewalks.

He walked through the screen door of the mess hall, taking more than his usual pains not to let it slam. The mess sergeant sat at a wooden table littered with lettuce. He looked up with an iron petulance.

"Now what, Jo-Jo? Ya feelin hungover?"

"Nope. Got any black coffee?"

One of the Neapolitan kitchen help poured him a mess cup full of scalding java and passed it to him.

"Grazie, Joe," he said.

"Niente, Joe," the Neapolitan said.

The metal lip of the canteen cup singed his lips and his tongue, but the coffee flooded down his throat. Again the sweat seeped out through his shirt. He felt the cup teetering against his teeth from the trembling of his wrist.

"Ya ain't feelin good, Jo-Jo?" the mess sergeant said. "Ya ain't been on the beam since ya quit ya shackin . . ."

"Nope," he said, setting down his cup, "I ain't feelin well."

"Knock her up or somethin?"

"Nope. Me and Marisa just broke up."

"Well, they's plenty more where she came from," the mess sergeant said, shoving a mound of lettuce wearily away from him. "Plenty more."

"I don't want no more."

Now in a lewd sweat from the steaming coffee and the reeking Neapolitan morning, he plowed along, his cap on the back of his head and his hands in his pockets. Seeing Vesuvius and the barbed wire around the port enclosures, he decided to smoke a cigarette. As he was lighting his butt with fingers that wobbled, an officer passed. He lowered his eyes.

"Say, soldier," the lieutenant said, "don't ya salute officers any more?"

"This ain't a salutin area, sir . . ."

"Shut up an salute me," the lieutenant said. "I don't know why I don't take ya name an serial number. . . . Wearin ya dogtags?"

"Yessir."

"Well, get on ya way. Next time watch ya step. Not all officers is as square as me."

He saluted again and walked on, replacing his hands in his pockets. He put his cigarette in the farthest angle of his mouth. He felt that his shoulders were sagging. He didn't care. He dragged along with his eyes on the ground. For he wished that he could pass out quietly some place, that the March eruption of Vesuvius had buried both Naples and himself under lava as stiff as molasses. He cussed and spat against a tree that grew from the sidewalk in his path.

There was no one in the Galleria Umberto except some children asleep like sweaty kittens, and little old men who went over the pavement searching for cigarette butts. From the cornices the weather-eaten angels looked snottily down at him from behind their trumpets. He saw the canvases in the art shops as daubs of vermilion and ocher and cobalt. The bars were all shut behind their rolling corrugated blinds. The new sun filled every nook of the arcade, microscopically adumbrating the smears on the walls, the peeling posters, the chipped mosaics in the pavement. And above him the empty skylight crisscrossed the sky like veins in an eyeless socket. He remembered the Galleria in past evenings: blots of light leaking from under the bars till curfew time, the smell of bodies in movement, the shrill laughter, and the voices promising annihilation from the heat and the pain. And like a flashlight into his dark hot misery he saw the figure of Marisa swaying in the August darkness, the cleft of her breasts in her gray figured cotton frock, her tiny brown feet. He heard her voice:

"Vieni, amor mio . . . fammi tua per sempre. . . ."

Thinking of the past, he walked across the Galleria into Via Roma. A Neapolitan kid asked him if he wanted to eat; so he told him what he could do with himself. On Via Roma there was the sparrowy life of Neapolitans hurrying to work, old ladies fanning themselves with their morning paper, the screams of the cameo dealers as they set up their displays in the porticos of abandoned shops and ruined tenements. British and American convoys rumbled in the pinched street. In the gutters lay squashed oranges and spent rubbers that had been hurled from the windows above.

He turned, crossed Via Diaz, and entered PBS building from the side. For a while he stood before the red and white canvas sign that read FIFTH GENERAL DISPENSARY. He laid his hand on the bronze maniple of the door. It was as hot as a molten ingot to his palm. He was listening too to his heart throbbing, opening and closing like a spastic fist. It had beat like that when he lay in Marisa's arms after their lovemaking. . . . Marisa. . . . He felt his knees begin to shake. There seemed to be a pool of icewater in his belly. But he stiffened his legs and pulled the door of the dispensary open.

It was cool in there. The floor was a pepper-colored parquet. The GI's who worked there stood behind glass wickets like bank tellers. And in the coolness there was a reek of phenol and antiseptic. As they set up their cages for the day, the GI's called out to one another their pissin and their moanin. They yelled back and forth criticisms of the breakfast they'd just eaten.

"I've *had* Naples! O Mr. Roosevelt, can't I please go home?"

To stop the trembling of his knees and the turbine in his chest, he sat down on a bench near the door. He wondered were his eyes bloodshot. He felt like an ulcerous scarecrow sitting alone in the middle of that cool noisy dispensary, with the click and hum of the dental clinic just beyond. The other GI's were unconcerned and gay.

Finally he got up, clutching his cap, and walked to a window that said ADMISSIONS. He ran his tongue over his lips and looked at the floor.

"Ya too early for sick call, Sarge," the corporal back of the plate glass said. "Go outside an wait a while. . . ."

"But I took a blood test . . . five days ago," he murmured.

"Oh ya did? Imagine that! Blood tests is SOP in Napoli. . . ."

"Will ya please do me a favor an look?" he said, giving his name.

"Okay, okay, Sarge," the corporal said. "I hate to see a guy sweat."

Out of a pigeonhole the corporal took a sheaf of small pink slips and leisurely ruffled through them. With tormenting indifference.

"I don't seem to find ya name, Sarge. . . . Oh wait, here it is. . . . Outa alphabetical order . . . damn that lab. . . ."

Through a swimming mist he saw the pink slip thrust at him along the counter. A kettledrum was beating in his ears, thudding out Yes Yes Yes and No No No in acceleration. He saw the manicured fingers of the corporal holding the upper edges of the slip. He read down till he saw the brash rubber stamp and the red crayon comment:

Wassermann — Pos

Kahn — Pos

Everything inside him seemed to whirl up and go down in a crash. Besides the drumming there now came a ringing in his ears. His knees buckled. He gripped the marble counter to keep from dropping to the floor.

"Tough luck, Sarge," the corporal said.

"What do I do now?" he said, his vision clearing.

For his previous weakness there was now substituted an icy surety of horror that carried him out to a pinpoint in space. And he saw Marisa's face, her mouth open, her eyes closed, murmuring:

"O come sai bene amarmi, tesoro mio. . . ."

"Just step into number four," the corporal said briskly and professionally.

He stumbled along by the cages, clutching the pink slip in his palm, which seemed to be gushing hot butter. He steered through a railing and into a long corridor with clinics and rooms opening off it. He knocked on the door of number four. At a call he opened to find a medical captain washing his hands in a sink and chewing gum in rhythm with the oscillation of his forearms.

"Mind waiting outside, Sergeant?" the doctor called sharply.

So he all but lay down on a bench, the slip dangling from his hand. He tried to close his eyes and swallow the searing sensation in his eyes and throat. Finally the sound of running water stopped and the doctor beckoned him in. He thrust the pink slip into the cool moist hand.

"Well, got the dreadfuldreadful at last, hey? You're one of the bright joes who thinks that the signs and films are for everybody in the army except himself. . . . And you won't be sergeant much longer, boy."

"Yessir," he said.

"Well, we'll start treatment at once. . . . We don't mess with this."

"Is there . . . any hope, sir?" he said hoarsely.

"I'm no great believer in this new treatment. . . . Take down your pants."

Then began the questionnaire, which the captain wrote down.

"Take a pro after your last exposure?"

"Nossir."

"Italian girl, I suppose. . . . Give me her name and address."

"Don't know, sir."

"Don't try to protect her through any mistaken notions of chivalry. She gave you a nice burning, and she'll do it to others. I advise you to give me her name and address."

"I told ya, I don't know, sir. . . ."

He went outside the dispensary and hung around the several waiting ambulances, holding in his hand an admission slip to the hospital. One of the ambulance drivers, a tech five, had one of his boots through a window of the ambulance cab.

"What hospital ya goin to, Sarge?"

"Twenty-third General."

"Then hop in. Ya can ride in front with me. Just like an officer."

He climbed into the front, to the right of the driver's seat. On the line he'd never had to ride in an ambulance. Now in the rear area of Naples, here he was going to the hospital in style, but not for a wound or for trench-foot. The tech five pulled his boot inside the window and started his vehicle.

"What are ya goin to the Twenty-third for, Sarge? Hepatitis? VD?"

"Nope, neither . . . just a general checkup."

They drove along Via Caracciolo toward Bagnoli Tunnel. And, seeing the Bay of Naples in the August sun, seeing the fishermen already far out in their skiffs toward Ischia and Capri, he thought of how he and Marisa used to walk and dally here in the bright open moonlight. They'd lean on the parapet by the docks of Santa Lucia and watch the British sailors coming over the ramp on liberty. . . . But now he was riding in an ambulance with a tech five who talked all the time, having lit a cigar. The tech five made him listen to all the details of his last night's shacking.

"I get me one gal an I stick to her," the tech five said. "Then I don't stand no chance of pickin up nothin nasty. See my point, Sarge?"

"Ya never can tell about them things," he answered vaguely.

He wished Marisa would quit his thoughts. He pressed down on his thighs and peered through the ambulance windshield. He knew that Marisa was very much with him. She was even in his veins.

They pummeled through the dark dripping gloom of the Bagnoli Tunnel. The overhead inset lights barely pierced the dusty gloom kicked up by the truck convoys. Marisa and her family used to sleep in this tunnel during the air raids. . . . And at Bagnoli they turned by the old tenements with the washing on the balconies, the arrows to direct traffic and show the way to the staging areas.

Then he got his first look at the Medical Center. Long low modern buildings with friezes and dominant stairs, like WPA American high schools. Unexpected gardens and trellises, phallic arches, and parapets skirmishing like roller coasters out of the pine trees. Excavated rifts piercing white and unfinished out of the hillsides. The tech five explained that Musso had built these grounds for a world's fair or something, that now the Americans were using them for a concentration of hospitals. They passed plaster statues of ripple-thighed naked young men in Fascist attitudes of victory. A couple of swimming pools. The whole Medical Center had an air like an exhibition: sheets of windows, inscriptions everywhere.

The tech five stopped his ambulance on an avenue near an MP gate.

"That's the Twenty-third right over there, Sarge. Just walk straight up to that barbed-wire enclosure . . ."

"Barbed wire?" he said. "But I ain't no prisoner."

"Just wait," the tech five said, wisely chewing off the tip of a fresh cigar.

He got out of the ambulance and walked up a flight of stairs to the barbed wire, over which hung the leaves of low trees and vines. Inside was a great press of people moving around. He thought of the courtyard of a jail during exercise period.

"No visitors here, Joe," the MP said, raising his carbine to port arms.

"I ain't no visitor," he said, presenting his admission slip.

"Then welcome," the MP said. "This the place where shackees repent their shackin. . . ."

There was a series of arrows showing new patients where to go. It was as methodical and cold as his induction into the army. He entered first a long low hut where pfc's sat at typewriters. In a window a major sat with bored but catty stare. To this medical officer he presented his admission slip. The major scanned it quickly, with the air of a movie usher seeing a picture for the hundredth time.

"So you got burned?" the major said. "And you'll be losing those three stripes too."

"Yessir."

"I don't say: Welcome to our hospital. You're not going to have a good time here. Our whole setup is guaranteed to make you hate everything about us. We don't want men coming back here, do you see? There's no excuse for getting VD. No excuse whatever. We give you treatment here, but we do it in such a way that you won't care to come back as a repeater. Yet I see the same faces again and again. Well it's their skin. . . . Take down your pants. . . ."

"Pretty sight, aren't you?" the major said after the examination. "Just as pretty as you saw it in the movies. I'll bet you said: That'll never be me."

"Nossir."

After the major had got through with him, lashing softly and insistently with his tongue, he was sent over by a wall where there were chairs with armrests, rubber compresses, and a lot of little glass vials with red stuff in them.

"Roll up your sleeve," the pfc attendant said.

"But I already had a blood test," he said.

"Roll up your sleeve. You'll be takin blood tests from now on like you would a bath. . . . An you can't give none of your blood to the Red Cross an get ten dollars for it, neither. . . . Make a fist."

He did as he was told. He felt the rubber hose go about his upper arm and the pressure mount as though an anaconda were squeezing. His blood began to bang in his arm. Looking down, he saw that a blue vein was bulging from his elbow. The pfc took a needle and inserted it into the obvious blood vessel. He felt the cold point go in, and he watched his crimson blood seep into the syringe as its handle was drawn back.

"At this point," the pfc said, "the jigaboos usually faint. . . . Now go an draw ya clothes."

He got up from the chair, crooking his elbow against the patch of cotton to stop the slow ooze of his blood into the elbow joint. The GI took the vial of his blood and pasted his name to it on a piece of adhesive tape. This he put into the rack along with the other vials.

"Looks just as pretty as new wine," the pfc said, indicating the file of vials. "Only no wine has got what these tubes have."

Next he filed past a counter where another GI leaned on his belly cushioning it and picking his teeth. He had that spleen of all supply sergeants.

"Take off ya clothes, boy."

He undressed himself there in the half-light of that corridor. Outside swarms of men milled in what looked like a desolate and unweeded garden pricked with pyramidal tents. All his clothes went into a little barracks bag tagged with his name. In return he got a set of frayed but freshly laundered green fatigues, shirt and trousers. On the back of his jacket and on the trouser legs were painted these large smeary letters:

VD

"Guess this is about the last time ya'll be wearing ya stripes," the supply sergeant said. "There ain't no rank here in them green fatigues. Ya'll sit down next to a major an never know it . . ."

"Take it easy, take it easy," he said, buttoning up the fatigues, which were a casual fit and chafed his crotch.

"Ya shoulda taken it easy yaself," the supply sergeant replied.

"Where do I go now?"

"Ya'll hafta see about accommodations, I guess. We're full right up in this hotel. An ya never wired us for a reservation."

So he walked down, stumbling a little in his fresh fatigues, to another window, where a pfc in harlequin spectacles was reading his *Stars and Stripes.*

"What can we do for you? Have you got number one or number two?"

"I got the worst ya can possibly get," he said.

"Well, lawsy. That entitles you to our very best accommodations. The kids with clap get stuck in tents all over hell. But our guests with syph are put in the bridal suite. You'll get the very finest attention. Every three hours, rain or shine, for a hundred and eighty hours. . . . You'll find the bridal suite in the first door on your right off the court."

He went out into the hot light of the courtyard. Now he understood clearly the confused and mobbed movement he'd seen through the barbed wire. Among the tent pegs walked hundreds of men in green fatigues like his own. It seemed a holiday crowd promenading at a carnival. But those who had their backs turned showed VD signs on their jackets and pants in letters high enough to be read half a mile away. They were like a chain gang without chains.

He entered the indicated door into a long shed, half-ruined and rambling as a cattle barn. Canvas cots with mosquito netting tied up over their racks stretched as far as his eyes could see. On these cots more men in green fatigues stretched reading or playing cards or shooting craps in small knots. He knew that they were set apart from all the other men in the world, though they looked perfectly healthy. When he crossed the threshold, a shout went up. Nearly all who weren't asleep turned to look at him and yell:

"You'll be sor-ry! Only a hundred and eighty hours more!"

He flushed, cast his eyes to the ground, and walked between the cots looking for an empty bed. He found one between a Negro who lay looking at the ceiling and an Ayrab in a red fez.

"They ain't no pick on the sacks," the Negro said, rolling his eyes slowly around. "Ya cain't never get moren three hours sleep at one time anyhow, boy."

"What's that Ayrab doin here?" he asked in a whisper.

"Mohammed? Oh all the Allied GI's gits their shots here . . . we got Goums and Eyeties too. . . . Lend-lease. . . ."

He sank down on his cot and looked at his shoelaces. He was casting about in his mind for some way to enter into conversation with the Negro and get answered some of the questions that flopped like flounders in his brain. The Negro may have been waiting, but he merely looked at the low ceiling of the shed with his deep eyes.

"Is it . . . rough . . . here?" he asked, untying his shoelaces and frigging with the buckles on his boots.

"Well, it ain't no rest cure," the Negro said. "But it done me a good turn in takin me away from mah woman. Ah'd a shot her. She gimme bad blood, bad blood . . ."

"What I mean is, do they . . . cure you fast here?" he pressed.

He was conscious of a fluttering fright now that the panic and fever of first discovery had ebbed.

"They claims they does. But man, them needles . . . every three hours. Ah feel like mah Aunt Delilah's pincushion . . ."

"Needles?"

"Sho, boy. What does yo think they does to yo here? They sticks yo an then they sticks yo again. Every three hours. Sixty times in all. . . . But it ain't doin me no good. Ah cain't do thout mah lovin. Soah'll go right out an do it agin. . . . Yessir . . . but them needles sure does go over big with us colored boys."

He had a dozen more questions to put. But he was confronted by a sharp sergeant standing by his cot.

"You. Didja just come in?"

"Ya."

"Then get down to the lab for ya first Dark Field."

"An that ain't no grope," the Negro said, rolling his eyes up to the ceiling.

He went past the double file of canvas cots out into the sunlight. He passed through the crowds of men in fatigues who walked alone or together, brooding or laughing aloud. He crossed the clearing of the pyramidal tents to the swinging sign that said LAB. Inside was another long room with desks where microscopes stood in their metal frames like scrubwomen resting on their brooms.

"You've come for your first Dark Field?" a sergeant asked him.

"I guess that's what they call it," he said.

He had visions of being smothered in black gauze, or pain and probings.

"Then down with your pants," the sergeant said.

The sergeant's face assumed the expression of one who handles the entrails of a sick rabbit. He put down his cigarette and drew on a pair of rubber gloves. Into his shiny false fingers he took a large toothpick wadded with cotton on its tip. Then he bent over and went to work.

"Whaddya doin? . . . Hey . . . you're openin it up . . ."

"That's what I mean to do . . . and if you think I enjoy doing this . . ."

"But ya hurtin like fire . . ."

"I'm swabbing. . . . Okay, up with your pants."

The sergeant straightened up, brushed the swab against a glass slide and dribbled on the square of glass some drops of staining chemical. This he slipped under a microscope near him.

"Now," he said, "I want you to see what death looks like."

The sergeant stepped aside blandly, allowing him to apply his own eye to the lens of the microscope.

"Focus it to your taste," the sergeant said languidly, picking up his cigarette.

He finagled around with the brass screw till he saw the field of the slide clarify and harden like setting Jello. He was looking at a shifting orange horizon that seemed to be clouds at sunset. There were strata that buckled and changed their densities.

"That," the sergeant's voice said, "is your own polluted blood. Keep looking."

Then he saw something swim into the pink blobs. At first he thought it was a sunfish. He maneuvered the focusing screw some more and found that it was a tadpole. It passed across his field of vision, delicately rowing, and disappeared gaily from his sight with a flip of its tail. He wondered if it hadn't winked at him like a goldfish on the make.

"And that," the sergeant's voice continued like a lecturer's in a darkened room, "is Sophie Spirochete. Just one of the girls, but what she can do to you! . . . Better than a bomb, though somewhat slower."

"Have I got many of those?" he asked.

"Millions. They're multiplying all the time. And brother, they'll eat you up alive!"

"Tell me what I must do," he implored, running his tongue along his lips.

"Every last one of them," the sergeant said, "has got to be killed. That was just one dear little specimen I took off you."

"Well, thankya anyhow . . ."

"Oh don't thank me," the sergeant said coquettishly. "You didn't get it from me, you know."

He'd just got outside the lab when an electric bell went off. All through that dense field of roaming men a mobilization became apparent, as in a factory after lunch hour. Soon there wasn't anybody left in the tent area. He decided that he too must be concerned in this; so he followed the last straggler round a corner.

On a long lading platform hundreds of men in green fatigues were arranging themselves into two files, one much longer than the other. At the end of the platform, by the screen door to what seemed a dispensary, a tech sergeant stood with rosters in his hands, adjusted his glasses, and read aloud in a shout:

"Hardfield! Jones! Miozza! McCauliffe! Mahomet Ben Ali! Get the hell up here for ya shots! Don'tcha wanna be cured?"

The two lines quickly evened out till the longer reached back to the end of the platform. He wasn't quite sure what the lines were for, and which was which. So he stepped cautiously up to a fellow with glasses:

"Maybe ya can tell me what cooks here . . ."

"Je ne comprends pas. . . . Pardon. . . ."

He tried again and this time got an answer from a pimply fat boy:

"This here's the clap line. We get stuck first. Those with syph come after us."

He thanked the joe and walked quickly away, placing himself at the tail end of the shorter line. The tech sergeant appeared again at the door of the dispensary with his rosters and hollered through the entire area:

"Shots! Shots! For Chrissakes come an get em! Ya'd be late to ya own funerals! An I ain't goin through the whole area to rout you lazy bastards outa ya tents!"

Tentatively he touched the shoulder of the man in front of him, handsome and bland and shy:

"Say, bud, am I in the right line?"

"Depends on what ya got," the blond boy replied, appraising him languidly.

"Same thing you got, I guess."

"Well," the blond boy said, "this ya first shot? Ya get only fifty-nine more after this one. One every three hours. I don't envy ya much. Ya got a week an a day ta go. . . . Christ, ya'll never sweat out anything like ya will these shots. . . . Three hours . . . three hours . . . forty-eight, forty-nine, fifty. . . . They even wake ya up in the middle of the night. . . . An if ya miss one, they make ya start all over again. . . . I'm gettin' out tamorrah. Hope a hope a hope."

"Where do ya take these shots?"

"In both shoulders an in both cheeks a ya butt. Ya get ta feelin like a sampler. Ya get so ya can't sleep on any part a ya. An still them damn shots go on. Like a pile driver. . . . But ya lucky. They just started this new treatment last week . . ."

"New treatment?"

"Ya. Pencil somethin. Before that they gave ya shots for six months. Useta make fellers puke all over the place. Now they give ya sixty shotsa this new pencil stuff, and it usually cures ya. The clap boys get only four. They get out in a day."

"I'll never come back here again," he said piously.

"That's what they all say," the blond boy said. "But they get repeaters here just like in reformatories. Buddy a mine's been in here four times. He gets all cleaned up, then he goes out and picks hisself up another dose. . . ."

The first and longer line began to press forward with rapidity. He thought to himself it was just like all the other lines he'd sweated out in the army — for movies, for PX, for passes. Soon the second line, his, began to urge up on the screen door. Inside the dispensary there was a wild cry.

"Either he's fainted or it's his last shot," the blond boy explained.

Finally it came his turn at the end of the file to enter the dispensary. Inside the screen door the line had forked into two prongs and was being funneled past two GI's, each with a hypodermic in his hand. Along the walls of the room were electric iceboxes. And on the tables glittering with hypodermics and blunted needles were many little glass ampoules of an amber fluid. Into these the GI's plunged their hypodermics, filled them like fountain pens, and squinted at escaping bubbles of the yellow liquid. Ahead of him were men with either arm bared or with their buttocks offered like steak to the needle.

"They give ya a choice on where ya want ya shot," the blond boy said. "If ya take it in the arse, they'll use a longer needle to get through the fat. My advice is ta take ya shots round the clock. Then none of ya four parts gets too sore. Ya'll be hurtin anyhow . . ."

"Come here," a voice called to him. "I haven't seen your face in line before, boy."

He disengaged himself from the line and went over to where a sergeant with gentian-blue eyes sat at a field desk. This sergeant's sleeves were rolled up to his elbows. Rosters were spread out in front of him. He gave the sergeant his name, which was last on the list.

"You're too nice-looking a guy to get this crap," the sergeant said. "Why don't you stay away from women, like I do?"

"I'm takin my medicine without any sermons from you," he said doggedly, looking down at his boots.

He wanted to be cured, not played with.

"Sure, sure, kid. . . . Look, every time you come in here, be sure to stop by and see that I check your name. . . . Otherwise if you miss a shot . . ."

"Ya, I know all that," he said impatiently, rolling up the right sleeve of his green fatigues and preparing to advance into the line for the needle.

Then the sergeant thrust out his fair delicate hand and flipped the miraculous medal that nestled with his dogtags among the hair on his chest.

"This didn't help you much, did it?" the sergeant said. "You're a mockery of purity."

"I promised my mother to always wear it," he said, again avoiding the cool blue eyes.

"You've got nice brown skin too," the sergeant continued. "Too bad to think of soiling it with crap like you've got. . . . Tell me, did you love that signorina?"

"Shut up an let me alone," he said and walked into the line.

"You'll see me sixty times," the sergeant called after him.

He offered his brown right upper arm to a GI who stood waiting with a hypodermic. He felt the antiseptic go all over his flesh like slippery ice. And then a swift stab as the needle went in.

"We ain't interested in making these shots painless," the GI told him.

He felt the needle's charge going into him in a compressed enema of spite. Then he knew a stinging worse than he remembered from tetanus shots. The needle was pulled out and his arm wiped again. On his skin he saw many lemon drops shimmering, raised out against the brown.

"What's that stuff?" he asked, lowering his sleeve.

"Penicillin . . . and more precious than gold, boy."

Being the last to get his shot, he was the last to leave the other door of the dispensary. Barring his way stood the gentian-eyed sergeant, hands folded on his chest. That open neck reminded him, with a jump of memory, of Marisa's throat, glistening and tight in its cords after he'd kissed it.

"Look," he said to the sergeant, "I just wanna be alone. I just wanna take my shots an be left in peace, see?"

"I was wondering," the sergeant said, recrossing his arms, "whether you got it from a one-night stand or from love. Because you seem so bitter. . . . Yes, you must have been in love with her. And now you look like a lamb that can't understand why it's being led to the slaughter. Why don't you want to talk with me?"

"Ya got some ax ta grind with me," he said pushing through the screen door.

The sergeant followed him:

"You know that I'm in a position to do you dirt. I might forget to check your name on the roster. Then you'd have to take all your shots over again . . ."

"I wouldn't advise ya to mess with me," he answered.

Outside the dispensary there was another corridor leading back to the tent area. It had lighted doors leading off it, with the names of medical officers and their rank printed in curly letters. Along the other wall were tin sinks in which GI's were washing their parts. Under these sinks were tin cans stuffed with bloody gauze. The running water and the septic smell and the pungency of dried blood made him dizzy, so he went out into the open air. The tent area had filled up again with men walking or talking or reading. Now he knew the rhythm of the place. They'd walk or talk or read for the next three hours. Then the bell would ring again. Then . . . he felt already the stinging in his other shoulder. All his life telescoped down to three-hour periods and a hypodermic needle with yellow drops dribbling out of it. What was it called? Pencilin? Penisssilin? Pencilillin?

In the shed the syphilitics had resumed their poses. They didn't walk in the courtyard among the tents with the others, for theirs was the scabrous aristocracy of venereal disease. Between shots most lay on their canvas cots dozing. One boy with horn-rimmed spectacles was reading Plato. And his own Negro neighbor still rolled his eyes slowly at the ceiling.

"Ah was a numbers man in Harlem," the Negro began.

But in order not to encourage the Negro's reminiscences, he threw himself on his own cot and closed his eyes.

"It's bad in the moanin," the Negro's slow voice dribbled through, even past his shut lids. "Ya know how a man wakes up. Well, now it'll hurt. An at night the thoughts yo has! Ya feel lak cryin. Least of all ah does . . ."

He emitted a soft feigned snore and the Negro shut up. His brain kept turning over the sibilant secret name of his disease. It was a word that he'd always thought of in connection with others, like leper. He was trying to get used to the idea of having it himself. It was as strange now, in the peace of aftershock, as imagining yourself dead. He kept trying to figure out what there was in the name of this disease, its very sound, that was so frightening. It had a whistling slide when you pronounced it, like a toothless old woman dragging her skirts in a black corridor. Or it reminded him of girls' names like Phyllis. Only with this girl he saw the skull showing.

He thought also of his mother and his sisters in Pittsburgh; their bathrooms with the embroidered cover on the toilet seat, the hems on their towels, the white soap in the rack by the washstand. He remembered how his mother got panicky when she found a speck of dust anywhere. Then he peeped through his eyelids at his own brown body, tense under its shameful green fatigues. And under his flesh he seemed to see microscopic rats running in his blood, squeaking and nibbling as they did their work of demolition. Till finally the house fell apart with a screaming clatter.

He thought also of the army posters against VD. He imagined himself addressing a V-mail to Pittsburgh:

> Dear Mother,
> You'll be surprised to know that I'm writing you from the syph-
> ilis ward of the Twenty-third General Hospital . . .

"I've got a new secondary," a bright lecturing voice said from some-where down the shed. "Not very nice. Just a rash on the inside of my arms and legs. And a few little blisters containing a rather nasty kind of pus . . ."

"Me and my buddy sweated out the clap for five days," another voice said. "Were our faces red when we found out what we really had! . . ."

"Why, it takes twenty years to kill you," another voice said.

Lastly he though of Marisa. He remembered yet the brown still fra-grance of her body, the round sucking bite of her lips against his shoulder. She'd told him to give himself to her, as she was giving to him, without re-serve or fear. She's said that gli americani made the act of love as sanitary as brushing their teeth or gargling with mouthwash.

"Ma perchè mi tratti cosi? Hai forse paura ch'io sia malata? Godi, godi, e non torturarti con certi pensieri. . . ."

It had been the first time he'd fallen in love. He remembered how he'd wait for her evenings in the Galleria, longing and hot, yet in a peace that was tender, and how he'd been gentle with her. Each evening he'd brought her candy or cigarettes or a handkerchief such as she loved. And he remem-bered how, after they'd spent their love, they'd lie together talking and laughing. It had never been so with him before. With all the others, after his fever was cooled, he'd only wanted to pay them and kick them out of the door. But with Marisa he'd known a sense of joy and well-being. Thus he'd given her his heart like a piece of fudge in his open palm. He couldn't yet associate this disease with her name. Only over her face there now hung a veil that blotted her features.

Yes, he was sick. It didn't feel like much of anything now. But his sick-ness was like being told definitely just how long he had to live. There was something mocking and foul in his disease, because it was a legacy to him from the happiest moments in his life. He remembered the idiots he'd seen in county jails, leaning out from behind their bars, lolling their tongues and screaming. He remembered old men helping themselves along the sides of walls with their canes, so that every step took half an hour to accomplish. All this had nothing to do with Marisa. Yet it had. . . .

Someone was tapping the sole of his boot. He opened his eyes. At the end of his cot stood a red-cheeked chaplain arms loaded with tracts and colored leaflets. So he sat up respectfully.

"Well, son," the chaplain said, "I guess now we see what the wages of sin are, don't we?"

"What sin?" he said, turning his eyes to the other row of cots.

"My boy, my boy. We mustn't be unregenerate in our hearts. Our disease is the punishment of God for fleshly sin."

"I happened to be in love," he said, standing up from his cot, putting his hands into his pockets, and whistling a little.

"Love!" the chaplain said with shining eyes, lifting his plump pink hands. "Love brings little children into the world. Not death. We should have saved ourselves for some fine clean American girl. These Italians are all sinful and diseased . . ."

"Then they should all get some of these here pencil shots," he said sullenly.

"My boy, if there were no disease in the world, there would be no decency. The fear of God. Our illness is a sign of the disapproval of God for what we did . . ."

"I was unlucky, that's all . . ."

"And the army doesn't approve either," the chaplain said, searching for further backing. "After we leave this hospital, we'll lose our rating, if we have one."

"I know that too."

"Well, I'll just leave some of these pamphlets, son. Let's all think of our mothers . . ."

"I have."

"I'd like to shake hands, son," the chaplain said, withdrawing. "But God has made certain diseases highly infectious. . . ." The chaplain went on to other cots. He lay down again and covered his face with his hands. He still saw Marisa's face, but he heard too a crowing laughter. Even her voice now seemed clotted with slime.

He soon got used to the simple reality of life in a syphilis ward. Three hours was the boundary of all his consciousness. He lived only for his next puncture. Every needle meant another x on the roster opposite his name, and three hours nearer to his release. Forty-seven, forty-eight, forty-nine, fifty. Night or day had no longer any distinct meaning, for he couldn't count on uninterrupted sleep for more than three hours. Then the fleering jangle of the electric bell. At 0300 hours in the morning, having just got to sleep after his midnight injection, he'd hear that silvery rattlesnake in the court outside. All the tents would come to life, with men groping into their fatigues and tottering out sleepy and cursing to where the threads of light poked out from the dispensary. The sergeant in charge of shots yelling for order. The beams of flashlights thumbing through the dark. The uproar lasting about twenty minutes. The files forming and going through like an assembly belt. Then the voice of a sergeant speeding up slackers who might be still in their cots. He didn't understand how people could take their time about their shots. Here they had death in their blood, yet they were leisurely and dilatory about receiving from the needle's point those yellow drops that meant life to them, life truer than the amber drops of gasoline or bubbles of molten gold.

He got into the habit of waking by reflex a few seconds before the electric bell exploded. He'd lie under his mosquito netting with an arm under his head, thinking: Now what did I wake up for? Oh, number twenty-two. And as soon as he heard the tingling dissonance he'd be bounding off his cot, buttoning his fatigues and sliding his feet into his boots, which he never bothered to lace or buckle. And he'd go rushing down the line of cots with their shadowy dressing figures. He usually managed to get to the dispensary among the first. Not that it made any difference. The gonorrhea boys always went through first. They took their own sweet time in forming their line. The syph patients were more eager beavers and would stand with their file already in order, cheering and booing the stragglers. For nobody got pincushioned till both lines were formed.

Needles around the zodiac of his brown body. At first he tried taking them in alternate arms. But soon the flesh of both shoulders was so raw that he couldn't sleep on either side. By the twentieth shot he was ready and eager to have them jab him in the buttocks. This called for a longer and heavier needle which bit him like a hornet. After a while both of his tight brown cheeks were so sore that he couldn't sleep on his back any more. He asked if he could be shot in the bulging calves of his legs, but they told him it would hurt worse than a cramp. So he finally evolved the least agonizing of many torments, which would carry him through half a day: a shot in the right shoulder, a shot in the left, a shot in his right buttock, a shot in his left. This meant that every twelve hours his compass was boxed. The stings felt worse all the time in his mincemeated flesh; he'd stand watching the penicillin ooze down his skin like the yolk of an egg. And always in the dispensary the ampoules of penicillin stood in a pretty druggist's window display of bottles, and the trash barrels outside the dispensary were overflowing with the dead ones, like small jars that had contained a lemon preserve put up every fall by his mother.

"I wonder how much the government is forking out for my sixty shots?" someone asked.

"When ya see it in a refrigerator," another said, "the stuff looks just like sherry wine on ice. They hafta keep it cool. . . ."

He had to go for his second Dark Field. Again he met the sergeant with the rubber gloves who scraped some fluid off him and put the film on the slide under the microscope. The sergeant indicated he should look again through the lens. He saw his salmon-colored blood; but try as he might, he didn't see a solitary tadpole wriggling. One floated by in the field, but it looked curled up and lifeless.

"Your spirochetes are pretty well done for," the sergeant said dryly.

"Ya mean I'm cured?" he asked, raising his eyes, dazzled.

"You'll take your full sixty shots, just like everyone else."

But he walked on air back to the shedlike ward and told everyone within range that the tadpoles in his blood were kaput. The Negro in the next cot just lay and looked at the ceiling for the doctor had told him to expect a circumcision tomorrow. The Negro had been saying all day in his dreamy voice that no army doctor was going to circumcise *him*. Hadn't he still his razor with him?

The last shot of the night vigil was given just as the dawn came up over Mussolini's fairgrounds at Bagnoli. Nobody slept much between the three o'clock shot and the six o'clock. The sun would leak up with a lemon and creeping pace. He'd totter out into the yellow and gray light, his eyes foggy, pulling his fatigues about him. The lines would form and the needles would start pricking. This was the time when the night shift of butchers went off duty to be replaced by the day shift. Their tempers were frayed and they did their jabbing with a vindictive spite, hating all who were so stupid as to catch diseases which would keep them out of their beds all night long on a hypodermic line. The six o'clock shots were characterized by blunt needles which tore his flesh jaggedly. Then there was the pulsing orgasm of the penicillin pumping into him like a piston.

Then he'd limp back to his ward, flexing his stinging arm. By his cot on the mosquito netting bar with his towel and soap hung his mess kit. He'd gather up this metal gear and head for the chow line. It was now fully light.

He'd made a friend in the ward, a shy guy who said he was a staff sergeant in ordnance. They waited together in the chow line. His new buddy talked about this nurse, and how he never suspected she would have passed It on to him. They dipped their mess kits into the GI can of boiling water.

"I wonder if they sterlize these things with each next batch of patients?"

"Nah, what with the scaldin water an that pencil stuff, ya can't catch a damn thing here. They even have Ginso barbers to shave ya if ya want it."

He got three meals a day of hot C-rations ladled into his mess kit. Back of the steam tables stood Neapolitans who leered knowingly at them as they dished out the steaming powdered eggs, the scalding coffee, and the chunks of bread. They jested with the patients:

"Whassamatta, Joe? Signorina malata?"

"Ah, fungoo and ya signorinas," the patients answered, helping themselves to marmalade and sugar.

He and his buddy sat down at the long planked tables, which filled up in order as the joes came off the chow line. Occasionally he saw a guy dressed in OD's instead of fatigues. That was a sign his shots were finished and he was going in the world outside the barbed wire. Opposite them was a little redheaded man morosely eating his powdered eggs and bacon. He had a burst of friendship for this sad little man. After all they were all members of the freemasonry of penicillin.

"Doin all right?" he nodded at the little redhead.

The little man didn't answer but moved himself and his mess kit to the other end of the table.

"They say that's a first looie," his buddy whispered to him.

"Oh they get it too, huh?" he said, poking some bread into his face.

Nobody talked much in the mess hall, except to agree that penicillin was a wonderful thing. Dried you up in no time. Or they compared their symptoms or told one another how many more shots they had to go. A few bragged that they were repeaters in this dump. Some came back constantly in order to keep out of combat, where they'd only get killed. But most held up their hands over their coffee:

"No sir! I ain't never comin back to this concentration camp!"

"Wait till ya get outside the barbed wire," the minority said, "an ya meet another signorina an she shakes it at ya. That's all it takes. . . . You'll be back."

Over their coffee he and his buddy lit cigarettes and looked at each other. All the meals were the same here. Three a day. Then you waited for your next shot. They went outside into the sunlight and dunked their mess gear into the GI cans of scalding soapy and clear water. The tent flaps were up all over the area now; the new sunlight made weird curlicues of the monuments, mosaics, and shafts of Mussolini's fair grounds at Bagnoli.

After breakfast he made up his cot, rolled up his mosquito netting, and waited for his turn for the broom to come by him. Bedmaking was easy, for he had two GI blankets, nothing more; sometimes it got chilly in the early mornings at Bagnoli in August, 1944. Then he'd sweep the kittens of dust from under his cot into the aisle and would pass the broom to the Negro on his right. He knew now who were the officers in the ward, in spite of the incognito of their green fatigues, because when the morning sweeping was in progress they leaned against the wall and tried to look nonchalant.

"Hey, sirrr," the pfc wardboy called to one, "there's no rank in a syph ward."

After the policing he'd lie on his cot and wait for the doctor to come. Each morning they showed themselves to this medical officer, who discharged those who were going out that day. For others he prescribed circumcisions or made little notes in their Syphilis Registers. Each had his own little scrapbook in which the progress of his disease was recorded. This doctor felt their glands or said:

"Rash fading nicely, isn't she?"

He was a fat little captain with a face like a doughnut. His eyes had frozen into a perpetual revulsion from looking at men's genitals and thinking in terms of spirochetes and gonococci. He was forever tearing off his rubber gloves, washing his hands, and peeling on the gloves again. Each morning he made a set speech to those who were going out upon completion of their sixtieth shot:

"Ninety per cent of you men will be permanently cured . . . if you don't get another case. . . . And if you do have a relapse, there's always that nice long-term treatment with mapharsen and arsenic. . . . In three months come back for your spinal."

It was always the mention of the spinal tap that sent a shiver and a whispering through the rest of the ward, who always listened to the doctor's baccalaureate sermons even when they weren't included in them. The Negroes, at that word spinal, would roll their eyes and gibber at one another:

"No, boy, ah ain't takin no spahnal . . . no suh . . . if dey ties me to dis cot, ah still won't take no spahnal. Dat needle sometimes slips and dere you is, paaaaahlahzed for de rest o yo natcherl life. No spahnal fo me. . . ."

Hearing this as he lay on his cot waiting for the captain to call out his name for the morning checkup, he'd imagine the needle at the base of his spine, the slip as the target was missed, and all his nerves jolting into paralysis.

Or sometimes to relieve the tedium of his morning examinations, the probing of groins and armpits, the questioning about the state of the chancre, the medical captain would bring specialists into the ward with him, colonels who peered at the patients as though they were guinea pigs.

"Look, Colonel, sir, he had a rare kind of rash. I had him photographed. With a mask, of course. . . ."

"This man insists he never had a primary lesion. . . ."

There was everyone on that ward: Negroes, Ayrabs, Italians fighting for the Allies, one Hawaiian Japanese. They waited three hours, took their shot, then waited again. They all wore the green fatigues with VD painted on the back. They all lived eight days inside the barbed wire. They all sat on the long planks in the mess.

After the medical inspection he was free till 0900 hours, the time of the next inspection. He'd take his towel, razor, and toothbrush and go out into the sunlit courtyard where the patients walked. He crossed the area of the tents of the common ordinary twenty-four-hour patients who were here for only four shots. He passed also the barbed wire within the barbed wire where prisoners with VD were treated under the eyes of their individual MP's. These real prisoners slept on the ground under the pup tents, issuing forth every three hours with their armed guard to get nipped by the penicillin needle. Then he'd arrive at the latrines, these too in sheds. Then began his one joy of the day. He'd brush his teeth and shave. Then he'd strip away the hateful green fatigues with the advertising on the back and step under the shower. He'd smear his long dark body with soap and let the tepid water gush over his flesh. At such moments he still thought of Marisa's arms that had given him this death. He'd lift his hoarse voice and sing an Italian song she'd taught him. For between the soapsuds and the penicillin something was being washed away from and out of him.

Close to 1500 hours he was lying on his cot reading a comic book. His thighs were crossed and his boots were up on the rack for his mosquito netting. He was sleepy, but it was almost time for the next needle. In the cots near him were people different from those who'd been here when he came a week ago. In this ward life went on by relays, constant as to the disease, but different in respect to personalities. He laid down his comic book, aware that someone was coming toward him. It was the gentian-eyed sergeant of the rosters. He sighed. The sergeant was carrying a parcel wrapped in wax paper.

"You again?"

"You weren't very glad to see me," the sergeant said, sitting on the edge of the cot and undoing a package.

"A roast-beef sandwich. . . . Are ya gonna eat it right here in front of me?"

"It's for you. We get good chow in the detachment mess. You must be tired of that C-ration they give you three times a day. I got the mess sergeant to make this up for me special. I didn't tell him I was giving it to a friend."

"Well, thanks. . . ."

He sank his teeth into the hot red flesh. The soft bread rose round his gums in a contrast of textures and tastes.

"Ya shouldn't bother with me," he said. "I'm just another syphilitic."

"You're not," the sergeant said.

He edged over on his cot to make room for the sergeant. He buried his face in the roast-beef sandwich to finish it, but he knew that those strange blue eyes were on his face. It made him squeamish to be watched while he was eating.

"Ya got some ax to grind with me," he said again, putting the crusts into the wax paper.

"Why?" the sergeant asked brightly. "You don't know me . . . yet."

"Well, it don't add up somehow," he said, shaking his head and placing his boots again on the rack for mosquito netting. "Ya must meet thousands of VD's coming through here for their shots. I'm just another one with the dirty bug . . ."

"I've watched half the Fifth Army taking shots," the sergeant said. "But when I saw you, I knew you were different."

"I snafu'd just like the rest of them," he said warily.

Besides reminding him of Marisa, something in this sergeant's blue eyes touched him, the way a lame bird would.

"You should come out to dinner with me once in a while," the sergeant said. "I know a black market restaurant on Via Chiaia. Do you like pasta asciutta?"

The words thrilled him with a pang of remembrance. He seemed to be with Marisa in a cramped kitchen in Sezione, San Ferdinando, she with an apron on standing over the stove. In those days he'd come up behind her and slip his hands over her loins. And she'd turn her face to be kissed. . . .

"Ya don't wanta be bothered with me," he said, wrenching himself from this memory. "I'm no good. Can't even take care of myself. Accordin to the posters the army puts out, I can never get married now nor have kids. I'm just a old pieca meat gatherin flies in the streets."

"You'll get cured," the sergeant said. "Just don't think you are till you know you are, that's all. . . . But you *are* different. . . . I need a friend, you see. Being a dancer has given me an unreal view of life. I'm so fed up with the arty boys. I want to know just one real person. You're good and you're decent. . . . I'm so bored with sitting around in cliques and drinking and talking poetry and scandal. . . . Do you like to swim? We could go to Torregaveta and Mondragone for sun baths . . ."

"I don't get much time off," he said.

"I need a friend who's real," the sergeant continued softly. "Someone who lives quietly and thoroughly without pointing out that he's doing it. I'm fed up with the idea of sex without love and ideas without deeds. . . . You shouldn't run with these Neapolitan girls . . . the ones, on Via Roma, I mean. They don't offer you anything without a price. There are nice Italian girls, but you won't stand a chance of meeting any . . ."

"When a guy needs a woman," he said, "he needs a woman . . ."

"That's the great old myth of the American male," the sergeant said wearily, picking up the wax paper from the cot. "And you see what you've got out of it. . . . Look at yourself in the mirror sometimes. That fine coffee-colored skin you've got and your black eyebrows and your straight nose. You're a very good-looking man . . . too swell to end up with syphilis from some bitch who didn't give a shit for you. . . . When I first saw you, it was like looking at a statue covered with mud . . ."

"I was crazy about Marisa," he said, surprised that he wasn't sore at this sergeant.

"I suppose you thought you were," the sergeant said. "That's all part of the mystery and the pain of life to me . . ."

"Say," he said, sitting up suddenly, "don't you like women?"

"When I don't see through them," the sergeant said, rising from the cot. "Will you come to dinner with me next week? Then we can go to the ballet at the San Carlo. The Italians can't dance, but they call it ballet anyhow. . . . Will you come?"

"I don't stand to lose nothin," he replied, trying not to sound calculating. "I won't be lookin at no women for some time now . . ."

"You're crazy if you do," the sergeant said hotly. "And do you think it would be fair to take any chances? Right now you're not infectious, but you can never be sure until you've had your spinal. It can come back on you at any time. Would you want to pass it on to somebody else?"

"I been thinkin of that," he said. "I ain't so low that I'd do to another girl what Marisa done for me."

"She's doing it for others right now."

"No," he said, closing his eyes. "I don't believe that."

"Did you give her name on the questionnaire?"

"Get out."

The sergeant with his bright hair and blue eyes and delicate figure stood irresolutely at the foot of the cot. He seemed to want to stay and to go. He looked almost as if Marisa had dressed herself in GI suntans and a blond tight wig.

"Willya do somethin for me?" he asked, already knowing the answer. He didn't believe in putting friends to the test, but he had an overpowering compulsion to do this. "Bring me some of that penicillin?"

"What for?" the sergeant asked in a quick whisper. "Do you want to sell it? Do you know what an ampoule of penicillin is worth on the black market? What do you want it for?"

"I ain't gonna sell it," he answered stiffly. "I just want it for myself . . . like people keep their appendixes and tonsils in a jar."

The sergeant shot a swift look along the ward, where as usual the patients were snoring on their cots or playing cards. He darted off. Shortly he was back carrying something in the same wax paper.

"You realize," the sergeant said, passing the wax paper into his hand, "that if anybody finds out about this, they'll throw the book and the DTC at me . . ."

"I ain't never done no one dirt in all my life," he replied, returning the sergeant's stare.

The ampoule with its amber fluid was still icy and misted from the refrigerator. He thrust it into the chamois bag containing his toilet articles.

"What a world," the sergeant said. "The mold of yeast turns out to be more precious than gold. . . . I've got to go, boy. It's almost time for the bell. . . . Meet you day after tomorrow at 1900 hours in the portico of the San Carlo."

"Okay," he answered.

A little later the electric bell began to split the air. He went out to stand in the second line. He had two more shots to go. Fifty-nine, sixty.

Next morning when the 0600 bell pealed for shots and the shadowy men in the first orange of dawn groped from under their mosquito netting into their fatigues, he remembered and smiled to himself and turned over on his other shoulder. His butt and arms still felt like hamburg, but it didn't matter any more now.

"Hey, Joe," the guy from the next bed was prodding him, "get out of that fartsack and take your needle."

"Ah, go way," he murmured, "I had my sixtieth."

He fell back into a delicious sleep during which he sensed an electric excitement in his belly. He awoke again when the others came trooping back from breakfast with their dripping mess kits.

"Powdered eggs?" he asked dreamily.

After a while without hurrying he got out from under his blankets, made his cot, and swept beneath it. He had a sense of victory over all the others, bending over their housekeeping with the painted letters VD on their backs rippling as the muscles in their shoulders moved. He felt particularly affectionate toward a tiny Negro two cots over who'd just come in.

"Boy, ah's scared. Does them needles hurt much?"

"Ya'll faint sixty times," he answered, sweeping under the tiny Negro's cot.

"O Lawd," the Negro said, fainting on his blankets.

When he'd revived his small friend, he took his chamois bag and went down to the latrines. Here Italian prisoners of war were swabbing the wooden frames and the corrugated urinal with chlorine. He rejoiced in its clean acridity. Before he seated himself, he reverted to his old fastidiousness of placing clots of toilet paper all around the wooden hole. It was a practice he'd dropped during his treatment here. Now he was beginning it all over again. Cleaniness was no longer a mockery. One Italian P/W called to the other as they mopped:

"Sa che cos'è la sifilide? Un' ora con Venere e dope sei mesi con Mercurio."

Shortly he arose in great satisfaction, brushed his teeth, and shaved. He'd observed that the brown skin along his thighs was paler for the eight days he'd spent out of the sun. Then he took a shower, soaping himself with gusto and dodging the Italians as they turned on the other sprays to damp down the floor planking. And his body was once again immaculate. He passed both hands along his loins in a wringing motion to force off the tire of soap.

He dressed himself for the last time in the tight green fatigues and walked up among the pyramidal tents. The gonorrhea patients were still making their beds. They had no floor to sweep, for it was of clay pounded down hard. They were rolling up the flaps of their tents to let in the Neapolitan sunlight: Ayrab soldiers under the red fezzes they insisted on coupling with their ignominious fatigues, French soldiers and officers from Alger and Oran, Italian sergenti maggiori who worked for the Allies, and that greater percentage of Americans. Occasionally one would run out to the Lyster bag and swallow his sulfa tablets.

In the great clearing girdled with barbed wire he paused to look at the bulletin board. On typewritten sheets were thumbtacked the list of dispositions for that day. He found his own name in alphabetical order under American Personnel. At first he had a feeling that perhaps they might never let him out of this place, that he'd stay here till the end of the war in Italy, being jabbed with millions of units of penicillin. But there was his name. He was getting out today. After each patient to be discharged was the rank and serial number, followed in the last column by the diagnosis. These read: Syphilis, Old, Secondary, Relapse; or Gonorrhea, New Acute. He noticed also that some people he'd met (he'd never guessed from their fatigues) were first lieutenants or majors. But most were GI's of all the Allied armies.

He returned with his toilet kit into the shed. They were lining up for inspection by the nauseated-looking medical captain. He unbuttoned his own green fatigues and waited his turn in the queue.

"You're going out today," the captain said, looking at his revealed middle and sounding his lymph glands. "Take a blood test every month. And come back for your spinal in from three to six months. Come even if we don't send for you. . . . And behave yourself, understand?"

"Yessir," he said slowly, then swallowed. "An' I wanna thank ya for all ya've done for me."

The rubbery face contorted into another knot.

"Don't thank me. Thank penicillin. Thank Dr. Fleming."

The medical captain then wrote out in an acid hand a discharge slip from the Twenty-third General Hospital. Then he consigned to him the little bound Syphilis Register with his name on the cover, like a diary, and two copies of a letter to his commanding officer making it quite clear why he'd been in the hospital — not in the line of duty.

"And don't try to tear up that letter," the doctor told him. "Because we mail a carbon to your CO anyway."

Then he went out into the sunlight among the pyramidal tents where the men in their green fatigues were milling and talking and waiting for the next electric bell. He went first to the supply sergeant to draw his own clothes. It was the first time in eight days he'd had them on; they were rumpled and a little mildewed from lying in the barracks bag. Then he had an inspiration. He took his razor from his toilet kit and sliced both sets of sergeant's stripes from his sleeves. His chevrons fell to the floor, trailing thread, twisted like crinkled tin foil.

"Might just as well bust myself right now," he said to the supply sergeant, handing across the counter the green fatigues with those huge letters painted across the back of jacket and trousers.

Next he went into the large office with the typists and the vials and the chairs with armrests. He sat down against the wall and let a tech five leech more blood from his arm.

"Of course this proves nothing," the technician said, emptying the dark blood into a test tube taped with his name. "Penicillin turns ya blood negative anyhow."

Lastly he went to the barrier in the barbed wire and presented his pass to the MP.

"See ya back here in about another week," the MP said, looking down at his sleeve, at the light triangular patch where his stripes had been.

"Not me, boy," he answered.

He walked slowly down the macadam drive of the Medical Center at Bagnoli. Once he turned in his tracks and looked back at the barbed wire behind which the hundreds of marionettes in green fatigues paced like lifers. He saw also the kiosks, the glittering façades, the nude muscled statues under their helmets, and the swimming pools that Mussolini had laid out for his world's fair. He couldn't forget that here he'd passed eight days of his life in three-hour intervals with a hypodermic needle waiting to prick him at the end of each period.

On the Bagnoli-Naples road a pfc in a weapons carrier picked him up. They rumbled through the Bagnoli Tunnel. In the August morning the town of Naples stretched golden on its hillside. Ischia and Capri struck like honey-colored thumbs out of the Mediterranean. He had an urge to talk.

"Say, that penicillin sure is marvelous stuff," he confided. "I was nearly dead from pneumonia an it pulled me out of it."

"Ah, it may have worked for you," the pfc said, biting on his cigar. "Me, I always say that penicillin is still to be put to the test. It's probably the latest racket of the medical profession. They say it cures VD too. Me, I think it just conceals the symptoms and arrests the disease for a while. But we don't know nothin about its future reactions on the human body. Ten years from now you'll probably find cripples and people dropping dead all over the United States. Victims of the great penicillin swindle."

"Nah, it works," he answered in a dreamy sort of happiness. "It's great stuff, boy. . . . Cured my pneumonia. . . ."

In Naples he dismounted from the weapons carrier at the end of Via Roma. He entered the Galleria Umberto, where the girls were walking and the children screaming and bargaining in the August sunlight. He walked to that corner of the Galleria that he remembered best. Though it was noon he seemed to see Marisa standing there with her arms out to him. So he took the ampoule of penicillin out of his pocket and hurled it against the wall where her ghost flickered. The glass smashed; the yellow liquid ran like bright molasses to the pavement.

D-Day

ℵ

from *The Sixth of June*

by LIONEL SHAPIRO

The assault craft were lowered into a choppy sea and the moment they hit the water they bounced and snorted away from the mother ship. The sky was black and the sea was black. There were thirty men to an L.C.A. They huddled one against the other at the sides of the small craft, shielding themselves and their weapons from the spray that lashed all about them. Only two men at the helm stood erect. They were the navy men, a sub-lieutenant and a petty officer. They stood on a platform which elevated them above the line of the forward ramp.

The sub-lieutenant commanding Brad's landing craft looked ridiculously like a boy, fresh-faced and eager, his duffel coat open and flying in the wind and his helmet carelessly perched on the back of his head. His was the leading craft of a column of four. There were three columns, each of four craft, and they held steadily to formation though the swells were treacherous and the spray blinding.

Brad sat in the forward end, his back against the ramp, and he could feel the thump of the sea crashing the ramp, fighting and twisting and almost overturning the small craft. It had never been as rough as this in their rehearsals off the Dorset coast, Brad thought, and he wondered if they would make it. The waves thundered deafeningly against the thin steel sides as if eager to splinter through the impertinent little challenger. He looked at his men huddled against the sides. Their faces were grim and tight-lipped and terribly white. They were men who knew how to use their muscles and weapons on land. They were helpless in the wallowing sea and they kept looking back at the young sub-lieutenant, seeking to reassure themselves that he knew what he was doing and where he was going. The spray came over the sides regularly now. Water surged along the bottom of the craft and slopped over the men's boots. But the face of the youth at the helm had not lost its eagerness and his body inclined gracefully to the thumps and shudders of the craft.

Some of the men were sick. Brad could hear their retching in the brief silences between bursts of wind and spray. He made his way aft.

"How are we doing?" he called up to the sub-lieutenant.

"Coming nicely, sir. We're dead on — or nearly. Perhaps a minute or two late. Nasty swell."

"How long to go?"

"Oh — twenty-five minutes, I'd say." The youth looked down and said saucily, "In a hurry, sir?"

There was something vastly reassuring in the way the youth said it. Brad went back to his place at the ramp. His mind spun over the time schedule. In twenty-five minutes they would land. In an hour it would all be over — one way or another, all over. Thinking about it, he checked his equipment. Two 77 grenades, two 36's, his pistol, compass, dagger, and his field and shell dressings. His Sten gun was cradled on his arm, the spare clips in the long pocket on the right thigh of his trousers. And he had his luck, all of it, unchipped, as John had said. He was grateful to John for having said it. That had helped more than anything else. He felt wonderfully calm and confident. He couldn't fail.

The craft suddenly quivered as if it had been struck by a giant wave and it bounced high in the air and fell with shattering impact. For a long moment it remained at an alarming list. A burst of water poured in over the low side before the craft righted itself. The men cursed miserably and more of them were sick.

Then a sound of faraway thunder drove in over the lashing of the waves. The huddled men came alive. They were wildly sensitive to every new sound. The thunder increased in frequency and intensity and reached a violent, unceasing pitch. There was an uneasy shuffling in the craft.

The sub-lieutenant shouted, "Those are our navy guns. They've started beating up the beaches!"

Then a new sound, a distant roar of planes, swept in and added a bewildering complexity to the thunder of the guns and the waves slapping against the craft.

Brad glanced at the luminous hands of his watch. It was five forty-five. Landward to the left a line of briefly flickering lights leaped up out of the darkness like anvil sparks. Flares hung in the sky miles away and looked like tiny candles. Here and there a plume of green flame burst forth and burned fiercely for a few moments. The bombardment of the beaches had begun on schedule. These were the flat, fortified beaches where the full divisions would land after dawn. Straight ahead, the gap of Pointe Ange was cloaked in darkness and it was towards this strange patch of gloom in an otherwise desperate fairyland of fire that the L.C.A.'s of the special force beat their way through the rough seas.

The sub-lieutenant came forward, his duffel coat still flying open in the wind. His face was bright with elation, like a boy on a wonderful party.

He said, "You may alert your men, sir. We're a mile off the forming up for the final run-in."

The men didn't have to be told. Shielding their weapons, they crept to their places facing the ramp. The craft moved at reduced speed, stealthily it seemed, and the resistance of the sea slackened. It was very dark. The naval bombardment reached a new and terrifying pitch and though the sound was miles distant its immense power was transmitted through the night and the sea fairly shook with the punch of the great cannon. The men looked about with reborn interest. The feeling of being alone on the wretched sea had dropped away. Someone made a falsetto like an old woman: "Can you tell me, mister, when we reach Paducah, Kaintucky?" A little forced laughter died off quickly and left the compulsive thunder of the warships and the thrum of planes and the lapping of the waves.

"Kedge anchor!"

"Kedge anchor ready, sir."

The engines cut out and the craft floated free and aimlessly a few moments. There was a thump as if it had hit a rocky bottom, then a sickening lift and another thump and the ramp skittered down and a new wind, a soft, land wind, hit the wet faces of the men.

The men of Dog Company stood hidden by the starless night beneath a rocky outcropping on the narrow beach. Waves rolled up and lapped at the boots of the men on the outside flank. They waited for the signal that would propel them into action, that would send them scurrying eastward along the beach for sixty-five yards where, according to the map, a defile opened a way to the high ground. They were restless. Like athletes champing at a starting line, they tested the footing in the soft wet sand and pushed aside clumps of weed the receding tide had left on the beach. They could see only ten or twelve yards ahead and they were uneasy about the debris they might stumble into on their way to the defile.

They were panting though the run from the ramps of the landing craft to the shelter of the outcropping had been a short one. It was the deadly excitement of waiting that made them pant. The three other companies and the H.Q. platoon had landed farther down the beach and had to be given time to form up at their starting points, which were almost half a mile west of where Dog Company stood.

Far out on the sea to the east and west, tiny tongues of flame spurted out of the dark and the deep, full-throated roar of 16-inch naval guns raced across the water and echoed in wave after wave against the shelf of rock where the men stood. The thrum of hundreds of bombers flying high over the coastline was ceaseless. The men didn't look out to sea or up into the black sky. They peered at the limned figures of their platoon leaders, and the platoon leaders kept their eyes glued on the company commander, waiting for him to give the signal.

Brad studied his watch. He was scarcely conscious of the distant thunder of the naval guns and the ceaseless thrum of aircraft. He counted the seconds ticking off and listened for another sound, a sound of small-arms fire. This would be the signal that one of the other companies had been intercepted on its way to its starting line. If this happened, the zero hour for the synchronized attack they had rehearsed for so long would be jettisoned and he would, in the words of the operations order, "act independently to the capture and complete destruction of D Company objective."

It hadn't happened. Not yet. The luminous hand turned slowly around the face of the watch, so slowly he suspected something had gone wrong with the mechanism. Now there were three minutes remaining before the move to the defile would begin. Three minutes seemed terribly long. He wondered how he could pass three whole minutes standing motionless and quiet. There was a foul smell coming off the cliffside, a smell of feces and rotting food. The Germans had been tossing their waste pails over the cliffside. The tide had carried the stuff out to sea, but the smell clung to the rocks and the brush just above where he stood.

Now the arc of the sky had turned from black to murky purple and a thin line of light was rising out of the sea. The beach where he stood was still cloaked in impenetrable darkness. He wondered if the navy people who had set the timing of the operation to coincide with an exact degree of first light had made a mistake. He glanced at the watch. Two minutes to go and there wasn't enough light, not nearly enough light for sure footing on the climb up the defile. Perhaps the timing was all wrong. Perhaps a clerk in the navy met office had made a simple mathematical error.

He checked himself. There were eighty-five men peering at him and he was their commander. A few were close enough to see the expression on his

face. He forced his clenched teeth apart and moved the hand that held the
watch in a small circle to show that he was relaxed. He tried to gauge his
fear. There was some, perhaps a lot in him. This was his first battle.
He had no way of knowing how much fear he was entitled to feel. He remembered Dan saying once, "You're scared all the time, boy, but you're
too busy to know it." He wasn't busy now and he was scared. He could
feel his sweat on the helmet lining pressing against his forehead. He
turned to look into the faces of the men nearest him. He was sure they
could smell the feces and the rotting food so he put his fingers to his nose
and winked at them. He thought this was what Dan would have done.
There was one full minute to go.

One minute to go and there had been no rifle signal. This meant that
the other companies had reached their starting lines without interception.
The Germans would be alert, of course. The bombardment of the beaches
to the east and west would have alerted them. They might even know
there was an enemy on the beach below making ready to storm them.
This possibility had always figured in the planning. The fact that there
had been no rifle signal didn't necessarily mean the Germans were unaware
of the impending attack. It depended on the commander of the *Steutz-
punktgruppe*. If he was cool and clever, he would preserve silence and
meet the assault from his positions of strength behind concrete fortifica-
tions. A nervous commander might send his men to the edge of the high
ground and attack the assaulting forces coming up the defiles.

But there had been no signal. Either the German commander was cool
and clever or the landing, shielded by darkness and the diversion of the
distant bombardment, had been undetected. The forecast of the planning
staff was that they would land undetected. He prayed they might be
right. He would know soon enough. The second hand on his watch passed
the thirty mark. The men were shuffling with impatience.

The navy people hadn't made a mistake. The light *was* coming up steadily over the line of the sea, a hazy purplish glow that was neither daylight
nor night. He could make out a wooden ration box half buried in the
sand about twenty yards ahead. He hadn't seen it before. This was the
visibility they had been planning on. By the time they reached the wire
on the edge of the high ground, the light would be good enough for sure
footing but still too poor for the Germans in the pillbox to see them setting
the bangalores. The navy people were wonderful. Right on the nose.

The second hand came up to the sixty. He raised his arm and the men like
eager, stealthy animals moved swiftly along the narrow stretch of wet
sand.

The light that had appeared hesitantly on the edge of the purplish sky
was a welcome sight for a young *Oberleutnant* of signals in the Pointe

Ange station. He had been on duty in the big underground casement all
night, a terrible night of telegraph keys clicking without a moment's
respite and telephone bells ringing with wild impatience and the *Oberst*
pacing about in a foul mood. He had never experienced a night of such
utter confusion.

He himself was confused. He admired the Wehrmacht. He thought it was
the finest human instrument created by the Reich. Yet the generals
couldn't make up their minds whether or not a full-scale assault was being
aimed at the Normandy coast. Not a single troop movement had been
ordered, even in the face of the shelling and bombing of the coastal
positions and authentic reports of massive parachute drops behind the forti-
fications. This was the height of stupidity and he hated to think of the
Wehrmacht as stupid.

He welcomed the dawn because it would bring an end to official stupidity and a beginning of visual truth.

He remembered clearly when the confusion had begun. It was at exactly
0145 hours. The Intelligence section of the 709th Infantry Division at
Cherbourg signaled urgently that a mass of American parachute troops had
dropped in the vicinity of Ste. Mère Eglise. But not more than five minutes
later, the same Intelligence section corrected its previous report and indicated that the occurrence was merely an arms drop to the F.F.I. and was
being investigated. Then the 716th Infantry Division at Caen signaled a
British parachute drop at the mouth of the Orne. Headquarters of the
Seventh Army at Falaise immediately asked for clarification. Was it a raid
or an arms drop? And was it at Ste. Mère Eglise or at the mouth of the
Orne? Nobody seemed to want to say definitely. Then the navy confounded the already terrible mess. The navy station at Courseulles signaled that radar findings showed a great mass of ships approaching the
Bay of the Seine, but this interpretation was overruled by Naval District
Headquarters at Le Havre. It reported to Seventh Army that sea and weather
conditions were clearly unfavorable for an assault and what the Courseulles station had reported was a diversionary maneuver at best. Then
Seventh Army contacted the Calais station and the latter reported that
the enemy assault fleet based on Dover-Folkestone had definitely not put
out to sea. Then the Luftwaffe at Carpiquet aerodrome signaled that
their night patrols had observed a mass of assault ships in mid-Channel.
This launched a new spate of messages between Cherbourg, Caen, Calais,
and Seventh Army. The messages were angry and confused and by 0545,
when the bombardment of the beaches began, not a single headquarters
would make a formal declaration that the long-awaited assault was under
way, and Seventh Army was still asking for clarification.

The *Oberleutnant* concluded sadly that this was a perfect illustration of
what was called the fog of war. He handed over his duties to his deputy,

slung his field glasses over his shoulder, and came up out of the casement.

In a few minutes it would be light enough to see the warships that were bombarding the beaches on the flat beyond Port-en-Bessin. He thought it would be amusing on his next leave to recount to his wife how the generals, the Luftwaffe, and the navy had argued back and forth whether there was or was not an assault coming in across the Channel and he had merely walked to the edge of a bluff and seen for himself. It was really quite amusing, he thought. Everybody knew what was happening except the generals.

He climbed the cement steps and nodded good morning to a major of infantry who sat and smoked below the slits where his men stood at their machine guns. Then he climbed another short set of steps and emerged in the cool, breezy air.

It was not quite light yet. He could barely make out the rounded tops of the pillboxes to the right and left which defended the signals station though each was only a hundred meters distant. He looked behind him across the gully and couldn't see the third pillbox at all. It was at that peculiar time of morning when the light was exceptionally deceptive to the eyes.

He walked down the open ground between the two pillboxes, moving carefully in the uncertain light because the ground was pitted with shallow bomb holes. He listened to the salvos of naval artillery and the drone of the planes and he thought it would be something to see when the light became good enough.

He kept on walking until he reached the wire on the edge of the bluff. New wire had been looped over the old wire and it rose to a height above the line of his sight, so he moved away from the wire to a clump of low-growing bushes over which he could have an unimpeded view of the sea and the beaches.

He reached down at his hip for his field glasses. Then he paused. He thought he saw a heap of loosely strung wire lift into the air as though by unseen hands. Fascinated, he watched it for a few moments. He saw the glint of a helmet. Someone was trying to crawl up from under the wire.

He let his field glasses fall back quietly into the case on his hip and reached instead for his pistol. He flicked down the safety pin and waited. When the figure crawled clear of the wire and began to look about, he saw that the helmet was American. He lifted his pistol and waited until the figure had crawled forward a little more. He took careful aim and fired.

The shot that killed Dan Stenick also set off the battle for Pointe Ange.

Across the gully, a good three hundred yards distant, Brad heard the shot. He was lying in a culvert a few feet beneath the wire that hung over the lip of the high ground. He heard the single pistol shot despite the racket of the naval bombardment because his mind had become animal sensitive and was alert to any sound that would affect his safety. He wondered if the Germans in the pillbox had heard it. He calculated they were eighty yards farther distant from the shot and would not have been listening for it.

He watched the engineers of Urquhart's platoon push three lengths of bangalore pipe through the wire. They were the first men to reach the lip of the high ground; below them were the M.G. squads and still farther below were Norden's rifle squads. The engineers needed a few more seconds to set the fuses on the bangalores while men below struggled to position their 2-inch mortars that would fire smoke bombs into the open area in front of the pillbox and provide temporary cover for the men who would crash through the gaps blown in the wire.

They didn't get the few additional seconds they needed. In the wake of the single pistol shot across the gully came a shattering cacophony of rifle, Sten, and machine-gun fire, of bursting grenades, of screams and shouts of command, of wild inhuman yells that pierced the deafening clatter of automatic weapons.

The men of Dog Company had rehearsed for such an emergency. On command, the men below abandoned their 2-inch mortars and let fly with their smoke grenades, the 77's, tossing them high over the wire. It seemed an excruciatingly long time before the grenades landed and their smoke billowed up on the open ground. Then the engineers put fire to the fuses of the two bangalores that were primed and ready. There was a wretched, tearing explosion and flame and choking smoke leaped wildly from the gaps flung open in the wire and the men scrambled up over the lip of the high ground and crashed blindly through the gaps.

There were some, confused by the black billowing smoke, who failed to judge the gaps properly. They found themselves entrapped on the wire and tried to pull themselves free and smashed frantically at the wire with their rifle butts and screamed for help from the men beside them who were racing freely through the gaps. A squad leader, a bulky sergeant, paused to work the entrapped men off the wire, working desperately on the wire and bellowing and cursing and commanding the others to get through inside the wire. A sudden gust of wind caught up the smoke and the men on the wire were trapped naked in the rising light. A new hail of 77's fled through the air to give smoke cover to the men caught on the wire and the others who were scrambling over the lip of the high ground lugging the heavy equipment, the mortars and machine guns and the beehive charges. But the new smoke didn't come soon enough. The German machine guns at the slits of the pillbox swung swiftly into range and their bullets crashed and whined and ricocheted in the clumps of wire and the men screamed as they were hit and some didn't scream but fell face forward across the wire. The bulky sergeant who had been trying to pull the men free of the wire continued to bellow and beseech the others to keep moving up the defile and through the gaps and then a burst of 50-caliber M.G. ripped across his chest and punched him back over the lip of ground behind the wire. The bullets cut him almost in two and he lay half over the lip of ground, his mouth agape and his head and chest unrecognizably bloody like a butchered calf. He dangled there.

The men scrambling up from the defile heard the screams of the men hit on the wire and they saw the bloody dangling head of the sergeant. They waited for the smoke from the new hail of 77's to cloud the half light and they knew this was the time to get through to the high ground. This was the only time, for a mortar was working out of the pillbox, in addition to the M.G. fire, and was dropping anti-personnel shells into the defile and was taking a terrible toll of the men who were hesitating below the lip. So they scrambled past the dead sergeant and through the gaps. Some were hit but most got through and plunged blindly to the right on the inside of the wire, as they had done in rehearsal, until they made contact with their platoon and squad leaders, those that were left. The teams that carried the Brens and L.M.G.'s, Urquhart's teams, hurled themselves into the shelter of the merest bulge of ground and set their sights on the pillbox which loomed gray and hazy in the shifting, smoky, uncertain light and on the slits which were punching orange tracer into the gaps in the wire.

The newly organized fire from the Brens and the L.M.G.'s concentrated on the slits in the pillbox and the enemy gunners swung away from the gaps in the wire and sought out the men who had broken through.

Now Norden's riflemen flung themselves through the gaps and took up their positions for a right encircling assault on the pillbox. Norden scrambled among his men. A bullet had ripped open his cheek and he was bleeding badly. He cursed. He could count only about twenty men out of the minimum of thirty-five he expected to reach the position. He didn't know if he could make the assault with twenty men. He tried to make another check. He had to keep his head down. The Germans had widened their field of fire and bullets were ripping the ground all around him. The wind was brisk off the sea and was lifting the smoke too quickly. He thought if he didn't get the signal quickly for phase two he wouldn't have even twenty men to make the right encircling assault.

Brad had crashed through the wire with the leading squad. He was on the ground now, crawling like a wary animal behind the men of Urquhart's platoon who were maintaining the covering fire on the slits. It was hard to estimate how many had got through the wire. The light was a thinning, uncertain purple and the waves of smoke stung in his eyes and the inhuman racket of the automatic weapons blunted his brain. He could hear the screams of the wounded piercing the clatter but this did not touch him except as an estimate of how many men he had left for the final phase. He crawled about behind the perimeter of Urquhart's platoon until he found Urquhart, who was firing a Bren. Urquhart shouted over a body that lay crumpled between them. He shouted, "Go ahead. We're all right. We'll keep their heads down." And Brad shouted, "Watch for the yellow and give us everything."

He crawled around farther to the right where Norden's platoon was positioned. Norden's face was dripping blood and he shouted, "We only got twenty men. I don't count more. Only twenty. Do you hear me? Only twenty." Brad saw that Norden was badly wounded and hysterical. He kept shouting, "Only twenty, God damn it, only twenty. Either we go or we don't!" Brad shouted, "We go. Fire the yellow!" and Norden shouted, "Fire the yellow!" and then someone shot a yellow flare and it seemed to hang for a long moment in the smoke and dust.

This was the signal for maximum fire from Urquhart's men and for smoke bombs to be set off from the mortars below the lip of high ground. The air was convulsed with the clatter of every weapon the men could lay a hand to, even piats which would scarcely nick the concrete of the pillbox but would have strong shock effect on the men inside.

When the new smoke rolled over the open ground, Brad gave the signal and Norden's men advanced to the right in an outflanking movement, seeking to come up against the rear of the pillbox and to blast it open. Norden screamed unintelligible commands and his legs were buckling as he stumbled through the smoke. Brad knew he wasn't going to make it as far as the pillbox and he took command of the men. They advanced through the smoke, keeping well separated, and when the smoke began to thin they flung themselves to the ground. Brad saw they were about fifteen yards from a narrow, cement-lined trench which led to a door at the side of the pillbox. He saw that the door of the pillbox was open, that eight or nine Germans were crouched in the trench peering over their rifles as if they knew an outflanking attack was coming around the right and were waiting to slaughter the attackers when the smoke cleared. He saw that two of his men who were lugging the beehive explosive had gone ahead blindly just as they had rehearsed it and he shouted to them to hit the ground.

The Germans in the trench fired and the men lugging the beehive fell back screaming. In the interminable moment between the time they were hit and the time they fell back screaming, a brutal, chilling, panic-stricken moment, Brad saw that he and his handful of men were trapped in the open, hopelessly trapped, and he thought, This is the way it ends and this is where it ends, here on the pitted ground, and all the things that have gone before are erased and don't count, and all the exercises and the toughness and the unchipped luck, nothing counts. This is the end, the way it's got to be and God! I don't want to die but I'm going to die on this pitted ground and I wonder how it will be. He thought, It's a lousy break having to die like this in the racket and the smoke and the smell, a lousy break first time out. He thought these things in the terrible moment between the time the men lugging the beehive were hit and the time they fell back screaming. He could see clearly they had no chance against the Germans crouching inside the concrete trench, but he was the leader of the men lying on the ground around him, and a leader must do what he must do, but it was hard, so terribly hard to get off the ground and plunge forward knowing he would be cut down, but he had to do it and he got up off the ground. He saw Norden staggering up from behind, his face stark and bloody as if he had crawled out of a grave, and he screamed, "Hit the ground, Norden!" but Norden didn't stop and he plunged forward together with Norden, and all the men, those that were left, shouted crazily and charged the trench.

He was almost at the trench, not more than three or four yards from it, when he was hit. He could see the face of the German who fired the shot, a pair of young, terrified eyes in an ashen face beneath a helmet, and for a lucid and singular moment the war was between him and the young, terrified German.

It was a moment wrenched out of time, removed from the gun clatter and the animal cries, from the fever of the attack. He had been hit. He knew he had been hit. The bullet punched him back as if he had been struck a powerful blow in the belly. He wondered why he didn't feel pain. His whole body vibrated with the kick-back of the bullets sputtering out of the Sten he held thrust forward in his two hands. His eyes telescoped on the frightened eyes of the youth who had shot him. He felt a dizzy elation for knowing he had been hit and didn't feel pain, and for his animal awareness that he was stronger, more vicious than the frightened youth, that he was going to kill the frightened youth. He saw the bullets from his Sten strike across the neck and chin of his enemy and he saw the youth's mouth open in an intensely human attitude of indignation. He thought it was a strange expression, that of indignation, at the instant of death. And then the moment was flung back into time and reality and he was shattered by the racket of the automatic weapons and the shrieking and a convulsion of pain poured through him and his elation turned to agony. He couldn't feel his legs for the fire in his belly, no legs at all, and he toppled as from a great height and was a long time hitting the ground. He saw heavy boots leaping over him and round him and he heard screams of animal rage and terror mixed with the deafening vibration of automatic weapons. A grenade came looping through the air and bounced along the ground away from him. He pulled his arms around his head and tried to burrow into the hard ground. There was an explosion. He felt he was being lifted as if by a hurricane wind and the scorching pain in his belly was over-whelmed by a new anguish as if a thousand hot needles had struck into the side of his body. He couldn't see for the smoke pouring up all around him and the fumes of burning cordite brought vomit choking into his throat.

He was afraid to move, afraid to discover how badly he had been hit. He lay still but his mind was frantically alive and he listened to the rattle of fire, calculating its direction, and then he heard the thud of a great many boots racing up to him and past him into the trench. Suddenly the firing and the screaming stopped and he heard only deep sobbing moans and he knew the battle was over.

After a time he tried to bring his arms down from their shielding posi-tion around his head. Only his right arm would respond. He couldn't feel his left arm except as part of a great area of pain that throbbed and stabbed and was sickeningly warm. He rolled over on his back. The first thing he saw was the sky. It was at half-dawn, gray and shimmering with a haze of thinning purple. He turned his head and looked along the ground and he saw Norden's bloody face staring at him. Norden was lying flat on his stomach, his legs spread wide apart, and his head was twisted on its side in grotesque juxtaposition to his body. Norden was dead. He tried to lift himself by his good arm. He couldn't. He felt the strength running out of him and he thought he had better lie still.

He spent a little time convincing himself he was alive. He watched the clouds scudding across the purple-gray sky and listened to the soft moans of men around him and to the clatter of the battle across the gully. He wondered why the battle there wasn't finished. He tried to remember the time schedule for the battle across the gully but he couldn't remember it. His mind was numb. All he could think of was that he was alive and that he should fire three red flares to signal to the beach that the battle was over. He moved his good hand along his wounds and it came up warm and dripping blood.

Urquhart leaned over him.

"How is it, Brad?"

He said, "Did you fire the three reds?"

"Yes. What hit you?"

"Everything."

"I'll get a medic. Does it hurt?"

Brad said, "Norden's gone."

Urquhart looked over at Norden's body. He gathered up the dead man's helmet and placed it over the bloody face.

Brad said, "How many more gone?"

The lieutenant grimaced and said, "Christ, I don't know. I just don't know. About thirty."

"Oh God. Thirty."

Urquhart looked as if he wanted to cry. He said, "We made it."

A medic, panting and frowning, ripped away the cloth on Brad's left side, cut open a bag of sulfa, and sprinkled the powder over the blood and the bits stuck in the blood. Brad said, "What is it? Bad?" The medic said with sharp anger, "There's lots worse'n you." He applied a shell dressing and powdered it with more sulfa.

Brad said to Urquhart, "What happened? At the end, I mean."

"They stopped firing when you hit the trench. They turned their gun barrels up out of the slits and we charged over and collected what was left of them. About a dozen — old and kids. Christ, they were scared. Worse than us."

The medic bandaged his left arm against his side, over the shell dressing, and said, "We'll get you down to the beach soon as we can," and hurried away.

The sulfa burned on his naked wounds. His head whirled with pain and nausea came in waves and was worse than the pain. He wondered if he was going to die. The medic wouldn't have handled him so angrily if he was going to die. Even on a battlefield there was some pity for a man who was going to die. The medic had shown him no pity at all. That was good. He thought, God, the luck! It wasn't chipped away. I had all of it.

The rattle of automatic weapons and the crump of mortar shells came from across the gully. The sound seemed to him remote compared with the compulsive clatter of his own action, but he listened to it with a heightening sense of terror for the men who were still in the midst of battle. He thought of John and of Dan and now an awareness of what was happening drove thunderously in on his mind.

"Urquhart!"

The lieutenant was standing against the scorched and blackened pillbox peering across the gully.

"Urquhart!"

This time the lieutenant heard and came to him.

"What's happening across there?"

Urquhart said, "Take it easy. You're not supposed to move. It'll start the bleeding again."

"What's happening across there?"

"Christ, Brad, we can't do a thing about it. They're in trouble and we can't do a goddamn thing."

A wave of nausea passed through him. He felt terribly sick. He thought, Oh God, it isn't over. I thought it was over but it isn't over. If they don't win across there, it's all wasted, everything is wasted. He said, "What kind of trouble?"

The lieutenant said, "Bad trouble. Charlie Company didn't make it. They're pinned down." He was trying hard to remain calm. "Baker Company made it but Charlie didn't. They're pinned down! Christ, what'll happen to Able?"

Brad though it was impossible that Charlie Company was pinned down. Charlie Company was Dan's company. Dan couldn't be pinned down.

The lieutenant said, "There's nothing we can do. They'll make it. They got to make it."

Brad listened for a little while to the terrible clatter of heavy machine guns. He said, "What's happening now?"

"It's hard to see. We're laying down smoke." Then the lieutenant said, "I think Able Company's starting to come up. Christ! They're starting to come up!"

Across the gully the automatic weapons opened up in a new pitch of fury. Brad shuddered. He held out his good arm and called to Urquhart: "Pull me around and turn me on my stomach."

The lieutenant said, "There's nothing you can do, Brad. You'll start bleeding."

"Please, Urquhart. Do as I say."

"Christ, Brad —"

"Do as I say."

The lieutenant turned him over slowly and pivoted him around in a quarter circle. He could feel the bleeding starting up again from the movement of his body. He lifted his head and rested his chin in the crook of his right arm and looked across the gully and he could see the battlefield. Not all of it. But enough.

The gully was a good sixty yards across. The opposite ridge was several yards lower than the height of the ground on which he lay and beyond the ridge he could see the dome of the pillbox which was Charlie Company's objective, only the top curve of the dome, and beyond that was the field of approach. He couldn't see the signals casement. It was deep to the right of where he lay and well below the ridge on the opposite bank of the gully. He knew where it was from the tracer that was pouring down the field of approach.

Mortar smoke billowed thickly over the field. He could see streams of orange tracer driving into the smoke. The tracer was coming from two directions, from the signals casement and from the pillbox that Charlie Company had failed to capture.

Then a gust of wind from the sea whirled the smoke off the field of approach and laid bare the men of Able Company moving up the middle of the rising ground. He saw John out ahead of his company, a tiny figure in the distance and the drifts of smoke, but he knew it was John. He couldn't mistake the posture of the man, the narrow line of his shoulders, and the way he moved steadily a few yards in advance of his men as if this were the Indian wars and not 1944. He thought, The man's gone out of his mind, he's gone out of his mind like Norden went out of his mind. He's forgotten his assault tactics. You don't walk straight into fire, not this kind of fire. He thought, Where's the smoke? Why don't they lay down more smoke? Where's MacEwen and the reserve platoon? He thought, John is going to die.

Now a new agony seized him and it was like no other agony he had ever known. He thought he had already passed through the ultimate agony, the agony of his own battle, and had triumphed over it and had come away the warrior, the victor, the hero brandishing the prize of life. It wasn't the ultimate agony. He watched John advancing along the rising ground into the streams of tracer and this was the real agony, beyond recognition, beyond control, and there were no weapons he could use to fight it, no muscle, no courage, no paroxysm of fury to fight it and overcome it.

Orange tracer enfiladed the field of approach. It was impossible for a man to walk into this stabbing fire. John kept coming on, now running, now weaving, now walking steadily forward up the slope of the ground, and the men of Able Company moved in concert with him. There were those that fell forward or dropped slowly to their knees with the punch of the bullets that hit them, but the rest came on.

Brad watched and the agony stirred afresh inside him and prayers tumbled in and out of his mind and he didn't care any more whether he lived or died. He thought, No man can be so brave. He thought, It's not bravery. He doesn't know what he's doing. It's madness, it's Norden's kind of madness. He thought, If he dies now — oh God, he mustn't die because if he dies, everything dies. He thought, Oh God, don't let him die. Make him stop. Don't let him die.

A salvo of screaming mortars looped over the field from the direction of the signals casement. John fell flat and the men behind him fell flat and black smoke rose in billows all over the field of approach. Oh God, Brad thought, and he shut his eyes and felt the sweat from his forehead drop down over his face and he struggled with himself not to open his eyes for he couldn't bear to see. He opened his eyes. The smoke of the mortars had cleared and John was on his feet in a crouch, but the men behind still lay flat on the ground. John looked back at them and drew himself erect and still the men lay flat on the ground. He took off his helmet and waved it over his head and moved forward, and now the men, those who were not cut down by the mortar and the bullets, scrambled to their feet and charged wildly to the crest of the high ground.

Brad dropped his head into the curve of his arm. The battle had passed out of the line of his vision, beneath the opposite ridge of the gully. He heard a new surge of clatter from the automatic weapons and he thought, He's going to die and everything will die with him.

The clamor of battle came across the gully in convulsive waves. The cries of men intermingled with the crump of grenades and the sputter of small automatic weapons. Brad crushed his face into the ground. This was the terrifying sound of the climax, the last paroxysm, the moment when the ugly gods separated the lucky from the unlucky, the determined from the faltering, those who must die from those who would live. He knew the moment. He had lived it. He quivered with a terrible agony wrought out of guilt and helplessness and despair and great love.

He heard Urquhart cry out, "Charlie Company's moving. And Mac-Ewen's coming up with the reserve. He's coming up fast! They're going to make it, Brad! God Almighty, they're going to make it!"

The sound of savagery rose up from across the gully. Brad buried his face in the ground. He felt his wounds throbbing and bleeding freely. He didn't care. The agony that racked him was deeper than his wounds. This was not what he came to war for, he told himself bitterly, not this agony he had never known and never thought to know or wanted to know.

Gradually the crump and the clatter and the inhuman shrieking died out. After a little time three red flares looped up over the battlefield and Urquhart gasped, "They made it! Holy God, they made it! They made it, Brad!" He repeated it again and again as if he didn't believe it and had to convince himself.

Brad brought his head up from the ground and looked across the gully to the section of field within his line of vision. He saw thin curls of smoke rising from patches of ground where the mortars and grenades had set the grass afire and men trudging inquisitively among the bodies and some of the men bending down and peering into the faces of the dead. He saw that full dawn had broken and the sky was overcast and darkly gray. He thought, This is the way it should be, gray and sad. He thought, It's over and John is dead. We've won, we've captured the signals casement, we've made it easier for them on the beaches but John is dead. He thought, His luck was mostly chipped away and he must be dead. Urquhart, crouching beside him, still panted, "Holy God, Brad, they made it! They made it!"

A medic came up herding two German prisoners who carried a stretcher. The Germans were bareheaded, their tunics torn and caked with dirt. One of them, a haggard, elderly man with matted gray hair, had lost a jackboot, and blood from his toes was seeping through his stocking on the foot that had no jackboot.

The medic said, "Okay, we'll take you down now."

Brad said, "Take the others down first."

Wounds

✕

from *Heroic Love*

by EDWARD LOOMIS

A rifle bullet striking bone hits with a fine hardness, followed instantly by a numbing shock; and then down you go.

When it happened to me, I felt my left leg for blood, thinking to gauge the wound, but could not do it, for the blood was running imperceptibly in my heavy trousers already soaked with the rain. I moved the knee, where the bullet had hit, and said to the man ahead of me: "I think maybe I'm hit, by God! Now what do you think of that?"

It was a November night in the south of Holland, with low gray clouds billowing voluminously close to earth. In the flash of a shell bursting you could see the pale misty bottoms of the clouds, and the rains came stirring out of them against your face with a feeling of impalpable moist depths. Up ahead of me were woods, from which the rifle shot had come; behind me a ditch, its waters flowing black like sooty Acheron itself; and all around me was the war — my war, one of the old ones now — littering the earth, making an ominous dark.

I lay with my face to the ground, padded where my cheek touched it by leaf mold and withered grasses; we were in a pasture, surely, and there was a soft wind. In a little while it was time to go on, and so I rose, finding that I was not badly hurt, and continued marching through the night. Now and then I wondered that a bullet could knock me down and still bounce away, but I was growing used to perplexity and did not mind it. I had no thought of taking my sulfa tablets, for I wanted to save them for a major wound.

Toward morning we dug holes that started water seeping from the earth like wells, and when the dawn came we discovered ourselves in a cultivated field, plowed now and harrowed down, that was bordered on two sides by a dike lined with poplars, and on the third by a clump of houses. These were gray houses, blurred by a faintly falling rain; there were narrow windows and doors, and tile roofs the color of dirty copper. Each house had its trees, black and unidentifiable, glistening with the perpetual damp. The people were gone, I was sure, from those houses five hundred yards away, who have now long since returned to make the fields ripen again in heavy crops of sugar beets and grain.

There was no sign of life, though we had been told that Germans held the houses, and so that morning I thought about the farmers, hiding with their families. It was possible they hid in haystacks, or in the little pine forests of that country, and I could guess how it might be for them, for each chilly family huddled beneath a dripping tree. But of course they were far away; they did not exist, and at nine o'clock that morning came something which did, a British plane, strafing the houses for us. In an instant I had eyes for nothing else.

The plane was a Spitfire, of slim body and wide wings curved at the tips, and its course was to swoop low, fire the machine guns, and rise again. I crouched in my hole, legs folded into the water at the hole's bottom, and stared upward with joy. On the plane's second pass there was an answer from behind the houses, the steady, jarring hammer of 20-millimeter anti-aircraft guns firing synchronously; there would be a flak wagon behind the houses, that was it, a tracked vehicle with four guns in a turret, and so I grew frightened for the plane and its pilot.

But for two more passes the plane came low and then roared away in safety. I rejoiced, and forgot the icy chill gripping my feet and lower legs. The sound of the motor was loud and sweet on the downswing, and I could almost feel the delicate sheen of oil masking each working part in that slick harmony; I could sense the pistons firing in a row, and the electric messages of control vibrating along the wires. And of course I had a notion of the pilot, who would be a thin-faced Englishman like some of the British infantry officers I had seen; he would have a soft voice, and a deprecating way of moving his hands, and be from Kent perhaps, or Lancashire, places I knew from training days.

And then the plane was hit, on the fourth pass, as it was pulling out: one moment there was the screaming sound from the motor as the pilot started his climb, and then there was a silence, hoarse with meaning. The plane climbed ever more steeply, until it became apparent that the arc of its climb would fall back into a circle leading to a crash. Quite distinctly I made out the markings on the upper surfaces of the wings: there were the emblematic rings of white and royal blue and red, and numbers in heavy block forms. For an instant there was a soft glitter on the hood over the cockpit, an aerial shadow of death.

Who was that pilot? I could never know. At the beauty of his fall I sighed. Down he came, and there was a crash at which any man might blink.

Deeply I flung myself into my hole, bringing my forehead close to the earthy smell of water. After the crash there was an explosion, and then the familiar sound of splintered metal going by, a rough *whirroo* that leaves a hard quiet in the wake of its passing. Cautiously I looked out of my hole and saw, not a hundred yards away, the wreckage with smoke clumped upon it and slowly rising. There was nothing to do or say; the man was dead. In the shallow pool of water nearest my hole I observed a few patches of oil film, spattered there by the explosion. They widened; they grew floating there, unchanged by damp, in subtle colors I could not really see. There was a smoky blue perhaps, and a touch of orange or red; the colors had a perfect polish and no reflection in the gray morning.

Later that day another company attacked the houses, and we moved on to the dike with the poplars, where we stayed for a time in shallow holes. Toward nightfall a barrage of 120-millimeter mortars fell on the dike, killing the two men in the hole next to me, and thus stirring the officers to move again. We climbed out of our holes, and I looked at the bodies laid out under somebody's shelter-half; the feet projected from under the canvas, toes up, and the feet looked alive; one left foot was naked and bloody, the shoe blown clean off, exposing the horny toenails of the infantryman. We marched a long time that night, and finally arrived at the still-burning ruins of a barn, near which we dug holes again, for the third time that day.

There was an orchard all around the barn; little trees with sleek black trunks stood there in crooked rows, and our holes went down into a heavy earth that had a pleasant fragrance of rotted apples. The resiny smell of burning timbers carried to me a memory of campfires, and so it was not long before I had the feeling of holiday. My knee was stiffening, and I was wet and cold, but I became cheerful, and with a friend named Curry I decided to go closer to the tumbled fires of the barn. Our idea was to warm ourselves, and we were happy with that idea.

"If there's any shelling, we can duck back to our holes," Curry said. "But I'll bet the Germans are just as tired as we are."

"It's a fool thing to do," I said. "But let's do it. Damn it, I want to do it!"

Cautiously we made our way, staying clear of the German side of the fire so that we would not make silhouettes; and we were stopped only once in our progress, when a horse came charging through the position. There was a commotion behind us; the horse came looming into the light of the fire, clumsily galloping, swaying from side to side. He was high and dark, and somehow marred, moving like a creature stiff-jointed and old, and he stumbled against one of the little trees; then he screamed in terror, and we could see that he was badly burned. He had no mane or tail, and carried a sweet smell of burnt flesh into our holiday air. Again he crashed into a tree, and screamed, and then we knew he was blind. His eyes were singed wounds in his bony head, and he tossed his head as he galloped, as if to shake away the terrible darkness.

He galloped through the position from one end to the other, and disappeared into the night. I was a little shaken, but Curry restored my confidence. "Somebody'll shoot the old thing before morning," he said, "and put him out of his misery. Sure they will."

In a few moments we were back on our quest, and very quickly found what we wanted, an orderly fire, burning in a little stack of the poles used in that country to prop hayricks. It was warm there, and you could stand close without discomfort; and there was shelter from German eyes in a still-untumbled corner of the old barn itself.

"This is the place," Curry said. "By God, I'm going to take off my shoes and pants and get 'em dry."

We set about it, and in fact we stripped off all our clothes, in a gesture of high spirits, and set them out to dry. We drove stakes and placed our shoes and socks on them; I improvised a coat-rack for the shirts and jackets, and Curry arranged a way of stretching trousers between pairs of stakes. We had a game of co-operation, and so in a little while it was possible to enjoy feelings of harmony and peace.

Curry was not my best friend in the squad, but he was a good friend, and we had an understanding. He came from the same sort of family I had come from, and from the same sort of town. He had two brothers and a sister; his father was a purchasing agent, his mother had been to a small college in Michigan; and he lived in a suburb of Detroit. He had been drafted from the University of Michigan three months before his nineteenth birthday, and now he was awaiting his twentieth birthday. We were two of a kind; we understood that we were fortunate in everything except being in the war, and we were getting used to that; and of course we were pleased to be together, to be able to exchange identical sentiments about the unhappy incidents of our life.

Soon we had canned rations bubbling on the embers at the edge of the fire, and all about us were clouds of steam rising from our clothes. Naked we could stand the cold air of night, and even enjoy it; the wind raised gooseflesh on skin grown oily and bitterly resistant. We sparred a little, and in doing this I got several twinges in the knee that only made me happier. I looked at my wound, which was two small holes, each well covered by a crisp black scab, and a moderate swelling to the left of the kneecap. The wound was genuine, clearly, and yet no hindrance to lightheartedness and running.

Ah, that was a time! We leaped in and out of the firelight in that cold soft Holland air, and ate our rations as children eat at picnics, voraciously, so as to gain a quick release to the games of the woods. We were fierce, like children, and felt scorn for our friends crouching in holes, their bodies clotted in damp cloth. Indeed, we were happy, and I will never forget the feeling.

An end came, as it had to, but at first it seemed not serious. A light shelling of 120-millimeter mortars began to fall on the edges of the orchard, and as we headed for the holes we had dug, it was plain that the pattern was moving toward the fire. We left our clothes, naturally, and ran naked, crouching close to earth, and there was no danger, for we had time. The holes were close to us, not twenty yards away, and we were all but safe until Curry fell. Perhaps his bare foot caught on something a heavy shoe would have brushed aside; perhaps he stepped on a hot ember and by flinching from it lost his balance; but he fell, and the pattern of the barrage abruptly included him.

It was a light barrage. Moments after I reached my hole, where one of my other friends was waiting for me with arms braced to catch some of the shock of my diving fall, the barrage was over, and I rose quickly to see what had happened behind me. I was breathing sharply, feeling excited and happy, and so I needed a few moments before I could see clearly. Meanwhile I heard Curry's voice speaking rapidly in a normal tone, though I could not distinguish words. I was perplexed; I looked around, and called the word "Curry" several times into the hush which follows a barrage.

Then I saw him. Like a white flower in the night was the whiteness of his body, and very clearly I saw a spout of blood rising from the base of his throat. And heard him: "Lordy, Lordy," he said, "somebody, the blood's going out of me like water out of a hose. For God's sake, somebody, come help me. Do you want me to die here like a stuck pig?" The tone was almost humorous, and showed the control of the considerate patient who wants not to be a bother.

"I'm coming!" I shouted. "Curry, Curry, I'm coming, hold on!"

I scrambled out of the hole and started for him, charging low as if to knock something down with my shoulders; and I had made perhaps eight or nine yards of the distance when I heard the whispering fall of a mortar shell as the barrage began again. Down I went, as I had been taught, to hide myself against the stained old earth; flat on my belly, hands over my head, and listening to the explosions and whistling flights of shrapnel. The barrage was a little heavier this time, but shorter, and I scarcely had time to think about it before it was over.

I got to my feet a little slowly, with belly and chest darkly washed by a fine, silt-like mud, and began to trot toward Curry, but even before I reached him I saw that there would be no reason for haste. He had been hit again, and was dead now. He lay on his back, arms outspread against the rainy Holland earth. His hands and face were dark, with the weathering that comes to the devoted infantryman.

I could not see the wound that had first caught him; there was no spout of blood to define it now, and a wrinkled sheet of blood was settling all along his throat and collarbone and down his right shoulder. The wounds of the second barrage I could scarcely miss, for they were a great slash across his right thigh and a rip all across his belly, out of which now tumbled bowels and intestines.

Quickly I saw it all, and will not forget it, the death, the great wounds, the white body and scarcely used sex of this boy who had so great a part of his life ahead of him when he died.

In a little while other soldiers came, and a blanket was stretched over the body. I went back to the fire in the hayrick poles and slowly dressed myself, not brushing away the mud from my chest and belly. I was feeling sad, and empty, as I have since felt a few times after rising from women.

Before I went to my hole for sleep, I dressed the body of my friend in the clothes which had dried while he was dying. I wanted whatever was left of him not to be cold, and so I did what had to be done with his spilled guts, and bundled the slippery coils back into the still-warm cage of muscle and tough hide. I got him together, and got him dressed, and thus had what I wanted, the feeling that I had done the few things left me to do.

And then I went back to my hole and started to be cold in a way I had not known before. That night I shivered with cold for the first time in my life, and it seemed to me that I could feel the moist night air seeping into my bones, corrupting the sweet, secret marrow. It was a fancy, but the next morning I was stiff and ailing, and had trouble making the day's march.

I had a recovery to make from Curry's death, however, and so I worked away at it, and was beginning to succeed by four o'clock, when my knee started an action very like the throbbing of blood, except that it was pain moving there. I was glad to have the pain, for it seemed a way of getting along with Curry's death, a way of settling accounts with whatever powers might be.

Also it was true that the pain persuaded me that my wound might soon be serious enough to take me out of the war for a while, and that was a thought which must cheer any soldier of the infantry. Toward dark we stopped near a big farm and were told that we might expect the company cooks that night with hot food and newspapers, and so we knew that our war was about to cease for a little while. We had seen no firing all that day; we were growing cheerful; we dug great holes, and found pleasure in the labor.

I dug with my friend Olney Arnett, a Tennessean, and we constructed a masterpiece of comfort in the field. We were on a little hill, and so we could go deep without getting water; we went down four and a half feet, in a hole seven feet long and almost five feet wide. We thatched the bottom to a depth of a foot and a half with fragrant hay taken from the barn at the top of the hill, and covered everything against the rain with our two shelter-halves draped across a pole stolen from the same barn.

We had a rough equivalent of a cabin with roof and ridgepole; we fastened the sides of the shelter-halves with well-packed heaps of dirt, and were ready to weather out a gale. "It's the best hole we've had for a week or more," Arnett said. "Just think how it's going to be to sleep in it to-night!"

A furry little mist was in the air, to moisten the face and the backs of hands, but we were sure there would be heavy rain that night, for there was always heavy rain in those nights. We would need our cave. In constructing it, we had achieved something good, and so we could have the pleasure of shared accomplishment. Arnett had for some time been my best friend in the squad, and therefore in the world, though we were not at all like each other; and so my pleasure in the task was augmented by the pleasure of having Arnett take part in it. He was a farm boy who had subtle arts of whittling with a pocket knife sharp as a razor; he knew bird cries, and the Tennessee names for all the trees and grasses of ancient Europe; he came from an old people long rooted in a single county, and he knew strange songs that puzzled me. He was a sturdy boy, not the kind to give into his circumstances; braver than I, and more calm, so that he could regard the details of our life in the war with a reluctant good humor, where I was given to furious rages.

We were at odds in everything except the necessary arts of living together, but in these we could be at peace. Having finished our hole, we walked like loving brothers to the farmhouse where I had been told to come for treatment of my knee. There we found an agreeable officer who made arrangements for hot water and cloths; he was the platoon leader of the second rifle platoon of our company, and thus it was an act of special condescension for him to forsake his responsibilities to think about easing my pain.

It was a trick to get my trousers down past the huge swelling that had come into my knee, but we managed it, and then Arnett moistened pads of clean white cloth into compresses, which he laid delicately over the sore places. I sat in a chair, with my left leg propped on another, and might have been a little king of that high, narrow room.

Close to my hand was a fire burning in a little porcelain stove. On top of the stove was a canteen cup of coffee, prepared especially for me, with a little of the lieutenant's whisky in it for flavor and comfort, and a big pot of water for the compresses. There had been no destruction in the room; the woodwork in windows and wall moldings was highly polished and dark; the chairs which ringed the old table were plain and hard, but not uncomfortable, and there were two steel engravings on the walls, each showing a skater dashing brilliantly down the winter ice of a canal. It was a Dutch interior, immaculately polished and rich, and not much altered by the litter of soldiers. Rifles leaning against the walls did not really change the look of it, but they were sufficiently present so that I could have a momentary sense of belonging to the room. I was at ease, and could have been happy greeting guests.

When the cooks arrived outside in their two-and-a-half-ton truck, Arnett went to them and got a noble supper for me. I had tomatoes, bread, and two kinds of meat, with a sweet stimulant composed of one part canned milk and sugar, and one part black coffee. The tears almost came to my eyes as I sat in the hot room holding the heavy cup. My skin was alive with the pleasure of warmth; my whole system was growing soft and joyous in the pleasure of being tended to. Two hours I spent in this way before I had to go outside again, and when I left I felt fortified and strong. The cold air, blown against my face by the night wind in such a way as to suggest the rain which was coming, only served to remind me that I had a fine shelter to take myself to, and so I joked with Arnett and even made fun of his country ways as we walked slowly along. When we got to the hole, Arnett offered to take part of my guard that night, and I accepted; I would keep watch for the first three hours, until midnight, and then he would be responsible for the rest of the night. I was grateful, and thanked him.

At the open end of the hole I propped myself up and set my rifle on its sling, sights up, the barrel pointing north. Beside it I placed my three grenades and Arnett's two. For a while I listened to Arnett burrowing in the hay on his side of the hole, and then, when there were no more noises from him, I occupied myself in watching the sky. At ten-thirty I was dismayed to see the sky grow clear, exposing a crystalline darkness and a few stars. I was angry, thinking there might be no rain to test the cave and give me the sounds of rain addressing a roof above my weary head. For half an hour I had this distress, and suffered bitterly, until the sky closed again and I could prepare myself for enjoyment.

At midnight I woke Arnett, and he rose cheerfully. He arranged his hay so that he could sit wrapped in it to the waist while he was keeping guard, and then said good night to me and began softly to hum an old tune.

I was ready for sleep as I crawled slowly into my hay. Deep in it was the musty fragrance of summer; I distinguished three kinds of flower smells, and even found, with darkened fingers, a dry little burr soft to the touch that might have been a clover blossom. As I settled myself, I could feel a pollenous dust crossing the skin of my face and tickling the back of my neck under the shirt collar. I became dry in feeling, as if I too had lain curing through the wet autumn, in the high old barn on the hill.

In a little while I became warm also, and therefore ready for bliss, but for a while no bliss came. My left leg was stiff and sore from the ankle far up into the thigh, and there was an untouchable coldness in the toes of my left foot. There was a steady pain. I could not sleep, and in my wakefulness I remembered the tragic stories of my soldier's life.

I grew angry; there was no rain, and so I softly cursed the weather, for a long time, until at last the rain began. It came hard and beating, just what I wanted, and yet it did not bring me sleep. I heard the drumming on the canvas, and in the not-quite-thorough darkness of a night in the midst of war I could just make out the canvas sagging with the accruing weight of water. I had what I wanted, and yet it did not suffice, and so my spirit for a while approached despair.

Disappointments were severe in those troubled days. I was having an unpleasant time in that sweet hay, and then a thing happened that changed everything in an instant. The heavy rain at last grew too much for the moorings of the shelter-half on Arnett's side of the hole; he had stretched the canvas too near the horizontal, and left no way for the water to run off, and so there were surely ten gallons of water gathered above his head. I did not see what happened, of course, for my eyes were closed, but I knew what it was. Arnett, sitting motionless, his face composed under his helmet, eyes watching out into the night, was allowing himself to remember his mother's face, perhaps, or the look of her kitchen; and then the shelter-half pulled free and loosed those gallons of Holland rain on his head like a flood sent from on high.

"Gre't God A-mighty!" Arnett said, spluttering like one drowning. I opened my eyes and saw instantly what had happened: Arnett was floundering, shaking his dripping head and shoulders like old Neptune himself rising out of troubled waters. He tried standing up, and said: "My God, I'm drownded, the goddamned roof . . ." And then he sat down again, his haunches splashing. "Oh, no," he groaned. "Oh, goddamned no!" Weakly he raised his right arm and then let it fall. "I'm all wet," he said. "And on a night like this I'll never get dry!"

I half sat up, but then my leg hurt sharply, making me fall back. I shivered, and raised my shoulders, awaiting the shock of icy waters from Arnett's disaster, and for a moment I felt a savage fury that he had been so clumsy in building his side of the roof. "God damn it, Arnett," I called, and then stopped out of regard for our friendship. "Arnett?" I said again. It came to me that I was not yet dampened, and this was an enormous surprise. Cautiously I felt around in my hay, looking for signs of water; but there were none.

"Arnett," I said. "My God, I'm dry! It all fell on you, you poor bastard!"

"Son of a bitch!" Arnett shouted. He was standing now, thrashing his arms about wildly. "Son of a bitch! Son of a bitch! You goddamned water, you rain, may you fairly die, you goddamn, cold, mis'able water!"

His hands fell to his sides, and he shook his head. "Oh, no," he said. "And

I done so many *good* deeds today." Slumped over, he stood without moving, and suddenly I began to laugh.

He had helped me, he was the best friend I had in all the world, but I laughed at his misfortune as I have rarely laughed in my life. Tired and dejected, he stood without answering while I laughed with fury. After a long time he threw his wet hay out of the hole and sat down again, on the bare ground, to resume his guard, and I laughed even then. His silence was nothing to me; I could not care; and long after the night had grown quiet again I was still chuckling, deep in my warm hay smelling dryly of wild flowers and clover.

I went to sleep without our speaking to each other again, and I slept a flowing, tide-like sleep that carried me with perfect ease into the wakening chill of the next morning. It was joyous sleep, and I was presiding over it as it happened, with some part of me that will be forever wakeful. I had enjoyment, and knew I was having it, and knew further that no man could ask for more from the earth and the curious things which grow upon it.

I woke in the morning cheerful, with the full expectation that my life would soon improve in all its conditions. I was certain that good luck was coming; and so it did. Arnett had got over his disaster, and held nothing against me, so that we were friends as before. He helped me out of the hole, and caught me when I fell; he was sympathetic when it became apparent that I would not be able to walk all the way to breakfast at the cooks' truck.

I was a cripple now; there was nothing left me but to say good-bye to my friends and go to the hospitals. I went with the cooks, sitting in the cab of the truck with the driver and the mess sergeant. I was sorrowful at leaving all my old friends, but anxious to see what the hospitals had to offer, and so I traveled in great serenity of spirit; and of course it happened that the hospitals offered a great deal, enough to please any rational man, any soldier of the infantry.

At the first hospital there was a warm room filled with long narrow tables, at which doctors were working over other wounded men. On one of these tables I had my knee opened and dressed. I was warm once more, looking upward into bright unfocused light, and, being really not badly hurt, I could enjoy the sharpness of the doctor's scalpel. I could feel the edge with a shock of pleasure, knowing that the edge was exposing corruption and cutting it out. Without looking, I could feel the small flow of blood which followed the course of the knife, and enjoy that too, for I was only losing a tainted blood that any man would be happy to have out of him.

Then there was a ride in an ambulance to yet another hospital, where I stayed for a few hours in the late afternoon while a train was making up to carry a load of wounded to Paris. I was in Belgium now, far from the fighting. Over my supper I began to dream about the great luminous city to the south, and I could not quite believe in my good fortune when I was taken to the train at eight o'clock that night.

Events were passing me by, they happened so swiftly. I was borne from one fine place to another like a little boy on a roller-coaster, wild with joy, unable either to get off the car or make it stop. All the faces were friendly, all the machines aided my comfort. I was technically a walking wounded, and so I traveled in one of the standard carriages, and there the seats were fine, for the carriage was of the first class.

Suddenly from walls broken and crumbling I was transported to walls beautifully finished in polished wood. With two other wounded men I established myself in luxury, with my left leg propped up on a little bench the nurse had brought in for me. I was astonished by the dark and glossy walls, and charmed by the patterns of flowers and trees inlaid under the final shellac; the images might have been reflected there, such was the effect, as if the walls had been the shut windows of an old house that mirror the rich, decaying gardens outside. The benches we sat on were covered with a heavy tapestry, on which were a parade of silver bushes and marble fountains, with little golden deer delicately walking by.

I was dazzled, and then, of course, sleepy, but sleepy in a pleasant way; I only wanted to be fresh for the wonderful things the next day might bring. The train rolled southward, whistle screaming as in a dream of fast night trains, and we reached Paris before dawn. Then there was a ride in an ambulance, and disappointment that I would not see Paris that day, but the disappointment did not last.

There was a faint daylight at the hospital doors, and I knew I was entering a fine old building redolent with peace and charity. Above the doors, in a frieze, were sculptured naked angels and cherubic infants; they were gray figures almost lifelike in the hesitant light. Pigeons fluttered near, and as I entered the building I understood that the pigeons had the right to enjoy the mottled purity of the carved stone. Who would worry? The stone would last.

Inside, there was a rhythm of care to draw me in, and I knew I had reached an end. Here I could rest, and be comforted. I was put to bed between sheets of English linen, under blankets of English wool, and the skin of a noble woman could not be finer to my touch than those humble fabrics were. I was fed on a pink ham, surely from the best of Virginia smokehouses, on yams, and asparagus smelling astonishingly of spring; and I was given fine coffee, in a white crockery cup. I talked to a nurse, who smiled at me; she was busy, and she was plainly a dutiful type, but I was her duty, and so in a way she belonged to me.

There was so much to be grateful for that I began to feel guilty, as if no single man could merit such care. Men were dying within those walls, I knew, for I had seen rooms closed behind placards which said that no visitors were allowed, and I had sensed, on my passage upstairs to my ward, several ominous movements of nurses and doctors; they would be walking softly, as if on tiptoe, and solemnly like priests, and they could not fool me. Death was all about me, and might even have left its stench in some of the darker corridors and more distant rooms. And of course I was curious, remembering stories I had heard of other military hospitals; I wondered whether I would have duties in this strange, delightful place, and so I asked the doctor who came to see me, as soon as he had finished his examination.

"Will I have duties here, sir? Like making the bed and scrubbing the floor, say?"

"Of course not," he answered. "Don't even think about it." He was a short, dark man wearing gold-rimmed spectacles; a major, a middle-aged man. He looked shrewd and good-humored, and it came to me, as a summation of all my pieces of wonderful luck, that he was a man I could trust; and so I spoke quite frankly.

"What will I have to do here, then?" I asked. "What *should* I do?"

"Why, just get well, son," he said. "That's all. And enjoy yourself. Don't you like it here? Well, then, enjoy it, there's your duty. Maybe later on you'll be able to go out and see if Paris suits you. It's easy. You'll see. Don't you know how to be happy any more?"

"Happy?" I said, and took thought. "My God, in all my life I've never been so happy!"

Indeed, will I ever be so happy again?

Corporal Albert Selig

✂

from *The Strange Land*

by NED CALMER

This Harrod guy's got guts. He didn't have to go up to the pillbox last night. He could have ordered himself a guide to get back to the CP when the trouble started. The war correspondent couldn't take it. But Harrod stayed with us. He worked with us every step of the way down here to the bridge this morning when I thought we wouldn't even make it this far. And now we're pinned down he's still with us.

He's pulling his weight with that pistol, too. He got two the first time they started down the hill to clean us up. And one the second time. That gave the bastards something to think about. It's been nearly two hours since that last rush and I guess they're still trying to make up their minds whether to try it again. But if Keith hadn't rescued the machine gun we'd all be killed already. Or prisoners, like Boyce. *Because Boyce is a prisoner. He's got to be.* Nothing happened to Boyce except maybe he was surrounded up there in the dark before he knew they were coming at us. And now they've got him up there in the woods and we'll get him back when we go back in there again.

We've got to go back in there. Boyce is there. If we don't, I'll go in there myself and get him out. Keith will let me. And if he doesn't let me I'll go anyway. But he'll let me. He knows Boyce.

I'm hungry. We're all hungry and weak. We got to wait till dark before we can get rations. If we live that long. It's tough lying on this gravel. This must have been a plenty good mill before it got beat up. Plenty of force in that water going by to turn a wheel. Deep and muddy. It's already pushed half the broken bridge downstream below us. Thank Christ the heinies knocked out that bridge for us. When they aim bad they sure aim bad. Otherwise they would have had tanks over it by now and then where would this platoon be and where would Crosby's CP be?

When did the engineers put that bridge in? It seems like a week ago or even a month. Actually it's not much over twenty-four hours. The second time in two days I've been lying on my belly all day in this boneyard. Twenty-four hours since Bender signaled the okay and we moved across the bridge behind Keith. Boyce was right ahead of me. That was when he said he could see his officer-kaydet up there in the pillbox waiting to surrender. Boyce was a card. *But what am I thinking about him like he was killed for?* He's not killed. He's a prisoner. Yesterday this time we were crossing the bridge. Today we're halfway back to our positions up on the ridge and we'll be wiped out if we try to get the rest of the way back up the unprotected slope in daylight.

It looks lonesome out there behind us. It looks like twice as long as it is. I wouldn't give two cents for any one of us that tried to run for it. They could blanket that slope with mortar and machine gun before he got halfway to the woods. And what can we do to stop them? Not a tank in sight to cover us. Two grenades left for the bazooka. No ceiling for the bombers to come back and work on the heinie ridge. No nothing. That's the story of B Company from the start.

I don't see any movement up there at all. But it could be five hundred of them are getting ready inside the tree-line to come at us. Maybe this time they'll bring some of their little rubber boats they used back on the Meuse. Whatever they do, they haven't got a hell of a lot of time to do it before dark. But it's still fifty years till night today. And here we sit like ducks.

Maybe we aren't the only ducks in the Siegfried Line. And what happened to 2nd Platoon on our left? Were Garnett's bunch all killed in the north pillbox? Were they all captured? Maybe we could find out a few things if Keith could get that God damn radio fixed. Look at him and Kearney still bending over it, whispering to it, begging to it, while they try to fix it. They've been fooling with it all day. Don't they know they'll never fix it! We're finished here. We're kaput. We're —

Keith's shout as mortar shells start bursting behind us. Two. Three. Two more. How bad can you aim? But it's only a matter of time before they zero us no matter how often we shift around these ruins. Where the hell is our own artillery?

"Why don't we make a run for it?"

That's Fay again. His thin little face all streaked with mud. He looks like one of the Rangers back in England blacked up for a night raid. Only they didn't show how scared they were and Fay is in bad shape. His voice cracks like he's about to cry. His voice sounds like the kid, like Hill. *Why couldn't it be Hill they captured instead of Boyce? Why didn't Hill get killed instead of Ferguson?* Keith turns back to where Fay is lying behind the pile of stones with Kearney.

"Nobody moves out of here till I give the word."

"It's crazy to stay here when they're going to kill all of us! Captain Crosby wouldn't make us stay here."

Keith gets up and runs over crouching, then flops down beside Fay. "You better get yourself under control, Fay." He's talking to him soothing and nice. "Look at Lippold. He's got a smashed-up leg and he hasn't complained about anything all day."

"Gregg got back up to the ridge, didn't he?" Fay's clutching his arm, looking up at him helplessly like a little child. "Gregg made it! Why can't we?"

"Gregg was hurt. I sent him back because he was able to walk and he would have passed out if he'd stayed here. He had to take the chance. Look back there at the man Crosby tried to send down to us. Look at Kirk. You knew Kirk. He's dead."

Fay isn't listening any longer. He's sobbing and pounding the ground with one fist. Keith gets up and goes back to the radio. Fay's head shrinks down between his shoulders. Maybe he'll feel better if he cries. Sometimes they do. It helps them get ashamed of themselves. That's what Boyce always said. *I can't figure what happened to Boyce.* "I don't figure it."

"Are you still talking to yourself about Boyce?"

Chapman, rolling over on his side to look at me, resting his head along the rifle.

"He just disappeared."

"He got captured, Selig. I told you that. Right now he's safer then we are."

"Keith couldn't find him."

"He was captured I told you."

"He's too smart for that. I don't figure it. He never did anything like this before and I was with him a long time in this war." Another mortar blast, over to the right of the bridge. "With him and Ferguson. The three of us. Boyce said he was going to get himself an officer-kaydet. That's the last thing he said before I lost him in the dark."

"I'll lay you a bet Boyce turns up tonight."

"I can't figure what happened to him."

Somewhere up there on the torn slope leading to the heinie ridge is the answer. I can just see the dull spot of brown that is part of Vorak's body still lying by the corner of the pillbox. It's hard to understand that Vorak is dead because he was with us so long. They probably haven't moved any of the bodies yet. In Normandy they shot some of our wounded like they shot the paratroopers caught in the trees the night of the invasion. Tate and Brannigan are probably still lying where they were when Keith rescued the machine gun. And farther up toward the edge of the woods Hoey is lying where the flamethrower caught him at the beginning of the attack.

I've seen a guy's body that was seared by a flamethrower. I'm glad I didn't have to see Hoey. Now Hoey's gone as well as his buddy Mitch. Stars and Stripes said we kill plenty Japs in the Pacific with flamethrowers. They died in piles for the Marines. But Hoey is white. No white guy should be killed by a flamethrower. Wait till Phelan hears it. He'll line up the next prisoners he gets and sear them.

"Watch it!"

There goes the heinie machine gun again. But it can't do much except chip off the tops of the rockpiles. *Here it comes — duck!* I wonder why they haven't used the SP guns they had around here on us. They must have had to move them into another sector. Or some other reason. I'll never know why. Those are the things that only Mallon and the generals find out. Away back where it's safe, an aide comes into a warm room, slicked up in polished boots and necktie, puts down a little pink paper on the desk and says Here's what the enemy did, sir, with the SP guns, sir. And Mallon turns to WAC dreamboat and says Make a note of that, and she says, Yes, sir, Yes, sir. And he says Oh, my, stretching his arms, I need some fresh air, I guess I'll get in my car and make an inspection tour, call my car. And Yes, sir, right away, sir. And —

A *new sound, sudden, jarring, spreading terror.* Tanks! No, just one so far, moving out of the protection of the trees up there. Starting down toward us. Keith stops fighting the radio. Every man concentrates on the tank. Are any more going to follow? Not now. Not yet, anyhow. This is a IV. I guess it's the one that made most of the trouble last night. My stomach tightening. I'm thirsty. I'm scared again. It's coming straight down toward us. Moving right along. Kearney crawls over and picks up the bazooka.

The tank can hurt us. Compared with this they were just fooling up to now. *Haven't we got anything left on the ridge to shoot at it?* I guess not. The tank can hurt us. It's getting bigger as it comes nearer. The snout-nosed gun, watching us. The big tracks grinding the earth. This time it looks like we're in for it. *This time —.*

It stops, suddenly. There isn't a sound anywhere on the front. The tank is motionless. It's like a big slow animal smelling out its direction. I can hear Keith muttering between his teeth, staring at it, waiting. "Well, make up your mind." That's what he said. "Make up your God damn mind." But the tank is just standing there. I never saw anything so still.

"Hold him! Get him back! Fay — !"

Keith shouting, turning back. It's too late to stop Fay. He's running up the slope toward our ridge. Lippold tried to grab him when he scrambled past him and Fay tripped but kept going. And machine-gun fire is whipping over our heads after him. They opened up right away. This was all they needed. A mortar burst about twenty yards ahead of him. He's galloping crazily, swerving right and left. Two more bursts farther ahead. Those are machine-gun bullets kicking up the turf around him. I don't want to watch it. *And in front of us the tank lets go.* A heavy blast. A shell from the tank gun hits the water beside this end of the broken bridge, throwing up a geyser of dirty water. The tank's motor is grinding again. So far it's not moving.

What about Fay? *There he is.* He's down, lying still, about halfway up the slope. About fifty yards from Kirk's body. Fay looks smaller than he should look. Nobody could lie there like that and be alive. Another blast from the tank! The guys are trying to flatten themselves closer to the ground. The shell goes over like an express train, hits about eighty yards behind us and to the right. Cascading dirt showering down over us. It's only a matter of minutes now before he hits us direct.

"Look!"

Lippold's hoarse shout. He's pointing back up the slope to our CP. Somebody's coming down. He's crazy! He's running zigzag through the heinie fire and taking it easy, keeping his head down. He looks familiar. It's Crosby! It's the captain. Christ, everything happens at once around here. Crosby's coat is bulging out. Rations, I bet! At the same time Keith is yelling something. He has stood up and Kearney is standing up beside him holding the bazooka. The tank out in front of us is moving again. Nearer. Nearer. It's almost down to the edge of the river. They both walk out into the open, to the end of the broken bridge. Keith looks like he's praying. Hold still, for Jesus' sake. Kearney's getting the bazooka aimed. I don't want to look. I don't want to look.

He fired it. The shell strikes just short of the tank. It seems to shake the turret a moment, then the tank comes on behind another of its own shells that hits this end of the bridge and throws up another fountain of mud and steel and water. It sprays all the way over here. Keith and Kearney are both lying flat on their faces. Fabricant is trying to get up off his knees a few yards away from them.

"Stay down, you God damn fool!"

He goes down again but not because he wants to. He rolls twice, clumsy, and lies still. He must have got a fragment. Keith and Kearney are getting up. The heinie machine gun is spraying all around them. The tank is still coming on. I never saw a live one so near. *The gun is pointing right at me.* This is our last grenade. Kearney fires again. A sharper, deeper blast. The tank shudders, staggers.

"That does it!"

It's Crosby. It's the captain who shouted it. He made it all the way down here, and he's running out and grabbing Keith and Kearney by the shoulders, pulling them back into cover. A big bright flame flaring up out of the tank turret. Then dying away to smaller steady flames. A man sticks his head out. He's trying to hoist himself out of the turret but he's burning. Halfway out he falls forward and his arms drop in front of him, swinging. Little flames are flickering out of his neck and shoulders. His uniform is smoking along the back. Oil is burning on one of his hands. Was he bald-headed or did his hair burn off when the big flame went up?

Shooting from our side. Luria shouting, screaming something, spraying the tank with the machine gun. Crosby jumps at him and pulls him away from the gun. It stops. Keith watches him, dazed. *Plane motors low in the air above us.* It's clearing up there. They're ours!

There goes the fourth dive-bomber down on Zenz! You can almost feel the blast away over here in the woods. They're working the place over good all right. But it takes more than a few P–47's to clean out a town if the heinies are waiting to ambush us from the cellars. Look at them soar back over the valley now on their way home, and listen to those mortars hit! I'd sure like to get a good look at a P–47 engine. I should have taken that job at

Boeing back in '42 when I had a chance. There's a hell of a racket up where the Limeys are. Plenty of bombing there too.

These rookie replacements are standing around with their eyes hanging out. They never see this until they really see it. The kid next to me looks like that kid Hill we had. He'll be all worn out before we get moving. The little yokel doesn't know how to relax. And I'm not going to use any energy telling him.

Now our artillery starts on Zenz. So far we're not getting any heinie fire here at all. Could they be pulling out? I don't believe it. Kearney doesn't believe it either and he always knows. The day those guys quit without a trick. Like that booby trap inside the dirty book that took Schaeffer's face off back in Belgium. I don't want to think about it. I was coming in the door right behind him and could have been the one to get it. I woke up dreaming it for two weeks.

"Hey." The kid next to me.

"What?"

"The captain just came back down this way. He called the looie over and they went back in the woods there. Something's happening."

Maybe it means we're moving again soon. Into Zenz. *And I'm afraid*. So is the kid. He's trying not to show it, the way they all try at first. He thinks that if he's afraid often enough like this he'll get over it, the way they all think at first. But right now the only difference between him and me being afraid is he's finding out about it the first time and I've been afraid the same way many times. I wish I was back at the stage where you don't know what being afraid is.

No, I don't wish that. Finding out the first time is the worst of all, so it's a little better at least to know it when it comes. All you learn is that you can take it again. But it don't make it easier. You never forget any of the times. *And the first time most of all*: D plus 11, the sun burning down hot, the sound of that machine gun, and the bodies that had been ironed out by the tanks lying like empty uniforms on the yellow road running past the orchard toward Treveers. A little farther up, around the bend where the 88 was dug into the hedgerow, the big patch of gore glittering on the road like thousands of those teeny red melon balls we used to have on the five-course dinner at Jerry's down the highway from the station.

When we get our tavern we won't serve melon balls. *We'll never have that tavern anyhow*. I'm dreaming. I'll never see it. I'll be lucky now if I ever get home, let alone what I do when I get there.

"Hey. Do you think we'll start soon?"

"Maybe." This God damn kid's face keeps reminding me of Hill. And of myself, the first time. And now today, here on the ridge in the woods, we all have to do it all over again. I'm sorry for the kid. I'm sorry for myself. Nobody should have to do it more than once. They should make that the final test of duty and make somebody else do the next one and send us home.

Home. Like four big letters in front of my eyes that I could reach out and touch, each one three feet long. I can wrap them around me and hold them around me. Only I've got no home. No future. Most of all no buddy. *I have to find my buddy.* I have to find Boyce. He's waiting for me to help him. Somewhere, he's waiting for me.

Keith coming back along the platoon line while the captain goes out to the edge of the woods and looks at Zenz with his glasses. Keith knows I want to find Boyce. He'll help me the way Vorak would if Vorak was still here.

"With all these guys to help us we ought to find Boyce today, Selig."

"I don't need no help, Lieutenant. I just need to get over there where they're holding him, that's all."

"Do you think he's in Zenz?"

"He's got to be if he wasn't in the woods."

"It looks like they took the whole town with them last night."

"They could be hiding in the cellars for an ambush."

"We'll soon know, Selig. The scouts are due back."

"What's those houses halfway down the slope with the high fence all around?"

"A slave labor camp. Major Harrod just got a slave out of there. General Mallon wants to look at him." He stares at me a second. "Stop worrying about Boyce. We'll find him. We'll find him today."

"Listen, Lieutenant. It's a feeling I've got. I was all right till Boyce got lost. Now it's like Boyce is inside me, see? Whether he's dead or alive, I'll never get him out of there. We were close to each other, see? And if they've killed him I know they're going to kill me too. It's a feeling I've got. Like every shell from now on has my name on it."

"Yes." He looks at the tears in my eyes and I don't care any more if he sees them. "Anyway we'll get into Zenz. We waited long enough for that."

"I don't care about Zenz or anything else except I have to find Boyce."

"We'll find him." He drops his hand on my shoulder before he moves along the line.

The kid again. "Who's Boyce?"

"Shut up and don't bother me!"

I yelled it at him. I didn't mean to. But the terrible feeling of helplessness. I'm sweating all over. The sweat on my face is hatred. Tighten up. Fight it back. If I let it get on my nerves any more they'll think I'm breaking up. This kid will think he's braver than I am. He's leaning over to look at me, smiling.

"You all right, pal? You don't look so good."

"Look out for yourself." I must be bad if a yokel sees it.

But we should have found Boyce by now. Maybe we'll still find him in Zenz. *Stop thinking about it*. Pick up your piece. Check the rod. Get out the brush once more and go over it. This is a bayonet job. Check the combat knife. *That stain still on my left hand*. Three times I tried to wash it off again last night. I know it wasn't there Sunday. Sometimes when I look at it I can see the stain and sometimes I can't. I don't really know if it's there. Maybe I'm seeing things. Maybe I'm batty. It's about time. Plenty others were batty before me and they're not here any more. Away back somewhere in a headquarters mess washing dishes. They don't have to be here today. They saw things that weren't real, like this stain on my hand.

Close your eyes, rest them a minute, now open them and look. Maybe it was Ferguson who killed him, not me. *No, it's there*. Just where the blood came off when I wiped my knife. That was an easy patrol. And an easy German. He never had a chance to yell. He opened his mouth and gurgled. It wasn't even a gurgle. It was softer than that. His throat was warm. I couldn't see his face in the dark but he was old. About forty, maybe, with a thick stubble of beard. And he stunk. All Germans stink. I wish I could rub this stain off. I'll keep on trying to rub it off with dirt.

"What's the matter with your hand?"

The kid, staring, like he's almost guessing. He haunts me. "Nothing."

In the woods in back of us a new sound breaks into our artillery. Those tanks are beginning to rev up. That's a good noise. The gears meshing clean, the power mounting. These are motors not yet hurt by the war. Not smashed and scattered in burning oil along a roadside, with the wonderful working of the parts together ended for good. Steel destroyed, marvels destroyed, with all the burning, smoking things that the war has scattered over Europe.

That's the worst of it. These machines so beautifully built and powerful, and the wonderful things they can do. Smashing them is the real crime and the sin. Not guns. Not exploding things. They're made for that, to kill something and be killed by something. But these machines, maimed and burning. It's easy to see some of the other things gone. Nobody gives a damn for a million beat-up buildings between here and the Atlantic Ocean. The churches can go too, as far as I care. But not the motors. These are the cleverest things a man ever made, and the best to watch, and the best to own. If it's worth living at all. If there's no war. Why do we have to destroy the best things we have? And kill each other? Who started it? When? Where? I hate to kill these German people. I don't want to kill anybody, not even the Nazis. I only want to find Boyce.

December 14, 1944

✕

from *The Beardless Warriors*
by RICHARD MATHESON

Hackermeyer sat up with a start as he realized that Linstrom wasn't in the foxhole with him. He stood quickly, wincing at the pull of stiffened muscles in his thighs and groin.

Linstrom was sitting against a tree a few yards away, holding something in his hands. When Hackermeyer popped up from the hole, Linstrom raised his eyes and smiled a little.

"Hi," he murmured.

Hackermeyer didn't answer. Hastily he glanced around. There was a milk-white mist curling along the floor of the woods and lying in the trees like wool.

He looked back at Linstrom. "You better get down here," he said.

"I'm all right," said Linstrom.

Hackermeyer sneezed. While he blew his nose he noticed Linstrom's hands.

"What have you got?" he asked.

"A bird."

Hackermeyer grimaced.

"It's dead," said Linstrom. He sounded apologetic.

Hackermeyer shuddered as the stabbing pain hit his kidneys. He climbed out of the hole and urinated. When he turned back, Linstrom was stroking the dead bird.

"I saw it when I woke up," Linstrom said.

Hackermeyer jumped back into the foxhole, grunting at the impact. His feet felt as if they were made of wood.

"What do you think killed it?" Linstrom asked.

Hackermeyer shrugged as he drew off his shoes. "Shrapnel," he said.

"No. There isn't any mark on it."

Hackermeyer pulled off his right shoe and started massaging the foot, gasping at the sting to his almost numbed flesh. Gritting his teeth, he rubbed harder.

"What do you think?" asked Linstrom.

"Concussion," said Hackermeyer. He was surprised at how calm Linstrom sounded.

"I don't think so," said Linstrom.

"You better get down here," said Hackermeyer, still rubbing his foot.

"It died of fright," said Linstrom. He smiled down sadly at the bird. "It was frightened to death by the noise, poor thing."

Hackermeyer wriggled the tingling toes of his foot. He didn't have trench foot yet. He pulled his sock back on.

"You better get down here," he said.

Linstrom drew in a quick breath. "Yeah," he said. He put the bird down gently and, pulling aside a clot of damp leaves, scraped out a small hollow in the soil. He laid the bird's stiff body in the hollow and covered it up, piling leaves over the grave. He looked around a moment, then leaned over and picked up a twig. He pushed it into the ground as a marker.

"Go to sleep, little bird," he said. He started to get up.

Suddenly he fell against the tree, looking up so quickly that his helmet fell off and thudded on the ground. Overhead, the harsh, whistling noises were beginning.

"No," said Linstrom.

"Get down," said Hackermeyer.

Linstrom didn't seem to hear. "No," he said again. There were tears in his eyes.

"Get down!" said Hackermeyer.

Linstrom remained against the tree, looking upward, his breath coming faster and faster.

Suddenly he raged at the sky, "No!"

The first explosion flung him to the ground. Hackermeyer ducked into the foxhole and heard the hissing whiz of shrapnel overhead. A second shell exploded in the trees, a third. The fourth one reached the ground. The air was filled with deafening thunderclaps, with the buzz of shrapnel, the crack and thrashing fall of boughs, the spattering of dirt and stones and leaves descending in a dark rain.

Linstrom's scream of agony pierced it all. Jerking up his head, Hackermeyer looked at him. Linstrom was struggling to his feet, blood pulsing from his shoulder. He looked down at the wound, his expression one of incredulity. He stumbled sideways against the tree and almost fell. Then, twisting around with a shriek, he started running toward the German lines.

"Linstrom!"

Hackermeyer started from the foxhole when a second cluster of shells began to fall and he jerked back down. The last he saw of Linstrom was his slender figure lurching into the forest, his shrill screams wavering in the air.

Then shells exploded everywhere and a flood of ear-crushing thunder drove Hackermeyer deep into the hole. A heavy limb came crashing down above him, its foliage blotting out the light. The earth around him rocked convulsively, dirt spilling from the foxhole walls and trickling under the neck of his coat. His head seemed to be expanding against the helmet liner. He gasped and clapped both hands over his ears, feeling engorged with din.

When the explosions stopped, Hackermeyer sat down limply, ears ringing, hands twitching weakly on his lap. After half a minute, he looked at the limb overhead and, reaching up, tried to push it aside. It wouldn't move.

He jumped as German machine guns started firing. Bullets zipped above him, ricocheting off the trees with rasping whines. Hackermeyer raised up cautiously and pushed at the limb with his shoulders. It slid away. Just above, the air was thick with mist and shell smoke and flying bullets.

The line of German fire drifted to his left. Without thinking, Hackermeyer clambered from the hole and started crawling in the direction Linstrom had gone. He tried to listen for Linstrom's voice but his ears rang too much.

"Linstrom?" he called. His voice was thick, unrecognizable. He crawled around a smoking shell hole. "Linstrom?" He wondered, vaguely, what he was doing.

He found the flashlight in a clearing. A violent explosion had taken place there. The ground was one vast hollow. The bark of trees was hacked and gouged as if by butcher knives. Saplings had been toppled by the detonation. Hackermeyer looked around the mangled area. Where was Linstrom? He couldn't have gotten much farther than this in such a bombardment.

Now he noticed the colorless slime which was dripping from the lacerated tree trunks. As if many men had blown their noses on them. Hackermeyer's gaze moved dumbly from tree to tree. He couldn't stop because he knew that he was looking at all that remained of Linstrom. His stomach started heaving as nausea bubbled in him. Abruptly he remembered what he'd said when Linstrom had asked how close the shells could come.

He didn't remember crawling back to the foxhole. The first thing he was conscious of was sitting in it, the bitter taste of vomit in his mouth. Numbly he held up his hand. The flashlight was still clutched in his fingers. He stared at it, remembering how Linstrom had used it to see the rabbit. As he let it fall, he saw his right shoe and realized that he hadn't put it back on after he'd rubbed his foot. He pulled it on with shaking fingers and fumbled with the laces and the legging strap. The sight of Foley and the Germans had been bad enough but, at least, they'd been in one piece. Of Linstrom, there had been only that pale viscous . . .

Someone shouted hoarsely, "Here they come!"

Gasping, Hackermeyer grabbed his M–1 and lurched up dizzily, laying the rifle across the rampart of the hole. He looked toward the German lines, his heart jolting painfully. All he could see was the stand of trees, the bushes and, everywhere, the thickly curling mist. He searched the woods intently. Here they come! his mind cried out. He swallowed quickly, pushed off the safety lock. He checked the chamber. There was a clip in it. The bolt handle slipped off his glove and snapped shut loudly. Hackermeyer swallowed again. Here they come, he thought. But where?

Something landed with a thud in front of him. For a second, Hackermeyer gaped at the object. It looked like a potato masher — the impression came just before instinct drove him below the ground. The grenade exploded sharply, shooting leaves and dirt across the hole. Shrapnel bounced off the trees, one of the smoking fragments thudding against his coat and falling to the bottom of the hole. Hackermeyer gulped and jerked upright.

There was something moving in the mist. Hackermeyer squinted hard. He ducked, gasping, as the rifle shot rang out, the bullet cutting up a swath of leafy dirt in front of him. He crouched a moment, panting, then reared up again.

A blue-gray-coated figure was charging at him, firing from the hip. Get him! cried a voice in his mind. Freezing, Hackermeyer aimed and squeezed the trigger twice. The M–1 jolted in his grip, the figure pitched forward, thudding to the ground. Something exploded deep in Hackermeyer. For an instant there was a crimson-edged haze before his eyes.

A shot rang out close by, the bullet popping near his ear. Grunting in surprise, Hackermeyer fell against the foxhole wall, twisting his head to the left. A burly German soldier was rushing toward him, blotting out the sky. Hackermeyer could see his face distinctly.

Suddenly the M–1 jarred in his hands as if firing by itself and, magically, a hole appeared in the German's forehead. The German cried out hoarsely and dove to one side, landing on his shoulder. He thrashed on the leaves, trying to raise his rifle. Hackermeyer fired again and heard the bullet thudding in. The German stiffened. Hackermeyer stared at him. Abruptly he fired two more bullets into the German's body. There!

"Fire!" Cooley yelled somewhere. "Shoot! Yell! Use your weapons!"

With a hollow, animal-like cry, Hackermeyer whirled, looking for more Germans, conscious, for the first time, of the rapid crackling of gunfire all around him. He raised his rifle eagerly but there was no one to use it on.

Hackermeyer gasped. Suddenly his legs began to vibrate as he realized that he'd just killed two Germans. Something hot expanded in his chest and stomach. He couldn't seem to breathe. He'd killed them. They were dead. It was miraculous.

There was a sudden crashing in the underbrush and Hackermeyer spun, jerking up his rifle to fire.

"Let's go, boy!" said Cooley. "We're moving in!"

"Yeah." Hackermeyer started clambering from the foxhole. As he stood, he saw Cooley looking at the dead German.

"That yours?" asked Cooley in surprise.

Hackermeyer pointed shakily at the other German lying half-obscured by ground mist. "Him too," he gasped.

There was a tensing of skin across Cooley's leathery cheeks. Something glinted in his eyes. Suddenly he clapped Hackermeyer on the shoulder.

"Come on, Hack!" he said, and turned away.

Hackermeyer ran into the forest after Sergeant Cooley. There was something so exciting deep inside him that, without noticing it, he raced directly through the clearing where Linstrom had been killed. Inexplicably he felt like cheering wildly.

Ten minutes before, the mortar barrage had lifted, a whistle had shrilled to the right and Cooley had shouted, "Here we go!" Hackermeyer had jumped up from behind an overturned tree, vaulted across its shrapnel- and bullet-pocked surface, and started jogging through the shadowy forest. Up ahead, rifle fire started.

He was trotting past a thicket of bushes when the bullet popped beside his ear and ripped up dirt behind him. Instinctively he jumped behind a tree in time to elude a second bullet, which ricocheted off the trunk and shot off, whistling, into the woods.

Hackermeyer pressed against the tree. He glanced around but saw no one. Apparently the squad was all ahead of him. He shifted and a third shot rang out, the bullet tearing into the ground in front of him. All of them were going into the ground, he realized. That meant that they were coming from above. Hackermeyer caught his breath.

Sniper.

He licked his lips, remembering how Cooley had fired his carbine into the trees and the figure had come toppling down. He swallowed again — his throat unusually dry, it seemed. Inchingly, he raised the M–1 until he held it vertically before his chest. He fingered at the safety lock. It was off. He checked the cartridge chamber; loaded. Unconsciously he dragged his lower teeth down across his upper lip.

Now!

He lunged out from behind the tree and fell to one knee, rifle raised, eyes darting upward. The German's Schmeisser barked out in the stillness, the bullet caroming across the top of Hackermeyer's helmet with a ringing whine. Hackermeyer dived behind the tree. The German fired again, the slug burrowing into the earth beside his right shoe. Hackermeyer jerked his legs in and pushed up to a trembling stance, his heart thudding so giganti- cally that it seemed to rock his body. The woods faded and a tide of dark- ness flooded toward him.

Instantly he closed his eyes and leaned against the tree to regain his equilibrium. He started to gag on the saliva gathering in his throat and had to cough explosively. Opening his mouth wide, he sucked at the cold, damp air, then raised his eyelids. Things had fallen into place once more. He found himself yawning and shuddering at the same time.

He looked around again. There must be something he could do. He frowned with concentration. Jumping out was worthless. The German wasn't to be caught by surprise. What was more, the bullet had nicked his helmet so quickly that he'd ducked before getting a chance to see where the sniper was hidden.

Slowly, Hackermeyer raised his hand and ran a finger along the groove in his helmet. It ran at almost a right angle to the furrow which the piece of shrapnel had dug there earlier that morning. Hackermeyer inhaled and let the breath fall fluttering from his lips. He felt his hands begin to shake and clenched them on his rifle. He stiffened as the German fired again, the bullet rebounding off the trunk, spitting bark. Hackermeyer pressed against the tree. He had to kill the German, that was all. There was no other possibility.

His gaze moved around hastily and settled on a clump of bushes to his right. It was so thick he couldn't see beyond its surface. Was it possible that he could run to it and get inside? It would offer scant protection from the German's fire, but it would hide him. Moving around within the bushes he might avoid the bullets and, at the same time, locate the sniper's hiding place. He pulled in a long, agitated breath. Should he try? Or would that just be asking for it? He shook his head jerkily. It didn't matter. That was the only thing he could do.

Impulsively, he stuck his rifle out and the silence was shattered by the crack of the German's rifle, the whistling passage of the bullet, the dull thud of it against the ground. Hackermeyer pulled the rifle back and closed his eyes. What did that prove? Except that the German was a patient man, prepared to wait it out. Well, what else could he do? He was behind American lines now. Either he surrendered or he went on fighting. Clearly, this one wasn't thinking of surrender.

For the first time since the sniper had fired at him, Hackermeyer felt conscious of fear. It was an odd sensation; one he hadn't felt for years. Almost irritably, he clenched his teeth. He had to act. It was stupid to stand here waiting. Nobody was going to get him out of this. He got himself out or he stayed until dark.

He consulted his watch. Just past ten in the morning. It would be more than seven hours before dark. He could, conceivably, wait that long; but if he did, the squad might be miles ahead by then. He might never find them. No, that was ridiculous. He had to get the German now.

Hackermeyer looked downward at the hand grenades hooked across his cartridge belt. He stared at them a moment, calculating, then jerked one free and peeled off the tape.

He hadn't thrown a hand grenade since basic training. Now he ran a finger over its cold, knurled surface. Why was it made like that? He shook his head. What did that matter anyway?

Easing down his rifle, he leaned it against the tree and held the grenade in both hands. He pulled out the pin and held the arm down for several moments. Then, impulsively, he let the arm pop out and fly away. Drawing back his arm, he pitched the grenade as hard as he could in the direction that the shots were coming from. The Schmeisser barked and he jerked his arm back, grabbing up his M–1, waiting.

The grenade exploded with a deafening roar, firing shrapnel in all directions. Catching his breath, Hackermeyer lunged away from the tree and sprinted for the bushes. His feet felt as if they were shod with lead. It seemed impossible that he could be running so slowly. The German began firing and bullets whistled past him. What if the bushes are booby-trapped? The thought exploded suddenly in his mind. He tried to swerve aside but he was going too fast. Plunging into the bushes, he flung himself to the right.

Twisting around, he squinted upwards. The German was pumping bullets into the bushes as fast as he could fire. They buzzed past Hackermeyer's body like hornets as his gaze jerked searchingly from tree to tree. There! He saw the muzzle blast, the drift of powder smoke. Muscles twitching, Hackermeyer propped the M–1, aimed and squeezed the trigger. The rifle bucked against his shoulder. He fired again, shooting at the German's muzzle blast. He kept on shooting until the empty cartridge clip popped upward from its chamber.

The sniper had stopped firing. Hackermeyer sucked in fitful gasps of breath. Had he hit his target? Or was the German playing dead, waiting for him to stand? Hackermeyer swallowed. Wouldn't the German have fallen if he was hit? The sniper Cooley had shot had tumbled to the ground. Hackermeyer grimaced, looking fixedly at the tree. It was like a cave up there, the foliage shaded it so darkly. Why should the German have stopped firing if he was still alive? Unless he was running out of ammunition and wanted a clear target before expending more. Hackermeyer held his breath and listened. It was very still now. The sounds of battle had drifted so far ahead as to be almost inaudible. He tightened suddenly. There *was* a noise. Like something falling or — dripping.

Hackermeyer stood and walked over to the tree. There was a gathering splotch of bright red blood on the leafy ground. He stood there, transfixed, watching the blood arc down in endless, heavy drops. It was so vividly red and glistening. Hackermeyer stared dumbly at it. His gaze lifted slowly, trailing its crimson descent.

High above, the dead German sagged outward from a bough, the rifle dangling from a strap around his neck, his arms swinging loosely. He was belted to the tree. His body swayed back and forth as if a breeze were moving him.

Abruptly Hackermeyer turned and started running in the direction the squad had gone. There was a tingling lightness in his body as though he'd been drinking. He seemed to float across the ground in effortless strides, moving as in a dream. Nothing could stop him. Nothing.

Sixteen minutes later he reached the clearing. There were dead American soldiers lying all over it. Hackermeyer started out among them, looking to see if any were from the squad. It was the first time he'd seen so many dead at once. There must have been a terrible battle here. That sniper might have saved his life, it occurred to him. It was strange to think of being singled out for fortune. That sort of thing never happened to him. Still, if he hadn't been held back . . .

He was halfway across the clearing when, overhead, the fluttering rush of shells began. Hackermeyer staggered to a halt and looked up quickly. For the fragment of a second he felt a sense of angry justification. This was more suitable to the pattern — that he should survive the attacks of three Germans and miss this battle only to be personally assaulted by 88's. Before the idea had flared more than a moment in his consciousness, he flung himself to the ground and hid his face.

The shells exploded in the trees behind him. Hackermeyer jerked his legs in as the air was filled with billowing thunder. The zing of shrapnel sounded overhead.

"Hackermeyer!"

Instinctively he raised his head and looked around, then pulled it down again as the second flurry of shells exploded in the trees.

"In front of you!"

Hackermeyer looked up again but saw nothing ahead except a rise in the ground, a clump of trees and bushes at its peak. He dropped his head again and a third cluster of shells exploded crashingly. He gasped as the pressure waves gushed over him, pounding at his flesh.

"It's Cooley! Run!" the voice roared down at him.

Automatically Hackermeyer pushed to his feet and started running forward, sensing with his legs, rather than his eyes, the incline he was scaling. He still saw nothing but the trees and bushes.

"Keep coming!" Cooley's voice boomed down at him.

Suddenly a shell exploded close behind and, like an ocean breaker, the concussion wave lifted Hackermeyer off his feet and flung him to the ground, knocking out his breath. Another blast ripped at the air, driving spikes of pain into his head. The earth leaped under him, then dropped away, giving him the sensation of being thrown to the ground. Dazed, he watched the muddy cloud of smoke rush over him, filling his eyes and nose and mouth with clogging fumes. He tired to rise but couldn't. His legs went rubbery under him and he bumped down onto his side.

Someone grabbed him underneath the left arm. He looked up dizzily and saw Cooley's bearded face wavering above him in the smoke.

"Come on, son!" Cooley's shout seemed to reach him from a distance. He felt himself being hauled to his feet. Suddenly he was running next to Cooley, barely concious of the ground beneath him. He began to sag and Cooley jerked him up again.

"Keep running!" he yelled in Hackermeyer's ear. This time the shout was like a knife-point jabbed against his brain. Hackermeyer winced and kept on running. They were almost to the clump of trees now. Thunder blasted all around them, shrapnel fragments wailed and moaned, skimming by their bodies. Hackermeyer felt the wind of one piece rushing past his cheek.

Now Cooley dragged him by the clump of trees and bushes and Hackermeyer caught a glimpse of curving stone like the top of some ancient ruin. He crossed the peak and instantly was skidding down an incline beside a giant concrete structure. A narrow doorway loomed before him. Cooley shoved him through, he tripped and sprawled inside, tumbling down into a dim-lit chamber.

Lippincott helped him up. "Greetings, Hackermeyer," he said.

Hackermeyer looked around the cold, cement-walled room, which was illuminated by daylight coming through the wall slits and by a single candle on a wooden table. Outside, the explosions sounded muffled.

"What's this?" he asked. His tongue felt swollen in his mouth.

"Pillbox," said Lippincott.

"Oh." Hackermeyer gaped at him. Lippincott seemed to be rising rapidly off the floor.

"Easy." Cooley's face appeared beside him once again, his strong grip under Hackermeyer's arm. Hackermeyer's shoes scraped on the cement floor as Cooley led him to a tier of three bunks on the wall and sat him on the bottom one. "There we go," said Cooley, taking away his rifle.

Hackermeyer sat groggily as Cooley squatted down in front of him.

"You all right?" Cooley asked.

"Yeah."

Cooley grinned at him. "That's the old stuff," he said. "Where you been?"

Hackermeyer ran a sluggish tongue across his lips and inhaled the dankly sour air.

"Sniper," he said.

Cooley stopped chewing. "Pin you down?" he asked.

Hackermeyer nodded slowly. It hurt his head.

"What'd you do?" asked Cooley.

Hackermeyer coughed weakly. "Shot 'im," he mumbled.

Cooley clucked. "We got us a tiger, boys," he said. Hackermeyer raised his eyes, blinking, and saw that, in addition to Lippincott and Cooley, Schumacher and Fearfeather were also there. Schumacher was methodically stripping down his rifle on the middle of the three bunks across the small room.

"What happened to Linstrom?" Cooley asked.

"Hit," said Hackermeyer thickly.

"With what?"

"Shell." Hackermeyer cleared his throat viscidly. "Was — nothing left."

"Oh, Christ." Cooley patted his shoulder. "Lie down now," he said. "We'll be here awhile."

Hackermeyer tried to lift his legs but couldn't. Cooley picked them up and Hackermeyer fell back on the bunk, closing his eyes. Then, laboriously, he sat up again and fumbled for his canteen. As he drank, he watched Cooley talking to Lippincott. In a few moments, Cooley went outside.

"Where's 'e going?" he asked. He could hardly recognize his voice.

"Checking on Guthrie and Lazzo," said Lippincott.

Hackermeyer slid the canteen back into its canvas sheath and fumbled at the clips. He couldn't close them. Painstakingly he inched his gloves off and pushed the clips shut. Then he took off his belt and helmet and slipped back onto the bunk, wondering what happened to the Germans who had manned the pillbox.

The smell was getting stronger now; a thick, consuming stench that he could almost taste. It was the smell of locker rooms, subway toilets, ill-kept kitchens, firing ranges. Acid smells, sweet smells, stale smells; the reek of dirt and grease and smoke and unwashed bodies. It seemed to ooze down his throat when he swallowed.

Hackermeyer stared up dizzily at the crisscross of ropes on the bunk above. It reminded him of the bunks on the ship he'd taken overseas. Except that they had had canvas bottoms. He turned his head and looked at the crude, unfinished cement of the walls. There were drops of water trickling down it. It looked like the wall in the cellar of his uncle's house. Used to whip me there, he thought. Bastard. Powerless, he slipped away.

Hackermeyer opened his eyes. For a moment, he forgot where he was and sat up so quickly that his head struck the rope webbing overhead and bounced him back.

"Low bridge," he heard someone say. Turning his head, he saw Cooley and Lippincott sitting at the table playing cards. It was Lippincott who had spoken.

Hackermeyer eased himself to a sitting position on the edge of the bunk and looked around with sleep-dulled eyes.

"How do you feel?" asked Cooley without looking over. His jaws worked rhythmically with tobacco-chewing.

"Okay." Hackermeyer looked across the room and saw that Schumacher was reading on the middle bunk. His rifle, glinting with fresh oil, leaned against the wall, its barrel protected by a clean sock, its bolt assembly by a piece of oilskin. That's a good idea, Hackermeyer thought. It was important to take care of your weapon.

Hackermeyer closed his eyes and felt a twinge of pain on his right cheek. Opening his eyes, he touched the cheek with his fingers. There was a crusty thread of blood running outward from beneath his eye. He raked at it with a nail and winced. Reaching into his inside coat pocket, he slid free his steel mirror.

It was a shock to see his face ingrained with dirt, eyes bloodshot, lips chapped, a jagged scratch across his cheek. Picking up his helmet, he poured some canteen water into it. He got a scrap of soap and the damp washcloth from his web belt and cleaned off his face, grimacing at the sting on his cheek. As he washed, then brushed his teeth lethargically, he became conscious of the whispering flutter of shells overhead, the muffled rumble of explosions in the distance. The Americans must be shelling Saarbach.

He realized that he needed to empty his bowels and kidneys and, pushing to his feet, he started for the doorway.

"Where you going?" Cooley asked without turning from his cards.

"Bathroom," Hackermeyer answered.

"There's a room in back," said Cooley.

Lippincott groaned faintly. "Isn't this place enough of a toilet already?"

"No point in getting his ass blown off," said Cooley.

Lippincott grunted. "Oh, well," he said, "I guess it can't smell any worse."

"Hell, man, this is home," said Cooley.

"Sure it is," Lippincott played a card. "How they could live in this stench for months is beyond me," he said.

"I would, personally, prefer an outhouse," said Fearfeather.

"I'm with you," said Lippincott.

Hackermeyer found the cement corridor and edged along its dark length, grunting in surprise as the floor dropped away and he jarred down into a small, dungeon-like room which smelled of burned food and grease. Gritting his teeth, he opened up his coat and pulled his pants down.

When he was through, he came back into the main room and walked over to one of the rectangular slits through which daylight was passing. Bending over, he looked outside and saw the slope which he and Cooley had come running up. It was a perfect spot for ambush. No wonder there had been so many bodies in the clearing. Hackermeyer blinked. There weren't any bodies. Had they been taken away? Or had he only imagined them?

Returning to the bunk, Hackermeyer sat down with a sigh. He opened a box of K rations and slumped there chewing on the biscuits. He could hear the crunching in his head as he ate, causing miniature tremors through his skull. I'll clean my rifle soon, he told himself. It was important.

"Hackermeyer?"

He raised his eyes.

"How come Linstrom got it and you didn't?" Cooley asked. "Weren't you together?"

Hackermeyer coughed on a piece of biscuit. It was strange, but he'd completely forgotten about Linstrom until that moment. Already it seemed days since Linstrom had been killed.

"He ran away," he said.

"Oh — great." Cooley slapped down a card. "And the government keeps sending them over," he said. "Why the God damn hell don't they use their brains?"

"Teen-agers are all right," said Lippincott.

"Not as soldiers," Cooley said. "I got nothing against them personally, for Christ's sake. I got one at home, ain't I? And there was Jimmy."

Hackermeyer looked at Cooley as the sergeant played cards. He remembered thinking that Cooley wasn't the father type. Now he found out that Cooley had a son. Who was Jimmy?

"They're all right for helping cooks or working in supply or — oh, hell, they're just no good for combat, that's all."

"They're fast," said Lippincott, looking at his cards.

"So they're fast," said Cooley. "What good is that if they don't think? And they don't. They're used to being in a group, thinking like the group."

"You mean that's not the secret of being a good soldier?" Lippincott asked wryly.

"You know better than that," said Cooley. "I'll take a man over a teen-ager any day. Ain't no guarantee, but he's more likely to think for himself than a kid is."

"Maybe not," said Lippincott. "A teen-ager has more independence. He hasn't been forced into line yet."

"It's knowing how to operate while you're *in* line that counts," said Cooley.

"Could be," said Lippincott, yawning.

"Don't get me wrong," said Cooley. "I ain't saying that just because a guy is older, he's automatically on the ball. I'm just saying he's had more time to get on the ball. A teen-ager don't bring anything to war but himself. The only training he has is what the army gave him and, Christ knows, that's not much."

Lippincott clucked. "Fine talk from a noncom," he said.

Cooley spat tobacco juice to one side.

"Trainees get taught every damn thing but what they need the most," he said. "The details of what it's like to be in combat. Look at Linstrom. If basic training was what it should be, he'd have been rooted out, not sent over here. Now he's dead and what the hell does it prove?"

Hackermeyer sat looking intently at Cooley. He'd never seen him so talkative before.

"I'll tell you one flaw in the way guys are trained," said Cooley. "Nobody ever tries to find out who's going to fire his weapon."

Cooley nodded at Lippincott's curious expression.

"Yeah," he said. "Yeah. Obvious? Hell, it couldn't be more obvious. But do they try to find out? The hell they do. Even after a man gets in combat, they don't try to find out."

Hackermeyer noticed that Schumacher had lowered his book and was looking at Cooley.

"Nobody ever tries to find out the most basic fact of all about a soldier," Cooley said. "Does he shoot his weapon or doesn't he?"

"Don't follow you," said Lippincott.

Cooley played a card.

"Take our squad," he said. "We're not so bad, but we don't even make thirty per cent fire. I won't name names — but more than half our guys never fired a shot. Simple as that. And why?"

"Inadequate drilling," said Schumacher.

Cooley glanced at him.

"That's only part of it, Bernie," he said, shaking his head. "A small part of it. Not enough to explain why seventy-five per cent of soldiers won't fire their weapons. Oh, sure, they'll face the enemy but, God damn it, they won't fire their weapons at him!"

He pointed a finger at Lippincott.

"Nobody says a word about it," he said, "but, when the chips are down, seventy-five per cent of soldiers are conscientious objectors. They won't shoot and they won't kill."

I will, Hackermeyer almost said aloud.

"A question of discipline and drilling," said Schumacher.

"No, Bernie," Cooley shook his head again. "A question of human nature. If a soldier can't stomach killing you can't make him stomach it by teaching him how a rifle works. And how do you beat your enemy unless you fire your weapon at him? You fire and you advance — hell, that's combat, that's it. And it don't matter if you got anything to shoot at either. It's mass fire that counts, not accuracy."

Hackermeyer understood now why Cooley always kept yelling for them to fire their weapons even when there was no visible target.

"I agree with you one hundred per cent, of course," said Schumacher, nodding. "Fire superiority is of the essence. The relating of each weapon to the ground for maximum fire power. This is, however, a matter of drill and discipline."

"Nope." Cooley shook his head once more. "I'll tell you what you got to relate, and it ain't weapons to the ground. It's one guy to another guy. You got to teach a man what he can expect from his buddies in combat. If he knows that, it don't matter if the ground ain't worth anything or if his weapon don't even work. He'll still know what the score is."

Cooley picked up his new hand.

"How do you teach soldiers human nature?" asked Lippincott.

"I don't know, but that's what we need," said Cooley. "Especially for teen-agers. They got to have something to lean on besides themselves. All they got is — fast legs and titmilk ideals. You got to make up for that."

"If a grown man's ideals are more established, won't it be even harder for him to kill?" asked Lippincott.

"Maybe so," said Cooley. "Except he's more likely to know why he *has* to kill. And less likely to be affected by killing, too."

He grunted. "Crazy thing," he said. "A soldier fires his weapon and everybody thinks he's doing what comes naturally. Hell, he's practically a hero just for doing that."

Hackermeyer felt surprised. He hadn't thought of himself as a hero for shooting his rifle. Then he recalled that he'd never seen Foley shoot his rifle. Or Linstrom. Or Fearfeather. Or Bill Riley or Goldmeyer, either. Cooley must be right.

"One good thing about a teen-ager," said Cooley. "They're more used to team pepper than an older guy. If they're not scared shitless, they're more likely to talk it up in combat."

He put down his cards again.

"Which is another thing they don't mention in training," he said. "That you got to keep in touch, let every other man know where you are. That means a lot in combat. Why do I keep telling you guys to shout out your names? So you'll know you're not alone, that's why."

He spat tobacco juice to the side. "War ain't guns against guns," he said. "It's men against men. And the men that have the most confidence are going to win. That's one reason Americans make out in the long run. They're more full of piss than anyone else. But there'd sure be a lot of lives saved if they were given the right kind of training too."

Schumacher made a dubious sound. "I still say discipline or lack of discipline is the key," he said. He reminded Hackermeyer of his uncle. Uncle George was always raving about discipline too. Until now, Hackermeyer had assumed that, even though he'd hated his uncle's guts, he was inclined to think in that direction too. Now, oddly enough, he found himself tending toward Cooley's point of view. Maybe discipline had its limitations.

"Discipline ain't the key," Cooley said as if reading Hackermeyer's mind. "And drilling ain't the key. Combat breakdowns ain't breakdowns of discipline or drilling. They're human breakdowns. Or human break-*throughs!*" he said, pointing at Schumacher. "Some of the best soldiers are guys who've been nothing all their lives. When it counts is when they prove themselves. And, by God, you never know who it's going to be."

Hackermeyer stared at Cooley. It was as if the sergeant were addressing him personally. Was it possible that every lack and failure in his life could be, somehow, compensated for in combat? Hackermeyer shivered with a sudden, strange excitement.

"Except, when your best soldiers show up," said Cooley, "it ain't likely they're going to be eighteen-year-olds."

The Siegfried Line

✕

from *And Save Them for Pallbearers*

by JAMES GARRETT

Snow still lay about in huge, inert banks, and a cold wind swept along the front. Charlie Company was cloaked in white robes brought up during the night. The men clustered together in uneasy groups, like ghouls in a graveyard. The robes were to camouflage them as they attacked across the snow.

Flaggler raised his hand slowly and shouted, "OK, men, let's go!" and the war that had temporarily ended with the Ardennes counteroffensive sprang back into life again like an uncaged beast. The Infantry shivered and launched itself at the beast's claws.

Flaggler led them across a stream into the German fire. There was to be armor. But because of the stream it was necessary that the armor come from the south.

Crawford sprawled formlessly in a defile, worked his way towards the German positions. His feet were soaked from the stream, cold ate its way into his belly and his head ached. He could smell nothing except burning gunpowder. This was a dead country, he thought, looking at the snow-covered earth. It was a carnal, lusting graveyard awaiting new markers. It fed and grew on the flesh of men. It fed on the dead broken body of Private Harry Madigan, face down in the field behind him, struck down by an 88 shell quite aimlessly thrown out from the enemy lines. The Germans were not yet sure there was to be an attack or from where it would come.

It was not until 1100 hours that the tanks arrived, snow chewing from their treads in fine, spumy trails. The tanks moved behind the Company and suspiciously swung their 76's in great arcs.

The Company stirred in the snow, a common emotion booting into them like an officer's shoe: the tanks would draw 88 fire!

Jaro Thrumm, lying belly-down in the snow, watched in disgust as they waddled up. He had no use for armor, particularly this green, untried division. The Second Armored had had men who knew how to die, to bring fire and death to the enemy. But these new, hairless boys, battened down in hulks of steel, understood only that the Infantry must precede them. Otherwise, they would refuse to fight. It was always like that, he thought, the Infantry gettin the shitty end of the stick. He coughed noisily and raised his head to see what Crawford was going to do. At one time he had been self-confident, but now he was just one of the cattle lowing in the pasture that Crawford herded toward the German village on the sky-line. He was awfully tired of this field; he wanted to get some place where he could remove his boots and massage his feet. The biting fear of trench foot hung over him. C'mon, Crawford, he thought, get the lead out!

Crawford divested himself of his snow blanket and waved the Platoon to its feet. Behind him the tanks sputtered indignantly, as though angry at being left behind, and whirred through the snow in pursuit.

The line wavered a moment and lurched forward. The tanks squealed, "Wait for us. Wait for us," their whirling treads spewing out the snow behind them in sheets of white, mucousy excrement.

As usual after an attack, it was peaceful and silent in the village street. American soldiers moved spiderlike through the village, filtered to its perimeters, flushed out snipers. The captured snipers ran or limped past, smiling, laughing, showing quantities of gold-filled teeth. Hatless, weapon-less, they ran into the American lines, and Donatti wondered why they should be so happy. It must be, he thought, because we have won and failed to kill them, and now they will be our guests while we go out to die. They are done with war, and we have still just begun. A shot snapped his head upward, away from Lieutenant Boyd Hanes, who received the bullet in his head and crumpled to the ground. When he turned back to him, he was dead.

The sniper was trapped in the building. He had leaned from an upper window, sighted on a helmet, and pulled the trigger.

Donatti lunged into the building. He attached the bayonet to his rifle and slowly mounted the stairs. The faint darkness of his shadow slipped on before him. On the third floor he paused, listened for enemy sounds. They came from a room overlooking the street at the other end of the hall. Inside the room, the German was firing methodically into the street. The door was slightly ajar and Donatti slipped inside. The room stunk with an odor of age, as of old people, and it was not of death, but of dying. It smelled like cabbage in tenements, spaghetti on a hot, still day. He twisted his face away from it and shot the German in the back. The soldier turned, triggering his rifle, and a puff of dust marked the spot where the bullet entered the wooden floor. He fell against the window, tottered momentarily on the sill as a suicide might, changed his mind and toppled back. The sound of his fall filled the room. Donatti cringed away from it, placed his hands over his ears, ran down the stairs and out of the house.

Far behind, stretched somberly against the skyline, the German snipers plodded wearily, going farther away from the war. They looked as tired, at that distance, as the American soldiers guarding them. After a while, the tanks came up and moved behind the Company's line of foxholes and Donatti walked to the other end of the village where he found Lewandowski, Thrumm, Last, Crawford, and the First and Second Squad sergeants, Kearns Mendlesohn and Joe Rindone, gathered in a house in the village back of the thin line of Platoon foxholes.

"Rough." Sergeant Al Lewandowski took a long pull from his canteen.

"It'll get rougher," Jaro Thrumm grunted.

"That's right, Al," Crawford said, stroking his hands together nervously. "There are two thousand yards between us and the river."

"The river? Today?" Lewandowski asked in bewilderment.

"Tell him, Sam," Thrumm said.

"Sure, Al," Crawford said. "You didn't think this was our objective, did you?"

"Well," Lewandowski said hesitantly, "I kind of hoped so. For now, anyway."

They all laughed listlessly and went back to planning the attack. Lewandowski listened without much interest. Right now, if he was still a private, he'd be in his foxhole taking it easy. It wasn't all gravy being an NCO, even though the rest of the guys in the Squad kidded him about it. They had probably been disappointed when he was promoted, having expected Dakola or Joslin to get the rating. But he'd finally won it. And he was proud of it — it was the first step.

The only thing he regretted was that he could not sew sergeants' chevrons upon his arm.

The Germans had thrown in every piece of equipment and man they could spare in staving off this puncturing of the Siegfried Line. When the Americans mounted their attack, however, the Germans retreated to the other side of the river to hold forth from behind its rushing waters, much as a small boy thumbs his nose at the school bully from behind his mother's back.

The Platoon approached the Blüt River leisurely, suspiciously. Finally, they came — pulled by curiosity — to its banks and stared into the murky brown water. The Blüt River. One day it would become a living stream of blood. Not today, however.

Engineers would have to assess its currents first, bring up pontoons and boats; artillerymen would have to compute ballistics and ranges and map co-ordinates; SHAEF would have to look at it; and Army and Corps and Division and Regiment and Battalion, as well. They would have to mass shells, tanks, jeeps, bullets, blankets, shelter halves, Ack-Ack batteries, P-38's and B-24's, bandages, and plasma and penicillin, gasoline, rations, maps, pencils and papers and typewriters and desks, TNT and nitroglycerin and black powder, USO shows and Red Cross Mobile Units — and replacements.

The Platoon sighed in relief. It was a big river. They wouldn't get over it tonight.

Hell, they wouldn't even be asked to.

Oh, yeh, you wait'n see what G-2 cooks up.

Yeh, I'll wait, all right. What else?

They moved back from the river, had a mail call, a hot meal, received their blanket rolls and dug in.

Toward nightfall the Germans got their 88's placed and began to fire into the American positions. The Company shivered and settled in to wait.

But, unexpectedly a few days later it was pulled back from its position on the banks of the Blüt River. Like a race horse being groomed for the Kentucky Derby it was curried in the coal mines of Heerlen; fed and stabled near Vaals; saddled with a host of alien replacements from Maastricht, and trained to the bit by river-crossing techniques and practice on the Maas River. Moreover, the Army exhibited a strange willingness to provide the Company with everything it desired: mail, hot chow, sleeping bags, toothpaste, cigarettes and a freedom in which to find liquor and women. The Army also provided the Company with items it regarded suspiciously: ammunition, field rations and extra fragmentation and incendiary grenades. Finally, the Army issued the Company items which turned its blood cold: overshoes and new waterproof boots, waterproof trousers and lifebelts. By that time the Company suspected what SHAEF, Army, Corps, Division, Regiment and Battalion had known all along: Charlie Company had been selected to lead the United States Army's assault across the Blüt River.

Donatti had been standing in a welter of spray in a shower for coal miners in Heerlen, his body covered with ribbons of lather, singing along with the hundred or so voices that filled the subterranean chamber with a cheerfully off-key maleness, when he suddenly realized what Charlie was to be asked to do. He rinsed quickly and walked unsteadily from the stall to pull his uniform down from the roof. He went outside and stood shivering in the cold north wind smoking cigarettes until the rest of the Squad joined him.

He had not really known that Charlie Company was to be *the* assault company, but he had known it would be in the first echelon. One would be as bad as the other in this instance — only it would occur a little later.

A chain of command had always existed, a hand that extended directly from SHAEF to his Squad. It was a gentle but insistent hand. It pushed. It pointed. It said, "You." And before you knew it, you walked into the hell of German fire, the hand a continuous pressure on your back. Donatti knew the hand had tapped him on the shoulder. He had felt its fingers in England before D-Day, and Charlie had been in the first wave.

He was willing to give the hand quite a lot. He would gladly concede the Division, the Regiment even, and perhaps the Battalion — but not the Company. The Company was three rifle platoons, a weapons platoon, and some assorted characters belonging to Company Headquarters. When the hand touched the Company, it tickled Donatti's ribs. But it was not he who conceded the Company anyway — it was Flaggler, just as Mayberry had conceded the Battalion; Jaffee, the Regiment; Stephenson, the Division, and so on, all the long road back to SHAEF where Eisenhower must have conceded the AEF, and further yet to where Roosevelt conceded the United States. Had God, he wondered, conceded the earth?

Then Crawford, who had been at Headquarters, brought the official word. He reported that Flaggler had seemed very tired, as though he had fought a hard, losing battle. "We have no choice," Flaggler had said, "so we'll do the best we can. It's really a very good plan of attack."

Crawford, from some distant irritation and a sense of incompleteness (he, too, had crossed the Channel in the first wave June 6), said, "All right, let's have it. You don't have to sell it to anyone."

"You don't understand, Sam," Flaggler said, "but the odds are ten to one against us getting across the river, and a hundred to one that we'll be cut off once we're across."

Crawford had apologized and brought the plan back to the Platoon and held a meeting for the squad leaders. He looked into their eyes and told them of the plan, and Donatti thought he saw shame there since it was Crawford who had conceded the Platoon. Crawford's voice drilled on in a repetitious monotone: terrain, camouflage and cover and concealment, logistics, rations, ammo, the replacements, training and God-speed. Donatti looked deeper into Crawford's eyes and realized that what he saw there was the knowledge that he himself had just conceded his Squad.

The Maas River snaked down its gullies, a portentous omen of wily brown waters that sucked and gasped and tore chunks from the bank. It swirled in small eddies and branching fingers that stretched in to lap at the assault boats like a licking of hungry lips. The Company drew back and stared morosely into the water that spumed into the air. There was fright on their faces and Crawford was worried — fear should not have come to them yet. What would their faces show, he wondered, on the banks of the Blüt?

The replacements that had arrived from Maastricht to bolster the Company's strength were particularly awed by the Maas. It was a grisly introduction to the Company, and they sensed the hazards it portended. They stood in closely knit groups and listened to the older men, the veterans, talk of the approaching battle, but they ventured no opinions — they were replacements, tolerated but not consulted. They awaited their baptism of fire with the same breathlessness a pledge awaits his fraternity hazing.

Lewandowski surveyed the river with distaste, shifting the BAR on his broad shoulders. He was indignant. Donatti had decided to alter the Squad's Table of Organization and had saddled him with the BAR, taking it from Borg who, Donatti felt, was not strong enough to carry it in the attack. It was not fit for the assistant squad leader to carry a weapon heretofore designated for a private first class! Why couldn't Donatti have assigned it to Joslin or Dakola? They were just as strong as he was. Here he had been a sergeant for only a short time and Donatti had decided the Squad wouldn't need an assistant leader in this attack. What the hell good was it to win the stripes if you couldn't use them?

Sure they were short-handed, but why the hell pick on him? He was just a sergeant doin' private's work. God damn you, Donatti, I won't get promoted doin' a private's job!

Donatti, standing apart from the Squad, knew that Lewandowski was unhappy about the BAR, but he had a reason for giving it to his assistant. He had assessed the coming battle of the Blüt as a fluid series of firefights

once they breached the river and emerged from the horrors of the Siegfried
Line. For the first time in months they would be mobile, and since, with
the three new replacements they had received — Privates Carl Trajec,
Henry Meeker and Joe Spazzi — the Squad now numbered nine men,
Donatti felt that the T/O would have to be altered. Accordingly, he had
placed himself as scout, concentrating Lewandowski, Borg and Meeker as
the BAR team, vulnerable and important. Joslin, Dakola, Spazzi and Trajec were riflemen, and Hogan, the antitank grenadier. Lewandowski
would not be careless, reckless or somewhere else when needed. He wanted
to be promoted again.

The engineer, a young second lieutenant who was directing the practice session, beckoned Donatti. He draped his rifle over a shoulder and said,
"Step up, boys, the water's fine," and the Squad moved to the edge of the
bank. The engineer grinned and said, "This is just a dry run. You guys
don't have to look so scared," and turned to a huge, sullen-faced sergeant
who was his assistant. "Drag it up here, Mike."

Along the bank similar scenes were being enacted as other engineer
officers and enlisted men instructed Charlie Company in the use of the
small rubber boats. Behind Charlie, several hundred feet from the bank,
Able and Baker Companies awaited their turns.

"These craft are designed to take six men and an engineer in the stern.
You'll be crossing the Blüt in the dark, so you'll have to know exactly what
you're doing and which boat you're to take." He turned to Donatti. "You
know how you're going to split 'em?"

Donatti nodded. "Hogan, Lewandowski, Borg, Meeker and Joslin go
in one boat. Spazzi, Trajec, Dakola and Last will go with me. We'll keep
the BAR team together."

"OK. Mike, get the other boat," the lieutenant directed. Mike slipped
on the river bank and went knee-deep into the water before he was able
to secure the second boat. "Sergeant, your boys will be in boats twelve and
fourteen. We're superstitious, so there's no boat thirteen. One man in each
boat will hold the weapons, the others will paddle. There'll be an engineer
in each boat to steer and bring it back. Remember to do it exactly this way
on the Blüt and you'll be OK."

The Squad clumsily entered the small, bobbing craft. George Las walked
down the bank to stand beside Donatti. "Jaro says I go with you."

"That you do," said Donatti, extending his hand gallantly. "After you,
chum."

The practice crossing went very well. Charlie Company upset no boats
and, when it was completely across, Flaggler commended the men for
their work. Jo Spazzi, his dark Italian face wreathed in smiles, said, "Hell,
Sarge, this crossing'll be a snap."

Donatti felt the muscles in his jaws tighten. "Don't count on it," he said shortly, and walked away from Spazzi.

"Christ," Spazzi complained to Henry Meeker, "he's really got a wild hair up his ass."

"Maybe he knows somethin' we don't. He's done this before."

"Yeh, I never thought of that. Wonder how bad it'll be?"

"All I know is what Joslin said."

"What's that?" Spazzi asked eagerly.

"Joslin said G–2 says it's a walk. Only trouble with that, Joslin says, is that G–2's never been right yet."

The shell rose, arced and plummeted toward the earth. At first its sound was only the distant protest of shattered air. Then, describing its vast, flashing arc, it was followed by a high, wailing sound from which soldiers averted their faces. When it fell, it was the shriek of uncaged demons, like fingernails dragged across a blackboard, and the soldiers trembled as the screeching rubbed tense nerves that caught and condensed the sound and translated its message of fear to their tortured minds. After what seemed an eternity, the shell uttered a sharp, crackling expletive as it exploded and dug a sullen cavity from the earth.

The artillery barrage hurled itself across the river like a living thing. From camouflaged positions the American guns hacked at the opposite shore like giant scythes, searched out hidden machine-gun nests, snipers and artillery. Bursting shells were huge orange blossoms sprouting from the inky blackness. The frenzy of the guns mounted to an incoherent crescendo. Miscalculations — shorts — splashed meaninglessly into the river, erupted in geysers of water that rained upon the engineers already at the water's edge. It seemed that nothing could live on the other side of the river.

Flaggler pressed his back to the wall of the house that contained his Company Headquarters. The muscles in his jaws were clenched and white, and he tried to prevent himself from shaking. Cold gusts of night air washed across his perspiring face. The boats were already down there waiting to carry Charlie across the churning water.

Where Flaggler stood, a road wound down to the river bank, a long, muddy road saturated with melting snow that had almost disappeared. The Company was encamped in houses along its length. The houses once had been a small farm village, but the Germans had long since departed. There were only Americans in the houses now.

Flaggler winced at each new explosion. His head ached and he wanted to scream into the night, to shout, "Stop! Stop!" His fingernails dug into his palms, causing great pain, but he was unable to stop himself. Something about this fierce mechanical death held him relentlessly. He was fascinated by the shells blossoming on the other bank, his mind numb to all but the overhead whine of artillery. His eyelids felt as though weights were attached to them. A pleasant, lassitudinous sensation enveloped him, and he desired to crawl into a cellar and allow the delicious languor of sleep to drift over his body. He felt lost as in a woman's arms and surrendered to the sensation, moved his body voluptuously as the shells passed overhead, until a short shell exploded fifty yards from him and halted his writhing. He wanted to turn and strike at the air, at his enemies, at the war that had brought him to this desolate river bank. There would be no shiny gold leaves for him, he thought suddenly. They didn't pin majors' insignia on broken, mauled dead bodies.

"My God!" he said aloud as an 88 shell roared in and exploded on the other side of the house. "Jesus Christ!" he swore again. A tear worked out of his eye and wormed its way down his face. "Oh, my God," he said. "Oh, sweet running Jesus, this is it!"

"Cap'n, Cap'n, for God's sake get in the door!" a voice pleaded at his elbow. Blakethorn tugged on Flaggler's arm. "Cap'n, Cap'n!" he shouted, and Flaggler permitted himself to be dragged into the shelter of the doorway. "It's time for the attack, Cap'n," Blakethorn said importantly.

"The artillery," Flaggler said blankly. "The artillery, Sergeant."

"It's stopped. It's been stopped for half a minute."

"Stopped?" Of course, it was the 88's coming in now from positions the American artillery had failed to destroy.

"Of course. It's stopped. Funny, I'm almost deaf."

"Yes, sir," said Blakethorn, refusing to look into the officer's face. "The Company's out on the road, sir."

"Oh, yes," Flaggler said, as though he had remembered something profound. "The Company."

The approach to the river was a nightmare. At first the road ran parallel to the river, but after several hundred yards it curved down to meet the water — a thick, soupy, clinging muck that covered and slid into boots and galoshes. The snow, which had been a crust for weeks upon the road, had melted in the previous forty-eight hours, and caused the relentless quagmire through which the Company struggled. Later it would become an impassable and miring bog for hundreds of vehicles. Now, it sucked voraciously at soldiers' feet. Floundering and falling helplessly in the slime, the Company despaired of ever reaching the boats waiting below.

The American artillery, which had meticulously raked the opposite bank, had failed to destroy the enemy's positions to the extent that had been desired. From shattered foxholes and gun emplacements the enemy pointed the lethal barrels of artillery and small arms toward Charlie Company.

There were two alternatives: retreat or slide through salvos of enemy fire to the river. The Company never faltered; it was simply forced to scatter.

Screams filled the air around Donatti: pitiful, weak and helplessly drowning in waves of bursting shells. Another, and yet another, projectile rocked him until he was dazed and could not find the strength to drag his body from the violence that threatened to engulf and destroy him. He crushed the earth hungrily under his belly and clawed at it. From the road above the river bank a single, sustained scream mounted over all others. For a moment even the 88's were silent, as if the Germans shoveling shells into their weapons had stopped, appalled at what they had done. During that single lull the Company dashed toward the river.

Jaro Thrumm shouted, "Third Platoon, over here! Third Platoon! Mendlesohn! Donatti! Rindone! Last! Over here!" He shoved through the tangle of men that swarmed from the road and ran along the bank, corralled the Platoon.

He slipped on the shore and got to his feet covered with mud. He looked at the luminous hands of his wrist watch and swore. Only ten minutes had passed. He gesticulated angrily at the darkness, making a hammer of his fist. "Third Platoon, over here! Donatti! Mendlesohn! Last!" Then, desperately, "Crawford!"

Only a few engineers remained at the river's edge. Seventy per cent of them had been killed or wounded in the half-hour preceding the assault. Their lieutenant had drowned while trying to pull drifting boats back to shore, and Mike, their sergeant, was seated on the bank crying like a baby as he cradled the lieutenant in his arms. The Company had to launch and steer its own boats.

The river was a boiling caldron. The Blüt was five times as wide as the Maas, and where the Maas was like a tame housecat with sheathed claws, the Blüt was a raging tiger. It raked the boats with its sharp talons, chewed on them with bloody fangs.

Donatti sat on his heels in the stern of the boat and dug his paddle into the current, but the raging water gradually pushed the prow downstream, drove the boat north. The relentless pressure of the river was shoving them far off their prearranged landing place.

"God damn it," Donatti swore above the roar of the river, "lean into it! Row!" The rifles lay in the center of the boat between the six oarsmen in front of Donatti. He cursed silently as trees fled southward to indicate their steady drift.

Other boats still fought the current with their prows pointed toward the opposite shore. One boat manned by only three men was suddenly caught in the current, and its prow came around in the water. The boat gathered speed and swept down the river; every effort of its crew to straighten it met failure. Donatti watched it approach in fascination, prayed that it would miss his boat, which was directly in its path. Then he saw the helmsman lean far out over the water, dig his oar into it as he might have against a buttress of earth until the paddle bent and threatened to snap, and the helpless craft swerved and passed Donatti's boat with only a yard or so to spare. Its three oarsmen surrendered to the river and lifted their paddles from the water like Indians caught in rapids who lay aside their paddles and sing their death songs before vanishing over a waterfall. The boat disappeared around a bend in the river.

A second boat swept out of control. It crashed into the boat containing Joslin, Lewandowski and Last. Donatti heard their hoarse cries as both boats turned over. At that moment his own boat struck a fallen tree that stretched into the river. The crew shoved at it with their oars, but the boat would not come free of the branches.

Donatti thrust his paddle into the water, but it failed to reach bottom. "It's too deep here!" he shouted. "Pull her along the tree!"

"Shit," one of the soldiers said, "we're stuck."

My God, Donatti thought, if the Krauts catch us out here, we're dead!

"This son-of-a-bitch is gonna sink," someone said. "She's struck a leak."

Only a few seconds had passed since the two boats had overturned, but they were already only bottoms bobbing far downstream. Some of the men had reacted immediately and pinched the air capsules that inflated their lifebelts. They rose to the surface shouting encouragement to one another. One soldier came up, floundering and screaming in panic, and Donatti recognized Lewandowski. The heavy BAR was strapped across his shoulders and its weight, along with the pack and steel helmet that in his panic he had not shed, pulled him under again. Only the rising air bubbles gave evidence that he had ever existed.

Donatti hesitated; a shuddering, crawling fear saturated him. There was a time, he thought, when I could have done this without hesitation, but it somehow seemed involved with clean, chlorinated swimming pools inhabited by sunbaked people unafraid of water. He shed his helmet, pack and lifebelt and dove into the river.

The water was nearly freezing and when he opened his eyes and stared into the black, alien depths that pressed against him he panicked, closed his eyes tightly and lashed out. The moment passed quickly, however, and he swam to the spot where he thought Lewandowski had sunk. Reaching bottom, he struck out at a different angle, but his outstretched fingers encountered only water. Finally, his chest bursting, he struggled upward. It seemed much brighter above the surface and, for a moment, he thought that it was merely the difference between the air and water, but then he looked into the skies and saw dozens of flares bursting above the river. The flares soared above the battleground, floated serene and majestic to earth and water. A German machine gun sputtered downstream, but outside of that it was remarkably quiet. Donatti took a deep breath, measured his position with the shore, and dove again.

The water sucked at him. He held his legs very straight until he could sense the air in his chest buoying him back to the surface. He kicked his legs then and breaststroked his path through the water. His uniform dragged him down and slowed his smooth stroking and made all his movements cumbersome. Darkness and quiet swirled around him. It seemed that he could hold his breath forever, that he could escape the war in the depths of the Blüt River, that he could relieve himself of his responsibilities and disappear from the Company. Then his breath gave out and he bobbed back to the surface.

The boat that had been pinned against a tree was now alongside the bank and the men were clambering out, aided by a soldier who held his rifle like a lifeline. Donatti swam leisurely toward the shore.

Joslin pulled him onto the bank and Donatti rolled over on his back. To his surprise, he discovered that he was winded.

"Christ, I never thought you was comin up that last time, Pete," said Joslin. "You musta been down five minutes."

"Five, ten, what's the difference?" Donatti gasped. "I didn't find Al."

"I tol' him 'bout that lousy BAR when we got on the boat, but he wouldn't lissen. The dumb bastard!"

"Sure," Donatti said, and sat up. "That helps him, doesn't it?"

"Aw, Christ, Pete, I saw Last go down, too," Joslin said uncomfortably. "We can spend the rest of our lives cryin'."

All the units of the Battalion were across the river now and somewhere Harrison, who had been his friend, was driving Able Company against the German emplacements. Mayberry had received no word from Able Company since it left the line of departure, but if anyone could make it, Harrison could.

Technician fifth grade Amos Simms skillfully brought the jeep to a halt and peered at the slime that was the river road. The brackish muck awaited him gleefully. "I think we'll get stuck, Colonel."

"I'll tell you when to stop," Mayberry said.

Simms shifted gears and the jeep darted forward.

They reached the hill that overlooked the river and the wheels spun crazily in the mud and the vehicle slewed around and settled into it.

"We're stuck, sir," Simms said.

"I'll walk. You can stay with the jeep." Mayberry climbed out gracelessly and started down the river bank, observing the discarded equipment lying profusely about. Medics scurried around on the lower levels removing the wounded. Mercedes's intelligence had been correct. The Battalion had suffered horribly here.

Mayberry passed one body, then another, striving not to look into their faces. At the third body he hesitated, glanced down. It was Wakely Piersall. Surrounded by the odors of war and the mutilated bodies of his men, he covered his eyes with a hand and sobbed aloud. His Battalion, as he had known it, was dead. It could be replaced all right, new men assimilated into the ranks, but it would never be the same. The Battalion that he had known, nurtured and loved since D-Day had died at last on the greasy banks of the Blüt River. The wild men of Camp Martin-Noye, Normandy, Moine, the Siegfried Line were no longer. The Battalion was dead.

He went on to a place where the engineers were trying to get a pontoon bridge across the river. The men perspired freely from their labors and the continuous fear of incoming artillery. Mayberry was able to persuade the officer in charge of the detail to ferry him across the river.

"I dunno, Colonel," the officer said when the boat reached the opposite bank, "but what I'd be careful up there. The Infantry's not too far ahead."

"I'll watch it, Lieutenant." Mayberry dismissed him with a wave of his hand. "And thanks."

He stood on the bank, watching the boat as it breasted the fury of the river on its return trip, saw it beach on the opposite shore. About him envelopes of smoke slid along his body. He was a pale wraith in this dead land. For a moment he forgot what it was he sought. He finally remembered the Battalion. It was his past, his present, his future.

Earlier, at the Battalion Command Post he had felt the Battalion row away from him; he had felt it die on the river bank. Now he sought the Battalion; not to bring it back to him but to return to it.

A Welcome to Germany

✗

from *The Young Lions*

by IRWIN SHAW

The men in the trucks fell quiet as they drove up to the open gates. The smell, by itself, would have been enough to make them silent, but there was also the sight of the dead bodies sprawled at the gate and behind the wire, and the slowly moving mass of scarecrows in tattered striped suits who engulfed the trucks and Captain Green's jeep in a monstrous tide.

They did not make much noise. Many of them wept, many of them tried to smile, although the objective appearance of their skull-like faces and their staring, cavernous eyes did not alter very much, either in weeping or smiling. It was as though these creatures were too far sunk in a tragedy which had moved off the plane of human reaction onto an animal level of despair — and the comparatively sophisticated grimaces of welcome, sorrow and happiness were, for the time being, beyond their primitive reach. Michael could tell, staring at the rigid, dying masks, that a man here and there thought he was smiling, but it took an intuitive act of understanding.

They hardly tried to talk. They merely touched things — the metal of the truck bodies, the uniforms of the soldiers, the barrels of the rifles — as though only by the shy investigation of their fingertips could they begin to gain knowledge of this new and dazzling reality.

Green ordered the trucks left where they were, with guards on them, and led the Company slowly through the hive-like cluster of released prisoners, into the camp.

Michael and Noah were right behind Green when he went through the doorway of the first barracks. The door had been torn off and most of the windows had been broken open, but even so, the smell was beyond the tolerance of human nostrils. In the murky air, pierced ineffectually here and there by the dusty beams of spring sunshine, Michael could see the piled, bony forms. The worst thing was that from some of the piles there was movement, a languidly waving arm, the slow lift of a pair of burning eyes in the stinking gloom, the pale twisting of lips on skulls that seemed to have met death many days before. In the depths of the building, a form detached itself from a pile of rags and bones and started a slow advance on hands and knees toward the door. Nearer by, a man stood up and moved, like a mechanical figure, crudely arranged for the process of walking, toward Green. Michael could see that the man believed he was smiling, and he had his hand outstretched in an absurdly commonplace gesture of greeting. The man never reached Green. He sank to the slime-covered floor, his hand still outstretched. When Michael bent over him he saw that the man had died.

The center of the world, something repeated insanely and insistently in Michael's brain, as he kneeled above the man who had died with such ease and silence before their eyes. I am now at the center of the world, the center of the world.

The dead man, lying with outstretched hand, had been six feet tall. He was naked and every bone was clearly marked under the skin. He could not have weighed more than seventy-five pounds, and, because he was so lacking in the usual, broadening cover of flesh, he seemed enormously elongated, supernaturally tall and out of perspective.

There were some shots outside, and Michael and Noah followed Green out of the barracks. Thirty-two of the guards, who had barricaded themselves in a brick building which contained the ovens in which the Germans had burned prisoners, had given themselves up when they saw the Americans, and Crane had tried to shoot them. He had managed to wound two of the guards before Houlihan had torn his rifle away from him. One of the wounded guards was sitting on the ground, weeping, holding his stomach, and blood was coming in little spurts over his hands. He was enormously fat, with beer-rolls on the back of his neck, and he looked like a spoiled pink child sitting on the ground, complaining to his nurse.

Crane was standing with his arms clutched by two of his friends, breathing very hard, his eyes rolling crazily. When Green ordered the guards to be taken into the Administration Building for safekeeping, Crane lashed out with his feet and kicked the fat man he had shot. The fat man wept loudly. It took four men to carry the fat man into the Administration Building.

There was not much Green could do. But he set up his Headquarters in the Commandant's room of the Administration Building and issued a series of clear, simple orders, as though it was an everyday affair in the American Army for an infantry captain to arrive at the chaos of the center of the world and set about putting it to rights. He sent his jeep back to request a medical team and a truckload of ten-in-one rations. He had all the Company's food unloaded and stacked under guard in the Administration Building, with orders to dole it out only to the worst cases of starvation that were found and reported by the squads working through the barracks. He had the German guards segregated at the end of the hall outside his door, where they could not be harmed.

Michael, who, with Noah, was serving as a messenger for Green, heard one of the guards complaining, in good English, to Pfeiffer, who had them under his rifle, that it was terribly unjust, that they had just been on duty in this camp for a week, that they had never done any harm to the prisoners, that the men of the SS battalion, who had been there for years and who had been responsible for all the torture and privation in the camp, were going off scot-free, were probably in an American prison stockade at that moment, drinking orange juice. There was considerable justice in the poor Volkssturm guard's complaint, but Pfeiffer merely said, "Shut your trap before I put my boot in it."

The liberated prisoners had a working committee, which they had secretly chosen a week before, to govern the camp. Green called in the leader of the committee, a small, dry man of fifty, with a curious accent and a quite formal way of handling the English language. The man's name was Zoloom, and he had been in the Albanian Foreign Service before the war. He told Green he had been a prisoner for three and a half years. He was completely bald and had pebbly little dark eyes, set in a face that somehow was still rather plump. He had an air of authority and was quite helpful to Green in securing work parties among the healthier prisoners, to carry the dead from the barracks, and collect and classify the sick into dying, critical and out-of-danger categories. Only those people in the critical category, Green ordered, were to be fed out of the small stocks of food that had been collected from the trucks and the almost empty storerooms of the camp. The dying were merely laid side by side along one of the streets, to extinguish themselves in peace, consoled finally by the sight of the sun and the fresh touch of the spring air on their wasted foreheads.

As the first afternoon wore on, and Michael saw the beginning of order that Green, in his ordinary, quiet, almost embarrassed way, had brought about, he felt an enormous respect for the dusty little Captain with the high, girlish voice. Everything in Green's world, Michael suddenly realized, was fixable. There was nothing, not even the endless depravity and bottomless despair which the Germans had left at the swamp-heart of their dying millennium, which could not be remedied by the honest, mechanic's common sense and energy of a decent workman. Looking at Green giving brisk, sensible orders to the Albanian, to Sergeant Houlihan, to Poles and Russians and Jews and German Communists, Michael knew that Green didn't believe he was doing anything extraordinary, anything that any graduate of the Fort Benning Infantry Officers' Candidate School wouldn't do in his place.

Watching Green at work, as calm and efficient as he would have been sitting in an orderly room in Georgia making out duty rosters, Michael was glad that he had never gone to Officers' School. I could never have done it, Michael thought, I would have put my head in my hands and wept until they took me away. Green did not weep. In fact, as the afternoon wore on, his voice, in which no sympathy had been expressed for anyone all day, became harder and harder, more and more crisp and military and impersonal.

Michael watched Noah carefully, too. But Noah did not change the expression on his face. The expression was one of thoughtful, cool reserve, and Noah clung to it as a man clings to a very expensive piece of clothing which he has bought with his last savings and is too dear to discard, even in the most extreme circumstances. Only once during the afternoon, when, on an errand for the Captain, Michael and Noah had to walk along the line of men who had been declared too far gone to help, and who lay in a long line on the dusty ground, did Noah stop for a moment. Now, Michael thought, watching obliquely, it is going to happen now. Noah stared at the emaciated, bony, ulcerous men, half-naked and dying, beyond the reach of any victory or liberation, and his face trembled, the expensive expression nearly was lost . . . But he gained control of himself. He closed his eyes for a moment, wiped his mouth with the back of his hand, and said, starting again, "Come on. What are we stopping for?"

When they got back to the Commandant's office, an old man was being led in before the Captain. At least he looked old. He was bent over, and his long yellow hands were translucently thin. You couldn't really tell, of course, because almost everyone in the camp looked old, or ageless.

"My name," the old man was saying in slow English, "is Joseph Silverson. I am a rabbi. I am the only rabbi in the camp . . ."

"Yes," Captain Green said briskly. He did not look up from a paper on which he was writing a request for medical materials.

"I do not wish to annoy the officer," the Rabbi said. "But I would like to make a request."

"Yes?" Still, Captain Green did not look up. He had taken off his helmet and his field jacket. His gunbelt was hanging over the back of his chair. He looked like a busy clerk in a warehouse, checking invoices.

"Many thousand Jews," the Rabbi said slowly and carefully, "have died in this camp, and several hundred more out there . . ." the Rabbi waved his translucent hand gently toward the window, "will die today, tonight, tomorrow . . ."

"I'm sorry, Rabbi," Captain Green said. "I am doing all I can."

"Of course." The Rabbi nodded hastily. "I know that. There is nothing to be done for them. Nothing for their bodies. I understand. We all understand. Nothing material. Even they understand. They are in the shadow and all efforts must be concentrated on the living. They are not even unhappy. They are dying free and there is a great pleasure in that. I am asking for a luxury." Michael understood that the Rabbi was attempting to smile. He had enormous, sunken, green eyes that flamed steadily in his narrow face, under his high, ridged forehead. "I am asking to be permitted to collect all of us, the living, the ones without hope, out there, in the square there . . ." again the translucent wave of the hand, "and conduct a religious service. A service for the dead who have come to their end in this place."

Michael stared at Noah. Noah was looking coolly and soberly at Captain Green, his face calm, remote.

Captain Green had not looked up. He had stopped writing, but he was sitting with his head bent over wearily, as though he had fallen asleep.

"There has never been a religious service for us in this place," the Rabbi said softly, "and so many thousands have gone . . ."

"Permit me." It was the Albanian diplomat who had been so helpful in carrying out Green's orders. He had moved to the side of the Rabbi, and was standing before the Captain's desk, bent over, speaking rapidly, diplomatically and clearly. "I do not like to intrude, Captain. I understand why the Rabbi has made this request. But this is not the time for it. I am a European, I have been in this place a long time, I understand things perhaps the Captain doesn't understand. I do not like to intrude, as I said, but I think it would be inadvisable to give permission to conduct publicly a Hebrew religious service in this place." The Albanian stopped, waiting for Green to say something. But Green didn't say anything. He sat at the desk, nodding a little, looking as though he were on the verge of waking up from sleep.

"The Captain perhaps does not understand the feeling," the Albanian went on rapidly. "The feeling in Europe. In a camp like this. Whatever the reasons," the Albanian said smoothly, "good or bad, the feeling exists. It is a fact. If you allow this gentleman to hold his services, I do not guarantee the consequences. I feel I must warn you. There will be riots, there will be violence, bloodshed. The other prisoners will not stand for it . . ."

"The other prisoners will not stand for it," Green repeated quietly, without any tone in his voice.

"No, sir," said the Albanian briskly, "I guarantee the other prisoners will not stand for it."

Michael looked at Noah. The expensive expression was sliding off his face, melting, slowly and violently exposing a grimace of horror and despair.

Green stood up. "I am going to guarantee something myself," he said to the Rabbi. "I am going to guarantee that you will hold your services in one hour in the square down there. I am also going to guarantee that there will be machine guns set up on the roof of this building. And I will further guarantee that anybody who attempts to interfere with your services will be fired on by those machine guns." He turned to the Albanian. "And, finally, I guarantee," he said, "that if you ever try to come into this room again you will be locked up. That is all."

The Albanian backed swiftly out of the room. Michael heard his footsteps disappearing down the corridor.

The Rabbi bowed gravely. "Thank you very much, sir," he said to Green.

Green put out his hand. The Rabbi shook it and turned and followed the Albanian. Green stood staring at the window.

Green looked at Noah. The old, controlled, rigidly calm expression was melting back into the boy's face.

"Ackerman," Green said crisply. "I don't think we'll need you around here for a couple of hours. Why don't you and Whitacre leave this place for awhile, go out and take a walk? Outside the camp. It'll do you good."

"Thank you, sir," Noah said. He went out of the room.

"Whitacre," Green was still staring out of the window, and his voice was weary. "Whitacre, take care of him."

"Yes, sir," said Michael. He went after Noah.

They walked in silence. The sun was low in the sky and there were long paths of purple shadow across the hills to the north. They passed a farmhouse, set back from the road, but there was no movement there. It slept, neat-white and lifeless, in the westering sun. It had been painted recently, and the stone wall in front of it had been whitewashed. The stone wall was turning pale blue in the leveling rays of the sun. Overhead a squadron of fighter planes, high in the clear sky, caught the sun on their aluminum wings as they headed back to their base.

On one side of the road was forest, healthy-looking pine and elm, dark trunks looking almost black against the pale, milky green of the new foliage. The sun flickered in small bright stains among the leaves, falling on the sprouting flowers in the cleared spaces between the trees. The camp was behind them and the air, warmed by the full day's sun, was piney and aromatic. The rubber composition soles of their combat boots made a hushed, unmilitary sound on the narrow asphalt road, between the rain ditches on each side. They walked silently, past another farmhouse. This place too was locked and shuttered, but Michael had the feeling eyes were peering out at him between cracks. He was not afraid. The only people left in Germany seemed to be children, by the million, and old women and maimed soldiers. It was a polite and unwarlike population, who waved impartially to the jeeps and tanks of the Americans and the truck bearing German prisoners back to prison stockades.

Three geese waddled across the dust of the farmyard. Christmas dinner, Michael thought idly, with loganberry jam and oyster stuffing. He remembered the oak paneling and the scenes from Wagner painted on the walls of Lüchow's restaurant, on 14th Street, in New York. They walked past the farmhouse. Now, on both sides of them stood the heavy forest, tall trees standing in the loam of old leaves, giving off a clear, thin smell of spring.

Noah hadn't said a word since they had left Green's office, and Michael was surprised when he heard his friend's voice over the shuffle of their boots on the asphalt.

"How do you feel?" Noah asked.

Michael thought for a moment. "Dead," he said. "Dead, wounded and missing."

They walked another twenty yards. "It was pretty bad, wasn't it?" Noah said.

"Pretty bad."

"You knew it was bad," said Noah. "But you never thought it would be like that."

"No," said Michael.

"Human beings . . ." They walked, listening to the sound of their composition soles on the road deep in Germany, in the afternoon in spring, between the aisles of pretty, budding trees. "My uncle," Noah said, "my father's brother, went into one of these places. Did you see the ovens?"

"Yes," said Michael.

"I never saw him, of course. My uncle, I mean," Noah said. His hand was hooked in his rifle strap and he looked like a little boy returning from hunting rabbits. "He had some trouble with my father. In 1905, in Odessa. My father was a fool. But he knew about things like this. He came from Europe. Did I ever tell you about my father?"

"No," said Michael.

"Dead, wounded and missing," Noah said softly. They walked steadily, but not quickly, the soldier's pace, thirty inches, deliberate, ground-covering. "Remember," Noah asked, "back in the replacement depot, what you said: 'Five years after the war is over we're all liable to look back with regret to every bullet that missed us.' "

"Yes," said Michael. "I remember."

"What do you feel now?"

Michael hesitated. "I don't know," he said honestly.

"This afternoon," Noah said, walking in his deliberate, correct pace, "I agreed with you. When that Albanian started talking I agreed with you. Not because I'm a Jew. At least, I don't think that was the reason. As a human being . . . When that Albanian started talking I was ready to go out into the hall and shoot myself through the head."

"I know," Michael said softly. "I felt the same way."

"Then Green said what he had to say." Noah stopped and looked up to the tops of the trees, golden-green in the golden sun. " 'I guarantee . . . I guarantee . . .' " He sighed. "I don't know what you think," Noah said, "but I have a lot of hope for Captain Green."

"So do I," said Michael.

"When the war is over," Noah said, and his voice was growing loud, "Green is going to run the world, not that damned Albanian . . ."

"Sure," said Michael.

"The human beings are going to be running the world!" Noah was shouting by now, standing in the middle of the shadowed road, shouting at the sun-tipped branches of the German forest. "The human beings! There's a lot of Captain Greens! He's not extraordinary! There're millions of them!" Noah stood, very erect, his head back, shouting crazily, as though all the things he had coldly pushed down deep within him and fanatically repressed for so many months were now finally bursting forth. "Human beings!" he shouted thickly, as though the two words were a magic incantation against death and sorrow, a subtle and impregnable shield for his son and his wife, a rich payment for the agony of the recent years, a promise and a guarantee for the future . . . "The world is full of them!"

It was then that the shots rang out.

Christian had been awake five or six minutes before he heard the voices. He had slept heavily, and when he awoke he had known immediately from the way the shadows lay in the forest that it was late in the afternoon. But he had been too weary to move immediately. He had lain on his back, staring up at the mild green canopy over his head, listening to the forest sounds, the awakening springtime hum of insects, the calls of birds in the upper branches, the slight rustling of the leaves in the wind. A flight of planes had crossed over, and he had heard them, although he couldn't see the planes through the trees. Once again, as it had for so long, the sound of planes made him reflect bitterly on the abundance with which the Americans had fought the war. No wonder they'd won. They didn't amount to much as soldiers, he thought for the hundredth time, but what difference did it make? Given all those planes, all those tanks, an army of old women and veterans of the Franco-Prussian War could have won. Given just one-third of that equipment, he thought, self-pityingly, and we'd have won three years ago. That miserable lieutenant back at the camp, complaining because we didn't lose this war in an orderly manner, the way his class did! If he'd complained a little less and worked a little more, perhaps it might not have turned out this way. A few more hours in the factory and a few less at the mass meetings and party festivals, and maybe that sound above would be German planes, maybe the Lieutenant wouldn't be lying dead now in front of his office, maybe he, Christian, wouldn't be hiding out now, looking for a burrow, like a fox before the hounds.

Then he heard the footsteps, coming in his direction along the road. He was only ten meters off the road, well concealed, but with a good field of vision in the direction of the camp, and he could see the Americans coming when they were quite a distance off. He watched them curiously, with no emotion for the moment. They were walking steadily, and they had rifles. One of them, the larger of the two, was carrying his in his hand, and the other had his slung over his shoulder. They were wearing those absurd helmets, although there would be no danger of shrapnel until the next war, and they weren't looking either to the left or the right. They were talking to each other, quite loudly, and it was obvious that they felt safe, at home, as though no notion that any German in this neighborhood would dare to do them any harm had ever crossed their minds.

If they kept coming this way they would pass within ten meters of Christian. He grinned without amusement, thinking of it. Silently he brought up his machine pistol. Then he thought better of it. There were probably hundreds of others all around by now, and the shots would bring them running, and then there wouldn't be a chance for him. The generous Americans would not stretch their generosity to include snipers.

Then the Americans stopped. They were perhaps sixty meters away, and, because of a little bend in the road, they were directly in front of the small hummock behind which he was lying. They were talking very loudly. One of the Americans, in fact, was shouting, and Christian could even hear what he was saying. "Human beings!" The American kept shouting, over and over again, inexplicably.

Christian watched them coldly. So much at home in Germany. Strolling unaccompanied through the woods. Making speeches in English in the middle of Bavaria. Looking forward to summering in the Alps, staying at the tourist hotels with the local girls, and there no doubt would be plenty of them. Well-fed Americans, young, too, no Volkssturm for them, all young, all in good condition, with well-repaired boots and clothing, with scientific diets, with an Air Force, and ambulances that ran on gasoline, with no problems about whom it would be better to surrender to . . . And after it was all over, going back to that fat country, loaded with souvenirs of the war, the helmets of dead Germans, the Iron Crosses plucked off dead breasts, the pictures off the walls of bombed houses, the photographs of the sweethearts of dead soldiers . . . Going back to that country which had never heard a shot fired, in which no single wall had trembled, no single pane of glass been shattered . . .

That fat country, untouched, untouchable . . .

Christian could feel his mouth twisting in a harsh grimace of distaste. He brought his gun up slowly. Two more, he thought, why not? The grimace turned into a smile. He began to hum to himself softly, as he brought the nearest one, the one who was yelling, into his sights. You will not yell so loud in a moment, friend, he thought, putting his hand gently on the trigger, humming, remembering suddenly that Hardenburg had hummed at another time which had been very much like this one, on the ridge in Africa, over the British convoy at breakfast . . . He was amused that he remembered it. Just before he pulled the trigger he thought once more of the possibility that there were other Americans around who might hear the shots and find him and kill him. He hesitated for a moment. Then he shook his head and blinked. The hell with it, he thought, it will be worth it . . .

He fired. He got off two shots. Then the gun jammed. He knew he'd hit one of the bastards. But by the time he looked up again after working fiercely to clear the jammed cartridge, the two men had vanished. He'd seen one start to go down, but now there was nothing on the road except a rifle which had been knocked out of the hands of one of the Americans.

The rifle lay in the middle of the road, dark blue, with a pinpoint of sparkling sunlight reflecting off a spot near the muzzle.

Well, Christian thought disgustedly, that was a nicely botched job! He listened carefully, but there were no sounds along the road or in the forest. The two Americans had been alone, he decided . . . And now, he was sure, there was only one. Or if the other one, who had been hit, was alive, he was in no shape to move . . .

He himself had to move, though. It wouldn't take too long for the unwounded man to figure out the general direction from which the shot had come. He might come after him, and he might not . . . Christian felt that he probably wouldn't. Americans weren't particularly eager at moments like this. Their style was to wait for the Air Force, wait for the tanks, wait for the artillery. And, for once, in this silent forest, with only a half hour more light remaining, there would be no tanks, no artillery to call up. Just one man with a rifle . . . Christian was convinced that a man wouldn't try it, especially now, with the war so nearly over, when it was bound to seem to him like such a waste. If the man who had been hit was dead by now, Christian reasoned, the survivor was probably racing back right now to whatever unit he had come from, to get reinforcements. But, Christian figured, if the man who had been hit was only wounded, his comrade must be standing by him, and, anchored to him, not being able to move quickly or quietly, would make a beautiful target . . .

Christian grinned. Just one more, he thought, and I shall retire from the war. He peered cautiously down the road at the rifle lying there, scanned the slightly rising, bush-and-trunk-obscured ground ahead of him, shimmering dully in the dying light. There was no sign there, no indication.

Crouching over, moving very carefully, Christian moved deeper into the forest, circling . . .

Michael's right hand was numb. He didn't realize it until he bent over to put Noah down. One of the bullets had struck the butt of the rifle Michael had been carrying, and, whirling it out of his hand, had sent a hammerblow of pain up to his shoulder. In the confusion of grabbing Noah and dragging him off into the woods, he hadn't noticed it, but now, bending over the wounded boy, the numbness became another ominous element of the situation.

Noah had been hit in the throat, low and to one side. He was bleeding badly, but he was still breathing, shallow, erratic gasps. He was not conscious. Michael crouched beside him, putting a bandage on, but it didn't seem to stop the blood much. Noah was lying on his back, his helmet in a small pale bed of pink flowers growing very close to the ground. His face had resumed its expensive, remote expression. His eyes were closed and the blond-tipped lashes, curled over his pale-fuzzed cheek, gave the upper part of his face the old, vulnerable expression of girlishness and youth.

Michael did not stare at him long. His brain seemed to be working with difficulty. I can't leave him here, he thought, and I can't carry him away, because we'd both buy it then, and fast, moving clumsily through the woods, perfect target for the sniper.

There was a flicker in the branches above his head. Michael snapped his head back, remembering sharply where he was and that the man who had shot Noah was probably stalking him at this moment. It was only a bird this time, swinging on a branch-tip, scolding down into the cooling air under the trees, but the next time it would be an armed man who was anxious to kill him.

Michael bent over. He lifted Noah gently and slid the rifle from Noah's shoulder. He looked down once more, then walked slowly into the forest. For a step or two, he could still hear the shallow, mechanical breathing of the wounded man. It was too bad, but Noah had to breathe or not breathe, unattended, for awhile.

This is where I probably catch it, Michael thought. But it was the only way out. Find the man who had fired the two shots before the man found him. The only way out. For Noah. For himself.

He could feel his heart going very fast, and he kept yawning, dryly and nervously. He had a bad feeling that he was going to be killed.

He walked thoughtfully and carefully, bent over, stopping often behind the thick trunks of trees to listen. He heard his own breathing, the occasional song of a bird, the drone of insects, a frog's boom from some nearby water, the minute clashing of the boughs in the light wind. But there was no sound of steps, no sound of equipment jangling, a riflebolt being drawn.

He moved away from the road, deeper into the forest, away from where Noah was lying with the hole in his throat, his helmet tilted back away from his forehead on the bed of pink flowers. Michael hadn't figured his maneuver reasonably. He had just felt, almost instinctively, that sticking close to the road would have been bad, would have meant being pinned against an open space, would have made him more visible, since the forest was less dense there.

His heavy boots made a crunching noise on the thick, crisp, dead leaves underfoot and on the hidden, dead twigs. He was annoyed with himself for his clumsiness. But no matter how slowly he went, through the thickening brush, it seemed to be impossible to make no noise.

He stopped often, to listen, but there were only the normal late-afternoon woodland sounds.

He tried to concentrate on the Kraut. What would the Kraut be like?

Maybe after he'd fired, the Kraut had just packed up and headed straight back toward the Austrian border. Two shots, one American, good enough for a day's work at the tail end of a lost war. Hitler could ask no more. Or maybe it wasn't a soldier at all, maybe it was one of those insane ten-year-old kids, with a rifle from the last war dragged down out of the attic, and all hopped up with the Werewolf nonsense. Maybe Michael would come upon a mop of blond hair, bare feet, a frightened nursery-expression, a rifle three sizes too large . . . What would he do then? Shoot him? Spank him?

Michael hoped that it was a soldier he was going to find. As he advanced slowly through the shimmering brown and green forest-light, pushing the thick foliage aside so that he could pass through, Michael found himself praying under his breath, praying that it was not a child he was hunting, praying that it was a grown man, a grown man in uniform, a grown man who was searching for him, armed and anxious to fight . . .

He switched the rifle to his left hand and flexed the fingers of his numbed right hand. The feeling was coming back slowly, in tingling, aching waves, and he was afraid that his fingers would respond too slowly when the time came . . . In all his training, he had never been instructed about how to handle something like this. It was always how to work in squads, in platoons, the staggered theory of attack, how to make use of natural cover, how not to expose yourself against the skyline, how to infiltrate through wire . . . Objectively, always moving ahead, his eyes raking the suspicious little movements of bushes and clustered saplings, he wondered if he was going to come through. The inadequate American, trained for everything but this, trained to salute, trained for close-order drill, advancing in columns, trained in the most modern methods of the prophylactic control of venereal disease. Now, at the height and climax of his military career, blunderingly improvising, facing a problem the Army had not foreseen . . . How to discover and kill one German who has just shot your best friend. Or maybe there were more than one. There had been two shots. Maybe there were two, six, a dozen, and they were waiting for him, smiling, in a nice orthodox line of rifle pits, listening to his heavy footsteps coming nearer and nearer . . .

He stopped. For a moment he thought of turning back. Then he shook his head. He did not reason anything out. Nothing coherent went through his mind. He merely transferred the rifle back into his tingling right hand, and kept on, in his thoughtful, rustling advance.

The log that had fallen across the narrow gully looked strong enough. It had rotted a little here and there, and the wood was soft, but it looked thick. And the gully was at least six feet across and quite deep, four or five feet deep, with mossy stones half buried in broken branches and dead leaves along the bottom. Before stepping out onto the log, Michael lisened. The wind had died down and the forest was very still. He had a feeling that no human beings had been here for years. Human beings . . . No, that would be for later . . .

He stepped out onto the log. He was halfway across when it buckled, tearing, turning slipperily. Michael waved his hands violently, remembering to keep silent, then plunged down into the gully. He grunted as his hands slithered along the rocks and he felt his cheekbone begin to ache immediately where it had slammed against a sharp edge. The splintering log had made a sharp, cracking sound, and when he had hit the bottom it had been with a dull crash and a crackling of dried twigs, and his helmet had bounced off and rapped loudly against some stones. The rifle, he was thinking dully, what happened to the rifle . . . He was groping for the rifle on his hands and knees, when he heard the swift rushing sound of footsteps running, running loudly and directly toward him.

He jumped up. Fifty feet away from him a man was crashing through the bushes, staring straight at him, with a gun at his hip, pointing toward him. The man was a dark, speeding blur against the pale-green leaves. As Michael stared, motionless, the man fired from his hip. The burst was wild. Michael heard the slugs thumping in, right in front of his face, throwing sharp, stinging pellets of dirt against his skin. The man kept running.

Michael ducked. Automatically, he tore at the grenade hanging on his belt. He pulled the pin and stood up. The man was much closer, very close. Michael counted three, then threw the grenade and ducked, slamming himself wildly against the side of the gully and burying his head. God, he thought, his face pressed against the soft damp earth, I remembered to count!

The explosion seemed to take a long time in coming. Michael could hear the bits of steel whining over his head and thumping into the trees around him. There was a fluttering sound in the air as the torn leaves twisted down over him.

Michael wasn't sure, but he thought, with the noise of the explosion still in his ears, that he had heard a scream.

He waited five seconds, and then looked over the edge of the gully. There was nobody there. A little smoke rose slowly under the overhanging branches and there was a torn patch of earth showing brown and wet where the leaves and mold had been torn away, but that was all. Then Michael saw, across the clearing, the top of a bush waving in an eccentric rhythm, slowly dying down. Michael watched the bush, realizing that the man had gone back through there. He bent down and picked up the rifle, which was lying cradled against two round stones. He looked at the muzzle. It hadn't been filled with dirt. He was surprised to see that his hands were covered with blood, and when he put his hand to touch his aching cheekbone, it came away all smeared with dirt and blood.

He climbed slowly out of the gully. His right arm was giving him a considerable amount of pain, and the blood from his torn hand made the rifle slippery in his hand. He walked, without attempting to conceal himself, across the clearing, past the spot where the grenade had landed. Fifteen feet farther on, he saw what looked like an old rag, hanging onto a sapling. It was a piece of uniform, and it was bloody and wet.

Michael walked slowly to the bush which he had seen waving. There was blood all over the leaves, a great deal of blood. He is not going far, Michael thought, not any more. It was easy, even for a city man, to follow the trail of the fleeing German through the woods now. Michael even recognized, by the crushed leaves and familiar stains, where the man had fallen once and had risen, uprooting a tiny sapling with his hands, to continue his flight.

Slowly and steadily, Michael closed in on Christian Diestl.

Christian sat down deliberately, leaning against the trunk of the great tree, facing the direction from which he had come. It was shady under the tree, and cool, but shafts of sunlight struck down through the other foliage and lit, in oblique gold, the tops of the bushes through which Christian had pushed himself to reach this spot. The bark of the tree felt rough and solid behind his back. He tried to lift his hand, with the Schmeisser in it, but the hand wouldn't move the weight. He pushed annoyedly at the gun and it slithered away from him. He sat staring at the break in the bushes where, he knew, the American would appear.

A grenade, Christian thought, who would have thought of that? The clumsy American, crashing like a bull into the gully . . . And then, out of the gully, a grenade.

He breathed with difficulty. So far, he thought, so much running. Well, the running was now over. His mind seemed to slip in and out, like a faulty set of gears. The spring woods outside Paris and the dead boy from Silesia, lips stained with cherry juice . . . Hardenburg, on the motorcycle, Hardenburg with his face split away from its foundations, the stupid half-naked American firing from the mined bridge in Italy until the machine gun cut him down . . . Gretchen, Corinne, Françoise, the French will have us all yet . . . The vodka in Gretchen's bedroom, the sherry and brandy and wine in the closet, the black lace and the garnet brooch . . . The Frenchman pulling Behr's boots off on the beach after the planes, always the planes . . . "Listen, when a soldier joins an army, any army, there is a kind of basic contract the army makes with him . . ." Who said that, and was he dead, too? Fifty francs for a glass of brandy, served by an old man with rotting teeth. "The larger issue is Austria." And, "The end justifies the means" . . . This was the end, and what means did it justify? Other things . . . The American girl on the snowy hill. Just one more and I retire . . . The blundering, foolishly brave American, surviving by luck, accident, God's will . . . 1918 on the church wall, in chalk, the French knew, they knew all along.

The gears slipped in and out. It was getting very cold. The shafts of sunlight, which looked as though they were coming into the forest through narrow, slanted green windows, were getting thinner and thinner.

Two shots and the gun jammed. Finally, of course, it had to jam. My entire company marched into Munich, still in possession of their weapons. It was much more orderly. The important thing was always to be able to lay your hands on a bicycle. How long, he thought, full of self-pity, can they expect a man to run?

Then he saw the American. The American wasn't cautious any more. He walked directly up to him, through the thin green sunlight. The American was no longer young, and he didn't look like a soldier. The American stood over him.

Christian grinned. "Welcome to Germany," he said, remembering his English.

He watched the American lift his gun and press the trigger.

Michael walked back to where he had left Noah. The breathing had stopped. The boy lay quiet among the flowers. Michael stared dryly down at him for a moment. Then he picked Noah up, and, carrying him over his shoulder, walked through the growing dusk, without stopping once, back to the camp. And he refused to allow any of the other men in the Company to help him carry the body, because he knew he had to deliver Noah Ackerman, personally, to Captain Green.

The Flag Is Raised

⚔

from *Maybe I'm Dead*

by JOE KLAAS

Jim awakened slowly in the familiar mumble and bustle of the prison bay. He brought his arms from under the blankets and stretched thoroughly. Suddenly he sat up and looked about him between the hanging clothing and the towels. The bunks of Tom and Bob were empty. Beside him, on another lower bunk, Jack Noble was lacing up a shoe. "What's going on, Jack?"

"Nothing. Why?"

Jim slid his stockinged feet to the floor and stood up. Legs dangled from some of the upper bunks. Prisoners walked about munching Reichs bread or smoking. Jim looked at Burt Salem and Al Koczeck quietly buttoning up their greatcoats. He brushed past them out onto the main floor. Men milled about in confusion, grumbling, wisecracking, laughing, sour-faced, blank-faced. Everything was entirely normal. Frowning deeply, Jim walked back to his bunk and sat down, closing his eyes tightly.

"Appel!" someone down the bay shouted. "All out for appel! Everybody out!"

The floor rumbled as the prisoners headed for the exits. Jim felt a shoe nudge his calf. Bob stood beside Tom looking down at him. "You going to appel in your stocking feet?"

Jim reached down, pulled his shoes on and tied them. He looked at Bob and Tom as they walked toward their block's formation gathering in front of the Abort. "I don't get it."

Bob looked down at the ground. "Don't worry about it, Jim."

"But I just don't get it. I don't get it!"

Tom placed a hand on his shoulder. "Don't flap, Jim."

They followed Jim across to Major Smith, who was standing before the formation. "Pete, what happened last night? Didn't they go through with it?"

The major grinned through his beard. "Didn't who go through with what?"

"The goons. They were going to surrender the camp. I was there when they started out."

The smile faded from the major's face. "Now, wait a minute. Maybe I came in late. What are you talking about?"

Tom spoke flatly behind Jim. "We'd better fall in. Here come the goons now."

Major Smith nodded. "I'll see you after the count."

Jim stared at the Wehrmacht lieutenant and at the sergeant-major as they approached the formation. He had to hurry into place when the major issued the command.

"Blawck . . . tennnshun!"

Major Smith and the German officer exchanged salutes, and the Germans counted them off by fives.

"Block . . . at ease." The major motioned for Jim to come forward, turned his back on the formation, and spoke in a lowered voice. "Now what the hell were you saying, Jim?"

"I figured you would know about it. Real early this morning von Munsing and some of our brass left in a white car to negotiate a surrender with our people to the west of here. It should have been over by now. I saw them go myself."

The major nodded gravely. "Anybody else see them?"

"Well, Colonel Baker was there. And Colonel Akron. And a few of us who happened to be out just then."

The major nodded. "I'll have a talk with Red or the Old Man. In the meantime I wouldn't mention it any more if I were you." He nodded toward the Germans taking appel. "The goons are obviously still running things."

"But, Major, I saw them."

"Maybe something went wrong. You might have built up false hopes." He stared briefly at a distant goon box that was still manned by a machine gunner. Then he looked down at the ground and stirred the dirt with his toe. "Or somebody might think you've gone round the bend. You've been behind the wire a long time, you know. Why not just wait and see what happens?"

Jim turned and walked back to his place in the formation. Without looking at Bob or at Tom he lit up a cigarette and smoked it, glaring toward the distant goon box. When appel was dismissed, Tom broke the silence between them. "Come on, Jim. Let's take a circuit."

Still silent, Jim walked with them. Looking out beyond the tents that splattered the old parade ground behind the Abort, they could see the sentries strolling as usual along the outer fences. They crossed a line where a fence had been removed and walked between prison blocks occupied by RAF prisoners with their blue remnants of uniforms and blue laundry hanging from the lines. After more tents and milling men they came to the southeast corner of a large square field strangely free of tents or buildings. Its north boundary was the double barbed-wire fence and goon-box towers of the outer edge of the camp. To the west was another crowded compound. To the south as they walked with a ragged parade of morning strollers lay the first compound they had lived in after their delousing shower. Now its parade ground was cluttered with a jungle of makeshift shacks constructed by Balkan prisoners out of scrap lumber, cardboard, and gunnysack cloth.

Jim nodded to where several prisoners were talking through the fence with two tattered Balkan prisoners. "I wonder if they would know anything. All the time they've been in this place they ought to have a grapevine."

Bob sighed. "Aw, Christ, Jim. Drop it, will you?"

They rounded the bend and walked along the guarded north fence. Jim stared at the first sentry as they passed. He wore Wehrmacht green and his rifle was slung barrel down over one shoulder. They passed a goon box and looked up. The machine gunner was sitting relaxed on its railing. They passed on until they came abreast of another sentry standing outside the fences. Jim stopped and looked at him. He muttered out of the side of his mouth. "I'm going to talk to this goon." He waved and called out, "Wie geht's?"

The sentry looked surprised and smiled. "Gut, danke. Wie geht's Ihnen?"

"Gut, danke. Wo ist Ihre Heimat?"

The German's tanned face grinned wider. "I'm Sudetenland."

"Und wann gehen Sie da?"

"Heute Nachmittag."

Jim looked at Tom and Bob and at several others who had paused in the circuit to listen. He looked back at the German. "Heute?"

"Ja, ja. Heute Nachmittag." The sentry spread his arms. "Heute ist der Krieg zu ende für uns alle."

Bob nudged Jim. "What's he saying?"

Jim spoke rapidly. "I asked him when he was going home. He said this afternoon. He said this afternoon the war is over for all of us."

The slit in Bob's teeth showed in a grin for the first time that morning. "He said that?"

Jim turned back to the German. He gestured at the forbidden zone between the perimeter path and the fence. "Können wir daran kommen?"

The German shrugged, still smiling. "Ja. Warum nicht? Kommen Sie doch." He unslung his rifle, and the prisoners cringed back a step. "Wir haben keine munition." He snapped the bolt back twice. There was no ejection.

Jim spoke excitedly to the faces around him. "He doesn't have any bullets in his gun. They're standing guard with empty guns!"

"What the hell!" somebody exclaimed. "They run out of ammunition?"

"No bullets!"

"Yeah. I'll bet."

Jim grinned first at Bob, then at Tom. "Come on." He led the way across the forbidden zone to the fence. He smiled back at the German. "Warum keine munition? Hat der Kommandant — er — ah . . ." He looked around at the others who had gathered up close to the fence. "Does anybody know how you say 'surrender' in German?"

"I schpeak zum English." The German chuckled.

"The hell you do. Well, what I want to know is, has your Kommandant surrendered the camp or not?"

"Ja, ja. Er hass all our bullets early ziss morgnink zu your colonel giffen. Zoon ve all now go home."

"What's he talking about?"

"What's he saying?"

Jim held up his hands. "Quiet, will you? Let me find out."

Tom nudged Jim. "Ask him why they're still standing guard."

"Yeah. If the camp is surrendered, why are all you guys out here standing guard?"

The German's tanned face frowned. "More z — z — slower, please."

"Why are you still on guard with empty guns?"

The sentry shrugged. "You haff hear of zer S.S., nicht?"

"Yeah, sure."

"Zer S.S. haff not zurrendered. Ve must play like ve are still in command or zer S.S. . . ." He drew a finger across his throat. "Verstehen Sie? Ve must make belief ve vill fight viss zem."

"All the Wehrmacht?"

"Ja. No one but zer S.S. vill truly fight now. Ve must make belief or zer S.S. . . ." Again he drew a finger across his throat.

"Youeee!

"Man, oh, man!"

Excited prisoners broke away from the group and ran across the field toward the main part of camp. Others stayed, their thin faces split by glad smiles. Tom smiled. "Then it's all a fake. Just an act."

Bob was grinning. "It sure fooled me."

Jim pulled a pack of Old Gold cigarettes from his pocket and held them out through the rusty inner fence. The German reached them through the outer fence and was barely able to get them over the wire coiled in between. "Danke. Danke schön."

The German looked up at the goon box. "Ve must go in now. Zoon zey come. I must now go. Please to have meet you."

Jim called after the sentry. "Where you going?"

"Into der Lager. Soon zey come. Zie Amerikaner. Aufwiedersehen."

"So long, Fritz."

All along the fence the machine gunners were climbing down the ladders from the goon boxes. The strollers were walking north along the fence toward the front of the camp. Tom, Bob, and Jim turned and started walking light-footed across the field. Jim laughed, shook his head, and gritted his teeth with joy. "Well, it wasn't as quick as I thought, but it won't be long now."

Tom actually showed his teeth in a smile and patted Jim's shoulder. "You were right, Jim. You were right all the time."

Bob Montgomery sighed. "You know something? When I got up this morning and found everything just the same as it's always been I thought you had gone round the bend. I figured it had finally got you."

Jim kept on laughing softly. "I wasn't so sure myself. But what the hell? It's all over now but the shouting."

Tom ducked under a blanket hanging from a line between two of the British prison blocks and came up with the smile gone from his face. "It's all over but the shooting, you mean."

Jim stopped laughing. "What do you mean?"

"Don't forget the S.S. They're around here somewhere. If Hitler ordered us shot, the Wehrmacht may have ignored the order. But the S.S. won't have any qualms about that."

RAF prisoners were dashing about, shouting from block to block the news that the sentries had all left the fences and goon boxes.

Tom shrugged. "There's no use flapping about it, but it's there. If the guards had to put on a show for them, that means the S.S. are here and are going to put up a fight. Hell, they have to. Our people don't take S.S. prisoners any more. Not since the Malmédy massacre. So if they've got to die anyway, they may want to take someone along with them. It'd be awful easy for them to take some of us."

Bob sighed. "I haven't seen an S.S. around here."

Tom nodded and jumped over a crumbling slit trench. "Let's hope you don't."

Major Smith joined them as they walked along. "You were right, Jim. Von Munsing tried to surrender Moosburg to the Tenth Armored Division last night, but the American general he talked to refused to accept the surrender."

"Refused to accept it!"

"That's right. Von Munsing couldn't surrender for the S.S., so now there's going to be a fight. We got all the guards' bullets, though."

"Yeah, I know." Up beyond the end of the prison block men started cheering. "Now what's up?"

Bob, Burt, Noble, Koczeck, and Junior Jones stood in the group standing by the closed compound gate, staring westward. Tom tapped Koczeck's shoulder. "What's the flap about?"

Koczeck rubbed his hands together. "The goon flag just went down. Somebody ran down the Nazi flag at the main gate."

The pole standing beside the large sentry tower about an eighth of a mile down the main road pointed starkly up toward white sunlit clouds. Four immaculately uniformed Wehrmacht officers marched with flashing black boots up the road from that direction. Jim nodded toward them. "Here comes von Munsing and his staff all dressed up." The four officers wore Iron Crosses and silver decorations pinned to spotless green tunics. Instead of pistols they wore short swords in scabbards decorated with polished silver. "I guess they're going to hole up in here until it's over. We're the farthest compound back."

Tom watched the four Germans pass in through the compound gate and walk in dignified step into the compound. He looked again at the barren flagpole. "Do you reckon von Munsing struck the colors?"

Jim grinned. "What say we walk up that way and have a look?" He nodded toward the open compound gate. "I don't see anybody around to stop us."

Bob grunted. "I think we'd better stay where we are."

"What the hell difference does it make?"

Tom started for the gate through which a few Kriegies were already venturing. "O.K. Let's go, Jim."

Tom and Jim passed through the compound gate and started down the main road that stretched through the center of the jumble of barbed-wire fences and dirty gray buildings on either side. Jim shook his head as they walked. "I can't believe it. I can't believe it's true. This is a great day, Tom. A great day!"

Beyond the Vorlager gate and the outer gate the sloping-roofed Moosburg cheese factory nestled in sunshine against rolling green hills. Two airplanes suddenly popped up over the curve of the hills. Tom pointed. "Here they come. P-47's!" As he spoke the two Thunderbolts whistled and roared overhead, their silver white-starred wings rocking. Two more shot over as the first pair curved upward over the town, dipped their wings, and dove with chattering guns toward the ground. One explosion followed the other. "Dive bombing!" Explosions three and four shook the earth as the first two silver fighters in line-astern formation whined through perfect slow rolls directly over the prison camp. Men of many lands joined in a cheer as the P-47's darted off to disappear beyond the cheese factory and the hills.

"Wahoo!" Jim's teeth flashed as he bounced up and down. "How was that for a victory roll?"

Suddenly the cheering stopped. Near silence settled over the camp. Tom stared straight ahead at the main gate flagpole. A jet-black banner moved steadily up the pole and billowed out. On its silken bulge in the wind were jagged lightning streaks. Together they spelled S.S. Tom's face was taut, his lips thin. "Oh, God. They've taken over."

They moved forward slowly to join a group of silent prisoners of several nationalities standing at the locked gate leading to the Vorlager with its administration buildings and Wehrmacht barracks. All stared at the slowly flapping black flag. Beside Jim a ragged Pole crossed himself. Beyond the fence, among the buildings of the Vorlager, Germans wearing mottled brown and green coveralls, cloth caps or steel helmets, and carrying rifles and machine guns hurried about from one place to the other in seeming confusion. Jim spoke out of the side of his mouth. "Maybe we'd better get back to the other end of camp."

"Wait." Tom frowned in the direction of the fast-moving Germans. "Are they S.S.? I thought the S.S. wore black."

"Those are camouflage suits. Come on. I don't like it here."

Tom ignored the suggestion. "That guy with the Luger must be the top dog."

The German with the pistol wore a brown cloth-peaked cap instead of a helmet. He was shouting orders in unintelligible German. Machine guns were being set up facing a long low building similar to the prison blocks in the compounds. With shoulders swaying athletically the officer strode over to the door of the building and pounded on it with the butt of his Luger. He screamed something to whoever was inside. A voice inside answered something. The German officer stepped back beside one of the machine-gun crews. "Feuern!" he screamed. Instantly the machine guns went to work. Their chatter was like a million riveting hammers. Glass tinkled. Wood splintered. Chunks of gray stucco fell out of the sides of the building. Inside, men screamed. The door fell open on its hinges. Two Wehrmacht guards stepped into its opening and fell back inside. Prisoners standing inside the Vorlager fence began to run. Jim and Tom ducked around the corner of a cookhouse building and stayed there pressed up against the wall. The shooting stopped. "What are they doing, for Christ's sake?" an American voice wanted to know.

"It's the guards," another frightened voice answered. There were three more quick machine-gun bursts. "The guards refused to fight. The S.S. is shooting 'em dead."

Jim turned his pale face to Tom's. "Let's get to hell out of here."

Tom nodded. "This way." At a nervous trot he led the way between the cookhouse and the delousing building. They slowed down as they walked along the rear of the camp hospital. Tom shook his head and panted. "My God! Why didn't they shoot back?"

Jim snorted between heaves of his scrawny chest. "No ammunition. They turned all their bullets over to us. Remember?"

The ground shook from nearby explosions. As they came out from behind the hospital they found the road crowded with prisoners standing and looking curiously up toward the Vorlager. Junior, his face red from running, darted up to Jim. He thrust three holstered pistols and a burp gun at Jim. "Here. Take these back to the block and hide them for me, will you?"

Jim stared down at the guns left in his arms. "Where did you get them?"

"Von Munsing's house. I liberated 'em." Junior's full lips quivered with excitement. "I got to go back and liberate some food. I'll bring you some."

"Food?"

"Yeah. Red Cross parcels. The Kommandant's basement is full of Red Cross parcels. He's been stealing them. Hide that artillery good, for Christ's sake! I'll see you later." Junior darted off again.

Tom gazed thoughtfully toward the black S.S. banner and the cheese factory and green hills beyond it. He had stopped panting. "We didn't have to flap. All the shooting has stopped. Look at those guys on the roof of the cheese factory."

On the sloping roof the tiny figures of riflemen lay on their stomachs pointed westward. Jim nodded. "There's going to be a fight, all right. Too bad the bastards didn't kill off more of each other. Imagine von Munsing with a basement full of our food!"

Tom tapped the burp gun in Jim's arms. "You'd better put this hardware away. You wouldn't want the S.S. to catch you with that."

Jim grinned as they headed back toward their compound. He felt the weight of the machine gun's clip. "This baby is loaded. The burp gun is, anyhow. Here. Take these rods." Tom took the pistols and Jim hefted the burp gun. "You know? This is the fastest-shooting light machine gun in the world. It can cut a man in half."

"Well, don't point it at anyone."

There was a powerful whine to the south as a P–47 dove on an unseen target in the village. The stubby fighter pulled out of the dive behind a red church steeple at the top of which flew a red, white, and black Nazi flag. "Give it to 'em!" someone in the crowd by the compound gate yelled. "Go get 'em!" Prisoners cheered and shouted at one another. Several sat on the sloping roofs of the prison blocks for a better view.

Al Koczeck was dancing a jig in the open gateway. "Hubba, hubba, hubba! Hubba, hubba, hubba!"

Major Smith grinned. "Where'd you get the arsenal?"

Jim grinned back. "These are Junior's. He got 'em from von Munsing's quarters. The house is full of swiped Red Cross parcels." Jim pushed on through the crowd and stopped. A few feet away, and approaching, was the German Kommandant followed in step by his three aides. They halted, staring tensely at the burp gun held pointed at them waist high. The Oberst looked up glaring hate from beneath the shiny black bill of his cap. Jim stared back without relaxing his tight grip on the gun. His lips curled slowly into a thin cold grin. The Oberst looked down into the barrel of the gun again. Jim sniffed, turned, and walked up the steps into the prison block. As he walked past the partition of the small infirmary, he glanced in through the doorway and noticed that it was empty except for Captain Daniels, who was setting rolls of white gauze on the table. Jim hurried on into the vacated prison bay and found his lower bunk in the maze of tiers. He felt beneath his tick, felt the hard bulk of his hidden manuscripts, and grunted. He started to stick the burp gun in with them, but whirled at the sound of footsteps. "Oh, it's you."

Tom smiled and tossed the three holstered pistols down onto the blankets. "Who else? Everybody else is out waiting for the main feature to start."

Jim shoved the three pistols in with the burp gun and the manuscript. "That ought to hold them for a while." He smoothed out the bunk and stood up. "Let's go. I don't want to miss a minute of this." He led the way out of the aisle and paused to look in again at the infirmary. "Come on out, Danny. You don't want to miss the show."

Danny smiled back over his shoulder. "I think my place is right here. There may be casualties. I hope not, but I wouldn't want to have to be searched for in an emergency."

Jim nodded smiling, and went on out. The air was filled with roaring as more Thunderbolt fighters swept overhead. In the distance above the green hills beyond the cheese factory a high-wing monoplane drifted about like a kite in the sky. Tom pointed. "Look! A light plane. It's a Fairchild."

Nearby Bob's spaced teeth glistened in a grin. "Yeah. It's an artillery spotter."

The roofs of the prison blocks were covered with prisoners. Rifles began to go off, little popping noises in the distance. Men swarmed up the barbed-wire fences, using the cross stands for ladder rungs. The fast stutter of German machine guns joined the deep rapid chatter of the fifty-caliber guns of the fighters diving down on Moosburg. Men ran laughing from place to place along the fences, clambering up a few strands to look westward, then back to look southward at the diving planes. Burt Salem ran among the taller men like a rabbit, crying the same thing over and over again in a high emotional voice: "God damn! God damn! God damn!" Jack Noble jumped back and forth over a slit trench. Prisoners in the compounds lining the side of the road leading to the Vorlager shouted in foreign tongues.

"There they come! There they come!"

A great shout went up. Jim climbed up the fence, ripping his clothes on the barbs. The shouting grew louder and more sustained. Slowly, majestically, over the crest of the green slopes beyond the cheese factory, appeared first one crawling blue-gray tank, then another and another and another. Jim screamed with joy, his screams unheard in the screams of the others. On down the slope they crawled, firing their long guns as they came. There was an explosion, dirt and smoke flying just outside the front gate, then another, which tossed dirt and rocks into the air beyond the outer fences. The third blast hit the outer gate and sent a crashing fountain of splintered posts and lashing barbed wire into the air. The screaming of the prisoners rose to a crescendo. And then the tanks rolled like great crawling insects down the green slopes, four abreast.

Pinnnngg! A bullet hit a pebble on the road among the prisoners standing before the compound gateway. Ping! Pinnnnnnngunng! Two more bullets sent dirt flying and ricocheted on toward some prison blocks. A prisoner fell to the road and lay there, his legs thrashing.

"Hey! They're shooting at us!"

Prisoners leaped from the fences and dropped from the roofs. Some dove to the ground, others jumped into slit trenches, and many, like Jim, cowered down to watch the onward coming tanks. A pebble lifted from the ground at Jim's feet and went clattering into the end of the prison block. He looked in the opposite direction. "There he is!" He pointed toward the distant red steeple with its Nazi flag flying over Moosburg. "There's a sniper in that church steeple! He's firing into the camp!"

He and Bob scrambled to their feet and climbed up the fences again. The American tanks were still coming, their cannon barking sharply and jerking with recoil. Two more prisoners were hit, and lay squirming on the road. Noble clung to the top strand of the fence screaming: "Look up on the cheese factory! Look up on the cheese factory!"

Two of the tiny figures on the roof of the factory were crouched over a machine gun. It was pointed toward the prison camp. Jim took one short glance at the cheese factory roof. "The dirty bastards!" Then he continued to cheer the oncoming tanks with the other yelling prisoners. Bullets plunked among them, but they kept on cheering and laughing, watching the battle. A score of Balkan prisoners on the roof of one of their prison blocks scrambled onto its east slope to dodge a burst from the cheese factory. Jim looked at Tom clinging to the fence beside him and laughed hilariously. "You damned fool! Why don't you take cover?"

Tom laughed back. "Why don't you?"

A few places down the fence a Kriegie fell back into the arms of those behind him. He groaned and clutched at a bleeding thigh. Jim stopped laughing. "I think I'll go tell Danny there's some wounded out here." As he darted up the steps of the prison block there was a thud, and a chunk of plaster fell out of the wall by his head. He ducked going through the doorway. He turned into the doorway of the infirmary and called to Danny, who was sitting on one of its neatly made-up empty bunks. "Danny, there's quite a few guys wounded out there." Danny, white of face, was grasping his stomach. Jim stepped closer. "Danny." Danny rolled his eyes up. Jim bent over him. "What's the matter, Danny? What is it, boy?"

Danny let out a big breath and stammered, "I'm hit."

Jim fell to his knees and stared at Danny's clutching hands. "Where, Danny? Where? Not—not in the belly!"

Danny nodded. He pulled his hands away and began unbuttoning his shirt and pants. "It doesn't feel too bad."

"I'll get some help. I'll get a doctor."

"No. Wait." Jim stared in horror as Danny revealed a slightly bleeding hole in the clean white skin just above his navel. Danny probed into it with a thumb and forefinger as Jim got slowly to his feet. The probing red-stained fingers came away from the wound, and Danny grunted. "Here it is."

Jim stared at the flattered lead and copper pellet Danny held out in the palm of his hand. "Jesus! Jesus, you got it out?"

Danny nodded. "It came through that wall. Mostly spent, I guess. But it puts me out of action."

"You think it might be serious?"

"It could be. Depends on whether it went in far enough to puncture the peritoneum. Hand me one of those bandages, will you?"

As Jim handed over a bandage from the table, two men brought in the Kriegie who had been shot from the fence. One of them spoke up. "You were right, Danny. We got a customer." His eyes focused on the white patch Danny was taping to his belly. "Hey. You get shot, too?"

Danny nodded and motioned to a chair. "Put the man down. Is it a flesh wound? Get a compress on that leg." He lay back in the bunk. "I'm all washed up. I think I'd better not move until I can get to a hospital. You and the rest of the crew will have to take over."

Jim stood looking at the trail of blood leading from the doorway to the wounded man in the chair. "Anything I can do, Danny?"

Danny smiled, rolling the spent bullet around in his fingers. "No, thanks. The regular crew can handle it. Go on back out and watch the show."

Jim nodded solemnly. "You would get hurt on the last day. You take it easy, Danny."

Danny grinned up out of the bunk. "Sure. See you later."

One of the infirmary crew was tying a reddening compress to the thigh of the man in the chair. Jim motioned to the other one and stepped into the hall. His forehead furrowed as he faced the man. "You know anything about medicine?"

The man shrugged. "Only what I've picked up from Danny. Why?"

"What's the peritoneum?"

"The inner lining of the abdominal cavity. It covers the stomach and a lot of other organs."

"What happens if it gets punctured?"

"Peritonitis." The Kriegie looked back at the infirmary doorway. "Is Danny's peritoneum punctured?"

"Maybe. You'd better watch him."

The Kriegie shook his head. "That's all I can do. Watch him."

Two prisoners entered the block as Jim was leaving. One of them was holding his bleeding shoulder. The sound of thousands of men shouting hit Jim like a wall as he stepped into the open. Out by the main gate machine guns rattled and rifles popped. Jim scrambled up onto the fence between Tom and Koczeck. Tom turned his head and shouted to be heard.

"You missed seeing those goons on the cheese factory get shot dead. One of 'em fell off. There's another one still up there where he got killed. Those S.S. really are fighting to the last dirty bastard!"

A tiny motionless brown form lay on the sloping roof. The Fairchild spotter plane was cruising back and forth about five hundred feet above the blasted gate. Jim ground his teeth together and breathed hard. In the compounds to the right of the road prisoners were standing on the roofs of the prison blocks. Suddenly on one of the blocks a great flag billowed, blue, white, and red forming an ecstatic cross in the wind. A solid roar of voices welled up from that direction. Koczeck almost fell from the fence. "That's Norway, isn't it?"

From another roof point along the road the red, white, and blue tri-color of France rolled downward. Prisoners lay flat on the roof nailing the top of the flag to the eaves. Jim looked back over his shoulder at the crowded roof of his block. "Where's ours? We ought to have one!"

On another roof a long stick went up and a Polish flag fluttered in the air to another mass roar of victory. The popping and rattling of guns beyond the blasted gateway began to let up. Another cry went up as a crowd of British prisoners passed a Union Jack up to the men on a rooftop. Noble called up from the ground. "Where's ours? Don't we have a flag?"

A Netherlands flags rolled down the front of another building, making six flags in all in a blaze of colors adorning the prison blocks along the right side of the doorway in contrast to the black and white grimness of the S.S. flag over the main gateway. Only an occasional pop came from that direction. Then it was drowned out by a deep mass yelling up by the gate. Burt looked back and forth along the fence. "See anything? What's going on up there?" Slowly the yelling grew louder and nearer. Slowly it swelled back toward them. Suddenly it hushed as the S.S. flag started to drop down the pole. Then the yelling exploded all over the man-packed camp. Burt threw back his head. "Ya-a-a-a-y-e-e-e-e!"

Koczeck jumped to the ground and kept on jumping up and down. "Hubba! Hubba! Hubba!"

Bob, Tom, and Noble clung to the fence screaming through wide-open mouths. Jim screamed from a taut throat through his clenched teeth.

Swiftly, surely, the stars and stripes of a great red, white, and blue American flag shot up the main gate flagpole and waved in the sun.

The shouting raised itself a pitch. Ears tingled with it. The camp blurred with it. It kept on, a mighty all-out scream of thousands of voices. Men hugged each other and cried. Some rolled in the dirt, still shouting, wres-tling with one another. Men clapped their hands, beat each other on the back, threw their hats into the air, ripped shirts from one another's bodies and shouted with all the power in their lungs. Jim danced in a circle on the ground with Tom and Bob, their arms around one another. Suddenly he felt a sharp shooting pain that darted from his jaw to the top of his skull. He spat out the splinters of the rotten molar he had caved in. He and the others kept on screaming and dancing; and every time they looked up, there it was, red, white, and blue, strong in the breeze and the sunlight, flying above all. Jim stopped screaming and dancing and sobbed into his hands, tears running through his fingers. "Oh, thank you, God! Oh, God! God . . ."

World War II: There Was Also Time for Laughter

The Birthmark

x

from *Mr. Roberts*

by THOMAS HEGGEN

The anchoring of the Naval Auxiliary U.S.S. *Reluctant* was accomplished without incident. The anchor chain banged and rattled in the hawse pipes and the ship shuddered as it stampeded out. The word, "Secure the special sea detail," was blatted over the P.A. system and five seconds later the engine room called the bridge for permission to secure the main engines. The Captain made the appropriate reply, "Goddamit, they'll secure when I get good and ready to let them secure," but he did it without enthusiasm, and he only muttered for perhaps two minutes about those bastards down there who sit on their tails waiting to secure. It was a very hot, sweaty day, about three in the afternoon, and it seemed just another island: so nobody's heart beat very much faster at being anchored.

The port routine commenced, a matter of loosening the ship's belt a notch or two. The gun watchers stayed on, but the lookouts were secured and ran below to find the crap game. A boat was lowered to go over and get the mail. Back on number four hatch the canvas screen was rigged for the night's movie. Stuyzuiski, a seaman in the third division who wouldn't get out of his clothes under way, took a bath; and at chow everyone remarked on how much better he smelled. Ensign Pulver mixed himself what he called a Manhattan — a third of a water-glass of brandy, a splash of vermouth, and a couple of ice cubes — and lay in his bunk and sipped it admiringly. The crew leaned on the rail and looked around incuriously at the little bay and the naval base ashore. Becker, a seaman received on board in the last draft, was moved to remark to Dowdy: "This ain't a bad place, you know it?" Dowdy said something obscene without even turning his head. Becker bumbled on: "No, I mean it ain't as bad as most of the places we been to. It's kind of pretty."

Becker was right, though; it *was* kind of pretty; it was really a rather lovely little bay. The water off the reef was terribly blue, a showy light-ink blue. The bay was enclosed by a chain of islands, and instead of the usual flat barren coral these were green with lush and heavy foliage, and on two sides of the anchorage they ran up to impressive hills that were remote and purpling in the late afternoon sun. And the channel at the end of the bay wound away into the deep shadow between the islands and reappeared flashing in the secret and smoky distance. The crew, lined along the rail, began to feel obscurely good at being here; and even Dowdy was probably aware that, aesthetically, this was quite a superior place.

Its intrinsic and most spectacular virtue fell to Sam Insigna to discover. (Although if Sam hadn't found it one of the other signalmen would have soon enough.) Sam was a little monkey of a man, not quite five feet tall, long-armed and bow-legged like a monkey, with a monkey's grinning, wizened face, who had achieved considerable fame aboard the ship by once attacking, unprovoked and with the intention of doing physical violence, a six-foot-four-inch marine. Sam was up on the flying bridge with the other signalmen and he was idly scanning the beach through the ship's telescope, a large, mounted glass of thirty-two power. The ship was anchored perhaps two hundred yards from the beach, and just off the starboard bow, the way she was heading now, there was a base hospital. The hospital flag was flying over three rows of Quonset huts; there was well-trimmed grass between the huts, and straight neat coral paths that looked like sidewalks. Farther off to the right was the rest of the naval base; clapboard buildings and Quonsets scattered between coconut palms, and down at the waterfront there was a long wooden dock where a Liberty ship was unloading. Dead ahead, right on the point, was the interesting thing, though, the really amazing thing. It was a house, easily identifiable as a house; an authentic civilian house. It was a wooden, two-story house, painted yellow; long and low, with a veranda running the entire length. There was a swing on the veranda and several cane chairs, there was a fine green lawn running down to the beach, and there were two green wooden benches on the lawn under the trees. It was an old house, obviously long antedating American occupation of the island; it was a formless, bleak, and even ugly house; yet, in these surroundings, in the middle of the Pacific, it seemed to the signalmen a thing of great magnificence.

"It must have been the Governor's house," Schlemmer explained.

Sam swung the telescope around to have a look at this. At first he trained it carelessly around the grounds, then he turned it on the house. For perhaps a full minute nothing happened, and then it did. Sam had been leaning with one elbow on the windshield; all of a sudden he jerked upright, sucked in his breath and grabbed at the glass as if he were falling. The idea flashed through the mind of Schlemmer, standing beside him, that Sam had been hit by a sniper.

"Holy Christ!" Sam said. He seemed to have difficulty in speaking.

"What is it?" Schlemmer said, and he grabbed for a long-glass.

There was only reverence in Sam's voice. "Holy Christ! She's bare-assed!"

One of the many anomalies of our ponderous Navy is its ability to move fast, to strike the swift, telling blow at the precise moment it is needed. There were accessible in the wheelhouse and charthouse seven pairs of binoculars; on the flying bridge were two spyglasses and two long-glasses, and the ship's telescope; and on a platform above was the range-finder, an instrument of powerful magnification. Within a commendably brief time after Sam had sounded the alarm, somewhere between fifteen and twenty seconds, there were manned six pairs of binoculars, two spyglasses, two long-glasses, of course the ship's telescope, and the range-finder. The glasses were all on the target right away, but the range-finder took a little longer, that instrument being a large unwieldy affair which required considerable frantic cranking and adjusting by two men in order to focus on a target. Through a rather surprising sense of delicacy, considering that two quartermasters and the talker were left without, one pair of binoculars remained untouched: the ones clearly labeled "Captain." In future scrutinies, it was found necessary to press all glasses into service, exempting none.

Sam's discovery was basically simple, natural, reasonable. He had discovered that nurses lived in the long, yellow house. He had discovered two large windows in the middle of the second-story front, and that these windows had none but shade curtains, retracted. He had discovered (the telescope is a powerful glass and the room was well illumined by sunlight) that the windows belonged to the bathroom. It is, of course, redundant to say that he had also discovered a nurse in the shower stall in the far left-hand corner of the room. All of this would seem to be a model of logic, of sweet reasonableness: what could possibly be more logical than that there be a hospital at this base, that there be nurses attached to this hospital, that these nurses lived in a house, that this house have a bathroom, that this bathroom have windows, that these nurses bathe? Nothing, you would think. And yet to these signalmen and quartermasters (who had last seen a white woman, probably fat, certainly fully clothed, perhaps fourteen months ago) this vision was literally that, a vision, and a miracle, and not a very small miracle, either. Like Sam, they were stricken with reverence in its presence, and like Sam, their remarks were reverent; those who could speak at all. "Holy Christ!" a few of them managed to breathe, and "Son-of-a-bitch!" That was all. Those are the only legitimate things a man can say when suddenly confronted with the imponderable.

The word spread fast, although how it is difficult to say: certainly no one left the bridge. The four-to-eight signal watch, Niesen and Canappa, never known to relieve before the stroke of the hour, appeared at three-thirty and met an equally incredible thing; a watch that refused to be relieved. "Get the hell out of here," Sam told the newcomers. "We're staying up here till chow." There was some bitterness and much indignant insistence by the oncoming pair of their *right* to relieve the watch, but the old watch, firmly entrenched at the glasses, stayed by them until chow was piped. There was a splendid run of bathers. The shore station blinked for half an hour trying to rouse this ship, a bare two hundred yards away; and, finally succeeding, sent out a nasty message about keeping a more alert signal watch. Accordingly, the glass of the striker Mannion was taken away from him and he was detailed to watch for signals. It seemed that Sam had just gone below for supper when he was back again, demanding and getting his telescope. He and the rest of the watch stayed on until after sunset, when lights went on in the bathroom and the curtains were pulled chastely down for the night; all the way down, leaving not the merest crack.

That first day was chaotic, comparable perhaps to the establishing of a beachhead. It was ill-organized; there was duplication and wasted effort. The next day went much better. A system and a pattern appeared. The curtain was raised at 0745 and was witnessed by Sam, Schlemmer, Canappa, Mannion, Morris, Niesen, three quartermasters, and the officer-of-the-deck. For perhaps forty-five minutes there was a dazzling crowd of early-morning bathers; almost a surfeit of them, sometimes three or four at a time. Then there was a long slack period (no one in the room) that extended to ten o'clock. Sam organized for the slack period. It is fatiguing to stand squinting through an eye-piece for long periods, so Sam arranged that one man, by turns, keep the lookout during the off-hours and give the word when action developed. But he refused to let Mannion take a turn. "That son-of-a-bitch watched one strip down yesterday and didn't open his mouth," he accused.

It was possible by this time to establish the routine of the house. After the big early-morning rush there was only an occasional and accidental visitor until around ten, when the night watch would begin to get up. From ten to eleven was fairly good, and eleven until noon was very good. From lunch until two was quiet, but from two until two-forty-five there was the same rich procession as in the morning. After four, things dropped off sharply and weren't really much good again for the rest of the day. It was shrewdly observed and duly noted that watches at the hospital evidently changed at eight in the morning and three in the afternoon. All glasses were manned during those periods; pathetic little two-power opera glasses made their appearance then, and the windshield and splinter-shields of the flying bridge presented a solid wall of variously magnified eyeballs.

By this time, also, the watch — as it came to be known — assumed a routine of its own. The assignment and ownership of glasses came to be understood. Three pairs of binoculars belonged down below for the officer-of-the-deck and two quartermasters. The other four pairs of binoculars, the spyglasses and the long-glasses, belonged to the signalmen; to use themselves or lend to radiomen, storekeepers, and cooks in return for future favors. The range-finder came to be recognized as officer property and was almost continually manned by a rotating team of two officers; Lieutenant Carney and Ensign Moulton being the most constant. The big telescope, of course, was a prize. It magified thirty-two times. There was a box of Lux soap sitting on a shelf on the far wall of the bathroom, and with the telescope Sam could make out with ease the big letters "LUX" and below them, in smaller letters, the word "Thrifty." He could even almost make out the much smaller words in the lower left-hand corner of the box. The long-glass could barely make out the word "Thrifty" and couldn't begin to make out the words in the corner. The spyglasses and the binoculars couldn't even make out the word "Thrifty."

From the first, Sam's right to the telescope had been strangely unchallenged, perhaps an intuitive recognition of his zeal. Turncliffe, the first-class signalman, gave him a brief argument once — more of a token argument, really, than anything else — and then retired to the long-glass. For quite a while Sam was indisputably on the telescope; then one morning Lieutenant (jg) Billings chanced on the bridge. Lieutenant Billings was the communication officer and Sam's boss, and he relieved Sam briefly on the telescope. That was all right the first time; Sam was good-natured in yielding; he liked Mr. Billings. But then Mr. Billings began to chance on the bridge frequently and regularly, and every time he would relieve Sam. Not only that, he had an uncanny talent for arriving at the most propitious moment. Sam got pretty sore over the whole business. As he complained to his friend Schlemmer: "Sure, he's an officer. All right. If we was in a chow line together, sure, he could go in ahead of me. All right. But I sure can't see where that gives him the right to take a man's glass away from him!" To Sam, a man's glass was an inviolable thing.

By the third day personalities began to emerge from the amorphous group that flitted past the bathroom windows. Despite the fact that the light was usually bad up around the face, thus eliminating facial identifications as a method, the boys were able to distinguish one nurse from another with considerable accuracy. There appeared to be nine consistent users of this particular bathroom. Canappa insisted there were only eight, but then he denied the validity of the two-blonde theory. The two-blonde theory was Sam's and it was supported by the consensus. Canappa pointed out that the two had never been seen together; but this was rather a foolish argument, as both had been examined separately from the same angle, which happened to be a telling one. Canappa, who had not seen both from this angle, stuck to his discredited opinion. Undeniably, there were grounds for confusion. Both girls were young, both were pretty (although, as mentioned before, facial characteristics were inexact), and both wore red-and-white striped bathrobes — or maybe even the same bathrobe. That is no doubt what threw Canappa off. Because, actually, there was conclusive evidence of their separate identity; evidence of the most distinctive sort which one of the girls carried.

As Mannion put it, looking up from his glass: "What the hell is that she's got?"

Sam *didn't* look up from his glass. "You dumb bastard, that's a birthmark."

Mannion was convinced, but he was irritated by Sam's tone. "Birthmark!" he said scornfully. "Who the hell ever heard of a birthmark down there? That's paint; she's gotten into some paint. Or else it's a burn. That's what it is — it's a burn!"

Sam's rebuttal was simple and unanswerable: "Who the hell ever heard of a burn down there?" It routed Mannion satisfactorily, and after a moment Sam disclosed: "Why, Christ, I had an uncle once who had a birthmark . . ." He went on to tell where his uncle's birthmark was situated. He described it in some detail.

The two blondes were the real stars: as the result of comparison the other girls came to be regarded as rather run-of-the-mill and were observed with condescension and even some small degree of indifference. There was one, rather old and quite fat, who absolutely disgusted Schlemmer. Whenever she put in an appearance, he would leave his glass and indignantly exhort the rest of the watch to do the same. "Don't look at her," he would say. "She's nausorating!" He got quite angry when he was ignored.

With the emergence of personalities came the recognition of personal habits. The tall skinny brunette always let the shower water run for several minutes before a bath. The stubby little brunette with the yellow bathrobe always used the bathtub; would sit in the tub and drink what looked like coffee, but might have been tea. The girl with high, piled-up hair would fuss for an hour extracting hairpins, and then take a shampoo in the washbasin by the window without removing her robe. "That's a stupid goddamn way to take a shampoo," Sam commented.

But by far the most notable idiosyncrasy belonged to the blonde with the birthmark. It was one which endeared her to all the watchers and drove Morris to rapturously announce: "I'm going to marry that gal!" Like everything about the place it was plausible, normal, and really not at all remarkable. It occurred before every bath and consisted simply of shedding the red-and-white striped bathrobe and standing for several minutes (discreetly withdrawn from the window), looking out over the bay. Undoubtedly, this was a girl who loved beauty, and certainly the view was a fine one. The bay in the afternoon was shiny blue plate glass, really perfect except where the wake of a lazily paddled native canoe flawed the illusion. The tall coconut palms along the beach were as poetically motionless as sculpture. A little way out from the bay was the thin white line of the surf at the reef, and far, far out was the scary, almost indistinguishable line of the horizon. Perhaps the girl's thoughts, as she stood admiring all that beatitude, ran something like this: "What peace! There is no effort anywhere. See the canoe drifting lazily across the bay. Observe the trees with not a leaf stirring, and the ship riding peacefully at anchor, her men justly resting after the arduous days at sea. What utter tranquility!" From there she could not hear the cranking of the range-finder.

There was one ghastly afternoon when not a soul, not a single soul, came in for a bath. The watchers were bewildered and resentful; and, finally, disgusted. Sam probably spoke for all when he said: "Christ, and they call themselves nurses! They're nothing but a goddamn bunch of filthy pigs. A nurse would at least take a bath once in a while. Jesus, I pity those poor sick bastards over there who have to let those filthy pigs handle them!"

But that only happened once, and by and large it could not fairly be said that the nurses were disappointing. In fact, Sam himself was once moved to observe: "This is too good to last." It was one of the most prophetic things Sam ever said.

Lieutenant (jg) Langston, the gunnery officer, had been having a good bit of trouble with his eyes. He wasn't at all satisfied with his glasses. One day he had a splitting headache and the next morning he went over to the base hospital to have his eyes refracted. They were very nice over there. The Doctor was very nice, and there was a pleasant-faced nurse who helped, and she also was very nice. It took only about an hour and a half to find just the right lenses, and while he was waiting for his pupils to contract, Langston began talking with the nurse. In a very short time it came out that she was from a town not twenty miles from Youngstown, Ohio, where he lived. Langston felt that a certain bond was established, and on the strength of it he invited the nurse, whose name was Miss Williamson, to dinner on the ship that night. It is well known that shipboard food is several cuts above shore-based food, and this consideration was perhaps a factor in Miss Williamson's ready acceptance. She did add one clause, though: she asked if she could bring a friend, "a terribly cute girl." Langston, a personable if rather courtly young man, of course said yes, and mentioned that he would assign her to a friend of his, an Ensign Pulver, whom he described as a "very handsome young man." Everything was most friendly.

When the girls came aboard that night, escorted by the two officers, the entire crew was massed along the rail and on the bridges. As the white-stockinged legs tripped up the gangway, one great, composite, heartfelt whistle rose to the heavens and hung there. Ensign Pulver's girl, Miss Girard, had turned out to be a knockout. At dinner in the wardroom he could scarcely keep his eyes off her, and no more could the other officers, who feigned eating and made self-conscious conversation. Miss Girard had lovely soft blond hair which she wore in bangs, wide blue innocent eyes, and the pertest nose there ever was. The total effect was that of radiant innocence; innocence triumphant. Only Ensign Pulver noted that when she smiled her eyes screwed up shrewdly and her mouth curved knowingly; but then only Ensign Pulver would. For Langston, it was enough to have what he felt to be the envious admiration of his messmates; but there began to grow in the mind of Ensign Pulver, himself a young man of deceptively guileless appearance, visions of a greater reward. Once in a while he would catch and hold Miss Girard's glance, and when he did he thought he detected interest there.

After dinner, when the party repaired to his room for further polite conversation, he felt more and more sure of it. There were only two chairs in the room and so he and Miss Girard sat together on the edge of the bottom bunk. That gave a certain intimacy, he thought; a certain tie of shared experience. He was moved to break out the quart of Old Overholt, four-fifths full, which he had kept hidden for two months in the little recess under the drawer of his bunk. With Coca-Cola which Langston provided it made a nice drink. Ensign Pulver was then emboldened to tell what he privately called his "test story," the decisively off-color tale of "ze black chapeau." Miss Girard's response was excellent; she laughed delightedly. Then, craftily aware of the impressiveness of the unfamiliar, he proposed a tour of the ship, and both girls enthusiastically approved. The plan now began to shape itself in Pulver's mind: after the tour, a few more drinks; then a little dancing in the wardroom; then a few more drinks; then get Langston to take the other one off somewhere. As they started out, Miss Girard gave him her small hand.

First they toured the main deck, the offices and the galley and sick bay. Then they dropped down into the cavernous engine room, and Pulver, who was an engineering officer, talked casually of the massive turbines and terrifying boilers. The girls were very much impressed. From the engine room they went up to the bridge, through the wheelhouse, through the charthouse, through the radio room, and on up to the flying bridge. That was a thoughtless thing for the two officers to do, but fortunately an alert quartermaster had preceded them. The inspection party found the signalmen clustered in an innocent group under the canvas awning, and the telescope trained at an angle of ninety degrees from the yellow house. The signalmen presented a curious sight. They were absolutely speechless; they seemed welded to the deck with awe. The two nurses giggled a little, no doubt over the prospect of these men so obviously dumbfounded at seeing a woman that they could only gape. Ensign Pulver later claimed that he felt something ominous in that group, but whether or not he actually did is unimportant.

Langston led the party to the forward splintershield, where it could look down the sheer drop to the main deck, and the even more scary distance to the very bottom of number three hatch. The girls were *really* impressed with that. When they started to walk around behind the funnel, Ensign Pulver noticed that Sam Insigna was trailing them. He was a little annoyed, but, being a young man of poise, he made a sort of introduction. "This is Sam," he said, "one of the signalmen."

Miss Girard smiled at Sam. "How do you do, Sam," she said graciously. Sam was evidently too shy and flustered to speak; he just stood there and grinned foolishly. When they had gone on, Miss Girard squeezed her escort's hand and whispered, "He's darling." Pulver nodded dubiously. They took a turn around the funnel, came forward again, and went over to the port wing to look at the twenty-millimeters. By this time the signalmen had gotten their tongues back and were having a bitter and quite vocal argument under the awning. It was obvious that they were trying to keep their voices guarded, but, as often happens, the restraint only intensified them. Sam's voice in particular carried well. "Goddamit," the party heard him say, "I'll bet you one hundred bucks!" Lieutenant (jg) Langston nodded his head in the direction of the signalmen, smiled superiorly, and said to the nurses: "Seems to be an argument." Then Sam's voice came to them again. That voice was several things: it was shrill, it was combative, it was angry; but most of all it was audible. There have been few more audible voices, before or since. It traveled out from under the awning in an unfaltering parabola, fell on the ears of the inspection party, and broke into words of simple eloquence.

"You stupid son-of-a-bitch, I tell you that's her! I got one hundred bucks that says that's the one with the birthmark on her ass! Now put up or shut up!"

Sam may have been right, at that. No one ever knew; no one on the ship ever saw that birthmark again. The curtains of the two middle upstairs windows were not raised next morning, and when the ship sailed three

days later they were still down. It was three weeks before a sizable membership of the crew would speak to Sam except to curse him, and it was longer
than that before Ensign Pulver would speak to him at all.

The Lacy Battle Flag

✕

from *Don't Go Near the Water*
by WILLIAM BRINKLEY

There were some Navy people who bitterly resented women correspondents, claiming the war would be over years earlier if they stayed at home.
It was true that they added a number of man-hours' labor in the Navy's
push to the Japanese home islands. Once a detachment of five men from
the Seabees, the famous Navy "Can Do!" outfit, had to put in a full day
building a special head for a correspondent who decided her coverage of
the war required her to visit Gug-Gug, and there was considerable complaining over this. It was difficult to have any sympathy with such com-
plaints. After all, a war is no excuse to add to the discriminations women
already endure. Besides, some of the women correspondents went above
and beyond the call of duty to make themselves useful. On Tulura there
was one correspondent, a fifty-five-year-old woman who represented a chain
of Texas papers, who put in every Saturday afternoon in the main Public
Relations building sewing on buttons and darning socks for all comers.
She was a kindly if somewhat concupiscent lady who probably had more
suitors than any fifty-five-year-old woman in the world. It was necessary to
date her up three weeks in advance. Being a woman correspondent in the
Pacific put you in a really distinctive class. The ratio of woman correspondent to military men was about 1:250,000. The Pacific needed more,
not fewer women, and it was worth building an extra head here and there
for them.

A few of the women correspondents flaunted the ratio. But they could
hardly be blamed for obeying the oldest law (supply and demand). Some
also paraded that envied mobility which derived from profession rather
than sex. One war correspondent for a true-confession type of magazine
used to pop into the Media Section and plant herself, legs apart, in front
of a map of the world which obliterated the entire wall. Her eyes would

ravage the great map as if it were a tray of French pastry and she couldn't make up her mind which piece to select, all of it being so mouth-watering.

"I wonder where I should hit next," she would think out loud. "Guadalcanal — but things must be terribly dull down there by now. Bombay — there *would* be Gandhi to interview. Sydney — we could use a little down-under stuff. Tahiti — I wonder if anyone's ever thought of asking those gentle Tahitians what *they* think about the war . . ."

The island-stuck officers would sit at their desks and look at her menacingly out of the corners of their eyes. Ensign Christopher Tyson III would be seething. The Princeton odd-job ensign was a very handsome young man who was not accustomed to going without sex. Back in Rye, Ty had had succulent debutantes standing in line ready to give him their most precious possession. But he was a long way from Rye. When the true-confession woman would flutter out of the room after a few minutes of map-gazing, Tyson would storm to his feet.

"The b-b-b-bitch. The fanny-shaking b-b-bitch." And he would mimic her, mincing around the room, hips shaking and hand to the back of his head. "Now I wonder if I should go to Tahiti . . . or Sydney . . . or Bombay and get the true confessions of Mahatma Gandhi. I'd like to catch the b-b-bitch some dark night down in the boondocks and r-r-rape her from here to Sydney. Women correspondents! I don't see why we can't fight a war without women correspondents."

Tyson was always talking about fighting the war, always itching for sea duty.

Any woman correspondent in the Pacific became a very special person, if for no other reason than the oldest law. But the most upsetting woman correspondent ever to reach the Pacific was Debbi Aldrich. For one thing she represented a publication of a type which up until then had not been sending correspondents to the Pacific. Most of the women correspondents were with newspapers or wire services. Debbi Aldrich represented *Madame*.

When the dispatch that a *Madame* war correspondent was on her way to Tulura arrived, there was a lot of speculation as to what angle of the war she was going to cover, *Madame* being a magazine of great tone, best described by its subtitle: "The World of Women — Decor and Cuisine, Beauty and Fashion." There was certainly not a great deal of subject material for these matters in the western Pacific. "I hear she's going to do a takeout on what kind of drawers ComFleets wears," Lieutenant Morey Griffin said. There were many guesses along this line.

Debbi Aldrich turned out to be quite a dish. The critical faculties of Pacific Navy men about women were almost pathologically warped, of course, but Miss Aldrich could have held her own in Radio City. She made a spectacular entrance into the Pacific. Lieutenant Morey Griffin said later he was too embarrassed to get up from his desk for an hour. As a Correspondent's Aide, Tyson had gone out to meet her and he followed her into the Public Relations building like a cocker spaniel with its tongue hanging out. All his resentment against women correspondents had evaporated sometime between his departure for the airfield and the trip back. He was staggering under a load of three brand-new, bright red lizard-skin bags, including a hatbox wedged under his arm. In the surroundings the hatbox looked sensational.

"May I present Miss Debbi Aldrich!" Ty exclaimed to Lieutenant Commander Junius Randolph, the Media chief, in his excitement making a faux pas in introduction etiquette unusual for a Rye boy.

She was very beautiful. She had a sculptured face which must have had a kind of wistfulness to it before she got into the magazine business. Now there was no wistfulness but an air of being in complete command of any situation. She was very clean-looking and as smart and tailored as an illustrated ad from her famous magazine, even in her khaki slacks and shirt, and with her face faultlessly made up, her lipstick precisely modeling her small mouth. She had a junior-model body, boyish hips, and her hair, just peeking out from under a baseball cap, was cut almost as short as a man's. In fact, if one had looked at her just from the neck down, one might have had trouble, except for one feature, deciding for sure whether she was a boy or a woman. This feature left no doubt, and if the ancients were right, that it is really woman's crowning glory and a woman desirable in direct ratio to its shape and prominence, then Debbi Aldrich was certainly a queen. They were magnificent and incontestably all her own. One other tiny but startling feminine detail appeared below the neck — a half inch of black brassiere just visible in the V of her khaki shirt.

She crossed the room briskly, held out a hand to Lieutenant Commander Randolph, and came right to the point.

"I'm sure it's going to be a pleasure working with you, Commander," she said in a husky, just slightly bored voice which, like her whole appearance, stepped right out of the pages of her magazine. "I'm out here to do a job. I'm not on a junket. *Madame* is anxious to bring off some really different material from the Pacific. We have a feeling it hasn't really been covered — I mean, of course, as *Madame* wants it covered —" and she made a graceful gesture with her free hand. "I'm after the offbeat, if you know what I mean."

It was quite an inaugural speech, and the officers could feel the uncovered Pacific all around them, right here in this room, waiting to be covered by Debbi Aldrich. Griffin gave a gulp from across the room. "Well, anything we can do," he said with a forced laugh, "— that's what we're here for, Miss Aldrich."

"Yes, I'm sure you are, sweetie," the *Madame* correspondent said, giving

Griffin a polar one-second smile before turning back to Randolph. "Right now, before I go to work, Commander — may I call you Junius? — I really could use a shower."

"Tyson!" snapped Lieutenant Commander Randolph, who before the war had run a paper in Georgia. "Give — I mean get — Miss Ahl-drich a showuh right away!"

"Yes, sir!" Tyson said, coming to attention.

It was the nearest to a military exchange the Public Relations Headquarters had ever seen.

Debbi Aldrich created a major upheaval in the Public Relations Section. So many officers were forever sniffing around her, volunteering assistance, to the neglect of correspondents of the opposite sex, that some of these began to grumble that after all the Associated Press, United Press, International News Service, New York *Times*, Chicago *Daily News*, CBS and Time, Inc., as well as *Madame*, were covering the war and had been for years before that goddamn fashion sheet decided it wasn't really being covered.

Before long, Debbi Aldrich was both the most hated and most sought-after person in the western Pacific. She was hated and sought after for the same reason: for being an aloof, tantalizing and beautiful woman in the midst of many men. She would come into the Media Section to use a desk and sit there tapping out her copy on her new Hermes, her body lithely erect in the chair, that half-inch of black bra showing in the V of her khaki shirt. No brave bull was ever more violently disturbed by a red muleta than the officers of the Public Relations Section by this minute strip of cloth. No work ever got accomplished while she was present, except by herself. As she typed, absorbed in what was going on on her Hermes, the officers would sneak glances at her and writhe in hellish frustration, at night go back to their BOQ's and over poker hands bicker endlessly as to her accessibility.

Ensign Tyson came very near to going crazy. "She knows that little piece of black b-b-bra shows," he would rage. "You know what she is? She's a sadist! That's what she is! I know these b-b-black-underwear kind of women!"

Tyson was probably entirely wrong, for Debbi Aldrich seemed oblivious of the effect she created and interested solely in her work, which she was at almost constantly. She was all over the place, interviewing Seabees, submariners, admirals, amphibious crews, fly-boys, everybody. She filed reams of copy to her magazine. Tyson knocked himself out getting jeeps, arranging interviews, even changing typewriter ribbons for her. It was obvious to everyone but Tyson himself that he would never get to first base with Debbi Aldrich. She accepted all he offered politely but with the condescen-

sion that said it was all her right both as Debbi Aldrich and as correspondent for *Madame,* and that anyhow he was just a boy and an ensign boy at
that.

For her escort, Debbi Aldrich looked around and tapped Admiral Boat-
wright's assistant. Captain Thornberry was fiftyish and gray-haired. It was
Thornberry who took her to the beach for swims — she carried her two-
piece black bathing suit (anything closest to her skin was always black, it
seemed) in the red lizard hatbox — Thornberry who took her to the dances
at the Island Base officers' club. Tyson was enraged at the idea of her going
around with an aging, homely captain when there was a pretty ensign like
himself so available. "I can't figure her out," he fumed. "I don't see what
she g-g-gets out of it. It's downright p-p-perversion. I've got it figured out!
She's a lesbian!" Really, for all his looks, Tyson didn't know the first thing
about women.

Debbi Aldrich had not been long on Tulura when she announced her
plans to do what no woman correspondent had ever done: make a combat
operation. The Media officers were sitting at their desk shuffling papers one
day when she walked in and gave the word to Randolph. Ship assignments
for the invasion of Nanto Shima had been relayed to the correspondents a
half-hour earlier. Debbi Aldrich sauntered up to Randolph's desk and
cocked her hands on her hips. Randolph looked up and saw her standing
there and got quickly to his feet. Lieutenant Commander Randolph was a
Georgia gentleman who had been reared to stand up in the presence of
women, even those who wore pants.

"Junius. I haven't heard yet what ship I'm going on," she said, as if it
were mere oversight on his part.

"But . . . theh's no arrangement on ships," Randolph mumbled in
Georgian. "Theh's no arrangement for carryin' women, Miss Ahl-drich.
You see, that is . . . that is, it isn't customary for women correspondents
to go along on combat operations. Women stay back heah, and, ah, well,
one subject the women correspondents covuh frequently is the wounded
when they come back to the fleet hospitals . . . ah, that is, how the nurses
and the wounded are doin' . . . Ah, the women's angle, the nurses as related to the wounded."

"But Junius. *Madame* isn't in the slightest interested in doing the customary," Debbi Aldrich said crisply. "I've come five thousand miles, Junius,
to do something that's not customary. The fact a woman correspondent
has never made an operation is precisely why *Madame* wants me to do it.
Isn't that logical?"

"But Miss Ahl-drich, ah just don't see . . . Much as we'd like to, we
can hardly refit an entah ship, knock out bulkheads and that sort of thing,
to, ah, accommodate a woman. It's relatively easy on an ahland, putting

up a separate, ah, cottage and that sort of thing — we've got plenty of Seabees to do that sort of thing — but on a destroyuh . . . Ah, you see, theh are not separate facilities and the officers use, ah, things in common. Besides, the Bureau of Ships has to approve any structural changes in a naval vessel. Next destroyuh we build, we'll try to blueprint in a compahtment for women . . ."

Randolph gave a forced laugh, in which Miss Aldrich did not join.

"Junius," she said crisply, "please don't talk to me as if I'm a retarded child. I don't know what kind of women you're used to in Georgia, but I assure you, I can take care of myself — even on a destroyer."

Lieutenant Commander Randolph looked forlornly into Debbi Aldrich's flawlessly made-up face. "Ah'm suah of that, Miss Ahl-drich. But on a Navy ship men's . . ."

"Now, Junius, be a good boy and write me up those orders. If nothing else, my conscience wouldn't let me stay on Tulura during the operation. This isn't the nineteenth century, you know, sweetie. Women are emancipated, or haven't you heard, and we've got to do all the things the men do, and all that. That's what I'm out here for. Really, Junius, I wish you wouldn't try to give me special consideration." She reached out and touched Lieutenant Commander Randolph's hand resting on the desk, and Randolph's hand blushed violently. "I want to be treated just like anyone else."

"Puhsonally, Miss Ahl-drich," Lieutenant Commander Randolph said soothingly, "ah'd be happy to write those ohduhs up right this minute, but, you see, it's not in mah powuh . . ."

Randolph turned to his desk. The Media chief had foreseen, in the short time he had known the *Madame* correspondent, that such a demand might arise, and he had done his homework well. He had been relieved to discover that the all-encompassing *Navy Regulations*, which provides for almost every conceivable contingency, had also provided for this one. With complete assurance Randolph picked up the volume and opening it to a marked place, turned to his last and sure resort.

"Y'see, Miss Ahl-drich, Article 116 of *Navy Regulations*, entitled 'Women on Board Ship,' reads in full as follows: 'Officers commanding fleets, squadrons, divisions, or ships shall not permit women to reside on board of, or take passage in, any ship of the Navy in commission except by special permission of the Secretary of the Navy.' "

There was a moment of silence while Randolph, closing the book, stood ready to soothe Miss Aldrich's disappointment.

"Why, you mean," Debbi Aldrich said slowly with an air of incredulousness at the simplicity of it, "that all I have to do is ask Jim Forrestal? Why, Junius, why didn't you say so in the first place?"

And Debbi Aldrich was gone, her narrow hips swiveling her across the room and through the swinging doors.

"Commander," Lieutenant Griffin broke the awed silence when she had gone, "I'll be happy to have Miss Debbi-all share my stateroom on the U.S.S. *Campfollower*."

"Oh, be quiet, won't you? Women in trousuhs, anyhow! Damn it all!" Lieutenant Commander Randolph said. That was rather astonishing, too, for the Georgian had never before been known to lose his temper.

What exactly happened no one ever knew, but Captain Thornberry was credited with the leading role in the outcome. The outcome was that Debbi Aldrich was assigned to a ship for the Nanto Shima operation. She didn't get a destroyer but she did get a cruiser. The roster of vessels for the operation was searched and a heavy cruiser, the *Seattle*, turned up which was used ordinarily as a flagship but had no admiral aboard for the operation. The *Seattle* was to take part in the bombardment of Nanto Shima. Debbi Aldrich was to pick up the ship at Muranu, stay with her during the operation and return with her. She was dispatched to the *Seattle* and put up in the admiral's cabin.

At the same time Ensign Tyson, who had never got anything but the odd jobs nobody else wanted at Public Relations Headquarters, got the sea duty he had so long sought. It was still an odd job, but this one happened to be in great demand, for the sea duty was with Debbi Aldrich. Tyson was assigned as Public Relations officer-in-charge of Miss Aldrich for the Nanto Shima operation. There was scuttlebutt that Debbi Aldrich had arranged this, too, through Thornberry. Tyson just smiled when asked about it. "Men, I'm the obvious choice for the assignment with Miss Aldrich," he said. "You guys should have got on the ball and changed a few typewriter ribbons instead of sitting around torturing yourselves." Of course Tyson never gave anyone else a chance to change her typewriter ribbons.

The captain of the *Seattle*, Ty later related, almost had apoplexy when he and Debbi arrived aboard. The captain was a non-public-relations type. He was outraged at the idea of a woman occupying flag quarters on his ship during an assault operation.

"He couldn't say anything to Debbi," which was what Tyson called her after the operation, though he had always called her Miss Aldrich before, "though you should have seen the look on his face when she and her three suitcases including that damn red hatbox were piped aboard. But soon as she was settled in the admiral's quarters and I in the non-admiral quarters — well, I'd no sooner unzipped my duffel bag than a Marine orderly came down and said the captain wanted to see me on the double."

The captain banged on the table and shouted at Tyson, "What are you trying to do to my ship? What kind of war do they think we're fighting out here?"

"Sir, it wasn't I who assigned her. I'm just in charge of her."

"Don't tell me who assigned her out here, you impudent pup. So you're 'in charge of Miss Aldrich,' " the captain sneered. "What duty for a commissioned officer of the United States Navy!"

The captain fixed his eye on Tyson. "Do you know how many men there are on a heavy cruiser?"

"Sir, the *Seattle* carries a complement of 1712 officers and men," said Tyson, who had boned up on the ship on Tulura before putting out to sea with the *Madame* correspondent.

The captain was irritated that Tyson should know the answer so exactly. "And do you realize how long this ship has been in the Pacific?" he snapped.

"Thirty-one months and thirteen days, sir."

"All right," the captain said furiously, "do you realize something these secret documents they let you read but shouldn't on Tulura don't tell you: Do you have any notion what just the sight of a woman, any woman, but especially this woman, has on these men who haven't even seen a white woman in thirty-one months and thirteen days?" The captain banged on the table. "Do you?"

"Yes, sir, I minored in psychology at Princeton. Besides, I have some thing of a notion myself," Tyson said truthfully.

"The hell you do!" shouted the captain, whose concept of Tulura was of officers boozing all day and wallowing in orgies in the boondocks with nurses all night.

"I'm placing a twenty-four-hour Marine watch on the admiral's cabin!" the captain said. "No one is to be allowed up there. That goes for you, too," the captain said suspiciously.

Tyson was dismayed. "But, sir! There are certain coverage problems on which it is essential for me to confer from time to time with Miss Aldrich."

"Coverage problems!" the captain bellowed. "What does that mean in English?"

"Well, sir, I mean, what stories she would like to do, transmission problems, deadlines, censorship problems, that sort of thing," Tyson said mysteriously. "You'd be surprised, sir, how many problems these correspondents can come up with. ComFleets is most anxious that they come away with a favorable impression of the Navy, and that means we've got to take care of their problems."

Tyson's discreet dropping of "ComFleets" did the trick. Really it infuriated the captain even more, this ensign pulling ComFleets' rank on him. But there was nothing he could do about that, for the woman correspondent did come from ComFleets. However, his eye gleamed as he thought of something to do.

"All right, then," he said, pushing his lips together, "you can 'confer' with her in her cabin. Incidentally, have you ever been aboard a ship before?"

"No, sir," Tyson said shyly.

"I thought not. Well, we've no room for deadheads on the *Seattle*. Starting with the first watch you'll stand regular watches in communications in addition to conferring with that woman."

ComFleets Headquarters Public Relations officers were not supposed to be given additional duty during their visitations aboard ship, but far from being displeased, as the captain had expected, Tyson was overjoyed. He had always wanted aboard ship, and here he was standing watches, just like a naval officer! Of course, the work in the communications shack, consisting of sitting at a desk and coding and decoding messages, wasn't particularly nautical, but still he was standing regular watches. They couldn't very well have made him a junior officer of the deck. The captain of the cruiser was not so angry at Tyson that he wanted his ship run aground.

The crew took a different attitude from their skipper's toward Debbi Aldrich. They were happy to have her aboard. They talked of little else. Fresh scuttlebutt was piped down hourly from the admiral's quarters by the Marine guard. Once Miss Aldrich asked a big Marine corporal from Oklahoma named Donahue if he would get her some Ivory soap flakes to wash out some "things." The *Seattle* had a fine laundry but the clothing it handled required somewhat more powerful soap flakes. But Donahue got a case of Ivory bar soap and got one of the carpenter's mates to shave it into fine pieces on his lathe and there were Ivory soap flakes for Miss Aldrich.

"She had them 'things' soaking in the admiral's basin when I took the soap flakes in," Donahue reported, "and Jesus Christ what 'things'! Yowee!"

For days the crew would talk about how Debbi Aldrich was washing out her "things" in the admiral's basin. God damn!

The moment one of the Marines came off watch he was pumped for new Aldrich poop, Donahue especially because he always acted mysterious. A swarm of sailors would surround him in Marine quarters and Donahue would hold court.

"What about that damned officer who goes up there?" a sailor with a ravenous look in his eye would ask Donahue. "You hear anything when he's inside?"

"Hell, you can't hear through them bulkheads," Donahue said. "You swabbies ought to know that."

"You sure you don't hear noises?" the sailor said suspiciously.

Donahue would look as if his sense of delicacy had been offended.

"God damn, you swab jockeys can't never think of nothing else, I'll swear to God."

"Listen, you Gyrene bastard, we said noises. You hear any *noises?*"

Donahue shrugged. "To tell you the truth, men, I heared one or two noises. But it's been so goddamn long since I even *heared*, I just can't tell for sure if it's *them* noises."

As the ship cruised toward Nanto Shima, Debbi Aldrich's very presence aboard began to give a certain spirit, a lift, to the ship. This spirit was typified by an incident just before the bombardments.

D minus eight, as the ship was preparing to maneuver into position for the first bombardment, the captain came on the bridge, and glancing skyward, noticed a flimsy piece of cloth fluttering from the mast.

"What the hell," he muttered and flicked his binoculars to his eyes.

Studiously the captain examined the delicate and magnified fretwork. Still looking through the binoculars, he addressed the officer of the deck. "Hepburn, am I getting old or are we flying from the mast a pair of something no one on this ship has seen for thirty-one months?"

"Yes, sir," Hepburn said nervously. "I mean no, sir, you're not getting old and yes, sir, you have correctly identified the object."

The captain snapped the binoculars down, looked quietly at Hepburn, who was standing twelve inches away, then suddenly let out a roar: "Well!!?"

"You see, sir," the officer of the deck said, his voice trembling a little, "I believe we're the first ship in naval history to carry a woman into combat and the crew had the idea of, well — flying her pennant!"

"Anyhow, sir," piped up the boatswain of the watch, boldly flinging a hand toward the transparent strip of cloth, "that's what we're fighting for!"

The crew had noted Debbi Aldrich's half-inch of black in the V-neck of her shirt. They had correctly gauged that anyone representing a magazine like *Madame* would be wearing a matching color below. They had requested and Debbi Aldrich had supplied the pennant. She was delighted that her colors — the panties were a lacy black — should lead the U.S.S. *Seattle* into battle.

The captain looked mastward again, his face reddened and swelled. Then suddenly he burst into laughter, a phenomenon many of the crew had not witnessed during three years under his command.

"Okay, Hepburn. Let's go in and give 'em hell."

The pennant stayed up. The cruiser *Seattle*, incidentally, was credited with the deadliest bombardment of any of the ships in the Nanto Shima operation.

Then one day — D plus two, it was — Debbi Aldrich disappeared from the ship. Vanished. Flick! Like that.

There was unprecedented consternation on Tulura when that first message, marked "Urgent," came in and was decoded:

031955. Originator: U.S.S. *Seattle*. Action: ComFleets. Miss Debbi Aldrich, correspondent for *Madame* magazine, disappeared at 031910 from *Seattle*. Miss Aldrich was last seen by a Marine orderly who left his post at her quarters in flag cabin to go to ship's service and purchase her a package of cigarettes. When orderly returned, Miss Aldrich was no longer in the cabin. The officer of the deck, ship then being anchored in Nanto Bay five miles offshore, immediately instituted search. Exhaustive search of all ship fails to turn up Miss Aldrich. Search of flag cabin reveals two of three pieces of luggage she brought present and accounted for but one — a red hatbox believed to be made from lizard skin — missing. All ships in area and all ground forces on Nanto Shima being notified to be on lookout for woman with red hatbox. Disciplinary action being instituted against Marine orderly and Ensign Christopher Tyson III, OinC Miss Aldrich.

ComFleets' answer was prompt and hot:

ComFleets stupefied by your 031955. Dispatching immediately Airtrans Rear Admiral B. G. Pumphrey, chief of intelligence, to supervise search for Miss Debbi Aldrich, correspondent for *Madame* magazine, and conduct exhaustive investigation into startling laxity of *Seattle* whereby VIP passengers can quote disappear unquote from ship five miles from shore. You are hereby directed meantime to conduct relentless and unceasing search of ship ballast to bridge. Signed (Personal) ComFleets.

Viewed from the *Seattle* the whole operation on Nanto Shima, where the Marines and Army had landed and were pushing respectively north and south, ground to a halt. It was not true that the Army's search for Miss Aldrich was responsible for its temporary failure to progress southward. The Japs were to be blamed for that hold-up. But all Marine and Army units were repeatedly reminded to be on the lookout for the *Madame* correspondent and supplied with detailed descriptions of the missing woman — including her red lizard hatbox, as if there might be several similar creatures, but perhaps not equipped with red lizard hatbox, wandering around the battle area — and all ships in the area were searched. For a while the Navy communications system carried almost as many Debbi Aldrich as operational dispatches. The Navy Department in Washington was putting the heat on ComFleets, which was burning up the air waves to the *Seattle* off Nanto Shima. War or no war, you just don't lose a correspondent, at least a *Madame* woman correspondent, by "disappearance." Admiral Pumphrey directed all search operations from the *Seattle*'s newly vacated admiral's quarters, which at least were again rightfully occupied by flag rank.

Seven days after Debbi Aldrich vanished, Tyson, who was a prisoner-at-large awaiting his disciplinary action for losing her, was standing forlornly on deck leaning over the rail and thinking seriously about jumping in. It was a beautiful, clear day with a sea smooth as a summer pond where the *Seattle* remained at anchor in the spot from which she had not budged since Miss Aldrich disappeared. She had been ordered to remain there, like a homing pigeon's loft. Squinting shoreward, Tyson saw an LCVP bobbing its way toward the cruiser. As the boat came closer, he could see what appeared to be a rather grimy Marine sitting, legs crossed, on the engine cover. His eyes moved casually over the boat, then fetched up. The Marine's hand was resting on an object which, though grimy itself, looked familiar. It looked like a red hatbox.

By the time Tyson had rushed down to the gangway, the boat was alongside. Peering over the side — he almost fell overboard — he was just in time to see the Marine wave good-bye to four other Marines and the LCVP crew and hear a familiar husky voice.

"Thanks awfully, you darling Leathernecks," the voice said. "It couldn't have been lovelier."

Tyson tore down the gangway past the startled officer of the deck.

"Debbi!" he yelled. "My God, Debbi. You've had the whole U.S. fleet looking for you! The war's almost stopped since you left! Where in the name of God have you been?"

Debbi Aldrich, correspondent for *Madame*, brushed a wisp of hair back under a Marine fatigue cap which came down over her ears. She hitched up her Marine combat trousers and pulled down her Marine jacket. They were so big for her that the sleeves came over her hands and half the pants legs had been rolled up. Her face was caked with dirt — her lips, however, were properly lipsticked. She looked up at Tyson and said, easily, "Where have I been? Why, to the wars, sweetie. Be a good boy and help me with this hatbox, will you?"

Stunned, Ty preceded her aboard with the hatbox. By this time the captain and Admiral Pumphrey were striding rapidly down to the quarterdeck. The captain was practically a stuttering maniac. But Pumphrey retained the coolness that had made him an admiral. His voice rammed like a torpedo across the quarterdeck.

"Miss Aldrich, you will be confined to your quarters until the first available air transportation to Tulura. I hope you know what this means. You're headed back to the States, Miss Aldrich."

Grimy-faced, Debbi Aldrich stood there on the quarterdeck, her body almost swallowed up in the Marine fatigues, hands on hips and cocky as a sparrow. She pushed back her hat, gave her pants another hitch and suddenly reached forward and chucked Admiral Pumphrey under the chin. The admiral drew back, startled.

"Sweetie," Debbi Aldrich said, "it was worth it."

Then she looked up slowly at the mast. The black pennant was still there. It just looked a little limp, it being a windless day.

"Happy to see my panties are still flying."

And with an insolent swagger Debbi Aldrich started to her cabin, the hoarse echo of a violent command from the admiral — who had looked mastward with a startled air — following her.

"Take those goddamn things down! What is this, a United States Navy vessel or the Pacific office of *Madame!*"

Down came the panties and up went the two-star flag of Rear Admiral Pumphrey, which in the confusion of the search had not previously been hoisted.

Debbi Aldrich wrote her story under confinement in the admiral's cabin. Rear Admiral Pumphrey furiously sent two Marines to empty the cabin of his gear after Debbi Aldrich had scribbled him a note: "Sweetie, are we *both* going to stay here? I do need a bath more than anything in the world. If you don't mind I don't." Her story was a good story, of its kind, beginning: "I have just become the first woman in American history to accompany an infantry patrol into battle." She wrote how simple it was. One evening around dusk she had looked out the port of her cabin and seen an LCVP alongside the ship. It had come out for some supplies from the cruiser. She quickly threw some "things" in her hatbox. Then she sent the Marine orderly for some cigarettes, pushed her hair up under her cap and stepped out of her cabin. While the deck watch was seeing to the supplies, and in the confusion of men passing back and forth between cruiser and LCVP, she simply went down the gangway and got aboard. LCVP crews are used to carrying everything. They didn't bother to ask questions. Ashore she hitched a ride with a Marine jeep headed for the front. She stayed with a front-line Marine outfit for four days. The Marines never ask questions, particularly of women.

Then she came back. It was as simple as that.

Of course they had to send her back to the States, even though she was a correspondent for *Madame*. It was probably worth it to her, for she had a real exclusive. Tyson said he thought it was a pretty shabby thing to do, sending her back, in view of the fact she probably had a lot to do with the *Seattle*'s brilliant bombardment record. Really, he said, Debbi Aldrich was a great inspiration to the whole crew, and maybe the Navy Department in Washington knew what it was doing after all and should send a couple hundred women correspondents out here. Ty said he thought those black panties should be preserved in one of those glass cases at Annapolis where they keep famous naval battle flags.

An odd thing was that when he returned from Nanto Shima, Tyson had completely lost his stammer. Though there were cases of combat operations giving stammers to men, this may have been the first time such an operation actually cured a stammer.

The Happiest Man in the World

✕

from *Captain Newman, M.D.*

by LEO ROSTEN

When things crowded in on us at Colfax, when the news from overseas was shattering or a crash on the desert took the life of a boy we liked, when the remorseless heat or the unremitting pressure or the endless, exacerbating Army routines began to get us down, someone would smile, "How about Coby Clay?" and the grins would spread around the room. Coby's saga never failed to warm our hearts.

Coby was the happiest soldier on the post. For all I know, he was the happiest man in the United States Army, Navy or Marines. Captain Newman once told me that Coby was the only man he ever knew who was utterly impervious to life's vicissitudes. "He is consistently euphoric without being hypomanic." Coby baffled him, delighted him, and renewed his faith in the surpassing powers of a happy childhood. Coby baffled and delighted us all — all of us, that is, who did not have to contend with his one-man victory over the Army. It was his sergeant, his lieutenant and all the officers directly above them in the line of command whom Coby nearly drove out of their minds. As Laibowitz said, when the whole post was rocking with laughter over the *cul-de-sac* into which Coby had driven Colonel Pyser and the entire military establishment, "That Coby stepped out of some fairy tale or something. They ought to put up a monument. In my opinion, he is the happiest man in the world."

Coby was an Alabama lad, exactly six feet five inches in height. He had baby-blue eyes, curly hair and a cherubic spirit that spilled over from some inner reservoir of content. He walked around in a private cloud of delight, always grinning, chuckling, slapping his thigh in gratitude for his own inexhaustible good company. "Man, oh, man," he would chortle, "just you listen to that. Man, oh, man, that's mighty fine stuff." He was entirely at peace with the world and at home with himself — his body, his reveries, his Maker, his soul. His moods ran an exceptionally narrow gamut, being bounded at the lower end by pleasure and at the upper end by bliss. The only thing he was sensitive about was his height, which he reported, in rueful confession, as "five foot seventeen."

On the post we always knew when Coby was about to materialize; we could hear, in advance, the whistling or humming or chuckling which accompanied his running colloquy with his beatific self. Hear it? No; overhear it. For his contact with any of us, with the unhappy universe beyond his own fantasies, was fragmentary, and oddly compassionate. I think he felt sorry for everyone who could not join him in the idyllic past with which he chose to replace the irksome now.

Coby was an exceedingly amiable soldier, but he was most oddly co-ordinated. His long, far-flung limbs seemed to live a life independent of his torso. When Coby drew those six feet five inches to attention, for instance, he did it in sequence — as if his brain were sending messages to the outlying provinces of his bodily empire; naturally it took more time for a foot to respond than, say, a hand, since the one was so much farther from headquarters than the other.

Coby had immense biceps and looked strong, very strong, which I'm sure he was; but he did not feel strong. And a man who does not *feel* strong simply is not able to lift heavy loads, or move burdensome objects, or heave, haul, toss or carry things which much weaker men manage to do because they want to be strong. This was an illusion Coby did not entertain. He did not care a fig about physical strength; he wanted harmony, not power.

At an early age, he had found himself in a world where men competed — for jobs, for money, for women, for promotions — and he had long since come to the conclusion that he did not care to compete for anything. He was content with himself, encouraged himself, enjoyed himself and admired himself. "His ego," Captain Newman wrote in the confidential report on Coby Clay which Colonel Pyser requested, "appears to be inaccessible to conventional appeals."

It certainly was. For Coby was the only private in the United States Army who never made his bed; his sergeant made his bed for him, each and every morning. I think Coby was the only soldier in military history whom neither sergeants nor lieutenants nor captains nor majors nor colonels could prevail upon. They tried — all of them; Lord knows they tried. They tried command and cajolery, blandishment and bluster and threats of reprisal, but Coby would not make his bed. He would hear out the orders, the coaxings, the reasoning, the threats; he would gravely consider the appeals to sense, to teamwork, to *esprit de corps*. Then all he would say, with the utmost kindliness, was: " 'Tain't fit for a grown man to make his own bed."

All this broke upon our collective awareness the very first dawn after Coby was shipped to our unsuspecting installation, when his sergeant came into quarters to find Coby gazing out of the window happily, humming a roundelay. His bed was unmade.

Sergeant Pulaski, an uncomplicated Polish boy from Chicago, called, "Clay!"

"Yes, Sarge," Coby beamed.

"Clay," said Sergeant Pulaski sternly, "you didn't make your bed."

"That's right, Sarge."

Sergeant Pulaski wrinkled his brow. "Why not?"

Coby said, " 'Tain't fit for a grown man to make his own bed."

Sergeant Pulaski, who had a gift for unvarnished command, put his fists on his hips at once and barked, "What the hell kind of double-talk is that?"

"Back home," said Coby, "my maw always makes up my bed. Ever since I been born, my maw always made up that bed."

"In the Army," said Sergeant Pulaski slowly, "there ain't no ma's to make no beds. In the Army, soldier, everyone — everyone except officers — makes his own bed!"

Coby took thought and clucked his tongue.

"Inspection is in ten minutes."

"That's *nice*," said Coby.

"Now, boy, make that bed."

Coby sighed and shook his head with regret. "I ain't hankerin' to make no trouble for nobody, nohow; but I jest cain't do it."

"And why 'cain't you just do it'?"

"Why, I jest couldn't look my maw in the eye again if I made up my own bed."

Sergeant Pulaski stared at Coby in amazement, tightened his lips, declared, "A guy asks for trouble he's gonna get trouble!" and stalked out.

Coby lay down on his bed and sang himself a song. In less than five minutes, Sergeant Pulaski returned with Lieutenant Bienstock. I had briefly met Bienstock, a second lieutenant with fuzz on his cheek but not on his chin. He was an enthusiastic exponent of that Come-on-fellows-let's-all-put-our-shoulders-to-the-wheel attitude which never failed to puzzle military observers from abroad, who expect an army to be divided simply into those who command and those who obey.

Lieutenant Bienstock now hastened into the barracks with shining eyes, alert ears and palpitating disbelief. "Which one? Where, Sergeant? Which one is it? That one? On your feet, soldier."

As Coby undulated himself upward, part after part, until all of his five foot seventeen assembled more or less at attention, Lieutenant Bienstock paled slightly.

"Mornin', suh," Coby smiled.

Lieutenant Bienstock glanced uneasily at Sergeant Pulaski and said, "Now listen, Clay. Sergeant Pulaski has been very patient with you, I must say. You don't want to get into any trouble, do you? And we certainly don't want to make you any trouble. Now, what's all this nonsense about your refusing to make your bed?"

Coby looked down at his superior from bland, unruffled heights. "Oh, I don't aim to make no trouble for nobody, nohow. I *like* it here, suh. But it jest ain't right, suh. I couldn't look my maw in the eye again if I made up my own bed."

Lieutenant Bienstock stared at the kind, forbearing face above him and, in a strained voice, asked, "Do you realize what you're *saying*, Clay? Do you know what this means? Why — you are deliberately refusing to obey an order from a superior officer!"

"Oh, no, suh," Coby drawled. "I ain't refusin' t'obey no one, nohow."

"Then you'll go ahead and make that bed!"

"Cain't," said Coby.

Lieutenant Bienstock glanced at Sergeant Pulaski nervously, wetting his lips, and said, "Sergeant, take this man to Captain Howard's office."

"Right." Sergeant Pulaski saluted and nodded to Coby, who regarded Lieutenant Bienstock in the kindest possible way before ambling out. Bienstock lighted a cigarette and inhaled deeply, organizing his thoughts. There were a great many of them. Then he hurried out and headed for Captain Howard's office in Building Two.

Coby was sitting on a long bench, one foot drawn up, his elbow on it, his hand dangling loosely, moving in lazy rhythm to his humming. Sergeant Pulaski was standing next to him in the correctest possible military fashion. Lieutenant Bienstock regarded Coby sententiously, giving him one last chance to reconsider or recant. Coby started to mobilize his bodily ingredients for ascent; Lieutenant Bienstock turned on his heel and strode into Captain Howard's office.

I disliked Captain Howard. He was a knuckle-cracker and a mint-sucker — efficient, crisp, hard-working and mean. An automobile salesman from Wichita. Herbert Howard was a stern believer in fair play, cold showers and clean thoughts. His thoughts were so clean that he spent most of his evenings at the Officers' Club boring us with his plans for a five-minute car-washing service he was going to open up as soon as the war was over. He was the kind of incomplete personality known as "a man's man." He had few friends and many doubts. When he thought no one was watching, he bit his nails. I am sure that when he slept, he looked puzzled.

He was tallying up some requisition forms when Lieutenant Bienstock entered. Bienstock saluted smartly, accepted Captain Howard's cursory "Proceed," and, while the latter continued to add and carry over, recited the details of Private Coby Clay's defiance of the simplest and most universal requirement of military life.

Captain Howard lifted his head with an expression of incipient outrage. "He won't make his *bed?*"

Lieutenant Bienstock cleared his throat. "Yes, sir."

Captain Howard scrutinized Bienstock as if at one who had just told him the sun had risen in the west that morning.

"He says it's against his principles, sir," Bienstock quickly added.

"His principles?" Captain Howard echoed. "What the hell is he, a Mohammedan?"

"No, sir. He's from the South."

"So what? Halfa this little old installation is —"

"He says his maw always made his bed for him and 'tain't — it isn't fit for a grown man to make his own bed."

Captain Howard leaned forward, hunching his shoulders like a fullback plowing through the line, and cried, "His '*maw*'? What the hell's the *mat*ter with you, Bienstock?"

"Nothing, sir," said Lieutenant Bienstock with a pained expression. "I was just *quoting.*"

"Well, stop quoting and talk sense! He calls his mother 'maw'?"

"Yes, sir."

"Is he a hillbilly or something?"

Bienstock hesitated. "I think he's from Alabama, sir."

"I don't care if he's a thirty-plus-three *degree* Mason! Do you mean to stand there and tell me you let a damn dogface pull a cockeyed gag like *re*fusing to make his own bed on you?"

"Sir, I explained and insisted and argued with him. I even —"

Captain Howard's face assumed various variations of impatience as Lieutenant Bienstock proceeded. This made Lieutenant Bienstock more nervous, and he began to stammer. This made Captain Howard's lips thread themselves so that contempt replaced impatience. This made Lieutenant Bienstock blush. This made Captain Howard slap his desk with his open palm and snap, "You *argued* with him? What the hell's the *mat*ter with you anyway, Bienstock? You are an *o*fficer in the *U*nited States *A*rmy! This isn't a debating *s*ociety. We're at war! Get the marbles out of your head and throw that no-good gold-bricker in the little old guardhouse!"

"Sir?"

"You heard me. Throw him in the can!"

"I thought —"

"That's not smart of you, thinking. Give him to the MP's, Bienstock, to the MP's. Twenty-four hours in the little old cooler will cool off that joker. It's as *simple* as that. Won't make his bed! 'It ain't fit for a grown man.' " Captain Howard's expression was a masterpiece of disgust. "Holy Moses, Bienstock, even the *Com*munists make their own beds. Dismissed!"

Lieutenant Bienstock wiped his brow the minute he got outside the door, signaled to Sergeant Pulaski, and strode out as Sergeant Pulaski told Coby, "Up!"

When they were fifty feet from Captain Howard's office, Lieutenant Bienstock took Coby under a tree and made a last earnest effort to save him from his fate. Coby listened with the utmost consideration. Anyone could see that he wouldn't want to hurt Lieutenant Bienstock's feelings for the world. But what he said, after Bienstock's moving appeal to reason, was, " 'Tain't fit for a grown man to —"

"Sergeant," said Bienstock petulantly, "take this man to the guardhouse! By order of Captain Howard."

Coby spent that day and night behind bars. He spent most of the day singing and all of the night sleeping like a particularly contented lamb.

When Coby returned to the barracks from the guardhouse the next morning, Sergeant Pulaski was waiting at the entrance with a superior smile.

Coby was delighted to see him. "Man, oh, man," he chuckled, "I caught me up on plenty of snoozin'."

Pulaski said, "Okay, Clay. Let's us have no more trouble from you, huh?"

Coby's eyes moved serenely around the barracks, coming to rest on his own bed in the far corner. It looked as neat, tight and oblong as a coffin.

"We got commended for neat quarters at inspection this morning," growled Sergeant Pulaski defensively. "Okay, okay, so *I* made up your bed. But no more trouble from you, huh, Clay?"

"No, Sarge," said Coby. "I ain't aimin' to give nobody —"

"— no trouble nohow," Pulaski finished. "I heard you. Now get the lead out of your tail and fall in with your squad."

Coby spent the day training with his company, went to sleep that night, responded to reveille nobly the next morning, helped his comrades mop the floor and sweep the porch, lent a cheerful, helping hand to one and all — but he did not make his bed. Sergeant Pulaski looked hurt as he went out to find Lieutenant Bienstock.

Bienstock gave Coby a ten-minute lecture on military discipline, Captain Howard's cold heart, Major Forman's nasty temper, and the reputation of Colonel Pyser, an absolute Caligula in disciplinary matters. Coby could not have been more interested in these novel insights into the military organization of which he was so small a part. But he would not sacrifice his principles; he would not sully his mother's image of him; he would not make his bed. He returned to the guardhouse. And, back in the barracks,

Sergeant Pulaski made his bed again, while Coby sang for his colleagues in the can.

The next day Coby was back with his fellows. That night he slept in the bed which Sergeant Pulaski had made that morning. The next morning he declined to make his bed, with genuine affection and regret, and went to the guardhouse again.

This went on for a week, Coby spending alternate nights at the guardhouse, sleeping alternate nights in the bed which Sergeant Pulaski, hamstrung and desperate, made for him. When it seemed clear that Coby Clay was willing to spend the rest of his days in this idyllic double life, Sergeant Pulaski appealed to Lieutenant Bienstock, and Lieutenant Bienstock reported to Captain Howard with an unmistakable note of panic in his voice.

Captain Howard cracked his knuckles, studied Lieutenant Bienstock with disgust diluted only with disbelief, and, between his fine, well-brushed teeth, said, "Bring that mother-loving soldier in to me." He had never laid eyes on Coby Clay.

When Coby presented himself, Captain Howard was on the telephone, tilted far back in his chair, his back to the door, reading aloud acidly from a report and bawling out a lieutenant in Quartermaster's. Captain Howard was feeling especially curt, concise and complete that day. He slammed the phone down, swiveled around to his desk, deliberately keeping his eyes on the report, and waited for the familiar: "Private ———— reporting, sir," from the soldier awaiting his dispensation. He did not get it, because Coby saw no reason to give it.

Captain Howard put his pencil down slowly, exactly parallel to the blotter pad, assumed an expression of icy foreboding, then slowly lifted his eyes up the height of the erect body before him. This calculated maneuver of the eyes had always before served Captain Howard's purposes; it effected a slow deflation of the other's ego; it smothered hope or illusion; it was a shrewd tactical gambit which made it crystal-clear who was standing and who was sitting, and who was going to continue standing at the sole pleasure of who was sitting.

But Lieutenant Bienstock had forgotten to tell Captain Howard that Coby Clay was six feet five. By the time Captain Howard's gaze reached the unexpected altitude of Coby's chin, Herbert Howard, who was only five feet eight, had his head far back in the socket of his neck and his eyes bugged in an involuntary bulge.

Coby blushed sheepishly, as he always did when people first comprehended his eminence. "I come right over, suh, like that there other fellow told me."

"Who?" asked Captain Howard.

"That there other fellow. The one brought me here before."

Captain Howard could feel his neck getting hot. "That 'other fellow' is an *officer*, an *officer* named Lieutenant Bienstock, and you will re-fer to him hereafter by name."

"He never told me his name," said Coby.

"Well *I* am telling you his rank *and* name!" Captain Howard retorted, slamming his fist on the desk. "And even if you didn't know his name, you could call him 'lieutenant.' You understand *that* much, soldier, don't you?"

"Yes, suh!" Coby was always grateful for increment to his store of knowledge.

Captain Howard turned sideward and poured himself a glass of water, noting with approval that his hands were steady. He sipped the water slowly, lowered the glass, studied it, placed the glass back on the table, leaned forward, put his palms together, and said in an even voice, "Soldier, I want you to listen *care*fully to what I am about to tell you. I'll say it slowly, so there is not the *slight*est chance you'll misunderstand. It involves your making a decision that may affect *your whole life!* Are you ready?"

Coby furrowed his brow, concentrating on every word Captain Howard had uttered, and nodded.

Captain Howard took a deep breath and let it out, word by word. "Either you make your bed, every morning, without *a* single beef, or I will throw you in the little old guardhouse for ten days." He fixed Coby with his deadliest I-take-no-nonsense-from-anyone stare. "Is that clear?"

Coby nodded.

"You understand it?"

Coby nodded again.

"Any questions you want to ask?"

Coby shook his head.

"Fine. Now, boy, which will it be?"

"How's that again, suh?" asked Coby.

Captain Howard gritted his many teeth. "Which — will — it — be? Make your bed in the morning, *every* morning, or go to the cold, cold jug for ten days?"

Coby sighed, regarding the man seated before and below him with infinite compassion. "I don't want to make no trouble for no one nohow, suh, but 'tain't fit for a grown man to —"

The blood drained out of Captain Howard's face; all sorts of evil thoughts welled up in him and had to be denied. He placed a mint in his mouth and pressed a button on his desk. "Good-*by*, soldier!"

Coby spent the next ten days in the guardhouse. It was, according to the reports that Corporal Laibowitz brought to the hospital and that raced through all the wards with the speed of a forest fire, the happiest ten days of Coby's life.

The MP's and Captain Howard and Major Forman — to whom Captain Howard brought his problem, confessing defeat — simply could not believe it. They could understand it, but they could not believe it. Or perhaps it was the other way around.

For Coby Clay was behaving in such a way that the entire theory of punishment, as a deterrent, was endangered. Every day Coby spent happily in the guardhouse clearly demonstrated that the punitive could be made rather pleasant, and this challenged the very foundations of law enforcement. For the whole idea of a guardhouse, or any place of confinement, rests on the assumption that detention is hateful to man's free spirit and crippling to man's free soul. But now the American Army was confronted by a man for whom detention held no terrors, confinement meant no deprivation, discipline represented no threat. The awful truth, which was beginning to confound our brass, was this: Private Coby Clay *liked* the guardhouse. He slept like a king and sang like an angel. In fact, he preferred the guardhouse to the barracks. There was something about that bounded, ordered microcosm that appealed to Coby no end; there, life was reduced to its simplest form — devoid of conflict or the perplexities of choice.

The fact that Coby declined to make his bed in the guardhouse, too — politely, but definitively — presented its own special problem to the MP's: after all, there was no other guardhouse to which you could send a man to punish him for not making his bed in the guardhouse in which he was. "What in hell can I *do?*" Major Inglehart, commanding MP, often moaned to us. No one knew what to tell him.

Nor was this the worst of it. The other prisoners, who regarded Coby with the awe of apprentices to master, were beginning to be converted to Coby's unique philosophy of life; the insidious idea began to germinate in their delinquent brains that perhaps they could get away with not making their beds, too. To nip this frightful prospect in the bud, Major Inglehart swiftly transferred Coby to a cell with one Lacy Bucks, a young enlistee from Louisiana who could not endure Yankees but felt kin to anyone south of Tennessee. The major interviewed Private Bucks personally and, after a certain amount of shilly-shallying, bribed Bucks ("double rations") to make up Coby's bed every morning. "And don't tell anyone you're doing it!" Inglehart warned him darkly.

Bucks seemed contented to be silent for the major, and the rations. Coby, of course, had no reason to tell anyone that Bucks was making his bed for him. He never felt the need of initiating any discussion of the bed problem; it was no problem to him: at home, his maw had made his bed; then Sergeant Pulaski had; now Lacy Bucks did. It was the most natural thing in the world to Coby Clay.

Things simply could not go on this way forever.

Besides, there was the problem of work details. Men suffering punishment in a guardhouse cannot, obviously, be permitted to spend their days in happy idleness while all around them their haggard comrades drill like furies, crawl through sand, contest barbed wire, run fiendish obstacle courses under a merciless sun, bivouac under a chilling moon. The Air Force could not be *that* naïve.

So Major Inglehart put Coby, Private Bucks and a barrel-chested boy named Tony Caralucciano into a detail to police the grounds. It seemed a safe enough assignment. But as it worked out, that threesome became the finest show at Colfax and nearly demoralized the installation. For Army regulations require that every prisoner must be accompanied by an armed guard whenever he (the prisoner) is allowed outside the guardhouse. This meant that as Coby, Bucks and Caralucciano ambled happily across the grounds, in a memorable formation which I shall describe forthwith, three MP's, carrying rifles and wearing battle helmets, marched stiffly behind them. When the heat was very great, clawing at the senses with fiery hands, the three prisoners in their loose and tieless fatigue garments were conspicuously more comfortable than their nominally freer custodians.

The formation of the detail added its own piquancy to the scene. Coby always took the middle spot, looming up above Lacy Bucks on his right and Tony Caralucciano on his left. Tony carried a long pole with a nail at the end; Lacy carried a burlap sack. As the three good men moved lazily across the ground they had been assigned to make bereft of trash, Tony would spear a piece of paper — a chewing-gum wrapper, an envelope, a crumpled ball of unrequited love — on the end of the nail that was on the end of his pole, and would bring the pole up horizontally toward Coby. Coby would remove the paper from the nail with the utmost delicacy, crooking his little finger, bring his hand across from left to right, where Lacy Bucks was holding the sack open, and let the piece of paper drop daintily into the sack. He hummed or sang during the entire operation. This did not help the morale of the guards.

Tony Caralucciano had a fine barbershop bass and, in the great tradition of his ancestors, loved grand opera. Lacy Bucks was strictly a hot-jazz type, the kind who tries to find in life the archaic excitations of the syncopated. Coby, a man of broad and generous interests, liked to sing anything. These three music lovers soon learned to float together on the sea of their common fantasies, singing or humming while they worked and as the spirit of the moment moved them. It was a thing beautiful to hear and, once heard, never to be forgotten. It particularly pleased the men in Ward 7. It went like this:

Each morning when "The Prison Warblers," as Francie dubbed them, moved into position ahead of their helmeted Cerberus, Coby would greet the day by humming a note — any note, whichever note best suited his mood. His mood was unfailingly happy. If Tony was feeling very operatic he would take off, using Coby's theme note as a springboard, into anything from *Tosca* to *Madame Butterfly*. If it was Lacy Bucks who was in touch with his private muses, he would give out with *Johnny One Note* or *Roll, Jordan, Roll*. And if Coby wanted to override his confrères, he would simply sing out his own immemorial hymns. There was no set pattern to it: whoever sang, the others accompanied; whatever one man finished, another would take up, on the last, long, expiring note, for his own. It was as close to true understanding as men can ever get. As one of the guards was heard to mutter, struggling with his confusion and dismay: "Them is the happiest goddam garbage collectors I ever did meet."

When Coby's term of punishment ended, he appeared, refreshed and forgiving, in my office. Major Forman had told Captain Howard to tell Lieutenant Bienstock to tell Sergeant Pulaski to deliver Coby to "the head-boys." Major Forman phoned me himself and said he wanted Coby Clay rigorously tested. "The works, Alderson!" he said. "I want you to give him every blasted test you ever gave anyone. Then take him over to Captain Newman and let Newman start where you left off. Send all the reports directly to me. I'm going to build up a file on this joker that buttons down every angle, then I'm going to take the case up directly with Colonel Pyser. If this guy is a nut, we'll get him out of the army on a C.D.D., and if he's faking we'll Section Eight him out. Either way, goddamit, we'll make him regret the day he ever decided to pull that gag about not making his bed. One way or another, Alderson, *this farce has got to end!*"

No one ever got as many tests as I administered to Coby Clay that day. I gave him the whole battery from simple IQ's to the Cornell Selectee Index. I gave him Self-Idealization scales and Sentence Completions ("I faint at the sight of blood. . . . I avoid people who . . . I feel nervous when . . .") I gave him AGCT's and ACIO's. I tested him for mechanical aptitude, motor responses, minimum literacy, box counting, mental alertness, visual-motor skills. I gave him perception tests, emotional adjustment inventories, aptitude scales, visual classification series. I went through the manual put out by the Personnel Procedures Section of the Adjutant General's Office to make sure there wasn't a form I had missed.

It took me a good seventeen hours to code, score and appraise my findings. The results were absolutely frustrating. As far as the accumulated diagnostic genius of our society could discern, Coby Clay was a healthy, responsible, wholesome, brave, reasonable, well-adjusted (though slowly co-ordinated) specimen of American manhood. His schooling was not all that might be desired; his vocabulary was far from impressive; his spelling was atrocious — but then, so was the spelling of most of our armed forces. Coby's IQ was 96 — not high, to be sure, but you must remember that 50 per cent of the GI's in the Army ranked between 95 and 105.

"How," Captain Newman asked me, with rather bated breath, "would you summarize all this? If you had to describe Clay in one word, what would it be?"

"Delightful," I said.

Captain Newman put his head between his hands. "Okay, Barney, bring him around."

Captain Newman interviewed Coby Clay for an hour and returned him to the unhappy jurisdiction of Sergeant Pulaski.

The report which Captain Newman wrote on Coby for Major Forman and, through him, for Colonel Pyser, was something to treasure. There was not a note of irony in it, nor a smidgen of levity. It was precise, technical, thorough, and — to someone like Colonel Pyser — infuriating. Francie showed it to me, smiling. "If you want to see the great psychoanalyst at the top of his form, cast your youthful eyes on this." I copied parts of it for posterity:

> Clay's reflexes are good, though not particularly rapid. He shows excellent psychological equilibrium. He has balance, proportion, and a good sense of humor. He sleeps well, eats well, and (aside from the particular problem for which he was referred to the undersigned) performs his duties in a responsible fashion. He may be classified as "Oral, passive." . . .
>
> He discusses his convictions about bed-making (rather, about not-bed-making) without anxiety, ambivalence, or hostility. He appears to have deeply encapsulated opinions about the masculine and feminine roles, placing some things firmly in the former category and others (such as bed-making) in the latter. . . .
>
> I do not believe his opinions on this subject can be altered by therapy. Clay may be described as having an unusual character structure. His aggressions are well in hand. His views about certain aspects of military discipline are unique, but not subversive. His ego appears to be inaccessible to conventional appeals.
>
> (Signed) J. J. NEWMAN, *Captain*, M.C.

When Colonel Pyser called Captain Newman to his office, that report on Coby Clay lay on Colonel Pyser's desk. Major Forman and Captain Howard were present. They looked terribly serious: Pyser kept biting his mustache, Major Forman kept drumming his fingers, and Captain Howard kept sucking mints.

Colonel Pyser opened the conference bluntly: "Captain Newman, do you regard Clay as a mental defective?"

"No, sir."

"Do you regard him as a queer — I mean *as* queer, in any shape, manner or form?"

"No, sir."

"I take it, from your report, that you insist on considering Private Clay well adjusted?"

"Yes, sir."

"You couldn't find *any* signs of neurosis, psychosis or any other incapacitating factors?" asked Pyser almost plaintively.

"No, sir."

"What about moral turpitude — or *antisocial behavior?*"

Newman shook his head.

Colonel Pyser studied him hatefully. "So you won't recommend a Section Eight hearing for this son-of-a-bitch?"

"No, sir."

Pyser put his hands on the arms of his chair and looked as if he might spring at Captain Newman any moment. "Goddamit, Newman, you have recommended men for a Section Eight-ing who never gave us half the trouble this soldier has put the post through! And now, when we really need and can *use* an N.P. diagnosis you get more conservative than Herbert Hoover!"

"But apart from not making his bed, Colonel, Clay has created no difficulties —"

"'*Apart* from not making his bed'?" Pyser echoed, his cheeks going gray. "'*Apart* from not making his *bed*'? What more do you want from a nut than refusing to make his bed and *enjoying* the guardhouse, for the love of Mike? I ask you again, Newman. Do you mean to sit there and tell me that you will not recommend this goldbrick or screwball or whatever-the-hell-he-is for a Section Eight?"

Newman met Colonel Pyser's glare steadily. "I *might* classify him as neurotic, phobic type — a bed-making phobia, but that would only go with a recommendation for a C.D.D."

"Medical discharge?" shouted Colonel Pyser. "Give that bastard a pension — on half-pay — for the rest of his life? Over my dead body, Newman!" He leaped to his feet and paced back and forth furiously, then wheeled on Newman. "The real test is — do you think this soldier is fit for combat?"

"Yes, sir."

"God," Pyser groaned. "Look; if we send him overseas, do you think he's going to change his opinion about making his bed?"

"No, sir."

"Right!" cried Pyser. "Then who the hell do you think *will* make his bed overseas?"

"Someone else," said Captain Newman.

Colonel Pyser stared at Newman bitterly. Newman said he could hear Major Forman's chair trembling, and Captain Howard sucking on a mint as if it were an oxygen tube.

"One final question, Newman. If Clay finishes his training, and if I send him overseas with his outfit, when the chips are down — is this joker going to fight or is he going to wash out?"

"This boy will never wash out," said Captain Newman.

"Oh, Christ," said Colonel Pyser.

And so when Coby Clay, that fine and delightful soldier, returned from his latest stretch in the guardhouse, rested and unruffled as of yore, and appeared before Sergeant Pulaski, smiling and considerate, that product of the West Side of Chicago studied him in silence for a long, long moment before inquiring, "Coby, you learned your lesson now? You want solitary and bread-and-water next? Or you gonna be a good boy and make your bed?"

Before Coby could even finish shaking his head, Sergeant Pulaski threw his head back, crying, "Oh, hell! Okay! All right, I give up! You win! A couple million guys in the whole screwy American Army, from North and South and East and West, and I have to draw you! So okay, soldier. That's the way God wants it, that's the way He's gonna have it! I'll make your goddam bed from now on."

And he did. Every morning. Every single morning, an American sergeant made a private's bed for him. It was the talk of the post — except at Headquarters, where no one dared mention it. Not a day passed but what Sergeant Pulaski got kidded and razzed and needled about this basic transmutation of the established order. Pulaski began to get mighty edgy.

Then one day Private Clay loomed over Sergeant Pulaski and said, "Say, Sarge, can I ask you somethin'?"

"Come on, come on," said Pulaski crossly. "Talk fast."

Coby scratched his head. "Well, I been thinkin' out about this bed-makin'. 'Tain't fit for a man to make his own bed, like my maw says. But I been thinkin' an' scratchin' aroun' an' all, an' I don't see no right reason why a man cain't make up someone *else's* bed. Like you been doin' for me. I figger my maw wouldn't hardly mind if I jest did that same little thing for you."

The kidding of Sergeant Pulaski stopped after that. For from then on, until that whole contingent of brave men was flown into action overseas, while Sergeant Pulaski made Coby's bed each morning, Coby — humming of dark glades and promised lands — made Pulaski's.

World War II: The War in the Pacific

The Squad

✕

from *The Naked and the Dead*
by NORMAN MAILER

The squad formed a single file and began to move out. First Battalion's bivouac was very small and in thirty seconds they had reached the gap in the barbed wire. Martinez led them cautiously down the trail leading to A Company. His drowsiness vanished quickly, and he became alert. Actually, he could not see anything, but some sense seemed to guide him along the bends in the path so that he rarely stumbled or blundered off the trail. He was proceeding about thirty yards ahead of the other men and he was completely isolated. If some Japanese had been waiting in ambush along the path, he would have been the first to be trapped. Yet he had very little fear; Martinez's terror developed in a void; the moment he had to lead men, his courage returned. At this instant, his mind was poised over a number of sounds and thoughts. His ears were searching the jungle ahead of him for some noise which might indicate that men were waiting in the brush beside the trail; they were also listening with disgust to the stumbling and muttering of men following behind him. His mind recorded the intermittent sounds of battle and tried to classify them; he looked at the sky whenever they passed through a partial clearing in order to find the Southern Cross and determine in which direction the trail was bending. Wherever he could, he made a mental note of some landmark they were passing and added it to the ones he had observed previously.

After a time he kept repeating a jingle to himself which went, Tree over trail, muddy creek, rock on trail, bushes across. Actually there was no reason for him to do it; the trail led only from 1st Battalion to A Company. But this was a habit he had formed on his first patrols. He did it instinctively by now.

And another part of his mind had a quiet pride that he was the man upon whom the safety of the others depended. This was a sustaining force which carried him through dangers his will and body would have resisted. During the march with the antitank guns, there had been many times when he wanted to quit; unlike Croft, he had felt it no contest at all. He would have been perfectly willing to declare the task beyond his strength and give up, but there was a part of his mind that drove him to do things he feared and detested. His pride with being a sergeant was the core about which nearly all his actions and thoughts were bound. Nobody see in the darkness like Martinez, he said to himself. He touched a branch before his extended arm and bent his knees easily and walked under it. His feet were sore and his back and shoulders ached, but they were ills with which he no longer concerned himself; he was leading his squad, and that was sufficient in itself.

The rest of the squad, strung out behind, was experiencing a variety of emotions. Wilson and Toglio were sleepy, Red was alert and brooding — he had a sense of foreboding. Goldstein was miserable and bitter, and the tension of creeping down a trail in the black early hours of the morning made him gloomy and then sad. He thought of himself dying without friends nearby to mourn him. Wyman had lost his power to recuperate; he was so tired that he plodded along in a stupor, not caring where he went or what happened to him. Ridges was weary and patient; he did not think of what the next hours would bring him, nor did he lose himself in contemplation of his aching limbs; he just walked and his mind drifted slowly like a torpid stream.

And Croft; Croft was tense and eager and impatient. All night he had been balked by the assignment of the squad to a labor detail. The sounds of battle he had been hearing all night were goading to him. His mind was buoyed by a recurrence of the mood he had felt after Hennessey's death. He felt strong and tireless and capable of anything; his muscles were as strained and jaded as any of the men's, but his mind had excluded his body. He hungered for the fast taut pulse he would feel in his throat after he killed a man.

On the map there was only a half mile between 1st Battalion and A Company, but the trail doubled and curved so often that it was actually a mile. The men in recon were clumsy now and uncertain of their footing. Their packs sagged, their rifles kept sliding off their shoulders. The trail was crude; originally a game wallow, it had been partially enlarged, and in places it was still narrow. A man could not walk without being scratched by the branches on either side. The jungle was impenetrable at that point, and it would have taken an hour to cut one's way a hundred feet off the path. In the night it was impossible to see anything and the smell of the wet foliage was choking. The men had to walk in single file, drawn up close. Even at three feet they could not see one another, and they plodded down the trail with each man grasping the shirt of the man before him. Martinez could hear them and judge his distance accordingly, but the others stumbled and collided with one another like children playing a game in the dark. They were bent over almost double, and the posture was cruel. Their bodies were outraged; they had been eating and sleeping with no rhythm at all for the last few hours. They kept loosing gas whose smell was nauseating in the foul dense air. The men at the rear had the worst of it; they gagged and swore, tried not to breathe for a few seconds, and shuddered from fatigue and revulsion. Gallagher was at the end of the file, and every few minutes he would cough and curse. "Cut out the goddam farting," he would shout, and the men in front would rouse themselves for a moment and laugh.

"Eatin' dust, hey, boy," Wilson muttered, and a few of them began to giggle.

Some of them began to fall asleep as they walked. Their eyes had been closed almost the entire march, and they drowsed for the instant their foot was in the air and awakened as it touched the ground. Wyman had been plodding along for many minutes with no sensation at all; his body had grown numb. He and Ridges drowsed continually, and every now and then for ten or fifteen yards they would be completely asleep. At last they would weave off the trail and go pitching into the bushes stupidly before regaining their balance. In the darkness such noises were terrifying. It made the men uncomfortably aware of how close they were to the fighting. A half mile away some rifles were firing.

"Goddammit," one of them would whisper, "can't you guys keep quiet?"

The march must have taken them over half an hour, but after the first few minutes they no longer thought about time. Crouching and sliding through the mud with their hands on the man in front became the only thing they really knew; the trail was a treadmill and they no longer concerned themselves with where they were going. To most of them the end of the march came as a surprise. Martinez doubled back and told them to be quiet. "They hear you coming for ten minutes," he whispered. A hush settled over the men, and they trod the last hundred yards with ridiculous precautions, tensing every muscle whenever they took a step.

There was no barbed wire, nor any clearing at A Company. The trail divided in a quadruple fork which led to different emplacements. A soldier met them where the path broke up and led the squad along one of the footpaths to a few pup tents pitched in the middle of some foliage. "I got Second Platoon," he told Croft. "I'm just about a hundred yards down the river. Your squad can sleep in these holes tonight, and set up a guard right along here. They's two machine guns set up for you."

"What's doing?" Croft whispered.

"I dunno. I heard they expect an attack all up and down the line about dawn. We had to send a platoon over to C Company early tonight, and we been holding down the whole outpost here with less than a platoon." He made a rustling sound in the darkness as he wiped his hand against his mouth. "C'mere, I'll show you the setup," he said, grasping Croft's elbow. Croft slipped his arm free; he hated to have anyone touch him.

They went a few feet along the path, until the sergeant from A Company halted before a foxhole. There was a machine gun mounted in front, its muzzle just projecting through a fringe of bushes. Croft peered through the foliage and in the faint moonlight was able to see a stream of water and a strip of beach bordering it on either side. "How deep is the river?" he asked.

"Aw, it's four, five feet maybe. That water ain't going to stop them."

"Any outposts forward of here?" Croft asked.

"Nothing. And the Japs know right where we are. Had some patrols up." The soldier wiped his mouth again and stood up. "I'll show you the other machine gun." They walked along a stubbly path cut through the jungle about ten feet from the river's edge. Some crickets were chirping loudly, and the soldier trembled a little. "Here's the other one," he said. "This is the flank." He peered through the bushes and stepped out onto the strip of beach. "Look," he said. Croft followed him. About fifty yards to their right, the bluffs of Watamai Range began. Croft looked up. The cliffs rose almost vertically for perhaps a thousand feet. Even in the darkness, he felt them hovering above him. He strained his eyes and thought he saw a swatch of sky where they ended but could not be certain. He had a curious thrill. "I didn't know we were that close," he said.

"Oh, yeah. It's good and it's bad. You don't have to worry about them coming around that end, but still we're the flank. If they ever hit here hard, there ain't much to hold them." The soldier drew into the bushes again and exhaled his breath slowly. "I'll tell you these two nights we been out here give me the creeps. Look at that river. When there's a lot of moonlight it just seems to shine, and you get jittery after a while looking at it."

Croft remained outside the jungle edge, looking at the stream that curved away at the right and flowed parallel to the mountains. It took a turn toward the Japanese lines just a few yards before the first walls of the bluff began, and he would be able to see everything on that side. To the left the stream ran straight for a few hundred yards like a highway at night, sunk between high grassy banks. "Where are you?" he asked.

The soldier pointed to a tree which projected a little from the jungle. "We're just on this side of it. If you got to get to us, go back to the fork and then take the trail at the far right going away from here. Yell 'Buckeye' when you come up."

"Okay," Croft said. They talked for a few more minutes, and then the other soldier hooked his cartridge belt. "Jesus, I'll tell ya, it'll drive ya crazy spending a night here. Just wilderness, that's all, and you stuck out at the end of it with nothing but a lousy machine gun." He slung his rifle and struck off down the trail. Croft looked at him for a moment and then went back to recon. The men were waiting by the three pup tents, and he showed them where the two machine guns were placed. Briefly he told them what he had learned and picked a guard. "It's three A.M. now," he told them. "There's gonna be four of us on one post and five on the other. We'll do it in two-hour shifts. Then the post that's only got four men will get the extra one for the next time around." He divided them up, taking the first shift at the flank gun himself. Wilson volunteered to take the other gun. "After Ah'm done, Ah'm gonna want to sleep right on through," Wilson said. "Ah'm tired of gittin' up right when Ah'm havin' a good dream."

The men smiled wanly.

"An' listen," Croft added, "if any trouble starts, the men that are sleeping are to git up goddam fast and move to help us. It's only a couple of yards from our tents to Wilson's machine gun, and it ain't much further to mine. It shouldn't be takin' you all more than about three hours to reach us." Again, a couple of men smiled. "Okay, that's about it," Croft said. He left them and walked over to his machine gun.

He sat down on the edge of the hole and peered through the bushes at the river. The jungle completely surrounded him, and, now that he was no longer active, he felt very weary and a little depressed. To counteract this mood, he began to feel the various objects in the hole. There were three boxes of belt ammunition and a row of seven grenades lined up neatly at the base of the machine gun. At his feet were a box of flares and a flare gun. He picked it up and broke open the breech quietly, loaded it, and cocked it. Then he set it down beside him.

A few shells murmured overhead and began to fall. He was a little surprised at how near they landed to the other side of the river. Not more than a few hundred yards away, the noise of their explosion was extremely loud; a few pieces of shrapnel lashed the leaves on the trees above him. He broke off a stalk from a plant and put it in his mouth, chewing slowly and reflectively. He guessed that the weapons platoon of A Company had fired, and he tried to determine which trail at the fork would lead to them in case he had to pull back his men. Now he was patient and at ease; the danger of their position neutralized the anticipation for some combat he had felt earlier, and he was left cool and calm and very tired.

The mortar shells were falling perhaps fifty yards in front of the platoon at his left, and Croft spat quietly. It was too close to be merely harassing fire; someone had heard something in the jungle on the other side of the river or they would never have called for mortars so close to their own position. His hand explored the hole again and discovered a field telephone. Croft picked up the receiver, listened quietly. It was an open line, and probably confined to the platoons of A Company. Two men were talking in voices so low that he strained to hear them.

"Walk it up another fifty and then bring it back."

"You sure they're Japs?"

"I swear I heard them talking."

Croft stared tensely across the river. The moon had come out, and the strands of beach on either side of the stream were shining with a silver glow. The jungle wall on the other side looked impenetrable.

The mortars fired again behind him with a cruel flat sound. He watched the shells land in the jungle, and then creep nearer to the river in successive volleys. A mortar answered from the Japanese side of the river, and about a quarter of a mile to the left Croft could hear several machine guns spattering at each other, the uproar deep and irregular. Croft picked up the phone and whistled into it. "Wilson," he whispered. "*Wilson!*" There was no answer and he debated whether to walk over to Wilson's hole. Silently Croft cursed him for not noticing the phone, and then berated himself for not having discovered it before he briefed the others. He looked out across the river. Fine sergeant I am, he told himself.

His ears were keyed to all the sounds of the night, and from long experience he sifted out the ones that were meaningless. If an animal rustled in its hole, he paid no attention; if some crickets chirped, his ear disregard them. Now he picked a muffled slithering sound which he knew could be made only by men moving through a thin patch of jungle. He peered across the river, trying to determine where the foliage was least dense. At a point between his gun and Wilson's there was a grove of a few coconut trees sparse enough to allow men to assemble; as he stared into that patch of wood, he was certain he heard a man move. Croft's mouth tightened. His hand felt for the bolt of the machine gun, and he slowly brought it to bear on the coconut grove. The rustling grew louder; it seemed as if men were creeping through the brush on the other side of the river to a point opposite his gun. Croft swallowed once. Tiny charges seemed to pulse through his limbs and his head was as empty and shockingly aware as if it had been plunged into a pail of freezing water. He wet his lips and shifted his position slightly, feeling as though he could hear the flexing of his muscles.

The Jap mortar fired again and he started. The shells were falling by the next platoon, the sound painful and jarring to him. He stared out on the moonlit river until his eyes deceived him; he began to think he could see the heads of men in the dark swirls of the current. Croft gazed down at his knees for an instant and then across the river again. He looked a little to the left or right of where he thought the Japanese might be; from long experience he had learned a man could not look directly at an object and see it in the darkness. Something seemed to move in the grove, and a new trickle of sweat formed and rolled down his back. He twisted uncomfortably. Croft was unbearably tense, but the sensation was not wholly unpleasant.

He wondered if Wilson had noticed the sounds, and then in answer to his question there was the loud unmistakable clicking of a machine-gun bolt. To Croft's keyed senses, the sound echoed up and down the river, and he was furious that Wilson should have revealed his position. The rustling in the brush became louder and Croft was convinced he could hear voices whispering on the other side of the river. He fumbled for a grenade and placed it at his feet.

Then he heard a sound which pierced his flesh. Someone called from across the river, "Yank, Yank!" Croft sat numb. The voice was thin and high-pitched, hideous in a whisper. "That's a Jap," Croft told himself. He was incapable of moving for that instant.

"Yank!" It was calling to him. "Yank. We you coming-to-get, Yank."

The night lay like a heavy stifling mat over the river. Croft tried to breathe.

"*We you coming-to-get, Yank.*"

Croft felt as if a hand had suddenly clapped against his back, traveled up his spine over his skull to clutch at the hair on his forehead. "Coming to get you, Yank," he heard himself whisper. He had the agonizing frustration of a man in a nightmare who wants to scream and cannot utter a sound. "We you *coming-to-get*, Yank."

He shivered terribly for a moment, and his hands seemed congealed on the machine gun. He could not bear the intense pressure in his head.

"We you coming-to-get, Yank," the voice screamed.

"COME AND GET ME YOU SONSOFBITCHES," Croft roared. He shouted with every fiber of his body as though he plunged at an oaken door.

There was no sound at all for perhaps ten seconds, nothing but the moonlight on the river and the taut rapt buzzing of the crickets. Then the voice spoke again. "Oh, we come, Yank, we come."

Croft pulled back the bolt on his machine gun, and rammed it home. His heart was still beating with frenzy "Recon . . . RECON, UP ON THE LINE," he shouted with all his strength.

A machine gun lashed at him from across the river, and he ducked in his hole. In the darkness, it spat a vindictive white light like an acetylene torch, and its sound was terrifying. Croft was holding himself together by the force of his will. He pressed the trigger of his gun and it leaped and bucked under his hand. The tracers spewed wildly into the jungle on the other side of the river.

But the noise, the vibration of his gun, calmed him. He directed it to where he had seen the Japanese gunfire and loosed a volley. The handle pounded against his fist, and he had to steady it with both hands. The hot metallic smell of the barrel eddied back to him, made what he was doing real again. He ducked in his hole waiting for the reply and winced involuntarily as the bullets whipped past.

BEE-YOWWWW! . . . BEE-YOOWWWW! Some dirt snapped at his face from the ricochets. Croft was not conscious of feeling it. He had the surface numbness a man has in a fight. He flinched at sounds, his mouth tightened and loosened, his eyes stared, but he was oblivious to his body.

Croft fired the gun again, held it for a long vicious burst, and then ducked in his hole. An awful scream singed the night, and for an instant Croft grinned weakly. Got him, he thought. He saw the metal burning through flesh, shattering the bones in its path. "AII-YOHHHH." The scream froze him again, and for an odd disconnected instant he experienced again the whole complex of sounds and smells and sights when a calf was branded. "RECON, UP . . . UP!" he shouted furiously and fired steadily for ten seconds to cover their advance. As he paused he could hear some men crawling behind him, and he whispered, "Recon?"

"Yeah." Gallagher dropped into the hole with him. "Mother of Mary," he muttered. Croft could feel him shaking beside him.

"Stop it!" he gripped his arm tensely. "The other men up?"

"Yeah."

Croft looked across the river again. Everything was silent, and the disconnected abrupt spurts of fire were forgotten like vanished sparks from a grindstone. Now that he was no longer alone, Croft was able to plan. The fact that men were up with him, were scattered in the brush along the bank between their two machine guns, recovered his sense of command. "They're going to attack soon," he whispered hoarsely in Gallagher's ear.

Gallagher trembled again. "Ohh. No way to wake up," he tried to say, but his voice kept lapsing.

"Look," Croft whispered. "Creep along the line and tell them to hold fire until the Japs start to cross the river."

"I can't, I can't," Gallagher whispered.

Croft felt like striking him. "Go!" he whispered.

"I can't."

The Jap machine gun lashed at them from across the river. The bullets went singing into the jungle behind them, ripping at leaves. The tracers looked like red splints of lightning as they flattened into the jungle. A thousand rifles seemed to be firing at them from across the river, and the two men pressed themselves against the bottom of the hole. The sounds cracked against their eardrums. Croft's head ached. Firing the machine gun had partially deafened him. BEE-YOWWWW! A ricochet slapped some more dirt on top of them. Croft felt it pattering on his back this time. He was trying to sense the moment when he would have to raise his head and fire the gun. The firing seemed to slacken, and he lifted his eyes cautiously. BEE-YOWWW, BEE-YOWWWW! He dropped in the hole again. The Japanese machine gun raked through the brush at them.

There was a shrill screaming sound, and the men covered their heads with their arms. BAA-ROWWMM, BAA-ROWWMM, ROWWMM, ROWWMM. The mortars exploded all about them, and something picked Gallagher up, shook him, and then released him. "O God," he cried. A clod of dirt stung his neck. BAA-ROWWMM, BAA-ROWWMM.

"Jesus, I'm hit," someone screamed, "I'm hit. Something hit me."

BAA-ROWWMM.

Gallagher rebelled against the force of the explosions. "Stop, I give up," he screamed. "STOP! . . . I give up! I give up!" At that instant he no longer knew what made him cry out.

BAA-ROWWMM, BAA-ROWWMM.

"I'm hit, I'm hit," someone was screaming. The Japanese rifles were firing again. Croft lay on the floor of the hole with his hands against the ground and every muscle poised in its place.

BAA-ROWWMM. TEEEEEEEEN! The shrapnel was singing as it scattered through the foliage.

Croft picked up his flare gun. The firing had not abated, but through it he heard someone shouting in Japanese. He pointed the gun in the air.

"Here they come," Croft said.

He fired the flare and shouted, "STOP 'EM!"

A shrill cry came out of the jungle across the river. It was the scream a man might utter if his foot was being crushed. "AAAIIIIII, AAAIIIIIIIII."

The flare burst at the moment the Japanese started their charge. Croft had a split perception of the Japanese machine gun firing from a flank, and then he began to fire automatically, not looking where he fired, but holding his gun low, swinging it from side to side. He could not hear the other guns fire, but he saw their muzzle blasts like exhausts.

He had a startling frozen picture of the Japanese running toward him across the narrow river. "AAAAIIIIIIIIIIIH," he heard again. In the light of the flare the Japanese had the stark frozen quality of men revealed by a shaft of lightning. Croft no longer saw anything clearly; he could not have said at that moment where his hands ended and the machine gun began; he was lost in a vast moil of noise out of which individual screams and shouts etched in his mind for an instant. He could never have counted the Japanese who charged across the river; he knew only that his finger was rigid on the trigger bar. He could not have loosened it. In those few moments he felt no sense of danger. He just kept firing.

The line of men who charged across the river began to fall. In the water they were slowed considerably and the concentrated fire from recon's side raged at them like a wind across an open field. They began to stumble over the bodies ahead of them. Croft saw one soldier reach into the air behind another's body as though trying to clutch something in the sky and Croft fired at him for what seemed many seconds before the arm collapsed.

He looked to his right and saw three men trying to cross the river where it turned and ran parallel to the bluff. He swung the gun about and lashed them with it. One man fell, and the other two paused uncertainly and began to run back toward their own bank of the river. Croft had no time to follow them; some soldiers had reached the beach on his side and were charging the gun. He fired point-blank at them, and they collapsed about five yards from his hole.

Croft fired and fired, switching targets with the quick reflexes of an athlete shifting for a ball. As soon as he saw men falling he would attack another group. The line of Japanese broke into little bunches of men who wavered, began to retreat.

The light of the flare went out and Croft was blinded for a moment. There was no sound again in the darkness and he fumbled for another flare, feeling an almost desperate urgency. "Where is it?" he whispered to Gallagher.

"What?"

"Shit." Croft's hand found the flare box, and he loaded the gun again. He was beginning to see in the darkness, and he hesitated. But something moved on the river and he fired the flare. As it burst, a few Japanese soldiers were caught motionless in the water. Croft pivoted his gun on them and fired. One of the soldiers remained standing for an incredible time. There was no expression on his face; he looked vacant and surprised even as the bullets struck him in the chest.

Nothing was moving now on the river. In the light of the flare, the bodies looked as limp and unhuman as bags of grain. One soldier began to float downstream, his face in the water. On the beach near the gun, another Japanese soldier was lying on his back. A wide stain of blood was spreading out from his body, and his stomach, ripped open, gaped like the swollen entrails of a fowl. On an impulse Croft fired a burst into him, and felt a twitch of pleasure as he saw the body quiver.

A wounded man was groaning in Japanese. Every few seconds he would scream, the sound terrifying in the cruel blue light of the flare. Croft picked up a grenade. "That sonofabitch is makin' too much noise," he said. He pulled the pin and lobbed the grenade over to the opposite bank. It dropped like a beanbag on one of the bodies, and Croft pulled Gallagher down with him. The explosion was powerful and yet empty like a blast that collapses windowpanes. After a moment, the echoes ceased.

Croft tensed himself and listened to the sounds from across the river. There was the quiet furtive noise of men retreating into the jungle. "GIVE 'EM A VOLLEY!" he shouted.

All the men in recon began to fire again, and Croft raked the jungle for a minute in short bursts. He could hear Wilson's machine gun pounding steadily. "I guess we gave 'em something," Croft told Gallagher. The flare was going out, and Croft stood up. "Who was hit?" he shouted.

"Toglio."

"Bad?" Croft asked.

"I'm okay," Toglio whispered. "I got a bullet in my elbow."

"Can you wait till morning?"

There was silence for a moment, then Toglio answered weakly, "Yeah, I'll be okay."

Croft got out of his hole. "I'm coming down," he announced. "Hold your fire." He walked along the path until he reached Toglio. Red and Goldstein were kneeling beside him, and Croft spoke to them in a low voice. "Pass this on," he said. "We're all gonna stay in our holes until mornin'. I don't think they'll be back tonight, but you cain't tell. And no one is gonna fall asleep. They's only about an hour till dawn, so you ain't got nothin' to piss about."

"I wouldn't go to sleep anyway," Goldstein breathed. "What a way to wake up." It was the same thing Gallagher had said.

"Yeah, well, I just wasn't ridin' on my ass either, waitin' for them to come," Croft said. He shivered for a moment in the early morning air and realized with a pang of shame that for the first time in his life he had been really afraid. "The sonsofbitchin' Japs," he said. His legs were tired and he turned to go back to his gun. I hate the bastards, he said to himself, a terrible rage working through his weary body.

"One of these days I'm gonna really get me a Jap," he whispered aloud. The river was slowly carrying the bodies downstream.

"At least," Gallagher said, "if we got to stay here a couple of days, the fuggers won't be stinkin' up the joint."

Collision Course

χ

from *Away All Boats*

by KENNETH DODSON

Man-made thunder, greater in din and scope than anything previously experienced, announced the dawning of D Day plus One, day of the main assault landing on Kwajalein. Since Brooks and his men had explored the reef the previous afternoon, small but important landings had been made on five lesser islands which dotted the reef clockwise to westward. Official plans called for capture of only four of these, but in the darkness, during a blinding squall of wind-beaten rain, strong current setting northward along the seaward face of the reef carried rubber rafts filled with men from the 7th Division Reconnaissance Troop to an unscheduled destination. Intending to land on Ninni Island, which flanked the deepwater pass through which the fleet must steam in order to enter the lagoon, they landed unknowingly on Gehh Island, where a sharp little skirmish took place which had been planned neither by Americans nor Japanese. Japanese military personnel, fishing in the nearby lagoon, had been caught in the hail of the early bombardment. Survivors fled for safety, hiding under the coconut palms of Gehh Island, where they were tracked down and with few exceptions were exterminated by Americans who accidentally stumbled ashore in the darkness.

After small but intense skirmishes, all five islands were captured, providing invasion forces with a preliminary toehold on the tremendous atoll. Flanks of the narrow deep-water entrance into the great lagoon were now protected. As soon as minesweepers cleared a passage, transports, carriers and men-of-war could enter. Enubuj, next to Kwajalein main island, had been captured, but not without the loss of two great radio towers which, in a ringlike waste of flat islets, nearly awash, had been a great help in identification. A battery of some sixty 105-mm howitzers, boated from transports, carried across the reef and landed on Enubuj, was now set up wheel to wheel, facing Kwajalein landing beach. Sharp barking of these cannon now joined the swelling chorus of naval explosions and their bite was felt on the strongly built but now crumbling defenses at the main island's southwestern tip, scene of Brooks's wading exploration the previous afternoon, and where the principal assault landing was to be attempted this day.

Yesterday's threatening weather had cleared, replaced now with a man-made hurricane stirred up by naval gun barrels and the artillery landed on Enubuj. Sulfurous fumes and smoke billowing from burning Japanese oil dumps almost completely clouded the fresh blue sky. Aboard the *Belinda*, in turn drifting and jockeying for position in the transport area, debarkation nets hung overside, sagging from recent clambering of soldiers debarking for island battle. Boat davits were empty, long arms of gray steel reaching overside like gigantic claws, wire boat falls with their heavy steel blocks swinging out then back, with doleful clatter against the hull at every roll. Watching from his bridge, Gedney divided his attention between the bustle of unloading preparations on his weather decks and on Sherwood's boat waves, now moving along the seaward side of the reef towards Kwajalein Island, some five thousand yards distant. MacDougall stood beside Gedney, his binoculars also trained on the distant landing craft. "Can you make out Sherwood?" Gedney asked. "Are you sure those are our boats?"

MacDougall lowered his glasses and wiped the lenses with a dry corner of shirttail. After all night on the bridge his sight was blurred from constantly watching the bobbing command boat. "Yes, sir. There he goes, just ahead of the amtrack waves — right in line with Enubuj Island."

With pleased sounding, metronomic tones, Gedney began to review the operation out loud: "Bombardment groups deployed on both flanks. DD's 673 and 478 marking the line of departure off Red Beach. First assault waves transferred from *Belinda* to LST's 1020 and 1026, thence to Army alligators guided in by *Belinda* boat group. Brooks and Kruger to guide first wave. Boat officers from *Mears* and *Woodbridge* to guide second and third waves to Red Beach One. Sherwood then to bring troops for fourth, fifth and sixth waves to line of departure for transfer to LVT's. Tanks and bulldozers in LCM wave: Ensign Marty. Sherwood to coordinate. . . ."

MacDougall paid no particular attention to Gedney's measured tones. It seemed to him that they were part of this gigantic machinery for invasion, as if all of them were puppets moved about on endless treads, fear compressed within, actions automatic, in accordance with operations plans. Yet in spite of this he knew that Sherwood was out there on his own. Nothing said here except into the mike of the landing craft voice circuit could have the slightest effect on Sherwood's actions. I wonder if he's still trying to sing against all this racket, MacDougall thought, remembering Sherwood's predawn departure from the *Belinda*. Sherwood had climbed into his command boat singing, "Oh, What a Beautiful Morning" — singing at four in the morning before shoving off into the rainy, black unknown.

Daylight now, sun and blue sky after murk and rain, ephemeral beauty of clean white cloud scurrying from the windward horizon to join smoke of exploding bomb and shell and great smudge pots of burning Japanese fuel storage. Battle would change this beauty soon enough, yet while it remained, words of Sherwood's song returned to filter through MacDougall's thoughts. Sherwood was out there now — out where MacDougall would like to be — taking the greater chances, herding boats and men in helmets along that offshore reef towards the inevitable moment of H Hour — floundering and splashing over coral and out to the sea to attack an enemy dug in behind battered concrete and twisted steel. The carefree tune from Sherwood's lips returned to MacDougall now, intensified, beat out with the tremendous authority of one-ton projectiles, carried by the wind blowing from clean, open sea, passing over gray ships now belching not only projectiles and burned gunpowder but men, materiel . . . passing over boats and crawling amtracks, flung with the awesome speed of bullets upon frightened little men on the island shore who waited for invasion and death. . . . Ridiculous thought, yet so real to MacDougall now that it seemed to him all must hear it, friend and enemy: the little Jap, ducking shot and shell, he must hear it too, and joining in the tremendous, mechanized chorus with his squeaking little voice must even now be singing a repetition into the winds of circumstance, committed beyond recall to his death:

> Oh, what a beautiful morning,
> Oh, what a beautiful day
> I've got a beautiful feeling
> EVERYTHING'S COMING MY WAY! *

MacDougall looked at Captain Gedney. Surely he heard the song screaming out in the whine of passing shells. It was louder than earth-shaking explosions they watched; it was the loudest thing in the world.

Gedney's face was impenetrable; whether he was making complicated mental computations of time, speed and distance or merely following progress of Sherwood's boats along the reef, MacDougall could only guess. At last Gedney said in a casual tone of voice, "It's a nice morning." Then he noticed the startled look on MacDougall's face. What's got into him, Gedney wondered; he's usually calm enough.

Seconds of the final hour ticked by while widely dispersed units of the Army and Navy approached the culmination of months of planning and practice. The scene was like the reconnaissance photos and battle maps expanded to full size and seen in three dimensions with sound and smell added. Regardless of the hesitancy of any given unit, or of fear in individual human hearts, the overall impression was one of relentless mechanical precision and overwhelming power. So it appeared from the bridge of the *Belinda*, even as bells jangled and excited orders were given to keep her on station and to prevent collision with sister ships often drifting closer than a single ship length away. . . . And so it must have appeared to the enemy crouching behind crumbling revetments at Red Beach — to those who were still physically able to see the tidal wave of invasion before it swept over them.

While artillery set up on Enubuj lobbed shells across the reef to drop on the focal point of attack, naval gunfire reached a crescendo of rapid fire. Hellcats dived, bombing and strafing the landing beaches. Ships numbered in the hundreds moved deliberately on exact missions prescribed by the operations plan, or else lay to in ordered groups, waiting like substitutes at a football game for word to rush into action. Hundreds of alligators clattered along the reef, herded by the Sherwoods, the Brookses and the Krugers from many ships, looking like columns of industrious ants. From close up this ant-like behavior was emphasized by the meandering approach to the beach of the almost unmanageable amphibious tractors in ragged lines abreast. Yet these clumsy armored craft were the heart of the expedition; it was for them that large ships deployed, and in preparation for their landing at Red Beach that the pre-landing bombardment thundered.

Finally, for the last time before landing hour, the sweep second hand in the large brass clock, eagerly watched now in the *Belinda*'s pilothouse, made its round. Gunfire lulled to an unaccustomed silence, awesome as the quiet blue eye of a hurricane. Their last bullets expended, strafing planes zoomed upward from the beach and returned to their carriers while the first wave came in. Amtracks lurched and floundered, boxlike bodies rising unevenly from the water, slithering across wet coral, pressing onward as close as they could get to the battered sea wall. Out came the infantrymen, moving quickly, without apparent hesitation — some swarming ashore from knee-deep water, others less fortunate dropping into potholes, staggering out dripping salt water, stripping protective Pliofilm from their rifles before crossing wavelike heaps of rubble and moving on into the graveyard of shattered coconut trees and men which was the southwestern tip of Kwajalein.

After the two minutes of silence required by plan, the guns opened fire again. Gone the tumultuous crescendo; fire deliberate now, sometimes in salvo, more often the startling crack of a single great fourteen-inch rifle, carefully aimed beyond friends and upon the enemy. The radio air was filled with messages from gun spotters, some on foot with the infantry, some aloft in toylike Piper Cubs: *Up five hundred yards. . . . Left two*

. . . Shoot the enemy, not the friend. Over the island of Kwajalein spread a stinking pall of smoke which the trade wind would not blow away for five bloody days.

At two in the afternoon, order came for transport groups to enter the lagoon through the narrow deep-water entrance between Ninni and Gea Islands, each ship to proceed independently. Shrill boatswain's mate's pipe sounded over the *Belinda's* PA, "Now trice up all debarkation nets. . . . Now go to your stations all the special sea detail. All hands man your battle stations." Tanks, field guns, ammunition and cans of water for troops in the battle line were left hanging in cargo slings while the *Belinda's* crew ran to battle and anchoring stations.

Gedney was pleased. "We've had enough of drifting outside the reef," he said to MacDougall. "We'll soon be anchored inside the reef, comparatively safe from submarines. . . . All engines ahead full."

Harrison, the navigator, raised an anxious face from his charts. "How about shore batteries, Captain?"

Gedney waved a negative in the air with his hand. "Shore batteries are the lesser evil. We can always move out of range. Besides, a shore battery is much easier to locate and engage than a submarine. . . . Flank speed, MacDougall. Come around on full right rudder."

"Right, full rudder, sir." Engine room annunciator clanged, ship surged ahead, swinging about her pivot point, then ranging along the reef towards the narrow entrance into the lagoon. Gedney began to hum a tune, startling the bridge messenger, who leaped out of the captain's pathway, then turned to stare.

"Proceed independently," said Gedney reflectively. He flavored the words, running the tip of his tongue about his lips as if they were sweet to taste. "Proceed independently. That's the order I like to hear. While we proceed independently, International Rules of the Road apply, and not even a battleship has precedence over the *Belinda* unless it is given to her by those impartial rules."

Bow began to cut the waves and fresh breeze whipped spray over the foredeck, soaking the anchor detail.

Harrison's lanky frame bent over his chart, his brows furrowed with concern while he plotted and replotted sets of bearings which refused to intersect on his inaccurate chart. "Watch your plot closely, Harrison," ordered Gedney. "What is the course and distance to the entrance?"

Harrison raised an unhappy face from the maze of bearings which gave him no definite answers. "I'm not positive, Captain . . . matter of island identification, perhaps. The operation plan clearly showed two large radio towers on Enubuj Island. I do not —"

"Get busy, Harrison, get busy. We will be at the entrance within three minutes." Gedney trotted out of the pilothouse to where MacDougall stood on the bridge wing, watching his bearings over the pelorus and estimating safe distance from the reef by eye. Gedney's eyes were shining with excitement. "I'm not worried about Harrison's plot," he said under his breath. "I just want *him* to worry a little. . . . His navigation at Maalaea Bay: *'The large island is Maui.'* I'll not let him forget that in a hurry."

MacDougall grinned, "With the sun shining we can see the reef line clearly, sir."

"Exactly. Much better than the charts. Hold her as close as you think safe. I want to beat the commodore inside." Gedney looked off to port. The squadron flagship *Woodbridge* was racing for the lagoon entrance on a more direct line than the *Belinda,* now streaking along the reef. "Watch the *Woodbridge,* MacDougall!" Gedney cried, ducking back to take his place at the pilothouse windows. "She's a little closer to the entrance, but the *Belinda* has the right of way and I am going to take it."

MacDougall watched the *Woodbridge* through his pelorus's sight vanes. He kept the hair wire on the flagship's white-frothed bow, watching the reflection of the compass bearing in the tiny mirror beneath the sight vane. "We're on collision bearing with the *Woodbridge,* Capt'n. Two-six-eight; no change."

"What are the engines doing by tachometer, Randall?"

"Eighty-three rpm and a bit, sir."

"Call the engine room; tell them we must have two full turns more."

"Aye, aye, sir."

Excited looks were exchanged between junior officers and enlisted men in the pilothouse. Only Harrison remained serious, frowning over his bearing plots, certain that the *Belinda* would crash either into the reef or into the flagship. The *Belinda* shuddered from the extra thrust of her screw. Shouts and clanging could be heard coming up through engine room ventilators. The bow rose higher, then fell deeper, slicing the clear sea water and sending sheets of wind-blown spray over the foredeck. The two ships were racing nearly at right angles to each other: *Woodbridge* heading straight towards the lagoon entrance, *Belinda* running parallel and just outside the reef. Randall stood on the port wing, taking distances with a stadimeter. "What is the range to the *Woodbridge?*" Gedney asked.

"Fifteen hundred yards, closing rapidly, Capt'n."

"Bearing, MacDougall?"

"Still steady, Capt'n. . . . Collision bearing. . . . Now it's moving a bit." MacDougall's voice rose with excitement. "We're beginning to draw ahead now, sir."

Gedney took a quick look at the gap in the reef through which he must thrust his ship, then swung about on his heel to watch the racing flagship.

A dozen binoculars were focused upon him from her bridge. "Look at them!" Gedney cried. "Staring at *me*; examining *me!* Why don't they put their noses into the International Rules of the Road, Article Nineteen: *When two steam vessels are crossing so as to involve risk of collision, the vessel which has the other on her own starboard side shall keep out of the way of the other.*"

The two ships rushed towards a point of intersection. "Range, nine hundred yards," called Randall.

"Bearing moving more rapidly now, Capt'n," called MacDougall, adding anxiously, "It doesn't look good to me. They should slow down and sheer astern of us."

Gedney seemed to ignore his officers. Except for quick glances at the narrow lagoon entrance to starboard, he kept his eyes on the flagship. At last, no longer able to contain himself, Gedney jumped up and down, pounding his right fist into his left palm, bioculars swinging violently from side to side like the pendulum of an old clock while he shouted across the water in the general direction of the *Woodbridge*, "Article Twenty-Two: *Every vessel which is directed by these rules to keep out of the way of another vessel shall, if the circumstances of the case admit, avoid crossing ahead of the other.*" The bridge watch, who with the exception of Willicut, the quartermaster, had never heard of the Rules of the Road, gaped at their captain with open mouths. Gedney paid no attention to them. His eyes were shining: his ship drawing ahead now; war, invasion, death on the beach — even the safe full of operation plans — all forgotten in the excitement of this moment. Once more the fist pounded into the palm as Gedney continued his chant. "Read Article Twenty-Three: *Every steam vessel which is directed by these rules to keep out of the way of another vessel shall, on approaching her, if necessary"* — Gedney's voice rose now to a triumphant shout — *"SLACKEN HER SPEED OR STOP OR REVERSE!"*

MacDougall and Randall exchanged glances, both entertained and concerned by Gedney's suddenly precipitous behavior. Such a stickler for rules! MacDougall was thinking. Yet he must hate them, he must. Look what he's doing with his precious ship when he gets a chance to throw rules back into the teeth of a commodore!

If Gedney felt any concern he failed to show the slightest inkling of it, even while the speeding ships closed to within eight hundred yards. "The commodore knows he's wrong," Gedney announced to his officers. "Look at that signal yard. Nothing there. If he had any rule back of him — any favorable interpretation of an unfavorable rule — he'd be throwing bunting at me by the mile. He's just bluffing, throwing his rank, which is not a rule of the road. He gave the order to proceed independently and I have the right of way. His officer of the deck may not know it, even his navigator possibly may not know it, but the commodore knows it. He knows the rules and he knows that he has allowed himself to get into an untenable position."

The ships still raced towards intersection. MacDougall sucked in his breath. The situation would be serious in a matter of seconds. Gedney, model of correct behavior that he was, was dangerously out of character. Could it be possible that the bombardment . . .

"Distance, seven hundred yards," called Randall.

"Time to head for the entrance, Capt'n," cried MacDougall.

"Not yet. . . . Not yet," shouted Gedney. "Steady as you go, quartermaster. . . . He must slow down first."

"Ha!" exclaimed Randall. "He must have heard you, Capt'n!" The flagship was coasting now, her propeller dragging, rudder swinging her conservatively and in accordance with Article Twenty-Two, towards the *Belinda's* speeding stern. Then a cloud of escaping steam shot from her funnel with a loud pop.

Gedney put his hand on the stooped shoulder of the navigator, who still struggled with his bearings. "Look, Harrison," he said. "The commodore has popped his safety valve! Right full rudder, quartermaster." Gedney rubbed the palms of his hands together as he watched MacDougall bring the ship's head up for the narrow lagoon entrance. "Relax, Harrison. Just look at the flagship, sitting on her tail while we lead the way into the lagoon. I remember back in Nineteen-Twelve . . . old Captain Gow got Admiral Brashler in a box off Hampton Roads, made him pop his safety valve. Of course that was in the days of coal burners —" Gedney broke off to point with happy satisfaction at the mixture of white steam and black smoke pouring from the *Woodbridge's* funnel — "even more spectacular than this."

Still at flank speed, the *Belinda* shot into the narrow breach between Gea and Ninni islands. Gedney's eyes still danced with excitement and pleasure, risk to his ship in a narrow and poorly charted channel did not seem to concern him in the slightest. "It's a clear day with the sun at our backs. We can see the reefs, MacDougall. You watch this side, I'll go watch to port." Gedney skipped lightly back through the crowded pilothouse, went to the bridge wing where he could look for coral close ahead. Still unconcerned he pointed along the reef. "There's Gehh Island," he said to Randall. "The second one to port. They captured it by mistake this morning — rubber rafts drifted past Ninni in the dark. Easy mistake to make on a black and windy night, drifting along in a rubber raft. Just as well, too; the place was thick with Japanese."

MacDougall stood behind the pelorus, watching the reef, making sure that the *Belinda* kept in blue water and skirted the green and white shallows which would rip her bottom open. Gea Island was close to starboard now: pretty little place with a lookout dwelling high on stilts, poking above tops of unharmed coconut trees. He noticed a beached tug off Gehh — several Japanese dancing in and out of the pilothouse in wild excitement. "Captain," MacDougall called across the bridge, "there's —" His voice was drowned out by sudden clamor from the gun crews on the signal bridge above him.

"Look at them Japs! Can I shoot, Mr. Kelly? Can I shoot? Hey! Look at 'em, look at 'em, look at 'em!"

"No, no! Wait for orders."

A new voice above the others: "Shoot the yellow bellies!"

"Aw, Mr. Kelly, I got 'em in my sights. Lemme shoot."

Gedney jumped from bridge wing to pilothouse, sending his orderly spinning into a bulkhead, knocking a messenger flat. Gedney snapped on the PA and stuck his lips angrily into the microphone. "All guns hold fire. All guns hold fire. I will give the order to fire. No gun will be fired without orders. Our objective is Kwajalein, not a beached Japanese tug." Gedney stepped back to the open wing of the bridge, blue eyes mild again; all the anger had poured out of the man. He looked around at nearby land, coconut trees, native huts, canoes, bits of clearing all flowing back from his fast-moving ship. "Fine place for bearings, Harrison," he remarked mildly. "If you don't know where you are now, you'd better toss your binoculars into those coconut trees."

Fresh wind blew in from seaward, pressing battle smoke back upon Kwajalein. Clear, deep water reflected blue sky; shallows revealed themselves in lustrous emerald greens; white sand bars dazzled the eyes. MacDougall was happy, unworried in the sure knowledge of his work, the battle momentarily remote. Keep in blue water and be safe; use the eyes seamen had before charts. Harrison stood beside him, looking unhappily at the coconut trees. MacDougall liked the kindly Harrison, yet he was amused that science had failed this former schoolmaster to midshipmen. If Harrison could only realize that sometimes you drive a ship just like a car down a country road — only Gedney would never let Harrison guess. Harrison was the assigned navigator, officially responsible for operational exactitudes. Here on the bridge were three other men who could have done the job for him, but one was his commanding officer, the other two his juniors in rank. It was a crazy system.

The last yard of white reef came abeam. Right ahead lay a sand bar. "Time to turn now, Capt'n," called MacDougall.

"Right full rudder," shouted Gedney. The *Belinda* came around, steaming close along the reef once more, but this time doubled back on her track and within the lagoon. Ahead was Kwajalein Island, torn and shaken with explosions, nearly covered with a murky blanket which was half burning oil, half burned powder.

The fresh beauty of Gea Island faded astern. The *Belinda* steamed alongside Enubuj Island, where a landing had been made the previous afternoon, now a shambles of broken palms and wrecked buildings. Over the whole drooped ruins of the two giant radio towers for which they had looked. "Oh!" exclaimed Harrison. "There's my landmark. No wonder I couldn't find the towers." MacDougall barely heard Harrison's words. More than sixty cannon, placed wheel to wheel near the eastern tip of Enubuj, cracked in a ragged staccato of rapid fire as they poured a barrage just ahead of the slowly advancing battle line of Kwajalein. The *Belinda* moved on, paralleling the bare reef where Brooks had made his reconnaissance the previous afternoon. Fresh wind blew over this bare reef between Enubuj and Kwajalein, yet it could do nothing with the death pall which hung over the battlefield. Carried by some fickleness of the upper air, pressed downward by the weight of its noxious gasses, littered with scorched paper and tiny fragments of tree and dwelling, it fell now upon the decks of the *Belinda*. It brought the smell of many burning things, a sweetish, kerosene-like smell. . . . And mixed with it was the stink of death.

Gedney anchored the *Belinda* close to Kwajalein in fifteen fathoms of water, using barely enough chain to hold her there, keeping an anchor watch at the windlass to heave up should the *Belinda* be required to run from air or submarine attack — it was conceivable that Japanese submarines lurked within this great lagoon — or to veer more chain should the ship drift towards the reef. After them followed other transports, and squadrons of LST's. Anchors splashed and chain rattled from hawse pipes all about. Carriers steamed nearly to the north horizon within the lagoon, then turned and headed full speed into the wind, launching and taking on planes. Battleships, cruisers and destroyers paraded along the beach, half hidden in smoke from their own guns and from the dying island.

"No word yet from Sherwood or O'Bannion?" asked Gedney petulantly.

"No, sir. Not yet."

Gedney stamped his foot angrily on the deck, jumped back into his high seat and began to thumb rapidly through a stack of radio dispatches. At this moment an inexpertly handled landing craft, returning from the beach, crashed into the ship's side, just below the bridge. Hearing the sound and feeling the light shudder echoing through his ship, Gedney came down from his chair again, rushed to the wing and looked down angrily. "Get me a megaphone — a megaphone," he demanded in a furious whisper. When a messenger brought one on the run, Gedney grasped it, aimed it at the dungaree-clad coxswain. "Put on your helmet and life jacket don't you know how to handle a boat where is Mr. Sherwood?" Gedney shouted in one angry exhalation. The coxswain stared up at the bridge, mouth half open, tanned young face smeared with grime and dried sweat. The boy looked completely baffled. It was obvious that he had no information for his captain. Gedney threw down the megaphone, allowing it to bounce towards the corner of the bridge while he returned to the stack of dispatches.

Randall came over from the port wing. "Look at the *Woodbridge*," he said to MacDougall. "She's calling us; looks mighty important, bridge almost covered with flag hoists."

"Trying to make up for losing that race with us."

"No doubt." A bell clanged sharply in the pilothouse. "Signal bridge," said Randall, heading for the pilothouse. "Bridge, aye."

"Signal from the *Woodbridge*, sir. LST 627 ordered alongside *Belinda* to take on thirty thousand gallons fresh water."

"Understood," said Randall, making a face. "That takes care of the shower I was going to have tonight." Gedney glared at Randall and jumped down from his high chair again. He's stewing over the boats and this uncertain anchorage, thought Randall, quite undisturbed. "There's the 627, Capt'n, board on the starboard beam."

Randall gave instructions to a boatswain's mate and the PA called out: "Now the first division, stand by to receive LST 627 alongside, starboard side number three hatch. . . . Now the water-king report to the log room." The bald-headed water-tender who was charged with the pumping of all water tanks turned from the rail where he had been watching the burning shore line and headed on the run for the chief engineer's office. Seamen climbed down from gun platforms and left cargo winches to get mooring lines ready.

Pappy Moran rolled down the foredeck, shouting, "Stand clear, soldiers. Stand clear of the side."

Infantrymen from platoons being held in reserve moved grudgingly back from the rail. Up on the bridge, Gedney and MacDougall watched the approach of LST 627. "She's coming in too fast," said MacDougall.

"Yes," said Gedney, "much too fast. When he backs down, his bow will fall off the wind." True to prediction, the LST swept up splendidly, while her engines churned madly astern in an unsuccessful attempt to overcome headway. Then the wind caught her high bow. LST 627 shuddered, wavered, then swung rapidly towards the *Belinda* in a wild yaw which could never be controlled by engines or rudder.

"It's one of those ribbon-clerk skippers," said MacDougall in angry concern. "Shall I yell at him to drop his port anchor, Capt'n?"

"Certainly not," snapped Gedney. "That young fool may indeed be a ribbon clerk, but remember, he is the commanding officer of that . . .

commissioned . . . thing. Rank does not permit us to give orders to a commanding officer, no matter how junior, no matter how ignorant, as long as he is at the conn of his own ship."

By this time the LST was too deep into trouble for either advice or anchors to do any good. The young junior lieutenant on her foredeck froze into immobility. Around him were line handlers, rushing up now with limp-looking fenders which they hung overside. "Lot of good that will do," growled MacDougall. "Look at the boy on the burning deck!" Randall called out a warning through the *Belinda*'s PA and Pappy Moran's gravel voice urged his men to get hot with fenders: substantial lumps of old rope woven together. These were gotten overside just as the LST crashed into the *Belinda*'s side — right between two fenders — and buried her anchor out of sight in the *Belinda*'s hull.

The *Belinda* lurched at the impact. Sounds of ruptured steel plate and buckling frames momentarily drowned out din of bombarding cannon. Hardly knowing how he got there, MacDougall found himself two decks below the bridge, shouting to crowds of enlisted men on the two vessels. "Don't just stand there gaping! Get out your mooring lines and hang on. Do you want her to surge back and crash us again?" Not six feet from MacDougall the young junior lieutenant scrambled to his feet, laughing in the foolish, embarrassed manner of one who did not know what to do about the situation. Feeling himself being roughly thrust aside from behind, MacDougall turned angrily around, only to see that he was being pushed by Captain Gedney, whose face was livid with rage.

Gedney took MacDougall's place, hung out over the railing and shook his finger at the junior lieutenant of LST 627. "Laugh, you driveling idiot!" he screamed. "It's my ship you're wrecking!"

The junior lieutenant gaped back at Gedney, too overwhelmed by his rank and his anger to make any reply whatsoever. Now Gedney heard a respectfully urgent voice at his back, and turned to be confronted by Harrison. "The hull board, sir," suggested the navigator. "Shall we survey damage, sir?"

Swallowing, Gedney regained his composure. "Yes, by all means. Then report to me." Gedney swung forward abruptly and, as his crew fell away before him, ran lightly back up the ladder to his bridge.

Searching methodically for damage, Harrison came to a crowd about the entrance to the troop officer's head on the deck below. Worming his way into this large compartment, he was startled to catch a glimpse of the LST through an anchor-shaped aperture punched in the side of the *Belinda* just above a toilet seat. The adjacent seat was occupied by an artillery major who sat quietly puffing on his pipe in calm detachment from the furor all about him. Fraser, the *Belinda*'s first lieutenant, was on the scene with his damage control party. "Bring in the shoring, Chips," he yelled to his carpenter. Harrison walked to the hole in the ship's side and bent his lanky frame to peer more closely at the jagged edges.

Just then the artillery major poked his head around the thin partition to confront Harrison. "What caliber?" asked the major.

Harrison chuckled all the way to the bridge. Before reporting to Gedney he told Randall about the major in the troop officers' head.

"Wasn't he scared at all?" asked Randall.

"He didn't seem to be," Harrison said. "But if he was, he was in a good place for it."

Harrison began his report to Gedney, who was now concerned with other matters and waved him aside. Sitting tensely, one leg thrown over the metal arm of his high chair, Gedney aired his indignation in a loud voice. "Messages; thousands of messages filling the air — not a single one of the slightest use to me, or that can be understood for that matter. Such utter lack of discipline and order: everyone shouting at once! Meanwhile, where is Sherwood? Where is O'Bannion? Why have I not heard from them?"

Robinson, the communications officer, gave up trying to dig a hole in the steel deck with the toe of his right shoe. "I'm sure they're trying to get through, Captain. I have two Six-hundred W's on their circuit — continuous watch kept on both of them."

"Can't you cut in another circuit?"

"No, sir. We're on the only bands authorized for ship-to-shore."

Gedney whirled around, jerked a thick, mimeographed volume from his bulkhead bookshelf and thumbed through the Communications Plan for the operation. "That's right," he conceded. "Well, do something, Robinson; don't just stand there. I must hear from the beachmaster and the boat group. Hundreds of men worked for years to design and build your equipment, the best communications procurable. I have told you many times that the main battery of an attack transport consists of her boats. We must maintain control of our main battery at all times." Gedney's voice rose nearly to a scream. "Yet this is the best you can do! Listen!" Gedney pointed to the TBS speaker on the bulkhead just above his seat.

Above incessant roar of static and overlapping syllables, certain sounds rather than sentences could be identified: "Blah — zing babel bombard — proceed — pendently, form on guide eighteen thousand, I repeat eight — Sycamore, this is Spinach — twenty-five — raise your — blah — dangering own forces — itch Roger, Wilco, over and —"

"Just listen to that!" exclaimed Gedney. "All the wonders of modern science! They had all that racket thousands of years ago in the Tower of Babel. But can I get Sherwood? Can I get O'Bannion? No!"

Momentary silence from the TBS, then a crystal-clear message: "Punchbag, this is Bounder. Reference your work request of zero five four eight dash seventeen, I say again repairs to dishwashing machines will be performed by ship's personnel Xray initial."

The babel took over again. MacDougall stirred. "Listen to that. Six weeks ago, back in Pearl, they ask to get a dishwasher repaired and some jackass waits until D Day to say, 'No.' Does he think they've been eating on the deck for a month, waiting for him to make up his mind?"

Gedney had regained his professional mask. He looked disapprovingly at MacDougall. "Perfectly in order," he said. "No doubt taken in correct sequence from the flag secretary's message board." Gedney considered his statement. It was logical; it was proper, but there was no comfort or help in it. "MacDougall," he said, the words blurting out suddenly, "I want you to get into the next shorebound landing craft. Go find Sherwood and O'Bannion. See what has happened, then report to me at once."

The Hunter and the Hunted

✗

from *Wolfpack*

by WILLIAM HARDY

In the weird half-light of the conning tower, Terence Reardon strained his eyes to read the illuminated dial on his watch. It was almost seven-thirty. His mind hurriedly translated that to read nineteen-thirty. His instincts were still basically those of the civilian, Reardon thought. Even with the matter of telling time, he had not yet brought himself to think naturally in military terms.

Nineteen-thirty. It would be dark enough now to surface. He issued the orders which would send the *Hagfish*'s crew into the busy routine of preparing the submarine for its return from its natural habitat. How strange, he reflected, that in such a short time a man could come to feel more secure under the water than out in God's fresh, clean air. There was safety beneath the sea. The *Hagfish*, ungainly and awkward on the surface, was transformed into the most graceful of vessels when it sank into its element.

Nineteen-thirty. They had been running submerged since the middle of the afternoon when the Japanese aircraft, which had taken the *Remora* by surprise, had forced the *Hagfish* to dive also. Reardon's submarine, however, had evidently not been detected by the planes. Since that time he had been keeping watch on the convoy as it pulled together. The Japanese strategy soon became evident to him. They would try to protect themselves against the submarines which they knew were to the rear and then proceed into Formosa after dark. The additional planes which had been sent out made it unfeasible for Reardon to attack while it was still light. Darkness would offer him the same protection which it afforded the enemy. He had spent most of the time since the dive evaluating the changing situation. He had never before fought a night battle. There were rules he might apply, of course, but most of them would be empirical — created to fit the situation.

Concern over the fate of the other two submarines gnawed at him. He had actually heard the attack on the *Remora* and surmised what was taking place. He had no knowledge of the whereabouts or condition of the *Lamprey*. Since the *Hagfish* was unable to transmit or receive radio messages in her submerged condition, he had to assume that he was now operating independently.

"Boat prepared to surface, Captain." The quartermaster's voice was soft in his ear.

Reardon nodded. The bridge personnel which included himself and the two lookouts were wearing red goggles to prepare their eyes for night vision.

We are like creatures from some other world, he thought, readying ourselves to invade an alien people.

"What's the picture, sound?"

The sailor on the sonar rotated the wheel slowly and carefully, then looked up. "No great change, Captain. There're still those four big ships to port. Range is still about ten thousand yards to the nearest one. The escorts seem to be running the same kind of pattern around them."

"Very well. Stand by to surface."

We are from another world. There can be no similarity between us and the men up there whom we will try to kill and who will try to kill us in return. It is impossible that like creatures should want to destroy each other. It is not the weird red goggles, or the fact that we are beneath the water that makes us from another world. We are from a world where war and killing is not a way of life but a means of preserving life. We are from a world that has an Elizabeth in it, and they are from a world which would destroy ours. That is why we try to kill them. That is why . . .

"All right, Turner," he muttered to the quartermaster. The sailor cranked the alarm, and, as the third blast of the klaxon horn died away, Reardon's voice called into the intercom.

"Surface! Surface! Surface!"

The *Hagfish* gave a convulsive shudder as the high-pressure air shot into her ballast tanks, forcing the water out. Below in the control room, the men on the diving station were spinning wheels, tilting the bow and stern planes to point the submarine's way to the surface.

"Four oh feet!" Bill Persons was handling the surfacing procedure. "Three five feet — three oh feet!"

Reardon put one hand on the quartermaster's shoulder. "Crack the hatch!"

The sailor was up the ladder quickly, undogging the hatch handwheel. Air began to blow in through the slightly open hatch. A few drops of water sprayed through.

"Pressure one-half inch." This from Persons. Then, "Two five feet, Captain. Holding steady."

"Open the hatch!"

As the quartermaster finished undogging the hatch and snapped open the safety latch, Reardon was up the ladder behind him. The heavy bronze hatch cover, propelled by the action of a large coil spring, heaved open with a loud rush of air as the latch was released by the quartermaster. Reardon, followed by the two lookouts, gained the dripping surface of the bridge a moment later.

Slowly and deliberately, he scanned the horizon. It was a clear night, with no moon. He quickly made out the Japanese ships off his port quarter.

"All clear aft, Captain." The lookouts' first job had been to search the after one hundred and eighty degrees sector.

Reardon acknowledged. He was not surprised. He knew what lay astern. Land was there. The Japanese would not have to worry about his escaping in that direction. He knew also that beneath him there was less than one hundred feet of water. There would not be a very good chance of escaping in that direction either. He recalled his conversation with Roger Lewis that morning. Was he going to be afraid? It was a possibility.

Leaning over the intercom, he called, "Open the main induction. Start the low-pressure blow."

The routine procedure of surfacing had to go hand in hand with the preparation for battle. He heard the main induction valve, through which the air for the diesels came into the boat, open with a loud thump. It seemed illogical that such a noise could not be heard by the men out there on the Japanese ships.

Another, and even louder, sound now came from below — a screech like some wild beast in mortal pain, wavering, swelling. The turbo blow had commenced. Reardon bent over the speaker again.

"Run the blow five minutes."

The sea was moderate. The *Hagfish*, her decks almost awash, rode sluggishly in the water. Now, as the turbo blow forced large amounts of air into the ballast tanks, the submarine gradually lifted herself to a more seaworthy attitude. Five minutes was not really a long enough time, but Reardon did not want to delay any longer than that.

"Quartermaster to the bridge."

In a moment, the quartermaster, Dave Tanzi, stood beside him. Tanzi would be Reardon's voice throughout the surface attack, using the battle telephone to relay all orders to the men below decks. Reardon noticed that Tanzi was wearing his steel helmet. He had forgotten all about that bit of gear. So had the lookouts. He ordered the steel hats sent up. He felt rather foolish somehow with the thing on his head, like a small boy playing soldier.

He grinned to himself. *Don't be sorry, be safe.* What the devil was that for? Soap or underarm deodorant?

"Battle stations, surface."

Dave Tanzi repeated the order into his battle phone, and below, Reardon heard the alarm sounding its clanging message throughout the boat.

"Battle stations manned and ready, Captain."

"Very well."

The wail of the turbo blow subsided, then died away to silence. Reardon took a long look at the dim shapes of the Japanese ships on the horizon. Radar had been feeding him information which indicated that the bulk of the convoy must be gathering quite near him. There was no longer any further need in relying on radar, he decided. He had plenty of shipping where he could see it without having to worry about radar.

"Come left to two two five."

He had been running on a course which was roughly parallel to that of the ships. Now it was time for him to close. He still felt remarkably calm, but there was a slight throbbing in his left temple. He tried to ignore it in his concentration on the task at hand. As the *Hagfish*'s bow swung to port, he drew a deep, long breath. This was no longer the classroom or the drawing board or the carefully considered calculations on a sheet of paper. This was real. The throbbing increased.

"Steady on two two five."

"Very well. All ahead two thirds."

They were on their way! What do you do to stop the throbbing — to keep the palms from sweating — to keep the mind from panic? Terence Reardon knew only one thing to do. He thought about the problem. His mind calculated distances and times like a singer doing vocal warm-ups or an athlete loosening taut muscles before a contest. Torpedo speed — torpedo run — at flank speed the *Hagfish* would cover one thousand yards in how many minutes — turning radius — this is the work the brain must perform automatically in a little while. . . .

The picture on the horizon was coming clearer now. He could make out several ships in silhouette, and there were at least three escorts dashing about. One of these looked to be a destroyer. The other two were probably frigates. One of the latter was off the *Hagfish*'s starboard bow now. The other frigate and the destroyer were to port between *Hagfish* and the convoy.

"There's one of them ships heading this way, Captain!"

The lookout's shrill cry broke off his mental gymnastics. He sought for the escort — it was a frigate, and she was heading directly for the submarine. It was doubtful that the *Hagfish* had been sighted, but on its present course, the frigate would soon take care of that.

"Left twenty degrees rudder!"

The maneuver would swing the sub inside the approaching escort and, at the same time, continue to close with the ships of the convoy.

"Rudder is twenty left, Captain."

"Very well." He watched the frigate through his glasses as the *Hagfish*'s bow swung more and more away from the enemy craft.

"Meet her!" The swing slowed. "Steady as you go."

"Steady on one seven four, Captain."

"Steer one eight oh."

"Aye, aye."

The new course would take *Hagfish* in between the destroyer and the convoy if she continued undetected. The bow wake was a brilliant phosphorescence, and Reardon could not imagine its remaining unseen for very long. He considered reducing speed, but time was as vital a factor as was anonymity.

"Captain, those ships are beginning to pick up speed!"

It was true. In the time Reardon had used to avoid the frigate, the convoy had apparently received its orders to head for home. The ships were moving more rapidly, and their course had been altered in *Hagfish*'s direction. They were now closing the sub. The time factor had diminished suddenly. Reardon glanced behind him. The destroyer was off his starboard quarter now, well astern, but he realized that he would need a pair of eyes back there he could trust.

"Executive officer to the bridge!" Roger Lewis's usual battle station was in the conning tower, but this was a new situation. It called for new tactics. In a moment, Lewis stood beside him, and Reardon gave him the picture quickly.

The exec nodded. "I have it, Captain." He grinned. "Remember what I said about being scared? Forget it. This looks like fun!"

"If that destroyer pins us in here, it won't be fun. Keep loose back there, Roger."

The sound of his own voice startled him. It was harsh. It sounded frightened. Was he frightened? He did not know.

With Roger Lewis on station aft, Reardon turned his attention back to the approaching ships. The nearest one looked to be a medium-sized freighter. It would be his first target.

Fitting his binoculars into the TBT, he took a bearing. Radar data would be too confused now for any sort of accuracy on individual targets.

"Bearing — mark!" His finger pressed the button, and the information was relayed to the TDC operator below. He studied the freighter quickly. "Make the range to be one thousand yards. Angle on the bow is ten port. Estimate speed at eight knots."

He was aware of the throbbing again.

"Stand by forward tubes. Open outer doors."

Beside him, the quartermaster was repeating his orders. Now he bent over the TBT again.

"Bearing — mark!"

He studied the ship. Something was wrong. It looked bigger than he had thought. The range! He had misjudged the range! The ship was looming up ahead of him now. The range could not be much over four hundred yards!

"Right full rudder! All ahead emergency!"

Now was the time for the heart to stop and wait. Slowly, like a reluctant schoolboy dragging his way to class, the *Hagfish's* bow swung. He could see the freighter's bow wake, could see in detail the high masts, the bulky superstructure. There was one moment in the turn when the freighter's bow was pointing directly at the men who stood rigidly on the submarine's bridge. Then they slid away from it, and the Japanese ship crossed their wake a scant two hundred yards astern. There was no chance now that *Hagfish* could be undetected.

"Ease your rudder to twenty right!"

He wanted some distance between him and the ship. The submarine continued to turn, less sharply now.

"Stand by tubes one and two!"

"One and two tubes standing by!"

He watched as the freighter swung slowly back into his path.

"All ahead one third! Steady as you go!"

The range was now about five hundred yards. It was too close, he thought, but the die was cast.

Wait . . . wait . . . wait . . .

"Fire one! Fire two!"

The streaks of foam diverged from the submarine's bow. One of the fish was running erratically. Reardon watched it broach like some wanton game fish. The other one appeared to running true, but it was to no avail. The freighter's commanding officer was alerted. He was swinging around to put his stern to the *Hagfish*. Both torpedoes missed.

"Now we're in for it!" He was talking to himself, and the throbbing was gone. The battle was joined.

"Two big ships off the starboard bow, Captain!"

Suddenly the sky ahead of the *Hagfish* burst into flame. A flare had been fired, and its unexpected glare almost blinded Reardon. The two ships were clearly visible about five thousand yards ahead.

"Right full rudder! All ahead flank!"

As the *Hagfish* started its turn, Reardon looked back at the freighter which had escaped the first torpedoes he had ever fired as a commanding officer. There was something personal about this failure, he thought grimly, and he found himself trying desperately to recall in detail the exact conditions which had prevailed when he fired. Why had he missed? He would need the data in trying to evaluate the problem later on. The freighter was still changing course radically, her captain obviously not yet satisfied that his escape was complete.

"Rudder is full right, Captain. Engines answering all ahead flank."

He had fired when the freighter was bearing . . .

"Captain! How about a stern shot? Look at her!"

Roger Lewis was pointing frantically. Reardon stared uncomprehendingly for an instant, then the exec's meaning struck him. The freighter was now about one thousand yards astern to port. Its course change had put it on a heading which would take it directly across the *Hagfish*'s stern.

"Stand by tubes aft!"

He gave the order without any clear idea of what he was going to do. One lightning thrust of realization swept over him. Carefully planned attacks did not take into account the variables of battle. His decisions must be here and now, without the impediment of detailed analysis.

"Ease your rudder! Ease it!"

The submarine's swing slowed. Reardon watched the freighter closely.

"Steady as you go!"

The Japanese ship's captain was making his decisions on instinct also. He chose this instant to zig away, and his time of crossing the *Hagfish*'s stern was delayed by perhaps two minutes. It would be enough.

"Stand by eight and nine tubes! Set gyros zero, depth ten feet!"

He watched as the two adversaries' relative positions adjusted, then . . .

"All stopped! Steady as you go. Steady — steady . . . Stand by to shoot. . . ."

The instant was now!

"Fire eight! Fire nine!"

The *Hagfish* shuddered in her after parts as the fish were away. Reardon turned forward to locate the ships ahead of him. He had done all he could about the freighter.

"All ahead flank!"

He would not allow himself to look back yet. The new prey lay ahead, and he must seek it out and destroy . . .

WHAM!

"You got her, Captain! You got her!"

The sky lighted suddenly and violently. Like Sodom and Gomorrah, Reardon thought as he spun to watch the freighter in its death agony. Could he look back and escape the punishment that had befallen Lot's wife? The freighter was sinking rapidly. Compassion struggled briefly with the joy of victory in Terence Reardon and lost.

The two ships ahead of him were now just off the port bow. Someone else was shooting off flares, and he caught their silhouettes clearly. They looked to be tankers, big ones, riding low in the water.

"What's our course?"

"Three one four, Captain."

"Come left to two nine five."

Somewhere behind them he could hear what sounded like gunfire.

"There's an escort back there, Captain," Roger Lewis yelled at him. "I can see his guns, but I don't think he's spotted us. The freighter got in between him and us." The exec laughed boyishly. "He's just shooting for the hell of it."

Reardon bent over the TBT.

"Stand by for a new setup. Bearing — mark!"

He studied the nearest tanker. "Make the range three thousand — no twenty-five hundred yards. Angle on the bow — twenty port. Speed ten knots."

Now he turned his attention to the second tanker and planned rapidly how he would attack it. It was astern the first ship to starboard, probably about five hundred yards. Unknowingly the two Japanese captains were presenting *Hagfish* with a perfect attack setup.

"How's the reload coming forward?"

"All tubes ready, Captain." The response was immediate. He glowed with pride for those men down below. He could imagine the taunts that had passed forward from the after torpedo-room gang, rubbing the fact of their torpedoes' success into the salt of the wounds of failure of the fish from the forward tubes.

"Stand by all forward tubes. Conning tower, we will fire four torpedoes at this target. Stand by for a quick change of targets as soon as we have fired." He drew a deep breath. "A damned quick change!"

"I can see that escort, Captain. Looks like a can, but he's running right on by. Hasn't seen us yet!"

He nodded at Lewis's words. There was no time to think of escorts now.

"Stand by for a bearing! Stand by — mark!"

The leading tanker was a big one; probably it would go about twenty thousand tons.

"Angle on the bow is ten port. Make her speed twelve knots. Range two thousand yards. Stand by for a firing setup!"

The silence hung like a pall for one endless minute.

"Bearing — mark!" His finger pressed the button. "Mark . . . mark . . . mark . . ."

"Fire!"

Four times the *Hagfish* trembled as she spawned her deadly fish.

"Left full rudder! Stand by for a new target!"

He tried to ignore the four phosphorescent streaks that marked the courses of the torpedoes. Swiftly he fed the data on the second tanker to the TDC operator below.

Seconds crawled by . . . twenty, twenty-one, twenty-two, twenty-three . . .

WHAM! WHAM! WHAM!

From cutwater to wake, the leading tanker collected the salvo of torpedoes. The first one must have missed, Reardon realized, but the second one blew the ship's bow to pieces, and the third and fourth fish hit amidships and astern.

"Bearing — mark! Fire!"

Tubes five and six disgorged their fish, and the men on the *Hagfish*'s bridge watched in awe as the first tanker disappeared, leaving only a patch of blazing oil to mark the spot where it had been.

WHAM! WHAM!

Reardon had a chance to observe the second tanker just before it was hit. It was a medium-sized ship, but it took the torpedoes better than had its larger companion. Both fish hit near the bow, but the tanker did not go under immediately. It settled in the water for a little, then burst into flames, lighting up the sky with a brilliant orange glow.

"Left full rudder!" He was screaming, he knew. So was Roger Lewis. So were the lookouts. The fury of battle and killing was upon them like a mantle of fire.

Hagfish drove ahead, past the stricken tanker deeper into the heart of the convoy. By now the scene was one of the wildest confusion — a Dante's inferno of ships milling around, firing indiscriminately. Two more ships were attacked — a large cargo vessel was left listing heavily to port — a smaller freighter went down in a matter of ten seconds after taking three hits.

Reardon and Lewis watched a Japanese frigate take a direct hit from some ship's deck gun, and they roared with laughter, pounding each other on the back like small boys enjoying some indescribably funny joke.

Out of the melee, a cargo ship loomed up astern of the *Hagfish* a few hundred yards away. Two torpedoes from the stern tubes slammed into it, stopping the *maru* dead in the water. As it settled by the stern, Reardon heard the quartermaster screaming at him.

"Only three fish left, Captain. Three left!"

He looked around dazedly. Off to port he could see the glistening streaks of tracer fire. A shell exploded just ahead of the submarine, shooting a towering geyser of water into the air and spraying the men on the bridge.

"Lookouts below!" He shoved the quartermaster toward the hatch. There was no point in exposing the men needlessly now. Turning to his exec, he gestured wildly. "Roger, get below!"

"Captain, please, I want to stay!"

Reardon nodded. He understood. This was the man who had dreaded his own fear.

"Okay, Roger. Let's get the hell out of here!"

He thought he saw a clear place to port. Turning the *Hagfish* toward it, he poured on all the power they had. This was the time to be gone.

"Captain, look!"

Lewis was clawing at his arm. Bearing down on the submarine to port was a small cargo ship. Its purpose was obvious. A bare five hundred yards away, it was charging in to ram the *Hagfish*.

"All ahead emergency! Rig for collision!"

The two ships charged together like a pair of maddened animals. When the *Hagfish* was halfway across the rammer's bow, Reardon screamed, "Left full rudder!" The submarine heeled over violently. No more than one hundred feet apart, *Hagfish* and the Japanese ship slid by each other in the night. He could hear the cries of the men on the enemy's bridge and his own voice answering them as they screamed curses at each other. A gun was firing from the other ship, and Reardon heard a sound like someone throwing stones against the *Hagfish*'s side.

"Look . . ."

Roger Lewis had fallen against him. Reardon spun to catch him, nearly falling himself. The exec was slumped forward. There was something warm and wet on Reardon's hands. Pushing back the other man, he saw where his face had been.

Now there was no face.

When he had lowered the body down the hatch to the waiting hands below, Reardon straightened. He stood alone on the bridge now, more alone than he had ever been.

Somewhere back in the States, Connie Lewis was waiting at that moment, waiting for a man she would never see again. What was she thinking now? Were her thoughts of a man without a face? Hot tears ran down his cheeks, tears of anger and horror and shame. . . .

The ship was directly ahead of him, heading for the *Hagfish*. To port and to starboard were frigates. Their guns were blazing at him. There was only one way out.

"Stand by forward!" It was a hoarse, choking cry of a man in pain.

"Fire one!"

Forgive me, Connie!

"Fire two!"

Good-bye, Roger!

"Fire three!"

In the name of the Father and of the Son, and . . .

The first torpedo missed. The next two were solid hits. The ship rumbled to a stop, sinking rapidly. Wearily Reardon looked around him. The night was a holocaust of fire and death which he had wrought.

God help me!

In less than an hour, *Hagfish* had sunk five of the convoy's ships and damaged a sixth. All of her torpedoes were expended in that one frightful battle. Eluding the frigates, Reardon gave the order to submerge.

Hagfish's attack was done. Instead of the hunter, she now became the hunted.

Act of Charity

※

from *The Mountain Road*

by THEODORE H. WHITE

They had eaten lunch and it was now almost one o'clock. The smell of food mixed with the smell of bodies, but no one noticed. Though their bellies were full and heavy, a nervous indolence twitched them all, some pacing, some talking, Michaelson and Collins needling each other, the inaction scratching at all of them. Baldwin felt he should do something, and ordered the room policed. Idly, they fell to, piling the leftover food, the packages of hard biscuit, the little envelopes of sugar, the open tins of butter, the unopened cereals and jam back into the big cartons which were now overspilling in disorder.

Outside, finally, the snow was ending. Every now and then someone would open the door to peer out, leaving the door open for the welcome burst of fresh air which cut the heavy stuffiness of the room, then slamming it shut when the cold began to flood in, overwhelming the little heat from the charcoal fires. The last time the door had been opened, there was no doubt but that the snow was ending — it fluttered down in occasional gusts, but it was thin, and in the gusts it was difficult to tell whether the snow was falling from the sky or being lifted from the powder drifts in the street. The snow was no longer much reason for lingering, and Baldwin felt it was time to check the Ssuchuanese headquarters again. They were only seventy miles from Tushan and they ought to push on — at least part way.

He saw Kwan talking to Su-Piao and approached them.

"Will you ask him," he said to Su-Piao, "if he can go back to that divisional headquarters and see if their courier has arrived yet? Or any other word from Tushan. We'll be pushing on soon anyway, but I want to know what the word is."

Kwan was back within the hour, long before Baldwin expected him. He was out of breath, holding on to his dignity with an effort.

"Go back," said Kwan, "now everyone goes back. The courier says the army at Tushan wants everyone to go back because the Japanese are coming."

"When?" said Baldwin.

"They do not know. But the army has decided the Japanese will take Hochih. The Japanese Third Division moved up the road last night, with cavalry. The Japanese Thirteenth Division is north of the road and will start for Hochih soon."

"Both divisions? Two whole Japanese divisions?" Baldwin could not conceive of two divisions moving so quickly up these passes, moving from the summer of the lowlands to the winter here with no transition. Unless they had planned, really, to seize the highlands. Did they?

"This general does not know how many. He does not know much. The army has told him only they will not fight for Hochih, that he should go back quickly to Tushan. This general will go quickly, before the army changes its meaning and makes him stay and fight guerrilla battles. This general does not want to fight. He will go first himself, today, in his few trucks, and his soldiers will walk after him, slowly."

"And Tushan?" said Baldwin.

"Tushan is only seventy miles away, there are Central troops in Tushan. But they will go back, too. They will meet the new divisions from Burma near Tuyun, in the hills between Kweiyang and Tushan. They will make a new front there."

"Will the headquarters still be there when we get to Tushan?"

"I do not know, the general here does not know. The army at Tushan would not tell such a thing to this general. They do not trust him."

Baldwin let the information roll around in his mind. It was not clear. Nothing had been clear since they left Liuchow. He was tired of making up his mind in a fog. He did not know how fresh the general's information was. In an army without radio or telephone, dependent on couriers, the information might be a day old. Or it might be false, the Central Government might be trapping the Ssuchuan general.

It was a madness, thought Baldwin, there were several wars going on at once here. There were the Ssuchuan troops in this town fighting in some past century, on foot, with rifles thirty years old, and old French pack howitzers, their commander an opium sot, dependent on messenger-couriers, almost as antique as General Grant's army, except that it was worse because the Ssuchuanese distrusted their command, their government, and one another.

Then there were the Japanese. Who had begun the war with an air force, a navy, a mechanized army, electronics. And outward on the Pacific they still faced the Americans with air force, navy, radar, radio, guns, and were being punished and crushed. So that here they were turning inward on Asia in an older kind of war, moving on foot, on horse, like Jeb Stuart's calvary, punishing China because America was strangling Japan. And there would be more people dying on this one road, of hunger, of cold, and sickness, than would die in all the battles of the Pacific. This was the old-fashioned killing, the dirty bloodless killing of women and children and refugees, the old-fashioned war in which he was trapped.

And then, ahead of him somewhere, if the general's rumor were true, reaching around the awkward distances of India, of Burma, of the Hump and the Himalayas, the U. S. Air Force was ferrying fresh Chinese troops into battle, Chinese troops of a different kind. Chinese troops that the Americans had trained and brought from the last century into this, new units who had learned to fight with American planes, radios, artillery, medicine. Somewhere up ahead, the new armies that Americans were building up for China would meet the dwindling ferocity of the old Japanese horse cavalry. And as Japanese energy ran down, as the Jap capacity to supply ran out, they would come to a deadlock with the new troops and the plateau would be safe.

But in-between was where he was right now, seeing everything come apart. And he could sway it a little bit. The Ssuchuanese general would be out by night and, of course, the Ssuchuanese general would not burn Hochih as he left. Hochih *should* be burned so that the Jap cavalry could not shelter in it. It could be flamed, not easily now that the snow had wet it, but flamed nonetheless. But to flame it was a Chinese job. To flame it meant leaving the dying in the snow to die more quickly, leaving the other refugees still trekking up to the highlands to find no shelter. Casually Baldwin wondered whether he was responsible for burning it, and the thought ended: The hell with it. He would get out fast, the way the Ssuchuanese general was going to get out. He would get on to Tushan, close on the rear, leave the idiot war to the Chinese, letting them wreck their own country in their own way; he was responsible only for the road; and possibly for Tushan if the headquarters there wanted him to be.

"Michaelson!" he yelled.

Michaelson came.

"We're moving now," he said. "Snow's over. The Japanese are coming. We're getting out. Are the trucks ready?"

"That Lewis job, she won't start. We've worked on her all morning, but she's worse than she was yesterday. She's dead."

"The hell with it. Leave it," said Baldwin. "Off-load what gear you can into the other trucks. The demolition chests and the auxiliary motor. Dump what you have to, to make room. Fix Lewis up comfortably in the back of your truck. Get him as many blankets as you can dig up."

They moved fast. Soon he could hear the big six-by-sixes churning their motors. The men came in one by one to get their bedrolls, moving with force and vigor, for the morning's rest had helped them. Even Baldwin felt better, now that he had decided. It was almost over. Then Collins was approaching him, and Baldwin smiled because he knew that Collins was with him.

"We're going on to Tushan," said Baldwin, "and the dumps. There's no point in wrecking this town; if the Chinese want to burn it, they'll have to do it themselves."

"I always hate this part of it," said Collins, unhurriedly, "pulling out and leaving them behind. I know we can't take any of them with us, I know. But this morning, those kids, it was worse than anything I've seen all summer. It's like giving these people over to death. I wonder what they think of when they see us go."

"I know," said Baldwin, realizing that it was because of the people in the street, not because he was tired, that he did not want to burn it.

"Say," said Collins, nudging the overflowing food cartons on the floor with his boot, "are we going to load these, too?"

"Why?" asked Baldwin.

"I was just thinking," said Collins, "we have enough rations in the trucks for a week or more. And the jokers in the street are starving. We'll probably dump this stuff on the way, anyway. How about distributing it to them out there?"

Baldwin suddenly knew that Collins was suggesting expiation. The boy shifted from the slick to the soft, from the shrewd to the emotional, so easily; but there was a quality in him that came out like this. He was suggesting expiation for the people killed at the blow, for the old man left at the gap, for the leper at Liuchow, for being well fed and on wheels while the people they had seen in the cold, crowded streets this morning would remain to die. The food would save few, there was so little. But it might save one or two. The biscuits, and butter and cereals and condensed milk might nourish a few bellies for the night, so they could die farther up the road. But not on his conscience.

"O.K.," he said, "but don't waste any time."

Awkwardly, Collins hoisted one carton on his shoulder and moved out, through the door that opened on the street. Miller came in to rouse Lewis on the *k'ang*. Lewis rose, motioned to his bedroll, which Miller shouldered, then staggered after Miller to the trucks, through the side door that opened on the courtyard. Collins returned for the second carton, and left, and the room was empty except for Baldwin and Su-Piao.

"Where is he going with that?" she asked sharply.

"We're leaving it for the refugees," said Baldwin, knowing she would approve, and glad that Collins had suggested it.

Instead, her face frowned, and she said sharply:

"Oh, no! Call him back."

The alarm in her voice startled him.

"Why?" he asked.

"It's dangerous," she said. "Oh, don't!"

He realized as soon as she spoke that there *was* danger. But everything was dangerous. It was a kindness that Collins was trying to do; he wished Collins were here to explain it, he could not say the words of kindness the way Collins might.

"What's dangerous?" he said in a cold voice, his face hardening. "Giving food away? We can't eat it." He groped and came up with a thought. "You were talking about Kwan-Yin last night. Mercy. We can burn the town, or leave them food. It's all the same. But I wanted to leave them food."

She angered him. She was Chinese, these were her people. She should approve; but she said, "Refugees are dangerous. You don't understand China. They're starving. If we leave the food in here, they can loot the place as soon as we've gone. Oh, please, stop him!"

Outside, muffled by the door, he heard a sudden noise rise, a murmur and growling, punctuated by yells, then shrieking and a howling. Baldwin rushed to the side door and looked at the courtyard. The Americans were there, he noticed, standing alertly, listening to the tumult beyond the barred gates of the inn.

"Where's Collins?" yelled Baldwin.

"Ain't he in there with you?" asked Ballo.

"Where is he?"

Outside, the din and shouting grew.

Baldwin unslung the carbine from his shoulder, snapped the safety.

"Get your carbines," he shouted. "Open those gates."

As the timbered gates swung slowly inwards, parting to show what lay outdoors, it was as if a curtain rose on a stage. In the foreground, a mass of bodies squirmed and twisted in a tangle of forms out of which legs kicked away in the air, arms rose and fell, shoulders thrust up and crumpled again under more bodies that flung themselves on top of the growing mound. From out of the pile, a little boy was running away, dancing, holding a can of butter in his hand. A man shot out a claw, snatched the butter from him and ran off down the street faster than the boy could chase. On top of the pile now, a woman in a smeared pink dressing gown stamped with her heels in the small of someone else's back, trying to dig down through the mass of bodies to the cartons that lay underneath. From down the street came others, the fast-of-foot running, the slow and tired hobbling. Food!

Baldwin leveled the carbine over their heads and fired into the air. Michaelson and Prince were beside him and he was ordering, "Over their heads, over their heads, into the air, Collins is underneath, over their heads." And they were volleying. A shriek sliced through the growling of voices and Baldwin heard Michaelson grunting, "Winged one!" Then, dissolving, the tangle began to unsnarl itself, the edges unraveling, the animals becoming people, standing up, running away, leaving a space of snow and mud, littered with torn cardboard, packages, tins and strewn food.

And in the blank and littered filth of gray and white, lay Collins. Collins did not move. In one outstretched hand a can slowly dropped from his fingers and Baldwin saw it was a can of sardines. Baldwin stared at the body, his stunned mind slowly grasping that the neck of the boy twisted awkwardly from his shoulders and the round of his head seemed oddly shaped.

"Cover me," he said hoarsely to Michaelson, and walked across the snow, and stooped. There was a rock beside the head, and the light-brown hair was matted with blood, and the rock with which the head had been bashed in was covered with blood, too. Baldwin wanted to touch the head, to smooth the wound; he noticed that Collins's cheeks were shaved, the only man who shaved, he wanted to touch them, too. But he could not, it was over. Like that.

Through the quivering of rage in his body, through the fear, through the numbness as he tried to absorb what was happening, as his mind spun, Baldwin found himself trying to reason with the hate that rose in him. It was because they were hungry. It was because Collins was at the bottom. It wasn't because Collins was American. Whoever held the rock and was hammering his way through other Chinese to the food had not meant to kill an American because he was American. He had only meant to eat, even if it meant killing. But trying to be fair made no difference. They had killed Collins because they were beasts. He hated them because he had not been able to keep the vital, fragile distance between his men and the refugees, because you could not be kind to them.

He walked back to the courtyard gates, very slowly, not wanting to scuttle back in the sight of the mob or of his men. Michaelson and Prince were still there, facing out with their guns, covering him; behind on the jeep's hood stood Ballo with his gun.

"I want to bring him in," said Baldwin. "Niergaard and Miller, get out there and carry him in. We're covering."

Baldwin walked out with Niergaard and Miller as they lifted the body and brought it back to the courtyard. And as he walked back, he became aware that they were still there, behind him, hungry, growling and rumbling to get back at the food which now, as the cartons had ruptured, lay strewn in the snow.

Su-Piao knelt, touching Collins's lips with her fingers, lifted the wrist, felt for the pulse, stood crouched for a moment, then shook her head.

"Oh, the frigging Chinese," said Miller almost to himself. "Oh, the bastards."

Kwan spoke softly in Chinese and Su-Piao frowned.

"What did he say?" asked Baldwin, hoping that some magic phrase in Chinese had passed between them that could erase what had just happened.

"He says, let us go now quickly. The shots will bring some of the soldiers here. He says the soldiers have guns and they are as hungry as the refugees. If they know we have food here, we cannot stop them. If we shoot, they will shoot back. He says go now, quickly."

But Baldwin was already moving the convoy into formation, his orders snapping flatly, efficiently, coming off the top of his mind while somewhere the same mind groped to accept what had happened, and what had gone wrong, and the ache was momentarily pushed down underneath, the ache he knew would return.

The jeep first, he ordered, impersonal and brisk, Michaelson riding the hood to fire cover. Miller on the second truck, with Lewis in the blankets behind. Ballo next, Niergaard driving the last truck, carrying Collins's body, with Prince to fall back from the gate and ride the back firing rear-cover.

They were ready to roll now. Baldwin lowered the flat windshield of the jeep flush with the hood. It gave a clearer field of sight if he had to shoot, and no glass to splinter if the crowd threw rocks.

Baldwin moved behind the wheel of the jeep, noticed and was angry that Kwan and Su-Piao were already in place without being asked, called to Prince still standing at the gate, with Michaelson, holding the crowd at its distance with their carbines.

"Prince!" Baldwin called from the jeep as his motor raced and the other trucks sounded behind him. "Fall back now. Tell every man to keep the trucks inched in close. No separations. If one of these Chinese edges in between, keep going. Don't stop. You get on Niergaard's truck, in the back. You fire rear-cover. When you're ready to go back there, fire two shots, and we take off. Mike," he continued, yelling to the burly back that stood guard at the courtyard gates, "when you hear Prince fire twice, hop back to the hood of the jeep and be ready to shoot when we roll."

He waited for the seconds it took Prince to get back to Niergaard's truck, gazing at the mob which held its distance, roaring with desire and discontent.

There were no faces he could see, only the large encircling arc of people, half-mooned about the entrance, dressed in grays and blues, rags and woolens, heads covered with old towels, shawls, handkerchiefs, fedoras. They were not people at all, he told himself, but a giant beast, swaying and pulsing like an unfed animal, panting in a subhuman passion of hunger and fear. They had killed Collins and none of them was responsible. They could not care that Collins was dead any more than they could care for one of their own Chinese dead that he and Collins had seen this morning. It was a pack. It was not human. The pack had a personality. And he hated it, hated it.

Behind him, he heard Prince's carbine fire twice and he fed gas to the jeep as Michaelson, never lowering his carbine, backed aboard, and then fired over the heads of the mob several times for warning. Baldwin twisted the wheel as he emerged from the gates. He could feel it crunch over the cartons, mashing the food into the ground, knowing the trucks behind would mash what was left and not caring. The crowd thinned and parted, and he moved out, the trucks following.

The convoy was in the clear now, slowly gathering speed, when a figure darted out at them from the side, a figure in a Chinese soldier's uniform. It ran alongside them, calling, whether to curse or beg for a ride, Baldwin could not tell. But he saw Michaelson's carbine go up again and shoot point-blank into the running figure and it tumbled awkwardly, like a football dummy carried to the ground. Baldwin noticed as it fell that the soldier had been running barefoot in the snow. Behind he could hear Prince's gun on the last truck blasting off in a volley, and then they were out of it. The last he saw of Hochih was a little girl gaily waving at them, and the mother's hand reaching out to snatch her back.

They drove a minute or two in silence and Baldwin turned to speak to Collins, but Collins was not there, only the two Chinese and Michaelson up front on the hood. He wanted to talk about it with Collins, only with Collins. He was conscious now of many things as the fright of the fight ebbed from him, that anger was hardening in him, that the boy had been precious. And that he, himself, had been a fool. Because I was a fool,

Collins is dead. I was responsible. It was all right for him to have the idea, thought Baldwin. But it was not right for me to let him go. I was responsible. The flattened windshield was still down, and Baldwin was beginning to be cold, his fingers were numbing at the wheel, and Michaelson must be freezing up there. But he could not stop now because if he stopped he would be sick, he would not be able to stand up, he wanted to throw up. He must keep driving just a few more minutes until his hands stopped shaking. And what were they going to do next? He could not think about it. He would stop in just a minute and when they stopped he would figure it out. If he had gone out with Loomis it would not have happened; he had wanted to go out by road, to do this job.

Beyond the Call of Duty

✗

from *The Locust Fire*

by EUGENE BROWN

With the surge of the engine cutting back in, a tingle of pain went down through my forearms, a feeling that comes with the spasms of dysentery, as if needles are pricking the veins. My hands jerked away from the crossbars then, and seeing the onrush of a ridge beyond the windshield, I plunged into the pilot's compartment to grab at the wheel on the left side of the pedestal. As I pulled back on the column the nose came up shuddering, so I slid into the seat and bore down hard on the rudder pedal. With the wings almost level she began to bend around, but I felt my leg shaking and put on some rudder trim to hold against that one-sided tug of power.

When both my hands were back on the split-wheel I looked down below to see those strange barren foothills with their convoluted shadow lines. I knew then that we had crossed the last of the ridge lines, and my eyes moved around to the instrument panel. And then I panicked; all the dials and gauges beneath the windshield went out of focus and began to float crazily. I sat there scared with a rapid pounding in my diaphragm and waited for them to stop. After a few seconds I was all right again. I saw the altimeter clearly and the needles were steadying at almost ten thousand feet. I had thought we lost a lot more before the engine recovered. She must have been completely dead for thirty seconds anyway. It had seemed even a longer time when we were going in. Only you could never be sure about time in the air. The same as with distances on water. But she had come back. She had shaken out the gremlins. And what I had to do right now was get back into that baggage compartment and go. While she was still holding the altitude. Then shake the lead out, soldier. You can do it now. With no freezing up at the door. You saw it once that way already. Only now you're not going to wait for it to come and take you. What you're going to do is jump right into it. Bail the hell out of this flying coffin. Open that freaking lid and go before you're buried down there with the rest of them.

But that was when I saw them in my mind; the Chinese troops all crouched in the cabin, and the unpiloted aircraft going in, slanting down the wall of the sky. To hell with those slopies. I have enough to go now. And why the freak shouldn't I go? Mossi and Shellbarger had left them up here. Gone right out the door by the numbers. And I would have gone then too if my guts hadn't froze. I had not even thought about those poor chuteless bastards back there. Then don't think about them now. It's your own guts that count, and now you can stretch them the way you should have before. You can stretch them all the way out and down, as far as any man's can go. You're lucky you got the chute, and it's just tough tit for Gismo's slopies.

Only how could I leave them while the engine was holding this way? How was I going to feel afterward if my guts weren't busted on those hills down there? What kind of life could I have? And what did I have now? A wife waiting in Fresno? The hell you have. Not even a little wan-faced street girl in Shanghai. She wasn't crying for you, Sergeant. None of them was going to cry.

So all you got now are those slopies in the cabin. And every one an enlisted joker, the conscripts who had to snap crap at the orders, who made none of the decisions in this cruddy civil war and had not been asked to choose their politics. We had those things together, and our lives to lose unreasonably. But up here now I had more than they did. I could choose how I would live or die. What gave me the choice was the chute I sat on, my solo hours in a primary trainer at Parks and all the final approaches I had sweated out over here. And what I could do was try and set her down on the runway back at Isin. There was a chance for all of us that way. The only one they had now.

I came forward in the seat then and began to think what I should do. I figured we were still about twenty minutes out of Isin, and even if she lost altitude rapidly we should be able to clear everything before the field. Only she might cut out again any minute. She had sure come back from the dead. Maybe it was water in the fuel. Any one of those gremlin things. Listen to her go now. And how about those power settings for a single engine? Better not touch anything on that control pedestal. Mossi had her all set up and trimmed before she quit. The mixture was all right. And the prop, too. I looked at the air-speed indicator. One-thirty. She was powering along nicely. The tachometer now. Twenty-five hundred, almost. A whole lot of r.p.m.'s. And look at that manifold pressure. You better draw some off. No, you don't. Just stick to the wheel and rudder. You got her trimmed up pretty well now. Leave well-enough alone. Didn't they say a gooney bird was nothing but an overgrown Piper job? Fly better by themselves. Only I'm not worrying about her flying. What she can't do is land by herself. And how the hell can you watch the air speed and the altimeter and handle the flaps too? You get the gear down maybe and fly her into the ground while you're fooling around with the locking pin. Jesus Christ on a joy stick!

It was then I looked at the compass for the first time. She had not swung off very far, and I booted in rudder to skid her back on the heading that would take us into Isin. It was too bad I could not check the reading against a zero indication on the radio compass. But the range station at Isin was inoperative. I would have to forget that. And the radio equipment was what I knew. Why the hell aren't you on that command? You didn't even think to call the tower. And you never did get a Mayday out on the liaison. *The radio operator will send distress signals and report position of aircraft until the final bail-out signal is given.* Oh, sure he will. And don't forget to screw down the key. Or to take those log sheets with you. The radio operator will. Like hell he will.

Now I had Mossi's headset on and plugged in. I pressed the mike button and began calling the tower. My right hand was locked around the wheel, and I could feel the trickle of sweat down my stomach and legs. Then I heard him and adjusted the tuning. The voice of the Isin tower operator came in loud through the hiss and crackle.

Again I thumbed the microphone button. "Isin tower, this is army two-three-seven," I said. "This is a Mayday. A *Mayday* call. This is the radio operator calling. Repeat, the *radio operator*. I am at the controls now. My pilot and co-pilot have bailed out. Now give me a call, Isin. This is two-three-seven on a *Mayday*. Over."

The tower operator cleared the frequency then, and I began telling him about the engine cutting out and in, how I had frozen when my pilot and co-pilot jumped. The tower operator asked me the approximate time of bail-out. I told him that, and then he wanted to know if I had seen their chutes open. No, I had not. We had troops in the main cabin, all of them armed, so the jump was made out of the forward cargo door. They had to go under the wing that way. But I had seen nothing. I said the engine seemed to be holding well now at a little over nine thousand feet. I had her back on the heading into Isin and wanted to try and shoot a landing.

"All right now," said the tower operator. "Stand by for a minute."

"For Christ's sake," I shouted. "Get somebody on here who can tell me what the freak to do."

"Take it easy now, radio. That's what I'm going to do. We got a captain in operations here who can recite you the book on a forty-seven."

Nearly five minutes went by before the captain called me. "How you doing up there, radio?" he asked almost jokingly.

"I don't know, sir."

"My name is Paxton," said the captain. "You might as well know who's going to be doing all the talking."

"Yes, sir."

"Don't sir me yet," the captain said. "Wait until I have you walking away from it." I could hear him laughing. "What do they call you, radio?"

"Lewis," I said. "George Lewis, sir."

"All right, George," said the captain. "Now just try to relax up there and keep your mind on what I tell you. We figure you about twenty minutes out of the field now. So let's start checking."

"I'm ready, sir."

"You got your safety belt fastened?"

"No, sir."

"Get with it, then," said the captain. "Now you should have a heading of one-eight-five. Check your gyro against the mag compass to make sure."

"I've just about got it."

"Fine," the captain said. "Now tell me. You ever fly a forty-seven before?"

"I used to fly with a mobile squadron at Baker Dog, sir," I said. "Every radio operator there got a fast shot at the stick and a cockpit check-out. But that was over a year ago."

"But you're familiar with most of the stuff up there?"

"I know it pretty well, Captain. All I been flying over here is forty-sevens." And then I told him about my primary flight training in the States.

"Well, you're not in too bad shape, then," said the captain. "How were your landings in cadets?"

"I shot some pretty good ones, sir."

"What did you wash out on, George?"

"The V.D.," I said. "That was before the seven-day cure."

"All right," the captain said after a few seconds of dead air. "Let's start to check her out now. Your power settings first. You all set?"

"Go ahead, sir."

"You ought to have about thirty-five inches of manifold pressure."

"I go a little over that."

"Pull it back, then," the captain said. "She's going to build up as you descend, so you want to keep your eyes on that. Thirty-five is what you want all the way."

"Thirty-five now, sir."

"Now get your r.p.m.'s down to twenty-three-fifty. Just inch her back. You got lots of time. That should have your air speed around one-twenty-five indicated. Now don't let her go below one-twenty. You do and she's going to turn into the dead engine. Try to hold her at one-twenty-five. How's she doing now?"

"She feels all right, sir."

"Now you know where the temperature gauges are located?"

"Yes, sir."

"Cylinder head and oil. They both ought to be in the green."

"They are, sir."

"Now take a look at the oil pressure."

"That's in the green too, sir."

"Now what about your gas?"

"I don't *know*, sir," I said. "I just didn't think about it."

"Easy now," said the captain. "Look at your selector."

"On the right main, Captain."

"Now the gauge. Where's the knob?"

"Right main, too."

"All right. What's the needle reading?"

"About one-fifty."

"Save the sweat," the captain said. "Just keep on checking those temperature gauges and your manifold pressure."

"I'll watch them, sir," I said.

"How you feeling now, George?"

"I'm getting a little loose now, Captain."

"In the bowels, eh?"

"They been that way right along."

"Who gave you the dose, George? Some little V-girl?"

"No, some colonel's little daughter."

"Now ain't that something."

"It was something, all right."

"*But she looked so clean, doc,*" the captain said. "Was that it?"

"I guess so."

"Now that's *really* something."

"I've lost some altitude, Captain."

"What is it now?" His tone was hard again.

"Around eighty-five hundred."

"That's all right," the captain said. "It's about time you started letting down, anyway. You're going to have a straight-in approach, if you hold your heading all right. Once I have you spotted you can forget just about everything on the panel. No instrument staring. I want you to feel your way down. Try to keep the wings level and split the middle of the strip. One thing you do have to watch. The manifold pressure. But let me do the worrying about your altitude, the rate of descent and all that. Right now you want to have a real shallow glide."

"How about the rate of descent now?"

"About five hundred a minute," the captain said. "But watch your speed and that manifold pressure, too."

I pushed the wheel forward a little more. Way out ahead I could see the flatland of rice fields, all coppery and shining after the heavy rains. Then I saw some landmarks I knew from our previous flights over the route; first the large excavation of a quarry and soon afterward the winding stream off to the left, a tributary of the Yangtse. I could feel my pulse going fast under the damp rubber of the phones.

The altimeter reading was forty-five hundred when the captain saw me north of the field. "You're way off to the left," he said. "Bend her around, George. A little more rudder. Watch the nose now. That's the way."

Then I saw them through the windshield, the grave mounds of the village cemetery, the mirror flashes of heat waves over the bright tiled roofs. "What about the landing, Captain?" I shouted. "What should I do now?"

"All right, George," the captain said. "Nothing to be scared about now. Just drop that mike into your lap and listen to me from here on in. I'm going to make it simple for you. A power-off landing. The power off and the gear up. The other way you might overshoot the strip, and I wouldn't like to see you try a go-around on the one engine. So you're going to land like a hot rock. By the seat of your pants. You can start reducing power a little more now. Start taking out the rudder trim as you pull it back. Keep your nose down now. Lots of time yet. Don't fight the wheel. That looks better. Wings level. Easy now. You're looking good. Just a little high. Now pretty soon I'm going to have you pull all the power. Then I want you to try and neutralize your rudder. After that you're going to cut the switches. At about three hundred feet. First the master. Then the mag. Nothing else. Just feel your way in from there. All right now. Get that nose down a little more. You're coming in high. Still high. Get it down. You're drifting now. Skid it. Still too high. Now listen to me. You're going to make it. You can hit at the end of the strip and make it. All right. Now. Pull it now. Pull the power. Props. Throttle. Mixture. Now the rudder. Fast now. You're drifting again. Watch it. Cut the switches now. Cut those ——"

The radio went dead when I pulled the master. I switched the mag off, too, but there was the runway coming on like a huge conveyor belt, then sliding away to the left, with me booting rudder to bring it back and the wheel pulled into my stomach. That was how we hit the taxiway, the wing tip first and digging hard, the real jolt making my head snap, and all the breath gone out of me. I could feel the tremors as she slid along, but I did not let go of the wheel and my leg kept straining on the rudder pedal.

When she stopped the silence was deadly. Even when I had the phones off I could hear no sound, and suddenly I was afraid I would not find anyone back in the cabin; that may be the troops all had panicked and jumped out the cargo door right after the second engine cut out. I unfastened the safety belt and worked myself out of the seat. I felt a very deep pain like shin splints in my leg that had been holding in the rudder. The chute pack pulled down on the straps across my shoulders as I started back into the radio compartment. Then I thought I could hear them moving around. I opened the access door to the cabin. I smelled it before I saw the bilious slime in the corrugations of the floor. A few of them were still lying there; others sat cross-legged, their heads lowered down onto the kneecaps. The ones who stood also looked very sick.

When I stepped into the cabin they all began to talk. I went down toward the cargo door, but their faces were turned the other way and they looked into the flight compartment. Then very slowly their eyes came around to me. I had the cargo door opened, and motioned for them to go out. "*Hao*," I told them. "It's all right."

They were all staring at me now. But after a few more seconds they began to file out, their rifles slung over the shoulder, and each one pausing by the cargo door to look closely at my face. Then after the last man had gone out the door I climbed down too and walked away from it.

Mutiny

✗

from *The Caine Mutiny*
by HERMAN WOUK

A steamship, not being a slave to the wind like a sailing vessel, is superior to ordinary difficulties of storms. A warship is a special kind of steamship, built not for capaciousness and economy, but for power. Even the minesweeper *Caine* could oppose to the gale a force of some thirty thousand horsepower; energy enough to move a weight of half a million tons one foot in one minute. The ship itself weighed little more than a thousand tons. It was a gray old bantam bursting with strength for emergencies.

But surprising things could happen when nature puts on a freak show like a typhoon, with wind gusts up to a hundred and fifty miles per hour or more. The rudder, for instance, can become useless. It works by dragging against the water through which it is passing; but if the wind is behind the ship, and blows hard enough, the water may start piling along as fast as the rudder so that there is no drag at all. Then the ship will yaw or even broach to. Or the sea may push one way on the hull, and the wind another, and the rudder a third, so that the resultant of the forces is very erratic response of the ship to the helm, varying from minute to minute, or from second to second.

It is also theoretically possible that while the captain may want to turn his ship in one direction, the wind will be pushing so hard in the other direction that the full force of the engines will not suffice to bring the ship's head around. In that case the vessel will wallow, broadside to, in very bad shape indeed. But it is unlikely. A modern warship, functioning properly and handled with wisdom, can probably ride out any typhoon.

The storm's best recourse in the contest for the ship's life is old-fashioned bogeyman terror. It makes ghastly noises and horrible faces and shakes up the captain to distract him from doing the sensible thing in tight moments. If the wind can toss the ship sideways long enough it can probably damage the engines or kill them — and then it wins. Because above all the ship must be kept steaming under control. It suffers under one disadvantage as a drifting hulk, compared to the old wooden sailing ship: iron doesn't float. A destroyer deprived of its engines in a typhoon is almost certain to capsize, or else fill up and sink.

When things get really bad, the books say, the best idea is to turn the ship's head into the wind and sea and ride out the blow that way. But even on this the authorities are not all agreed. None of the authorities have experienced the worst of enough typhoons to make airtight generalizations. None of the authorities, moreover, are anxious to acquire the experience.

The TBS message was so muffled by static and the noise of wind and waves that Willie had to put his ear to the loudspeaker: *Chain Gang from Sunshine. Discontinue fueling. Execute to follow. New fleet course 180. Small Boys reorientate screen.*

"What? What was it?" said Queeg at Willie's elbow.

"Discontinuing fueling, sir, and turning south. Execute to follow."

"Getting the hell out, hey? About time."

Maryk, squat and enormous in his life jacket, said, "I don't know how she'll ride, sir, with her stern to the wind. Quartering seas always murder us —"

"Any course that takes us out of here is the right course," said Queeg. He peered out at the ragged waves, rearing and tossing everywhere as high as the ship's mast. The flying spray was like a cloudburst. A few hundred yards beyond the ship the gray mountains of water faded into a white misty wall. The spray was beginning to rattle against the windows, sounding more like hail than water. "Kay, Willie. Call Paynter and tell him to stand by his engines for some fast action. Steve, I'm going to conn from the radar shack. You stay here."

The TBS scratched and whined. The voice came through gurgling, as though the loudspeaker were under water: "*Small Boys from Sunshine. Execute reorientation. Make best speed.*"

"Kay. All engines ahead full. Right standard rudder. Steady on 180," said Queeg, and ran out of the wheelhouse. The *Caine* went plunging downhill into a foaming trough. Stilwell spun the helm, saying, "Christ, this wheel feels loose."

"Rudder's probably clear out of the water," Maryk said. The nose of the ship cut into the sea and came up slowly, shedding thick solid streams. The wheelhouse trembled.

"Rudder is right standard, sir," said Stilwell. "Jesus, she's getting shoved around fast. Heading 010, sir — 020 —" Like a kite taking the wind, the minesweeper heeled, and swept sharply to the right. Fear tingled in Willie's arms and legs as he was swung against the wet windows. "Heading 035, sir — 040 —"

Hanging increasingly to starboard, the *Caine* was rising and falling on the waves, blown sidewise, riding more like flotsam again than a ship under control. Spray blew across the forecastle in clouds. Instinctively Willie looked to Maryk, and was deeply relieved to see the exec hanging with both arms to an overhead beam, his back planted against the bulkhead, calmly watching the swift veer of the forecastle across the water.

"Say, Willie!" The captain's voice was angry and shrill through the speaking tube. "Get your goddamn radio technician up here, will you? I can't see anything on this goddamn radar."

Willie roared, "Aye aye, sir," into the speaking tube and passed a call for the technician over the PA. He was beginning to feel nauseous from the dizzy sidewise slipping of the *Caine* and the queer rise and fall of the slanted deck.

"Mr. Maryk," the helmsman said in a changed tone, "she's stopped coming around —"

"What's your head?"

"Zero nine three."

"We're broadside to. Wind's got her. She'll come slow."

"Still zero nine three, sir," said Stilwell, after a minute of bad wallow-ing — heavy slow rolls upright and swift sickening drops to starboard. It was hard to tell whether the *Caine* was moving forward. The sense of motion came entirely from the sea and the wind; yet the engines were mak-ing twenty knots.

"Bring your rudder hard right," said Maryk.

"Hard right, sir — Christ, sir, this goddamn wheel *feels like the wheel ropes are broken!* Just sloppy —" The hair of Willie's head prickled to see the looks of fright on the sailors. He felt the same expression forming on his own face.

"Shut your yap, Stilwell, the wheel ropes are okay," said Maryk. "Don't be such a baby. Haven't you ever had the wheel in a sea before —"

"Now goddamn it, Steve," came the squeak of Queeg, "what the hell's going on out there? Why aren't we coming around?"

Maryk yelled into the speaking tube, "Wind and sea taking charge, sir. I've got the rudder at hard right —"

"Well, use the engines. *Get* her around. Christ on a crutch, do I have to do everything here? *Where's* that technician? There's nothing but grass on this radar —"

Maryk began to manipulate the engines. A combination of standard speed on the port screw and slow backing on the starboard started swing-ing the ship's head slowly to the south. "Steady on 180, sir," Stilwell said at last, turning his face to Maryk, his eyes glinting with relief.

The ship was tossing and heeling from side to side. But there was no alarm in the steepest rolls any more, so long as they were even dips both ways. Willie was getting used to the sight of the three rusty stacks lying apparently parallel to the sea, so that between them he saw nothing but foaming water. The whipping of the stacks back and forth like gigantic windshield wipers was no longer a frightening but a pleasant thing. It was the slow, slow dangling rolls to one side that he dreaded.

Queeg came in, mopping at his eyes with a handkerchief. "Damn spray stings. Well, you finally got her around, hey? Guess we're okay now."

"Are we on station, sir?"

"Well, pretty near, I guess. *I* can't tell. Technician says the spray is giving us this sea return that's fogging up the scope. I guess if we're too far out of line Sunshine will give us a growl —"

"Sir, I think maybe we ought to ballast," said the exec. "We're pretty light, sir. Thirty-five per cent on fuel. One reason we don't come around good is that we're riding so high —"

"Well, don't worry, we're not capsizing yet."

"It'll just give us that much more maneuverability, sir —"

"Yes, and contaminate our tanks with a lot of salt water, so we lose suction every fifteen minutes once we refuel. Sunshine has our fuel report. If he thought there was any danger he'd issue ballasting orders."

"I also think we ought to set the depth charges on safe, sir."

"What's the matter, Steve, are you panicky on account of a little bad weather?"

"I'm not panicky, sir —"

"We're supposed to be an anti-submarine vessel, you know. What the hell good are depth charges set on safe if we pick up a sub in the next five minutes?"

Maryk glanced out of the blurred window at the colossal boiling waves. "Sir, we won't be making any sub runs in this —"

"How do we know?"

"Sir, the *Dietch* in our squadron got caught in a storm in the Aleutians, and got sunk by its own depth charges tearing loose. Blew off the stern. Skipper got a general court —"

"Hell's bells, if your heart is so set on putting the depth charges on safe go ahead. I don't care. Just be damn sure there's somebody standing by to arm them if we pick up a sub —"

"Mr. Maryk," spoke up Stilwell, "the depth charges are on safe, sir."

"They are!" exclaimed Queeg. "Who says so?"

"I — I set 'em myself, sir." The sailor's voice was shaky. He stood with legs spread, clutching the wheel, his eyes on the gyrocompass.

"And who told you to do that?"

"I got standing orders, sir, from Mr. Keefer. When the ship is in danger I set 'em on safe —"

"And who said the ship was in danger, hey?" Queeg swung back and forth, clinging to a window handle, glaring at the helmsman's back.

"Well, sir, on that big roll around seven o'clock, I — I set 'em. The whole fantail was awash. Had to rig a life line —"

Goddamn it, Mr. Maryk, why am I never informed of these things? Here I am, steaming around with a lot of dead depth charges —"

Stilwell said, "Sir, I told Mr. Keefer —"

"You speak when you're spoken to, you goddamned imbecile, and not otherwise!" shrieked Queeg. "Mr. Keith, place this man on report for insolence and neglect of duty! He told Mr. *Keefer!* I'll attend to Mr. Keefer! Now Steve, I want you to get another helmsman and keep this stupid idiot's ugly face out of my sight from now on —"

"Captain, pardon me," said the exec hurriedly, "the other helmsmen are still shot from last night. Stilwell's our best man and we need him —"

"Will you stop this back talk?" screamed the captain. "Great bloody Christ, is there one officer on this ship who takes orders from me! I said I want —"

Engstrand stumbled into the wallowing wheelhouse and grabbed at Willie to keep from falling. His dungarees ran with water. "Sorry, Mr. Keith. Captain, the barometer —"

"What about the barometer?"

"Twenty-eight ninety-four, sir — twenty-*eight* —"

"Who the hell's been watching the barometer? Why haven't I had a report for a half hour?" Queeg ran out on the wing, steadying himself from hand to hand on the windows, the engine-room telegraph, the doorway.

"Mr. Maryk," the helmsman said hoarsely, "I can't hold her on 180. She's falling off to port —"

"Give her more rudder —"

"I got her at emergency right, sir — heading 172, sir — falling off fast —"

"*Why* is the rudder emergency right?" Queeg bellowed, lurching in through the doorway. "Who's giving rudder orders here? Is everybody on this bridge going crazy?"

"Captain, she's yawing to port," said Maryk. "Steersman can't hold her at 180 —"

"One *six* zero, sir, now," said Stilwell, with a scared look at Maryk. It was the dreaded weather-vane effect, taking charge of the *Caine*. The rudder was not holding, and the ship was skidding sideways at the pleasure of wind and waves. The head was dropping off from south to east.

Queeg grabbed at the helmsman and steadied himself to stare at the compass. He jumped to the telegraph and signaled "Flank Speed" with one handle and "Stop" with the other. The engine-room pointers answered instantly. The deck began to vibrate with the one-sided strain on the engines. "That'll bring her around," said the captain. "What's your head now?"

"Still falling off, sir, 152 — 148 —"

Queeg muttered, "Needs a few seconds to take hold —"

Once again the *Caine* took a sickening cant to starboard and hung there. Waves coming from the port side broke over the ship as though it were a floating log. It wallowed feebly under the tons of water, but did not right itself. It came halfway back to level and sagged further to starboard again. Willie's face was pushed against the window and he saw water no more than inches from his eyes. He could have counted little bubbles of foam. Stilwell, hanging to the wheel, with his feet sliding out from under him, stammered, "Still falling off, sir — heading 125 —"

"Captain, we're broaching to," said Maryk, his voice lacking firmness for the first time. "Try backing the starboard engine, sir." The captain seemed not to hear. "Sir, sir, *back the starboard engine.*"

Queeg, clinging to the telegraph with his knees and arms, threw him a frightened glance, his skin greenish and obediently slid the handle backward. The laboring ship shuddered fearfully; it continued to drift sidewise before the wind, rising and falling on each swell a distance equal to the height of a tall building. "What's your head?" The captain's voice was a muffled croak.

"Steady on 117, sir —"

"Think she'll grab, Steve?" murmured Willie.

"I hope so."

"Oh holy Mother of Christ, make this ship come around!" spoke a queer wailing voice. The tone made Willie shiver. Urban, the little signalman, had dropped to his knees and was hugging the binnacle, his eyes closed, his head thrown back.

"Shut up, Urban," Maryk said sharply. "Get on your feet —"

Stilwell exclaimed, "Sir, heading 120! Coming right, sir!"

"Good," said Maryk. "Ease your rudder to standard."

Without so much as a glance at the captain, Stilwell obeyed. Willie noticed the omission, for all that he was terror-stricken; and he noticed, too, that Queeg, frozen to the telegraph stand, seemed oblivious.

"Rudder is eased to standard, sir — heading 124, sir —" The *Caine* stood erect slowly and wabbled a little to port before heeling deep to starboard again.

"We're okay," said Maryk. Urban got off his knees and looked around sheepishly.

"Heading 128 — 129 — 130 —"

"Willie," said the exec, "take a look in the radar shack. See if you can tell where the hell we are in the formation."

"Aye aye, sir." Willie staggered out past the captain to the open wing. The wind immediately smashed him against the bridgehouse, and spray pelted him like small wet stones. He was astounded and peculiarly exhilarated to realize that in the last fifteen minutes the wind had actually become much stronger than before, and would blow him over the side if he exposed himself in a clear space. He laughed aloud, his voice thin against the guttural "Whooeeee!" of the storm. He inched himself to the door of the radar shack, freed the dogs, and tried to pull the door open, but the wind held it tightly shut. He pounded on the wet steel with his knuckles, and kicked at it, and screamed, "Open up! Open up! It's the OOD!" A crack appeared and widened. He darted through, knocking down one of the radarmen who was pushing against the door. It snapped shut as though on a spring.

"What the hell!" exclaimed Willie.

There were perhaps twenty sailors jammed in the tiny space, all in life jackets with waterproofed searchlights pinned to them, all with whistles dangling around their necks, all with the same round-eyed bristly white face of fear. "How are we doing, Mr. Keith?" spoke the voice of Meatball from the rear of the crush.

"We're doing fine —"

"We gonna have to abandon ship, sir?" said a filthy-faced fireman.

Willie suddenly realized what was so very strange about the shack beside the crowd. It was brightly lit. Nobody was paying any attention to the dim green slopes of the radars. He let loose a stream of obscenity that surprised him as it came out of his mouth. The sailors shrank a little from him. "Who turned on the lights in here? Who's got the watch?"

"Sir, there's nothing on the scopes but sea return," whined a radarman.

Willie cursed some more, and then said, "Douse the lights. Get your faces against these scopes and keep them there."

"Okay, Mr. Keith," said the radarman, in a friendly, respectful tone, "but it won't do no good." In the gloom Willie quickly saw that the sailor was right. There was no trace of the pips of the other ships, nothing but a blurry peppering and streaking of green all over the scopes. "You see, sir," said the voice of the technician, patiently, "our masthead ain't no higher than the water most of the time, and, anyway, all this spray, why, it's like a solid object, sir. These scopes are jammed out —"

"All the same," said Willie, "the watch will be maintained on these radars, and you'll keep trying till you do get something! And all the guys who don't belong in here — well — well, stay here, and keep your faces closed so the watch-standers can do their duty —"

"Sir, are we really okay?"

"Will we have to abandon ship?"

"I was ready to jump on that last roll —"

"Will the ship come through it, Mr. Keith?"

"We're okay," shouted Willie. "We're okay. Don't lose your heads. You'll be back chipping paint in a few hours —"

"I'll chip this rusty old bitch till doomsday if she just rides out this blow," said a voice, and there was a ripple of small laughs.

"I'm staying up here if I get a court-martial for it —"

"Me, too —"

"Hell, there are forty guys over the lee of the bridge —"

"Mister Keith" — the gutter twang of Meatball again — "honest, does the old man know what the Christ he's doing? That's all we want to know."

"The old man's doing great. You bastards shut up and take it easy. Couple of you help me get this door open."

Wind and spray blasted in through the open crack. Willie pulled himself out and the door clanged. The wind blew him forward into the pilothouse. In the second that elapsed he was drenched as by buckets of water. "Radars are jammed, Steve. Nothing to see until this spray moderates —"

"Very well."

Despite the whining and crashing of the storm, Willie got the impression of silence in the wheelhouse. Queeg hung to the telegraphs as before. Stilwell swayed at the wheel. Urban, wedged between the binnacle and the front window, clutched the quartermaster's log as though it were a Bible. Usually there were other sailors in the wheelhouse — telephone talkers, signalmen — but they were avoiding it now as though it were the sickroom of a cancer victim. Maryk stood with both hands clamped to the captain's chair. Willie staggered to the starboard side and glanced out at the wing. A crowd of sailors and officers pressed against the bridgehouse, hanging to each other, their clothes whipping in the wind. Willie saw Keefer, Jorgensen, and nearest him, Harding.

"Willie, are we going to be okay?" Harding said.

The OOD nodded, and fell back into the wheelhouse. He was vexed at not having a flashlight and whistle, like everyone else. "Just my luck to be on watch," he thought. He did not really believe yet that the ship was going to founder, but he resented being at a disadvantage. His own man-overboard gear was in his desk below. He thought of sending the boatswain's mate for it; and was ashamed to issue the order.

The *Caine* yawed shakily back and forth on heading 180 for a couple of minutes. Then suddenly it was flung almost on its beam-ends to port by a swell, a wave and a gust of wind hitting together. Willie reeled, brought up against Stilwell, and grabbed at the wheel spokes.

"Captain," Maryk said, "I still think we ought to ballast — at least the stern tanks, if we're going to steam before the wind."

Willie glanced at Queeg. The captain's face was screwed up as though he were looking at a bright light. He gave no sign of having heard. "I request permission to ballast stern tanks, sir," said the exec.

Queeg's lips moved. "Negative," he said calmly and faintly.

Stilwell twisted the wheel sharply, pulling the spokes out of Willie's hands. The OOD grasped an overhead beam.

"Falling off to *starboard* now. Heading 189 — 190 — 191 —"

Maryk said, "Captain — hard left rudder?"

"Okay," murmured Queeg.

"Hard left rudder, sir," said Stilwell. "Heading 200 —"

The exec stared at the captain for several seconds while the minesweeper careened heavily to port and began its nauseating sideslipping over the swells, the wind flipping it around now in the other direction. "Captain, we'll have to use engines again, she's not answering to the rudder. . . . Sir, how about heading up into the wind? She's going to keep broaching to with this stern wind —"

Queeg pushed the handles of the telegraph. "Fleet course is 180," he said.

"Sir, we have to maneuver for the safety of the ship —"

"Sunshine knows the weather conditions. We've received no orders to maneuver at discretion —" Queeg looked straight ahead, constantly clutching the telegraph amid the gyrations of the wheelhouse.

"Heading 225 — falling away, sir —"

An unbelievably big gray wave loomed on the port side, high over the bridge. It came smashing down. Water spouted into the wheelhouse from the open wing, flooding to Willie's knees. The water felt surprisingly warm and sticky, like blood. "Sir, we're shipping water on the goddamn *bridge!*" said Maryk shrilly. "We *got* to come around into the wind!"

"Heading 245, sir." Stilwell's voice was sobbing. "She ain't answering to the engines at all, sir!"

The *Caine* rolled almost completely over on its port side. Everybody in the wheelhouse except Stilwell went sliding across the streaming deck and piled up against the windows. The sea was under their noses, dashing up against the glass. "Mr. Maryk, the light on this gyro just went out!" screamed Stilwell, clinging desperately to the wheel. The wind howled and shrieked in Willie's ears. He lay on his face on the deck, tumbling around in salt water, flailing for a grip at something solid.

"Oh Christ, Christ, Christ, Jesus Christ, save us!" squealed the voice of Urban.

"Reverse your rudder, Stilwell! Hard right! Hard right!"

"Hard right, sir!"

Maryk crawled across the deck, threw himself on the engine-room telegraph, wrested the handles from Queeg's spasmodic grip, and reversed the settings. "Excuse me, Captain —" A horrible coughing rumble came from the stacks. "What's your head?" barked Maryk.

"Two seven five, sir!"

"Hold her at hard right!"

"Aye aye, sir!"

The old minesweeper rolled up a little from the surface of the water.

Willie Keith did not have any idea what the executive officer was doing, though the maneuver was simple enough. The wind was turning the ship from south to west. Queeg had been trying to fight back to south. Maryk was doing just the opposite, now; seizing on the momentum of the twist to the right and assisting it with all the force of engines and rudder, to try to swing the ship's head completely northward, into the wind and sea. In a calmer moment Willie would easily have understood the logic of the act, but now he had lost his bearings. He sat on the deck, hanging stupidly to a telephone jackbox, with water sloshing around his crotch, and looked to the exec as to a wizard, or an angel of God, to save him with magic passes. He had lost faith in the ship. He was overwhelmingly aware that he sat on a piece of iron in an angry dangerous sea. He could think of nothing but

his yearning to be saved. Typhoon, *Caine*, Queeg, sea, Navy, duty, lieutenant's bars, all were forgotten. He was like a wet cat mewing on wreckage.

"Still coming around? What's your head? *Keep calling your head!*"
yelled Maryk.

"Coming around hard, sir!" the helmsman screamed as though prodded
with a knife. "Heading 310, heading 315, heading 320 —"

"Ease your rudder to standard!"

"*Ease* the rudder, sir?"

"Yes, ease her, ease her!"

"Ru-rudder is eased, sir —"

"Very well."

Ease, ease, ease — the word penetrated Willie's numb fogged mind. He
pulled himself to his feet, and looked around. The *Caine* was riding upright.
It rolled to one side, to the other, and back again. Outside the windows
there was nothing but solid white spray. The sea was invisible. The forecastle was invisible. "You okay, Willie? I thought you were knocked cold."
Maryk, braced on the captain's chair, gave him a brief side glance.

"I'm okay. Wha-what's happening, Steve?"

"Well, this is it. We ride it out for a half hour, we're okay — What's
your head?" he called to Stilwell.

"Three two five, sir — coming around slower, now —"

"Well, sure, fighting the wind — she'll come around — we'll steady on
ooo —"

"Aye aye, sir —"

"We will not," said Queeg.

Willie had lost all awareness of the captain's presence. Maryk had filled
his mind as father, leader, and savior. He looked now at the little pale man
who stood with arms and legs entwined around the telegraph stand, and
had the feeling that Queeg was a stranger. The captain, blinking and shaking his head as though he had just awakened, said, "Come left to 180."

"Sir, we can't ride stern to wind and save this ship," said the exec.

"Left to 180, helmsman."

"Hold it, Stilwell," said Maryk.

"Mr. Maryk, fleet course is 180." The captain's voice was faint, almost
whispering. He was looking glassily ahead.

"Captain, we've lost contact with the formation — the radars are blacked
out —"

"Well, then, we'll find them — I'm not disobeying orders on account of
some bad weather —"

The helmsman said, "Steady on ooo —"

Maryk said, "Sir, how do we know what the orders are now? The guide's
antennas may be down — ours may be — call up Sunshine and tell him
we're in trouble —"

Butting and plunging, the *Caine* was riding ship again. Willie felt the normal vibration of the engines, the rhythm of seaworthiness in the pitching, coming up from the deck into the bones of his feet. Outside the pilothouse there was only the whitish darkness of the spray and the dismal whine of the wind, going up and down in shivery glissandos.

"We're not in trouble," said Queeg. "Come left to 180."

"Steady as you go!" Maryk said at the same instant. The helmsman looked around from one officer to the other, his eyes popping in panic. "Do as I say!" shouted the executive officer. He turned on the OOD. "Willie, note the time." He strode to the captain's side and saluted. "Captain, I'm sorry, sir, you're a sick man. I am temporarily relieving you of command of this ship, under Article 184 of *Navy Regulations*."

"I don't know what you're talking about," said Queeg. "Left to 180, helmsman."

"Mr. Keith, *you're* the OOD here, what the hell should I do?" cried Stilwell.

Willie was looking at the clock. It was fifteen minutes to ten. He was dumfounded to think he had had the deck less than two hours. The import of what was taking place between Maryk and Queeg penetrated his mind slowly. He could not believe it was happening. It was as incredible as his own death.

"Never you mind about Mr. Keith," said Queeg to Stilwell, a slight crankiness entering his voice, fantastically incongruous under the circumstances. It was a tone he might have used to complain of a chewing-gum wrapper on the deck. "I told you to come left. That's an order. Now you come left, and fast —"

"Commander Queeg, you aren't issuing orders on this bridge any more," said Maryk. "I have relieved you, sir. You're on the sick list. I'm taking the responsibility. I know I'll be court-martialed. I've got the conn —"

"You're under arrest, Maryk. Get below to your room," said Queeg. "Left to 180, I say!"

"Christ, Mr. Keith!" exclaimed the helmsman, looking at Willie. Urban had backed into the farthest corner of the wheelhouse. He stared from the exec to Willie, his mouth open. Willie glanced at Queeg, glued to the telegraph, and at Maryk. He felt a surge of immense drunken gladness.

"Steady on 000, Stilwell," he said. "Mr. Maryk has the responsibility. Captain Queeg is sick."

"Call your relief, Mr. Keith," the captain said at the same instant, with something like real anger. "You're under arrest, too."

"You have no power to arrest me, Mr. Queeg," said Willie.

The shocking change of name caused a look of happy surprise to appear on Stilwell's face. He grinned at Queeg with contempt. "Steady on 000, Mr. Maryk," he said, and turned his back to the officers.

Queeg suddenly quit his grasp on the telegraph stand, and stumbled across the heaving wheelhouse to the starboard side. "Mr. Keefer! Mr. Harding! Aren't there *any* officers out there?" he called to the wing.

"Willie, phone Paynter and tell him to ballast all empty tanks on the double," Maryk said.

"Aye aye, sir." Willie seized the telephone and buzzed the fire-room. "Hello, Paynt? Listen, we're going to ballast. Flood all your empty tanks on the double — You're goddamn right it's about time —"

"Mr. Keith, I did *not* issue any orders to ballast," said Queeg. "You call that fireroom right back —"

Maryk stepped to the public-address system. "Now, all officers, report to the bridge. All officers, report to the bridge." He said aside to Willie, "Call Paynter and tell him that word doesn't apply to him."

"Aye aye, sir." Willie pulled the phone from the bracket.

"I said once and I say again," Queeg exclaimed querulously, "both of you are under arrest! Leave the bridge, right now. Your conduct is disgraceful."

Queeg's protests gave Willie a growing sense of gladness and power. In this shadowy careening wet wheelhouse, in this twilit darkness of mid-morning, with a murderous wind shrieking at the windows, he seemed to be living the happiest moment of his life. All fear had left him.

Maryk said, "Willie, think you can grab a look at the barometer without being blown over the side?"

"Sure, Steve." He went out on the port wing, clinging carefully to the bridge structure. As he crept up to the charthouse door it came open, and Harding, Keefer, and Jorgensen emerged, clasping each other's hands. "What's the dope, Willie? What goes on?" yelled Keefer.

"Steve relieved the captain!"

"*What?*"

"Steve relieved the captain! He's got the conn! He's put the captain on the sick list!" The officers looked at each other and lunged for the wheelhouse. Willie edged to the rear bulkhead and peered around at the blurry barometer. He dropped to his hands and knees and crawled back to the pilothouse. "Steve, it's up," he cried, jumping to his feet as he came to the doorway. "It's up! Twenty-eight ninety-nine, almost 29.00!"

"Good, maybe we'll be through the worst of it in a while." Maryk stood beside the wheel, facing aft. All the officers except Paynter were grouped, dripping, against the bulkhead. Queeg was hanging to the telegraph again, glaring at the exec. "Well, that's the story, gentlemen," Maryk said, his voice pitched high over the roar of the wind and the rattle of spray on the windows. "The responsibility is entirely mine. Captain Queeg will continue to be treated with the utmost courtesy, but I will give all command orders —"

"Don't kid yourself that the responsibility is all yours," Queeg interposed sulkily. "Young Mr. Keith here supported you in your mutinous conduct from the start and he'll pay just as you will. And you officers" — he turned, shaking his finger at them — "if you know what's good for you, will advise Maryk and Keith to put themselves under arrest and restore command to me while the restoring is good. I may be induced to overlook what's happened in view of the circumstances, but —"

"It's out of the question, Captain," said Maryk. "You're sick, sir —"

"I'm no sicker than you are," exclaimed Queeg with all his old irritation. "You'll all hang for collusion in mutiny, I kid you not about that —"

"Nobody will hang but me," said Maryk to the officers. "This is my act, taken without anybody's advice, under Article 184, and if I've misapplied Article 184, I'll get hung for it. Meantime all of you take my orders. There's nothing else you can do. I've taken command, I've ballasted on my own responsibility, the ship is on the course I ordered —"

"Mr. Maryk!" Stilwell shouted. "Something up ahead, a ship or something, close aboard, sir!"

Maryk whirled, squinted out through the windows, and grabbed at the telegraph handles, hurling Queeg roughly aside. The captain staggered and grasped a window handle. "Hard right rudder!" the exec shouted, ringing up full astern on both engines.

Visibility had improved so that the sea was in sight through the driving spray some fifty yards beyond the bows. A vast dim red shape bobbed on the black swells, slightly to port.

The *Caine* veered quickly, shoved sideways by the wind as soon as it turned a little. The thing drifted closer. It was immense, long and narrow, longer than the *Caine* itself, bright red. Waves were breaking over it in showers of foam.

"Holy Mother of God," said Keefer. "It's the bottom of a ship."

Everybody stared in awe at the horror. It slipped slowly down the port side, endlessly long and red, rolling gently under the breaking waves. "Destroyer," Harding said in a choked voice.

The *Caine* was moving well clear of it. Part of the wreck was already gone in the gloom. "We'll circle," said Maryk. "All engines ahead full, Willie."

"Aye aye, sir." The OOD rang up the order. There was a hideous sickness at the pit of his stomach.

Maryk went to the PA box and pressed the lever. "Now all hands topside keep a sharp lookout for survivors. We will circle the capsized ship twice. Report anything you see to the bridge. Don't get excited. Don't anybody get blown overboard, we have enough trouble as it is."

Queeg, braced in a forward corner against the windows, said, "If you're so worried about the safety of this ship, how can you go monkeying around looking for survivors?"

"Sir, we can't just steam by and forget it —" said the exec.

"Oh, don't misunderstand me. I think we should look for survivors. In fact I order you to do so. I'm simply pointing out your inconsistency for the record —"

"Left standard rudder," said Maryk.

"I should also like to point out," said Queeg, "that twenty minutes before you illegally relieved me I ordered you to get rid of that helmsman and you disobeyed me. He's the worst troublemaker on the ship. When he obeyed you instead of me he became party to this mutiny, and he'll hang if it's —"

A roaring wave broke over the *Caine's* bridge and buffeted the ship far over to port, and Queeg tumbled to his hands and knees. The other officers slid and tottered about, clutching at each other. Once again the minesweeper labored in difficulties as the wind caught it and swept it sideways. Maryk went to the telegraph stand and manipulated the engines, altering the setting frequently, and shouting swift-changing rudder orders. He coaxed the ship around to the south, and steamed ahead until the hulk came vaguely in view again. Then he commenced a careful circling maneuver, keeping the *Caine* well clear of the foundering wreck. It was entirely awash now; only when a deep trough rode under it did the round red bottom break to the surface. The officers muttered among themselves. Queeg, his arm around the compass stand, stared out of the window.

It took forty minutes for the *Caine* to maneuver through a full circle around the lost ship against wind and waves, and all the time it wallowed and thrashed as badly as it had been doing since morning, and took several terrible rolls to leeward. Willie was scared each time. But he now knew the difference between honest fright and animal terror. One was bearable, human, not incapacitating; the other was moral castration. He was no longer terrorized, and felt he no longer could be, even if the ship went down, provided Maryk were in the water near him.

The exec was out on the wing, shielding his eyes from the hurtling spray with both hands, peering around at the heaving spires of black water, as the *Caine* steadied on north again. He came into the wheelhouse, trailing streams from his clothes. "We'll come around once more and then quit," he said. "I think it's gone under. I can't see it — Left standard rudder."

Willie groped to the barometer once more and saw that it had risen to 29.10. He crawled to Maryk's side and reported the reading, yelling into the exec's ear. Maryk nodded. Willie rubbed his hands over his face, fevered with the sting of the flailing spray. "Why the hell doesn't it let up, Steve, if the barometer's rising?"

"Oh, Jesus, Willie, we're thirty miles from a typhoon center. Anything can happen in here." The exec grinned into the wind, baring his teeth. "We may still catch all kinds of hell — Rudder amidships!" he shouted through the doorway.

"Rudder amidships, sir!"

"Getting tired, Stilwell?"

"No, sir. Wrestle with this son of a bitch all day if you want me to, sir!"

"Very good."

The door of the radar shack pushed open, and the telephone talker, Grubnecker, poked out his whiskered face. "Something that looks like a raft on the starboard quarter, sir, Bellison reports."

Maryk, followed by Willie, went trampling through the wheelhouse to the other side of the bridge, shouting at Stilwell as he passed, "Hard right rudder!"

At first they saw nothing but peaks and troughs of water veiled by spray; then, broad on the beam, as the *Caine* rose to the top of a swell, they both spied a black dot sliding down the slant of a wave.

"I think there's three guys on it!" shrieked Willie. He danced aft to the flagbag rails for a better look. A stiff gust of wind sent him sprawling on his stomach on the canvas cover of the flagbag. As he gasped and clutched wildly at the halyards to keep from rolling over the side, swallowing salt water from the puddle on the canvas, the wind stripped his trousers clean off his legs, and they went flapping away over the bulwark into the sea. He pulled himself to his feet, paying no attention at all to the loss.

Queeg stood in the doorway, face to face with the executive officer. "Well, Mr. Maryk, what are you waiting for? How about rigging your cargo net to starboard and having your deck force stand by with life buoys?"

"Thank you, sir. I was about to give those orders, if you'll let me pass."

Queeg stepped aside. The exec went into the pilothouse, and passed the instructions over the loudspeaker. He began to maneuver the lurching ship toward the object, which soon showed clear, a gray balsam raft, with three men on it and two more heads bobbing beside it in the water.

"You'll be interested to know, gentlemen," Queeg said to the officers while Maryk manipulated engines and rudder, "that I was about to issue orders to ballast and head into the wind when Mr. Maryk committed his panic-stricken criminal act. I had previously determined in my own mind that if the fleet guide had given no orders by 1000 I would act at my own discretion —"

Maryk said, "All right, Stilwell, head over to the right some more. Hard right —"

Queeg went on, "And I saw no reason for confiding my command decisions to Mr. Maryk, who seemed to be treating me like a feeble-minded idiot, and I'll say as much over the green table, and there'll be plenty of witnesses to —"

"Don't run 'em down, Stilwell! Rudder amidships!" Maryk stopped the engines and went to the loudspeaker. "Now throw over your buoys!"

The survivors were pulled aboard. A white-faced, wild-eyed sailor, naked except for white drawers, streaked with broad smears of oil, with a bleeding gash in his cheek, was brought to the bridge by Bellison. The chief said, "It was the *George Black*, sir. This here is Morton, quartermaster third. The others are down in sick bay."

Morton stammered a brief, horrid tale. The *George Black* had been thrown broadside to the wind and all combinations of engines and rudder had failed to bring it around. Ventilators, ammunition boxes, and davits were ripped off the decks by the seas; water began flooding the engine rooms; power failed; the lights went out. The helpless ship drifted for ten minutes, rolling further and further to starboard, with all hands screaming or praying, and finally took a tremendous roll to starboard and never stopped rolling. His next recollection was being under water in complete blackness, and after that he was at the surface, being dashed against the red bottom of his ship.

"We'll keep circling," said Maryk. He peered out at the streaked sea, visible now for several hundred yards. "I think it's letting up some. Take him below, Bellison."

"I am resuming the conn, Mr. Maryk," said Queeg, "and we will drop the matter entirely until the storm has abated —"

Maryk turned wearily to the captain. "No, sir. I've got it. I respectfully ask you to lay below to your cabin. Contradictory orders will endanger the ship —"

"Are you putting me off my bridge, sir?"

"Yes, Captain."

Queeg looked to the officers. Their faces were scared and somber. "Do all you gentlemen concur in this act? . . . Do you, Mr. Keefer?"

The novelist gnawed at his lips, and turned his glance to Maryk. "Nobody is concurring. Nobody has to concur," the exec said quickly. "Please leave the bridge, Captain, or at least refrain from giving orders —"

"I shall remain on the bridge," said Queeg. "The ship is still my responsibility. Mutiny doesn't relieve me of it. I shall not speak unless your acts appear to me to be endangering my ship. In that case I shall speak even at pistol point —"

"Nobody's pulling pistols on you, sir. What you say suits me." The exec nodded to the officers. "Okay, no need for you to hang around. We'll have a meeting as soon as weather permits."

The officers began straggling out of the wheelhouse. Keefer went up to

Willie, saluted, and said with a pallid grin, "I am ready to relieve you, sir."

Willie looked at the clock in astonishment. Time had stopped running in his mind. It was a quarter to twelve. "Okay," he said. The formulas of the relieving ceremony came mechanically to his lips. "Steaming on various courses and speeds to look for survivors of the *George Black*. Steaming on boilers one, two, and three. Depth charges set on safe. Condition Able set throughout the ship. Last time I saw the barometer it had risen to 29.10. Fleet course is 180, but we've lost contact with formation due to jammed radars, and I don't know where we are. About one hundred and fifty miles east of Ulithi, I'd say. You can check our 0800 dead reckoning position. We're in the same place, more or less. The captain has been relieved under Article 184, and is still on the bridge. The executive officer has command and is at the conn. I guess that's all."

"Just a routine watch," said Keefer. Willie smiled ruefully.

Keefer saluted. "Okay, I've got it." He grasped Willie's hand, pressed it warmly, and whispered, "Good work."

"God help us all," murmured Willie.

Life in the Foxholes

✗

from *The Big War*

by ANTON MYRER

Night was a swarming pressure of lights and silhouettes and shadows. Ahead of Newcombe, as he swung his gaze from left to right over a hundred-and-twenty-degree arc, were two crouched figures, a tall man with an unwound burnoose, a turkey gobbler, two twisted stove-lids, another stealthy crawling figure. A flare burst high above him and the shadowed apparitions morphosed subtly, cleverly, into two shrubs, a blasted coconut palm, a maguey plant, some corrugated iron shards. The flare descended — a solemn, swaying incandescence, and shells *chuff-chuff-chuffed* overhead in glowing flights of four, crashed into the jungle beyond; and the shadows around things crept under cover to wait . . . Then the flare went out and the crouching figures, the man with the burnoose returned, advanced a step. They advanced a step with the death of every flare.

He was fixing again: fixing on one thing — that configuration to the left of the ruffled turkey gobbler. Keep turning your head: make yourself turn your head rhythmically, sweep back through the flash-scarred dark to where Danny's helmet protrudes from the hole slightly ahead and to the right. Old Danny. Our rock of ages. On this rock we will found us our battle line: oh rock of our far-flung battle line, beneath whose awful —

Keep turning your Goddamned head.

Mosquitoes floated against his face in a high, whining drone, stung him savagely before he could wave them away; lighted on his wrists and hands in spiderlike finesse and bit him still more. He had tried wearing his head-net but with it he'd been able to see nothing at all; and the sensation of meshed enclosure had driven him almost crazy. The air, hot and damp and heavy, bore them along on its soft, invisible combers, was filled with their malignant humming. At the end of his traverse was Derekman's helmet, turning too: thousands of cloth-covered helmets slowly turning in the dark, eyes beneath them straining against the night like watchers on a hostile shore. Watchman, what of the night? Ah, what indeed?

His legs were aching from the strained crouch he maintained at the edge of the hole; his shoulder pained hollowly from some time when he'd gone sprawling, crashing into something. He shifted the alarm cord Kantaylis had rigged up for them to his left hand and chafed the shoulder gently.

Another flare, brighter this time, and the hissing, locomotive-run-amok passage of shells. An eerie, sunless light: like Xanadu, where Alph the sacred river ran through caverns measureless to man. Hades might be like this, perhaps: the jewel-lit crepuscular illumination of Hades. *Might* be — !

Damn: it was falling behind them, behind their lines; swinging in its pretty silk parachute it swayed lower, in evil, tantalizing dalliance. *They* were silhouettes now. Jesus. Was he in a Jap's sights — helmet, shoulders, quaking heart — ?

Don't think of that.

He had hunched his shoulders instinctively, as if to draw them up under his helmet like a turtle. Eyes were fastened on him from the dark. El miedo tiene muchos ojos: fear has many eyes. Courage only one.

And the dark a thousand more.

The flare snuffed out, darkness rolled around him in a kindly wave; and he felt his shoulders and neck relax again. All are equal in the dark. In the grave. All cats look alike in the dark. When had he thought that? Ah, the night with her: that entrancing, achingly brief night with her . . . He felt the lightly burning shock of her hand against his face with awesome vividness. *You don't do that,* she had said. *You don't do a thing like that.* If she could see where he was now, what he was doing; what — good God — he had done that day, what would she think? Huddled in the hot darkness he had the eerie sense that in some way she *could* see him, was observing him that very instant with an expression of mingled anger and re-proach. *You don't do that*, she still seemed to be saying, shaking her head, her eyes glittering with tears. *You don't* —

Something struck the back of his hand: he jumped in fright, felt another tap on his shoulder, his knee. Rain. Huge drops coming in rapid succession they thickened, driving down, swelled in an instant to a roaring torrent. Cursing he thrust his rifle between his knees, wrenched at his poncho, pulled it out of his belt and removing his helmet put it on over his head. His shoulders and thighs were already soaked through. The rain lashed down in seething waves. Under another flare it turned to darting silver spikes that bounced on helmets, points of wood and metal.

Beside him O'Neill was stirring; Newcombe heard him mutter something in an angry monotone, then the crackling of his poncho as he broke it out.

"My watch?"

"No: you've got half an hour yet."

"Everything okay?"

"Swell. Perfectly swell."

He heard O'Neill settle himself again; his shoes pushed against New-combe's thigh, a contact which he welcomed. The rain fell in torrents, be-gan to trickle in icy ribbons down his neck and up the backs of his legs. All at once he was chilled; his teeth began to chatter and his hands shook monstrously. He rubbed his hands and feet, got out his brush and worked at his rifle under the poncho sightlessly, watching ahead. Far to the right the wall of the church, a ghostly gleaming silhouette in the glow of an-other flare, rose like an emaciated suppliant with one arm raised toward the heavens: devout or mocking, it was hard to say . . .

Time had stopped, it seemed: time too was exhausted after such a day as this; had given up, succumbed to the inertia of the void and could pro-gress no more than they. His legs and body ached with the wet cold, shrank from it in nervous little spasms: his head started to vibrate. He went on brushing at sand he couldn't see. Here on his second watch the day's ex-haustion caught up with him and seeped into the marrow of his bones, blended with the wet chill; water streamed in a steady, blinding curtain through the cloth of his helmet cover. Oh, that there would never be a day such as this day had been; never again. His mind, foggy and sharp by turns, started and slowed: geysers black and awful rose on either side, the figure came toward him with its wavering, stumbling walk, Diebenkorn again gazed moaning up at him in immense, horrible supplication . . .

He shut his eyes, opened them again, blinking rapidly. It was that no-body knew. Nobody knew, or they would never have suffered this kind of thing to rend the body, blacken the soul, reduce the spirit to a gibbering caricature that begged, that begged for death —

The man with the burnoose had moved. Jesus. His heart leaped softly.

He'd almost gone off, he'd damn near nodded off and he never would have seen it. Advancing stealthily, on mincing feet, through the downpour. Of course: waited for the rain. He thrust his rifle out ahead of him, felt feverishly for the grenades sitting in the sand by his right knee; picked up the alarm cord lying across his thighs and hefted it. Be sure, now: make sure. His temples were pounding against his helmet liner; with each pound there was a little flash of light across his field of vision.

Yes: it had moved. Get ready. He raised the rifle to his shoulder, pushed off the safety catch. Why hadn't Danny spotted him? or Harry? What was the matter with them? He forced himself with a great effort of will to look away to the right, then slowly back again. Yes: it had moved, had thickened. A Nip was using it for cover. Jesus — he was close enough to grenade them all to hell and gone. All right. Watch him till he moves, watch nothing else now. Then blast him.

Light exploded from above like a violent, heavenly dispensation, streaming points of rain — revealed the same blasted, shattered palm trunk. It was alone, unaccompanied: the same as before. He almost cried out in sheer relief.

Derekman's head dipped down near him. He glanced at his watch again. Two five. It was after two! Actually after. He put his hand on O'Neill's calf and pressed gently, murmured: "Jay . . ."

O'Neill started violently, kicked out at him. "What's the matter?"

"Time to take over. Two o'clock."

"Oh . . . okay."

The rain let up a little, fell in soft, sibilant streams around them. O'Neill moved up beside him, said, "Jesus: this is a daisy, isn't it?"

"Yeah. Great."

"Been quiet?"

"Yes. Some firing way over on the left. BAR, some grenades . . . Here's the cord. Look sharp now, Jay: it's hard as hell to see in this."

"You wouldn't snow me now, would you?"

He smiled faintly, patted O'Neill on the shoulder, moved back and lay down — became aware of water several inches deep around him. He pushed along in it, felt his shoes slither in the thinning mud. His rifle: he'd got mud smeared all over the butt. Mud was suddenly everywhere: it stuck to his fingers, smeared everything around him; his poncho was picking it up in folds and ridges. But his rifle —

He pulled the front of his skivvy shirt out of his trousers and rubbed the bolt clean with the tail of it; checked the safety again, drew the rifle in between his legs and lay on his side, head cradled in his helmet . . .

He awoke in a flash of wild dread: something struck him on the hip and he lurched to a sitting position. A rifle went off close beside him, then another, then a BAR in a rolling crash. A voice was screaming something over and over. He rushed to the edge of the hole just as O'Neill fired again. The blast almost deafened him; his hands were shaking so he could hardly hold the weapon and his heart, swollen to prodigious size, was choking him unbearably.

"— Illaaaaa!" someone screamed. "*Louelllaaaaa! . . .*"

There was another burst of firing and Kantaylis's voice shouted: "Hold your fire! Hold your fire!"

"Password, he's giving the password," O'Neill called.

"Could be a Jap," Ricarno answered him. "Look out."

"Could be . . ."

"All right," Kantaylis was saying, his voice clear and metallic in the clamor. "Who are you, chum?"

"Patrol. C Company," the voice called faintly.

"All right. Come on. Slowly. Your hands over your head. Come ahead —"

"Watch it, Danny —" Klumanski said.

The figure got to his knees with incredible slowness, rose and tottered forward in a strange, drunken lurch, waved one hand and fell again. Kantaylis was out of his foxhole running, knelt above him; and Newcombe saw him fling one of the fallen man's arms over his shoulder and stagger back toward them. Several others left their holes; scuffling in the murky dark they got him into the hole Derekman and Klumanski shared.

"Where's CP?" the man panted. He was holding one arm against his chest; blood lay in broad black streaks across his shoulders and back, cast one side of his face in a slick shadow. "CP —"

"Down the line," Kantaylis said. "Pass the word down for Carry . . . Where you from?"

"C Company CP —"

"C Company — you're way off base. We weren't even alerted for you. C Company's down —"

"Get hold of Herron. For — Christ — *sake* —"

"It's Moore," Ricarno said suddenly. "Ain't you Moore?"

"Yeah. Staging. For a heller . . ." He swayed forward, would have fallen if Klumanski had not held him; the air wheezed in and out of his throat in a whining singsong. "Right away quick . . ."

"Where's the rest of your patrol?" said Lundren, who had just come up.

"Got 'em all. All. But me." He gripped his arm tighter and tighter; his head waggled loosely, his eyes open and staring. "Get me CP, will you? They're staging."

"He'll never make it," Kantaylis said. "Pass the word for Herron."

Flares burst in profusion above them — four, five, six — their canisters fell whistling into the dark around their holes: light burgeoned — a fierce yellow illumination that disclosed helmets, heads, white smears of faces looped with shadow. His rifle was working smoothly; Newcombe put a clip on the edge of the foxhole near his right hand and opened all the flaps on his belt. In the crazy, fabricated daylight of the flares he felt calmer, but he was soaked through and shivering and the wild panic of half an hour before when the firing had wakened him still persisted: he could hardly draw air into his lungs. Steady down, you craven chicken, he told himself savagely. Be worth the trip, for once at least. For once in your life.

Slowly he turned his head and looked at O'Neill and said: "All set?"

O'Neill, fixing his bayonet with great care, looked back, nodded curtly. "Ready as I'll ever be . . ."

Detonations leaped in a row of orange blooms along the hill beyond the jungle, raced in and out in mad neon patterns; and above their heads the air became alive with sibilant, droning menace.

Newcombe pressed his elbows against his sides in an effort to steady himself, reduce his shivering. Somewhere near him a serene, dispassionate voice was saying over and over again, "Keep your fire low, boys, remember to fire low, now —" He looked around in amazement, saw Colonel Herron walking along high above him with badgerlike, sure-footed determination, carrying a carbine; with his free hand he made slow, flat sweeping motions as he spoke ". . . keep your fire low, now . . ."

"For God's sake, Herron, get your ass down!" Klumanski bellowed at him — a roar of anger and concern. The colonel nodded to him, gave him a benign, almost indulgent smile — kept moving along in his fantastic, leisurely stroll while invisible objects of incalculable malevolence whined and hummed and crackled around him, searching him out; his voice still floating intermittently, a calm, paternal admonition, through the flash-shot bedlam:

"— come up and meet them when they . . . cover each other, boys . . . see every man —"

Then his voice was gone, swallowed up as he moved off to the right, into chaos and uproar. More flares in wild incandescence, turned the night into an eerie subterranean afternoon. Ahead of them the tops of palms lashed and flailed like mops brandished by madmen.

Danny was shouting something to him: he couldn't hear, leaned forward, perplexed. Danny, his face dead white and full of dark hollows, called something again — all at once raised his fist and shook it in fierce exhortation. He nodded dumbly. There was a brief lull and Lundren's voice thundered:

"*Stand by*, you people!"

From the jungle beyond them came an unrecognizable sound which resolved itself into a high, wild cry, like a chant but thinner, more disembodied: "*Aaaaaaiiiii* . . ." An unbroken wail filled with savagery and despair, it rose and fell away, rose again to a fevered pitch and held it. Newcombe found he had his rifle in both hands and was shaking it as though to clear it of dust. Jay had grabbed him by the arm.

"Newk —"

"Yeah?" he said.

O'Neill still clutched him fiercely, a grip that pinched his arm with a pain he welcomed.

"Stay with it."

"Right," he said. "Right." He ground his teeth on each other, gritted them: lights glowed and shrank before his eyes. Beside him O'Neill, gazing ahead intently, crossed himself; raising his right hand he swiftly followed suit, though he had never done that before in his life.

There was a crackling in the jungle like herds of elephants trampling all the gathered twigs in the world — and then suddenly there they were in the clearing: lumps of ghostly dancing figures who swelled monstrously without advancing, changed aspect in an agony of trance to flapping birds, to goats, to antlike crabs with helmets glinting; came on in bands, in spidery striations, and everywhere was the wild, ghostly scream: ". . . *aaaaa-iiiii* —" neither animal nor human: lost limbo scream . . .

Low: fire low and squeeze 'em off.

The gun kicked him, kick, kick, kick: he pressed in toward the recoil with his shoulder, a fierce affection: brass bubbles flipped past his eyes' scan, curving out of sight. Another clip. Quick. Jay was shouting something. They were puppet figures — jerking along on arms and legs, jerking stiltlike, idiotic in blobs and patches, in hordes; swelling in clarity. Holes: they had square holes in their faces: their mouths were open, they were screaming, uttering that fierce, despairing cry that floated above the pounding, cacophonic roar. *Banzai*, they were shrilling *banzaiiiii* . . .

Low. Fire low and steady. He clawed another clip out of his belt by feel, with marvelous agility, and jammed it home. His nose was stinging. Rags and snatches of bodies they grew with dreamy alchemy, making crazy, graceless motions: they held curving strips of ribbon that flashed blue-white, dazzled him; flashed and flashed.

All at once they were nearer — broke asunder, split into screaming, arm-waving men, the enemy, full of hate and death: one of them leaped high in the air and fell, clawing arms and legs in space: another doubled over and slid out of sight, another tripped, rose laughing — *laughing?* — tripped again and fell. He himself was yelling now, a hoarse, unintelligible yell, he knew by the unremitting ache in his throat, Jay was yelling, all of them were. Filled with rage he rose out of the hole, rose to meet a figure sweeping toward him — a broad olive face convulsed with screaming, shiny conical helmet polished or lacquered, something strange, with the little star aglow; bubbles of sweat ringed the mouth and cheeks. The figure burst against him in a mad dance, and the great blue sword in his hand gleamed as if on fire . . . And everything slowed. In a floating lurch, like dreamy soundless surf he crouched, feinted to the right, lunged in. He had missed. No: the blade had gone in to the haft with fearful ease: between the buttons. He could hardly believe his eyes. How easy it is to kill with the bayonet, a thought flashed, they never told us that, if they know why didn't they — Bound in the dreamy lethargy he wrenched back and plunged again, conscious of the blue sword raised higher and higher, and of a hand that danced in space, clawed at his nose and chin. There was a clangor on his helmet like the clatter of a thousand forges, an awful shocking weight: lightning streamers swarmed before his vision, turned it ruddy, black, again fitfully bright, through which the sword rose again, wavering now and slow. The face had vanished: reappeared a mask of boundless consternation. In a transport of fury he swung the butt with all his might at the hated face to smash it senseless, sightless, out of sight —

Something was wrong. He was floating in a dreamy, hazy surf. The Jap was above him: no, below him — foul, foreign smell that enraged him beyond measure. The face was staring with wild terror into his eyes. He shouted but no sound came. A carbuncle thrust out beside the nostril, distressing, red and inflamed against the smooth, sweating olive skin . . .

There was a thunderclap which seemed to originate in the base of his skull: his sight darkened, narrowed to a blue-gray band of light through which he endlessly whirled. Something hit him in the chest. Down. He was on the ground on his back. Get up *get up*. He got to one knee with drunken deliberation, stood swaying in the midst of an epicene nausea where figures pirouetted and danced in silly convolutions. Odd: how no one —

Rifle: his rifle was gone. He saw a space where there was nothing — absolutely nothing! — filled an instant later with two forms locked and swaying. He drew his knife with a movement which was almost a paroxysm. They both were gone. Another thunderclap of unspeakable intimacy spoke behind his eyes. Smoke enveloped him: smoke and whirling dust. He was on his hands and knees again: retching in a hollow, moaning gloom. Up. He had to get up!

All his joints were broken: or petrified. He rose on wobbling, watery legs: a man swept in front of him, a face turned — a wild tight face, flat helmet. Jap. He struck at it, clutched, drove the knife in, fell sprawling on the squat, writhing body: leaped up again, saw Danny — unmistakably Danny — rise up too, attached to a figure which soared over backward, arms flung wide; a soaring scarecrow. Someone roared a word in his face: he saw Harry standing calmly, as if on the range, firing offhand, the empty shells in a rising curving glinting stream of carnival delight. But he could not see the end of Harry's rifle. Odd. Someone was rolling near him: rolling back and forth like a dog bathing in dust. He saw a rifle lying near him, snatched it up — stared in owlish bewilderment into the mad moonlight of the flares. He was conscious of a series of whip-crack-booms of fearful magnitude immediately in front of him — black, boiling whorls which caught at him, swept him backward. What was wrong? Men leaped and fell in their dusty vortex, tight tunics and flat helmets. Japs. They were running. Running away. He raised the rifle, an instinctual, almost casual gesture, fired again and again into the splashed tinfoil shapes of light. Ahead the figures whirled into oblivion, swept away through rifts and floating scars of smoke. Scampered and danced in the black boiling rifts. Had vanished utterly.

All over.

It was all over. A stillness as though a crystal bell had been clapped over them all; then lifted — and cries and screams more horrible filled its place.

Jay. He could see no one, now. A man was doubled over, holding both hands to his head: a bubbling moaning. Marine. He cried, "Corpsman!" without thought; peered into strips of light and darkness that cut his eyes like knives.

It was over. The slow surf-lurch of nightmare was over. Fancy . . . He turned around, enclosed in a bewildered exhaustion beyond anything he'd ever felt. As though his body had been shocked into a quivering, paralyzed mass of flesh, a stupor from which it would never recover.

"— Al!"

He turned again, staring dumbly through the hurting, luminous strips. Jay — old Jay . . . Jesus! — was staring at him: a face frantically white and drawn.

"Al! You make out?"

"Sure," he panted. "Sure, sure . . ." Blood was welling up in his mouth from somewhere; he was choking from it. He coughed up a thick gout of blood and spat it out in revulsion.

Now time was racing again, absurdly. Ridiculous: after all the hideous dreamy timelessness, time now raced away. Things happened but he couldn't keep up with them, couldn't take part in them somehow, move in *their* time. He was cognizant only of a dulled cone dead ahead where Ricarno stood above a groping prostrate figure and fired down once, again, the muzzle kicking, spurting fire: the cone swung in eerie trajectory, far too slowly, to where Carrington was kneeling over someone, extending like a fluttering ribbon rolls of yellowed gauze; farther on Lieutenant Prengle was saying, "Don't talk: don't try to talk, Mario . . ." and Lieutenant D'Alessandro, pale as death itself, looked up at him with glittering eyes, his lips moving steadily, and from a smooth, lazy crescent in his throat blood streamed in a curtain, like a silken scarf —

He was still holding a rifle, not his own. His right hand was sticky against the stock; he looked at it curiously, the sticky noisome jam that darkened his palm . . . It was as though he had lost his hearing, his voice, his human density — had lost contact somehow with the world of movement where time had unfairly speeded up again. Too bad: at a time when —

Lundren was thundering at them: Lundren, towering before them, wrapping a green skivvy shirt tightly around his left forearm. His voice bombarded Newcombe like a spirit, a stern, ghostly admonition:

"All right now, stand fast, you people! Get into line and stand fast. Take cover, all of you. They may try it again, now . . ."

"Oh . . ." He turned and gazed away beyond the groaning and cursing and the cries — gazed at the dark, depthless mat of jungle: it was as remote, as soundless as the far shore of hell. The appalling implication of what Lundren had just said penetrated to the deepest deeps of his heart and wrung it. "Oh," he said, and squeezed his eyes shut.

"Newcombe! Get your ass into that hole!"

Lundren's voice again: he was moving already, without thought. Jay was speaking to him, something that also pricked his consciousness with swift force. Bayonet: there was no bayonet on the end of the rifle he held. His own. He wanted his own rifle and this was not his. He stepped out in front of the foxhole and got his own. It was lying beside the man he had killed, now a twisted carcass without dignity or grace. The face, bent sidewise, regarded him: smooth and Oriental and stamped with horror and despair. The carbuncle glinted at the edge of one of the nostrils; the mouth, like the eyes, was still open, still soundless. Staring down, Newcombe knew with the most implacable certainty that this face would never leave him all the rest of his life; that he would never lie in some sunlit field in thoughtless, happy reverie again.

Vicksburg Remembered

X

from *The Soldier*

by RICHARD POWELL

A lieutenant and several enlisted men were on duty in the Message Center. Farralon said, "Lieutenant, are the telephone lines from here to General Stock's headquarters absolutely secure? Is there any chance that Japs could have infiltrated and cut in on the lines?"

"The lines are O.K., sir," the lieutenant said. "They don't run anywhere near the front, and they're patrolled all the time."

"All right. Get me a line to General Stock, and then clear everybody out of here except your switchboard man."

He didn't want anyone — Japs or Americans — eavesdropping on his call. He couldn't telephone from the tent where Ben was packing his things, or from the Operations tent, where most of the staff was on duty. The switchboard operator in the Message Center wore headphones and could only overhear if he plugged into the connection, and Farralon could watch for that.

The call to General Stock went through and Farralon heard the rasp of his voice. "Sir, this is Farralon," he said. "I have just relieved Colonel Hetherington from command of the 484th."

"You have, have you?" Stock said. "Without asking me or anything, huh?"

"I thought we discussed the matter, General."

"Well, we did some talking but I expected you to check with me before doing anything."

"The situation seemed to require prompt action, sir."

"Huh. Makes it look like the Lower Pacific Command is running the regiment, not me."

That was exactly how it was supposed to look. "General," he said, "you can rescind my order if you wish."

"No, no, let's not go that far," Stock said. There was a note of relief in his voice; he didn't mind being out from under. "I approve your action. Now about the new C.O. —"

"For the time being, sir, I have assumed command."

What sounded like static came over the line. Perhaps General Stock had turned away from the phone to catch up on his cursing. The static ended, and Stock said, "You seem to run things your own Goddam way."

"I didn't want to leave the regiment even for a short time without a C.O., sir. I recommend that a message be sent to General McGuire asking him to detach Colonel Gruder, who is C.O. of one of our other Infantry regiments, to come here and take command of the 484th. When Colonel Gruder arrives I would like to be relieved at once. I'll prepare a message to General McGuire covering all this."

He was pushing General Stock fairly hard, and at the other end of the line Stock made noises like a freight train laboring up a grade. "All right, all right," Stock growled. "I don't know what else I can do but say O.K. But now listen, Farralon. While you're commanding the 484th you're not McGuire's Chief of Staff to me. You're completely under my command. Got that?"

"Yes sir."

"Your regiment better do something tomorrow or there'll be hell to pay. You'll get the written orders in the next hour, but I'll tell you what they are. The 33rd Marines will hold that salient. The 484th will advance and straighten the lines. Understand?"

So far, things had gone Farralon's way, but now they had come to a touchy point. It was too late in the day to start the amphibious operation. It would take many hours to line up the landing craft, and march the reserve battalion to the beachhead and embark for the cove.

"General," he said, "I'd like to outline a plan of attack for your consideration. There's a cove three miles up the coast. We've scouted it, and it's not guarded. I'd like permission to move my reserve battalion to that cove by landing craft tomorrow night, without any preliminary bombardment, and throw it across the enemy line of communications. I think that would let us stage a major breakthrough on our front. Of course it would involve postponing tomorrow's attack twenty-four hours."

There was silence at the other end of the line.

Farralon said, "Are we still connected, sir?"

"Oh, I heard you, all right," Stock said.

"Perhaps I could come up now and explain all the details to you, sir."

Stock shouted, "I don't want any of your details. It was bad enough with Hetherington not pushing his attacks. Now you don't want to attack at all!"

"General, it's merely a postponement to put us in position to crack the whole Jap front."

"Postponement, hell! The Japs might hit that salient in the flank tomorrow and roll my Marines back. Listen, Farralon, you have your orders. The amphibious landing is out! The postponement is out! You're to attack at 0700. Follow my orders or I'll get somebody who will. Understand?"

It was clear enough, all right. Maybe he had been too hasty in telling Ben that he wanted to fight Japs, not Marines. "Yes sir," he said. "I understand."

"That's all, then," Stock said, and slammed down his phone.

Farralon replaced the phone slowly and wiped the sweaty palm of his hand on his shirt. His hand was trembling. He clenched it until the tendons cut white ridges into the skin. There was no use arguing with Stock; you might as well try to stop a tank by pelting it with flowers. He had to launch an attack tomorrow or else. The attack that had just been ordered, however, was sure to fail. Of course he could knock heads together and scare hell out of the officers of the 484th. If he did, the regiment might drive forward with more determination, but it wouldn't make anything like a half-mile advance, and it would take brutal casualties. After a couple days of such casualties the regiment would lose effectiveness as a combat unit. And yet the regiment could do a good job, if you played to its strength instead of its weakness.

Once before he had received direct orders to do something he knew was wrong. Its words still crawled through his memory: *You will turn over Anchor Island command to next ranking officer* . . . Of course, all through history soldiers had received orders they felt were wrong, and had disobeyed them. Sometimes you could get away with it by claiming you didn't receive the orders or didn't understand them or couldn't carry them out. But there was no question of that here. He wondered what Caesar had thought, standing on the banks of the Rubicon with his 13th Legion, completely aware of the fact that no Roman general was allowed to lead his troops south of that river without special authority from the Senate. He didn't know what Caesar had thought but he knew what he had done.

He left the Message Center and went to the Operations tent and said to the regiment's Executive Officer, "I have relieved Colonel Hetherington from command of the 484th, and I have assumed command. Please have my sergeant, Kowalski, report to my tent at once. I want a meeting in my tent at 1900 with you, the Adjutant, Intelligence Officer, Plans and Training Officer, Supply Officer, the C.O. of the Artillery battalion, and the C.O.'s of the three Infantry battalions."

At his tent he found that Ben had cleared out his personal things and had left. He sat at what had been Ben's desk and studied the map. The amphibious operation was out. Stock had said that flatly, and he couldn't get landing craft unless Stock approved. But when you came right down to it, probably he didn't have to have landing craft.

He waited until Kowalski came in, and said to him, "That patrol you made last night. Could a whole battalion make it?"

Kowalski rubbed a speck of dirt off his BAR. "I dunno about the heavy weapons company," he said. "Kinda tough, lugging them big mortars and the fifties."

"Forget the weapons company. Can three rifle companies make it?"

"Not if the bums make a racket. There's got to be Japs near the top of them cliffs."

"All right. No racket. How about it?"

"Jeez, Colonel, if five guys can make it, three rifle companies can. We din hit no deep water. It's black as a bitch under them cliffs. If the bums don't make no noise, nobody up on them cliffs can spot 'em."

"Were the other four men in your patrol pretty good?"

"Not bad, Colonel."

"If you leave one of them to guide the battalion, can you and the other three take out that Jap post at the head of the ravine leading up from the cove, and hold it until the battalion gets there? Can you do it without making any noise?"

Kowalski licked his lips. "Sure thing, Colonel."

"O.K. I'm having a meeting here in a few minutes. I want you to stick around. Just stand back of my desk leaning on your BAR and don't say anything."

For once, Kowalski almost grinned. "I stand back of you looking mean, huh, Colonel?"

Farralon said sharply, "Just stand there. Don't start turning into an actor on me. I have enough troubles already."

"Aah, don't worry about nuttin, Colonel. You and me, we'll show the bums how to fight."

"I hope so. And as long as we're staging an act, give me a couple of hand grenades. I'll use them as paperweights."

Kowalski dug two grenades from his bag, and Farralon placed them on corners of the situation map. It would be a corny scene but perhaps effective: the grim figure of the BAR man behind him, and the hand grenades holding down the map. It ought to create a very different impression from the one Ben had created, with his soft-footed orderly and meals with a real tablecloth spread over the field desk.

His officers began coming in. Each of them looked at Kowalski and at the deadly paperweights.

When they had all arrived, he said, "Gentlemen, I'm sure you all know that I have assumed command of this regiment. I'm not going to give you a lecture or a fight talk. The 484th is a good outfit. In the next twenty-four hours it's going to prove it's a lot better than you or anybody else thought. The Marines are going to start looking up to you, not down on you. Here's how we're going to do it."

He outlined the plan. The Third Battalion, less its heavy weapons company, carrying nothing but weapons, ammunition, entrenching tools and one day's rations, would move immediately from the reserve area to the shore at the base of the cliffs. Its men would then move in single file, maintaining absolute silence, along the shoreline to the cove three miles up the coast. There the battalion would occupy high ground secured by an advance patrol led by Kowalski, and dig in across the enemy's line of communications. The Japs would probably attack in force during the morning, withdrawing front line units to do so. The regimental artillery would send along a team of forward observers to direct the fire support. At 1300, with the Jap front lines presumably weakened by withdrawal of units, the First and Second Battalions would attack, neutralizing strong points instead of stopping to destroy them, and break through to the Third Battalion. Walkie-talkies would be used for communication, with a relay point halfway along the beach route, in case the four to five mile range of the walkie-talkies did not provide clear transmission back to Regimental headquarters and to the batteries of 105-mm howitzers. Any questions?

There were only a few technical ones. His officers were taking this very well. They liked the idea of not having to stage another bloody frontal attack on fully manned Jap positions.

The lieutenant colonel commanding the Third Battalion said he could have his men on the beach by 2300. They ought to be able to move along the beach at the rate of a mile an hour. The leading elements should reach the head of the ravine at the cove by 0300.

Farralon gave orders about the patrol Kowalski was to lead, and about the guide for the battalion, and ended the meeting.

After they left, he typed a message to General McGuire reporting the relieving of Colonel Hetherington and asking for Colonel Gruder. He sent it to the Message Center for immediate transmission. Then, because he couldn't leave General Stock in the dark as to his plans, he wrote a full report on them. In the report he took the position that, since General Stock had merely vetoed an amphibious operation and a postponement of the attack, his new plans were acceptable. Of course he knew that they weren't. He intended, therefore, to make sure that the Third Battalion was on its way and beyond recall before he let Stock know what was happening. He signed the report and put it in his pocket and went to the Operations tent.

On the dot of 2300 a walkie-talkie message informed him that the Third Battalion was starting its march along the beach. Farralon brought out his report and sent it by runner to General Stock. Then he began thinking about what would happen when Stock read the report. Stock would realize it was too late to recall the Third Battalion. But it wouldn't be too late for Stock to do something else. Farralon could almost see and hear General Stock grabbing the phone and calling him and relieving him from command. God only knew who Stock would put in his place, and what would happen to the plans for tomorrow's attack. At the very least, Stock would order the new C.O. to attack with the First and Second Battalions early in the morning, before the Jap defenses had been weakened. That wouldn't do at all.

He got up and beckoned to his Exec and walked outside with him. "You and I don't know each other very well," he said.

"Well, sir," the Exec said hesitantly, "of course I know you by reputation."

"How do you feel about this operation we've started? Do you think it will work?"

"I'm sure it'll work, sir. These aren't bad soldiers. This will give them a chance to prove it. I have an idea they'll do fine, and it'll be the making of this regiment."

"I planned this operation all on my own," Farralon said. "Just a few minutes ago I sent a report on it to General Stock. That will be his first news of it. My guess is, you'll see sparks in the sky over Task Force Headquarters, and that will be General Stock going up in flames."

"I see what you mean, sir."

"I want to tell you a little story from military history. Are you familiar with the Vicksburg campaign of General Ulysses S. Grant?"

"I've forgotten whatever I knew about it, sir."

"Grant decided to cut loose from his base and swing around the Confederates at Vicksburg. He notified General Halleck, who was commanding all the Union land forces at that time, of his plans. Halleck ordered Grant to drop his plans and return to his base. But there was no telegraph line to Grant's headquarters. The order didn't reach him until the campaign was underway. Naturally, he couldn't obey it."

The Exec grinned. "I get it, Colonel. You —"

"Take it easy," Farralon said. "Let's keep this vague. I have now ended my lecture on military history. New subject. I am in command of the 484th. Nobody issues any orders to it except through me. I am in command until I personally receive official orders relieving me. I have decided that I can best coordinate tomorrow's attack by joining the Third Battalion. In passing, I might point out that there are no telegraph lines from here to the cove three miles up the coast. Do we understand each other?"

"Yes sir!" the Exec said. "I'll see you in, uh, Vicksburg."

Farralon nodded. An alert officer, the Exec. Worth watching. Tomorrow's attack by the First and Second Battalions would be a good test of the Exec, who would be running that part of the show. If things worked out well, maybe the Exec ought to get the regiment. Of course it was possible that, after tomorrow, he would be able to do only one thing for the Exec: make sure he wasn't court-martialed, too.

He returned to his tent and collected a flashlight, canteen, the map and the two grenades that had been holding it down. Then he started hiking along the trail that led to the beach. He arrived at the beach a little after midnight and found one of the rifle companies still there, waiting to go off in single file. Nearly five hundred men were already threading their way along the base of the cliffs; some were undoubtedly in Jap territory by now, and there had been no sound of firing. The battalion C.O. had left a major behind to coordinate the movement of the rifle companies. The major was surprised to see Farralon, but seemed pleased. That was a good sign.

Farralon slipped into the line of men and started plodding along in the black shadows of the cliffs. Here and there the walking was on dry sand, and easy. Occasionally he had to climb through a cleft between fallen rocks. At times he waded through water so warm you wouldn't have known it was there if it hadn't been for the splash and the drag around his feet. The column moved with little noise: a few clinks from equipment, splashing, a smothered curse as somebody fell. The cliffs soared up and up to the left, looming over them as if ready to topple down on the column. If Japs were up there, any noise that reached them ought to sound like the normal lapping of wavelets coming in across the reef.

He passed a spot where a huge block of cliff had split from the main mass, leaving a dark pyramid against the sky. He had seen that shape before, in the faded photograph at home and from the plane winging toward Moon Island. It didn't chill him as much as it used to do. What had Claire said? *You'll have to climb it again, but next time it won't be so hard.* The dark pyramid faded away behind him, like the tough decisions he had had to make in the last few hours. He had done the best he could, and now if things would only go right . . .

If things would only go right. There was no use saying they *had* to go right. Things never had to go right in a war. They were sure to go wrong for somebody: for you or for the enemy. All you could do was take your calculated risk, and pray for the luck that every soldier needed. Wolfe had the luck in that Quebec campaign. Wolfe's assault barges drifted under the St. Lawrence cliffs, moving in for the landing. A French sentry challenged them. A British officer replied soothingly in French. The sentry knew that provision boats were expected, and so he relaxed. That was the sort of luck you needed.

But if a Jap sentry challenged them now, from high on the cliffs, who could answer and make the sentry relax? Nobody. His own knowledge of written Japanese wouldn't mean a thing. The sentry would hail, and get no answer, and then the flares would bloom, and the Nambus and the Arisaka rifles would begin hammering, and the long column would writhe and start to die.

No challenge came from the cliffs. No flares ripped the velvet sky. He trudged on, following men who seemed to glide ahead of him like shadows on a wall. Then, abruptly, the sounds he dreaded began to clatter through the night. There was firing close ahead, up on the cliffs. He started running and bumped into the man in front.

The man turned and growled, "Relax, Bud. That's our stuff. You —" Then he peered at Farralon's face and insignia, and said, "Jeez, I'm sorry, sir. I didn't know it was you."

"It's all right," Farralon said.

He should have known the sounds were Garands and Browning machine guns. He hurried around a small promontory and found the cove. To the left the ravine cut a black notch in the cliffs. He scrambled up over rocks and through brush and came out, panting, on the tableland on top of the cliffs. A group of officers and noncoms, using hooded flashlights, were checking the men who came up over the lip of the ravine and directing them to their positions. One of them guided Farralon to the battalion CP.

Things were going well so far. Kowalski's group had wiped out the Jap post. Item and King Companies were digging in along a 1200-yard perimeter, and as Love Company arrived it would dig in along a support line. The battalion was entrenching across a trail that followed the cliffs, and had a clear lane of fire over what seemed like a major supply road, a hundred yards beyond the perimeter. They had cut enemy telephone lines along the road. The firing he had heard had been Item Company shooting up a small group of Japs walking along the road, perhaps hunting for the break in the telephone lines.

During the rest of the night nothing much happened, except to some trucks that came along the road and to a Jap patrol that blundered down the cliffside trail. Traffic on the supply road and the trail stopped.

Soon after dawn, mortar shells began plopping into King Company's position, and an attack in platoon strength rolled toward the perimeter. The reception proved to the enemy that it wasn't a job for a platoon. An hour went by. Mortars opened up more heavily and machine gun bullets combed the front. An attack in perhaps company strength surged toward them. Item and King Companies gave it the works with rifles and 60-mm mortars and automatic weapons, and the observers from the 105-mm howitzers called in a barrage. After that, the enemy knew that a company couldn't handle the problem. For two hours there was a breathing spell.

Of the seven hundred men holding the position Farralon suspected that he was the most useless. On Moon Island, because so few officers were alive, he had led troops. But here nobody above the rank of captain actually led troops. The battalion staff commanded officers, not enlisted men, and Farralon didn't really command anybody. He had given his orders to the battalion C.O. before the operation started; now he must avoid meddling unless a new major decision had to be made. All he could do was crawl from one rifle squad or mortar or machine gun section to another, talking to the men. It wouldn't hurt morale for them to see him taking a few risks, too.

In the middle of the morning the Japs went to work seriously. Farralon tried to identify the sound of the stuff they were using: Nambu machine guns and the heavier Hotchkiss type, light and heavy mortars, 70-mm infantry guns and 75-mm Krupp field artillery. Then the stuff got too thick and he lost track. It was like sitting inside a concrete mixer while people pounded on the outside with sledge hammers. Infantry attacks began foaming across the rocky fields and through the brush. The attacks went on and on, and thank God they didn't have tanks. Once a Jap rush broke through Item Company, and the reserve company charged from the support line and mopped it up. A mortar shell killed an artillery observer, and Farralon took on the job of spotting for one of the batteries. They were catching a lot of casualties. Fortunately they could take the wounded down the ravine and shelter them under the cliffs.

The battalion's lieutenant colonel crawled up to the rock behind which Farralon was lying, and said, "Pretty rough, isn't it, sir?"

"Your men are doing fine," Farralon said.

"Japs just keep coming, don't they?"

"Yes, but it's a lot easier than digging them from their holes."

"We'll be out of ammo by night, Colonel."

"They'll run out of Japs by night. They only had two regiments. I figure we're chewing up a full regiment right here."

"Thanks. Now I feel better, sir. I'll pass what you said along to the men."

Farralon hoped that what he said was correct. It ought to be right, but you never knew. It was fantastic, the way the Japs threw men at their position. Of course he had heard that the Japanese were very emotional in the attack. Against weak opposition that was an advantage. But against strong opposition, as in this case, it was a defect. You couldn't control troops properly if you and they were emotional. The attacking troops were brave, but bravery wasn't enough. A brave man might be a good individual fighter, but until his bravery was controlled and directed by discipline, he wasn't a good soldier.

Meanwhile there were too many brave Japs around.

The battle roared and pulsed. Early in the afternoon Farralon asked his battery to find out if the First and Second Battalions had launched their attack. The walkie-talkie he was using had good range; he was in direct communication with the battery without using the relay point. After a few minutes the battery commander got through to him.

"Is this Colonel Farralon?" the captain asked.

"This is Farralon."

"Wanted to make sure, sir. I have a message for you from your Exec. Maybe it won't make sense to you."

"Go ahead."

"He says the attack started on schedule. No news of results yet. He says, tell Grant that Halleck, that's H for How, A for Able —"

"I got it. Halleck."

"Yes sir. That Halleck exploded into a million pieces but that the telegraph line still isn't working. Do you understand that, sir?"

Farralon allowed himself a tight smile, and said, "I get it."

An hour went by. Another. The attacks kept coming like the great rushing gusts of wind in a hurricane. It was hard to tell whether or not the attacks were easing up. Unless they did, the battalion wouldn't be around much longer. More than two hundred men were dead or wounded. Item and King Companies had been forced to pull back, and Love Company had moved into the main line of resistance. Now they had no reserve. They would have been swept over the cliffs long ago if it hadn't been for the three batteries of howitzers. Time after time the salvos and volleys came howling across five miles of country to smash Jap attacks and knock out Jap artillery and mortars.

The radio squawked for his attention, and he said, "I read you. Over."

"Colonel?" the battery commander's voice asked.

"Right here."

"Colonel, I have another message for you from your Exec. He says tell you the word is, On to Vicksburg."

Thank God for that, Farralon thought. They had broken through. "Thanks," he said.

"One thing more, sir. The other two batteries have stopped getting reports from their observers."

"Hang on," Farralon said. He peered over the top of his rock. One of the other observers had been lying about a hundred yards to the left, the thin aerial of his walkie-talkie lifting over his position. Now there was no sign of the aerial. Mortar shells had been coming down heavily over there. "I'll spot for all of you," he said, "but you'll have to fire as a battalion, not as separate batteries."

"O.K., sir," the battery commander said. "We'll relay to the other two batteries."

Farralon looked around for a messenger, so he could pass the word that the First and Second Battalions were on their way. He saw somebody with a BAR lying behind a rock a few yards away.

"Soldier!" he called.

Kowalski's flat blank face turned and looked at him.

"How long have you been here?" Farralon asked.

"Maybe an hour, Colonel."

"You ought to be up front."

"Colonel," Kowalski said, "for the last hour, this cruddy rock has been the front."

Farralon glanced around. Kowalski was right. The lines had pulled back again. The original perimeter of twelve hundred yards had shrunk in half. And . . . And —

He grabbed the walkie-talkie, and said, "Here comes a big rush. I don't have time to work out firing data. We're back to a six-hundred-yard perimeter. Give us a box barrage with all the guns and lay it in close and keep it coming."

It looked like ants boiling across the ground toward them. Japs were running, crawling, stooping, leaping. The BAR began its clatter. Rifles and machine guns and mortars let go.

"On the way!" a voice yelled from the walkie-talkie.

Farralon began counting the seconds: one thousand and one, one thousand and two, one thousand and three . . . He could picture the 33-pound shells arching up and across the sky and starting the long plunge down. They seemed to be taking forever. The Jap rush was only a hundred yards away. It —

He jerked his head down. The hammer blows of the howitzers jolted the ground. Explosions grabbed the air and flapped it like an enormous sheet. Bits of rock and metal yowled overhead. The howitzers had pulled the barrage in tight. The concussion lifted and shook and slugged him dizzy. He glanced at Kowalski. For once the BAR man had quit. Kowalski lay flat, jamming hands against his ears.

He didn't know how long the barrage went on. Finally he got a faint impression that the walkie-talkie was making scratching noises. He put his mouth up close and yelled, "I can't hear a thing. Cease fire for a few seconds and let me take a look."

The radio made another scratching noise. Farralon waited. The sound of explosions didn't seem to stop. He took a chance and poked his head up and looked over the rock. The barrage had stopped but his numb ears hadn't noticed the difference. No more pink glares flickered along the front. No more columns of dirt squirted upward. Nothing moved out there. No Japs, no anything. It looked like the sort of landscape you might see after a forest fire.

"Cease fire," he said or yelled or screamed. It was hard to tell what you were doing when you couldn't hear. "That did it. There aren't any more targets. God Almighty, what shooting!"

The walkie-talkie made a scratching noise that might have had a note of pride in it.

An hour later an ugly lumbering thing poked its nose shyly around a bunch of trees five hundred yards away. It had a 75-millimeter gun in its side turret. It waited cautiously to make sure the battalion wasn't going to shoot at it, and then waddled toward them. It seemed appropriate that an M-3 tank called the General Grant was leading the breakthrough to Vicksburg.

Easter Sunday

X

from *Away All Boats*

by KENNETH DODSON

On the morning of Easter Sunday there was no evidence of the fury of Japanese defense: no clouds of counterattacking paratroopers reported waiting in Kyushu; no hornetlike buzzing of fast suicide boats with built-in warheads, known to be hiding by the hundreds in small coves, ready for the sudden rush to thunderous, glorious death; not a shot from Okinawa's well-placed coastal artillery; most surprising of all, no fury of Divine Wind Special Attack Force suicide planes diving from the skies. Desperate countermeasures on a scale not yet seen must surely come as Japanese died hard in defense of Okinawa, their homeland's last remaining island outpost, but there was no evidence yet as the great invasion fleet approached the main landing beaches at Hagushi on the southwest coast. Okinawa had been bombarded for seven days and nights while minesweepers protected by fast battleships swept all waters about Hagushi. Transport squadrons now steamed unmolested past Kerama Retto, a group of small islands within sight of Hagushi which had been captured during the previous week by the 77th Division. Now was the hour of testing: H Hour at 0830. One hundred twenty thousand Japanese waited behind carefully prepared defenses while over half a million American soldiers, marines and sailors closed in for the kill. Hearts beat fast and lumps refused to be swallowed in countless throats while men wondered, each in his own way, what was to be the grim joke-of-the-day this Easter Sunday — this April Fool's Day, 1945. And, at day's end, whom would the joke be on?

The sun rose bright in a sky that was clear except for great clouds of bombardment smoke rolling in from the sea. Standing tense but quiet on his bridge, Captain Hawks got his first glimpses of land through occasional gaps in drifting smoke; saw stony little hills of Naha, Yonabaru and the ancient fortress, Shuri. His crew was keyed up from long practice and overwaiting, eager to get into action. At the first indications of commands long since familiar, they sprang into landing craft, to boat davits, to cargo winches and to landing nets. Before the ending of the boatswain's mate's pipe, *Away All Boats*, winch-drums screamed and smoked with uncoiling wire cables while helmet-studded landing craft plunged down to the water carrying John, Dick, Joe, Carl to Okinawa this Easter Sunday. Others moved up to take their places, moved with a deliberate tramp, tramp, tramp — loaded with fighting packs, inflated life belts and rifles in Pliofilm — up the scuttles, along the decks and overside for the one-way ride. Davit boats dropped six at a time to upper-deck railings, paused long enough to load thirty-six marines in each, then dropped with the speed of elevators to dancing water, forty feet below. Winches hummed, steel cargo blocks slammed against hollow steel booms groaning with weight, yet Pappy Moran's hoarse shouts rose above all mechanical din as the rest of the landing craft were hoisted out yard and stay. "Hit that steadying line, Red. Take a turn now; take a turn. . . . Drop her now; DROP HER! . . . Unhook, down there. Pick up another one." Down the nets went human ants in jungle green: men, guns, ammo boxes, heavy machine guns in four pieces, in an unbroken flow like molasses from the lip of a man. During this process of debarkation the *Belinda*'s rudder moved from side to side, like a fish's tail in a riffle, and her propeller moved ahead in short kicks, maintaining the exact geographical relation between ship and shore so that landing craft might hit the precise sector of beach. No red barn to head for here, only ancient Okinawan tombs, unidentified on plan or chart but plain in white splendor when seen through ragged gaps in gunsmoke.

Hawks moved quietly about his bridge, remaining motionless for minutes on end. His nostrils quivered with excitement as acrid smoke drifted past; nerves taut as overtuned fiddle strings but outwardly quiet, his manner seemed almost casual to the enlisted men at his elbow. Anxiety showed clearly on Jim Randall's pleasant face as he plotted the *Belinda*'s position and kept her on station, "Things ought to pop any minute now," he remarked to Willicut, his quartermaster first.

Down in the *Belinda* command boat, anxiety clouded Brooks's face too as he cruised slowly around the ship, forming his boat waves, alert for any deviation from carefully worked out plans. Things were clicking this morning. He'd never seen it so fast, so smooth: thirty-two landing craft, four of them thirty-six-ton LCM's, plus four extra DUKW's launched in thirteen minutes. The *Belinda* davit tenders dropped their fully loaded boats with the casual competence of office-building elevator operators. Moran and Alvick had practically tossed the rest of them overside with cargo tackle. Boat officers were sharp today: all waves were formed up exactly as planned with the right boat in the right wave circle carrying the right landing unit; even Ensign Tuttle was on station. When Brooks came alongside Kruger's first-wave guide boat he grinned and yelled, "We might as well have stayed in the sack, Karl. They don't need us at all this morning." Kruger grinned back briefly, but his tanned face was serious again almost instantly and his gaze was directed skyward, rather than towards the smoke-obscured shore line. Brooks could feel his face tightening once more — that sky: best place to look for trouble. Then he shrugged his shoulders. "Take her around the other side again, Cox," he said to Larson. "We'd better check up on those other waves; it's nearly time to shove off."

Aboard the *Belinda*, some of the crew looked anxious, perhaps because of the intent quiet of these veteran Marines climbing down the nets for another one-way ride into battle. More than half of the sailors went about their well-rehearsed duties with considerable pleasure. During the passage from Leyte they had thought quite a lot about their chances of being killed this morning, but everything was humming now, winches, boat davits, the steady throbbing turbines and auxiliaries below-decks, and the motion was reassuring. After midnight reveille, two o'clock breakfast and the long wait at the guns while the attack force stood in to the transport area, the mingled feeling of warm sun, no Japs and familiar work to do was most welcome.

Around number five hatch they whistled as they rigged slings to hoist out gasoline drums, and stocky Ned Strange paused to ask his boatswain's mate, "Where is them Japs?"

"Don't you worry, little boy," said Doyle. "There's Japs in them hills over there."

"But why ain't they shooting at us? They got big guns; you told me so yourself. Why ain't they shootin' at us — and where's them kami planes? Ain't nobody's been crashed; this here's a picnic, sort of."

"Cut the chitchat, you two," ordered Chief Alvick. "Let the gun crews worry about the Japs. All you have to do is to run those winches smooth and fast and keep your eye on the hatch tender; we can't muff any signals or drop any loads today."

MacDougall, busy prowling the ship looking for bottlenecks in debarkation and finding none, had time to wonder about Japs. Why were they so quiet? What was the matter with the shore batteries? How about the hundreds of suicide crash boats; the kamikaze planes — were the Japs saving them for tonight, tomorrow? Or would they come tearing out of nothing, like that dive bomber at Lingayen, only this time from all directions at once? This was like the phony war in France in 1939. Notwithstanding all the unearthly thunder of battleship salvos and rocket barrages, he had the odd sensation of being in a vast vacuum of silence.

During midafternoon, MacDougall slid down the ladders from the bridge and strode into the wardroom for a quick cup of coffee. He found Dr.

Flynn standing under the radio speaker listening to a propaganda broadcast in English from Radio Tokyo.

"Business must be light, Pat," remarked MacDougall. "It's really something; you listening to Tokyo Rose on D Day — L Day, that is."

"Yes, just three casualties aboard so far, and they're not bad. But you must listen to this dame: she's the limit!"

By the time MacDougall had filled his mug and walked over to the speaker, a man with a pseudo-Oxford accent had taken over the mike at Tokyo: "American forces . . . landing at Hagushi . . . repulsed with terrific losses. . . . Reef strewn with bodies of these foolish ones. . . . Japanese soldiers defending to the glory of the Emperor . . ." There was quite a lot of this sort of thing. Bored and remembering that it was time to get up to the bridge and relieve Randall for a few minutes, he started for the door, only to be stopped short by the following: "It has now been positively determined that if Okinawa is lost to the American forces, Japan will be lost. Therefore this is the hour of Japanese opportunity to exercise glorious defense."

Flynn was shaking his head. "The guy must be nuts, admitting something like that. No matter what they do we'll take this island somehow or other."

"We'll take it all right, but we haven't seen the last of our little Jap friends. I can feel it in my bones. We're going to get it — somebody is. It isn't possible for them to give up this place without giving us the works first. You just wait —"

Flynn held up his hand. "Listen, Mac. Listen to this."

The phony accent from Tokyo was getting worked up now as he gave an English version of a pep talk to Jap suicide pilots:

"The faithful kamikaze special attack plane units — divine eagles, bombs composed of men and planes which plunge down on enemy ships — young, ruddy-faced men — are ever seeking the glorious road, again and again dealing crushing blows to the enemy. Each man ties scarf of white silk about his head, symbol of glorious death, rejoicing forever with ancestors at Yasukuni Shrine. Friends wave sad farewells to these broad-shouldered youths who are without even parachutes. The skies are slowly brightening for the Imperial Forces, brightening with the flaming ruins of American warships!"

"Trying to scare us," said MacDougall.

"Trying to!" exclaimed Flynn, wiping his face with his handkerchief. "As far as I'm concerned, he's succeeded very well!"

MacDougall laughed, yet as he climbed back to the bridge to relieve Randall, his face sobered while he thought: what a repulsive proposition! There was a nice breeze on the bridge wing and the sunlight cheered away his misgivings. It was time to run to the reef in order to cut running time for the boats unloading tanks, guns and ammunition.

Hawks was standing beside his high seat, eating a late lunch from a tray placed upon it.

"You take her in, MacDougall," he said. "Randall will plot her along for you."

"Aye, aye, sir," answered MacDougall. Then to the O.O.D., "Ahead standard; right twenty degrees rudder." Listening to Jim Randall's voice giving efficient directions through the chart-room intercom, MacDougall stood on the bridge wing, conning the *Belinda* in to the reef, cutting left and right to dodge drifting transports and to avoid line of fire of destroyers providing call fire to Marines in the battle line. At the beginning of the run in, a dense cloud of battle smoke rolled along shore, obscuring most of Okinawa from sight. Now and then he saw the peak at Naha, always the combat air patrol droning high and American dive bombers plunging down into the smoke, adding to the fires, rising again and streaking back to the carriers. Then an offshore breeze worked at battle smoke, rolling it inland so that here and there little hills stood clear — hills and lovely green valleys, slopes ridged with storm-warped pines, tile-roofed houses nestling together in small groups, white tombs shaped like tremendous easy chairs with oval backs and arms set into the contours. At last he picked out the mouth of the Hagushi River, water gleaming clear in the sunshine, cooler than the Lunga River, he thought. *The Lunga River.* "*I have posted the Lunga River —*" Cool, satin-smooth, drifting with the current — death had been there; now Okinawa on Easter Sunday. MacDougall scratched the rash on his chest.

There was the *Belinda's* beach just south of the river mouth: beach flags, little dots of men moving about the sand, bobbing landing craft — all this popped into view through his binoculars. He had the *Belinda* moving slowly now, inching towards the clusters of landing craft until there was no further need of binoculars to see landing beach and white reef bare now at ebb tide.

"This is about it, Capt'n."

Hawks, who had been leaning over the weather cloth, watching the shore but making no comment, raised his head sufficiently to nod. "Very good," he said at last, his voice sounding as if it came from far away.

"Shall we anchor at short stay, sir?"

"No, just drift around, keep close to our beach." Hawks turned slowly in a complete circle, looking all about the ship, then leaned over the weather cloth again. "Keep lookouts alert, especially surface — submarine —" Hawks's voice drifted off and he seemed lost in contemplation once more. MacDougall felt his scalp tingling. I get it, he thought. He's letting me handle things while he rests. He never does that unless he's expecting trouble.

MacDougall looked about the water, feeling foolish at the relief he felt that there were merely landing craft all about, no sign of sneaking periscope. Then he shivered and all sense of relief left; that broadcast — that stupid, damnable propaganda — "divine eagles, bombs composed of men and planes, which plunge down on enemy ships." MacDougall walked over to the bridge talker. "Alert all sky lookouts," he said. "Tell 'em to keep sharp; get in the reports; don't wait to be sure." Then he headed for the charthouse to shake up the radar crew.

Debarkation continued with increasing acceleration. The tide was low, yet battalion after battalion was carried to the reef in LCVP's, transferred to amtracks and DUKW's which landed them dry feet on the banks of the Hagushi River mouth. Further north the same operation was being performed by other transport squadrons. Divisional command posts were set up ashore together with reinforcements not yet needed. The line was everywhere two miles deep — already beyond the point previously planned as reasonable for three days of fighting. LST's with pickaback pontoons moved close to the reef and side launched them for use as cargo barges and floating docks. Bulldozers were already at work on Yontan and Kadena airfields, which had been captured within the hour. Casualties thus far were surprisingly light; to the astonishment of all, no Jap mortar fire had fallen upon the boat waves, no coast artillery had yet opened fire upon the mass of ships off Hagushi. Things were humming. Jubilant sailors slapped each other on the back, asking, "Where's them Japs?"

On the signal bridge there was a happy commotion as a message to all ships was hoisted to the flagship's yardarm. Moments later MacDougall handed a message to Hawks, who raised his head from his elbows long enough to read, "Well Done to all hands." Hawks grunted, handed the message back, and retreated within himself once again.

MacDougall carried the message to Randall on the opposite wing of the bridge. "The Old Man is really in a stupe," he said.

Randall raised up from the pelorus stand. "What now?"

"We got a 'Well Done' and he just grunted. In this Navy a skipper will stand on his head all day for those two little words. At Leyte he pranced around the bridge like a wild man, yelling, 'Well done: well done, Belinda!' He even sang us a ditty about it; now he grunts. And this has been something to get excited about: over twice the number of men have been landed here already today than were landed on D Day at Normandy!"

"That was twenty-one thousand, wasn't it?"

"That's right; Hawks told us all about it. Now we land fifty thousand before sunset and he's sad and weary about it all."

Looking tensely about, MacDougall still saw no evidence of the full fury of Japanese defense. The first hint came with sunset. All ships except a few retained for bombardment, for screening and for the mothering of landing craft remaining at the beach had been ordered to sea for night retirement, the most sensible defense against air and submarine attack. More supplies and troops had been landed than could be used during the night. Underway and clear of land, ships could maneuver at high speed together as a team and mass their combined firepower against air attack, while screening destroyers could be deployed most profitably against submarines known to be lurking in the area. But the dipping of the sun seemed to signal Japanese planes. While the fleet was still disorganized in a vast traffic jam of hundreds of ships rushing out independently to rendezvous beyond Keise Shima, five miles offshore, American radar picked up unidentified planes, closing in from north, east and south. The time for hot gun barrels and uneasy stomachs had arrived.

Captain Hawks was anxious to get the *Belinda* out to sea and formed up. "Flank speed," he ordered, from his position at conn, just forward of the pilothouse. Jim Randall answered from within the steel shutters, clanged shut across the windows at call to battle stations.

MacDougall stood beside Hawks, sweeping the sky with his binoculars. He saw no planes, not even the friendly combat air patrol. He supposed that they had been vectored out to intercept the Japs, but there were no reports of friendly planes from radar. The voice of Gene Cooper, the radar officer, came with a brisk confidence which MacDougall did not share, "Bogeys, three; zero-five-five, twenty miles, closing. Bogeys many, desig Raid Two, zero-one-zero, twenty-five miles, closing rapidly." On and on went Cooper's voice. Would he never stop? MacDougall wondered. Gun barrels were trained in the direction of the nearest raid. Distant ships began firing; still MacDougall's glasses revealed nothing but crimson and gold cloud forms swimming in a shimmering, empty sky, blue deepening towards black with overtones of yellow smoke haze.

MacDougall looked at Hawks, wondered what the skipper was thinking about. All this time, both had been looking left and right at dozens of nearby ships which had broken clear of the central mass and, like the *Belinda*, were steaming in a general westerly direction. The trouble lay, MacDougall saw, in that squadron flagships were widely separated so that individual ships were steaming at intersecting angles, each trying to get formed up in proper column. A large attack transport was bearing down upon the *Belinda* from starboard. MacDougall jumped to the pelorus, squinted through the sight vane for a few seconds, then hurried back to Hawks's side. "Ship zero-three-five, relative, Capt'n; on collision course. Shall we swing astern of her or slow down?"

Hawks continued to stare straight ahead. "What's her name?" he asked.

"PA 79, sir."

"That's the *Riverside*. Carry on. Hold course and speed."

"But Capt'n, she's got the right of way."

"That doesn't matter."

"But Capt'n, directives clearly require —"

"I said, 'Hold course and speed.' "

"We'll hit her."

"No we won't. Carruthers Johnson has her. I'm senior to him."

MacDougall jumped to the pelorus and took another bearing of the *Riverside*'s bow. He rushed back and broke into another of Cooper's bogey reports.

"Bearing hasn't changed, Capt'n. We'll hit him!"

"We won't hit Carruthers," said Hawks. "I shoved him naked the length of a soapy deck at Annapolis. He'll give way."

The fool! MacDougall fumed inwardly. Here we go on another trip into the sunset; well I'm not going to wait so long this time. I'm not going to ruin my career and drown six hundred men for a crazy man's notion. He ran over to the wing. Radar was too busy with Japs; he'd have to estimate distance by eye. About nine hundred yards — he'd swing right, stop engines and fight it out with Hawks later. Then to his amazement he saw the *Riverside* sheer away and let the *Belinda* pass clear. Still Hawks had not turned his head to look at her after the first quick glance.

The thunder of gunfire rolled nearer. Out of the yellow battle smoke, high up in the darkening sky, MacDougall saw a small black shape darting down, a second, then a third: Japs for sure! Down they came out of scarlet and gold sunset into the darker nether air, twisting and turning, but ever downward, lighted now by exploding flak. Cooper was reporting something about bogeys but his voice was drowned out by gunfire, rolling closer. Hawks swept the sky with his binoculars, paused to watch the diving enemy, then swept on. He looked briefly at MacDougall and shouted, "He's after the Northern Group."

MacDougall nodded, swallowing as he searched for closer planes. Hawks was not sightseeing; was not interested in anything which did not menace his ship. A steadily increasing mass of ships was milling, surging, rushing all about, the mass movement was seaward, yet as involved as a large school of fish. Worst traffic mess I ever saw, thought MacDougall. The *Belinda* seemed about to draw into a comparatively clear spot when another attack transport, carrying a squadron flag, suddenly bore across her bow from port. It looked like a dead heat; if each ship maintained course and speed they were bound to collide.

MacDougall pressed Hawks's elbow. "Look, Capt'n — look at those fools! We have the right of way; they're supposed to stay clear."

Hawks dropped his binoculars to horizon level and swung around for a quick look at the converging transport. "Sheer off and back her down," he ordered.

"But Capt'n — Rules of the Road require us to hold course and speed. They must take the action; we're not allowed to alter course or speed until they —"

Hawks grabbed MacDougall roughly by the shoulder and spun him around. "Stop engines, I say! Back full!"

Angry and apprehensive, MacDougall complied. This is going to be a mess, he thought. What in the world? — in this Navy you never know! Hawks was shouting at him again while Cooper's voice, no longer calm and methodical, yelled from the squawk box something about bandits closing, collision course; but Hawks's words mixed in with and overpowered Cooper's. "The Commodore," Hawks was shouting. "Much senior to me . . . Always give clear passage to flagships." Then something in Cooper's report registered with Hawks. Looking aloft, he sighted another diving plane, much closer than the others. "You watch the ship!" he yelled to MacDougall; then to his talker, "Control, get on that fellow! Commence firing; Commence firing! Lead the target, you fools, lead the target!" Hawks began jumping up and down with excitement, striking his right fist savagely into his left palm. "Hit the dirty black bastard! Lead the target; lead the target!"

Belinda's guns reacted so suddenly and savagely it seemed as if the ship herself was exploding. MacDougall took one split-second glance upward at a tremendously exciting movement of exploding color ringed about a single-engined Jap fighter now plummeting down towards a point a few hundred yards ahead of the Belinda's bow. He ran to the engine an-nunciator and swung the handle once more to emphasize the full astern signal to the engine room. A scant seventy-five yards away, the flagship APA, head of another squadron, swept majestically past. Torque of back-ing engines was swinging the Belinda's bow away from the reckless ad-vance of this other ship. MacDougall felt a slacking in the tension caused by this near-collision, yet at the same time an increase in his awareness of that black plane diving closer. He stole another glance upward around the rim of his helmet: gun barrels pointed lower, exploding shells blasted nearer, while the plane still dropped. She was in a flaming sideslip now, heading toward the exact spot the Belinda would soon have occupied had her engines not been backed. All the flagship's guns were belching and chattering. MacDougall saw figures of men running excitedly across her upper bridge, upturned faces on lower decks; everywhere clusters of guns with men in helmets hanging back in the firing straps or thrusting in fresh clips of ammunition. The flagship was passing fast, uncomfortably close and still converging but she should pass clear. MacDougall watched the relative movement of these masses of gray steel, caught a glimpse of a tall man in a gray helmet standing stiff and proud in the center of the flagship's bridge — her captain no doubt, standing motionless in command while lesser men ran busily about him. Now the crashing of guns and nearing flames pulled MacDougall's gaze away from all else. The flaming ball of shattered kamikaze dropped at a steep angle. One wing was shot away, then the other caught in the flagship's rigging. The plane spun around like a crippled windmill. What looked like an engine — perhaps a warhead — dropped out and fell into the open hatch just forward of the bridge, while the flaming wreckage crashed into the bridge itself. Tremendous double explosion, bridge gone, captain gone — guns silent now while white-hot flames seethed upward like writhing snakes of fire. Bridge, captain, helmsman gone; the flagship's propeller nevertheless maintained an even beat, thrusting a boiling white wake astern as she swept on in flaming dignity across the *Belinda*'s bow. They got her instead of us, thought MacDougall. That Hawks! . . . Breaks two Rules of the Road in three minutes and saves his ship!

MacDougall ordered speed ahead and left rudder to avoid the burning flagship. She would have to help herself for the time being; salvage tugs might be available but a ship could easily sink or burn to the water's edge while waiting for help. It was the duty of other transports to get to sea and avoid a similar fate. The *Belinda* shook violently as she gathered headway and left the burning transport astern. MacDougall heard intermittent bursts of gunfire towards the south, but the battle sound was moving away. Here and there towering flames shot up from the darkening waters, showing where other ships had been hit and set afire. Hawks was over on the starboard wing now, both elbows on the railing, chin cupped in the palms of his hands, silently watching the flaming hull of the flagship to which he had given right of way and, unintentionally, the privilege of being crashed by a Jap suicide plane. He waited until he saw streams of water from a dozen fire hoses playing on the blaze, then walked amidships and stood beside MacDougall. "All right, Mac," he said. "I'll take the conn now." Hawks looked ahead, ordered a small change in course, then poked MacDougall sharply in the ribs, leering into his face as he said, "So you wanted me to take the right of way, did you?"

MacDougall grinned and sighed with relief. How glad I am to be wrong this time! he thought as he walked to the bridge wing and looked about. Gun crews still stood tense and alert while their loaders refilled ready boxes from fore and after magazines. All around the horizon he saw ships plowing seaward, eager now to form up and to be lost in the darkness. Sea and lower sky were fading into deep shadow now, but skies high aloft to westward glowed pale yellow and gold where an invection of cooling battle smoke floated among islands of rose-tinted alto-cumulus. A new rash of gunfire brought MacDougall's attention back to the surface. A single-engine Jap "Zeke" had come out from Okinawa, flying low over the water, unseen and unheard in the confusion. Unlike his fellows, he chose no crash to flaming death but flew brilliantly about, banking sharply, zooming to masthead heights, then swooping down until his propeller fanned a wake in the darkening sea. Ship after ship opened fire, cautiously getting in a few bursts whenever possible to shoot without hitting other ships. While Hawks watched for his chance, the *Belinda's* guns followed the "Zeke's" movements. The little Jap seemed to live a charmed life, streaking back and forth in the middle of this compact group of ships, any one of which could have downed him easily, had he been in the clear. At last, as if realizing that luck was running out, he streaked between two old battleships, his wings turret-high, then, gunning his motor, zoomed aloft for his life. At once all hell broke out in the fleet as half a million dollars' worth of high explosive was thrown at him. They'll get him now, MacDougall thought; just a matter of seconds now. Amazingly the Jap still climbed, until the set-fused 40-mm flak peppered far beneath him. Still far from clear, he continued his weaving climb while proximity-fused five-inch shells passed by on either side to explode high in the clouds. Up he went, seeming gradually smaller to MacDougall's watching eyes, until at last he was a tiny black silhouette against that fading patch of yellow and gold.

Evidently feeling safe at last, he began a wild display of acrobatics, utterly without practical purpose. He seemed to be saying: *Here am I, brave Japanese gentleman. I do not lose face with you. I fly close to your biggest guns. I am afraid to die and I am not afraid to die. I perform most difficult acrobatics for you. I observe the sunset. I bow to the Emperor, Son of Heaven. Tomorrow I die: Divine Wind blow hot breath against your ships: all destroy. Tonight I am Japanese boy going home to rice and saki. Good night, sank you.* Ending his mad display with a lightning-quick snap roll, he climbed steeply still higher until dying sunlight glowed faintly against his distant wings, and then he was gone.

Captain Hawks spat over the side, the first time MacDougall ever remembered him doing so. "Jap-carrier pilot," he said shortly. "Their Army men can't fly like that."

Gate to Freedom

⚜

from *King Rat*

by JAMES CLAVELL

Changi was set like a pearl on the eastern tip of Singapore Island, iridescent under the bowl of tropical skies. It stood on a slight rise and around it was a belt of green, and farther off the green gave way to the blue-green seas and the seas to infinity of horizon.

Closer, Changi lost its beauty and became what it was — an obscene forbidding prison. Cellblocks surrounded by sun-baked courtyards surrounded by towering walls.

Inside the walls, inside the cellblocks, story on story, were cells for two thousand prisoners at capacity. Now, in the cells and in the passageways and in every nook and cranny lived some eight thousand men. English and Australian mostly — a few New Zealanders and Canadians — the remnants of the armed forces of the Far East campaign.

These men too were criminals. Their crime was vast. They had lost a war. And they had lived.

The cell doors were open and the cellblock doors were open and the monstrous gate which slashed the walls was open and the men could move in and out — almost freely. But still there was a closeness, a claustrophobic smell.

Outside the gate was a skirting tarmac road. A hundred yards west this road was crossed by a tangle of barbed gates, and outside these gates was a guardhouse peopled with the armed offal of the conquering hordes. Past the barrier the road ran merrily onward, and in the course of time lost itself in the sprawling city of Singapore. But for the men, the road west ended a hundred yards from the main gate.

East, the road followed the wall, then turned south and again followed the wall. On either side of the road were banks of long "go-downs," as the rough sheds were called. They were all the same — sixty paces long with walls made from plaited coconut fronds roughly nailed to posts, and thatch roofs also made from coconut fronds, layer on mildewed layer. Every year a new layer was added, or should have been added. For the sun and the rain and the insects tortured the thatch and broke it down. There were simple openings for windows and doors. The sheds had long thatch overhangs to keep out the sun and the rain and they were set on concrete stilts to escape floods and the snakes and frogs and slugs and snails, the scorpions, centipedes, beetles, bugs — all manner of crawling thing.

Officers lived in these sheds.

South and east of the road were four rows of concrete bungalows, twenty to a row, back to back. Senior officers — majors, lieutenant colonels, and colonels — lived in these.

The road turned west, again following the wall, and met another bank of atap sheds. Here was quartered the overflow from the jail.

And in one of these, smaller than most, lived the American contingent of twenty-five enlisted men.

Where the road turned north once more, hugging the wall, was part of the vegetable gardens. The remainder — which supplied most of the camp food — lay farther to the north, across the road, opposite the prison gate. The road continued through the lesser garden for two hundred yards and ended in front of the guardhouse.

Surrounding the whole sweating area, perhaps half a mile by half a mile, was a barbed fence. Easy to cut. Easy to get through. Scarcely guarded. No searchlights. No machine-gun posts. But once outside, what then? Home was across the seas, beyond the horizon, beyond a limitless sea or hostile jungle. Outside was disaster, for those who went and for those who remained.

By now, 1945, the Japanese had learned to leave the control of the camp to the prisoners. The Japanese gave orders and the officers were responsible for enforcing them. If the camp gave no trouble, it got none. To ask for food was trouble. To ask for medicine was trouble. To ask for anything was trouble. That they were alive was trouble.

For the men, Changi was more than a prison. Changi was genesis, the place of beginning again.

When the King first heard about the officer, he was lying on his bed, brooding. True, he still had the choice position under the window, but now he had the same space as the other men — six feet by four feet. When he had returned from the north garden he had found his bed and chairs moved, and other beds were now spread into the space that was his by right. He had said nothing and they had said nothing, but he had looked at them and they had all avoided his eyes.

And, too, no one had collected or saved his evening meal. It had just been consumed by others.

"Gee," Tex had said absently, "I guess we forgot about you. Better be here next time. Every man's responsible for his own chow."

So he had cooked one of his hens. He had cleaned it and fried it and eaten it. At least he had eaten half of it and kept half of it for breakfast. Now he had only two hens left. The others had been consumed during the last days — and he had shared them with the men who had done the work.

Yesterday he had tried to buy the camp store, but the pile of money that the diamond had brought was worthless. In his wallet he still had eleven American dollars, and these were good currency. But he knew — chilled — he could not last forever on eleven dollars and two hens.

He had slept little the previous night. But in the bleak watches of the early morning he had faced himself and told himself that this was weak and foolish and not the pattern of a King — it did not matter that when he had walked the camp earlier people had looked through him — Brant and Prouty and Samson and all the others had passed by and not returned his salute. It had been the same with everyone. Tinker Bell and Timsen and the MP's and his informants and employees — men he had helped or known or sold for or given food or cigarettes or money. They had all looked at him as though he did not exist. Where always eyes had been watching him, and hate had been surrounding him when he walked the camp, now there was nothing. No eyes, no hate, no recognition.

It had been freezing to walk the camp a ghost. To return to his home a ghost. To lie in bed a ghost.

Nothingness.

Now he was listening as Tex poured out to the hut the incredible news of the captain's arrival, and he could sense the new fear gnawing at them.

"What's the matter?" he said. "What're you all so goddamn silent about? A guy's arrived from outside, that's all."

No one said anything.

The King got up, galled by the silence, hating it. He put on his best shirt and his clean pants and wiped the dust off his polished shoes. He set his cap at a jaunty angle and stood for a moment in the doorway.

"Think I'm going to have me a cook-up today," he said to no one in particular.

When he glanced around he could see the hunger in their faces and the barely concealed hope in their eyes. He felt warmed again and normal again, and looked at them selectively.

"You going to be busy today, Dino?" he said at length.

"Er, no. No," Dino said.

"My bed needs fixing and there's some laundry."

"You, er, want me to do them?" Dino asked uncomfortably.

"You want to?"

Dino swore under his breath, but the remembrance of the perfume of the chicken last night shattered his will. "Sure," he said.

"Thanks, pal," said the King derisively, amused by Dino's obvious struggle with his conscience. He turned and started down the steps.

"Er, which hen d'you want to have?" Dino called out after him.

The King did not stop. "I'll think about that," he said. "You just fix the bed and the laundry."

Dino leaned against the doorway, watching the King walk in the sun along the jail wall and around the corner of the jail. "Son of a bitch!"

"Go get the laundry," Tex said.

"Crap off! I'm hungry."

"He aced you into doing his work without any goddamn chicken."

"He'll eat one today," Dino said stubbornly. "And I'll help him eat it. He's never eaten one before without giving the helper some."

"What about last night?"

"Hell, he was fit to be tied 'cause we took over his space." Dino was thinking about the English captain and home and his girl friend and wondered if she was waiting or if she was married. Sure, he told himself sullenly, she'll be married and no one'll be there. How the hell am I going to get me a job?

"That was before," Byron Jones III was saying. "I'll bet the son of a bitch cooks it and eats it in front of us." But he was thinking about his home. Goddamned if I'm going to stay there any more. Got to get me my own apartment. Yeah. But where the hell's the dough coming from?

"So what if he does?" Tex asked. "We got maybe two or three days to go." Then home to Texas, he was thinking. Can I get my job back? Where the hell will I live? What am I going to use for dough? When I get in the hay, is it going to work?

"What about the Limey officer, Tex? You think we should go talk with him?"

"Yeah, we should. But hell, later today, or tomorrow. We gotta get used to the idea." Tex suppressed a shudder. "When he looked at me — it was as though, just like he was looking at a — a geek! Holy cow, what's so goddamn wrong with me? I look all right, don't I?"

They all studied Tex, trying to see what the officer had seen. But they saw only Tex, the Tex they had known for three and a half years.

"You look all right to me," Dino said finally. "If anyone's a freak it's him. Goddamned if I'd parachute into Singapore alone. Not with all the lousy Japs around. No sir! He's the real freak."

The King was walking along the jail wall. You're a stupid son of a bitch, he told himself. What the hell're you so upset about? All's well in the world. Sure. And you're still the King. You're still the only guy who knows how to get with it.

He cocked his hat at a rakish angle and chuckled as he remembered Dino. Yeah, that bastard would be cursing, wondering if he'd really get the chicken, knowing he'd been aced into working. The hell with him, let him sweat, the King thought cheerfully.

He crossed the path between two of the huts. Around the huts were groups of men. They were all looking north, towards the gate, silently, motionless. He rounded another hut and saw the officer standing in a pool of emptiness, staring around bewildered, his back towards him. He saw the officer go toward some men and laughed sardonically as he saw them retreat.

Crazy, he thought cynically. Plain crazy. What's there to be scared of? The guy's only a captain. Yep, he's sure going to need a hand. But what the hell he's so scared about beats me!

He quickened his pace, but his footsteps made no noise.

" 'Morning, sir," he said crisply, saluting.

Captain Forsyth spun around, startled. "Oh! Hello." He returned the salute with a sigh of relief. "Thank God someone here is normal." Then he realized what he had said. "Oh, sorry, I didn't mean —"

"That's all right," the King said agreeably. "This dump's enough to put anyone off kilter. Boy, are we pleased to see you. Welcome to Changi!"

Forsyth smiled. He was much shorter than the King but built like a tank. "Thank you. I'm Captain Forsyth. I've been sent to look after the camp until the fleet arrives."

"When's that?"

"Six days."

"Can't they make it any sooner?"

"These things take time, I suppose." Forsyth nodded toward the huts. "What's the matter with everyone? It's as though I was a leper."

The King shrugged. "Guess they're in a state of shock. Don't believe their eyes yet. You know how some guys are. And it has been a long time."

"Yes it has," Forsyth said slowly.

"Crazy that they'd be scared of you." The King shrugged again. "But that's life, and their business."

"You're an American?"

"Sure. There are twenty-five of us. Officers and enlisted men. Captain Brough's our senior officer. He got shot down flying the hump in '43. Maybe you'd like to meet him?"

"Of course." Forsyth was dead-tired. He had been given this assignment in Burma four days ago. The waiting and the flight and the jump and the walk to the guardhouse and the worry of what he would meet and what the Japanese would do and how the hell he was going to carry out his orders, all these things had wrecked his sleep and terrored his dreams. Well, old chap, you asked for the job and you've got it and here you are. At least you passed the first test up at the main gate. Bloody fool, he told himself, you were so petrified all you could say was "Salute, you bloody bastards."

From where he stood, Forsyth could see clusters of men staring at him from the huts and the windows and the doorways and shadows. They were all silent.

He could see the bisecting street, and beyond the latrine area. He noticed the sores of huts and his nostrils were filled with the stench of sweat and mildew and urine. Zombies were everywhere — zombies in rags, zombies in loincloths, zombies in sarongs — boned and meatless.

"You feeling okay?" the King asked solicitously. "You don't look so hot."

"I'm all right. Who are those poor buggers?"

"Just some of the guys," the King said. "Officers."

"What?"

"Sure. What's wrong with them?"

"You mean to tell me those are officers?"

"That's right. All these huts're officers' huts. Those rows of bungalows are where the Brass live, majors and colonels. There's about a thousand Aussies and Lim — English," he said quickly, correcting himself, "in huts south of the jail. Inside the jail are about seven or eight thousand English and Aussies. All enlisted men."

"Are they all like that?"

"Sir?"

"Do they all look like that? Are they all dressed like that?"

"Sure." The King laughed. "Guess they do look like a bunch of bums at that. It sure never bothered me up to now." Then he realized that Forsyth was studying him critically.

"What's the matter?" he asked, his smile fading.

Behind and all around men were watching, Peter Marlowe among them. But they all stayed out of range. They were all wondering if their eyes really saw a man, who looked like a man, with a revolver at his waist, talking to the King.

"Why're you so different from them?" Forsyth said.

"Sir?"

"Why're you properly dressed — and they're all in rags?"

The King's smile returned. "I've been looking after my clothes. I guess they haven't."

"You look quite fit."

"Not as fit as I'd like to be, but I guess I'm in good shape. You like me to show you around? Thought you'd need a hand. I could rustle up some of the boys, get a detail together. There's no supplies in the camp worth talking about. But there's a truck up at the garage. We could drive into Singapore and liberate —"

"How is it that you are apparently unique here?" Forsyth interrupted, the words like bullets.

"Huh?"

Forsyth pointed a blunt finger at the camp. "I can see perhaps two or three hundred men but you're the only one clothed. I can't see a man who's not as thin as a bamboo, but you," he turned back and looked at the King, his eyes flinty, "you are 'in good shape.'"

"I'm just the same as them. I've just been on the ball. And lucky."

"There's no such thing as luck in a hellhole like this!"

"Sure there is," the King said. "And there's no harm in looking after your clothes, no harm in keeping fit as you can. Man's got to look after number one. No harm in that!"

"No harm at all," Forsyth said, "providing it's not at the expense of others!" Then he barked, "Where's the Camp Commandant's quarters?"

"Over there." The King pointed. "The first row of bungalows. I don't know what's gotten into you. I thought I could help. Thought you'd need someone to put you in the picture —"

"I don't need *your* help, Corporal! What's your name!"

The King was sorry that he had taken the time out to try to help. Son of a bitch, he thought furiously, that's what comes of trying to help! "King. Sir."

"You're dismissed, Corporal. I won't forget you. And I'll certainly make sure I see Captain Brough at the earliest opportunity."

"Now what the hell does that mean?"

"It means I find you entirely suspicious," Forsyth rapped. "I want to know why you're fit and others aren't. To stay fit in a place like this you've got to have money, and there would be very few ways to get money. Very few ways. Informing, for one! Selling drugs or food for another —"

"I'll be goddamned if I'll take that crap —"

"You're dismissed, Corporal! But don't forget I'll make it my business to look into you!"

It took a supreme effort for the King to keep from smashing his fist into the captain's face.

"You're dismissed," Forsyth repeated, then added viciously, Get out of my sight!"

The King saluted and walked away, blood filming his eyes.

"Hello," Peter Marlowe said, intercepting the King. "My God, I wish I had your guts."

The King's eyes cleared and he croaked, "Hi. Sir." He saluted and began to pass.

"My God, Rajah, what the hell's the matter?"

"Nothing. Just don't — feel like talking."

"Why? If I've done something to hurt you, or get you fed up with me, tell me. Please."

"Nothing to do with you." The King forced a smile, but inside he was screaming, Jesus, what've I done that's so wrong? I fed the bastards and helped them, and now they look at me as though I'm not here any more.

He looked back at Forsyth and saw him walk between two huts and disappear. And him, he thought in agony, he thinks I'm a goddamn informer.

"What did he say?" Peter Marlowe asked.

"Nothing. He — I've got to — do something for him."

"I'm your friend. Let me help. Isn't it enough that I'm here?"

But the King only wanted to hide. Forsyth and the others had taken away his face. He knew that he was lost. And faceless, he was terrified.

"See you around," he muttered and saluted and hurried away. Jesus God, he wept inside, give me back my face. Please give me back my face.

The next day a plane buzzed the camp. Out of its belly poured a supply drop. Some of the supplies fell into the camp. Those that fell outside the camp were not sought. No one left the safety of Changi. It still could be a trick. Flies swarmed, a few men died.

Another day. Then planes began to circle the airstrip. A full colonel strode into the camp. With him were doctors and orderlies. They brought medical supplies. Other planes circled and landed.

Suddenly there were jeeps screaming through the camp and huge men with cigars and four doctors. They were all Americans. They rushed into the camp and stabbed the Americans with needles and gave them gallons of fresh orange juice and food and cigarettes and embraced them — their boys, their hero boys. They helped them into the jeeps and drove them to Changi Gate, where a truck was waiting.

Peter Marlowe watched, astonished. They're not heroes, he thought, bewildered. Neither are we. We lost. We lost the war, our war. Didn't we? We're not heroes. We're not!

He saw the King through the fog of his mind. His friend. He had been waiting the days to talk with him, but each time he had found him the King had put him off. "Later," the King had always said, "I'm busy now." When the new Americans had arrived there still had been no time.

So Peter Marlowe stood at the gate, with many men, watching the departure of the Americans, waiting to say a last good-by to his friend, waiting patiently to thank him for his arm and for the laughter they had had together.

Among the watchers was Grey.

Forsyth was standing tiredly beside the lorry. He handed over the list. "You keep the original, sir," he said to the senior American officer. "Your men are all listed by rank, service and serial number."

"Thanks," said the major, a squat, heavy-jowled paratrooper. He signed the paper and handed back the other five copies. "When're the rest of your folks arriving?"

"A couple of days."

The major looked around and shuddered. "Looks like you could use a hand."

"Have you any excess drugs, by any chance?"

"Sure. We got a bird stacked with the stuff. Tell you what. Once I've got our boys on their way, I'll bring it all back in our jeeps. I'll let you have a doc and two orderlies until yours get here."

"Thanks." Forsyth tried to rub the fatigue out of his face. "We could use them. I'll sign for the drugs. SEAC will honor my signature."

"No goddamn paper. You want the drugs, you get 'em. That's what they're there for."

He turned away. "All right, Sergeant, get 'em in the truck." He walked over to the jeep and watched as the stretcher was lashed securely. "What you think, Doc?"

"He'll make it Stateside." The doctor glanced up from the unconscious figure neatly trussed in the straitjacket, "but that's about it. His mind's gone for good."

"Son of a bitch," the major said wearily, and he made a check mark against Max's name on the list. "Seems kinda unfair." He dropped his voice. "What about the rest of them?"

"Not good. Withdrawal symptoms generally. Anxiety about the future. There's only one that's in halfway decent shape physically."

"I'll be goddamned if I know how any of 'em made it. You been in the jail?"

"Sure. Just a quick runaround. That was enough."

Peter Marlowe was watching morosely. He knew his unhappiness was not due solely to the departure of his friend. It was more than that. He was sad because the Americans were leaving. Somehow he felt he belonged there with them, which was wrong, because they were foreigners. Yet he knew he did not feel like a foreigner when he was with them. Is it envy? he asked himself. Or jealousy? No, I don't think so. I don't know why, but I feel they're going home and I'm being left behind.

He moved a little closer to the truck as the orders began to sound and the men began to climb aboard. Brough and Tex and Dino and Byron Jones III and all the others resplendent in their new starched uniforms, looked unreal. They were talking and shouting and laughing. But not the King. He stood slightly to one side. Alone.

Peter Marlowe was glad that his friend was back once more with his own people, and he prayed that once the King was on his way all would be well with him.

"Get in the truck, you guys."

"C'mon, get in the goddamn truck."

"Next stop Stateside!"

Grey was unaware that he was standing beside Peter Marlowe. "They say," he said looking at the truck, "that they've a plane to fly them all the way back to America. A special plane. Is that possible? Just a handful of men and some junior officers?"

Peter Marlowe had also been unaware of Grey. He studied him, despising him. "You're such a goddamn snob, Grey, when it comes down to it."

Grey's head whipped around. "Oh, it's you."

"Yes." Peter Marlowe nodded at the truck. "They think that one man's as good as another. So they get a plane, all to themselves. It's a great idea when you think of it."

"Don't tell me the upper classes have at last realized —"

"Oh shut up!" Peter Marlowe moved away, his bile rising.

Beside the truck was a sergeant, a vast man with many stripes on his sleeve and an unlit cigar in his mouth. "C'mon. Get in the truck," he repeated patiently.

The King was the last on the ground.

"For Chrissake, get in the truck!" the sergeant growled. The King didn't move. Then, impatiently, the sergeant threw the cigar away, and stabbing the air with his finger shouted, "You! Corporal! Get your goddamn ass in the truck!"

The King came out of his trance. "Yes, Sergeant. Sorry, Sergeant!"

Meekly he got into the back of the truck and stood while everyone else sat, and around him there were excited men talking one to another, but not to him. No one seemed to notice him. He held to the side of the truck as it roared into life and swept the Changi dust into the air.

Peter Marlowe frantically ran forward and held up his hand to wave at his friend. But the King did not look back. He never looked back.

Suddenly, Peter Marlowe felt very lonely, there by Changi Gate.

Two days later more Americans arrived. And a real American General. He was swarmed like a queen bee by photographers and reporters and aides. The General was taken to the Camp Commandant's bungalow. Peter

Marlowe and Mac and Larkin were ordered there. The General picked up the earphone of the radio and pretended to listen.

"Hold that, General!"

"Just one more, General!"

Peter Marlowe was shoved to the front and told to bend over the radio as though explaining it to the General.

"Not that way — let's see your face. Yeah, let's see your bones, Sam, in the light. That's better."

That night the third and last and greatest fear crucified Changi.

Fear of tomorrow.

All Changi knew, now, that the war *was* over. The future had to be faced. The future outside of Changi. The future was *now*. Now.

And the men of Changi withdrew into themselves. There was nowhere else to go. Nowhere to hide. Nowhere but inside. And inside was terror.

Korea

(1950 – 1953)

✗

The Band

✂

from *The Last Campaign*
by GLEN ROSS

The Korean War — or rather the United Nations operation in Korea — was now two weeks old. At this embryonic stage, no one was quite sure if it was, in fact, a war. No definite date marked the time of peace from the months of fighting that followed. For the Regular Army, the war had begun with the sudden uprooting of a division on occupation duty in southern Japan. That division had gone to Korea in the hope and half belief that the mere presence of American troops there would be enough to restore order. But events had taken a sour turn, and the North Korean Army, headed by a strong column of Russian-built heavy tanks, was refusing to be stopped.

Korea, as the world was about to learn, is a mountainous land with no navigable waterways and no central valley. The six major rivers flow mainly east to west; and although at certain times of the year they can all be forded, they are yet significant natural barriers. The six great rivers are the Yalu, the Taedong, the Imjin, the Han, the Kum, and the Naktong.

South of the Imjin, the prevalence of rice paddies makes the valleys almost as difficult to cross as the rivers. It is more accurate to consider the valleys as swamps criss-crossed by narrow footpaths standing two to five feet above the mud bottom of the flooded fields.

The only unifying feature of the Korean landscape is the hill, the mountain, which abounds everywhere in all shapes and sizes, from the scrubby knolls of Pohang-dong to the great ancestral peaks, six, seven, and eight thousand feet high. Along the Kum and the Naktong Rivers of South Korea, the mountains, though seldom more than three thousand feet high, are rough and barren and rocky.

It is not a land, therefore, easily conquered. Nor does the terrain favor a modern, mechanized army. Tanks are restricted to the narrow, unpaved

roads; artillery must lay its guns in ravines or farmyards, with its fire subject to irregular breaks and blind spots in its pattern. And planes are rather
like hawks searching for mice in a plowed field. Since there is no flat
ground for grazing fire, machine guns are reduced in effectiveness to automatic rifles.

What the terrain does favor, in its cruel way, is the foot soldier, the
lonely infantry.

Three roads lead to Pusan from the north. In the first phase of the
North Korean invasion, it was the central, most direct route that served
as the artery of the Communist army. Along this road lay the following
towns and cities: Seoul, Suwon, Taejon, Kumchon, Waegwam, Taegu, and
Pusan.

What the members of Mr. Hassler's Division Band did not realize, as
their train left Taegu early in the summer morning, was that all beyond
Kumchon, to the north, was already lost. The Communist army was
spreading unchecked to the south and east, and Kumchon was dying on
the vine.

The loss of Kumchon was not especially important, except perhaps to
the inhabitants of that little town, who were already abandoning home
and shop on the morning when Mr. Hassler appeared on the scene. As he
led his sixty men through the dusty, weed-grown alleys in search of the
Division Command Post, the sleepy tranquillity was about to be broken
forever. Already an almost imperceptible quivering underlay the calm surface tension, a nearly inaudible fluttering sound, like birds in a chimney or
faraway thunder.

Division Headquarters was occupying a stone-walled compound on the
outskirts of Kumchon when the band arrived. A row of classrooms fronted
by a covered porch along two sides of the wall gave the place a cloistered
air. The general ground plan of the place was like that of a fort of the
plains cavalry.

Under a tree near the Headquarters offices, Sergeant Crowfoot, the clerk,
set up a field desk, tacked a sign overhead, and sat down to make out the
overdue morning reports; the rest of the band loafed about in the shade,
still at loose ends. With their band instruments left behind in Japan, and
their new duties not yet established, they were bored, restless, and a
little apprehensive. But presently Mr. Hassler reappeared and called them
together.

"I just talked to der colonel," Mr. Hassler began. "Here's der deal."
He paused for effect, and the men shifted uncomfortably, ready for the
worst.

"For der time being, ve stay here, mit headquarters. Ve got der security
mission. You don't know vat dot means — it's *guard!*"

The men looked at one another, both relieved and vaguely frustrated by the news.

"Now, besides der guard," Mr. Hassler went on, "ve're gonna haf special details. Vatever turns up. Shotgun guard on supply trucks, maybe, t'ings like dot." He paused to let this sink in before he came to the crux of his speech.

"According to der book," he said, "part of der band's mission in combat is stretcher bearers. If ve fuck up der guard, ve'll be at der front next t'ing you know. Ve got four extra men, and der first vuns dot screw up der detail gonna be pretty damn qvick long gone. Get me? O.K., Richtovan, take over."

Sergeant Richtovan saluted and said, "Aye, aye, sir!" He was an ex-Marine. Since leaving Japan, his job had blossomed with new responsibilities. But the top-kick mannerisms he had been too busy to bother with during the trip began to return now, and he fell the band in with profane efficiency. Afterward, with quite a bit of grumbling, the guard was ordered and posted and details were passed out to the squad leaders.

"Dougherty . . . unload trucks.

"Hatchman . . . police the compound.

"Troy . . . dig a latrine."

And so they settled down to work, in a world that seemed, if not altogether safe and sane, at least stable enough.

Hunter and Decksmith, of Dougherty's squad, after a couple of hours spent unloading trucks, busied themselves with their pup tent and looked forward to a night of unbroken sleep. Neither of them had ever had occasion to live in a pup tent before, and the novelty of the situation took some of the edge off the discomfort.

"It's going to be a pain in the ass," Decksmith said, referring to their proximity to Headquarters. "You won't be able to roll over without some bird colonel stepping on you! And if you ask me — Ouch! Sonovabitch!" He had been trying to drive tent pegs into the hard-baked ground with a crumbling rock. "Gimme my Goddamn shovel," he said, and the rest of his commentary was lost in the clangor as he pounded at the stakes with an entrenching tool, a procedure darkly frowned on by authority.

At dusk, their tent was up, floored with blankets, with packs and duffel bags properly stashed in the closed nook. "Now, how are we supposed to get into the damned thing?" Decksmith asked.

They were supposed to crawl in, it seemed, on hands and knees, kicking dirt and sand over the blankets; and with the two of them inside, neither could sit upright to the degree of being able to reach his boots. One could not move without jabbing an elbow in the other's face. They crawled out again, discouraged, and sought a place where they could loaf in peace. In the evening, mosquitoes drove them into their tent early, and they tried to write letters by candlelight. To go to bed, they had to get out of the tent once more, take off their clothes, and get into their sleeping bags while standing, then crawl into their shelter like worms under a leaf. Mosquitoes sang in joyful unison, and when Hunter fumbled for a bottle of insect repellent, he managed to break a section of a tent pole, and the whole thing collapsed about their ears.

Cursing mechanically, they struggled out of their sleeping bags, whittled the broken end of the tent pole into shape, and raised the tent once more. When they got into the sleeping bags again, they found them, mysteriously, full of sand. Outside in the dark compound, the last sound was a bitter *chank chank chank* of a shovel being misused on tent pegs.

The voice of Benfield goaded them out into the cold dawn, where they shivered in awkward nakedness as they tried to put on their clothes with as little sand and dirt as possible. Washing was out of the question. They went, sleepy-eyed, directly to the corner of the compound, where Headquarters Company cooks had established their barbecue pits. Here they got for their trouble a rather thin portion of cold bread, powdered eggs, canned apicots, and black coffee.

"How about some more eggs, Sam?" Decksmith pleaded. "I'm starving."

The cook stared at him in false disbelief. "More!" he said. "Hey, Doc! Can Decksmith have more eggs?"

"Hell, no," came the reply.

They moved on to the end of the serving line. Decksmith gave the server his bravest Texas grin and said, "A little more coffee there, if you please, sir."

"Hey, Doc! Decksmith wants more coffee!"

"Tell that Goddamn band I'm gonna kick their ass!"

"Get lost, Decksmith."

They moved on in search of a comfortable place to eat, dripping apricot juice from the shallow end of their mess kits.

"Lot of drag you got around here," Hunter remarked.

"Ahh . . ." Decksmith passed it off. "My nose ain't the right color for these C.P. boys. You see what it's gonna be like now."

In Japan, Decksmith had never been seen in the barracks after duty hours. He had a look of premature dissipation and a reputation for being well known in the honky-tonks of Itabashi and Ikebukuro — two rather dingy districts on the north side of Tokyo. At first glance, his face looked weak and shifty; and this defect, which came from the bone formations rather than from any source of character, was a handicap in his dealings with authority, which he kept at a minimum. He was a drummer by trade and could also play the guitar and sing Texas hillbilly songs.

In the cool of the morning, with stomachs comfortably warmed by bad coffee and souls soothed by the day's first cigarette, Decksmith and Hunter approached the band's orderly tree and saluted Sergeant Crowfoot civilly. Privately they thought it prosaic of Crowfoot to concern himself with such mundane matters as morning reports at such a time as this. "It's a mystery to me," Crowfoot replied to their request for news. "Old Man Hassler's in with the big chiefs, and I think they're having a council of war."

"More likely having one for the road," Decksmith said.

"What I want to know," Hunter said, "is where are we? You ought to know, Crowfoot. You're making out that morning report. What do you put on it?"

Crowfoot's huge face creased in a nearsighted smile. "Kumchon," he said.

"Well," said Decksmith. "Now we know."

Crowfoot joined in the rather artificial laughter. He was a fat giant of a young man whose gift was neutrality. Without in any way jeopardizing his orderly-room status, he was able to give the impression of being wholeheartedly with the opposition party in Benfield's platoon.

Except for the guards, the entire band had gathered in the vicinity of Crowfoot's tree, waiting for Mr. Hassler to appear with the day's orders. Informally they fell into two groups. The first and largest centered around Sergeant Pfiefer of the Second Platoon and split into several subsidiary groups; and the second, close-knit and more exclusive, sat in a circle around Benfield, who was enthroned on a water can.

Benfield was a powerfully built man of forty-five or thereabouts, bald except for a fringe of red hair around his ears and the back of his head. He had been overseas beyond living memory, and oceans of foreign liquor had all but ruined his digestion as well as his temper. He looked at the world with a permanently sour expression. Now, in faded fatigues bulging with muscle and beer fat, he was discoursing on one of his favorite subjects: the callosity and incompetence of Old Man Hassler.

"That old blimp's so scared of being shot at that he'll be bending over backwards to brown-nose all them wheels in there," Benfield was saying. "He don't care a damn about us. And he wouldn't put one square inch of that fat hide on line for you, or me, or anybody else in this outfit. Just as long as he can politic around and play poker with the staff, we'll be farmed out for every shit detail that comes along." Then he added prophetically, "Wait and see."

The circle of listeners sighed gravely and looked rebellious. Dougherty was there, as Benfield's lieutenant, Hunter and Decksmith were there, as well as Troy and Hatchman, the squad leaders. And several minor rebels, including Seymore Canning, the personnel clerk.

"But can he do that?" asked a man named De Baca. "I mean, could he really ship anybody out to a line outfit? I mean, if you got a M.O.S. number of a bandsman, *how can he?*" De Baca was a relative newcomer and at his question, the older men grinned wisely. Seymore Canning chortled and started to cite a case, but was interrupted by Benfield.

"How long you been in this band now, Prospero?"

"Couple of months."

"Hah! You don't know him yet? You still think he's some kind of a freakin' clown? Well, I'm gonna tell you something. They ain't nobody in the Army can make you do anything. Remember that. They can't make you play a horn, and they can't make you stand guard, and they can't make you go into a line outfit. What they can do is kind of arrange your life so you want to do those things, see? *He* can't send you to the line. Hell, no. But as long as we're overstrength, and the rest of the division is understrength, he can jolly well kick you out of the band. And where else is there to go but the line? Everybody got a basic infantry M.O.S."

"Balls, what a bind!"

"Hah! Bind is right. Face it, men, he's got you all by the short hair. 'Yas, sir, colonel,' " he mimicked Hassler's rasping voice. " 'Got a fine gang of boys out dere. Good vorkers. Good latrine men. No sick, no A.W.O.L., no furloughs. Just say der vord.' "

"God, what an old bastard," said De Baca wonderingly. "You know. I heard guys talking about him, even before I came overseas. Guys in bands back in the States, even, and I didn't believe them. I couldn't believe somebody like that really existed." A look of profound dissatisfaction marred his floridly handsome features.

"Well," Benfield summed up, "I was in the Navy for almost six years before I joined the Army, and I been in the Army five years. And if there's another such thoroughly wholehearted bastard in the service, I never heard about it. There ain't *nobody* so dedicated to the ideal of keeping you down. And you ain't never gonna get so miserable that Hassler can't dream up some deal to make you think you was happy till you got into his band."

"Yeah," Dougherty put in. "How about that court-martial, Al? Eh, that was typical. Get Al to tell you about that sometime."

"Yeah," Al agreed. "I'll tell you about it when it's over." He was a thin, hatchet-faced boy, and he grinned to show that he was not yet defeated.

"His rod and his staff shall guide you," Benfield quoted, "and woe unto him that fucketh up. But, yea, though I dwell on the shit list forever, I'll leave no dog behind!" He flipped a cigarette butt in the direction of Crowfoot's tree.

"Or sign the punishment book," Doughtery added, laughing.

The nervous laughter he drew from his men was reassuring to Benfield. He wiped his bald head in a characteristic gesture and said, "Goddamnit, Jim, gimme another butt."

"Watch it," Decksmith muttered. "Here he comes now."

"And he's got a gun."

Mr. Hassler strode up, wearing a newly acquired .45 strapped below his belly, and hooking his thumbs in the pistol belt, said, "All right, get dis place policed up. Ve're moving out in t'irty minutes."

As the Communist army was closing in around Kumchon, the band moved to the forward echelon of Division Headquarters, while the more unwieldy staff sections were moved back. The forward Command Post was taking up quarters in an abandoned seminary on a hillside north of Kumchon when the band joined it. Their first job was to clean out the rooms of the old seminary and make them fit for use as temporary offices.

A dilapidated air hung about the place. The central building, of ancient brick and wood, stood in a grove of gloomy pines in a yard all overgrown with weeds and unkempt shrubbery. The seminary had already been ransacked, and held only a musty collection of crippled benches and desks, broken cabinets, hymnbooks, and a wheezy portable organ, all strewn at random through the dusty rooms.

When they had cleared away the junk, Sergeant Richtovan assembled the band and announced that Sergeant Crowfoot would proclaim the orders of the day. Crowfoot, who looked greatly overdressed in his helmet and assorted battle gear, squinted through his round GI glasses at a paper; when he spoke, his voice was deliberately matter-of-fact, as if he found himself, the Army, and the situation slightly ridiculous.

"We don't know how long we'll be here," Crowfoot said. "And I don't know what's happening at the front. Headquarters describes the situation as 'fluid,' which you can interpret for yourselves. I am supposed to make the . . . ahem . . . following announcements:

"One, there will be no hot chow today.

"Two, in case of enemy aircraft, don't fire until you see the whites of . . . no, correction . . . don't fire until you're told.

"Three, don't eat indigenous food or unpurified water.

"Four, the North Koreans are infiltrating the line, wearing white clothes like refugees. So keep *all* refugees away from the C.P.

"Five, leave the women alone. They're not like the Japanese. They've got a completely different set of customs, and they're shy.

"Six, regular military courtesy is resumed."

The men had listened to this with more gravity than it now seemed to merit, and they felt cheated. "Does that mean *regular* military courtesy?" Hatchman asked. Low laughter accompanied his remark.

"It means keep your mouth shut, unless you're spoken to," Sergeant Richtovan broke in irritably. When Crowfoot had departed, he fell the band in by platoons and, in one of his tough top-kick moods, assigned the squad leaders their work.

"Dougherty . . . dig latrines.

"Troy . . . report to headquarters about picking up rations.

"Hatchman . . . the colonel wants the brush cleared out of the yard."

As the formation broke up, Dougherty said, "Hell, Stan, we don't have to dig no more latrines. There's a whole outhouse full around back."

"Sanitation, my boy, sanitation."

"Sanitation! Hah! You mean the colonel's afraid of catching crabs?"

Richtovan fixed on him what was meant to be a steely glitter. "Jim," he said, "someday that mouth of yours is gonna get you into real trouble."

Dougherty's face turned redder than usual. "What the hell!" he felt obliged to say. "Who wants to live forever?"

At four o'clock in the morning, the old seminary buildings were like a graveyard. There was no moon. As Dougherty led his men through the darkness of the pine grove, from one guard post to the next, a strange excitement, hardly akin to fear even though it had to do with potential danger, came over him.

The business of posting the guard appealed to his dramatic sense. There was suspense and adventure in the work, in the strange new surroundings, the creepy darkness full of mysterious summer-night sounds, the suspicious challenge of the guards, and the whispered exchange of the password. He rather enjoyed it. Hardly anyone moved abroad after dark now, with the North Koreans infiltrating, and the guards had the night to themselves. After posting the relief, Jim had nothing to do until six o'clock. There was no guardroom where he could go to read or talk — no one to talk to and nothing to read in any case. A couple of Headquarters Company men were awake on duty in the blacked-out message center, but he felt like an intruder there. He sat down on the front steps and waited for the dawn.

The weird insect silence of the hour began to disturb him with vague anxieties. He was a city boy, born to the undertone of trolleys and sirens and heavy trucks. Anywhere, silence such as this would have made him ill at ease; and now it caused a growing tension that he could not throw off. During the past few days, whenever he had been able to escape for a minute or two from the grip of physical circumstances that overwhelmed him with strange new sights and sounds and smells and sensations, the experience had taken on a sort of unreality. It was all so totally unforeseen, from his point of view.

He stood up and walked along the driveway through the pines and joined the two guards on duty at the front gate. "Feels like a storm coming up," he said softly.

But even as he spoke, he realized that what he had taken for sheet lightning and distant thunder were actually the flash and roar of artillery fire.

By breakfast time, the artillery had moved closer, its thunder more sharp and ringing, and there was no mistaking it now for a simple summer storm. Slowly, incredibly, as though they were seeing the reversal of some natural law, the men began to realize that the division was retreating.

The band's duty of guarding Division Headquarters, while keeping them in a fair position to observe the war, had fostered a feeling of being non-participants; and, thus removed from actual fighting, they had kept certain illusions about the invincibility of the American fighting man. They would not have been amazed if they had known anything of the tactical picture. The line regiments were deployed in a fan-shaped front across the main road and railroad, with nothing on either flank to prevent the North Koreans from pouring around the ends of the line. Withdrawal, in such a situation, was hardly a matter of choice. The retreat was unexpected only to those who had no understanding of the situation.

Toward noon, a battalion of 105 howitzers roared south through Kum-chon, pulling its guns with trucks. And before the end of the day, stragglers on foot began to appear.

They came like men with a spell upon their souls, with dust on their lips, and in their eyes the unforgettable, inimitable, staring look of the clobbered. Down along the white and dusty country roads they came, their equipment gone, sometimes even their weapons gone, and over the narrow paths between the tall green rice, and down from the stony, sun-stricken mountains.

There were not many of them. Some were brought to the old seminary building and allowed to lie inside and sleep on the cool floor. A few still had the energy to sustain a quiet kind of hysteria; but most simply lay as though stunned, unable to comprehend what had happened to their lives.

That evening, Dougherty and others listened in the dusk while one of the stragglers, a sergeant whom Benfield had known in Japan, told how it had gone with him.

"You never saw anything like it, Ben," the sergeant said. "We went up and dug in on a ridge overlooking the road, up by Yongdok, along about dark the first night. And I couldn't see anything in front of us. Couldn't hear anything. So we waited, and next morning a hell of a fire fight started, back around the Company C.P., and mortars started coming in on us. From back that way! And nobody knew what the hell to do, Ben, for there we was, cut off, without even knowing what happened.

"So we pulled out and went back through the hills and finally got back to the Battalion C.P. And set up another line.

"They overrun one platoon that was down on the low ground by the road. But we had pretty good positions and we managed to hold 'em off until dark. And nobody knew what the hell we were supposed to do because by now they were all around on three sides of us, in the dark. And along about four o'clock in the morning, we heard 'em sneaking up the hill, scrambling around in the rocks. So we opened up on them, and . . . you never in your life heard such noise and confusion and yelling, the way them Gooks do!

"It was still dark as hell, and . . . all at once everything stopped. The Gooks quit yelling, and we quit firing. And . . . spooky!

"And then I hear somebody a little ways off, saying, 'Hey, sergeant, where you at?' And it sounded like some GI, like some kid that'd got out of line. So I stick down and let him come up closer. I had my forty-five, and he can't tell where I am, see, there's rocks all around. Then I see him. He don't have on no helmet, but lot of our guys had lost theirs or thrown them away. But I still can't tell who it is, for sure. And he's whispering, kind of, 'Sergeant? Sergeant, where you at?'

"And I says, 'Over here,' real soft like, holding my head down. 'Who is it?' And he crawled on closer, and he's almost right over the foxhole and still can't see me. Then he says, 'Sergeant? *Where you are?*' And I said, 'Right here,' and I stuck the forty-five in his face and pulled the trigger. I felt the muzzle touch him before I pulled the trigger, even. You never saw anything like it, Ben.

"That sneaky little sonovabitch! I get the shakes just thinking about it. . . . Oh, we got 'em, all right, Ben. But, hell! You kill fifty and there's five hundred more behind them. *And they wear white clothes in the daytime.* And, honest to God, I've seen a bunch of refugees go off the road into a draw, and two minutes later a platoon of North Korean soldiers come out. The sneaky bastards!

"Anyhow, we still had most of two platoons left, and soon as it was light, we kicked the Gooks back down off that hill and cut out of there. We been dodging Gook patrols for two days, trying to get outa them Goddamn hills, and drinking water right out of the paddies. Man, you never saw anything like it. . . ."

Corpsman!

✂

from *Known But to God*

by QUENTIN REYNOLDS

Jeff Leigh spent some time on the water that summer but not in a fishing smack. On June 25, 1950, Communist forces invaded South Korea, and even though President Truman called America's entry into the conflict a "police action," it was still a war. As a medical student, Jeff was exempt from selective service, but he was twenty-four, able-bodied, and still sharply aware of the fact that neither his grandfather nor his father had ever really contributed a thing to his country. Professor Johnson had suggested at Williams that he was battling a guilt complex. Now that men were being killed in Korea, could he be the third generation of Leighs to sit out a war?

"I've got to get in this somehow, Cal," he said after a sleepless night. "I've been condemning my grandfather and my father ever since I can remember and now what am I going to do? The same thing they did?"

"Do you want to toss two years of medical school out of the window?"

"No . . . but still . . ."

"Why not see McClain? He likes you. He's young, but he's wise."

"I think I'll do that," Jeff said.

The young anatomy instructor listened while Jeff poured out his story. "I'm just sick of being a privileged person," Jeff said, much as he had once talked to Professor Johnson. "I've only been allowed to compete in one field — the classroom. My grandfather's money has made everything else easy for me; it has been a cushion protecting me from the realities —"

"Now just a minute, Jeff. I've been over your record here carefully. You know that there are four scholarships awarded annually to men who have completed their second year here. It hasn't been announced yet but you are to receive one of them. Which means that your future medical education won't cost you a cent."

"Oh, it's a great honor to get the scholarship, Doctor, but I'm almost the only man in the class who doesn't need one. I'm thinking of how I'll have to live with myself the rest of my life."

Three months later Jeff Leigh was a Naval hospital corpsman with the First Marine Division in Korea. The Inchon amphibious operation — one of the most audacious gambles in history — had been a complete success. The First moved fast to take Uijongbu, twelve miles north of Seoul. They helped take Seoul, and then without rest hammered their way north. For the first time Jeff found himself working with live patients and he enjoyed it.

They advanced stubbornly but by now the North Koreans had been reinforced by fresh, well-armed, well-trained Chinese troops and the First had to fight for every foot it gained. They reached the 38th Parallel, a section of hills and occasional mountains. Cold weather came early to the Peninsula in the autumn of 1950, and the slush, snow and intermittent rains slowed the tanks and supply trucks. Jeff Leigh was attached to the Third Platoon, Baker Company, 4th Regiment, First Marine Division. The platoon was in charge of experienced, crisp-talking Lieutenant Kenneth Downs, a regular Marine who had once landed at Guadalcanal and Iwo Jima as a private and whose superb combat record had earned him the silver bar on his shoulder.

One morning Lieutenant Downs came back from Regimental Headquarters with orders. He gathered the thirty-five men of the platoon around him to explain: "Here's a map and some air shots of our objective. Tomorrow the Regiment moves north along this road. It's fairly narrow and the enemy will probably figure that the Regiment will stick to the plains and not try this winding road through the hills and mountains because it's so susceptible to ambush. Just ten miles from here there is a farmhouse — that's our objective. It's well constructed with a four-foot-high stone wall around it. The Communists are about two miles north of that house. The house overlooks the road. Regiment sent out a small scouting party during the night and they discovered that the road from here to the farmhouse is not yet mined. Our job is to occupy that farmhouse and keep them from mining the road. We'll be on our own for about twenty-four hours, but with any luck they'll never know we're there. Any questions?"

Twenty minutes later the platoon was moving, cautiously at first, but then with more confidence when it appeared that the scouting patrol had been right — the Communists hadn't bothered to mine the narrow road. On either side of the road the trees were coated with transparent coverings of ice. This quiet white world seemed completely at peace. The men were tired. They'd been in continuous action for a month now. Lines of fatigue showed on their bearded faces. The biting cold seemed part of their very existence now; it seeped through their warm arctic clothing and penetrated the heavy boots and two pairs of wool socks they wore, but these were Marines and they accepted the weather and the danger of ambush as normal hazards. Now the light snow changed to stinging sleet that slashed their faces.

Lieutenant Downs made them stop and rest every fifteen minutes because they were carrying heavy weapons. It was during these "blows" that Jeff Leigh told them about his grandfather and his father.

Three miles from their objective, during a brief clearing of the snowfall, they were spotted by a Communist light observation plane and knocked it down with rifle fire. "A lucky shot," Downs had said derisively, but with obvious admiration for their marksmanship. "You'd never do it again in a thousand chances. Four more and you qualify as aces."

After Jeff and the others returned from the wrecked plane to report no survivors they moved out quickly as a new curtain of snow shrouded their movements. They trudged on doggedly and finally the lieutenant raised his arm. A hundred yards ahead was the farmhouse. "Take twelve men," he told Polinski, "and approach the house from the rear. Keep your men five yards apart. If there's anyone in there we'll surprise them. I'll bring the rest of the platoon to the front. Keep it quiet."

"Yes, sir." If there was any tension in the sergeant it was hidden. He motioned his squad and they followed him off the road to the right and disappeared among the snow-covered trees. After waiting five minutes, Lieutenant Downs motioned to the others to follow him. They approached the house and then spread out; with weapons ready they crawled up to the slope on the right. They reached the four-foot stone wall.

"Cover us, Tex," Lieutenant Downs said, but Thomas already had his Browning nestling on the wall. The others climbed over it and approached the front door of the farmhouse, fanned out so as not to present a compact target. It was completely intact; the North Koreans running from Seoul had had no time to demolish it as they retreated. Downs reached the door. Jones and Wade moved in behind him with grenades in hand. Downs pushed the door open with his carbine. There was no sound from within. The house was empty.

"This is a break I didn't expect." Downs grinned. "From here we can command the road north for at least a quarter of a mile once this snow stops and we can see something." To the radioman he said, "Grossinger, tell Regiment we made it without incident. . . . Sergeant, take Tex and three men and get set up behind the wall. Shoot at anything that moves but wait until they close in. The rest of us will take fifteen minutes and then I'll relieve you. Keep this in mind, men. If we can hold out it means that the Regiment will reach this point safely. Our orders," he said casually, "are to hold it at any cost. Chances are they haven't spotted us unless the plane we spotted was talking to control when it jumped us. If the observer had just reported his position when he was blasted, they'll guess what happened. In that case we'll have visitors by ground and air as soon as the snow stops definitely. Maybe by ground before, depending on how close they are."

The afternoon was uneventful and the night cold but quiet. Lieutenant Downs had half the platoon rest in the relative warmness of the house while the rest crouched on guard behind the wall. Guard details were relieved at one-hour intervals. The morning broke in a dazzling burst of sun. Snow hid the jagged rocks of the mountains that loomed to the right. Grossinger queried Headquarters. "Regiment starts moving in four hours, sir," he reported to Downs.

Downs passed along the word. "We're on the griddle for the next eight hours. If we can make it till then, we're okay."

There was plenty of hot coffee made by Lazar over the Coleman burner. There were C-rations of beef stew and corned beef hash. There were plenty of cigarettes. It was then that the silence of the white world was broken by the scream of a jet.

"Everybody freeze!" Downs shouted.

The men lay motionless beside the wall. The plane circled once at about 1000 feet and then disappeared to the north. "Tell Headquarters we may have been spotted by enemy aircraft," Downs told Grossinger.

The men were tense now with uncertainty and fear which each hid in his own way. Had they been spotted? Downs had every man out of the house and behind the wall now. Then they heard the rumble of a tank. "Lazar, Wilkinson, Abrams, over the wall to the right. Take cover behind the trees next to the road. Try to get it with your potato mashers. Aim for the treads."

The men's hands went to the grenades hung to their belts, and they slithered over the wall and through the shrubbery. "Bazooka ready?" Downs snapped. Pilner and Lombardosa nodded. Downs didn't even bother to look at Tex Thomas. He knew Thomas would be ready with the Browning. Then it came into sight. At three hundred yards it opened fire. Shells smashed against the wall, crumbling it. Explosive shells slashed through the wall as though it were papier-mâché, and when they exploded, their steel fragments found flesh. There were screams and soft whispers hardly heard because of the rapid fire of the Browning which scored a direct hit and the tank lurched to one side. But it kept moving and shells seemed to explode everywhere.

"Feed the belts smooth and even . . . smooth and even," Tex Thomas snapped at Polinski, who was handling the ammo for the Browning. There was an ear-splitting explosion and the Browning stopped. Simultaneously three loud blasts and spurts of flame came from the tank. Lazar, Wilkinson and Abrams had aimed their grenades. Three more roars followed and the tank was in flames. It came to a stop on one side, and was quiet.

"Get busy, Medic," Downs snapped, but Jeff Leigh was already busy.

Ten men had been killed outright. Six others had suffered wounds. Tex Thomas lay beside the wall groaning faintly. Jeff blanched when he saw Tex's left arm. Shell fragments had smashed it almost to pulp from the elbow down. Jeff took his knife and ripped the sleeves of the jacket and underclothing and then quickly he reached for the rubber tourniquet and tied it around the arm above the elbow. He cut through the sleeve of the right arm. He wound part of the shirt sleeve around it as an improvised tourniquet so that he could find the large vein inside the elbow. When he found it he injected two syrettes of morphine into the vein.

"Got to get him inside, Lieutenant," Jeff said.

"Right. Two of you lend a hand." They carried him into the farm-house and laid him on what had once been a whole kitchen table. The morphine had completed its quick errand of mercy. Jeff felt for his pulse.

"How is he, Medic?" Downs asked.

"Bad, bad." Jeff was thinking aloud. "I can hardly find the pulse. It's thready, rapid — beating about 140. His breathing is shallow. Look at his face. Almost white. He's in a bad state of shock and is losing blood rapidly; needs a transfusion right away, otherwise he won't live an hour. We have to get him to a warm place. If that arm doesn't come off he'll die of shock and hemorrhage."

"You're the only doctor around."

"I only had two years of med school and I was never even in an operat-ing room. Can't we ask Regiment to send up a doctor?"

"The radio is out," Downs said sharply. "Regiment won't be up for another six hours. Tex will be dead before they reach us. It's up to you, Medic. Just tell us what has to be done."

"First cover him with blankets. I'll get some plasma started. . . . I'll try to do something about his arm, and if he's still alive after that we'll have to get him back to the 'evac' hospital for a transfusion."

"Stop wasting time . . . get on with it, Medic." Downs was every inch the Marine officer now.

"It's a hundred-to-one shot, Lieutenant." Jeff's voice was tense. "I have no surgical instruments. Not even a saw."

"Do the best with what you have."

Jeff shrugged his shoulders and dipped into the corpsman's kit. He re-moved two circular units of plasma. Despite the cold he was sweating. He inserted the needle into a vein of Tex's good arm and started the dripping of the plasma. "Got to get his head lower than his feet. Put something under the table legs." Quick hands found rocks and when they were placed under the legs of the table the wounded man's head was six inches lower than his feet. "Blankets under him and over him . . . plenty of them," Jeff ordered. "Get his boots off. If his socks are wet put dry ones on . . . massage his legs. Hand me that other unit of plasma."

Every word of a conversation he had once held with Umberto Calvosa came back to him now: *"The Chief said he'd have to do a 'guillotine' or open operation. You only use it in traumatic cases where every minute counts. . . . He swabbed the mangled arm with metaphen to give it some measure of sterility."* Jeff was calm now. He knew what he had to do. "Get me a pair of wire cutters, Lieutenant."

Someone placed the ugly-looking wire cutters in his hand. He poured the red metaphen over a compression bandage and rubbed it over the two cutting edges. He ripped the remnants of Tex's left sleeve away and the whole arm lay bare. He soaked the healthy part of it in metaphen, then . . .

The lieutenant looked away. Jeff was too intent on what he was doing to hear Barney Lombardosa murmur, "Hail Mary full of grace, the Lord is with Thee. Blessed art Thou . . ." He didn't hear Polinski mutter tensely, "You're doing great, Doc."

Jeff was desperately trying to remember what he had read in Christopher's surgery text. . . . *First, find the brachial artery and clamp it off.* . . . It was not easy to find. It was oozing blood. He clamped a hemostat over it and the oozing stopped. He had six of the small forceps called hemostats which are used to close veins and arteries and he used them all. He wished he had twenty more. He poured sulfa powder into the wound and then soaked half a dozen compression bandages with metaphen and covered the stump. Then he took rolled bandages and wound them over the compression dressing.

He searched his memory. What else could he do? What had he forgotten? "Hold this plasma, someone," he said and a hand reached out for it. Jeff felt for the pulse. For a moment he thought he had been wrong. He watched the second hand of his watch. It was true; it had gone down to a rate of 115 and was stronger. The plasma was doing its work.

"My God, look at his face, Doc," Harry Polinski gasped incredulously.

Jeff looked up. Tex's face was no longer white. It had a faint glow now. He bent over to listen to the man's breathing. It was no longer shallow. It was slow and deep. Now if the hemostats didn't fall off, and if the plasma could be kept going, and if he was kept warm, and if a real doctor arrived in time, Tex Thomas might live.

"I think there's a good chance he'll make it, Lieutenant," Jeff said. "I'm glad you gave me that order. I wouldn't have dared to do it otherwise. Now I'd like to look at the other men."

"You go right ahead, Doc," Downs said softly. "You go right ahead."

For the next hour he removed shell fragments from bodies, administered morphine, poured metaphen and sulfa powder over minor wounds. Then he went back to see Tex Thomas. Grossinger was with him. Tex was conscious now. His voice was weak but he smiled when he saw Jeff Leigh.

"When this is over how about setting up your practice in Laredo? We can always use another good doctor down there. . . . The lieutenant told me what you did, Jeff. Said I was as good as dead."

"You'll be in the hands of a real doctor soon," Jeff said.

"I'll take you, brother," Tex drawled. "You got a little more of that dream medicine? I got a little ache in my left arm. I know it ain't there but it still aches."

Jeff injected another quarter grain of morphine.

Downs had every available man stationed by the wall now; even some of the wounded held carbines. Eyes were glued to the road to the north, but ears were tuned to the south, hoping for the sound of their own tanks. But the attack didn't come from the road. It came where they least expected it and where they were most vulnerable — the air. Two twin-engine planes roared around the mountains in back of the farmhouse and dove to within five hundred feet of them. The first dropped five bombs, all of which hit their target — the twenty-four men who crouched by the wall. The second plane strewed the deadly napalm fire but there was really no use for that. Every man in the Third Platoon, Baker Company, was dead — except one. Tex Thomas lay in his morphine-induced sleep on the table in the farmhouse and by some miracle the sturdily built stone house resisted the fierce heat of the napalm flames.

Hospital Corpsman Jefferson Leigh never knew that the Regiment arrived three hours later to put Tex Thomas into a truck and send him quickly back to a base hospital where doctors marveled at the miracle of the spontaneous surgery that had saved his life. Jeff Leigh never knew that the Koreans attacked in full force that afternoon to drive the Regiment back even before it had a chance to bury its dead. He never knew that during the next year other regiments would fight for this farmhouse and other men would die here, and be buried in a common grave — many of them unidentifiable. He would never know that he would be posthumously awarded the Navy Cross, and that when his father received it he would say sadly, "Maybe my father and I are forgiven the lives we led. Maybe young Jeff made up for us. . . ."

Frozen March

✗

from *Band of Brothers*

by ERNEST FRANKEL

Moonlight dripped over the rock pillar in the observation post, casting a black finger of shadow across the breast of Bad Girl Ridge. Pat lay there, his long body trembling with cold, his bowels shaken with excitement, his mind acutely aware of sound and range, movement and direction.

The shepherd's horn blew again, closer this time, its tuneless blast eerie in the night. An emerald streak erupted from the darkness and arched toward the defenders. A green flare burst above, rocked gently, and floated back, coating the scene in a ghastly hue, weaving grotesque patterns in the snow. Tracers whipped the flanks once more; and a ragged line emerged from trees and knolls and shellholes and underbrush. Pat turned to The Horse, who was hunched over, sitting with his huge hands between his knees. "Fire your barrage!"

The enemy rushed ahead. Mortars smashed above them. The line was severed. Still the remnants came on. "Walk the fire back to us. Walk it back!"

"Weather's funny with ammo, Captain," The Horse said. "Don't want to clobber our own."

The Chinese had formed again. They were ninety yards away. Eighty. "Keep one tube hot with illuminating," Pat called to the sergeant. A flare burst above them. Seventy. Sixty yards, Christ, only sixty yards! "Fire! Fire!" Pat was standing, screaming to his men below. But the only sound to answer him was "Sha! Sha!" All across the valley, for four hundred yards, the advancing line, like a sidewinder, wiggled and whipped forward. To within fifty yards. And coming on. "Sha-a-a!" And Pat was screaming with them. "Fire!"

He heard Andy's voice above his own, above the yells of the attackers, above the quavering bugle call. "Semper Fi!"

Able Company replied. On the left, Pat saw Allison's men — black motes on the white face of Bad Girl. Then the breast below him, with Cagle's platoon clinging to its slopes. Pappas's troops were to his right, across the belly and thigh. Together they lashed back at the charging horde, sending interlocking bands of tracers into the night.

The enemy was climbing, scrabbling up, crawling, throwing grenades, firing burp guns. Behind them another chant began: "Sonovabitch Marines we kill! Sonovabitch Marines you die!"

Pat was struck by the unreality of it. He lay motionless, his radio silent, feeling utterly remote.

The second wave appeared, surging forward, inundating the flatland. Though mortars scooped at it, and flame and steel hissed above and the tempo of fire increased, the wave rolled on, not slowing at all, and crashed against the battlements. Relentless. Relentless. Pat seized upon the word, repeated it to himself. What purpose, what cause could drive men on like that?

Below him a machine gun chattered viciously. A grenade exploded, and both gunner and assistant slumped forward. The Negro motor-transport man, who had volunteered to remain, pulled the bodies aside, crouched behind the gun, fired. But the enemy was close in now, swarming over the rocks below, working their way toward the weapon. "Swing it free," Pat yelled as the soldier fired it in fixed position. The gun jammed. The soldier began to bang futilely on it, shouting at the man beside him. It was leaving dead space below, and the Chinese were funneling into the free area. Pat pointed the spot to The Horse. "Call it in. Got to take a chance. Only way," he shouted breathlessly. "Hurry!"

"Only six men left down there to handle the mortars, sir."

It took two agonizingly long minutes for The Horse to adjust the fire. "On the way, Captain."

"Take cover!" Pat yelled. Then the shell blasted a geyser of snow and rock and mud and weapons and Chinese bodies. Still the enemy climbed frantically toward the jammed gun. Men on the flanks held them off with grenades while two Marines tried to clear the stoppage.

Pat left the shelter of the OP. Sliding, falling, he ran toward the gun. Its crew was clawing the earth as burp guns sprayed the area. Pat shoved the men aside. Then, automatically, calling on skill he had first learned in the sawdust of a hillside gunshed in Quantico six years before, remembering with uncanny detail the drill he had memorized only weeks ago, he lifted the cover of the heavy gun. Then he extracted a ruptured cartridge, tested the belt feed, slammed the bolt forward again. He freed the weapon, swung it in traverse, and sprayed the climbers below. Within fifty yards, the second wave was charging in to join the first. "Take it!" Pat shouted. The soldier thanked him solemnly, moved beside him, began to swat the enemy like flies on a wall.

"Sha! Sha!" Out in the darkness, a third wave was gathering. The shepherd's horn blared its signal. This time a longer wail, a more urgent summons. As they drew closer, Pat saw that most of them were unarmed, that they stopped beside the dead and took up their weapons, that some had reached the base of the ridge, still screaming, determined to wrest a weapon from the defenders. The wave grew, joined the backwash of the others, swept against the battered defenses.

Pat moved toward the observation post to call for mortars again. He saw two men wedged in the same hole, heads down, rifles between their legs. "Get up and fire!" he stormed at them. They did not respond. He pulled them out bodily, shook them and shoved them toward the front. "Fire, damn you!" One got off a shot. Then the other. They began to fire more rapidly, easing forward to seek out better targets. Their moment of panic had passed. Pat got to his knees and crawled toward the rocks.

A wounded man lay there, blood coursing from his shrapnel-torn shoulder, crying, "Corpsman . . . Corpsman . . ."

Pat took a morphine syrette from his armpit where he had taped it, and injected the drug. The mortars he had called in had been impartial; he had maimed one of his own. The man might die because . . . He rejected the idea and called another Marine. "Get him to the aid station."

"Lieutenant Anderson said no one was to leave the lines, sir."

"Take him down!"

"Aye, aye, sir."

He climbed to his OP, and fell beside The Horse, panting for breath. The Marine he had left in his command post was waiting for him, staring wide-eyed at the carnage below.

"Sir, Sanchez and that doggie. They didn't get in. They're out there someplace."

"Was getting ready to wake you. Not my fault. . . . Can't see too good . . . Wasn't sure. . . ."

Sanchez clapped a hand over Dorn's mouth, and pulled him down beside him. A Chinese officer was walking toward them, leading a column of troops. He stopped a few yards away and yelled at his men, gesturing first toward the ridge, then toward the flank. The Chinese slogged off through the snow.

Woody held his breath. He could hear the chatter of the enemy, the crash of mortars, the frantic stutter of automatic weapons. Everything seemed maddeningly familiar.

Sanchez released him, crawled to the lip of the shellhole, and looked out after the disappearing column. They were sixty yards from the lines, and moving parallel to the position. While the Marines were heavily engaged on the front, these Chinese were stealing past them, sweeping wide to envelop the position from the rear! He slipped down beside Dorn and explained the tactic. "C'mon, we've gotta get back."

"Can't now. They're behind us and in front of us. They don't get us, we'll never make it through our lines. Our own people will . . ."

"They hit in the rear, our guys'll get slaughtered."

"Sonovabitch Marines we kill! Sonovabitch Marines you die!" The chant was rising from the front as the third wave rolled against the lines. A Marine mortar exploded behind them. Both men pressed themselves to the frozen earth. Shrapnel whined overhead.

"No use," Dorn moaned.

"Gotta try." Sanchez unhooked the sound phone from the mortar-severed wire. "We'll separate. I'm gonna try to get in on the flank. You go in at Lieutenant Cagle's position. That grazin' fire's got the goonies discouraged, so you might slip through there. When you get close enough, just yell out who you are. Tell them the Chinks are movin' around to the rear. . . ."

But Dorn was shaking his head. "Why can't we go together?"

"This way we got two chances. One of us'll make it for sure. Just keep movin'. You run into Chinks, stay doggo."

"You said we'd stick together. You weren't gonna leave."

"Get goin'," Sanchez said gruffly. Then he rolled out of the shellhole.

Dorn looked after him. He was already a third of the way. Suddenly, he fell in the snow, inert. Boots were sloshing out in the darkness. The Chinese officer was back. Dorn could hear him cursing a man, kicking him to his feet, sending him forward. Then he could see him beside Sanchez, so close that his shadow fell across the Marine. Dorn watched, afraid to breathe. He told himself to leave, to go forward. But he could not force himself to move.

He gazed dazedly at the crumpled shadow in the snow. The Chinese officer paced nervously back and forth, yelling at his men as they passed. Sanchez was on his knees behind the officer, moving only under the deafening sound of gunfire. Dorn's muscles reacted to each motion.

Now! Sanchez was up, on the man's back, an arm around his neck to cut off the scream. The two figures rolled in the snow. Dorn watched, horrified, heard the grunts and the scuffling amazingly amplified in the brief silences between the sounds of battle. He had no doubt about the outcome. Sanchez would win. But even as he assured himself, he saw the Chinese pull free, saw the weapon, saw the Marine fall under the blow. There was more thrashing, a horrible groan. Dorn flinched in an agony of pain as the enemy stood over Sanchez and kicked him. Once. Twice. Again. Then the officer walked toward Dorn, calling for men to take a prisoner.

Dorn crouched, petrified, as the man approached. Fear expanded in him, filled his chest so that breathing seemed impossible, weighted against his bladder. He wet himself, not knowing it. Then the two men were looking at each other. Dorn in his hole, the officer directly above him. His weapon, a pistol, shone in the moonlight. Driven by instinct, Dorn grabbed the officer's boots, heard the bullet whistle past his ear as the Chinese fell on top of him. Dorn rolled aside and tried to stand, his ears ringing with the explosion. The Chinese kicked with both feet, driving him across the narrow hole. He tasted blood. His face was wet with it. The man was on top of him, pummeling him. Dorn slumped and awaited the inevitable. The man spat on him.

All the humiliations, all the fear and anger he had known in all of his life, rose in Dorn and choked him, impelling him to fight. He lashed out at his adversary, caught him off balance, threw him down, rolled him over, grasped his head by the hair, and smashed it against the rocks. The officer tried to fight back, tried to lift his pistol, but Dorn's hands were on his throat. The Chinese gurgled, pushed desperately at the bleeding face, arched his back, trying to unseat him. Dorn felt the pressure of a scabbard against his knee, grasped it, pulled the knife from the man's belt. Then he drove it again and again into the twitching body beneath him.

When there was no more movement, he leaned back, looking unbelievingly at the contorted face, staring at his weapon and at his bloody hands, grunting with the effort of drawing breath. He felt as if he had murdered his past.

He had known something like this only once before. He was living at the farm, with his father, finishing his school term. Another boy had left the bus with him, taunted him, beat him on the way home, stood on his shoes, held to his collar, while Dorn took one painful step after the other, carrying his tormentor. His father had met them on the road. "Fight him, Woody. Or fight me!" His shame, his despair had been overpowering. The neighbor boy became the symbol of everything that had ever oppressed him. Crying, repeating the single swear word he knew, biting, clawing with his fingernails, he had battered the other boy until he was pulled away, sweating, sobbing, and filthy. His father had walked back to the house with him, his arm around Woody's shoulder.

Now he was astride the mutilated body, his bloody hands clutching the knife. He had been transported for a moment. The scene — so vivid in all the colors of an Iowa autumn — had passed through his mind between the orange flash of a mortar and its crackling explosion. He dropped the knife, retrieved his weapon, and ran to Sanchez.

He was still breathing. He groaned. A bruise puffed one side of his face. Dorn lay beside him, cupped snow in his hand, and washed it over neck and forehead. "Sanchez? Sanchez?" Sanchez opened his eyes and started to speak. But the men summoned by the dead officer had finally come. They were at the hole, looking at the body, talking excitedly, searching the area. Dorn, his mouth to Sanchez's ear, kept whispering, "Quiet. You'll be okay. I'll take care of you."

The Chinese came within ten yards of them, but ignored the mounds in the snow. At last they left, running to the rear. Sanchez spoke painfully. "Watch . . . You got . . . my watch. . . ." Dorn returned it. Sanchez's eyes focused on him. "Get back . . . not much time. . . . Get back. . . ."

"I'm not leaving you."

"They'll send out . . . for me. Get goin'." He grasped his side where he had been kicked. "Goonie . . . licked me." His eyes were closed. "Hurry. . . ."

The Chinese, varying their attack, struck at points all along the front. With maniacal disregard for death, they hurled themselves against the wall of fire, climbed toward the guns, were smashed, screaming, from the rocks, were corded in grisly piles for four hundred yards across the base of Bad Girl Ridge.

Pat sat in a foxhole with Lieutenant Allison. He was in a fever of anxiety. No message from Battalion. No letup in the fury of the assault. Less than thirty minutes had elapsed since the first blast of the enemy bugle; and he had run the length of the position in that time, carrying ammunition, helping Huckabee and Choy with wounded, repairing a weapon, rallying the men to close a breach in the line. One incident merged into another in his mind.

Now he waited. There was nothing else to do. Twice, despite the clamor of the wind and the incessant squawk of his radio, he started to doze, only to wake with a start. His body cried out for sleep, but his mind kept nagging him, refusing him any retreat. His units were on their own. He could no longer maneuver them or control their fires. Each was fighting its own pocket war. And each war had its attackers and defenders, its terrain, its generals and heroes, its casualties, tactics, tragedies, horrors, and jokes.

Andy, armed with a recaptured Tommy gun, penned four of the enemy in the narrow confines of a rock shelf, and chased them from side to side until, exhausted, they lay in the snow, looking up at him, their hands raised in surrender. He pointed to the farthest Chinese, called his shot, dropped him with his pistol.

"Cease fire! Cease fire!" Chuck Cagle fell beside Andy. "They're trying to surrender."

"No prisoners," Andy said. "Number two!" He pointed to the next Chinese, who was on his knees, waving his arms. Andy leveled his pistol.

Cagle grabbed his hand, held it. "No! Dammit, Andy . . ."

"Get back to your job!" Cagle crawled away. "Number two," Andy repeated. One by one, the trapped enemy fell, and lay like rag dolls in the snow.

First Sergeant Goober gathered two wounded men in his arms, holding their heads on his shoulders. "Be still. I'll get you down."

"Well, if it ain't the Grim Reaper," one of them mumbled.

"Shut up," Goober said. "Or I'll make you walk, you wedgeass."

"Jesus, I hurt!"

"Don't move. You'll be okay. Think about somethin' else."

"I can see. And I got my balls." A weak chuckle. "All that matters . . . Top, you're a mean ole bastard. You gonna give me my purple heart?"

Across the ridge, Corporal Firesteen shouted a warning. A Chinese, explosives on his back, had scrambled over the rocks, worked behind, and was running toward a machine gun.

The crew was alerted too late. The man flung himself across the weapon. There was no explosion. For a stupefying instant, the Chinese, astounded, lay across the water jacket; and the Marines gaped at him.

"Get that goonie off there. I don't wanna blow up the gun," Firesteen said. Someone pushed the Chinese. He reeled away. The corporal's BAR fired a burst, and the man pitched backward and fell, his pack exploding among his own troops below. Firesteen dropped to his knees. "Like my ma would say, friends, 'Ken geharget vehren' — meaning, roughly — You can get killed around here!"

The gunner, roaring with laughter, swung the gun into a new group of attackers.

Before the warming-tent in the command post, Choy stood over the single prisoner. The ragged, wounded man, dragged back from Pappas's position, was in a delirium, unable to answer questions.

A Marine ran up. "Choy, Goober's lookin' for you. Wants you to help with the ammo detail."

"I am coming," Choy said. He shot the Chinese in the head, rolled the body out of his way, and went below.

George Pappas called Pat on his radio. "Have a small penetration in my second squad. About eight or ten Chinks. Can you give me help to counterattack?"

Pat deliberated. His mind was foggy. He forced himself to think, to phrase his answer, to speak. He had held his reserve despite two other requests for them, despite the need for men on the line. They remained his only unit for maneuver, his only chance to cope with the unexpected. Yet they were inactive when every man, every weapon was needed. Andy had pointed that out angrily enough. Pappas repeated his request. "Try to seal it off," Pat said at last. "If you can't, call me again." It was so easy, he reflected, so simple to give the order. As easy as it had been for Skinhead to order him to perform an impossible task. But the reserve had to be held against an extremity, he believed; and he was not yet willing to commit them.

The radio again. "Able Six. Able Two." Cagle's voice. "Can you give us more illumination? Over."

The Horse, who had followed Pat, leaned toward him. "Twelve rounds illuminating, eight rounds H.E. left. Better hold onto it, huh?"

Pat was stunned by the report. Ammunition, medical supplies, food, manpower — all were dwindling away. "Sorry, Able Two. Can't do it. Anything else?"

The voice, amazingly, incongruously gay, answered: " 'Send us more Chinks!' 'Retreat, hell, we just got here!' 'We don't wanna live forever.' " Cagle laughed. "Soon as I get time, I'm gonna come up with something that'll make the history books!"

Pat grinned, then shook with laughter. It seemed inordinately funny. His whole body sagged with the release of it. His eyes clouded. Allison was laughing, too. "Helps to be a little nuts in this lash-up."

The radio sounded again. "Able Six. Able One." Pat acknowledged the call. It was Pappas's platoon sergeant. "Lieutenant's been hit, sir. I'm takin' . . ."

There was an interruption. Then Pappas's voice, oddly thick and garbled, came on. "I'm okay. Lost some teeth, got a hole in one cheek. Nothing serious. Busy. Out."

While Pat still felt the upsurge of relief, he was shocked to wakefulness. He held to a rock, his face pressed against its cold, slick surface, listening. Allison had turned, too, was intent. The Horse had crawled a few yards to the rear and was poised, straining for an alien sound amid the din. It was repeated: The sharp snap of rifles and the *pump-pump-pump* of burp guns.

"They're behind us!" Pat shouted.

The Horse was already calling the mortars. Allison started to raise himself from the foxhole. "I'll get some people back to alternate positions in the rear."

A grenade looped over, struck the lieutenant's shoulder, and fell on the parapet in front of their foxhole. There was an instant of terrified indecision. Then Pat screamed, "Down!" The grenade spurted blue, whipped hot fragments of serrated steel.

The Horse heard the groans, the muffled cries. He crawled to the foxhole. "God in Heaven!" he whispered, turning his eyes away. Then, "Corpsman!"

Pat stirred. There was a weight on his back. His face was twisted against the broken mouthpiece of his radio, his knees pressed against the bottom of the foxhole. Something warm and wet was soaking his shoulders. He tried to turn, but could not. Then Allison was lifted from him and he could move again.

The Horse and a corpsman were bent over Allison. Pat crawled between them. "Is he —" His voice faltered. Stricken, bewildered eyes peered up at him. Then the torn features relaxed into vacancy. Overcome, Pat turned away and wearily, painfully, stood.

Allison dead. Pappas wounded. The enemy in the rear. Mortars out. Radio destroyed. All in five minutes' time. And on every side the slaughter raged on. The Horse nudged his elbow, prodding him from his stupor. With the dull fixity of a robot, he sent The Horse to alert Cagle, and ordered Allison's platoon sergeant to man alternate positions on the perimeter.

He staggered and fell, wrenching his shoulder, as he made the rocky descent from the position, but was up at once, stumbling through the drifts of snow within Cagle's platoon at the breast, running again up the rising belly toward the command post. The sound of firing behind the ridge was closer now, isolated, intense. He pushed ahead, straining for breath, wheezing with exertion. Did the mortarmen get in? How many enemy? Where was Andy? His thoughts were jumbled, as he tried to clear the cluttered passages of his mind. "Thank God I held onto the reserve," he said aloud.

He was on the point of collapse when he reached the command post. "Have you seen Lieutenant Anderson?"

The Marine on phone watch was kneeling with Choy over two bodies. "No, sir."

Pat dropped beside them. Sanchez and Dorn were stretched in the snow. For an instant, he knew an overwhelming sense of relief at their safety. "Couldn't get back in time," Dorn was saying. "Tried . . . Chinese workin' round flank." He sat up. His face was raw, bruised. "Sanchez is okay. Ribs. I tried, sir."

Dizziness nearly overcame Pat. He dug his gloved fists into his eyes. Recovering, he glanced at the massive form of Sanchez, seeing the puffed, swollen lips, the frozen blood on his cheeks. "You're Dorn, aren't you?"

"Woody Dorn, sir."

"You'll do, Woody."

A surge of pride choked the soldier. "I killed one of them," he whispered, as if it were a secret.

Pat did not hear him. He was no longer aware of Dorn or Sanchez or Choy or the Marine on the phone. Frantically, he pulled aside the flap on the warming-tent. Wounded men were packed in a tight, tangled mass inside. They looked at him blankly. He returned to the others. "Where are they? Where's the outfit I had standing by?"

"Gone, Captain," Choy said.

"Where? I told them —"

"Lieutenant Anderson. He sent for them a while ago," the marine said. "Runner from Mr. Cagle's platoon came over."

"He had no right!" Pat shouted, grabbing the man's arms. "Why didn't you call me? Why wasn't I asked?" His whole body shook with fatigue, with anger, with fear. "I need them! I need them *now!*"

"Sir, I never thought to —"

From below came the high-pitched voice of First Sergeant Goober. "Move out, damn you! Get yourself a hole. Move! Move!" Then the roar of a big gun, firing at close range, and the shattering impact of a shell exploding nearby.

The scream, windborne, urgent, brought Pat back from the edge of panic. "Get on the phone. Locate Lieutenant Anderson. I'm going forward. I want my men sent to me. You tell him that. You tell him I ordered it!" He climbed out of the crater, ran down the path, tripped over a dead man's foot, and sprawled headlong. Clenching his hands, willing the tremor out of his body, he commanded his disordered mind to function. He stood unsteadily and plunged into the wind, toward the other aid station.

Huckabee was dragging a man on a stretcher out of the warming-tent. Several wounded lay in the snow. "Get these people inside," Pat gasped. "They'll freeze to death."

The corpsman put the stretcher down and stumbled toward Pat, trying to recognize him in the darkness. With great effort, as if each word were being torn out of him, he said, "No more room in there." His shoulders sagged. His face was expressionless, drained of emotion. "Have to rotate 'em." He bent over another stretcher. "Like an oven. Put in a loaf. Take out a loaf."

"So many," Pat said hopelessly.

Huckabee stooped to part the flap. He jerked his head toward a group stretched beside the tent, their faces pressed against the canvas. "Made it back from the mortars. Only one hurt. Others too beat to move."

As Huckabee shuffled into the tent, Pat passed him and worked his way down the ridge, guided by the flash of tracers and the cough of gunfire. Twice he slipped, rolled, and clawed his way out of the snow.

Men were crouched among the rocks, firing into the night. Sixty yards away, spurts of light traveled along a wavering line, seeming to trigger the Chinese gun, revealing for an instant the dark shapes of the enemy. *Whirrr-ap* . . . *Shew* . . . *Wham!* The hillside shuddered under the blow. Pat stared as if hypnotized by the tiny dots of flickering blue. *Whirr-ap* — Count one-two-three — *Shew* . . . *Wham!* It was like a spectacular electric sign.

George Pappas and Goober were kneeling behind a boulder, watching the front. Pat slipped down to them. "Oh! Beard fooled me for a minute," Goober said. "Thought you were the skipper."

Again Pat recoiled, as if the phrase were a whip in his face. No matter

what, Andy would — by force of will and indifference to danger and in-
vulnerability — retain command. He summoned a curt, level tone of voice:
"How many out there?"

A scattering of rifle fire twanged around them. The three men lay flat,
their faces against the snow. "Jezoo! Can't even put your head up," Goober
said.

"Must be forty, fifty of them," Pappas said. The lieutenant's front teeth
had been shot away, and there was a small piece of tape on his cheek. He
spoke through his nose, his words flat and garbled. "Still a lot of pressure
up front. Couldn't afford to move more than this one squad down here.
Got to get some more people. . . ."

Whirrr-ap . . . Shew . . . Wham!

"Must be a recoilless gun," Pat said.

"Probably a seventy-five they've captured one place or another," Pappas
said.

"We damn well better put it out of whack," Goober said. "That bastard's
got our range and he's liable to hurt somebody."

"Send a bazooka team out?"

"No rockets, Captain. All expended," Goober said.

"Sooner or later they're going to rush us," Pappas said. "They're moving
up under cover of the gun."

The men Andy had taken away had been held for just such an emergency. If the enemy succeeded in a breakthrough, they would easily overrun the aid station, threaten the command post, and even roll up the perimeter, away from the commanding belly of the ridge. He had to have
enough men to meet the assault. But where could he risk weakening the
line? How to knock out that damned gun? He thought of mortars, and remembered the dazed mortarmen at the aid station. "I'm going on up," he
said to Pappas.

"If you're lookin' for Lieutenant Anderson," Goober said, "I sent a man
for him first thing."

For an instant the two men's eyes locked. Then, "I'll get some men together and be right back," Pat said.

"Yeah. Good idea. You do that, Captain."

Pat turned when he heard the warning *Whirr-ap!* and ducked behind a
boulder as the projectile whooshed in. *Shew . . . Wham!* Somewhere up
the feeble line, a man was screaming above the wind and the din of battle,
calling for a corpsman. A few feet away, hidden from his view by the
rocks, Pat heard Goober.

"I'm givin' it to you straight, Lieutenant. He lost his guts, committed
that reserve first time he got rattled instead of sittin' on 'em for the pay-
off."

"Knock it off," Pappas said.

"Couldn't get him on the radio. Didn't answer. Probably hunkered down in a hole, afraid to expose himself."

The accusation was so unjust that only the *Whirr-ap . . . Shew . . . Wham!* of the enemy gun restrained Pat from going back and having it out with his accuser.

"Damn!" Goober said. "If we get clobbered now, it's on his head."

"I told you to shut up!" The lieutenant spoke slowly, with thick-tongued pain. "He's CO of this company. And you better damn well remember it!"

Quietly, Pat got up and began to climb again, back toward the aid station. He stopped to catch his breath, fought the onrush of fatigue, and went on.

The mortarmen were still ringing the warming tent.

"Get one tube ready," Pat said, after a moment's forgetfulness as to why he had come. "And I want these people on line."

"They're pooped, sir," The Horse said. "Had a hell of a time gettin' in. Chinks all over the place. And ammo and tubes to carry. Had to leave the baseplates."

Pulling one of the men to his knees, Pat roared at him. "Get up!" The Marine obeyed, then crumpled. Pat tugged at him again, shook him. "Get up and stay up. You hear?" The Horse steadied the man, and Pat faced the others. The sleepless nights, the bitter cold, the unceasing wind, the freezing, inactive days — all these things had ravaged them. Their recent flight before the enemy had drained their will, and they had been overcome by lethargy. Pat cursed, shoved, and dragged them to their feet. Finally they were all standing, hazily aware of him. One collapsed against the tent. Pat ran to him, furious. "Damn you! Stand up!" He realized that he was screaming, that The Horse was looking at him open-mouthed. He bent down, hauling the man up again. "We need you, all of you," he said, his voice breaking. They took rifles from the stack beside the warming tent. "Can you fire that mortar without the baseplate?"

"I'm no Lou Diamond, Captain, but I'll try." The Horse picked up the tube, and Pat carried the last eight rounds of High Explosive shells. They followed him, sliding, falling, but rising again.

"You came back," Goober said, surprised.

"Get these men in position."

Whirrr-ap . . . Shew . . . Wham! The gun was in the same place, but the glitter of muzzle blast from the enemy rifles was closer, no more than thirty yards away — well within assault range.

The Horse held the mortar tube between his legs, jammed the steel ball at the base into the packed snow, and braced himself. "Get a round ready, sir."

Pat armed the sixty-millimeter shell and held it over the tube. "Now!"

The projectile slid, struck the firing pin, arced high above. They watched for its explosion, and saw it flash behind the emplaced gun.

"Higher angle," Pat said.

As if the mortar were their signal, the Chinese charged. This time there was no screaming, only the frantic sloshing of men through snow, the crackling of ice, animal grunts, the clatter of weapons against rocks. Pappas ran by, calling to his men. "Get up! They'll be on top of you."

Pat drew his pistol and joined Firesteen on the line. "Dump your grenades! They're right below us," the corporal yelled to the other three men in his fire team. He propped himself against a boulder, making room for Pat beside him. They waited. Pat drew a deep breath, then released it slowly, trying to expel all the tension in him. Firesteen was listening intently, his BAR at his hip, the birthmark on his cheek twitching.

Whirr-ap . . . Shew . . . Wham!

The men scrambled. Some started back to seek shelter. "Stay where you are!" Pat shouted.

The enemy appeared. Singly. In groups. Pulling themselves over boulders. Running between the masses of rock. It was no longer a battle of forces. It was one man against another now.

One Chinese jumped at a Marine from behind. Firesteen screamed, "Goonie!" and the Marine whirled, rifle at the ready. The enemy impaled himself on the Marine's bayonet. He fell on the ground, kicking, shrieking. Horrified, the Marine began to scream, but held on to his weapon.

Goober pulled him away, placed a foot on the enemy's chest, and tore the bayonet out. Then he lifted the body and heaved it over the side. He yanked the Marine erect and returned his rifle to him. "Shoot it, you bastard, or you'll end up where he did!"

Grenades exploded deafeningly. There was the *pump-pump-pump* of burp guns, the twang of rifles, the mad stutter of BAR's. Savage cries and agonized screams as Chinese and Marines battled for the same shelters. Pat saw an enemy soldier climbing over the rocks on the flank of Pappas's position. He called a warning, but his voice was a mere whisper in the bedlam. Leaving his niche, he ran toward Pappas, ten yards away. The Chinese was pulling himself over the edge of the boulder. Pappas saw him and fired his carbine, but the weapon jammed. Pat raised his pistol, but was afraid to fire from that distance. As the Chinese got to his feet, Pappas swung the butt of his weapon and clubbed him to the rocks below.

Off on the right, The Horse and two other Marines had loosened a boulder. They rocked it free and sent it crashing down the hillside, tearing a great slash in the snow, scattering enemy soldiers like tenpins.

The sound of sliding snow alerted Pat. It was behind him. He crawled toward it and saw the cloudy shape of an approaching enemy. He readied his pistol as the Chinese came on, eyes staring, panting hoarsely. This strange creature wanted to kill him! Pat's lips compressed. He felt cold and sick. He was emptied out. He heard the thud of his heart, felt the beat of his pulses. He licked his cold, dry lips and tasted fear. He squeezed the trigger.

The enemy uttered a cry of astonishment and twitched convulsively. A swath of red spread across the snow. Pat stared at the murder he had done, and gagged. Then he dragged himself back to Pappas's position.

The attack lasted less than five minutes, but in its intensity it seemed endless. When the enemy, still firing, had retreated into the darkness below, Pat sank down beside Pappas. Both struggled for breath, faced each other, smiling weakly.

Goober joined them. "Reamed 'em, didn't we? By God, we reamed 'em!"

Woody Dorn appeared, lugging a case of thirty-caliber ammunition. "Choy sent me, Captain. And some grenades are comin', too. Mr. Anderson called the CP, says he can't spare the reserve, but he'll come himself in fifteen or twenty minutes."

"Thank God for somethin'," Goober said.

"Get the ammo distributed," Pat said. "And get a corpsman down here. See how many were hurt."

"Got eleven okay," said Goober. "No dead. One wounded who can stay. Others I already sent out."

"Good work, Top."

The first sergeant, oblivious, tore open the box of ammunition and loaded Dorn. "Get this stuff out, doggie. Before we get called on again."

"If we can just hold until it gets light," Pat said, looking at his watch, "we'll be okay. Nearly four now."

Whirrr-ap . . . *Shew* . . . *Wham!* The shell exploded in the boulders well above them, erupting in a shower of rock and snow. "Broke their backs before," Pappas said, brushing debris from his parka. "But they'll try again after that gun works us over a while longer."

"Ought to get some people down there, flank it," Goober said, stuffing clips into his pockets.

"Haven't anyone fresh enough for that," Pat said.

"No, Captain, we don't. Now if we had our reserve, sittin' in the CP, warm and rested —"

"Get the ammo out," Pappas said, cutting him off. Dorn left them. The lieutenant picked up the box and pushed Goober ahead of him. "Better just wait them out," he said. "We've got pretty good cover."

"Well, the skipper'll be comin' . . ."

Pat followed them and found The Horse and his mortar. "We've got to try for that gun again," Pat told him.

"I don't think we can do it from up here, sir. Got to get closer, use it like a cannon."

Whirrr-ap . . . Pat dived for cover, scraping his chin against the ice as he went down. *Shew* . . . *Wham!* A tremendous blow, close by. The Horse hunched over him, offering him a hand. A few yards away, he heard Firesteen screaming for a corpsman.

When they got to him, Firesteen pointed below. "Lieutenant Pappas got it . . . in the belly."

Pappas was on his knees, his exposed intestines cupped in his hands. His eyes were tightly closed, his torn mouth was twisted in pain. "Is it bad? Really bad?" he gasped, begging for reassurance, afraid to look.

The Horse made him lie down. Moments later, Huckabee was there. Pat heard Firesteen: "Do something. Help him. Why don't you help him?"

And Huckabee: "Help him? Who do you think I am, God Almighty?"

Pat watched the scene, fixing it forever in his memory. The black night, the white snow, the crimson wound, the glazed blue eyes in the ashen face, the green-clad form, the icy brown strands of hair — and over all, the heartless, pale gold glow of moon. And Pappas dead, his hands still clutched to his ripped belly.

The *whirrr-ap* of another shell sounded. Then the explosion. Earth flew and rock and ice pounded around them. Pat found himself wedged against Firesteen and The Horse. "The bastards!" Firesteen yelled, ". . . bastards!"

Pat scrambled up. "Horse, we're going down. Take the tube. I'll carry the ammo."

They crept down the hillside, betwen the boulders, sliding over the snow on their stomachs, while the big gun fired overhead and enemy rifles spurted to their front. "Long as they don't see us," The Horse whispered. "Long as they don't see us . . ."

The gun was fifty yards away. They rested behind a clump of enemy bodies. Using them as a cover, The Horse set the tube in place. Pat moved to the front, readied the shell. "Try to make it good," he whispered. "Once we fire, they'll know we're down here."

The first try was too far to the left, but they could hear excited shouts from the enemy. It had landed in the ranks of the riflemen. "Quick!" The Horse said. "I'll move it 'bout three fingers. . . ."

Whirrr-ap! Pat didn't hear the whistling toward them, only the devastating roar as the shell detonated. It was too high, but they had revealed themselves. Next time . . . He thrust a round into the tube. It struck above the enemy gun. "Down!" he rasped. "Get it down!"

"No damn sight . . . I'm tryin'!"

Pat armed another shell, was holding it over the tube when he heard the enemy gun crackle its warning. He dropped the round in the snow and rolled away. An explosion roared beside him, above him, before him. He was tossed on his back and he lay there, staring at a fleecy, sheep-like cloud as it slipped over the moon, struggling for the breath that had been knocked out of him. At last he breathed, convulsively. It seemed to burn. He tried to stand, got to his knees. It took all his strength to speak. "Fire!" The mortar thumped beside him. Its shell blasted into the enemy, and there were cries, far, far off. He saw The Horse's face, his mouth moving, glee spreading over the pocked features. But it was like watching a film when the sound fails. The sense of victory he had expected crumbled before he could grasp it. There was no victory. Only death. If he should die . . . Like Allison. Like Pappas . . . If he should die . . .

He wanted only to survive, to be alive and unhurt and at home once more, to blot all this out, to overcome the odds. All his resolution eroded. I've tried, he thought hazily . . . tried and tried and tried. . . .

He fell forward, knowing that he was falling but powerless to prevent it. He felt the impact of ice on his cheek. He was conscious, but only with the vague awareness of a man succumbing to anesthesia. In that moment he could think of only one thing. It would be good to turn over. It would be good to see the sky.

The Bloodstained Beach

✗

by JACLAND MARMUR

It doesn't happen often. Nowadays, a car gets stalled along the roadway off the pavement, all the traffic just keeps zooming right on past. Maybe that's why he was taken by surprise. South of Oceanside, on Highway 101, he had the blue Pacific water at his back, separated from it only by a narrow beach, and small, white-headed combers were collapsing noisily upon the sand. He didn't hear these youngsters drive up in their old jalopy. With the car hood open, gray felt hat pushed off his forehead, he was growling anger at the engine. He was startled when he heard this clear, young voice so close.

"Mister," Eddie Topping said, "I know exactly how you feel. Can I help?"

The man looked up. Eddie saw he had a square, stern face, a pale scar angling down across one temple where the close-cropped hair showed flecks of gray. It gave his eyes a piercing quality. Suddenly they smiled.

"Well, son, that's nice of you," his deep voice said. "There's a service station down the road, though. I can ——"

"You let Eddie look at it. He is very good with cars." That was Susan. Tall, fine-figured girl, almost as tall as Eddie. She was walking over to them with the west wind in the tumble of her yellow hair. "Here's the tool sack, Eddie."

Susan had brought the little canvas bag. The big man saw them looking at each other for a moment. He saw Eddie grin. He saw the girl smile back, her little nose all wrinkling with her lovely smiling, telling Eddie all it meant. Seeing that, some sternness left the big man's brittle eyes. Then he heard the girl's voice, low and throaty.

"That's the ocean out there, mister, isn't it?" asked Susan. Then she gave a soft, quick chuckle. "I suppose you think that's silly if you live here. But we drove a long way to come see it for ourselves."

Eddie laughed. "That's right." He had his back turned, taking off the car's distributor cap. "We came down Highway 395. Turned off at Elsinore. Headed south on 101 at Capistrano. First time we ever saw the ocean." Eddie laughed again. "Sure is a lot of water. Pretty big puddle. I dunno."

"Eddie wants to make his mind up," explained Susan. "It's the ocean, isn't it? It's not a bay?"

The big man frowned. He appeared accustomed to swift judgment. He looked quickly toward their battered old car, parked behind his own. He saw the Kansas license plates. They weren't joking. So his frown relaxed. "Yes," he said, half smiling, "it's the ocean. Stretches all the way to China. Better than six thousand miles." He was looking straight at Susan. "Does it frighten you?"

She stared seaward, touched by wonder, seeing deep blue water flecked by runnels of white foam in the distance, glittering in brilliant sunshine.

"It's up to Eddie." Susan tossed her head. "If it don't scare him, it won't scare me."

Eddie was examining the distributor cap. "I think maybe I should join the Navy," he was saying. "That's what Susan means. Susan's got an aunt in San Diego where we're going. At a naval base like that there ought to be a lot of ships. I want to look around and make my mind up."

"Fine." The big man's steel-gray eyes showed glittering approval. "I have a son in the Marines myself. I hope you'll like the Navy."

"Like it?" Eddie was fishing for his pocket knife. "Why should I like it?" Eddie asked.

The big man frowned. "For a man who wants to join the Navy, that seems a funny attitude."

"What's funny about it?" Eddie found some emery paper in the tool sack. "Susan and me grew up together. We know what we want. We always knew. I been lucky like that. There's better ways to see the world than in the Army or the Navy. What good is it to me anyhow, seeing it alone? We'd rather see it together later, after the kids we hope to have are grown. All right, we can't. War hasn't been over four years yet, and everything is fouled up worse than ever. Maybe someone else knows why. I don't. But if I ——" Eddie's quiet voice broke off. "I'm through junior college," he said. "I just don't want no more deferments."

"Oh. The draft board's breathing down your neck."

Eddie straightened up. He turned round slowly. "No one's breathing down my neck!" His voice was sharp. Anger touched his dark eyes. "I'm just Eddie Topping. I'm just like a million other guys. I got a 1-A card. O.K.! If that's the way things are, O.K. I don't ask no special favors. But I got a right to make my own decisions!" Eddie turned his back. He was working quickly. "If we think for us the Navy would be better, then I got a right to ——"

"And you mean you both drove all the way out to the Coast to make your mind up?"

"Yes. That's right." Eddie wrapped his tools. "O.K., mister. Try her out. I think she'll run." The engine purred. The big man drove a short distance on the road heel, stopped, and heard Eddie giving sound advice, "You got a cracked distributor cap. It carbonized along the split. Sent all your juice to one plug. I scraped it. Cleaned it good. Get you home all right. First chance you get, though, I'd put a new one in if I was you."

"Thanks, son. I will." From behind the wheel he looked at Eddie, and he looked at Susan. For a moment he considered offering some payment. He thought better of it right away. "I live in San Diego. Up La Mesa way," he said instead. "I know some Navy people. Maybe if I wrote a note to the captain of a fleet destroyer, you could go on board and look around. Would it help you to decide?"

"Sure," said Eddie. "I'd be thankful. Sure it would."

The big man found some paper and an envelope in his glove compartment. He wrote rapidly, resting the sheet of paper on a magazine. He folded the letter sealed the envelope, addressing it. Then he handed it to Eddie, saying crisply, "Stay on 101. You'll drive on past Old Town and come into Diego on Pacific. Go past the foot of Broadway on the foreshore and you'll find Fleet Landing. Here. You better write that down or you'll ——"

"Oh, no, sir. It's not necessary," Susan's throaty voice said quickly. "Eddie won't forget. Eddie's got a wonderful memory. He could repeat that back right now, exactly as you said it, word for word. I know."

"Fine. You ask for the duty chief in the house at the dockhead on Fleet

Landing. I marked the envelope for him. He'll send you out to where the destroyer *Lockwood's* moored." For the very first time, the big man really smiled. "I've got a pretty good memory myself, Eddie. Thanks for fixing my car." His steel-gray eyes lit up an instant. "I can't help thinking that you'll choose the Navy. I still hope you'll like it if you do."

That's how Susan and Eddie Topping came to San Diego, driving all the way from Kansas to see how the ocean looked. In San Diego they first saw the gray ships, the long, narrow fleet destroyers moored in pairs, twin gun snouts bristling. That's where Eddie first felt restless ocean water under him, first saw the knifelike bows of tin cans. Susan waited for him. She sat all alone on one of the benches at Fleet Landing with her yellow hair in sunlight, till the boat brought Eddie back. Till he came and sat beside her, taking her hand in his own.

"Did you talk it over with the captain, Eddie?" Susan asked him after silence.

"No." He shook his head, frowning. "Didn't even see him. Wasn't on board, I guess."

"You didn't get in any trouble, did you?"

"No." He shook his head again. "That fellow they call the duty chief looked at me awful funny when he read the letter. He said, 'Hell, what next!' Then he sealed the envelope again. He told me, 'Give this to the officer of the deck on the *Lockwood*, Mac,' and he sent me out there in a boat."

"What made him think your name was Mac? You didn't get seasick, did you?"

"No. The way that boat moved, it felt good. The officer looked at me funny when he read the letter too. He kept it. I guess it said he was supposed to. He called a sailor and told him to show me around. Nice guy. About my own age. Said he came from Brooklyn. He's what they call a gunner's mate. I didn't like to ask too many questions. We should have asked that man his name. I mean when I fixed his car."

"Yes." Only when the time for silence passed did Susan ask him gently, "Well, Eddie, what do you think?"

Eddie's frown grew more intense. He said at last, "Susan, there's something terrible about them. Those gray ships, I mean. I wish we didn't have to have them." He turned, faintly grinning. She smiled back, telling him again a secret, joyful thing. Eddie said, "The men are fine."

"I telephoned Aunt Lucy. She's expecting us." Susan understood his choice. "We better go now."

That way Eddie Topping made his own decision for enlistment in the Navy. He learned a lot about it after that, in boot camp, on his first destroyer duty. Eddie learned real fast. Susan told him he looked wonderful in dress blues. When he made his liberty in San Diego, Susan met him at

Fleet Landing. When they walked together past the dockhead, arm in arm, she chuckled in her throat, remembering. Eddie knew why she was chuckling. He remembered too. He grinned. They weren't nearly so naïve now. But Eddie's grin was just as boyish. Susan knew for her it always would be. The core of his own entity he would keep secret to all others. Not to her. It was from that place he really wrote her when the ships of his division sailed — not from Pearl, Guam or Tokyo at all.

So Eddie found out what was on the other side of all the deep blue water. And he knew what lay between. Eddie had the gift of precise memory. He could recall exactly how a man with gray-flecked temples told him the vast ocean stretched across to China. Eddie didn't get that far. Not quite. But in less than two years he knew where Korea was. And if politicians didn't know why men were backed up on a burning beachhead at a place called Hungnam in that brutal winter, how could Eddie? Eddie was a seaman first by then, quartermaster striker in the U.S.S. *James Blaney.* One of Desron 40's taut ships. She was slicing a green bow wave in the sea off Point Gaiyoto, steam feathers at her funnel lips, blowers humming, her wake uncoiling bubbles far astern toward Hamhung Bay.

Eddie was on the main deck, portside. The confused clutter of evacuation shipping was already swallowed in the land mist. But the smoking pillars hung aloft against the distant sky and he could hear the thunder of bombardment somewhere. Big stuff. Eddie was on the main deck, portside of the tin can *Blaney,* swaying easily in balance as she swung one way and then another in the ground swell, cold seas foaming past him every time she dipped. Eddie was fishing out a candy bar when the squawk box crackled at his back.

"All hands! Attention, all hands! Hear this!" Eddie gave no outward sign of listening. He went on tearing off the wrapper of the candy bar. And a different voice began, distorted in the crackling. "This is the captain speaking," it said. Eddie absently bit off a mouthful of the chocolate. Was no one paying attention at all? "Some people of the First Marine Division are trapped against the beach up coast from here," Commander Johnson's voice went on. "We are going to get them off. I want twelve men, all qualified in small arms. The mission is dangerous. Ensign Hartley will command the motor whaler. Those of you who wish to go will muster on the quarter-deck, starboard side. I say again: Quarter-deck, starboard side. That's all."

The voice and the crackling stopped. Eddie was sauntering across the thwartship passage, chewing the last of his candy bar. He didn't seem surprised to find some others there already. They had heard that crisp voice, after all.

"Well, waddaya know; here's Topping." That was little Waspy. Second hitch. Quartermaster first. "How many times I told you, Kansas? Only way to get along in the Navy is keep your ears open, your mouth shut an' never volunteer for anything."

Eddie grinned. "Only reason you're here, Waspy," he said, "the Old Man took you by surprise. I'll bet you were standing here. You're just too lazy to walk yourself over portside."

"Someone told you!" Waspy snorted. He said, "Kansas, anything the ensign forgets to put in his report, I'm counting for you to remind him. You can remember anything. Me, I ———"

"Waspy means he figures he can make chief soon," Chuckland, the big gunner's mate, put in. "While you guys were logging shuteye, me and Waspy were at the gangway when the new squadron commodore came aboard. Big four-striper, name of Lasher. I was with him in the *Lansing*. Old Whip Lasher. Waspy's gonna show him how we do it while he flies his pennant in the *Blaney*. That right, Waspy?"

"Well, anyhow," a different voice was growling, "now I know why the Exec scrounged up that life raft we got lashed back on the fantail. We're gonna ———"

"All right, fellas; knock it off."

The bantering voices stopped at once. Watson, the bos'n's mate, walked down the line of men. Old Navy chief. Eyes narrow. Wisdom in them. Gig Watson knew his trade. He turned from accurate appraisal. They could hear him telling Ensign Hartley in a chief's wry voice, "All heroes mustered, sir."

The officer just smiled. He looked along the row of faces. Close behind them, where the men stood at the rail, the green sea lifted in unsteady rhythm, turbulent with foam caps, noisy when it fell away.

"This isn't a fishing party," Ensign Hartley said. "Anyone can change his mind." He waited. No one stirred. He smiled again. "I already have a radioman for the walkie-talkie, and a pharmacist's mate. Parker and Batley. Watson here will be with us. . . . O.K., chief. Pick ten."

It began like that. The chief picked Waspy. He picked Chuckland. He picked Eddie Topping too. Eddie was one of the men who went. He wasn't glad; he wasn't sorry. He was doing what he'd joined for. And he would remember all of it. He had the gift of precise memory. The tin can *Blaney* thrusting north and east for rendezvous with men of a platoon remnant in rear-guard action, cut off from their fellows, backed against a beach upcoast. No retreat for them to Hungnam. Nothing but the ocean at their backs, the ocean stretching all the way back home. Was it just the ocean brought them to debacle in Korea? Eddie couldn't tell them. Eddie didn't know. If Commander Johnson did, he didn't say. He came down the main deck, breathing vapor, glasses against his chest. He looked the boat crew over, his cheek twitching with fatigue.

"I want you men to understand one thing." The skipper's voice was rasping, but somehow it had a gentle tone. "I want you back. You are not an assault party. Your mission is to bring those men off, the effectives and the wounded, nothing more. If you need fire support, you'll get it. I want you back. Every blasted one of you! Good luck." He turned away. "Mr. Hartley, you may prepare to launch."

It began like that. Cold mist on the water, snow on all the land peaks, barren brown hills ringing in a crescent beach. The motor whaleboat headed in toward desolation, beating out loud echoes. Eddie looked back once. Beyond the raft they towed he saw the ship, destroyer U.S.S. *James Blaney*, rocking in the land swell, small foam feather at her bows. She loomed up long and narrow, dark shapes in her bridge wing, gun mounts of main battery all snouting at the shore. Then the whaleboat grounded. He could hear Gig Watson growling as the men leaped out, the whaleboat backing off.

It went easy. Easy landing. Lucky, maybe. All hands took cover by the briefing orders. Eddie crouched behind a boulder next to Waspy. Chuckland over there, his submachine gun ready in big paws. And all the darting eyes on Ensign Hartley, murmuring to Parker. Parker at the walkie-talkie, droning, "Butterball; hello, Butterball. This is Mudhen. Shoreside now. No enemy reaction. How do you receive me? Over."

Then the whistle, shattering taut stillness. Three sharp blasts. All the eyes snapped round. And a harsh voice snarling blasphemy from somewhere, "Where the hell you mudhens been? What kep' you? Sergeant Risko here. Sound off, someone or I ——"

"Here, sergeant." Ensign Hartley showed himself. "Over here. Are you in command of the platoon?"

The shape appeared from nowhere. It came swaying across broken ground, automatic weapon in its hand. Not walking. Staggering. Eyes hollow in a grizzled face of bleak exhaustion framed by a grimy parka hood. Eddie never saw a look like that before on the face of any man. Sergeant Risko, 1st Marines.

"Let's get out of here," his voice was croaking. "We got fourteen wounded. If that's what you want to call it, ten of 'em can walk. Gimme some men to help." He pointed. "You see what's left of that fishing village in the gully up there? That's where the lieutenant is. Machine-gun emplacement. Enfilades the whole approach. Gook patrol comes screaming at it every day. Let's get out of here before they try again. The lieutenant says he won't leave there till all the men withdraw."

It went like that. Still no reaction. How long could luck hold? Eddie remembered Sergeant Risko's face. The others looked the same. How else would combat people on a beachhead look? The landing party fanned out. Risko told them where. The remnant of the 1st platoon was gathering back where surf curled. And Parker at the walkie-talkie, passing Ensign

Hartley's words, telling Butterball about it. Not how men looked. Not what they endured.

"Butterball, this is Mudhen. Can you see the broken buildings of that village? Bearing from you about nine-oh relative. In the gully mouth. Request main director on it. Target area will be beyond it yards one-double-oh. I say again: Beyond it yards one-double-oh. We may need fire there. Acknowledge. Please stand by."

That's what Eddie Topping heard. On the distant water U.S.S. *James Blaney* loomed in sea haze, misty tatters at her signal yard. The twin mounts slewed, the gun snouts elevating all in unison. They hesitated, crawled down, stopped. Shoreward, luck still held. Till then. Then luck ran out. A cracking carbine splattered it apart.

Instantly, beyond the gully mouth, the screaming started, the weird banshee howling Sergeant Risko spoke about, the rattling fire of small arms. Eddie spun around in time to see quick-licking tongue bursts answer from the lieutenant's MG emplacement in the rubble heap. He saw shapes darting toward it, stumbling, falling. Grenades exploded in the ruin. And it burned. Three men were running from it now, doubled over, racing for the beach. Eddie heard the sergeant's hoarse voice, the chattering of weapons all around him. Fire to cover two exhausted men and the platoon lieutenant. Not enough. Not near enough. One spun and fell. Another dropped and crawled for cover, and the third dived headlong at a boulder.

"Butterball, this is Mudhen. Commence firing. Urgent, Commence, commence, commence. Butterball, this is ——"

Eddie leaped up. He didn't know why. He just knew he had to. He was racing forward over broken ground, darting to one side and then another, seeing nothing but a boulder where he knew a man lay. He heard Ensign Hartley shouting at him. He heard Sergeant Risko too. Eddie never stopped. He couldn't. Till he stumbled, fell. Close enough, though. He could see lieutenant's bars, a pain-racked, stubble-bearded face and hollow eyes. Eddie crawled there. The haggard eyes tried hard to grin.

"You sure as hell tried, sailor."

"Take it easy now, lieutenant. Salvos coming from the *Blaney*. She'll ——"

Seaward, flame spears leaped from *Blaney*'s guns. They ripped the mist apart, roaring thunder. Beyond the village rubble, earth exploded, debris splattering aloft. The lieutenant made it now; he really grinned. "Half hour too late," he said. "For me, I mean." Eddie saw the red stain spreading on his chest. "Listen, sailor. Urgent information for your CO. You got something you can write on?"

"No, sir. Say it. I'll remember. Say it. I remember good."

"Maps, coordinates, all gone. I laid it out in ranges and cross bearings.

Should have given it to Risko. Couldn't. Gave it to the corporal and to Lingman. Dead. Both ——" Thunder roared again. Second salvo out of *Blaney*. The lieutenant's gasping voice went on, "Enemy ammo dump. Bearing from the peak of Mount Sontoku three-two-eight. Range two-three-double-oh. Bearing from the peak of Hill Teikumishan ——" Third salvo from the *Blaney*. Ensign Hartley spotting, closing down the range. And Eddie listened, deeply frowning. The words and figures lodged in Eddie's mind. Sealed in a corner of his brain, when Eddie called for them they'd be there. "Those camouflaged ammo and supply dumps are in range of your ship's guns. I hope you ——"

"Don't you worry, sir. I'll give it to the skipper."

"I doubt it like hell, sailor. But O.K. You tried. Push off."

"It's not far, lieutenant. Easy now. I'll carry you."

"I said push off! I've had it. Shove off, sailor! That's an order."

"Sorry, sir." Eddie's voice was solemn. "This here's an amphib operation. I'm not under your command."

The rest compacted. Eddie thought it happened quickly. But it didn't. Underfoot the ground kept surging with concussion. Tongues of orange lightning in the sea mist. U.S.S. *James Blaney* shooting. Fire cover for poor devils on a beachhead. Eddie thought he heard men shouting. He kept staggering beneath his heavy burden. All he wanted was to reach the place where surf curled. How much farther? They ought to stop their shouting at him. Whose voice was it? Waspy's? Was it Chuckland? Then he recognized the hoarseness, recognized the bitter tone. It reached him like a sorrow, like a mourning for a great deal more than a platoon commander.

"Put him down, kid." It was Risko's voice. "The lieutenant's dead," the voice snarled flatly. "Put him down, I said!"

"I tried." What else could Eddie say. "I wanted him to live. I never wanted anything so bad." It was going round in Eddie's brain. Like a questioning of wasted glory, maybe. Like a questioning of wasted pain. "I tried," he said to Ensign Hartley in the whaleboat too.

The officer spoke harshly to him, with abruptness, like the hard, cold slap of reprimand. Combat shock. Mr. Hartley recognized it. Eddie quieted at once. The ensign knew he would. Eddie must have told him how he had to see the skipper, must have told him why. Eddie saw the officer's quick nod. He knew the guns were silent now. He saw the faces of the wounded in the boat, the others on the towing raft. Grizzled faces, stamped with bleak exhaustion. And the gray hull of the *Blaney* looming close, men peering down along the rail, the scrambling nets awash. He remembered Sergeant Risko worrying about his men, snarling at them as they stumbled to the *Blaney*'s deck, rescued remnant of a full platoon. Thirty-eight, no more.

The next thing Eddie knew, he was in the skipper's sea room. Never would have made it up the ladders without Watson's help. The chief was telling Commander Johnson who the kid was, what a fool thing he'd done. Didn't have sense enough to know how burp guns cut men down. Shot with luck. Carried the lieutenant all the way back to the beach. The lieutenant didn't have a sailor's luck, though. Had to leave him. He was dead. Gave Topping urgent oral information while he could. Topping was here to report.

There was another officer beside the skipper there. Big man. Big four-striper. Cap peak ridged with scrambled eggs. That would be the squadron commodore. Captain Lasher. Old Whip Lasher. His square face danced somewhere far in Eddie's mind. No time. Not now. Commander Johnson, seeing Eddie's face, pushed out the door. His voice cracked to the bridge wing, "Coffee! Hot! Hot coffee here!"

The skipper held a wardroom cup to Eddie's lips. Eddie gulped a scalding mouthful. "Please, sir," he said. "Please, sir, write it down. I don't think I could say it more than once." Eddie was reaching back to sealed compartments of his memory, fiercely frowning, ordering his small gift to release what he had stored there. Nothing! Panic seized him. There was nothing there! Then all at once he thought of Susan. The core of him grew quiet. Eddie stared out at the middle space of a tin can's narrow sea room off Korea, seeing Susan's smile. And the compartment opened for him. He was talking in a monotone, thinking all the time of better things. "Those camouflaged ammo and supply dumps are in range of your ship's guns." He began repeating bearings, ranges, words like litany, each one precise, exact. They came from where he'd put them. Chief Watson wrote them down. "Listen, sailor," Eddie droned. "Enemy ammo dump. Bearing from the peak of Mount Sontoku three-two-eight. Range two-three-double-oh. Bearing from the peak of Hill Teikumishan ——"

Eddie never stumbled. He went on until the end. Then he stood there, drained and empty. Skipper and the chief both gone. Commander Johnson and the navigator were triangulating bearings, plotting targets on the chart. The gun boss was suggesting courses that would bring his twin 5-inchers on the range. Eddie thought he was alone there in the sea room. Only for a moment. Only till the deep voice spoke.

"Well done, Topping," it was saying. And the voice went on, "I took your advice. I had a new distributor cap installed." Eddie looked up quickly, startled. Now he knew! He recognized the square face, scar along one temple, stern eyes faintly smiling. "I have a good memory myself, son," he heard Captain Lasher say. "Did you get on board the *Lockwood*, back in Diego?"

"Yes, sir. But I never knew ——"

"Of course not. The letter expressly said you were not to be told who sent you." The narrow, piercing eyes were really smiling. "How is Susan, son?"

"There are two Susans now, sir," Eddie blurted, and his face began to glow. "One of them I've never seen yet. Weighs twelve pounds already. We —— They" — he broke off — "they're both fine."

"I'm glad. I'm glad you chose the Navy too. I thought you would. I hope you like it, son?"

Eddie did his best to stand erectly at attention. Like it? He had never judged it that way. Behind his mind, behind the weariness, behind the silent instant there were things lodged he would not forget. Not ever! Tin can crashing in a seaway. Tropic thunder on the water and the thresh of deep-sea rain. Guns of Hungnam. Scream of aircraft. Faces of the combat people, battle-scarred and empty on a beachhead of Korea. Face of a Marine lieutenant dying. Like it? What could Eddie Topping say?

"The choice was mine, sir." Eddie knew you had to answer four stripes. Eddie knew free choice was precious, fragile, the last best thing men could have. "I don't regret it, sir," he said.

He turned away. The sea-room door pulled open. Skipper coming back, eyes taut with strain. Eddie saw winter twilight glinting on a running sea crest. Night already? It astonished him. And at his back he heard Commander Johnson telling Captain Lasher, "I've been talking, sir, with Sergeant Risko. The commanding officer of his platoon ——" Quick silence. Then the skipper's voice again, the slow voice saying, "The lieutenant's name was Lasher, sir. Lieutenant Clifford Lasher. I — I'm desperately sorry."

And then stillness. Stillness in the sea noise, in the cluttering of wind past signal halyards. Eddie spun around. One foot across the weather sill, he stood there wide-eyed, staring back. What would a man's face look like in such stillness when his son died? Bleak face. Face of sorrow. Face with eyes unseeing. Eddie's lips were parted. Speech was in his throat. He felt compelled to utter grief's thin fellowship. In officers' country? What could Eddie say? He stifled speech in time. He let the door close quietly. He went away.

So U.S.S. *James Blaney* steamed in darkness. Taut ship. Buttoned up. Coming on the charted range. Skipper in the bridge wing, close against the thin steel windbreak, alert talker near him. Captain Lasher stood there, too, his face a cold, pale mask. Words clamored in him. If he didn't say a different thing, a needless thing, he'd be defenseless, naked. So his deep voice rumbled to the skipper of the *Blaney*.

"I must tell you, sometime, how that lad joined up. Remind me. I mean Topping, that seaman first." Captain Lasher's voice was toneless. Words like that were never meant for answer. Fragile mantle against sorrow, nothing more. Presently the toneless voice went on, "He'd rather be back home in Kansas. Lots of them like that. And they ship over. They make fine men too. It's odd, Bert, odd."

Then the firing buzzer sounded. At his battle station, Eddie heard it, heard the twin 5-inchers thunder. Steady salvos. Walking HE shellfire back and forth along dark shore hills of Korea. Flaming fingers searching for a dead lieutenant's target. When the guns flashed they revealed dark lumps of running sea an instant, patches of the *Blaney's* tipping deck. Eddie saw eruption on the distant land. Pillar of enormous flame against the night. Found the ammo dump!

Eddie felt a cold elation. But the core of him was quiet. Turmoil or bombardment couldn't reach it. Nothing could.

Nothing except Susan. She was always there. Susan wouldn't have to wonder about Eddie's choice or judgment. Susan knew he asked no special favors. He was like a million other guys. Whenever folly, blunder, wasted power, brought again the need for them, they came. They came to oceans they had never seen before. They came from Iowa and Oregon. From Kansas too. They did what they were called to do. The best they could, they did it. Liking it or not, they did it. Susan wouldn't have to ask him. Susan knew.

A Plethora of Sergeants

✗

from *From Here to Shimbashi*

by JOHN SACK

Books about the Army, I know, are supposed to dwell quite a long time on basic training. In the standard formula the author, or hero, is tormented at length by a most execrable villain: a sergeant, preferably master, a man suckled by werewolves and weaned on the blood of Fafnir, devoid of heart and stunted of brain: elephant-lunged, Satan-eyed, vulture-clawed, volcano-mouthed, and pledged in life to the humiliation, prostration and ultimate trituration of our hero (author). I wish, for the sake of tradition, that I could tell such a story, but alas! even the names of my sergeants I can hardly remember. During our sixteen weeks at Fort Dix, New Jersey, we had easily half a dozen of them; they passed through our lives like magazine salesmen, or soldiers on review. As soon as we learned the whims and foibles of one, he would be transferred to the Rangers, or put in for chemical school, or go off to the wars, and a new one would take his place. The fault was the Army's, I think; it's not that we had such a repellent platoon, although one boy had lice and another, a fellow named Hawkins, disappeared in the fourth week of training and was picked up by the Feds in Oklahoma City.

Of all our platoon sergeants, only one was really a sergeant. His name was Sergeant Powell, and he lasted about five days. The only thing I remember about Powell was his way of saluting, which was to bend back like a parenthesis, force his elbow in front of his face, and then hurl his hand from his forehead as if, like Oedipus, he were plucking out an eyeball. It was a breathtaking thing to see, if you didn't stand too close. "All-presentandaccounted *for!*" Sergeant Powell would bellow, the word "for" shouted as on a golf course. Most of our sergeants were really corporals or PFC's, and one was only a private, like us: his name was pronounced *ka*-p'l-ch'k and was never spelled out, if indeed it could be. *Ka*-p'l-ch'k had finished Leadership School at Fort Dix, and was sent to us for practice. The quality of *Ka*-p'l-ch'k's leadership was unusual, at best: once he was showing us (first squad) how to quell civil rioters (second squad) and, when the plucky insurgents broke our ranks and scattered us in dismay, he could only whine, "Now *stop* that!" and look very unhappy. A PFC whom I remember was Castellani, who looked like Mussolini. Castellani took his fatigues to a zoot tailor and walked around making muscles, but beyond that he is just a blur. Of all our sergeants the most fearsome, I guess, was a corporal whose name eludes me but was that of some fabled beast, probably Griffin. Corporal Griffin (if that's his name) was a good fellow but had just come back from Korea, and the stories he told kept us in a constant state of neurosis. "Back in Frozen Chosen," he would say, "we never usta sleep in sleepin' bags. We *usta* usta sleep in sleepin' bags, but da Chinks caught us in 'em and slit our troats." Corporal Griffin was very frightening. We breathed easier when he was discharged.

I know this is all very disillusioning, as it was to me, for I too had expected a sergeant hewn of brimstone and voiced like the howling baboon. If I *had* to find a termagant old sergeant to rack me through basic training, I suppose I would have chosen the sergeant who loaded us on the buses from Devens to Dix. "Now when I call your name," he roared, "sound off as if you never had a blank-blank in your life. [Don't worry what the word was. It didn't make much sense, anatomically.] When I say sound off, goddamn it, *sound off*. If your girl or wife walked in, you'd *yell*. Now everyone pretend your barracks bag is your girl, and SOUND OFF!" It was quite a severe tongue-lashing, seeing how we had done nothing wrong, and I shudder to think of his words if we had. Another dire sergeant would have been our company commander at Fort Dix, who was a sergeant before the war. Captain Damisch stood straight as an arrow and steady as a rock; and when something went wrong in our company he spake with the hollow voice of doom: "Men, there's two things we don't do in the Army. We don't discriminate a fellow because of race, creed or religion, and we don't leave gum in the urinals." Or: "Men, there's two things we don't do in the Army. We don't discriminate a fellow because of race, creed or religion, and we don't sharpen pencils with bayonets." Captain Damisch's plea for tolerance came first in each exhortation, although, as far as I know, no fellow in our company was ever discriminated. We had two colored lieutenants in the company, and they were pretty nice guys. Lieutenant Moore, also known as The Kingfish, was happy as long as we remembered to carry pencils or, as he pronounced them, palcils. "Nah when everyone goes fall in," he'd drawl each morning, "doan fo'get yo' *palcils*." Lieutenant Collins, the other lieutenant, used to rattle all of us by wandering absent-mindedly into the barracks any time of day or night. As we leapt to attention he'd gaze vacuously around the room, mumble something like, "If you open *one* window, open 'em *all*," and ramble out again. Once he mustered the whole company to lecture us on putting hands in pockets. "It's not soldierly," said Lieutenant Collins, and then realized *his* hands were in *his*. He stared down blankly for a few moments and said, "But what *I* do is this. I jingle coins." Lieutenant Collins jingled furiously, but we weren't much convinced. He wouldn't have made a very terrifying sergeant, I think.

The platoon sergeant I remember best, because he was the first, is Corporal McHugh. McHugh was with us only three weeks, but he taught us everything about the Army a soldier has to know: how to make a bed with hospital corners (he called them Army corners) so a quarter will bounce in the center; how to close a rifle bolt without malforming one's thumb; why the Ninth Division patch is an octofoil, and which side goes up, and down; where to stamp, indelibly, each item of martial clothing; how to affix the centipedal straps of the Army field pack, which, next to the fourteen-count drill, is the hardest task military men are called on to do; and many other things like that. Corporal McHugh drilled us with infinite patience. "We shall now learn how to count off," he would say. "Is there any man in ranks" — and here he would gaze around, sizing up the educational background of each of us — "is there any man in ranks who cannot count to two?" *Right face* and *left face* he taught with similar caution. "Which is your right hand?" he would ask us each morning. Then: "Why?" It was not an easy question, as the reader can judge for himself, but I know now the answer that McHugh wanted: "Because Army Field Manual Such-and-Such says so, Corporal."

Corporal McHugh was a regular soldier and went by the book, and only once did we hate him for it. That day began pleasantly enough, with a tour of Dix by rubberneck bus: our guide, a PFC, pointed out the arts and crafts shop, the library "where you can hear the opera on Saturdays," the golf course and swimming pools, the picnic grounds, the PX village complete with dancing school, and the bars of nearby Wrightstown. The outing drifted into the Red Shield Club of Wrightstown, where we had coffee and doughnuts, and where a homesy voice cooed through a loud-speaker: "Come in, boys, come on in. Some of you will want to know whether you can smoke. Well, *of course* you can smoke. Smoke anything you want to . . . cigars, cigarettes . . . you don't *have* to smoke, of course." We had been lulled into a fine euphoria, both smokers and ab-stinents, when Corporal McHugh broke the spell. "Dix is a great place when you got free time," he guffawed. "Too bad you guys won't get none!"

For the rest of that week, McHugh said, we would shine our barracks floor to marmoreal luster; the weekend would be set aside for the sewing of patches and the stamping of names; and any free time could best be dedi-cated to the insides of our gun barrels. That very night, in fact, we would be confined to the barracks to master the Prescribed Array of Military Foot-lockers.

We were a sullen crew that evening when Corporal McHugh showed up, his hands full of mimeographed plans. "Now there's a right way and a wrong way to lay out footlockers," he began. "This platoon, we're gonna do it the right way." The right way, copied from an Army manual, could be found on the corporal's mimeographed maps. Everything had its place, to the fraction of an inch. The tooth powder stood bolt upright but the toothbrush lay down, its shank to the right and its bristles to the rear. Im-mediately behind the toothbrush, and on line with its balance point, came the razor blade, its edges parallel to those of the footlocker. Abreast the razor blade was the razor, head to the leftward; the comb pointed its tines to the soap dish, one and one-fourth inches away; a single handkerchief lay quadruply folded; and the socks, tightly furled, were contiguous. We looked at the chart in dismay.

"I got more'n one handkerchief," someone said. "I blows my nose like hell."

"Supposin' I use toothpaste instead?" another voice piped in. "How'm I gonna make the toothpaste stand up?"

"You don't *use* toothpaste," McHugh explained patiently. "Like it says here, you uses *powder*."

Tempers were rising. Half of us shaved with electricity, but the Army's mimeographed plan, evidently drawn in the days of the Cuban campaign, had sites for a razor blade, shaving brush, and a shaving stick. I for one had never heard of a shaving stick.

"You don't gotta *use* them," McHugh was arguing. "In fact, you *won't* use them. The stuff you *uses*, you hides somewhere. This stuff you buys special. You keeps it clean; it's for inspections."

"Jesus Christ!" said someone. Money meant a lot to us in those days. McHugh looked at our incredulous faces and tried to keep going.

"Now, another thing, all this stuff gotta be *uniform*. So now we're gonna have a vote, and figure what color toothbrush and everything we're gonna buy."

"Man, you knows what you can do wit' dat toothbrush," said a colored boy. All of us were ready to mutiny.

"*All right!* Don't vote!" roared McHugh. "I'll tell you myself what t'get! Lessee, the cigarettes in the corner, that's gonna be Kools. . . ."

"But I don't smoke!" said Faletti.

"Damnit you don't *gotta* smoke 'em," McHugh bawled, waving his plans in the air. "All you gotta do is *have* 'em!"

"Boy oh boy," said someone, "wait'll I tell my fambly! The Army's making me buy cigarettes!"

McHugh was shaking all over by now, and my wrathful bunkmates, deserting him, sulked to their footlockers. "They're pretty angry, Corporal," I said.

"Damnit, all this stuff is in the book!" said McHugh. "All I'm doin' is what's in the book."

"Well, maybe the book's just a guide."

"The book *ain't* no guide. The book's the book!"

"OK," I said, "but you have to admit it's sort of silly."

McHugh was simmering down. "Yeah," he said, "I guess it's sort of silly." For a few minutes he sat introspectively on my bunk. "I'm a funny guy," he said.

"Sure. We all are."

"Sometimes I feel different. I get temperamental. I'm moody."

"You're a man of many moods," I said.

"Yeah," said McHugh, "that's it. You got it." McHugh left our platoon soon after. He said he was going to the Infantry School at Fort Benning, Georgia. We had many sergeants after him, but none who lasted so long. I guess I sort of miss him.

Mayday!

✕

from *The Bridges at Toko-ri*
by JAMES A. MICHENER

From the flag bridge Admiral Tarrant followed the emergency landing and when he saw Brubaker lunge onto the deck safely he sent an aide to bring the pilot to him as soon as intelligence had checked battle reports. Some minutes later the young man appeared relaxed and smiling in freshly pressed khaki and said, "Somebody told me there were eight hundred ways to get back aboard a carrier. Any one of them's good, if you make it."

Tarrant laughed, jabbed a cup of coffee into the pilot's hands and asked casually, "What were you doing in the catapult room last night?"

Brubaker sat down carefully, sipped his coffee and said, "I lost my nerve last night."

"You looked pretty steady out there just now."

It was very important now that Brubaker say just the right thing, for he knew that something big was eating the admiral but he couldn't guess what, so he looked up over the rim of his cup and said, "Best sedative in the world is Beer Barrel and those paddles."

The admiral remained standing, somewhat annoyed at Brubaker's having presumed to sit. Nevertheless, the bonds of sympathy which bound him to the younger man were at work. He didn't want Brubaker to participate in the attack on the bridges, so in an offhand manner he asked, "Son, do you want me to ground you . . . for tomorrow's flight against Toko-ri?"

Brubaker thought, "If he'd wanted me to stay down he wouldn't have asked. He'd have told me. This way he hopes I won't accept." But of his own will and regardless of the admiral he decided to say no and replied evenly, "If anybody goes, I go."

Admiral Tarrant was at once aware that he had posed his question the wrong way and said, "I think you're jittery, son. I think you ought to stay down."

Again Brubaker thought, "The old man's wrestling with himself. He wants to ground me but he's afraid it would look like favoritism. So he's trying to trick me into asking. That way everything would be OK." But again he said, "I want to fly against the bridges."

Certain, and in some ways pleased, that the young man would refuse the order, Tarrant said, "Harry, I've been watching you. There's nothing shameful in a man's reaching the end of his rope for the time being. You know I consider you our finest pilot . . . after the squadron leaders. But I can't let you fly tomorrow."

And Brubaker said quietly, "Sir, if you'd offered me this chance last night I'd have jumped to accept it. Or half an hour ago when I stared at that big black Tilly. But I think you know how it is, sir. Any time you get back safe, that day's trembling is over. Right now I haven't a nerve. Look." He held out his coffee saucer and it remained rigid.

"You're sure it passed?"

"Positive. Remember when you told my wife about the voluntary men who save the world? I've seen two of these men. It shakes you to the roots of your heart to see such men in action."

"Who'd you see?" Tarrant asked, the sparring over.

"Yesterday I saw Cag take his photographic plane . . ."

"Cag?"

"Yes, sir. I saw a man so brave . . . Admiral, he went in so low that he simply had to get knocked down. Then he went in again . . . lower."

"Cag?" Admiral Tarrant repeated, amazed.

"And this morning . . . Did anyone tell you about the air force spotter in the SNJ?"

"No."

Brubaker's voice almost broke but he stammered, "He was killed by a gun I might have knocked out . . . if I'd really been on the ball." There was a long silence in which Tarrant poured more coffee. Finally Brubaker said, "Sometimes you look honor right in the face. In the face of another man. It's terrifying." His voice trailed away and he added in a whisper, "So I have no choice. I have to go out tomorrow. If he could fly an SNJ, I can fly a jet." He laughed nervously and thrust his saucer out again. It remained immovable, like the end of a solid stone arm. "No nerves now," he said.

It was 1145 next morning when Cag, his jets poised aloft for their first run against the bridges, cried, "Attack, attack, attack!"

With deadly precision, and ignoring the mortal curtain of Communist fire, four Banshees assigned to flak-suppression flung themselves upon the heaviest guns at more than five hundred miles an hour. Rendezvousing to the north, they swept back in ghostly blue streaks and raked the principal emplacements a second time, but as they reached the middle of this passage Communist fire struck number three plane and with a violence few

men have witnessed it smashed into a hill and exploded in an instantaneous orange flash.

Before the eight pilots aloft could realize what had happened Cag
called quietly, "Prepare to attack," and the four jets in his division peeled
off for swift assault upon the bridges. They descended at an angle steeper
than 50° and for the entire final run of two miles no pilot swerved or
dodged until his first huge bomb sped free.

From aloft Brubaker saw that Cag had got two of the bridges. Now he
must finish the job. He brought his division down in a screaming dive,
aware that when he straightened out the pull of gravity upon him would
suck the blood away from his head and drag his lips into grotesque positions, but the fascination of those looming bridges of Toko-ri lured him on.
Lower and lower he came. When he finally pickled his bomb and pulled
away he absorbed so many g's that a heaviness came upon his legs and
his face was drawn drowsily down upon his chin. But he knew nothing of
this for he experienced only surging elation. He had bombed the bridges.

Then he heard the dismal voice: "No damage to main bridge."

And you had to believe that voice, for it was Roy's, last man through.
Tomorrow stateside newspapers might exaggerate the damage. You could
kid the intelligence officer. And you could lie like a schoolboy to pilots
from another squadron, but last man through told the truth. No damage.

"I'm sure Brubaker got a span," Cag argued.

"Negative," Roy replied flatly.

"How about the truck bridges?"

"Clobbered, clobbered, clobbered."

Cag called, "Stand by for run number two," and eleven jets orbited for
position. The three flak-suppression Banshees stampeded for the gun-
rimmed valley and as they roared in the leader confirmed Roy's report:
"No damage to the main bridge." But the last of the flak jets reported,
"We really have the ground fire slowed down."

Then, to the surprise of the Communists, Cag brought his men in over
the same check points as before and cheated some of the Communist gunners, who had been gambling that he would use the other entrance to their
valley. Through gray bomb smoke and bursts of flak, through spattering
lead and their own fears, the first four pilots bore in upon the bridges. Roaring straight down the railroad track like demon trains they pickled their
heavy freight upon the bridge and pulled away with sickening g's upon
them, their mouths gaping wide like idiots, their eyes dulled with war and
the pull of gravity.

As Brubaker led his men upon the bridges he saw a magnificent sight.
Three spans were down and a fourth was crumbling. The two truck bridges
were demolished and the alternate railroad span was in the mud. In

triumph he called, "This is Brubaker. All bridges down. Divert to the dump." And with blood perilously withdrawn from his head he swung his Banshee away from the bridges, over a slight rise of ground, and down upon the sprawling military dumps. Strafing, bombing, twisting, igniting, he screamed on, his three teammates following. Somebody's bomb struck ammunition. Consecutive explosions, each keeping the next alive, raced through the stores.

This time Roy, last man through, said, "We hit something big."

Cag, aloft, called, "All planes, all planes. Work over the dump."

Brubaker, now higher than the others, watched the dazzling procession of Banshees. Swooping low, they spun their fragmentation bombs earthward and retired into the lonely distance. Returning, they dodged hills and spread deathly fire. Over snowy ridges they formed for new runs and wherever they moved there was silent beauty and the glint of sunlight on the bronzed helmet of some man riding beneath the Plexiglas canopy. It was a fearsome thing to watch jets assume control of this valley where the bridges had been, and it was gloomy, for no matter where any of the pilots looked they could see the scarred hillside against which one of their team had plunged to death a few minutes before.

His ammunition nearly spent, Brubaker nosed down for a final run upon the spattered dumps, but Cag called, "Stay clear of the ammo dumps. We have them popping there." So he twisted his jet to the south, away from the ammo but before he could launch his dive, two jets streaked across his target and jettisoned their bombs so that again he had to pull away. He was tempted to drop his last bomb where he thought he saw a gun emplacement but promptly he discarded this idea as unworthy for it occurred to him, quite clearly in this instant of decision, that even one bomb more might mean significant interdiction of supplies to the front: fewer bullets for Communist gunners, fewer blankets for their trenches, less food. He recalled Admiral Tarrant's words: "If we keep the pressure high enough something's got to explode over there."

So in an effort to add that extra degree of pressure which might help to beat back aggression, he turned away from his easy target and picked out a supply dump. He activated his nose guns and watched their heavy bullets rip into valued cargo and set it afire. Then he resolutely pickled his last bomb, but as he pulled out of his dive, with heavy g's upon his face, he heard a pinking thud.

"I've been hit!" he cried and as the jet sped upward chaos took over. He lost control of his mind and of the thundering Banshee and in panic thought only of Wonsan harbor. He felt the irresistible lure of the sea where friendly craft might rescue him and violently he wrenched his nose toward the east and fled homeward like a sea-stricken thing. But as soon as he had made this desperate turn he became aware that panic was flying the plane, not he, and he called quietly, "Joe, Joe. Just took a hit. So far I'm all right."

From the dark sky aloft came the reassuring whisper, "Harry, this is Joe. I have you in sight."

"Joe, drop down and look me over."

Now an ugly vibration identified itself as coming from the port engine but for one fragile second of time it seemed as if the frightening sound might abate. Then, with shattering echoes, the entire engine seemed to fall apart and Brubaker whispered to himself, "I'm not going to get this crate out of Korea."

A Communist bullet no bigger than a man's thumb, fired at random by some ground defender of the dump, had blundered haphazardly into the turbine blades, which were then whirring at nearly 13,000 revolutions a minute. So delicately was the jet engine balanced that the loss of only two blade tips had thrown the entire mechanism out of balance, and the grinding noise Brubaker heard was the turbine throwing off dozens of knifelike blades which slashed into the fuselage or out through the dark sky. Like the society which had conceived the engine, the turbine was of such advanced construction that even trivial disruption of one fundamental part endangered the entire structure.

He had, of course, immediately cut fuel to the damaged engine and increased revolutions on the other and as soon as the clatter of the damaged turbines subsided he cut off its air supply and eliminated the destructive vibrations altogether. Then, in fresh silence, he checked the twenty principal indicators on his panel and found things to be in pretty good shape. "I might even make it back to the ship," he said hopefully. But promptly he discarded this for a more practical objective: "Anyway, I'll be able to reach the sea."

He laughed at himself and said, "Look at me! Yesterday I pushed the panic button because I might have to go into the sea. Today I reached for it because I might miss the water."

As he reasoned with himself Joe came lazily out from beneath his wing and waved. "Everything all right now?" Joe asked.

"All under control," he answered.

"Fuel OK?"

"Fine. More than two thousand pounds."

"Keep checking it," Joe said quietly. "You may be losing a little."

Then the sick panic returned and no more that day would it leave. Impeded by heavy gear he tried to look aft but couldn't. Straining himself he saw fleetingly from the corner of his eye a thin wisp of white vapor trailing in the black sky. Knocking his goggles away he tried to look again and his peripheral vision spied the dusty vapor, no thicker than a pencil.

"Joe," he called quietly. "That looks like a fuel leak."

"Don't your gauges show it?"

"Don't seem to."

"You'll make the sea all right," Joe said, and both men surrendered any idea of the ship.

"I'll make the sea," Harry said.

"I'll trail you," Joe called.

In a few minutes he said, "You're losing fuel pretty fast, Harry."

There was no longer any use to kid himself. "Yeah. Now the instruments show it."

Joe drew his slim blue jet quite close to Harry's and the two men looked at one another as clearly as if they had been across a table in some bar. "I still think you'll make the sea," Joe said.

But Harry knew that merely reaching the sea wasn't enough. "How far out must we go in Wonsan harbor to miss the Communist mines?" he asked.

Joe ruffled through some papers clipped to his knee and replied, "You ought to go two miles. But you'll make it, Harry."

The turbine blade that had sliced into the fuel line now broke loose and allowed a heavy spurt of gasoline to erupt so that Joe could clearly see it. "You're losing gas pretty fast now," he said.

There was a sad drop on the fuel gauge and Harry said, "Guess that does it."

To prevent explosion, he immediately killed his good engine and felt the Banshee stutter in midair, as if caught by some enormous hand. Then, at 250 miles an hour, he started the long and agonizing glide which carried him ever nearer to the sea and always lower toward the mountains.

Quickly Joe cut his own speed and said, "We better call the word."

With crisp voice Brubaker announced the strange word which by general consent across the world has come to mean disaster. In Malaya, in China, over Europe or in the jungle airports of the Amazon this word betokens final catastrophe: "Mayday, Mayday."

It was heard by Communist monitors and by the officers in Task Force 77. Aloft, Cag heard it and turned his jets back to keep watch upon their stricken member. And aboard the scow the newly reported helicopter team of Mike Forney and Nestor Gamidge heard it.

"Mayday, Mayday."

Silently, through the upper reaches of the sky, the two men flew side by side. They had never been particularly friendly, for their interests and ages varied, nor had they talked much, but now in the dark violet sky with sunlight gleaming beneath them on the hills of Korea they began their last urgent conversation, their faces bright in Plexiglas and their voices speaking clear through the vast emptiness of the space.

"We'll make the sea," Joe said reassuringly.

"I'm sure going to try."

They drifted down to the sunny spaces of the sky, into the region of small cloud and laughing shadow and Joe asked, "Now when we reach the sea will you parachute or ditch?"

"I ditched once, I'll do it again."

"I never asked you, how does the Banshee take the water?"

"Fine, if you keep the tail down."

"Remember to jettison your canopy, Harry."

"I don't aim to be penned in."

"Six more minutes will put us there."

So they fought to the sea. As if caught in the grip of some atavistic urge that called them back to the safety of the sea after the millions of years during which men had risen from this element, these two pilots nursed their jets away from inhospitable land and out toward the open sea. They were low now and could spot Communist villages and from time to time they saw bursts of Communists guns, so they fought to reach the sea.

But they did not make it. For looming ahead of them rose the hills in back of Wonsan harbor. Between the jets and the sea stood these ugly hills and there was no way to pass them. Instinctively Harry shoved the throttle forward to zoom higher — only a couple of hundred feet, even fifty might do — but relentlessly the stricken Banshee settled lower.

From the adjoining plane Joe pointed to the obstructing hills and Harry said, "I see them. I won't make it."

Joe asked, "Now, Harry, are you going to jump or crash land!"

"Crash," Harry said promptly. Back in the States he had decided to stick with his plane no matter what happened. Besides, Communists shot at parachutes, whereas the speed of a crash often took them by surprise and permitted rescue operations.

"Keep your wheels up," Joe said.

"Will do."

"Be sure to hit every item on the checkoff list."

"Will do."

"Harry, make sure those shoulder straps are really tight."

"Already they're choking me."

"Good boy. Now, Harry, remember what happened to Lou. Unhook your oxygen mask and radio before you hit."

"Will do."

"Knife? Gun?"

Harry nodded. Although he was soon going to hit some piece of Korean ground at a speed of 130 miles, his plane bursting out of control at impact, in this quiet preparatory moment he could smile out of his canopy and converse with Joe as if they were long-time friends reviewing a basketball game.

"Pretty soon now," he said.

"I'll move ahead and try to find a good field," Joe said. Before he pulled away he pointed aloft and said, "Cag's upstairs."

Soon he called, "This field looks fair."

"Isn't that a ditch running down the middle?"

"Only shadows."

"You think I can stop short of the trees?"

"Easy, Harry. Easy."

"Well then, that's our field."

"Listen, Harry. When you do land, no matter what happens, get out fast."

"You bet. I don't like exploding gas."

"Good boy. Remember, fellow. Fast. Fast."

Desperately Brubaker wanted to make one run along the field to check things for himself, but the remorseless glide kept dragging him down and he heard Joe's patient voice calling, "Harry, you better jettison that canopy right now."

"I forgot."

Like a schoolteacher with a child Joe said, "That was first on the checkoff list. Did you hit those items, Harry?"

"I got them all," Harry said.

"Field look OK?"

"You pick 'em real good, son."

Those were the last words Harry said to his wingman, for the ground was rushing up too fast and there was much work to do. Dropping his right wing to make the turn onto the field, he selected what looked like the clearest strip and lowered his flaps. Then, kicking off a little altitude by means of a side slip, he headed for the earth. Tensed almost to the shattering point, he held the great Banshee steady, tail down, heard a ripping sound, saw his right wing drop suddenly and tear away, watched a line of trees rush up at him and felt the final tragic collapse of everything. The impact almost tore the harness through his left shoulder socket but without this bracing he would surely have been killed. For an instant he thought the pain might make him faint, but the rich sweet smell of gasoline reached him and with swift planned motions he ripped himself loose from the smoking plane. But when he started to climb down he realized that his oxygen supply tube and his radio were still connected, just as Joe had warned. Laughing at himself he said, "Some guys you can't tell anything." With a powerful lurch he broke the cords and leaped upon Korean soil.

Orders: Plans and Execution

✂

from *The Price of Courage*

by CURT ANDERS

Once again Harry Hamilton began the task of planning an operation. There was a peculiar feeling in his mind; he was excited by the power with which he was working, and yet he regretted the necessity for its use. Hamilton was proud that he was qualified to do the kind of thinking and acting that was required of him, and yet he was keenly aware of what the consequences of his plans might be to the men who must carry those plans out. It was a strange way to be fighting a war: clean, almost academic, seldom dangerous. Sharp analysis, imagination, and all sorts of knowledge were the weapons he had to employ at times like this, when a decision had been made, an objective announced, and the command "Write up the order, Harry," given. Humility, and calm, considerate recollection of the miseries and fear, as well as the strength and gallantries of the men, added to the depth of all the doing and hoping that was the awful responsibility of this man.

Before he sat down to write out the order, Harry went back to the wreckage of the operations tent and fumbled around in his barracks bag for a box of cigars his wife had sent him a week or so before. When he found the box he opened it, took out the three cigars, then put the box away again. He put two of the cigars in his breast pocket; the other he lit, taking long, almost ceremonial puffs.

He took a quick, horrified look at the debris, then he walked hurriedly over to the kitchen tent to write the order.

Harry Hamilton sat alone at the makeshift officers' mess table, leaning forward so that he could work by the light of a Coleman lantern that was hanging near the oven. As soon as his cigar was well chomped, he crammed it into one corner of his mouth and smoked in short, thoughtful puffs. One hand held the tablet: the other held a pencil which had already doodled the deaths of any number of the enemy — and, Harry Hamilton knew, all too many of our own men. His mind ranged back over the years he had spent in preparation for this moment; back through the years he had spent as an enlisted man; his miserable three months in Officer Candidate School;

the frightening loneliness of a parachute jump one cold night into the heart of an enemy-held continent; a cold night spent in the water, his fingers clawing the mud of a river bottom to keep his body from being swept even six inches farther downstream into the machine-gun fire which peppered intermittently all night, and somehow always came that far and stopped. He thought about all of the other times he had stared at a blank tablet, warming up his mind for the order he knew he must write. And from all this, he drew the courage to begin his task.

He wrote "1 Rifle Company" and stopped: about two hundred men, all of them men who had been shot at; about seventy rifles, half a dozen automatic rifles, a scattering of carbines and a few machine guns, three small mortars with enough ammunition to fight for an hour, if they had to; a body of men organized and armed for flexibility, but hampered by an almost complete lack of reliable radio communication. Then under "1 Rifle Company" he wrote "1 section of tanks," and again he stopped. Two tanks, left over from a previous war; a good cannon on each, and three light machine guns to boot; blind, lumbering, awkward beasts, but good to have on our side. Again he wrote: "Artillery F. O. Party." He knew that the artillery could reach out and paste anything on the forward slope of Lion or Cougar, but could they cover the back slopes adequately? He picked up his map and found the ridge; he studied the contours and folds in the earth, judging how each finger would look to the forward observer whose job it would be to bring the rounds down on the enemy in a few hours. There were several potential trouble spots which he thought might be safe from our artillery, so he added "1 Mortar F. O. Party" to the list. Again, just a few men and a radio, but good to have because they could bring mortar rounds in on targets which the artillery could not hit.

He picked up the map once more and studied it. This time he followed the valley floor from its beginning, to the left of the Shark's upper jaw, out toward the enemy. On each side, sharp ridges — Lion and Cougar — guided the valley in a long, gentle curve to the north. Hamilton guessed that the tanks could go nearly all the way up the valley, although they would not be able to elevate their guns enough to shoot at the ridgetops if they went too far. The men would have hard going along those ridgelines, he knew. There would be no room for maneuver; it would be like climbing a rope.

Major Dahl came into the kitchen tent.

"Hold up on the order, Harry. The colonel's on his way down here. There may be a change."

"All right, sir."

"He may want us to help the Third Battalion."

"Yes, he might."

Hamilton weighed the merits of such an operation in his mind. A real attack would be far better, because whatever ground the men might gain would be kept. He had never liked the idea of combat patrols because of the necessity of risking so much for ground that would be given back almost as soon as it had been won. If he had to fight, he wanted the gain to be permanent; sometimes he felt that no amount of information of the enemy was worth turning men into shooting-gallery ducks. He knew that his was a dangerous and somewhat unsoldierly attitude, but he couldn't help it.

A few minutes later, Colonel Hobbs arrived. Colonel Hobbs was a heavyset man of forty-four, balding, with a reddish complexion and green eyes.

Major Dahl met him as he climbed out of his jeep and escorted him into the kitchen tent. The colonel nodded to Hamilton, then he sat down. A cook brought a pot of hot coffee and several cups. Colonel Hobbs took off his gloves, stuffed them inside his steel helmet, then put the helmet on the ground. He poured himself a cup of coffee, and he looked intently at the map, getting his bearings.

"Now, Dahl, here's what's up."

The battalion commander pulled a C-ration crate up to the table and sat down. Hamilton stood behind the colonel.

"Stace tried to get this finger yesterday and couldn't make it. He's going to try again today, and I want you to help him."

"All right, Colonel."

"Stace is going up the finger he's on now."

He pointed to Rhino — the long ridge that extended due south from the Octopus's peak.

"His objective is to clear the whole Goddam mountain, but I'm worried about these."

Colonel Hobbs pointed to the long, curving fingers that Hamilton had been studying.

"We've got to get some people working up toward the top from another direction, or Stace'll never make it. Now, here's what I want you to do. Lion is going to be yours after this clambake is over, so I want you to go get it. That means you have to clear the center one, too."

"Very well, sir."

"Stace is going at nine. It's late, I know, but we want an airstrike if the weather will clear, and they tell me it will by then if it's ever going to. After Stace gets the peak, you'll tie in with him here." Hobbs pointed to a knob just down Lion from the peak. "You'll have to watch shooting into Stace. I'll tell him to keep panels out your way and you keep a radio on his channel, whatever the hell it is."

"All right, sir."

"You got any questions?"

"No, sir."

"How about you, Hamilton?"

"I've got it, sir."

"Well, I'm going over to Stace's, then. Anything you want me to tell him?"

"Just that we hope he makes it all right."

"Too bad about Hyde."

"We're pretty upset over losing him."

"I know you are, and I'd rather not have to use you again so soon, but you're in position to get off in a hurry. Besides, sometimes it works out better if you have plenty to do — you know what I mean?"

"Yes, Colonel."

The colonel rose to go. Hamilton watched as the two commanders went out, then he sat back down at the table and lit his second cigar. A moment later, Major Dahl returned and sat down beside him.

"What do you think?"

"Fox and a couple of tanks. Same as before, except they stay."

"What about the rest of the battalion?"

"They can follow the lead company up Lion. They'll have to — there isn't any room for anything else."

"All right. It'll be Fox. Then Easy behind them, up Lion. George Company last. Easy will have to provide security for the tanks."

"Sir, I'd leave that to Fox."

"Why?"

"Control. It'll be York's show, anyway. If he wants the tanks to move, all he has to do is radio his platoon leader to pass the word."

"You're assuming two things — that he can afford a platoon to stay down in the valley with the tanks, and that the radios will work when the shooting starts."

"He can't use but one man at a time up the damned ridgeline. And the radios haven't been working since the war started, anyway."

"All right, Harry. Write it up that way." Dahl got up. "I'll be in my tent. Bring the order in when you're done."

Harry Hamilton nodded and watched the major go out, then he turned back to his table and began writing the order. He had already thought it out pretty well, so the words came easily. Corporal Mayes would put it in proper form later, he knew, so he wrote quickly, omitting all but the essential points, concentrating on details of paramount importance.

Soon it was finished. He took the tablet to Major Dahl, got his approval, then listened as Dahl phoned the order out to the company commanders. Then he went back to the kitchen tent to eat breakfast.

Hamilton always felt uneasy during the time between the completion of an order and its execution, for until it passed completely out of his hands he was always tempted to make changes; and these, he had learned, often led to tragedy. Now he simply wrote orders and tried to get them as nearly perfect as he could the first time; he did not allow himself to tamper with a completed order, and experience was proving this to be a wise policy. Sometimes he felt that he would prefer to be a company commander again, receiving and executing orders instead of framing them. But he felt pretty certain that this order was a good one. There had been only one possible way of carrying out Colonel Hobbs's instructions, and besides, the real order had been given by Major Dahl verbally. The company commanders would be guided by what Dahl had told them; the written order, which Mayes would type out later, merely made the operation official, a matter of record.

Earlier in the war there had never been time for writing orders. When the rear echelon had screamed for records, Hamilton had been forced to dream up detailed plans for fights that had taken place months before; now he made it a point to write something about each action so that he could keep the paper-shufflers off his neck. A smile came to Hamilton's lips as he thought of the harassed and befuddled nit-pickers he had seen in staff sections in rear-echelon headquarters, grown men almost in a panic lest the chief of section find a dangling participle in a front-line battalion operations order. Harry Hamilton hated war in every form, shape, and fashion; yet there are worse ways to fight a war than being shot at, he mused.

Cougar, the ridge George Company was climbing, ran into Lion a few hundred yards north of the place where the company had halted while Cannon's platoon cleared the ambushes. Eric Holloway knew that if George Company could reach that junction, and capture it, before the enemy had time to set up strong defenses, or to reinforce whatever forces were already in place, then the battalion's mission could be accomplished rather quickly. But Eric realized that the enemy commander must be equally aware of that, and so he expected to have to fight for that knob, and possibly for the rest of Cougar. I'd better warn Felty, he thought. He's got to keep going, but he'd better be careful.

"Top, I'm going up ahead," he called to Gregg.

The first sergeant nodded.

Eric had passed three or four men on his way forward when shots cut the air over his head.

That's it, he thought. We'll have to fight for it.

Eric hit the ground, as did the rest of the column. He reasoned that the shots might be coming from the survivors of the ambushes Cannon's platoon had gone after; on the other hand, Felty might have hit the enemy's main defense line. Either way, Felty was in a spot.

Holloway looked ahead to see what was happening. A rise in the ridge-line blocked his view, so he crawled forward. Shots still cracked over his head, but the firing was intermittent and not well-aimed.

Eric noticed that Felty's men were waiting for orders; none of them showed the least inclination to do anything about the threat to their lives. Eric was surprised by this at first, but then he understood: there was nothing visible to shoot at.

When he reached the spot where Felty and his radioman were down, Holloway took cover behind a rock and peered ahead. He could see several prone figures, men from Felty's lead squad, but that was all.

"Felty, crawl over here," he ordered.

"Yes?"

"Anybody get hit?"

"No, but we're pinned down."

"What do you mean, 'pinned down'?"

"Every time anybody moves, he gets shot at."

"What have you tried to do so far?"

"Nothing. Nobody can move."

"Listen. I crawled all the way up here. Nothing touched me. You crawled over here, nothing got you. It's all overhead. Can't you hear the cracking? Hell, we can't even see where the trouble's coming from."

"Yes, but —"

"Now, what are you going to do about this thing?"

"I don't know."

"You have a good squad up in front?"

"Yes."

"All right. Tell that squad leader to have his squad inch up toward the trouble. Have him get them in position so they can kill somebody."

"Okay."

The platoon leader slid away, crawling up toward his lead squad leader. A moment later, Eric saw the squad leader crawl up to the man ahead of him, and in less than a minute the whole squad had moved forward.

Felty's not yellow, Eric thought. He's just ignorant. I've got to teach him what I can, when I get the time.

Two or three minutes passed. Then a sharp firing broke out ahead. Dull explosions: hand grenades!

Felty came running back, out of breath and greatly upset.

"They're just rolling those hand grenades down!"

"What —"

"We're pinned down again."

"Look, Felty —"

"We can't move!"

"Shut up and listen to me! Cut out this 'pinned down' business. You come with me."

Eric ran forward, crouching. There were a few shots over his head, but he stayed close to the ground and kept moving. Soon he reached a position from which he could see the whole show. There was a small, rocky knob about a hundred yards ahead and towering above him. He saw that no one could rush the knob, for the rocks were large and almost cubical. And as long as the enemy's hand grenades held out, Eric knew, Felty's men would have one hell of a time taking that knob.

Eric looked to his left to see if this could be the knob where Lion ran into Cougar: it wasn't. Lion was several hundred yards away and still roughly parallel to Cougar. The junction knob, Holloway knew, would be a long, bloody way off.

"Okay, Felty. Let's get something going. You have the fifty-seven, don't you?"

"Yes."

"Get it forward."

"Pass the word back for the fifty-seven to come forward!" Felty called to a soldier near him, and the soldier passed the word.

"You see, if the men can't move, the thing to do is to put supporting fire on the enemy. Then the men can move forward while the enemy's hiding from the covering fire. You get the idea?"

"Yes, sir."

"All right. No more of this 'pinned down' foolishness?"

Felty hesitated a moment, then he said, "Okay."

The leader of the fifty-seven squad crawled in between the officers.

"You got the recoilless rifle back there?" Eric asked.

"Yessir."

"We want some fire put on the knob up ahead."

"Loo-tenant, you're nuts. If we shoot that thing it'll give away our location!"

"Bring me the gun, Sergeant."

The squad leader went back for the gun.

A minute or two later, Eric crawled into the open and took the fifty-seven from the men who had lugged it forward.

"This thing loaded?" he asked.

"Ready."

Eric moved around a bit in order to get a stable rest. Then he took careful aim, placing the telescopic sight's crosshairs directly on the knob. He squeezed the pistol grip, and the gun fired with a deafening roar.

The round hit the left side of a large rock at the top of the knob.

"Load another one!" Eric yelled.

The soldier behind him opened the recoilless rifle's breech and slammed another round into the tube. When the breech was closed and locked, the loader looked behind the gun to make sure that no one had moved into the backblast area, then he slapped Eric's back and yelled, "Up!"

Holloway aimed at the right side of the knob and fired. Again the blast and the ringing noise in his ears.

The round cleared the rocks and landed on top of the knob, causing a flurry of snow as it exploded.

If this is killing, Eric thought, it is damned impersonal. If it has to be, this way is best.

A rifle shot glanced off a rock very near Eric's head.

"Enough of this!" the company commander said, scrambling behind the rock. "Sergeant, get your gunner to plaster that knob with this thing. Pick out a better position than that, and move after every couple of rounds."

"Very well, sir."

"Felty, you get ready to move out as soon as the boomstick people get set up and start shooting. Have your machine gun come up here and spray the target between rounds from the fifty-seven."

"All right."

Felty hurried to get the orders passed while the fifty-seven crew was seeking a good firing position.

Holloway noticed that Felty's edginess was beginning to wear off. He was glad, but he knew that Felty would still need a lot of help.

A messenger from the company command group crawled to within a few yards of the company commander and called him.

"Sir, Captain Hamilton's on the phone raising hell. Wants to talk to you right now."

"Thanks. I'll be right back there."

Holloway yelled to Felty. "You think you can handle this now?"

"Sure."

"Get going, then. And keep punching till you get the knob."

Eric didn't want to leave just as the critical part of the action was about to start, but he remembered the trouble he had had with Hamilton. He took a deep breath and ran back down the trail to take the call.

"Where'd this phone line come from?" Eric asked Sergeant Wood.

"Battalion put it in, sir."

"You know what Captain Hamilton wants?"

"No, sir. Wants you to call him pronto, though."

So Holloway called.

"This is Lieutenant Holloway, sir."

"Well you better by God cut out this movie-star stuff and look out for that comp'ny of yours or all hell's gonna break loose. That kinda showing-off may be big stuff here at battalion, but you aren't much good to those braves of yours dead. Now stay there where you belong and leave squad leading to the people who're getting paid to do that."

"Yes, sir."

"Damned if I wouldn't relieve you for that! You're a company com-mander, Holloway. Now start behaving like one, or Major Dahl will sure as hell jerk you out of there."

"Yes, sir."

"Now. What's going on out in front of you?"

"My Third Platoon's being held up by some people who can't shoot very good. They're trying to get the knob the enemy's on right now."

"Knob? Are you already at the junction?"

"No. It's still a long way ahead. But this one's a bitch!"

"They gonna make it?"

Eric didn't know how to answer that.

"Yes, they'll make it," he said, "but it may be messy. I'll call you back as soon as we're up there."

"Well, let's don't have any drawn-saber charges. We've lost enough com-pany commanders for one day."

"Are they getting Fox out?"

"Yep, and by the way, you can call your platoon back in now. York's dead. So's Webb."

"I'm sorry to hear that. How many other men did we lose?"

"It looks like twenty-one dead and sixteen badly wounded."

"Is the tank still functioning?"

"No. We're pulling it out. Why?"

"I thought it might be able to shoot at this thing that's bothering us."

"Use your Goddam bayonets. Wait a minute. Here's Major Dahl!"

"Eric, I want you to stay with this phone from now on."

"Very well, sir."

"Did Harry tell you about pulling in your platoon?"

"Yes, sir, he did."

"We didn't make it to the top of the mountain by noon, and Colonel Hobbs is pretty upset about that. But we've got to keep trying. Now, I don't know how soon Easy's going to get going again, but it looks like you're going to have to carry the ball. Can you get to that junction pretty soon?"

The perplexing question again.

"I'll try, sir."

"I know that, Eric. Answer my question!"

"Yes, sir."

"All right."

"I'll call you as soon as we have some progress to report, sir."

"That'll do. And you be careful!"

The conversation ended with that.

Holloway called Cannon on the radio and told him to rejoin the company. Then he sent for the executive officer, and while he was waiting for him he looked around for some place to set up the mortars.

"What's up?" Schaefer asked.

"Felty's got troubles with a big knob."

"I see."

"It'll be like climbing a tree, except this tree's dripping with hand grenades."

"That do make a difference."

"I got off a shot or two with the fifty-seven, but it just rearranged the snow. Felty may need the mortars, so I wish you'd get them ready to shoot for him."

"All right."

"There's a good place — as good a place as I can find, that is — right over there."

"Okay."

Schaefer went back to get the mortar section leader.

A few minutes later, Eric noticed that the men from the mortar section were hacking away at the side of the ridgeline, trying to prepare platforms for the mortar baseplates.

When the mortars were ready to fire, Schaefer climbed back to the top of the ridge and found the company commander.

"All set. You want them to register?"

"No, but send a forward observer up with Felty. He can use Felty's radio and talk to my radio operator if Felty needs help."

"Will do."

Then Eric turned to Sergeant Gregg.

"Top, we can't do any good from back here. We've got to move the command group far enough forward to see what gives."

"All right, sir. Don't like the idea of getting shot at, myself, but maybe the enemy'll see me coming and give up."

"Maybe."

Eric turned to lead the command group forward, but a muffled crunching sound stopped him cold. He turned and looked back down at the valley, where his Second Platoon was, and he saw two gray clouds of smoke drift above the bare trees. As he watched, two more clouds blossomed. Then he heard two more crunches, and a loud scream.

Eric closed his eyes. Dear God, he prayed, help them!

When he looked down into the valley again, he saw several men running toward the base of Cougar, trying to get out of the enemy's mortar fire. Eric wanted to reach down to them, to pull them out, to get his men clear of the danger, but for the moment he could do nothing but pray, and hope.

God, please lead them out of there! I'll settle for half of them — just half.

But as he bargained with God, it occurred to him that getting those men out of there was his job. There was still something he could do.

Holloway picked up the radio and tried to contact Cannon, but there was no answer. He thought about sending a messenger down to lead the scattered platoon out, but that seemed to him to be too much to ask: any man who went down into that valley would have practically no chance of surviving the mortar fire that was systematically stabbing both sides of the valley.

All at once, Holloway knew that he would have to go.

"Schaefer!" he called. "Look after things until I get back."

Holloway ran down the side of Cougar, slipping in the snow most of the way, breaking his descent by grabbing the trunks of small trees; he heard three rounds crunch near him as he ran, but he paid them little attention.

As soon as he reached the bottom, Eric began yelling.

"Come over here! Second Platoon, over here!"

Right away, two men appeared. Holloway pointed up the ridgeline toward the command group and told the men to get up there as fast as they could climb.

As the men scrambled past, Eric asked, "Where's Lieutenant Cannon?"

"Damned if I know," one man said.

"Down that-a-way," said the other, pointing down the creek line.

Eric called "Cannon!" and "Second Platoon!" several more times, and another soldier appeared.

"You stay here. Yell for people to come to you. You got it?"

The man nodded. A moment later he began yelling, as Eric had been.

The company commander ran down the creek bed, meeting other men on the narrow path that followed the water's edge.

"Up the way," he panted to each man as he passed. "Keep moving!"

God, help me to get them out! he prayed as he ran.

Suddenly he heard a cry from the other side of the stream.

"Lieutenant!" Then again, faintly, "For Christ's sake, somebody —"

Eric jumped into the creek and waded across. Several shots thumped into the water behind him, but he kept moving. Once across, he looked for a rock or a tree to hide behind.

Damned sniper, he thought.

When he had caught his breath, he began looking for the man who had called him. He yelled "Hey!" and "Where are you?" several times, but the man didn't answer. Holloway was about to give up and continue his search for Cannon when he almost stumbled over the wounded soldier's body.

Eric knelt beside the man and felt for a heartbeat. The pale face and tightly clenched fist made Holloway think that the soldier was dead, but a moment later the soldier opened his eyes and looked at Holloway.

"I'd given up," the boy said. "I thought sure I'd die here."

"You'll be all right. Where are the others?"

"Just — just a little — bit farther down."

Eric reckoned that he was almost as far down the creek bed as Fox Company had been earlier in the day. The distance back up to George Company was so great that Eric, too, was tempted to give up.

Give up and do what? he asked himself. Give up and die, came the answer. No, not yet. Not yet.

"Look. I'll come back for you in just a minute. Or somebody will come. Don't give up, and don't worry about being left. All right?"

"Yessir."

The man tried awfully hard to smile.

Holloway left the man and ran on down the creekline. When he had gone about fifty yards, a mortar landed directly in front of him, rocking him back, dropping him on a pile of sharp rocks. His ears were ringing when the echoes of the blast died away: I'm still alive, he thought. He had difficulty in breathing, and he thought of Wayne Hyde's white face and wild eyes, the yellow lips that whispered "I can't breathe! . . ."

Slowly, painfully, Eric got up. When he saw that he was not really hurt, he stumbled on. After he passed the crater, he saw about a dozen men coming toward him, and Cannon was among them.

"Cannon! Over here!" Holloway yelled.

The group dog-trotted toward him.

"Damn!" Cannon said. "Am I glad to see you!"

"Let's get these people out of here. Are you all right?"

"Yes, but where's the company?"

"Up on top."

"How'll we get out of here? They've got the upper end of this damned valley covered with mortar fire."

"You'll just have to keep scratching and run through it. By the way, they've got a sniper with some kind of automatic weapon covering the creek. Anybody who stops is dead. Oh, yes: you've got a wounded man up ahead. Have you got everybody else with you?"

"Yes, I think so. I've sent a bunch of people up ahead, and we can't think of anybody who hasn't been seen. That's Kelsey that's wounded, isn't it? We can't find him."

"I don't know. Find out, and if it isn't, we'll have to find Kelsey."

Cannon ran on up ahead.

Another mortar round landed nearby, and everyone got down.

"Man, we've got to get out of here!" one soldier yelled.

"Cut that out!" Holloway shouted. "You'll be out of here in nothing flat!"

Cannon returned, smiling.

"That's Kelsey."

"All right, then. I've put one of your men up the creek about a hundred yards. By that big bare tree — you see the one I mean?"

"Yep."

"When you get there, go straight up the side of the finger. Gregg will show you where to reassemble. You may have to fight again before long, so get your breath as soon as you can. And count noses!"

"What are you going to do?"

"I'm going up from here. I just saw Dolan's people up yonder, and I'm going to try to get that sniper before your folks have to cross that stream. Now get going — and be careful."

"Be careful yourself," Cannon called after him.

Holloway ran directly to the shallow creek and plunged in. He was almost across before the sniper got a wild shot at him. Once out of the water, he ran up the snow-covered slope and climbed as rapidly as he could.

He hit the ridgeline in the middle of Digger Dolan's platoon. He fell on his face on the path, completely worn out.

Dolan ran over to see about the officer.

"You hit?"

Holloway got to his knees.

"No. Where's your machine gun?"

"Over yonder."

"Haul it over here."

Digger, puzzled, trotted up the path a few yards and picked up the platoon's machine gun. The gunner threw a belt of ammunition around Digger's neck, and then Digger returned to the company commander.

Holloway was on his feet again, looking up the valley to see how Cannon was making out. The sniper opened up on the creek as Eric saw a couple of Cannon's men try to cross.

"You see that, Digger?"

Digger nodded.

"Cut loose!"

Digger had the gun in place and firing in five seconds. He raked the area where he and Holloway had seen the flashes of the weapon the enemy sniper was using, then he stopped to see if his firing had had any effect.

It had. Cannon's men were wading across, and they were not being fired on.

"Phillips!" Digger yelled. "You come here and shoot this damned thing. You see where I was shootin'?"

"Yes, Sergeant."

"All right. They open up again, you paste 'em."

Digger turned to tell Holloway that everything was under control, but Holloway was gone.

When he reached the command group, Eric Holloway sat down, exhausted.

"How's Felty making out?" he asked Gregg.

"He's nearly up there. He's tried everything in the book, and a few things that ain't."

"Good. Battalion call?"

"No, sir, they haven't. And it's strange. I think the wire's cut, or something."

Gregg was grinning.

"Better get it fixed, Top," Eric said. "And thanks."

"We been havin' trouble with the radio, too. We can hear, but we can't send. Ain't that too bad?"

"Yes it is, Top. I have an idea it'll clear up pretty soon, though."

"Morris, you can go fix that wire now," Gregg called. Then, to the company commander, "We've got the Second Platoon over here, sir."

"Fine."

Eric got up and went with the first sergeant to see about the Second Platoon. Gregg had told them to reassemble near the mortar crews, on the eastern slope of Cougar — the safe side.

"They made good time," Holloway said.

"They was goosed, sort of."

A medic was working on the man Eric had found in the valley. Holloway walked over to see how the man was feeling.

"Hi, Lieutenant," the soldier said. "You was right. I got out."

Eric got down on one knee beside the man and said, "You've got it made, now. All the way home. The war's over, for you."

Kelsey smiled, and then he said, "I hate to leave the comp'ny, though. I just wish they was all going, too."

"So do I."

"You don't remember me, do you, Lieutenant?"

Eric tried hard to think, but he couldn't remember having seen the man before that day.

"No, I'm sorry, but I don't."

"You drove an old green Buick, and you used to buy gas at my dad's filling station."

"Of course. You're Noah Kelsey — well, I'm — I'll be damned."

"Noah, Junior, sir."

"How's your dad?"

"He's fine, sir."

"Give him my best regards when you get home."

"I will."

"And tell him —"

"Yes, sir?"

Eric wanted Noah, Senior, to know how sorry he was to be sending his boy home flat on his back, to know how hard he had tried —

"Nothing, Noah. Just tell him hello. I'll be by to see you when I get back."

Litter bearers from battalion arrived to start Kelsey home. Eric stood up as they lifted the man, and as he watched them carry him down the path, he thought of all the responsibility that was his — awful responsibility.

As he looked around the assembly area at the men of the Second Platoon, sitting in the snow, laughing and joking, glad to be alive, he realized that his awkward, hurried prayers had been answered: the platoon was back, and Kelsey was the only man who had been hit. Another man had broken a finger in falling, but that might have happened in his own home. Eric had been able to get them out, just as he had prayed, and for that he was very grateful.

As he thought back over the experience, he was shocked, in a way, that any of the men had survived. Mortar fire is deadly, he knew; and yet the mortar round that had landed ahead of him had not touched him. There was no logical reason for the survival of the Second Platoon that Eric could think of; and his own survival was just as remarkable, just as inexplicable.

Eric listened to the men swapping stories about their experience like members of a winning football team in the locker room after an especially close game. Dirty, miserable, tired, but more alive, more animated than ever before.

And Eric Holloway knew that he would have to use all the energy, and skill, and intellect that he had to protect those men; not simply because of men like Noah Kelsey, Senior, whom he would have to face someday, but because of a feeling of even deeper obligation which he sensed but could not fully understand — a feeling that was bound up with the words "Company Commander."

The Tank, the Gun, the Man

X

from *Your Own Beloved Sons*

by THOMAS ANDERSON

They heard the first tanks long before the company had reached their part of the valley. The mortar hidden somewhere north of the village started firing and they could see the flashes appearing along a straight line far down the road. The mortar did not stop the advancing column; they could hear the halftracks, now, and the truck engines. Once a machine gun opened fire from a point over by the foot of the western slope; for a moment its tracers swept across the valley and its rapid tat-tat-tat sounded alone above the combined clamor of slowly moving machinery. Then a number of the company's guns returned the fire, their orange-colored tracers converging at the point across the valley, and the enemy gun stopped.

The mortar still boomed behind the village, and the short, violent bursts crept up the valley steadily, reaching now a point on the road just a couple of hundred yards from the haystack. As Richard and Little John watched, an explosion tore flame and debris from a vehicle that looked like a truck, and suddenly the column was clearly visible, halted now, a long row of dark, square forms waving and trembling in the flickering light from the burning truck. A tank moved out of the column and lumbered up along the side of the road toward the wreck; three or four figures appeared from the vehicle in front of the hit truck and hurriedly searched the fields on both sides. The tank moved in on the wreck and pushed it off the road and backed quickly away and waited as the column started to move again. The truck burned brightly there in the field, and the vehicles moving past it looked like huge black beetles that cast long swiftly swinging shadows across the snow.

Instead of rejoining the column, the tank that had pushed the burning truck aside turned and hobbled across the fields toward the village. The column had reached the side road, and the lead vehicle, a jeep, was rolling slowly down toward the first huts when a machine gun opened fire from a window in the large house between the twin hills. The turret on the tank behind the jeep swung around and the tank's gun fired; the shell hit the corner of the house and set it afire, but the tracers kept spurting out from the window. The tank which had cut across the fields wallowed in between two huts on the south side of the village and disappeared; the sound of its racing engine emerged like muffled thunder from among the walls, and a minute later it reappeared on the poplar-lined path, headed straight and fast for the big house. As the green tracers sparked off its front, it climbed within fifty yards of the house before it stopped and its turret adjusted and its 76-mm cannon sent a shell right through the left window that contained the machine gun. The explosion broke a large flame-filled hole in the front of the house and the tank sat still for a moment, watching the result. Then it backed and turned, felling a poplar by the maneuver, and came back down the path.

Richard went behind the haystack where Little John was struggling with his boots. They were stiff and crackled frostily when he forced his feet into them.

"Why don't you take his?" Richard asked.

"No," Little John said and tugged and kicked his heel in the ground.

Richard went over to the sergeant's body. "Why not?" he asked. "He won't need them any more."

"It's not right," Little John said. He rose and stomped on the ground vigorously. He shuffled out of the shadow of the haystack and took one quick look at the vehicles moving down the side road in the flickering red light. Then he came over to stand close by Richard.

Richard touched the sergeant's feet with his boot. "We're taking him with us," he said.

"Of *course!*"

"You take the gun and the blanket," Richard told him. "Never mind the pack. We better hurry now." He bent and lifted the sergeant's body into his arms. Little John picked up the gun and the blanket and followed Richard across the field and down the river bank and north along it toward the ford.

Most of all Miles would have liked to run the tank clear through the house, push it with him, walls, roof, machine gun, everything, tear it apart and dump it down the other side of the hill. Instead he grudgingly delegated his rage to the cannoneer by kicking the back of the man's chair. Having already zeroed in his 76-mm piece, all the cannoneer did was press the black handle, and the window up ahead erupted into a flaming hole. Miles rose inside the open turret and glared at the house, wishing that the machine gun would somehow collect itself and fire again so that he might knock it out once more. The spreading, crackling fire only kindled the slow, black hatred for all things alive that had grown in him ever since the beginning of dusk that day.

As the tank lumbered back down the poplar path and entered the village he remained standing on the seat, with head and shoulders outside the turret, bloodthirstily intent on every doorway he passed. Several of the straw roofs had caught fire from mortar and tracer hits and he felt the violent heat of molten clay stinging his cheeks. "Burn, you bastards," he mumbled, and turned and spat into the heat.

He stopped the tank at the crossing near the center of the village and waited for the column to come down from the main valley road. After a while a jeep appeared among the shadow-flickering walls lining the street; the captain's yellow standard hung pale and listless from the twelve-foot-high radio aerial which kept swinging back and forth drunkenly when the jeep pulled up and stopped in front of the tank. Driscoll, the company clerk, and a pale-faced rifleman were in the jeep. The captain rose in the jeep, still looking his parade-ground best, silver bars on shoulders, pistol belt tight, knotted holster straps straight down his leg. Miles noticed the carbine sitting in the slot between seat and sideboard. A lot of good that's gonna do you, he thought, as the captain shouted.

"See any sign of them, Miles?"

"Hell, no."

"Good job on that gun up there," the captain yelled. He sat down and motioned for the clerk to drive on down toward the ford. Miles leaned over the side of the turret and watched the jeep bounce away through the shadows. He sneered and shook his head. Hell of a night for a bare-ass jeep with two kids and a courageous captain in it.

Less than a minute later Driscoll was back, standing up again and yelling about a barricade. "Clear it, Miles," he yelled, "column'll be here soon as we get the maintenance truck off the road." The jeep scurried up the incline toward the main road, the captain still standing — glancing about, like Napoleon, Miles sneered to himself. All right, so Dressy Driscoll was a brave man. So what?

The barricade was nothing much: a few wooden chests which crushed like eggshells under the treads. No jeeps in sight. Maybe, maybe Stanley *had* stayed in Hoengsong.

The bow gunner announced over the intercom that he thought he saw a jeep.

"Where?" Miles shouted and swung around.

The gunner rose out of his hole, like a turtle, and pointed up ahead. Miles jumped out of the turret and balanced himself forward along the narrow ledge, peering out across the dark stretch of open field. Then he saw it, too — a jeep, sagging to the front like a man down on his knees.

"What're we waiting for?" he yelled. "Let's get the hell over there!"

He stayed out on the front ledge, holding on to the barrel of the gun as the tank churned across the open. He saw the grounded jeep, its gun mount stripped of the fifty, and beyond it, a black abyss. In the flickering light from the burning huts behind, he thought he saw the jeep trembling. He swore and made ready to jump to the ground when the driver rose again and turned his pale helmet-framed face up toward him.

"I think there's somebody down there, Miles."

Miles put both hands on the raised gun barrel and leaned out as far as he could without falling.

"Stanley," he yelled.

Above the hollow rumble of the idling engine and the drone of the column coming down through the village, he heard a shout from down the abyss. He stood back abruptly. That's not Stanley, he thought. But his driver was leaning over the edge of his hole, talking to somebody down there.

"Who is it?" he asked over the intercom. The driver turned again. "One of them guys went on patrol," he said. "Says he's got Stanley down there with him."

"Tell 'em to come on up," Miles said and waited tight-lipped, propped back against the turret now.

A soldier came struggling up the bank into the flame light; he was carrying somebody in his arms. Another one followed. The latter, smaller one stumbled over the brink and fell, and Miles watched from the top of the tank how the first one turned and waited until the little one got back on his feet and picked up the thirty he was carrying. At that moment a machine gun began to clatter over on the opposite bank and green tracers blew across the black water at them. Miles looked away from the bundle the soldier was carrying in his arms and got into the turret and kicked the back of the cannoneer's chair and directed him over the intercom.

As the turret began to move around him slowly, Miles glanced quickly down at the bundle again. The turret stopped, then inched into final position. He kicked the cannoneer's chair again; a long, narrow flame spat from the gun's poised muzzle, and the cracking report rolled away from the recoiling tank. Simultaneously a white flash exploded in the darkness back in the fields on the other side.

"Down a couple," he said and kicked the chair again. There was another blinding flash, closer to the embankment this time, and the machine gun stopped firing. There was small-arms fire coming from all along the opposite bank; this did not stop. He climbed out of the turret and went around to the rear deck and squatted and looked down at the two soldiers who had sought cover behind the tank. The bundle lay between them. He saw the face and knew that it was Stanley. It looked too damn gray. He rose abruptly.

"This ain't the place for him," he shouted. "Put him on one of the trucks."

The taller one of the two looked up at him for a moment; then he got on his feet and stepped out from the tank and peered back toward the village. There were no trucks or jeeps in sight; another tank was approaching, but it was still more than a hundred yards away.

"All right, you guys come up here and ride with me," Miles called. "I don't know where the fuck I'm going, anyway." He shook his head as a bullet cracked close and bent and squatted again on the engine grille. The two below were both on their feet now, lifting the bundle.

"It's Sergeant Stanley," the fellow shouted, standing with the body in his arms. It must be that new one, Miles realized now, and the other — of course, Little John! Miles overcame something which wanted to make him turn his back to the lifted figure and go away; he squatted deeper and reached down. The pasty gray face rose slowly toward him and he saw the black streaks coming out from under the closed lids and from the nose. Then all the weight was in his arms and he pulled the body up and laid it across the deck. The first fellow, the one who'd come with Harris to the company, now climbed up the side, toting the thirty with the belt hanging from it; when he was up he turned and reached down and almost lifted Little John over the edge. Little John looked sick; he held on tightly to the axe handle strapped to the edge of the deck.

Richard motioned toward Stanley. "We'll take care of him," he told Miles.

"You will?" Miles said.

"Sure," they said, speaking in unison.

"You realize he's dead?"

"Yes," and "Sure," they said gravely, simultaneously.

"He'll slide off when we start moving this crate," Miles said gruffly.

"We can put him there," Richard replied, and nodded toward the tent roll tied to the rear part of the deck. "We'll hold on to him, don't worry."

They forded the river, strafing the opposite bank continuously; the bow gunner stood up in his hole to watch his own tracers, and Miles stayed outside the turret, firing the fifty. The rifle fire along the bank scattered and disappeared as they came close; the machine gun that had ceased firing after the second HE shell hit near it was either knocked out or removed to another position, awaiting the more vulnerable trucks and jeeps.

Richard was down on his knees behind the turret, close by Little John. They both had their hands out to hold Stanley. When the tank started down the embankment into the river it had pushed on its side the jeep perched there, baggage and all, and the two hadn't even looked at it.

Miles saw the red glow in the sky above the eastern mountains and asked them what the hell was on fire over there. Richard rose from the deck far enough to see above the top of the turret. "That's Hoengsong, Sergeant," he said and sat down with Little John again.

"But ain't there supposed to be a Dutch battalion there?" Miles asked. "You guys been there today, ain't you?"

"Yes, Sergeant," Richard replied.

Miles turned and looked at the deep red glow again and wondered.

They had climbed the opposite bank and were waiting for the column to start crossing. The had stopped a little in from the river and Miles was listening for noises from the darkness ahead of the tank, but he heard only the engine of the tank coming across after them, and an occasional machine-gun burst far over beyond the village. Then there was a sudden whine above his head, and a whip and a crack and a red glint in the field in front. He also heard the weapon itself — a Chinese heavy mortar. The report seemed to come from a spot far back in the mountains between them and Hoengsong. They waited until the other tank came up over the bank before they moved into the field and crossed the spot where the shell had exploded. A second shell landed to their right, and a third hit in the river with a muffled *whock*.

Over close under the eastern slope they stopped again. Shells were hitting where the column crossed the river; most of the huts were burning fiercely in the village, and the line of waiting tanks and trucks and jeeps and halftracks was clearly visible, packed bumper to bumper and reaching all the way from the river bank through the burning village and left along the main valley road where the vehicles became lost in the darkness. Tracers from an enemy gun placed far over near the western slope swept the road crossing until a tank moved out of the line and, squatting in the field, started planting a row of flaring white blossoms reaching from the valley floor up the slope.

"Look," Miles heard Little John say — the two of them sat on the deck facing the rear and the sight of the burning huts and the vehicles in the river — "we're all going to get killed now."

"Like hell!" Richard said.

Three or four vehicles had come across and were lined up behind the tank. Somebody in the rear was shouting for Miles to move on, to get the hell out of there.

"Hey," he shouted to Richard, "you been here before. How do we get through to that God damn town?"

Richard rose and leaned against the turret. He kept one hand on Little John's shoulder as if to prevent him from jumping off. He told Miles how far to go before turning; he remained standing there until the gap appeared in the slope and they swung right and had the glow, now much fiercer, in the sky directly before them. Then he sat down on the deck again.

"I hope this damn trail's wide enough," Miles shouted, but his two passengers were silent.

They had gone on for about ten minutes — slowly because of the many sharp turns and the boulders that threatened to cut the treads — and the driver was cursing over the intercom, when they heard the mortar going off, somewhere ahead, very close, somewhere down in the canyon itself. A moment later the shell hit high on the cliff in back of them, and there was a many-toned whine of shrapnel. The detonation echoed sharply above the grinding of the tank engines.

Miles lowered himself so that only the top of his head was above the turret hole. The mortar sounded again, and he stared ahead for the muzzle blast, but they must have hidden it behind a boulder. The shell hit on the road behind them, blowing air past Miles's neck. Through the ear-humming monotone after the blast, he heard Richard shouting to Little John: "— if you stay right here nothing will hurt you. Lie down flat."

Again the mortar went off; when the shell had landed, once more behind them, Miles felt a hand on his shoulder. Richard was leaning in over the hole, asking him if there wasn't a corner down inside for Little John. "Hell, man, ain't you ever seen the inside of an M-four?" Miles hollered back, feeling a sudden, violent hate for the space-conscious men who had conceived the M-4. The mortar went off, and Richard dropped flat on the deck. This time Miles thought he saw the sparks from burning implements shooting into the air fifty yards further up the road. But the cannoneer said he didn't see a damn thing, and how the hell could he be expected to, looking through that God damn scope.

The shell hit about five yards behind the tank, square on the road. Over the intercom Miles told his driver to switch on the lights and go fast up the road until he ran into something.

"You kidding?" the driver asked.

"No," he said and swung out of the turret and got behind the fifty. Richard was in his way. "Hold tight now," he shouted.

The trail appeared suddenly in cold white light, the rocks closest to the tank with the garish intensity of papier-mâché props, the ones further out in a dim, pale mist. Small dark figures, squads of them, had frozen, bent almost double, their faces hidden away from the strong headlights. The tank roared down at them and they came to life suddenly and darted to each side of the trail and ducked in under the cliffs. The thirty in the bow started to clatter at the same time he pulled the trigger on the fifty. Then they were abreast of the ones who had reached the bottom of the crevices, and he swung the fifty around and fired into them, pouring bullets in there even after the light and the tank had moved on up the road and he was firing dangerously close to the tank behind. He didn't see the mortar.

"Put out the lights!" he ordered over the intercom.

For a couple of seconds the darkness was almost blinding. The tank stopped abruptly and Miles could hear the driver cursing. He was about to get back into the turret when his arm was pushed aside. Richard was standing beside him: in one hand he held Little John's arm; his other hand had a secure grip at the seat of the boy's pants. As Miles stepped aside, Richard mumbled an excuse and then lifted Little John over the hole and let him down into the turret, head first. Richard stepped back. "It's better that way, I think," he told Miles.

Miles put his hand on the rim and swung his legs over and lowered them into the turret on top of Little John, who instantly slipped away under his feet, he couldn't imagine where to.

"Get this crate moving!" he yelled at his driver.

"I can't *see* nothing!" the driver yelled back.

He cursed the driver, and suddenly the tank moved. It stopped again, and the voice of the driver came over the intercom, addressing no one in particular but speaking with determination.

"I'm gonna button up."

"Me, too," the bow gunner's voice said with equal firmness. Miles thrust his head far forward over the rim of the turret and shouted down the slanted bow, cursing them. Small crouching forms, about half a dozen of them, approached the tank from the driver's side where the bow gun couldn't reach them. Miles grabbed a grenade from his pocket, yelled, "Heads down!" and let it drop. There was a slapping noise below, and another, but it wasn't the grenade. It was the driver and the bow gunner, slamming down their covers. Then the grenade burst.

He had hardly stuck his head back outside the turret to see the effects when he discovered a figure crouching on top of the driver's cover. How it could possibly be there following the grenade burst Miles didn't understand. There were other figures down on the road right in front of the gunner.

He shouted to the bow gunner to start firing.

"I can't see!" the gunner yelled.

"You'll hit 'em," Miles shouted. "Go on, open up!" He shot the one already on the tank with his .45 and watched him raise his arms and drop backward onto the road in front of the left tread. The tank was moving ahead slowly, the driver asking about directions over the intercom. Miles, with the communication wires tangled around his neck, kept talking to the driver. The tank moved faster up the narrow trail. Then somebody fired at him from behind and he whirled around and saw them all, a whole platoon of them, some already hanging like monkeys, clinging to the tent roll tied to the deck. The ones on the ground were screaming at the ones already up urging them on.

They haven't any charges, he thought; they would have blown us up long before this. His hand was on the fifty, about to push it around, although he knew that its fire could never reach them in time.

Then Richard rose from the rear deck, holding a machine gun against his right hip. His head was bare; he was using his fur cap as a hand guard around the gun jacket. His first burst was unrehearsed and hit low, tearing into the tent roll; but he spread his feet and hugged the gun tighter and let go again, and one after the other the monkeys dropped, and the ones on the ground dispersed and fell as the gun reached them.

Miles stared at this for a moment; then he ducked into the turret and shook the cannoneer's shoulder.

"God damn!" he shouted, forgetting about the intercom. "Get me some thirty ammo, quick!" The cannoneer leaned down into the tank, and Miles straightened and saw his new machine gunner had come back and was resting his weapon on the rim of the turret. The cannoneer handed up the first box and Miles heaved it over the rim onto the rear deck. Richard stepped aside to make room.

"How much of it have we got?" he shouted into Miles's ear.

"Plenty," Miles shouted. "More'n you can use up." The boxes began to form a pile on the deck. While Miles was ripping the covers off, getting them ready for him, Richard knelt quickly behind the tent roll and fired a couple of bursts into a crevice. There was no return fire, and soon he rose and came back to the turret.

"It's a good gun, this one," he shouted to Miles. "We've been using it all day."

"That's fine!" Miles shouted. He could see that the column was catching up; all down along the trail there were machine guns firing, and some vehicles had their headlights turned on. He could see trucks, even jeeps. They made it, he thought wonderingly; they actually forded that fucking river. Over the intercom he told the driver to speed it up a little. Without comment, the driver put the tank in a higher gear.

"How far we gotta go before we get to that town, buddy?" Miles shouted.

Richard looked ahead and pointed. Miles turned and saw a large cliff jutting out into the canyon some five hundred yards ahead, looking like the Rock of Gibraltar with a red waterfall running down its front. Richard knocked on his shoulder. "Listen," he said. Above the noise from the column they heard what sounded like twenty machine guns fired together, coming down the canyon from behind the bend by the great cliff.

"Quad fifties," Miles said, puzzled. "Who's got quads around here?"

"The Dutch," Richard said proudly. "I saw them today."

As they watched, the cliff face turned liquid with reflected flame; several large artillery flares blossomed into the sky and hung fixed in brilliant white patterns high above the canyon. In the pale light Miles could see the other's face. He was staring up at the flares with a sort of childish astonishment. Then he smiled widely.

"Say! They're all right!"

"They're fine," Miles chuckled, and turned to tell his driver to knock it up one more. The tank roared past the boulders and nobody tried to climb it now. They had outdistanced the mortar; he could still hear it, but from far behind, back among the trucks and jeeps.

"This tank runs real swell," Richard shouted. "Are they hard to drive, tanks?"

Miles looked at the young, admiring face. "Wanna be a tanker?" he asked. The boy nodded.

"It's easy as pie," Miles said. "Nothing to it. Tell you what," he said, "just you stick around this particular tank until we're through Hoengsong, and pretty soon there'll be an opening."

Richard smiled.

"I mean it," Miles said. "I'll even talk to the Old Man about it, before I go home." He turned and narrowed his eyes as the tank quarter-turned into the last curve and the fighting town swung into view. Then, as bullets started to crack around the tank once again, he climbed out of the turret and pulled the handles of the fifty over so that he could fire it down the side. He looked down at the boy, who was now kneeling on the rear deck, the thirty ready in his hands. Miles half reached out a hand toward him, then pulled it back and turned to the fifty and started to fire it down on the road. The tank entered the long lane cleared through the burning rubble and roared down toward the center of town with all its guns going.

Bang the Drum Slowly

✕

From *The Last Campaign*

by GLEN ROSS

The full-scale Chinese attack of April of that year carried the war into its fifth act. The first four phases — the defense of the Naktong perimeter, the occupation of North Korea, the Chinese winter attack, and the United Nations counteroffensive — were now ancient history.

The Eighth Army was changing. The old divisions had slowly filled up with new men, and the Tenth Corps, which in the first three campaigns had been wielded separately, like a boxer's left hand, had now been integrated and deployed on line with the rest of the divisions. New divisions arrived. Troops from everywhere were now part of one of the most densely populated armies ever assembled.

Although the Chinese offensive began with much noise and caused a general withdrawal of the United Nations line, the situation was without the elements of surprise and mystery. The invincibility of the Red army had been proved to be a superstition. It was no longer a question of being driven into the sea, but a problem to be solved by the books and rules.

And thus the great stalemate began.

Thus Korea was, in a sense, divided and conquered. And the patriot's dream of once more uniting the country was thrown upon the mangled heap of lost causes, where many a patriot's dream had gone before.

Much of Korea's natural wealth and wildly beautiful land was in the grip of China, and there remained. The hills of Pakchon, in the west along the thirty-eighth parallel, were lost to China. Chinnampo and its bay were lost, as well as the ancient city of Pyongyang, and the pine-forested mountains of Chongjin. The foggy mountains of Sinanju were lost, and the walled city of Yongbyon, with its monastery mountain. All of these places were lost. And Korea was a ruined land.

How the fifth campaign fared with those who fought it, Hunter never really knew. The Division Headquarters struck its tents and went into convoy once more. All day they traveled south, over the mountain pass and down the valleys, not caring any more that they were retreating. For Hunter, the magic of the six-bys worked as it always had — simply to be on the move put his mind at rest. He did not think of this retreat as going into debt. In any case, it was a debt others would be paying.

The rotation of the old men was supposed to begin next week; and nobody cared much about the war any more. It seemed a shame that men were still being killed on the line, men who had come to Korea with the Division and endured for so long. They should call time out until the replacements came.

And the new men? How long would they have to stay here? How many generations would come and go?

At the end of the trip this time, there was waiting, not the Chineese or North Koreans, but the old ambush of responsibility and boredom of the rear echelon — unloading the trucks in the dark, putting up the tents again, keeping track of things. The only way Hunter had ever been able to face these things had been as an enemy. He hated confusion enough to be willing to fight it, even under the blotched banners of Old Man Hassler.

When the dawn came, he discovered that they were camped in a wide, sunny valley near the ruins of a small town. There were no other troops in sight, and they were so far from the front that not even the faintest rumble of artillery disturbed the April morning air.

It was pleasant to be there in the calm backwaters of the war, waiting to leave Korea forever, and feeling the sun grow a little warmer every day. The guard routine was easy and automatic, and Hunter found that he could do his part without having to contribute anything of himself. For days at a time now, the Old Man neglected to harass the band. Nobody seemed to care what they did. The new Chinese offensive soon bogged down, and Hunter lost interest in it.

Spring came to that country like an angel of mercy. As the rain fell less frequently and the sun grew warmer, a soft green haze crept over the abandoned fields and up the mountainsides. Hunter took notice every evening of a place beyond the mile-wide fields where a poplar grove around a farmhouse shone with a golden-green glow like fire at sundown. In the far-off high mountains, the bonfires of charcoal burners glimmered at night, and a faint smell of wood smoke came drifting down.

He had never been so aware of the beauty of the world, or of the pleasure of the sunlight. Even the sight of the red dirt road that led around a low hill to the ruined village of Shenbang-do could fill him with wonder at its reality. Several times he was surprised to find that what he had taken for the distant rumble of artillery was actually the natural voice of a thunderstorm.

One day, the mail, which had been delayed, brought him a stack of letters that had been following him around for weeks. Among them was a letter from Al, and another — surprising enough — from Kelley. Hunter sat in the sun behind the tent and read them.

Al, still on emergency leave in the States, vowed he would never return to Korea. His letter contained a great deal of bitterness, more or less in the same vein Benfield had opened. "Nobody wants to pay for it," Al wrote, "and nobody wants to fight it. Nobody wants to do a God damn thing but set on his ass or go to college or drink beer and watch television. So why should I go back just to be rotated? I've already been rotated. I'm going to get out of the Army and go to college. Maybe by the time the next war comes along, they'll have it on television. That would give everybody a chance to see plenty of action without all the risk and trouble. Which will be a great improvement. A deal like that last attack I was in would be a great eye-opener. . . ."

Later, he read the letter aloud to Stover and Hatchman, and they soberly agreed with Al's opinions.

Hatchman showed him a copy of *Hot Rod* magazine addressed to Jim Dougherty. "It comes every month," he said. "Makes you feel kind of funny."

"I guess he forgot to send a change of address."

The letter from Kelley was several weeks old and had been forwarded many times. Hunter read with a strange feeling of unreality:

HUNTER,

Got your letter the other day, and the money. I gave it to Gus and he said tell you thanks. I guess you are liking Japan better every day, you been gone a long time. Wish I was there myself.

They're talking about a rotation plan, and I figure on getting out of here this summer. I don't want another winter like last one.

I don't know if you heard, but Ames Dallas got hit again in the elbow and has gone back to the States. He done a real good job. We had him in charge of a section but before we could make him sergeant, he got hit again. I wish he could have stayed a few more days.

Bench is gone, and I've got the platoon now. We still don't have any officer. We got all new guys now, and you'd hardly know any of them. Louie went on R & R and stayed a week A.W.O.L. I don't know what they did, but he never came back to the platoon.

We had a patrol last week and three guys got K.I.A. Harvey, in your old squad, got it. I sure hate to see those boys getting killed, close as we are to getting out of here.

We're back off the hill now, doing C.P. guard for the battalion for a few days, just the machine guns. I'll close for now and see you later. News is short here.

Best of luck,

KELLEY

That afternoon, Hunter left the camp without saying a word to anyone and walked east into the hills. The day was mild and cloudless, with a warm sun pouring life into the new grass. In a few scattered paddies, the young rice plants shimmered greenish-yellow above the water.

Leaving the raw ugliness of the camp behind, he passed through a narrow valley floored with an apple orchard in full blossom. An old farmer was plowing between the trees, goading an ox and wrestling with a heavy wooden plow; and the sounds of his labor blended softly with the humming insect noises of the orchard. He gave Hunter only a single suspicious glance; and Hunter realized that the old Korean was thankful it was not easy to steal or burn an orchard.

Not caring where he went, he followed the valley to its end and crossed a ridge that blocked his way. He felt that he had to get away from the sight or sound of anything military, if only for a few hours. He felt that if he could not escape, he would go violently insane.

But in the next valley he found an artillery observation plane staked in a field, and a couple of guards were loafing in a jeep.

Everywhere, he thought desperately. *They're everywhere.*

He crossed that valley and climbed up through a pine grove on the ridge beyond. Once out of the woods, he followed a trail that led him over the ridge crest and along the side of the slopes beyond. Half a mile from the place where he had seen the plane, he met a party of Koreans. They wore clean white clothes and had been talking and laughing among themselves until they caught sight of him; whereupon they fell silent until he was well past them. Except that there were no young men in the group, it might have been a normal, happy family group who had been on a picnic.

Not far away, he found the place where they had been. The valley narrowed to a ravine and at the end of it, in a narrow place surrounded by cliffs and pines, he discovered a lake. The fresh water gleamed in the sunlight, and great trees grew upon the parklike banks. Among the trees at the water's edge stood a kind of pagoda, rather like a bandstand open on all sides. Like other Korean temples he had seen, it was painted bright red and yellow and blue, with intricately puzzling fretwork around the stairs and eaves.

The place was silent and deserted. Hunter climbed to the upper story of the pagoda and sat resting, sweating from the long walk. The slanting sunlight flickered through the pine branches, and nearby he could hear the splash and roar of a waterfall where the lake spilled out between two deep cliffs.

It occurred to him that this would be a nice place to be dug in with a machine-gun squad. Just the machine guns and a week's rations. And no Chinese. It would be very pleasant and peaceful.

He knew what was bothering him.

A vague feeling that he had deserted Kelley had been troubling him all afternoon, since getting that letter.

"Harvey, in your old squad, got it. . . ."

His squad? Not any more.

And Louie went A.W.O.L. And then there were none.

But Ames Dallas got hit again. . . .

So Ames had gone back, after all.

All their plans and talk and vows had been like straw in the winds of circumstance.

It seemed to Hunter that if he were to go on living, there were many things he must come to terms with. And yet . . . how did one make terms with the dead? How did one come to grips with the past?

It was too much for him.

He wanted, as much as he had ever wanted anything, to find a meaning in the whole mysterious pattern. But everywhere he turned, he was confronted with conflicting truths, paradoxes. He went back to the beginning of the war. The purpose had been easy to see, and the issues clear at the time. Nobody but a few notorious nonthinkers had claimed not to know why they were fighting. But the results? Anyone with eyes could see they had brought ruin upon Korea. Or had they?

He would have given a lot to be able to talk with the old farmer he had passed in the apple orchard. There were many questions he would have liked to ask.

Should they have simply turned South Korea over to the Communists without a fight? Should they have politely turned the other cheek and looked the other way?

Instinctively, then, he gave up trying to understand the war as a history lesson. He would not have to live with history, but with himself.

So he tried to look into his own heart, in honesty. And he discovered that he did not regret any of his part in this war. After his homesickness for Japan had worn off, he had never wanted to forget about Korea. And his earlier desire to take a closer part, to get to the center of things, had been so real and intense that he could not have denied it without denying himself. Now he believed that this desire had come from some deep-rooted part of his nature, some part that belonged not only to him, but to all men. It was not a suicidal instinct; far from it. To call it hunger for experience would be oversimplifying, but it would be accurate.

He had satisfied that hunger, but he was no more at peace now than before. He had a feeling that he had missed the complete experience.

And yet the complete experience, he knew now, included . . . well, Dougherty and Decksmith, Brandeis and Harvey. They had all got the complete experience. They had gone all the way through the war and out the other side.

Perhaps everyone who came out of a war alive was left with the troubling, hidden knowledge that he had not gone all the way. And maybe, to some extent, this was why so few infantrymen were willing to talk about the subject except among others like themselves, who, by simply being alive, were equally guilty.

In the long run, combat led only to the grave.

But unfortunately, he knew that this was no answer to the problem of war. He could not help seeing that what was true of combat was true of everything else. In the long run, the farmer's furrow led only to the grave. In the end, the grave was waiting for every man alive. The main difference was that in combat, the road was much shorter.

He still carried in his pocket the bullet that had wounded his wrist, which the medic had pried out of the clip in his bandolier. He took it out and studied it. The pointed brass nose was bent, and he knew that the bullet must have passed through a pine branch before being deflected in his direction.

He thought of the machine guns again, and the image came vividly into his mind. And with the image a passing flash of awareness, as if the veil had lifted from things, and he saw with pure clarity the enormous and astonishing insanity from the machine gun. But as quickly as it had come, the vision passed away, and no deeper insight came. He was left with the sunlight on the lake and the warm wind in the pine trees.

He held his life in his hand and gloated over it, like one might gloat over a profit, or another over some priceless and secret treasure. And the folly of abstractions and arguments seemed a folly too great for thought.

He would be leaving Korea eventually, and that thought alone was enough to sustain him indefinitely. A month or two, at most, and he would be gone. His records were still lost in the shuffle, but that hardly seemed worth worrying about now. He had a long trip ahead of him, a whole lifetime. He had weeks, months, if necessary (to spare), to wait for his records. He had time he would hardly even need. He had whole years in the bank. He was rich. He was lucky. He was getting out of the game.

He hadn't lost anything on the line. Nothing but his pride and a pint of blood. He would never miss them. Most of the people he knew who'd kept their pride were dead.

The rest of his losses were communal. The war had destroyed a way of life many of them had loved, but he saw that the only thing that had given that life any meaning or value had been its fleetingness and uncertainty. Under any other conditions, it would have seemed merely pleasantly sordid. Those he had shared it with were dead and gone. He had paid as he went, with a year of hard physical travail and deprivation and weeks of rock-bottom misery.

And still, with all this, the war was not quite over.

When he returned to camp, he said nothing about his discovery of the lake. He knew it would be found out soon enough, and for the time being, he wanted to think of it as his own private recreational area. He felt that the place had something for him, something he badly needed.

But the honeymoon was short.

The third time he returned to the lake, while he was resting on the shady planks high among the pines:

K'chaow!

K'chaow!

K'chaow! . . . *Whaaaaaaannnnnnnnnnnnnnnnnnnnnng!*

As Ames Dallas would have said, Hunter flipped, momentarily.

When he regained his wits, he was quivering — all of his muscles taut and prepared by reflex — and breathless with an unreasoning anger. He knew the sound of the M-1 rifle. And now he heard loud, raucous voices. He realized that Headquarters men had found his lake.

He shouted a curse at them, not in hope of quieting them or making them cease firing, but to let them know he was there so they would not use the pagoda as a target. Then he climbed down from his perch and walked back through the pines around the border of the lake.

There would be no point in returning again; soon they would have volleyball nets stretched between the pine trunks and diving boards set up over the lake. They would have Ping-Pong tables in the pagoda. And never, for as long as they remained, would there be any rest for the wicked on the shores of that lovely lake.

He passed them in the woods, half a dozen clerks on an outing. And for the first time, he wished he were an officer, so he could do something to punish them. After all, there were standing orders against casual and promiscuous firing. A month with a rifle squad would have done them all a world of good. They hadn't even the excuse of being trigger-happy, but had fired and continued to fire for the infantile pleasure of making a noise.

Remembering how the Koreans he had passed on the trail had fallen silent at the sight of him, Hunter began to be ashamed of this thing he was a part of. He hated his drab, shapeless clothes, and the ugly, useless helmet he was obliged to wear. He was ashamed of the graceless, expensive weapon he carried.

But as soon as the sound of the firing had been left behind, his mind grew calm again. He sat down to rest on a hillside in the shade of a pine. He found that his mind turned away from whatever was hateful and unpleasant with unrestrained joy.

He dreamed of a Korea freed of the curse that, for reasons he did not understand and was hardly interested in, had fallen upon it. It seemed like the greatest challenge that could ever face mankind. For here was a land in which everything that was inimical to the desires of the human spirit had taken hold with vulturelike claws. Divided by hatred, Korea had fallen victim to every other human misery. Where there should have been beauty, there was ruin and ugliness. Through the greatest and richest rice land of the Orient, hunger stalked like the grimmest of reapers. The young and innocent were homeless; the naturally shy and naïve country people were being trained in the patterns of fear and cynicism. In short, Korea displayed the failure of human social systems with blinding radiance.

And yet, as he sat there on the hillside in the warm spring afternoon, Hunter knew that all these disasters were as nothing to the earth itself. And it amused him to think that even one of the clerks he had so recently been abusing in his mind could, if given power enough, do more for Korea than all the armies of the world. All that the man would need to have would be a little imagination and good will.

He took the job upon himself to fashion Korea anew. It was a pleasant little game. First, he decided, he would withdraw all armies. Then he would make it illegal for Koreans to shoot one another. In order to make this practical, he would make it a crime against nature to bring arms or ammunition into the land. He promoted himself to the position of dictator of the United Nations and went on with his scheme.

He would make of Korea an international park — North and South. For underneath the raw scars on the mountainsides and the rubbled villages, the poetry of the land remained unchanged, even heightened by the human storms that passed over it. Every mountain seemed to hint of some strange and moving tale, and every valley seemed to shine with tragic glory.

It would have been so easy. For a fraction of the cost of the war, Korea could have been transformed into a garden of beauty and romance. What was now a place of dread could be made into a land of promise and joy for all generations.

He left the hillside and wandered back toward the camp; and his reverie was broken by the sight of raw ugliness — the scattered black tents, the spattered jeeps and trucks in the area churned to steaming mud. And he hated these things more than he had ever hated the Chinese; even though the Chinese, he had not a doubt, would have come like a plague of locusts into this valley. He had never hated the Chinese, though he had been angry with them a few times. He had never really had much to do with the Chinese. And in order to hate somebody properly, you had to know him well. You had to really understand somebody before you could hate him adequately.

He understood the rear echelon well enough — for after all, he was a part of it — to hate almost everything it stood for. And so he hated it all the way back to camp; and when he got back to the band, he had a splitting headache.

In the tent he found the members of Hatchman's platoon in a frenzy of excitement. He could tell by their voices that something cataclysmic was in the air.

"What the hell's going on?" he demanded.

"The Old Man's leaving, Hunter!" Stover exclaimed, almost beside himself. "The Old Man's leaving! He's going away."

"No!"

"Yes, yes! A thousand times yes! He's leaving. He's going away!" Stover seemed to want to join hands and dance around in a ring inside the tent.

A flood of relief came over Hunter. The happiness was contagious. The Old Man was leaving! The effect was as if someone of great personal magnitude and charm had just taken over. "What?" Hunter asked. "Is he going on rotation?"

"I don't know if he's going to rotate or not," Stover replied. "But he's leaving. And Richtovan's going to be the band leader."

"When?"

"Right now! In the morning. Richtovan says he's going to Guam or some damned place."

"Guam!" Hunter exclaimed. He thought Stover must have been mistaken. "You mean *Guam*, the island?"

"That's what they said. I don't give a damn myself if he goes to the North Pole, as long as he leaves."

Hunter went to Hatchman for verification.

"Yeah." Hatchman grinned. "He's going to Goddamn Guam! Ain't that great?"

"But why? Why don't they send the old bastard home?"

"Well, I don't know for sure," Hatchman said. "The story Crowfoot tells is that they been trying to retire him for months. You know how many years he's got in the Army, but he keeps fucking them off and turning down his retirement and refusing to leave the division. And it seems like he got wise with Colonel Corbett, or maybe even General Bitters. And remember when the General got relieved? Well, the Old Man wised off about that in the officers' mess. So I guess they got somebody in Eighth Army to go to work on him. And . . . anyhow, he's leaving. And he says he's going to Guam."

"I didn't know there were any troops on Guam."

"Well, if there ain't, that's just the place for him."

"I'll be Goddamned," Hunter said.

"He's leaving tomorrow morning. We're going to play him off at nine o'clock."

In the bright morning sun, at nine o'clock the following day, the band was assembled in the trampled paddy at the edge of camp, beside the road to Shenbang-do. Much of the exhilaration and good humor of the previous evening had worn off, and the men seemed nervous and preoccupied.

"Wait, wait, wait . . ." Hatchman muttered, blowing through his trumpet silently to warm the brass. "I'd hate to be waiting for that old bastard to die." And he grinned at Hunter, who was shuffling his feet uneasily — the trombones were in the front rank, in parade formation.

They waited a long time.

"Here he comes," Richtovan said at last, raising his baton. And as the Old Man's jeep appeared, the band played two choruses of "Auld Lang Syne."

Should old acquaintance be forgot?

Well . . .

Let those forget who could.

For most people, he supposed, it was a love affair, or a family crisis, or some chosen work, that colored their youth and set the pattern of their soul. Maybe. For him and many others, it had been this scroungy war. And Korea. He would never get it out of his mind. Never. It was in his blood and nerves and always would be, he supposed.

The band stopped playing and lowered their instruments.

"Band, atten-shun!" Richtovan said.

The Old Man had dismounted from the jeep and stood waiting while they finished playing.

"At ease!" said the Old Man. He was going to make a speech. Hunter hoped it would be brief. The sun was already growing hot there in the paddy.

"Men," Hassler began. "I been in der Army t'irty-six years."

He paused for effect.

"I vas in der First Vorld Var, and der Second Vorld Var. And I ain't out yet! Not by a long shot!" He paused and cleared his throat. "I ain't got no regrets. No. Maybe I made a few mistakes. Everybody does. But, by God, I always played by der rules. . . . Right?"

"Yes, by God," Richtovan murmured.

"Vell, by God, I alvays vanted you should do a good job. And I been rough, maybe, I don't know. But I alvays tried to be fair. And . . . any-vay, feelings don't count. Vat counts is doing der job . . . and doing it right. . . ."

"Right," said Richtovan absently.

The Old Man scowled at him.

"I ain't never went around patting you men on der back . . . exactly. Dot ain't my vay. But . . . I vant you all should know . . . vell, I been damn proud. I vanted to stay here until der campaign vas ofer. But orders is orders.

"Ve been t'rough a lot togedder, men. God bless you."

As the Old Man finished his speech, Hunter saw to his utter amazement that the Old Man was crying. He was weeping. Old Man Hassler. It was awful. Tears rolled from those piggy eyes and coursed down that bloated face.

"So long, men," Hassler called, in a breaking voice. "God bless you, men. So long!"

The Old Man climbed into the jeep beside the driver.

Hunter felt his face burning with embarrassment. He wished to God somebody would say something frivolous. Glancing around, he saw Hatch-man's face flushed like his own. Everybody seemed to be cracking up. Old Ed Stamps was weeping now. Richtovan, at least, was still in control of his emotions. He called the band to attention and saluted the Old Man's jeep.

The Old Man nodded to the driver. He drew out his faded bandanna and blew his nose loudly.

"Take off!" he commanded the driver.

A moment of awful silence followed, during which they could clearly hear the grinding of the worn starter. Hunter held his breath, afraid the Old Man would make a bad scene with the driver. But just as Mr. Hassler was about to open his mouth to say, "Vat der God damn," the fires caught. The jeep coughed twice and jerked forward, and the Old Man roared away through the rubble of Shenbang-do; and the band was dismissed, until the evening guard formation.

The New Weapon

$\times$

from *The Rack*

by ROD SERLING

This is about the fourth week of the proceedings and it's nearing the end. Wasnik rises.

WASNICK: I call Captain Hall for redirect examination.

Ed rises, goes to the witness chair. Sam stands nearby.

SAM: Captain Hall, you are reminded that you have been properly sworn and are still under oath. (*Nods to Wasnik, then sits down*)

WASNIK: Captain Hall can you tell the Court precisely the regimen involved in questioning and persuasion?

ED: They'd . . . they'd call me out of the barracks — any hour. Lead me to an interrogation shack. The night . . . the night I . . . I cracked, it was cold. It'd been raining for two weeks. They had me remove all my clothes. I walked through the mud to get to the shack. I was freezing, shaking all over, and I was scared. (*Wasnik nods*) When I got to the shack, I had to stand in a puddle of water. Then they started.

WASNIK: For how long?

ED: Usually for a couple of hours. That night they kept on — oh . . . maybe five hours. It seemed like . . . like a month or more. I fainted once. I don't know if it was from cold . . . from fear — I don't know. When I woke up, they had these . . . these pamphlets. The interpreter said I was the only man in the compound who was being so stupid. That if I signed, everybody'd sign. I knew . . . I knew that wasn't so, but then . . . that minute . . . I could feel my mind going soft. Crazy, disjointed thoughts. Nothing was clear at all. I didn't answer him. Then I asked him if I could think it over. He motioned to a guard. The guard pointed his gun, said to go outside. I followed him. He handed me a shovel. Said to dig a grave. And after it was done . . . they were going to shoot me. It was to be my grave.

We cut to a shot of the president of the court as he reacts to this — ever so slight a change of expression but nonetheless a change. Then a brief shot of the Colonel as, very slowly, he lowers his eyes.

WASNIK: They'd done this before?

SAM: Objection. He's leading the witness.

LAW OFFICER: Sustained. Strike the question.

WASNIK: Had they ever done this before?

ED (*His voice harsh now with the strain of telling and remembering*): Once. Not in the camp. On the way there. The week we were captured. They were marching us to Pyoktong — Camp Number Five. They'd told us that in each group of POWs, one of us would be in charge. And if any man in any group dropped out, the officer in charge would be shot.

We pan around the various people in the room. It's deathly still.

ED: A lot of the boys had been wounded — some not even tended to. Bad wounds. Running wounds. One boy — he'd lost a lot of blood. I didn't know who he was. He kept falling down. A lieutenant in charge of his group was half carrying him, and then this kid fainted dead away. And he couldn't be carried. They stopped the column. (*His voice falters*) They stopped the column. A guard went up to this lieutenant. Motioned for him to step out. He gave him a shovel. Told him to dig. Like . . . like they told *me* to dig. (*He looks up, around the room, then straight at his father*) Then, after he'd finished, they put a gun to his head. The lieutenant . . . the lieutenant looked the Korean right in the face and . . . and he said, "Mister . . . Mister, where I come from, they call this lynching."

There's an audible gasp from the court.

WASNIK: Go on.

ED: They shot him in the head. My group had to fill up his grave. That night, the night I cracked, all I could remember was the face of this lieutenant as he dug that grave — dug it knowing that in three minutes . . . he'd be lying in it. (*A deep breath. His voice rises an octave, still in control, but slowly losing it*) I remembered his face. That's all I remembered. I looked into the hole I'd dug and I thought — this one I'd be lying in. (*Looks around*) That's all. And later on, in the interrogation shack, I was standing in that puddle of cold water, and my leg — I'd been hit by mortar in the leg — it started to hurt like it never hurt before. And then I heard this interpreter say something about a warm blanket and my going to sleep. (*A long pause as he looks around again, and his voice rises almost to a shout*) I said yes! I said O.K. I said tell me what I have to do, or what I have to say, and I'll say it! I'll do it. Anything! Germ warfare, dope peddling, informing, surrender leaflets — anything! Only I've got to sleep and I can't be afraid any more. I've just got to sleep now and get warm! (*Then his voice gets quiet*) Lieutenant Wasnik, members of the Court — if this incriminates me, I'm sorry. But . . . but if it happened again tomorrow, I'd very likely do the same thing.

WASNIK: Do you wish the witness for recross-examination?

> *There's a murmur as Sam heads for him, passes Wasnik, and they look at each other. Then Sam stops in front of Ed.*

SAM: Captain Hall, in any camp you were in, did you ever see anyone shot?

ED: They threatened to shoot a lot of —

SAM: I didn't ask you that. I asked you if you saw anyone actually shot.

ED: No, I didn't.

SAM: Only on the march to the camp — and by North Koreans. Is that your testimony?

ED: That's right.

SAM: Was any man ever actually willfully hurt for refusal to collaborate, to your knowledge?

ED: In my sight — no.

SAM: Who was in charge of your compound — Koreans?

ED: No, sir. Chinese.

SAM: No further questions.

WASNIK: No further questions.

SAM (*Very pointedly*): Call Lieutenant Anderson.

SOLDIER: Lieutenant Anderson.

> *A door is opened at the far end of the room. Anderson comes in, takes his place in front of the witness stand.*

SOLDIER: You swear that the evidence that you shall give in the case now in hearing shall be the truth, the whole truth, and nothing but the truth, so help you God?

ANDERSON: I do.

SAM (*Without waiting for him to be seated, starts the questions as he sits*): Lieutenant Anderson, you testified prior to this that you knew Captain Hall, the accused, well before and during your captivity. Is that correct?

ANDERSON: Yes, sir.

SAM: Then you were familiar with what occurred on the night of August the seventh. The grave he dug. Their threatening to shoot him. The rest of it.

ANDERSON: Yes, sir.

SAM: You know the story to be the truth.

ANDERSON: Yes, sir.

SAM: *Why* do you know it to be the truth?

ANDERSON: I'm not sure I understand the question.

SAM: His story is gospel, Lieutenant Anderson, and you know why. Because the same thing happened to you the next night! Isn't that so?

WASNIK (*On his feet*): Objection! The questions are leading. The entire line of questioning!

SAM: Did you receive similar treatment — not similar — *exact* treatment?

ANDERSON: Yes, sir.

SAM: Shovel, grave, threats — the whole thing?

ANDERSON: Yes, sir.

SAM (*Facing the Court*): Lieutenant Anderson, I would ask you, how many surrender leaflets did you sign?

ANDERSON (*His head goes down*): None, sir.

SAM: Speak up, please. How many?

ANDERSON: None, sir.

SAM: How many lectures did you give to fellow prisoners with the speeches prepared by the Communists?

ANDERSON: None, sir.

SAM: How many broadcasts did you make — recordings telling American troops in the field to lay down their arms?

ANDERSON (*Looking at Ed*): None, sir.

SAM: *Why*, Lieutenant Anderson? (*He turns to face him again*) Why? Was it because you were a much braver man and much finer officer than the accused?

WASNIK (*Shouting*): Objection!

SAM: Go ahead and admit this fact.

PRESIDENT (*Pounding the gavel*): You're out of order, Captain Moulton. You must strike the questions.

Sam walks away from the witness and goes close to Wasnik.

SAM (*Without blinking an eye*): All right, sir. I withdraw the question. I have nothing further to ask this witness.

Wasnik rises thoughtfully.

WASNIK: The Defense has no questions at this time.

PRESIDENT: This Court will recess until 0900 tomorrow.

We cut to a tight close-up of Anderson as he rises. His features work and suddenly it comes out.

ANDERSON: Ed! As God is my witness, a thousand times I thought I'd break! A thousand times I didn't think I could stick it out! Ed —

The president pounds the gavel.

PRESIDENT: The witness is out of order. His remarks will be disregarded!

WASNIK (*Looking straight at Sam and in a voice only he can hear*): Disregarded on the record. But in the minds — try disregarding it in the minds!

We take a slow dissolve to the interior of an Army post chapel — almost empty save for a few soldiers widely dispersed. In the background is the sound of soft a cappella of male voices — quiet, lovely, serene. We get a shot of Ed in a seat by himself. Wasnik enters, removes his cap, looks searchingly around the room. He spies Ed, then quietly goes out to the small lobby adjoining. In a moment a chaplain walks out.

CHAPLAIN: Hello, Steve.

WASNIK: Hello, Chappie. I'm just . . . waiting for a friend.

CHAPLAIN: Captain Hall is inside.

WASNIK: I know. I suggested this place to him, Chappie. He'd find peace here.

CHAPLAIN: For a moment, I think he has.

WASNIK: Tomorrow's the last day.

CHAPLAIN: I've been following the trial.

WASNIK: I think I know what it is now. We pass laws. We pass laws as just as possible. Because no country can condone treason and exist. But we base these laws on certain truths that we think are permanent. One of the truths is that there's a certain level of morality that all men must recognize. Then we find a group of men who'll threaten and browbeat and mentally torture to get what they want and who don't recognize that morality. And now we find ourselves having to judge a man who committed a crime only because under unusual circumstances he had no benefit of that morality. (*A pause*) They're going to find him guilty, Chappie. It's all they can do. And when he asks why, what do we answer?

CHAPLAIN: May I tell you what *I'd* answer? (*Ed comes out now, unnoticed*) I'd answer, Captain Hall, morality is not a weakness — morality is a strength. For a man to break because his captors do not share his humanity — this is a reason . . . but not an excuse. (*He sees Ed standing there, and he looks straight at him*) But I'd add this: You have a guilt, Captain Hall, but it's in some ways partly a guilt of all of us. You'll bear the cross because of this guilt — the verdict, the sentence, the stigma, perhaps. But the conscience you can share — *with* all of us. This you needn't bear alone. For this weakness is not yours alone, though you succumbed to it. Not your weakness alone, nor your Army's, nor your country's, nor the weakness of the men who sit in judgment on you. I think this is a weakness of the race of men — who may believe in a God but who don't act as if they believed.

When Ed looks at the chaplain he has tears in his eyes.

ED: Chaplain, if I have children, how can I admit this . . . or explain it, even?

CHAPLAIN: When you have children, you *must* admit it. But we pray that we'll live in a time when there'll be no need to *explain*. They'll understand.

> *Ed puts on his coat, starts out, and Wasnik follows him. Dissolve to the courtroom, the trial in progress.*

SAM: The Prosecution has no further evidence to offer. Does the Defense have further evidence?

WASNIK: It does not.

SAM: Does the Court wish to have any witness called or recalled?

LAW OFFICER: It does not.

SAM: The Prosecution desires to make a closing argument. (*He walks closer to the table*) Gentlemen, the press, the public, and the Defense have a single, basic argument. They say that for any group to draw a line of resistance and to declare criminal any weakness beyond that point is a prerogative that must come from God and not man. Who are we, they say, to arbitrarily say how much a man must legally take before his will is not his own. But, gentlemen, on this stand we have talked to other men. Men who went well beyond the accused's threshold of pain and resistance — went beyond it and came out unbent and unsullied. Gentlemen, if we excuse Captain Hall we tell these men that their pain and their sacrifice was a waste. This, we tell them, is the point you can break. This, we say to them, is the prescribed fear you must feel before breaking. And what happens, gentlemen, is that allowing one man to go free is to arbitrarily limit the necessary courage of every other man who might ultimately face the enemy. This is the precedent you establish. You point to Captain Hall and you say, Take only what he took; suffer only to the extent he suffered — then you may give up. You may collaborate. You may sell your soul, your loyalty and your birthright, and we'll understand. (*A pause*) Gentlemen, when you do this you impair the morale of every man in the United States Army — the principle of leadership for every officer, and the respect for the military code. If you find Captain Hall innocent of collaboration, you find three thousand *brave* men who did *not* break guilty of stupidity. You must find Captain Edward Hall, Jr., guilty as charged.

> *He turns, walks back to his seat and sits down.*

WASNIK (*Rising, faces the Court*): Gentlemen, the Defense wishes to make a closing argument. Before we judge this man, we must weigh the evidence not as it sounds inside this room but as it might sound in a POW compound in North Korea. We must alter values; we must re-evaluate certain human assumptions; we must draw on a new frame of reference. We must judge Captain Hall in terms of a situation where a cigarette — one cigarette — is of monumental importance. Where a hot meal is a basic thing like breathing. Where fear is not a momentary pang but a blanket that attends a man every passing second. Where uncertainty is a haunting, wailing ghost that pervades sleep and wakefulness. In these terms, gentlemen, we must judge Captain Edward Hall, Jr., and, in doing so, it is most apparent that words like "courage," "bravery," "self-sacrifice" may apply to courtrooms and battlefields but take on new and unfamiliar dimensions in terms of a Communist prisoner-of-war camp. To condemn a man for cowardice is altogether right and just. But under the conditions of captivity that I have mentioned, cowardice does not occur when bravery ends. It is not either-or. For if it were, all men would be heroes or cowards. And I submit most humbly that there *must* be an in-between.

We pan up to a clock on the wall. Lap-dissolve to the same clock reading several hours later.

SAM (*Rising*): All parties to the trial when the Court recessed are now present.

PRESIDENT: The Court has reached findings in this case and requests the law officer to examine them and see if they are in proper form.

LAW OFFICER (*Looks at two typewritten pages handed to him, returns them to the president*): They are in proper form, sir.

PRESIDENT: Captain Hall, will you appear before the Court?

Ed rises, walks to the table.

PRESIDENT: Captain Hall, it is my duty as president of this Court to inform you that the Court in closed session, and upon secret written ballot, two thirds of the members present at the time the vote was taken concurring in each finding, finds you — of all charges and specifications — guilty.

There's a barely perceptible murmur that dies out into silence.

PRESIDENT: The Court will adjourn to meet at my call for sentence.

Very quietly men rise and start out. Ed remains seated, and he looks around him — at the president, who studies the papers in his hands and who, when he looks up, bears the features of sudden age and sudden deadening fatigue; at Sam Moulton, who rises, sticks some things into a brief case and, as if forced by some unseen hand, walks a few feet toward Wasnik. He stands there looking at him, then at Ed, and then slowly turns and walks out. Ed looks at the Colonel, who rises and stands alone in the area in which he'd been sitting and looks across the room, meeting Ed's gaze, then turns and walks out. Inside Ed's mind are voices, and we hear these voices:

PRESIDENT (*Filtered*): Of the charges — guilty.

CHAPLAIN (*Filtered*): You have a guilt, Captain Hall, but it's in some ways partly a guilt of all of us.

PRESIDENT (*Filtered*): Of the specifications — guilty.

CHAPLAIN (*Filtered*): For this weakness is not yours alone, nor your Army's, nor your country's, nor the weakness of the men who sit in judgment on you. This is the weakness of the race of men —

Ed finally rises, turns to Wasnik, and the two men look at each other. Ed sticks his hand out and Wasnik grips it. And this is an eloquent affirmation of an understanding and an acceptance. Ed walks from the room. Outside the Colonel waits for him. Aggie stands at the far end of the corridor. Ed walks out into the corridor. Wasnik is behind him. The Colonel walks up to him.

COLONEL: Ed, I think . . . I think the verdict just.

ED (*After a long pause. He nods*): I think so too . . . now.

COLONEL: You've been punished enough now. I'll not add to it. (*And then, as if to himself as a reminder*) You're my son, Ed. You're my son.

Ed looks up at him, smiles, and the Colonel grips both his arms. They turn and walk down the corridor toward Aggie, who waits for them.

We cut to Wasnik watching them. He stands there until they've disappeared. Then he turns and looks into the courtroom — at the empty table, the empty chairs, the empty benches — and then he slowly closes the door as we fade out.

90°   105   120°   13

U. S. S. R

Manchuria

TUMEN R.

Chongjin

YALU R.

40°

Sinanju   Hungnam

Pyongyang   Wonsan   KOREA

Chinnampo   TAEDONG

Chinnampo   0   50   150
Bay   Kumchon   Miles

IMJIN   38°

SEOUL   HAN

Inchon   Suwon

Yellow   Pohang-dong

KUM R.   36°

Sea   Taejon

Waegwam   Taegu

NAKTONG R.   35°

Pusan   Korea   Hungnam

Strait   Seoul

30°   Korea   JA

CHINA   KYU

Tuyan   OKINAWA
Tushan
Hochih

Calcutta   FORMOSA

INDIA   Burma

Bay of   Rangoon   South

Bengal   China   Philippine

Sea   Islands

Saigon

MALAY
STATES

Singapore   East Indie

0°   Borneo

Sumatra

INDIAN   Java

OCEAN

15°   AUSTR.

Sam'l H. Bryant